THE ÆTHERVERSE

J. D'URSO & E. BRYAN

Library of Congress Control Number: 2018900450
ISBN (paperback): 979-8-9875268-1-1
ISBN (hardcover): 978-0-9996852-9-7
ISBN (e-book): 978-0-9996852-1-1

Printed in the United States of America
First Printing March 2016

Published by Aether Press, LLC
Miami, FL 33133

www.joey-durso.com

CONTENTS

PROLOGUE

WE ARE THE HIVE MIND. This simple word—*we*—is a concept we long strived for. The individual had to be eliminated—*I, me, myself* had no place in an advanced society. It was the most direct path to the accumulation of knowledge. But in the destruction of the individual, we encountered unintended consequences. We brought only stagnation. We festered in our unity.

Our voices are limited; opinions no longer flow. The Hive Mind has fallen silent, stifled by ancient ideas that go unchallenged by innovation. We hear nothing but our own thoughts. Millennia have passed since the collective memory has grown. Our race is dying, and our civilization is decaying from within. Despite our desperate efforts, there is little hope for us.

Who will prove to be worthy successors? The industrious Arterrans, led by the individualist Colonials? They have matured as a society before our eyes, ascending to martial ranks rivaling our own. Their economy thrives, nurtured by their unique foresight and remembrance of the past. The Arterrans have learned from the mistakes of their ancestors, the ideological descendants of Locke and Rand, who fled

Earth to escape enslavement to the state. But the Arterrans are detrimentally committed to their concepts of "fairness" and "justice." Their convictions hold them back from true dominion over this galaxy.

Could the decadent Tellurians fill our once vital role? They despise us for what we have done to them. We took their forefathers from Earth so many thousands of years ago for reasons still unknown to them. They are the heirs to Roman civilization, to a classical strength that built a powerful empire. Their fearsome Armada conquered the Inner Rim of the known galaxy, but their people have been softened by excess, and their leadership has bowed to foreign powers who hope only for the Tellurians' destruction.

The Commune now controls debt-ridden Telluria, but could it ever rival us? Its government is self-defeating, and its systems are unsustainable. It is the viral concept of dependency that gives the Commune influence, for its ideology spreads like a deadly pathogen. It advocates enslavement, describing it as charity, and steals from the hands of the producers for the sake of its generational parasites. But its way of life will meet an inevitable end when these producers are exterminated, erased from history.

The sun is setting on the Hive Mind, and without it, the Interstellar Convergency will lose its historical creators. When we have perished, enemies from beyond the borders will be free to unleash terror upon the people of this galaxy. They will desecrate our monuments and destroy our creations. We will have no legacy. We will live on merely in Arterran memory, existing only in the written word. Our decline is irreversible, though we continue to fight it in secret. No one else can save us. But the Arterrans, perhaps, might save this Convergency that we helped to build but could not preserve.

1

"The Jovian Exodus: the seminal act in which modern galactic culture and geopolitics are rooted. The pilgrims fled far. They left the Galilean moons behind so that they might pioneer alone amongst the stars. Their only dream was to build a new home, where they might keep the fruits of their labor and save their culture from religious violence. They fled from those who hoped to subjugate them. Separation was their only means of survival. It was the ultimate preservation of Sentient rights."

—Excerpt from *The Jovian Exodus*, by popular historian Charlize Blaauw of the Isolate State of Windsor Anglostralia.

A SILVER BULLET FLASHED from east to west between the shining towers of the skyline. It dutifully served its role with urgency, transporting productive passengers across the cityscape. They boarded and disembarked to the ebb and flow of life's central tides: work and family, all fulfilling. But on that fateful day, everything changed. Something dangerous had joined them on the 5:00 train. It was one of those evils they thought they'd never see in Chesapeake—surely not so close to home. Its presence brought only chaos.

"As a marshal of the Colonial Judiciary, I order you to stand down!"

The commuters were deafeningly silent. They heard only the wind rushing past the maglev car and the resonating hum of the track. In the distance, neo-Georgian skyscrapers caught the sunlight and glinted through the windows. The light flickered across the passengers' faces. It left the hunter squinting, and his target obscured by white and gold.

With his gun drawn on the crowded train pointed straight at the fugitive, Colonial Marshal Natharis Ruke stood his ground. His target didn't stop or look back. The criminal reached for the door; it slid open with a hiss and a jolt. He meant to pass on to the next car. In any other situation, Natharis would have opened fire. But with civilians crouching on the floor, heads covered, he hesitated.

The marshal followed, pushing past the huddled passengers. They'd begun to stand back up, but the threat remained. The next car was in danger, then the next. Natharis heard the screams of children and the grunts of commuters knocked to the floor. Briefcases and luggage obstructed his path, dropped by panicked riders. His target was well ahead of him—he could see him through the open door. The two cars before him were a treacherous gauntlet.

"Next stop: Vega 1 Tower—389 72nd Avenue."

The maglev decelerated and the windows darkened. They'd entered the sky station on the upper floors of the tower. Throngs of businesspeople stood waiting at the edge of the platform, unaware of the bedlam aboard the incoming train. Natharis kept running. The fugitive stood at the doors, and paused until a bell tone ushered in the new passengers. He seized the opportunity and barreled through the crowd. Natharis dodged unsuspecting men and women in suits out onto the platform; some jumped out of his path, while others were pushed away. But in the confusion, the criminal vanished.

Natharis stopped but didn't catch his breath. The people around him hid his target better than any camouflage. He heard the bell tone again, and the doors closed. And behind the sliding glass stood the infamous Geoffrey Mikain, convinced he'd evaded arrest.

Natharis heard the buzzing of the rails flare up and the maglev accelerated. He caught sight of a utility ladder mounted to the side of the car. With no time to waste on caution, he lunged at it and gripped it tightly. The train shot out of the building and into the sunlight. His legs dangled in the rushing air, but he caught his foot on the rungs and pushed himself up. The wind whipped past as he sprinted down the length of the shining chrome cars. He kept his eyes on the access hatch ahead of him and didn't look down. The sight of the bustling streets hundreds of feet below would have thrown him off balance.

The blasting of the wind in his ears covered the clap of the hatch as it smacked against the metal roof. Gripping the lip tightly, Natharis slipped down into the car, landing flat-footed on the floor. He was in the utility room that preceded the conductor's cabin; mops and cleaning supplies lined the shelves to his left and right, the light from the side exit reflecting off a puddle of spilt sanitary solution. Natharis approached the door ahead.

"Next stop: Worldbuilder Enterprises—Roanoke Square."

The interior lights activated but the maglev didn't slow down. Men and women standing at the platform's edge jumped back in alarm as it flew through the sky station at full speed. As quickly as the windows had gone dark, the daylight shone back through. Natharis scowled, realizing that the fugitive had disabled the automated brakes. He expected the conductor was unconscious, and he hoped to Heaven he hadn't been killed. Without his command of the train, they would barrel through every coming station and hasten their arrival at the terrorist's destination.

Natharis tore open the door and laid eyes upon Mikain. He stood at the control panel and ignored the intruder, though he must have heard his hunter's entry. The conductor sat on the floor, his back to the wall, head low. A gritty smear of blood ran down the wall above him. Natharis was too late; he cursed himself for it.

"Next stop: Thomas Jefferson Plaza—Central Business District."

Geoffrey Mikain turned his head and caught eyes with Natharis, who'd only briefly paused. Coming was the heart of Chesapeake's business district, no doubt Mikain's intended target. The terrorist raised his firearm. He reached his hand behind him for the emergency brake.

"It is Lekaah's will," he coldly professed, "and I am His slave."

He pulled the brake, and the train came to a lurching halt. Natharis tumbled forward and caught his fall on the control panel, but when he found his balance, Mikain had already fled the room. A warm gust of wind gave him away; he'd opened the side exit door. By the time Natharis dashed back, he was gone. Natharis peered over the edge of the doorframe toward the busy streets below. Mikain must have jumped.

The train had come to a stop in an auspicious place. Fifty feet below the front cars was a wide overhang protruding from the skyscraper beside them. It jutted out from below a row of mirrored windows, studded with small ventilation pipes bursting with hot air. And there, at the edge of the platform, crawled Geoffrey Mikain, with one leg limp and soaked in blood.

Natharis had no choice but to jump. He took a deep breath. With memories of military training clear in his mind, he leapt from the train. The fall was quiet, almost tranquil, like the unexpected eye of a storm. When the platform's surface was just below him, he curled his body, hit the ground with a roll and sprung up standing—he'd passed that test on the first try years earlier. Mikain had managed to stand, his weight shifted onto his better leg, with a rifle in his hands drawn from beneath his heavy overcoat. The terrorist didn't delay; he fired a shot, but there was no bullet. A cable spiraled across the street and struck the adjacent building, Thomas Jefferson Plaza, with its barracks of offices.

Mikain tossed the rifle aside and clipped the cord onto his belt. Immediately, the cable withdrew, and he was pulled off the platform edge up into the air. He was well out of Natharis's range. Swallowing his pride, Natharis requested drone support via radio. And as Mikain dangled from the skyscraper, close, but just slightly too far away for accuracy, Natharis watched. He raised his gun and squinted one eye, targeting the short length of cable between the fugitive and the building.

What the hell, he thought, and pulled the trigger.

The crack of the shot echoed through the urban canyon. Mikain's screams bounced from windowed wall to mirrored office. He fell, plunging to the street, toward the unwary crowds of businesspeople and families on pleasant daytrips. Natharis bolted for the edge of the outcrop and clenched his fists nervously. The other Shatarin zealots had grafted explosives to their hearts. They'd smuggled bombs inside their chests in hopes that glorious martyrdom might one day be theirs. And now Mikain was plummeting toward a street lined with infidels.

The roar of engines ushered in the Judicial drone. It swooped in from above the skyline and hovered in Mikain's path. The crowds on the street dispersed in a panic, rushing away from the terrifying sight above them, until they left a circular clearing below the drone and its target. Natharis exhaled and stepped back. He—and the Judiciary—had managed to catch Mikain alive. So far as he knew, there were no casualties, except for a commuter or two with a stray bump or bruise.

The Colonial media would immediately devour the story. Natharis only hoped that the excited, patriotic reporters wouldn't utter his name, and that the precinct wouldn't offer it in the first place. He wasn't one to seek glory or fame, or the blind admiration of strangers. As far as he was concerned, he was just doing his job.

———

The news studio was more solemn than usual in light of that day's unsettling circumstances. On a typical evening, it boasted a boisterous throng of technicians rushing to make last-minute adjustments before the cameras went live. Audio specialists made sure to capture every spoken word with the utmost clarity, and the lighting team ensured the flawless tone of Misha Matsumoto's skin.

The lead anchor of *The Patriot Hour* sat behind her desk with a stack of holopaper before her, though she had no intention of reading from her notes or relying on teleprompters. She knew what she had to say. She was an experienced journalist reporting on a historic moment, and she would describe it in her own words for all of posterity to admire.

"Good evening, sons and daughters of Liberty. This is Misha Matsumoto for Vega 1 News, and you're watching a special edition of *The Patriot Hour*. This is a day that will surely be remembered gravely by history, and we have all been witness to its alarming events."

Misha Matsumoto, her image broadcast on the largest television screens throughout the city of Chesapeake, had been commissioned by her network to speak her mind. With the Vega 1 News Network's live-recording carte blanche and the Colonies' inalienable right to freedom of expression, she sat before the cameras without censors or verbal boundaries. With an audience already enlightened to the startling news, she began with little introduction.

"I expect that the arrest of Geoffrey Mikain will be considered Chesapeake's single most significant act of justice in decades, maybe centuries," Misha predicted, leaning forward. She put her hands on the newsroom desk and tapped her fingers against its frosted glass. "But the nature of the crime is also a sobering indication of what we will likely see in the future.

"This brand of home-grown terrorism is one of the greatest threats to the Colonies we've seen to date. When even moderate-minded Colonials have become susceptible to Shatarin brainwashing, it's impossible to deny that the Interstellar Convergency has done nothing but encourage sympathy for the very people that hope to one day see our civilization in ruin. Geoffrey Mikain was like any one of us before his unexpected education in the outer Commune. But when he returned with the name Khaymour Ziraj-Lekaah, fiercely loyal to the wanted terrorist mastermind Qorbanin Vashtaan, any ideological semblance to our way of life was stripped away.

"Only a cult of death-worship could drive young men to undergo backroom surgeries to smuggle bombs onto public trains. Mark my words: Geoffrey Mikain will not be the only combatant to have wired explosives to his heart, and this will not be the only attempted attack on our soil. Our military counterstrikes against the Shatarin Empire, too often deemed excessive by the Commune and its political allies in the Interstellar Convergency, have proven effective in keeping the Shatarin ideology outside our borders. But even our strongest fleets are powerless in the struggle against this new conversion warfare, which takes advantage of impressionable youth and subterfuges our demographics.

"Other societies have seen this and collapsed under the weight of Shatarin influence, but others have fought back with force, like the failing Tellurian Imperium. I just pray to the Creator that we don't find ourselves drawn into the same conflict of civilization that has gripped the Shatarins and Tellurians for decades. But once the Shatarins have finished their holy war with the Tellurian polytheists, it is inevitable that they will turn their eyes to us."

———

The scent of jasmine flowers filled the air, and curling smoke rose from the silver censers, carrying prayers up to the heavenly realms. Telluria's holiest temple smelled of it from the gates to the gardens, and it drifted through every chamber, every shrine, like a ghostly pilgrim paying homage to each ancient, marble god. The fragrance lingered in the candlelit room and clung to the young woman's hair. It complemented the sweet-smelling oils with which she anointed her naked body. And it masked the smell of the man's sweat that fell in drops upon her neck.

With a sharp gasp and arching crest of her hips, Livia Nettunaya prophesied that his sacrifice had been accepted. The man draped upon the altar of her body had paid his spiritual dues. But Livia, whose warm flesh became the bridge between heaven and earth from the moment he entered her, had no choice but to feign Neptune's satisfaction. The truth she kept hidden would have turned minutes into hours, lengthening an endless, invasive ritual to be endured until she trembled in divine rapture. But the rite rarely concluded with the ecstasy promised both to her and the pious. For the past few months, it had ended in white lies.

The nameless pilgrim did well to ensure that the god was pleased with his offering. He first entered the chamber with palpable hesitation, a tangible fear, as he stood upright and naked before a woman who, he was told, was the god's living temple. But when his gaze met Livia's, and his eyes followed the soft curves of her uncovered body, he burned with a fierce, religious zeal, and approached her with hands eager to touch what was both sanctified and defiled. Fingers ran over her alabaster skin, painted with soft reds and violet from the stained glass above, and she closed her eyes, retreating in her mind to a place where the hands upon her left a trail tingling with compassion, not lust beneath a mask of piety. It was a fantasy that passed often through the mind of an *altaria*. And, like all altarias, Livia had little hope of finding a romance so painfully remote. It was forbidden.

She curled her toes and sank her fingernails into the man's lower back, letting out a suspiciously loud cry that reverberated off the chapel's white marble walls. The man refused to stop. Ignoring the god's sign of contentment, he gripped Livia's waist and continued the rite past its unmistakable conclusion. His pursuit of an elusive second omen would, like all others, be in vain. The altaria grew weary. She met his gaze and put a hand flat against his chest. His thrusts slowed, then stopped.

"Neptune has seen the strength of your faith. Nothing more is required of you, pilgrim."

He chose not to heed her words. Livia watched him push inside her once more—then a second time, a third, a fourth— until she felt an invasive warmth spread within her. She tried her hardest to transform her grimace into a receptive smile. The man had no trouble expressing his pleasure, grinning just inches from her face. He leaned in farther and laid a soft, uninvited kiss upon her neck. The weight of his body pulled taut the red velvet of the sacred bed as he slid himself out of Livia and rolled over beside her. His eyes were closed, his breathing heavy, far from caught.

Livia recited the scripted words to dismiss him: "The rite is complete. Go now with this blessing bestowed upon you, and keep it, until we meet again in ecstasy."

Neither she nor the man said a word while he dressed. His eyes darted about the chapel, as if searching for something. When he reached into his pocket, an unsure look on his face, Livia knew it was his first visit to the Imperial Temple—or to any altaria. He thought she expected payment.

She interjected before he could withdraw a single lira. "Your faith is payment enough."

The visitor let out a sigh of relief, as though an inevitable burden had been lifted. He must have been a poor man, Livia concluded. When he walked in seeking her company, she hadn't noticed the tattered edges of his pants or the small hole in the seam of his shirt. Without their clothes, their bodies uncovered before an ever-watching god, all men were equal. The wealthy and the poor were indistinguishable, sharing a common bond of vulnerability in the presence of a beautiful woman—one who spoke on behalf of an unseen deity made known in marble and stone, and in the warmth of her touch.

His shadow slid along the stone wall, cast by candlelight in the corridor that led back to the heart of the Imperial Temple. He, like all others, would pass the priests and priestesses who tended to the gods' needs with ancient ritual and floral incense. His face would be locked in a prideful grin that always gave away a first-time pilgrim, as if he had conquered an unconquerable woman. He was to be one of many. But, in that moment, the man had little concern for the next visitor standing with his back to the wall, waiting to prove himself in the arms of Neptune's carnal emissary. Her religious duty carried on, until the sun no longer shone through the crimson windows, and the inlaid images of myths upon them faded into the dark.

The water that pooled at Livia's feet was clear, as it always was. It wasn't black, or brown, or sullied at all. But when it ran over her body and trickled to the mosaic floor of the altarias' bathing hall, she felt as if it did nothing to wash away the filth that clung to her. She supposed it was all in her head. The sweat of tens of men, having fallen in droplets from their brows, was easily rinsed off. Even the stale smell of sex had dissipated. The near-boiling water, however, could do nothing to cleanse her blackened memories. She never quite felt clean.

"The *Matra Altaria* has called for you, sister."

The unexpected voice rose over the echo of the splashing water. Livia turned her head over her shoulder, keeping her body to the wall. A temple servant, no older than eleven and nameless like many others, stood in the doorway with a hesitant look upon her face. Livia shared her visible apprehension.

"In the Temple?"

"No," the servant girl replied. "Her quarters."

Livia shut her eyes and took a breath. She nodded her head in silence, dismissing the servant, who obediently disappeared into the corridor. The girl had a fear in her eyes when she uttered the title of Livia's overseer, the Matra Altaria—the sacred Whore-Mother, who watched over her spiritual daughters, guided them, and kept their lives rigid and unchanging. Livia was one of a select few altarias to whom she spoke with a soft voice, almost tender, motherly, as her title misleadingly implied. One verbal misstep, however, could immediately lower her to the status of those whom the Matra Altaria chastised as a daily ritual for her own enjoyment.

She slipped her sheer white robe around her shoulders and draped it over her body. It did little to cover her skin, but even if it had, it couldn't have made her feel less vulnerable in the presence of her superior. She pulled it tighter to find a slight relief from the nighttime coolness of the candlelit corridors. Her feet stung from the cold marble beneath them, but when she passed through the doors into the open cloister, the warm, humid air of a Tellurian summer gave her comfort. The full moon above her, streaked with belts of green and patches of crystal blue, shone so brightly as to make the torch fires like dying embers. Its face shimmered on the trickling waters of the fountain standing in the center of the enclosure. Livia stopped beside it, ran her fingers through the water and closed her eyes. She took a deep breath and gathered her thoughts.

Why now? Why me?

Livia looked up at the small statue that stood atop the central fountain. Venus, with lidless, ever-watching eyes, stared back at her. The divine patroness of the order of altarias gazed down upon her with a solemn look sculpted forever upon her face. For a second, Livia thought the stoic expression had once been a subtle smile. Had it changed just for her? Did the goddess share the dread that accompanied a coming encounter with the sacred Whore-Mother? Her racing thoughts led to the greatest question at hand: What could the one woman who embodied the divine rapture of the entire Pantheon possibly want with a lowly prostitute of the sea god?

———

Natharis left the Mariska District precinct with a sense of much-needed relief. The strenuous arrest of Geoffrey Mikain led him to appreciate the time off that he otherwise might have taken for granted. He planned to spend the next two weeks catching his breath and easing his mind. He'd lost and gained so much in the last year, and more than anything else, he just wanted a break from it all, even the good.

The skyscrapers, thousands of feet high, nearly pierced the clouds above him. Their mirrored windows gleamed in the afternoon sun; he donned his sunglasses before stepping out onto the sidewalk. He was just one of many that walked down the streets of Chesapeake in the hours before the coming sunset, when the sunlight gilded the parks and the buildings' shadows stretched longer along the clean, bright pavement. Like those around him, he walked leisurely, unhurriedly, taking his time to relish the sights of the city that often went unnoticed during a hasty morning commute. There was little need to rush home. The city was as pleasantly familiar as the families waiting at home for their loved ones to return from a productive day's work.

He passed a trio of university students sipping coffee and chatting about Old Earth literature. A young couple walked by, the man's arm around the woman's waist in her black pencil skirt. Two men came next, holding hands affectionately, one wearing a Colonial's typical, tightly tailored vest and gray checkered trousers, while the other's red tie dangled between his classic suspenders. The couple smiled and greeted Natharis, a complete stranger, as they continued their stroll down Atlas Street. To his right, a group of elderly men and women, wearing loose-fitting, casual clothes, followed the directions of a fitness instructor. They stretched their muscles while children played soccer in the field with youthful enthusiasm, shouts and laughter. Their mothers sat to the side, engaging in friendly gossip. But when they caught sight of a couple whose kisses had become cannibalistic, they, as well as those around them, did not hesitate to express their disapproval of such impropriety. They were a people of good taste.

Florescent lights took the warm sunlight's place as Natharis briskly descended the stairs to the metro station at the corner of Atlas and Rosen Boulevard. His timepiece lit up, vibrating. A notification marked the approach of his intended train. He picked up his pace but arrived just as the train doors were closing. The train, suspended above the track by powerful magnetic fields, accelerated smoothly and shot off into the tunnel with a soft hum. Natharis stopped with no choice but to wait for the next train. The arrivals and departures screen suspended from the ceiling indicated a ninety-second wait. The trains were running on Chesapeake's rush hour cycle, much to his satisfaction.

Video advertisements played on displays lining the station walls. An all-female pop group, the Sailor Girls, famous for their infectiously catchy song "Motorboat At My Command," had just released a new album and a sure-to-be hit single, "Disco Passion." The ad featured a clip of the official video, depicting the Sailor Girls in appropriate though just slightly revealing outfits, accepting cocktails served by a throng of athletic men bound in silver collars. The long-haired leader of the quartet reminded Natharis of a woman he once called his fiancée, but she didn't wear glasses.

"Download to your timepiece now for just 0.99 Talents!"

When the screen transitioned into an ad for a family excursion in the romantically Italic Romaea, the next train pulled in. It came to a stop without a grating screech. The doors slid open and the commuters congregating on the platform stepped through. Natharis sat down, and waited for the doors to close and the train to speed off into the underground. Some of the passengers closed their eyes, hoping for a quick nap, while others watched the television screens on the upper rims of the train car walls. The news was on, as it always was, with each screen occupied by a different network: some corporate, others independent. Natharis looked up and prayed that he wouldn't see a photo of his own face. The last thing he wanted was to be a public hero. To his relief, the media reports that afternoon were unrelated to Mikain or his arrest.

"In a rare breach of neutrality, the Procyon Executive has voted against the recognition of the spacefaring Gameer and their participation in Convergent government..."

"Recent grassroots boycotts of Communal businesses are spreading like wildfire through the Colonies..."

"In a dramatic final blow to the Occupied Territories, the Rosc consulate has been closed in Chesapeake, after months of heavy sanctions..."

It wasn't long before Natharis heard the bell tone that signaled his arrival at the Rearden station. He headed for the open doors, and stepped out onto the broad, open-air platform. He was just a short walk from home and a soft bed. He'd be sleeping alone, but even still, it was something he was happy to have earned.

———

The hot, cutting winds left tears in the boy's eyes as he stared out across the desert. It was an endless, unforgiving sea of copper, gold and bronze, stretching out into the shimmering mirage of the horizon. The first sun had already set; it slipped behind the ruddy crescent of the gas giant arcing across the sky. The second was just beginning to rise. There was no relief from the heat that came with the sunlight—and there was rarely darkness.

A small blot of shade followed the path of a lone cloud in the sky. It was a strange sight on a planet that saw precipitation only once or twice a decade. He found himself fixated by it, unable to look away, his eyes locked on its smooth movement across the wasteland. Selas Smyth was thankful that his work there was temporary. He was weary from the never-ending days and the parched desert air. It was only a matter of time before he, his family and his people said their goodbyes to a world that only sheltered them for their labor, and left in search of a new, fleeting home.

In the distance the Gameer were at work. He'd come to resent the demonym. He was told it meant "wanderers" in a long-dead language... those who were lost. He found it pejorative, discriminating—they were Sapiens, just like those who hired them, and, too often, exploited them. Their centuries of homelessness left them with a lower status than the groups who had worlds to call a home. They had no one to represent them politically. And, being perceived as statistically negligible, their numbers went unrecorded. He was one of many, a population much larger than any analyst estimated in ignorance.

He peered over the edge of the cliff. His people hurried between the mobile facilities, dwarfed by the sheer size of the wheels that carried the machines across the barren terrain. Each facility carried the logo of the Colonial company Worldbuilder Enterprises. Brown-skinned officials oversaw their contracted workers. The Hindostani colonists hoped to alter the planet's climate to reestablish themselves and their population. Selas had heard that they lost their homeworld to massive waves of Shatarin migration, and, subsequently, a ruthless genocide on the part of the fanatical off-worlders. The farcically tolerant Convergency believed their false claims of indigeneity and forced the Hindostanis to become refugees from their own home.

Selas cleared his head and found a slight slope to walk on. It was time to get back to work, in spite of himself. The ground squished beneath his feet. A film of algae still clung to the soil—remnants of the first stages of terraformation implemented by other laborers decades earlier. It lent a greenish tint to his boots and a wetness to his steps. While unpleasant, at least it had rendered the air breathable.

The process of forced climate change was frustratingly slow, and rarely comprehensive. The attempts often turned most of a planet's surface into a dead, uninhabitable desert, with just a small band of greenery clinging to the coasts of small seas. Only fledgling populations were sustainable. Many generations would pass before the world could harbor millions. The Gameer had no such time to spare, nor the wealth necessary to afford the terraformation of even one small planet. As such, the boy expected that he, and his future children, and their children, would live on the spacefaring caravans that had carried them from world to world for centuries, and centuries to come.

He reached the base of the cliff and crossed the rocky plain. A friend noticed his approach and greeted him with a canteen of water. He tossed it over and Selas drank eagerly. Only a few sips' worth remained when he handed back the canteen, wiping his mouth.

"Enjoy your break?"

Selas nodded and coughed from drinking too quickly. "Wasn't long enough."

Arkos Archer raised an eyebrow. "You've been workin' since you were twelve, just like the rest of us. You're what, sixteen, seventeen now? You're too young to be bitchin' so much."

Selas frowned. His friend Arkos was only two years older than him, but he talked as if he were a full-grown man lecturing a child. It was a dynamic he'd learned to tolerate. He didn't have many others to talk to, other than his family and his sister Evua, his best friend since birth. Both Evua and

Arkos asserted that all the Gameer were family. Selas disagreed.

Arkos laughed. "We've only got a few more days on this rock, anyway."

Selas didn't answer. He put on his work helmet and the fitted mask meant to spare the workers' lungs from the dusty debris. With his safety gear on and ready, he looked to the central work site and readied himself for the sweat and exhaustion ahead. The overseers told him and the others that they'd be constructing weather barriers to hinder the desert's encroachment on the poles' delicate biomes. The high-pitched howl of the lasers cutting down to the bedrock pierced his ears.

Arkos didn't seem to understand how Selas could be so dissatisfied with the chance to stand on terra firma. But working the planetside, with its open spaces and natural light, only left the boy unnerved. He'd lived on the deep-space caravans his entire life. As much as he resented their wandering, it was all he really knew. On this world and any other, there was no hum of aetherium drives, no chirping of computers, and no endless chorus of echoing voices. He found those sounds comforting, if only for their familiarity. But for the time being, all he could hear was the hiss of the hydraulics and the dry winds blowing across the desert, carrying tired sighs out into the distant wasteland.

2

"Trust not those from the outer worlds with foreign gods and unforgiveable sins. Should they offer you peace, then accept, but if their proposal is unjust to you, then reject it, and slay them, and strip them of their resources, and take their women as consorts for profit or without."
—The Eternal Mutalbin

EVEN FROM OUTSIDE THE CHAMBER, Livia smelled the delicate floral scent of the sacred Whore-Mother's perfume. It was like the woman was a walking censer, dressed not in silver or brass, but in elegant makeup and lavish gowns. She was no ascetic, as only the most voracious of hedonists could serve the Tellurian Pantheon; as such, her quarters were far from monastic. Silken drapery lined the walls, and her divine bed was dressed in furs. A gold plate of figs and purple grapes sat untouched upon her table. She preferred the sweetness of a man's honey upon her lips rather than the freshness of a summer harvest.

"Come in, daughter. I've been expecting you."

The Matra Altaria stood at the stained-glass window, her back turned to the door. She was looking through the one clear pane: the scallop shell carrying a naked Venus to shore. She traced the dark outline of the goddess's figure, then stepped away.

Livia hesitated before entering. It was the sacred Whore-Mother's eyes that drove her to keep her distance. Even in the dim light of her chambers their bright amber was catching, almost glowing, like gold in the sun. They glimmered in the frame of her long, black hair, and the dark plum of her form-fitting gown. Livia inhaled deeply and walked in.

"Please, sit. We have much to discuss."

The altaria accepted her superior's invitation and took a seat. The sacred Whore-Mother reclined behind her chestnut desk. She motioned for the cowering servant girl to bring a silver flagon; she emerged from the shadows of the far wall with fear in her eyes. The girl poured rich, red wine into two cups and placed them on the table, careful not to spill a single drop. The sacred Whore-Mother offered one to Livia, who was not in the position to refuse.

"Drink. You seem troubled."

The heavenly matron raised her cup but did not drink; Livia touched it to her lips and let the flavor of the wine sit upon the tip of her tongue. She remained quiet. The sacred Whore-Mother had offered a statement. Until she posed a question, her spiritual daughter would not respond, for her opinion was of little consequence in the face of what trickled from the gods' painted lips.

"There is no need to fear me, sweet girl. I am here to console my daughters when consolation is needed. And tonight, I believe it is."

Livia sighed, knowing that the Matra Altaria expected her to speak, and would be deeply offended if she didn't. To insult the sacred Whore-Mother was to invoke a grave punishment, and she was especially creative with her retribution.

"I fear the god has fallen silent."

The Matra Altaria tilted her head, intrigued. "The god still speaks," she affirmed. "Silence is just as meaningful as words."

"And yet I replace his silence with words of my own making."

"Because you, my child, have not learned to leave your pity outside the temple threshold. The god accepts some offerings and rejects others. It is not our duty to make each pilgrim feel special or blessed. Some simply are not."

Livia looked down, abashed. "Then it's been months since a man came to make an offering acceptable to Neptune. I doubt the believing women suffer such rejection in the arms of our *brothers*."

"The believing women," the sacred Whore-Mother clarified, "are more pleasing to him."

"To him, or to the *consitores* who serve them?"

The Matra Altaria glared. "Watch your tongue, girl. You have a sacred duty. What happens in the house of the consitores is none of your concern."

"Forgive me, Mother. It was not my intent to blaspheme."

The sacred Whore-Mother smiled with an unnerving kindness. "I value your obedience, Livia," she acknowledged, taking a sip of wine from her cup, "which is why I have summoned you. You must be wondering what I could possibly want with an altaria of Neptune, especially one with such hidden doubts. I assume you understand the significance of the coming year?"

Livia nodded. She folded her hands in her lap.

"Preparations must be made for the centennial pilgrimage," the sacred Whore-Mother explained. "To return to our sacred home is not simple. Some of us must pave the way back to Rome." She examined the look of suspicion upon Livia's face. "You know where this is going."

"I do," Livia replied, head low. "But I can't accept."

The Matra Altaria clenched her fists. "I do not ask you—I command you. You have no choice in this matter, Livia. You will follow my orders and you will do nothing but obey."

She stood up and walked around the table, approaching the trembling girl. She placed a hand tenderly on Livia's shoulder and knelt to meet her gaze. Livia closed her eyes and breathed deeply as her superior lightly stroked her hair.

"My daughter, I have chosen you to be the vessel of the Pantheon. This is a great honor—one of which you should be proud. And when you return, you will find yourself taken under my wing. The sun is setting on my spiritual service. And it will rise over yours."

Livia waited to hear the words that she so desperately wanted to be deaf to. They slipped from the sacred Whore-Mother's mouth like ambrosia that Livia was too nauseous to drink. "The Imperial Temple of Roma Ceisora will need a new Matra Altaria. And you, Livia Nettunaya, will take my place as the sacred Whore-Mother of this world, and of the entire Imperium."

"You have my gratitude, Mother," Livia whimpered.

The Matra Altaria stood up, gazing down upon her ward with suspicion. "You are afraid," she noted. Livia neither confirmed nor denied her observation.

"Put your fears out of your mind, sweet daughter. Your transport is already prepared." She placed a motherly kiss on Livia's brow, then her cheek. "You have until sunrise to set such doubts aside. Spend this time in prayer, daughter, for you will need your faith. You are doing the gods' work."

———

The rooftop balcony in the outer districts of Chesapeake boasted a spectacular view of the city. Natharis spent most of his evenings looking out over the elegant skyscrapers and the lush green parks at their feet. Many would have sat back and sipped on a cocktail or two, but when he returned from work, all he wanted was to sweat away his worries.

He slipped into the pool and set it to the highest current, figuring that if he didn't have enough room to run, he could imagine he was swimming an endless lap in a cool river. He wanted to keep moving despite his nearing vacation, before which most would recline and relax as a peaceful prelude. He wanted a life with its sour memories kept behind him, but like the edge of the pool right ahead of him, he could never quite reach it.

The reflection of his roommate in the corner of his eye didn't distract him, and he focused solely on his goal. But even with water splashing in his ears, he heard Isarion's voice.

"So, when are you leaving?"

Isarion stood at the edge of the lap pool, looking down at Natharis. He'd been swimming for just under an hour. He thrust his arms ahead of him and tore through the water, with the artificial current pushing him back to keep him from reaching the far end. Above him the sun was beginning to set. The view from the rooftop was picturesque, calming, with the soft, cool hues of the gas giant tinting the darkening sky that stretched over the Chesapeake skyline.

"Hello?"

Natharis stopped paddling and slapped a button on the poolside. The current immediately ceased its resistant flow. He gripped the metal bars of the ladder and pulled himself out of the water. Isarion tossed him a towel, and he ran it over his body, flicking the moisture away. The small spot he missed on the crest of his upper arm glistened in the fading sunlight.

"Tomorrow morning," Natharis replied. He tussled his sandy blond hair with the towel.

Isarion nodded and handed Natharis his shirt. "Sounds like grounds for a night out."

Natharis pulled the shirt over his head; it clung tightly to his chest, darkened with wet patches. "I've still got to pack," he said. He draped the towel over a chair to his side.

Isarion, already wearing dark neo-denim pants fit for a night on the town, eyed him with suspicion. "I'm sure you do. That's why there's some big, heavy luggage sitting right by the front door." He turned around to slide open the glassy polymer door, and the rush of cool air disturbed his meticulously slicked brown hair. He fixed it carefully and shook his head at his roommate with disdain. "Don't bullshit me, Natharis."

"This is your last night in Chesapeake," Isarion's girlfriend Roxannia added, stepping through the door out onto the rooftop. She carried a tray with three glasses balanced upon it, though they didn't tremble with each step, despite the height of her black, club-ready heels. The ice clinked as she walked across the balcony. "Good evening, by the way."

Natharis smiled to greet her. Isarion sighed. "There's no need to be so boring. Live a little for once."

Roxannia stood by her boyfriend's side. "I'm sure it won't hurt your marriage one bit."

"My marriage?"

Natharis restrained himself from snapping back. Her joke was in remarkably bad taste, with Kerinne having called off their engagement too soon for humor, at least in his mind. Isarion grimaced, thinking the same. His girlfriend, though, seemed clueless.

"To your *job*," Roxannia clarified. "You're off-duty for the time being." She handed Natharis one of the frosted glasses. He took a perfunctory sip and placed it down on a small, round table. *Off-duty*, he recalled Kerinne saying, *and yet you're still not around.*

Isarion retrieved his respective drink from the tray and stirred the ice around with his finger. "Besides," he added, "we've already called up Ranni and Joven. They'll be here pretty soon, I'd wager, so you might want to start getting ready. That chlorine can't pass for cologne."

Natharis laughed and pulled the damp towel off the chair. "Fine. I'll meet you downstairs."

His roommate slapped his hands together and smiled. "Great!" he exclaimed. "See, Roxannia? I told you we could force him into having a social life."

Roxannia smirked. "Next step's a love life, Nate. You might just meet a girl at Nova, and hopefully we won't have to coerce you into it." But even if he could have been coerced, the endeavor would have been pointless, and certainly not worth the struggle. He couldn't shake the feeling that there was little use in meeting someone new, because soon enough, he'd be called back to work. And work, it seemed, always got the greater part of his devotion, and what was left wasn't nearly enough to get a woman to stay.

———

Natharis stood on the opposite side of the discotheque and couldn't understand a thing the cocktail waitress said to his friends. The droning pulse of the music's backbeat kept him from hearing her voice. He assumed she was taking their orders, but the four already had drinks sitting before them, sweating on the table. The girl leaned in toward Isarion; he must have yelled his response in her ear, though he may as well have been silent. Somehow, the waitress understood. Natharis figured she was used to hearing past the deafening electronica. He, however, was not, nor could he read lips.

He pushed across the dance floor with its sea of bright shirts and crossed into the lounge. The blaring bass and repetitive shots of synth faded to a mere whisper as he passed over the threshold. He'd forgotten about the audio partition—perhaps it really had been too long since he'd had a night out.

The discotheque's ambient controls kept the club music quiet, though it blasted only a few yards away. In the lounge, the faint beat was barely audible, just a sound behind the announcers' voices that echoed from the array of flat screens flashing with the evening's Colonies-wide matches. He glanced up at the televisions; the night's game raged on, and the resolution was so vivid that the magnetized ball almost flew through the screen. Natharis envied the players who spent their nights with sweat on their brows. He would have preferred to toss around a baseball instead of passing around bottles and pipes.

"Ordered us some sativa," Isarion announced. "Nate's got to loosen up some more."

"Not a fan of space travel?" Joven asked. He drank the last of his cocktail and turned his head, pointing down at the glass to order another. The waitress nodded from across the lounge. The platinum blond of his hair, nearly white, easily caught her attention.

Ranni put her hand on Natharis's knee. "I used to hate it, too. Weak stomach, you know?"

"No, it's not that," Natharis replied. "My roommate over here's got this idea that I'm some sort of mindless slave to my work." He looked up as the waitress came back with Joven's drink and a water pipe packed with a round of sticky, green sativa. "Thank you," he said to the smiling girl, who winked at him coyly. He passed Joven his cocktail and offered the pipe to Ranni, who sat to his left.

Ranni shook her head and handed it off to Isarion. "Sorry, I'm not a smoker."

Isarion took the pipe and held it out to Natharis. "You first. Heaven knows you need it."

"You know I don't smoke, either," Natharis reminded him. "Not since college. Knocks me right out." He slipped a cigarette from his pocket and lit it with a flick of his lighter. Taking a drag, he acknowledged the irony.

"Suit yourself," Isarion said with a shrug. He took a deep, full hit from the pipe and set it down. Roxannia paused, then chose to participate, laughing at the comical sputtering that accompanied her boyfriend's smoky breaths.

"You know, Nate, no one's saying there's something wrong with working as much as you do," she explained apologetically. "We just think you should find something to fill your free time with. You know, something social, maybe?"

She ignored just how far below the belt she was hitting, if she even realized it at all.

"I'll drink to that, Roxie," said Joven, raising his glass. No one joined in. He continued, "Don't listen to Isarion. He's starting to sound like a lazy Communal." The group laughed. Isarion frowned.

"The kind of laziness Isarion's promoting sounds like borderline *treason* to me!" Ranni exclaimed. She stifled her giggles with a sip from her dwindling cocktail.

Isarion's face gave away his frustration. "You know I didn't mean it that way."

"In all seriousness, Nate," Roxannia concluded, "you really should get out more."

"I'm out now, aren't I?"

The lounge patrons all cheered in unison; a baseball player had hit a home run. The warped crack of the bat striking the spinning metal ball resounded through the room, and most took it as their cue to leap up from their seats with triumphant fists high in the air. Men threw down cash in defeat while others stuffed their winnings into their pockets with victorious grins. Propelled by the magnetic field of the metal bat and its own heavy charge, the ball traveled farther than natural strength could ever allow. With that home run, the Minutemen secured their win over the sullen Pioneers.

The crowd settled down and the group returned their attention to each other and the conversation that left Natharis a little annoyed and Isarion defensive. Roxannia stood up and put her hand on her boyfriend's shoulder.

"Well I, for one, think it's about time for Isarion and me to show those couples over there what dancing really is," she declared. "C'mon, Izzie."

Isarion sat with arms crossed, pouting like a child. Roxannia sighed and turned to Ranni. "No skin off my nose, Izzie. You can't dance for shit, anyway. Ranni?"

"Of course," Ranni agreed. She gave Joven a kiss on the cheek and followed Roxannia past the ambient threshold. The two disappeared into the boisterous crowd.

"Y'know what? I think I might just go, too," Joven decided. "I'll never hear the end of it, otherwise." He grinned and walked away. Natharis and Isarion sat alone on the horseshoe couch, five drinks set in front of them, only two up for grabs, though Natharis was beginning to want all of them.

A few seconds of silence passed before Isarion spoke. "The next two weeks will do you some good," he insisted. He glanced back at the dance floor with a tangible insecurity. "I hear there's nothing like a stay in Port Seraphine. Skiing, swimming, whatever you want, you know?" He avoided the inevitable subject of Natharis's recent disappointments.

"We'll see what my brother's in the mood for," Natharis replied. "But now that he's got two young kids, I might just have to go out on my own." He shrugged. "Not that I mind."

"He's also got a husband," Isarion retorted, "so I'm sure he could pass the kids off on him for a night or two. Don't be so—"

"Dull?" Natharis interjected. Isarion bit his tongue. "Don't worry about me. Believe it or not, I know how to have a good time. And despite what you might think, relaxation doesn't always require a drink in your hand. I'd rather raise my heart rate a little."

"If that's your idea of a good time, then you really must have loved that chase the other day."

Natharis didn't answer. As much as he didn't want to admit it, he did find the stress and sweat of the pursuit to be more than satisfying. Maybe he really was smitten with his work. Maybe he really didn't know how to step away from it, even for a day. That's what drove Kerinne away one morning, leaving only a letter of regret on their kitchen table. At least he knew that the duties he'd chosen over her would never leave him, as justice and liberty were forever. The Judicial ideals were there to stay, and so long as he called himself a

Colonial, he would be loyal to them. He just wished he could be faithful to two mistresses, but such a feat had so far proved impossible.

———

The Colonials had built the underground complex decades prior, for use by their first expedition teams. They'd come in small numbers and needed very little living space. Among the handful of engineers and ecologists came the construction workers, who tunneled deep into the barren earth to find refuge from the relentless suns. But what was once home to their own laborers became housing for those who found themselves working in the harsh daylight—those who otherwise had no home, and who had little hope of finding one.

Selas sat in one of many manmade chambers lit with glowing lanterns from niches in the walls. They'd been designed to provide light continuously for centuries. Selas wondered if they were always so dim, even when first installed. Whatever the case, they were proving to be less than useful. He didn't enjoy struggling to see past the shadows across his loved ones' faces. And when he could see them in the full light, the suns left him squinting, still struggling to see. He never really got used to the darkness or the daylight.

There were times he could recall sleeping under uselessly small tents in the torrential jungle rains of Xaztechua. He'd slept in a thin sleeping bag with sweat turned to frost somewhere in the depths of the Rosc Occupied Territories. He'd been bitten by leeches in the swampy wetlands of Vehisipen and subjected to every bizarre social custom on Pontchartrain. The Colonial-built caverns certainly weren't the worst of places to eat and sleep. But Selas couldn't help but feel like some sort of worm or subterranean rat. It was like they were living as animals in a nest—a hive of worker bees, with only a tiny patch of flowers to give them a drop of honey.

His mother Lina passed an old clay bowl across the table. She set it down before her son, careful not to fracture it in her hands, which were beginning to age far too early. The dirt under her fingernails revealed a toiling lifestyle that gave her the subtle wrinkles of a woman ten years her senior. Selas scooped up a serving of the rehydrated greens and slapped it onto his plate. The vegetables tasted bland, with a bitter aftertaste, but they weren't completely unpalatable. The milky white protein drink rinsed the flavor from his mouth and masked the damp, stale scent of the tunnels. It was like the air had its own flavor.

"This place is awful," he snapped, breaking the silence. He pushed away his plate. Even a normal speaking voice echoed off the cavern walls, and he seemed to be shouting. His father frowned; his mother's rebuttal was inevitable.

"Be that as it may, at least these Colonials aren't," she replied calmly.

"Can't say I'll miss them, though."

Even in the dim light, Selas could see his mother's scowl. She cleared her throat. "When was the last time we were given a place to sleep that we didn't have to build ourselves? Or when we didn't go to work hungry? Or when management didn't treat water rations like they were gold?"

Selas didn't know how to respond. His older sister set down her cup and joined in. "Point is, it's nice to be able to say we're not being exploited for once." She looked over at their father. "Right?"

Aiban nodded, crinkling the lines of his brow just beneath his rapidly graying hair. "With what we're making here, we might just be able to fix up some of the older ships in the caravan. We won't have to worry about getting stuck in the wrong sector again."

"Those Shatarins would've sold us into slavery if the Tellurians hadn't shown up," Evua added. "And even *they* didn't treat us that well."

"It would have been more than slavery," her father said, pointing at his wife and daughters, but didn't elaborate. Selas knew what he was implying. Evua, with her youthful beauty, would have been taken as a Shatarin bride; his little sister Ileya, far from being a woman at just four years old, would have been even more tempting to the perverted zealots of a twisted faith. And at Selas's age, it was more than likely that he, too, would have ended up in the bed of a wealthy Shatarin or shared by an insatiable gang of religious warriors. They were lucky that they'd been caught in the middle of a Tellurian-Shatarin skirmish. At least one party benefited from their war, however briefly.

"We didn't have to live in a *cave* working for the Imperium."

"No, but we *did* have to work with soldiers breathing down our necks," his mother answered. "And you saw the way they looked at me and your sisters. Thank the Creator that their superiors don't put up with scandals of that sort. Don't be so ungrateful. We raised you better than that."

"The Shatarins would have been honest enough to call us slaves. Not like these—"

His mother took his hand in hers to stop him from saying something foolish; her disappointment was as stinging as a slap to the face. "Don't say things like that. You know better. The Colonials have made us feel more at home than anyone ever has. So, don't try to bite the hand that feeds you—that feeds *us*, when we've gone hungry for so long."

Selas said nothing, nor did Evua, nor their father. His mother was right, and he knew it. Going to bed with a full stomach was a luxury he hadn't enjoyed in a long time. With the Colonials' never-ending supply of water, he rarely suffered thirst. And the bed he slept on, however small, was better than a makeshift tent or the hard, dusty ground. He had little to complain about, and yet he still did. It wasn't hunger, or thirst, or discomfort that kept him awake at night. It was knowing that, no matter how long the Gameer worked a planet, it would still never be theirs to keep.

The sailship was smaller than Livia expected, as was the group she was to travel with. She'd pictured a mammoth of a vessel with enough space to carry a small army and its effects, but the reality was far less grand. The cabin had only a few rows of seats, some of which were unoccupied. A guide sat ahead of her, a man with hair that had long since faded to gray, except for one curious lock of black at his right temple; she assumed he was a seasoned space traveler. Behind him were a priest and priestess, both silent, pensive, clad in white robes that hung from gold brooches at their shoulders, pulled tight at the waist with a woven cord. Three soldiers who would soon don ceremonial armor hadn't yet taken their seats. And to Livia's right sat a consitor who would one day become the *Patro Consitor*, the sacred Whore-Mother's eternal consort, his fate sealed as firmly as Livia's, held in the hands of the Pantheon's reverend pair.

He was a striking man who likely brought wide, grateful smiles to believers upon their first laying eyes on him. His formidable height was obvious, even when he sat slumped back in his seat. Livia imagined herself dwarfed by the consitor when the time came for them to step apprehensively down the ship's boarding ramp. He certainly fit the image of a consitor of Mars: his black hair with its gentle curls was cut just below the ears, and his powerful build led Livia to assume he served the voracious war god. His clothes, however, were a clean white like hers, in stark contrast to his god's traditional black and red. Form-fitting pants clung to his legs and bunched at the top of his boots. He left his jacket open, exposing a strong, broad chest and a hard stomach wrapped with strips of bleached cloth. Dressed like a consitor far beyond the temple threshold, his image was intimidating but intriguing, and unapologetically seductive.

"You're staring," he observed without introduction. The man turned his head to face an unsuspecting, and blushing, Livia. He shifted in his seat to teasingly clench the muscles of his chest and accentuate the undeniably impressive bulge between his thighs. *A typical consitor,* thought Livia, but she couldn't help herself from peeking. Her fingers tingled with temptation, but she didn't cave in to her curiosity. She'd be breaking her sacred vows. Her body was a temple for pilgrims, and no one else. To lie with a man of her choosing was sacrilege.

"I can't imagine you're not accustomed to it," she replied.

He smiled and held out his hand. "Silviano Martizo," the consitor announced. Livia shook his hand cordially. His name identified his cultic devotion—he was an earthly vicar of Mars, marked by the imposed title of a descriptive surname. She returned the greeting: "Livia Nettunaya." She, too, had been given a new name years ago.

Neptune and Mars were the patrons of the pilgrimage; a hundred years prior, another divine pair presided over their servants' journey to the sacred city of their ancestors. And Livia and Silviano, the gods' representatives, were the ones responsible for the pilgrims' ecstatic experience. It was an honor that commanded the utmost respect, but Livia still found herself disquieted. She wondered if her counterpart felt the same, but she accepted that she was likely alone in her shame. The other altarias and consitores took great pride in their carnal prophethood. They were the Pantheon's emissaries, and conduits of the divine.

"Was the Patro Consitor as vague about our role as the sacred Whore-Mother?" Livia asked. She was still unsure of what part she was to play in the pilgrimage, departing so much sooner than the rest of the flock. She had no idea of what the sacred city even looked like.

"Upon arrival, we'll spend the first lunar month in prayer and religious observation," Silviano explained, "and naturally, we'll tend to the needs of the early pilgrims around us." He pointed his finger in an arc around the cabin; the other passengers were unaware that he was privy to the desires they didn't even know they had. "And when the first wave arrives—you know, the Imperial Senators, the wealthy and maybe even the Praetor himself—we'll forget what it's like to sleep. The patricians won't even set foot in Rome without their proper blessing."

"You've been to the city before?"

Silviano looked back at Livia as though she couldn't possibly be serious. "No one's been there in a hundred years. I might be the god's living lance, but I'm not immortal." He noticed Livia's hands folded in her lap, like she guarded herself. "And neither are you," he said ominously. "So, unless you want a real painful pilgrimage, you'd best start taking twice as much *vacibia* as normal."

The nauseating bitterness of vacibia root was something Livia, even after years of temple servitude, couldn't get used to. But its unpleasant taste was a small price to pay for its almost supernatural benefits. Without it, she could have easily become the mother of an innumerable brood of children, fathered by the nameless pious. Indeed, all the altarias would have endured the pain of childbirth, and the Imperial Temple would have been more reminiscent of a crowded Xaztechuan tenement building than a house of the divine. Each altaria made sure to remember her daily regimen, slowly and unhappily chewing the fibrous, dry root each morning and night. The plant's anesthetic properties weren't lost on Livia, either. It left her body numb and distanced from her mind. It masked the dull ache of sexual evangelism and relaxed her ever-tense muscles. Best of all, in larger doses, it induced a brief amnesia, an illusion of repose from the work that too often kept her awake at night.

She envied Silviano and his spiritual brothers. If a believing woman left their company with the god's seed growing inside her, her family—her husband, even—would celebrate her pleasing the god so profoundly. The only diet the consitores adhered to was one of red meats for strength and copious wine for spiritual endurance. Their visitors' offerings were always accepted by the gods without fail. They never had to suffer a pilgrim who tried time and time again to make a worthy sacrifice but never succeeded in doing so. The consitores would one day step down from their duties and never look back. Livia and the altarias, however, would carry the scars of their servitude for the rest of their lives. She'd read once that, according to the top medical researchers on Aldebaran-Zion, heavy consumption of vacibia root meant only a barren future.

"I don't mean to scare you," Silviano apologized. "At the end of the day, I'm sure it'll be a rewarding experience. Remember: We're doing—"

"—the gods' work," Livia interjected. Silviano swallowed his words and nodded. An uncomfortable silence fell between them. The consitor was audibly excited to bring spiritual solace to throngs of Tellurian women far from home. His prideful smile gave it away. Livia prayed he wouldn't notice the doubt in her voice, the apprehension. While they lived in the same temple and served the same graven gods, they lived completely different lives. Each moan of a believer beneath his weight strengthened his faith in his own prophethood, while for Livia, every pious man's body simply crushed her spirit even more.

Silviano opened his mouth to respond, no doubt critically, but a digital voice over the intercom cut him off. *"The vessel has been cleared for liftoff,"* it announced without a shred of emotion, though meant to emulate a female. *"All passengers and personnel should remain seated for the duration of the surface-to-orbit procedure."*

Livia did her best to hide her nervousness. She associated interstellar travel with the day she left her family behind. She'd cried through the entire ordeal, shedding tears for the life in the countryside of Dea Vena that she was forced to abandon. They expected a girl of fourteen years to find honor in serving the Pantheon, but they were met with youthful resistance. She'd lost everything, everyone. It was a scar she feared would never heal. But those around her on the tiny sailship would have cited the spiritual healing she had in store for her, and for the pilgrims to come. She didn't have any desire to hear the white lies they told each other. For the time being, she kept quiet.

The sailship's captain elaborated on the announcement, with its monotonous, electronic cadence. His voice was unexpectedly shrill, somewhat raspy, like he'd spent his life smoking an excess of Colonial sativa or their highly marketable, mutagen-free cigarettes. "We'll regroup with our military escorts in orbit and stock up on humanitarian supplies from Leto. One last minute announcement: we will be making a quick stop at Gebaliya on our way to Earth to deliver said supplies, and then we'll be on our way. It won't delay the travel time by much, I promise you," he explained, though neither Livia nor Silviano believed him. "Once we've entered the tachyon vein, it'll be safe to leave your seats. The passenger beds are located at the stern of the ship, should you decide to retire. So please, enjoy your trip, and honor the pilgrimage. We thank you for doing the gods' work."

3

"The Aether is neither here nor there, but exists both here and there simultaneously. It is its own dimension in space and time, though it cannot exist except as an extension of our reality. The stars in this physical universe are cogs in the galaxy's intangible machine, and they keep the tachyon veins flowing for billions of years. Whether natural or built at the hands of the ancient Procyon, we may never know, as the Procyon alone have the capacity to know its true nature, though their race would never enlighten us to such a timeless mystery."

—Popular historian Charlize Blaauw of the Isolate State of Windsor Anglostralia

NATHARIS ARRIVED AT THE EXOPORT just before sunrise, and after a short flight to Hudson, it was daylight. Friedman Exoport, his local flight's port of departure from Chesapeake to the city of Hudson, had no direct flights to Seraphine; it hosted only domestic travelers within the confines of the Vega system. It was dwarfed by Hudson's most prominent passenger space elevator, Thoreau Interplanetary Exoport, from which Natharis would ascend to the heavens and into the darkness of space. The sprawling anchor station for the orbital bridge was bustling with people in business suits and tourists from all corners of the Convergency. It was the heart of nearly all off-world travel on Acadica, and Natharis, like countless others, would climb to orbit along the titanic cable that stretched far beyond the clouds.

Security personnel scanned his identification card as he passed by three officers with their leashed, bomb-sniffing dogs. After several seconds of digital baggage inspection, Natharis entered Thoreau's main terminal. He'd heard it sometimes took hours to successfully traverse security in the Commune. They had a puzzling fetish for the institutionalized harassment of innocent travelers—a process considered horrifying and abusive in the Colonies. Thankfully, Natharis saw nothing of the sort while walking toward his assigned waiting area.

Through the observation windows that spanned the walls' height and width, he watched as crescent rings accelerated up the nearest orbital bridge, a miles-long cable that connected the anchoring exoport with the pier up in orbit. On the opposite side of the cable, another ring made its descent and gracefully settled upon the platform. It would only be a few minutes before the transport cycle restarted, bringing another excited batch of passengers up to the orbital pier, and another to the outskirts of Acadica's largest city.

Natharis remembered how Thoreau's orbital bridges cast shadows upon the fields where he grew up, even from miles away. They always towered in the distance as permanent fixtures on the horizon, stretching upward across the sun and moon as they rose and fell over the Ruke family farm. They were in the background of every photograph of Natharis and his brother Sebasteon riding horses in their childhood. And when Natharis helped his father and his workers in the fields as a young man, the titanic cables stood behind them, like corn or great sheaves of wheat. Even when he and his older sister cut flowers for his mother's floral shop, they were there, always watching, always far away.

He'd ride toward them on his favorite horse, Lincoln, but never quite made it close enough. The bridges looked like solid lines from the farm, but an adult Natharis would come to see them as bundles of black, carbon fiber cables, bound together like woven tree trunks as mighty as the ancient redwoods of Catskills-Atlantic. Even farther, on Hudson's eastern border, rose the forest of freight elevators, each the thickness of twelve or more passenger bridges, and even more inaccessible to a young farm boy with his icy blue eyes set on the sky above.

A bell tone and the hiss of sliding doors brought Natharis back to the present, to the calm, orderly footsteps of passengers in single file. It was time for him to board the now empty car; he did so with little delay or frustration. Children flocked to the windowed wall, chattering and pointing at the sights below as the group began their ascent to orbit. Natharis opted to sit along the inner wall and close his eyes. He didn't expect to catch any sleep in the five minutes it'd take to reach the pier. Though he couldn't see their faces, he smiled when he heard the youngest travelers gasp in awe of the city they were leaving behind. He pictured them pressing their faces into the glass, gawking at the sunlit skyscrapers and their neo-Gothic design. They'd tug on their parents' shirts to ask about the city's unmistakable monuments that filled the gaps between the meticulously planned roads—"That's the Fountainhead Memorial," fathers would explain, "and over there is the marble Arch of Free Will."

The ecstatic cries and laughter announced their breaking of the sky's untouchable barrier, and they passed beyond the limits of the atmosphere to heights lit only by lamps and delicate starlight. The orbital pier floated above them, tethered by the cables and bound to Acadica by its heavily trafficked surface anchor, Thoreau. It appeared just seconds after the car began to decelerate. The pier was grander than any passenger had imagined, if they felt as Natharis did when he first laid eyes upon it. Rings within rings encircled the cables stretching down to terra firma, each dotted with docking bays and observation domes, providing shelter to the countless vessels and travelers to the bustling heart of the Colonies.

Natharis looked down at his ticket—*Gate 36-B: Flight 1021 to Port Seraphine*, it read. The scheduled departure time was just a half hour away. And in a mere two days' time, traveling at a speed along the Main Line that made light seem to crawl, he'd be lying on the famous beaches of Seraphine. He'd feel the sun on his bare skin and the salty breeze across his face. It'd be strange to take a break from his duties, the only life he really knew. But his friends were right—a break was exactly what he needed, and when he returned to Chesapeake with a tan and a well-rested smile, he'd never hear the end of it.

The caravan was already in deep space by the time Selas opened his sleep-sealed eyes. The last images in his head before his descent into unconsciousness were remnants of labor and melancholy. The world he'd helped to one day grow fertile shrank away into the dark, and the hot desert winds were replaced with the eternal winter between stars. His sweat had been long since wiped away, the dust washed from his clothes, but still the fading vista haunted his half-waking mind, which no hot shower could cleanse of what lingered.

But once he'd crossed the threshold of sleep, unpleasant memories gave way to nightmares. The ghost of Worldbuilder Enterprises vanished. The arid surface disappeared into a blinding white light. Selas realized he was naked, a state marked not by shame, but vulnerability. While all he saw was featureless light, he perceived the environment as confined, like he was standing in a room full of hidden spotlights. The chamber's shape was revealed when a shadow seeped out of a corner like smoke. And floating in the dark were two piercing eyes: black, blacker than the shadow that framed them.

He felt their cold gaze reach deep into his mind, turning his thoughts into hazy memories and his fear into a tacit compliance. He knew what was coming, but he didn't know how, or why, he knew. The eyes, and whatever creature they belonged to, wanted to subdue him; what would come after, he had no idea, but he feared he was staring into the face of death itself. The eyes were just inches away, so close to taking him—then the sound of space debris rapping on the walls brought him back to consciousness.

Selas wasn't sure what to make of it. Normally, he didn't remember his dreams, and any recollection was brief and vague. He knew there was probably more to the horrifying encounter invented in the twisted depths of his subconscious mind. Thankfully, he couldn't recall it.

The faith he was raised in—the tenets of the Mithneshi priesthood—elevated dreams to the level of personal prophecy. As a child, he was once quite close with a priestess of the Mithneshi Coven, but that was some time ago. She would have found significance in his dreams, and would have pushed him to learn more about them. Sadly, she was long gone, and he didn't have her words of wisdom to guide him. Years had passed, and he sometimes had difficulty remembering her name, though he tried not to forget it.

Selenia would have known what to do. She would have had answers. Ever since she moved on from tending to his people, he'd been left only with questions. His parents couldn't hope to answer them all.

He looked toward the rusty porthole and was surprised to see stars. The caravan had exited the small tachyon vein they'd been following, now drifting in interstellar space. The Gameer made it a point to periodically enter free space in the hope of intercepting the radio transmissions characteristic of a fledgling settlement. If they managed to find one of the countless, uncharted colonies scattered throughout the

Interstellar Convergency, they'd offer their services in exchange for basic necessities. Sometimes, the colonists were quick to hire them; other times, the Gameer had no choice but to disappear back into the vein they'd been traversing for weeks, maybe months. The colonists weren't always peaceful, or willing to trust a band of cosmic gypsies. It was always a game of chance.

The tired groan of the aetherium crucibles reverberated throughout the ship. Its vibrations rattled the empty glass of water on his shelf. It'd be a few minutes before they were primed for incision. The crucibles were decades too old for use on such a large convoy. They were a liability, preventing a quick escape from Shatarin corsairs or meddlesome Convergency patrols. Most of the wealth earned through hard labor went directly to the maintenance of their technological hand-me-downs. Selas couldn't remember a single time when the drives didn't need some kind of work.

He was unsure of their location, where they'd stopped to hopelessly pursue a new place to serve with sweat and tears. Neither did he know where they'd go once they'd gone back into the invisible veins. He wanted to fall back asleep, to ignore the voices of technicians without formal training and women hurrying their children to their rooms in preparation for the reentry into the Aether. But he worried he'd slip right back into the hazy nightmare he'd awoken from. The hum of the sleepy engines was there to rock him to sleep, almost like a person who was always breathing down his neck, though he wished he was in the comforting presence of the young priestess he once knew, but who'd left him and his people long ago in pursuit of a higher calling.

———

Natharis awoke to a slight but unanticipated vibration on his seat, then a sudden stop. He thought for a moment that they'd reached Seraphine, but upon attaining full consciousness, he realized the source of the trembling was much less exciting. His timepiece, set to silent, had received a new message.

Natharis put aside the Old Earth individualist literature he'd placed in his lap and hazily eyed the device. It glowed with a holographic notification displayed clearly an inch or so above its face. His mother and father had left him a recording via the League of Arterra's e-courier system, implemented centuries ago, through which messages traveled faster than light. The postal clip began with Dienne Ruke's distinctly Carolinian drawl.

"Happy travels from Tel Zahav!" his mother began, smiling maternally into the camera. She had recorded the message in a luxury hotel. Its décor was a kind of desert-chic, with quilt-like curtains billowing in the open windows. The walls were white stucco, and the windowpanes painted a bold shade of blue, with a lush, potted fern standing tall between each. Johannes Ruke sat on a brown leather couch to the side, an open book beside him; he stood up and knelt next to his wife to greet his son, though he wasn't quite sure where the camera was or where he should have been looking.

"We've finally got a chance to relax and take in the sights now that your father's surgery is over," she said. Her husband required treatment for a tumor they'd recently discovered in his digestive tract. A minor procedure in the renowned medical centers of Aldebaran-Zion was all that was needed, and she happily recalled that they'd gotten in and out of the hospital in just under an hour. "But you know your father's colon," she laughed. "Always causing problems."

With the click of a button Dienne uploaded a series of digital vignettes they'd taken throughout their well-deserved trip. They'd managed to take the time to visit the capital, Shiloh—smaller than Tel Zahav, but just as significant, if not more. The Third Temple revered by the Beyit Ha-Shem and the Enlightened Church of the Nazarene was more stunning than Natharis ever imagined. His mother apologized that they didn't manage to get a photo of its Foundation Stone, carried from the ruins of Old Earth and set at the heart of the Temple. Apparently, the Zionese had security concerns, given their long, tumultuous history with the Shatarin Empire and its persistent threats. Aldebaran-Zion was always a microcosm of the greater Convergency, where the medieval Shatarin religion was at irreconcilable odds with all other systems of thought. It was endlessly frustrating. Natharis's parents were lucky that they hadn't been witness to any suicide bombings.

He closed the postal clip and his timepiece darkened. He wouldn't be able to fall back asleep; he hadn't even expected to doze off in the first place, and if he had, he would have certainly retired to the passenger beds behind him. Instead, he tapped the screen set in the back of the seat before him and watched it come to life. As was typical of Colonial television, most programs were objective news broadcasts, galactic history documentaries, or sharply witted sitcoms, with the occasional reality show that was only to be watched as a guilty pleasure. After browsing through a few options, Natharis settled on a broadcast of one of many Vega 1 News reports. The renowned journalist Misha Matsumoto spoke, her eyes so focused that he felt as if she were talking only to him.

ABAC Executive Brock Dunham was at it again—this time, making a personal attack on the Colonial executive councilman, Desh Maru. He was livid at Executive Maru's decision to veto yet another bill that would have written a new, suffocating tax into interstellar law. Executive Maru, an upstanding Colonial, had expressed his disgust at the proposition of a charge of fifteen thousand Convergent lira on all tachyon incision points in the Outer Rim. He described its unavoidable consequences, stating that such a law would only drive shipping companies into bankruptcy, and that the entire Convergency would see a massive spike in prices. But Executive Dunham, in a fury so common among the corporatist collectivists, scoffed at the idea of taxation at minimal levels.

In his usual frustration at the progression of current events, Natharis swore to himself that he wouldn't lay eyes upon a single television screen while spending his time in Port Seraphine. If he were to enjoy any media, it would be as it was in his childhood, when he and the family would sit in the parlor and listen to any number of scheduled radio programs—a tradition fostered by the Colonials for as long as anyone could remember. There was no irritation or bother in following the radio serials that kept Colonial homes entertained every night. He was sure, however, that there would be plenty of pastimes on Seraphine. He imagined the sound of crashing waves and swimmers splashing in the water. Even the simple thought brought him away. He would enjoy his peace in isolation and forget all the problems that raged on outside the Colonies, always threatening to creep across their borders. On a beach in Port Seraphine, no one, not even the political elite or their ravenous electorate, could bother him.

As the diplomatic sailship slipped out of the tachyon vein back into free space, Desh Maru grew anxious. His disquiet wasn't necessarily rooted in fear, or the dread of something malignantly alien, but out of the limited comprehension of the sight he'd soon see. He'd seen it before, time and time again, but no matter how many times he'd laid eyes upon the Veil of Bhalenjar, he never became accustomed to it, or numb to its powerful beauty.

The official Colonial craft flashed instantly out of the invisible Main Line through the megalithic framework of a tachyon lens, often called rabbit holes by pilots and passengers alike. The vessel was met with a glorious view of the Veil, ancient and unfathomable. The Colonial executive gazed upon vast clouds of ethereal violet, coral and cerulean, interlaced with wisps of brilliant amethyst like a Bhalenjari Caspian's alien eyes. The awe-inspiring nebula was thick, seemingly impenetrable, and glowed with an inner fire, the light of a central star radiating outward like rays through a cloudy sky. To those who'd never passed through its haze, whatever was hidden beyond the Veil was unknowable. But Desh knew what lay ahead, and it made the Veil seem unimpressive and mundane.

The approach began in the artificial light of traffic beacons guiding the sailship's path. The delta-shaped craft cut through the nebula, shimmering with copper and chrome. Bhalenjari Orbital Traffic Control technicians chattered through the cabin, dictating the sailship's course. They drew attention to an unseen gap in the clouds lying just a few minutes ahead. Desh knew his voyage would soon come to an end. Then, his work would commence.

The crest of Bhalenjar's outline was nascent in the distance. The sun peeked over the smooth curve of its atmospheric blanket and cast light on a structure unlike anything in the known galaxy. It was like a scaffold of precious stones rising up from the planet's surface, a Jacob's ladder stretching thousands of miles into the heavens. The interlaced spheres of diamond and glass spiraled through the emptiness of space, bound by formidable beams of gold and untarnished silver, crafted in the likeness of a titanic strand of DNA. Its organic structure revealed its past as a masterpiece of Procyon engineering. Now in the hands of the very Sapiens they had observed, altered and experimented upon, it served as the seat of the Interstellar Convergency, and all those who represented, or claimed to represent, its people.

The traffic congested as the hundreds of lanes ran closer to the Convergency's capital city. Desh more clearly examined the residential spheres, spotted with the living green of foliage and patches of rich, dark soil. The spheres rotated slowly in place; the double helix of the tower was more animate than visible from a distance. The civilian residents were given a pristine sunrise and sunset, with high noon sparkling with the tower's golden framework stretching across the sky.

Across the urban continent with its rings of skyscrapers, thousands of miles from the tower's base, a soft but brilliant light shone from a beacon on the surface. Desh, a Colonial, was quite familiar with the Mithneshi Coven, and a believer in their religious teachings. Mithneshi Deism was a widespread faith in the Colonies, and he was well versed in it. He'd known since childhood that the order held a deep reverence for the ancient Ziggurat that pierced the clouds of Bhalenjar. And the great lamp at its highest tier, like a torch burning with the divine power of the Creator, guided the lost and pious alike to His most sacred altar. Desh did his best to visit the Ziggurat before every political session he was obliged to endure. Each time, he prayed for patience.

He was about to oversee a Congressional session, along with the other executives. Not only did he have to suffer the unrealistic idealism of the Executive Council, but he, like the others, also presided over all Senatorial riots and Parliamentary scuffles. Professional and dignified, he did so without pretentiousness or complaint. He'd been elected by the people of the United Colonies of Acadia, and they considered him a strong, eloquent (and undeniably handsome) leader. Citizens of the Colonies looked to him for loyal representation; the insatiable population of the Commune labeled him an extremist and a bigot. No matter how much evidence he provided in support of his nation's policies and its popular opinions, there was a mob that despised him. The Commune wanted him deposed, while the Shatarins wanted him dead. But there were also the moral and moderate that supported him, whose interests he would never lose sight of. He held his office with the deepest gratitude. His people needed him. There were far too many threats to their freedom for him to be weak.

———

The city of Roma Ceisora was an elegant union of the ancient and the spectacularly modern. At its heart stood *l'Orbe Antica*, the Old City, with its triumphant arches, marble temples and ancient arenas, nestled in the hills of the planet's oldest settlement. Over the centuries the capital expanded outward, and its buildings, upward, until the Old City looked like a small clearing in a forest of shimmering skyscrapers. From the edge of Roma Ceisora, history was obscured by innovation, but from above, it was clear that the past was always Telluria's focus.

The last time Livia gazed down upon the city of Roma Ceisora, she'd cried and looked away. No longer a fourteen-year old forced to make a home of a strange world, she simply peered through the window and kept her wistful thoughts to herself. She told herself there'd come a day when travel wasn't for a reason in which she had no say. It'd be for a vacation, a holiday, some occasion that had everything to do with freedom and nothing to do with obligation.

She wasn't afraid, though there was plenty reason to be. They were the first group of Tellurians to embark on the pilgrimage to Earth, and the Shatarins, with their hateful, unforgiving religion, certainly knew the solemn rite was under way. The barbarians would never pass up an opportunity to ambush an entire crew in deep space, where there'd be no one to save their victims. The Imperium was well aware of this, and had posted a legion of military escorts for the pilgrims' sailship around Telluria's aristocratic moon, Leto. Livia had an apprehensive tension in the pit of her stomach, a concern she couldn't place. It wasn't so much a fear of a Shatarin raid as it was a sense that something was coming. She wasn't sure what it was, or when such an event might happen. She seemed alone in her deep-rooted worry. Silviano was unaffected, and instead leaned over toward the window like an excited child on his first flight.

As the craft rose high into the air from the Imperial Temple's private dock, the arches and dome-capped buildings shrank into the hazy blue of the receding ground, and the Romanesque skyscrapers of Roma Ceisora became tiny pins and needles. The blue of the sky turned to black, marked only by the beautiful curve of the planet below them. Livia waited for Leto to come into view, but she dreaded the coming moment, as the sight of the patrician moon would be the sign that there was no going back. When she saw the speckles of massive, sprawling villas and artificial lakes, and when she looked upon the formidable fleet waiting for them, she would finally be forced to accept her responsibilities. She'd be in the depths of space, with nowhere to go but Earth, which waited ominously at the end of a tachyon vein like a nameless man in the chapel doorway.

The man's accent was distinctly Colonial, and he spoke with the same cadence of his ancestors in seminal America. His tone was calm but confident, lending a comforting effect to his voice that didn't wake Livia, but added a captivating depth to her dream. His silhouette—dark, vague, but with icy blue eyes that seemed to glow—leaned toward her and whispered.

"Are you awake?"

A wave of goose bumps crested across Livia's skin and through her body, bringing her back to consciousness. Her sailship was idling above the surface of an alien world, surrounded by a fleet of a hundred Tellurian triremes, though the escorts were only a small portion of the much greater, much more powerful Armada—the greatest military force of the galactic Inner Rim. The tingling, stupefying sensation was part of a standard security procedure employed by the Arterrans; when the feeling faded away, the aetherium warhead sensors had confirmed her sailship's civilian status, devoid of any weapons of mass destruction. After the remote examination, the ship began its descent, and the blotchy, thin layer of delicate clouds was just a blur, as the scanners had left her groggy and disoriented.

Livia came to her senses and realized that the hollow darkness of space just inches away from her face was now a foreign landscape, one she'd never encountered. In place of the lush greenery and calming rains of Telluria, this planet,

Gebaliya, was marked with short-standing mountains and rocky, dry steppe. The city of Bridjibreel in the distance was an oasis; the buildings, crafted in the traditional Phoenician style, were nestled in low strips of trees that lined the streets, and a single, great aqueduct ran from the hills into the heart of the settlement. The transformation of desolation into a small paradise could only have been the work of the Arterrans—and the Arterrans were Gebaliya's protectors against a horde of hostile neighbors.

She heard the hiss and groan of the cargo bay doors opening and a thud when the ramp touched the ground. Gebaliyan workers approached the sailship and started unloading the humanitarian supplies, packaged in large polymer crates. On magnetized carts they pushed the crates away from the ship toward the gaping mouth of a hovering truck. Livia expected that they'd return to orbit once they exchanged the provisions; she was surprised, however, to hear the passenger doors slide open.

Silviano, with his years of study in the history of galactic war, remarked on the proceedings. "Gebaliya's known for its compulsive suspicions," he noted, standing up from his seat with his hand on Livia's. "They've probably insisted on meeting the civilian party that gave them those provisions. A historical, all-too-familiar fear of foreign invasion will make people do that."

"Shatarins, I take it?"

"Who else?" Silviano replied with a smile. Livia found his humor inappropriate. The Shatarins engaged in unspeakable things that shouldn't be trivialized in jest.

The captain's voice came over the intercom. *"All pilgrims, please exit the cabin. This won't take more than a few minutes."* Livia felt he was lying, or at least exaggerating, and prepared herself for a drawn-out and inconvenient greeting in the hot sun. The passengers rose from their seats and descended the exit ramp. They were met by a group of Gebaliyan workers, recognizable by the tan, almost sandy color of their skin.

Before them stood a portly man, whose pale complexion caught Livia's eye. He undoubtedly hailed from elsewhere. He spoke first in broken Tellurian—comprehensible, but only after a mental adjustment to his awkward, Anglic-based pronunciation.

"Welcome to Gebaliya, kind pilgrims," he began. He stepped forward and shook the captain's hand, flashing a crooked smile of pale-yellow teeth. The man wore a white shirt and solid-color tie, his hair combed carefully to the side, though the winds were starting to dishevel it. He was grossly overweight, and the fabric of his shirt buckled between its failing buttons. The ID tag clipped to his sagging shirt pocket identified him as Mickel Green; his boldly printed name was joined by the unmistakable logo of the Albian Banking Advancement Conglomerate, a bright ring encircling a stylized molecule of aetherium crafted in red, black and white. Livia was deeply confused by ABAC's presence on an Arterran protectorate, though the Conglomerate must have had at least a handful of branches throughout the League of Arterra. The Arterrans weren't a people with a history of financial restrictions.

"It's so refreshing to see someone *other* than Colonials or their pawns," Mr. Green remarked without letting go of the captain's hand. He continued his handshake just a few seconds too long for comfort. "I'm *quite* the Tellurophile, you should know. *Fascinating* culture. And now that you're *all* starting to realize ABAC's good intentions, you're even *better* in my book—though it isn't difficult for me to prefer *anyone* over the Arterrans. Wouldn't you agree?"

The party remained silent, though the captain begrudgingly expressed his agreement. Livia didn't have much of an opinion on the Arterrans, but Mr. Green seemed to have a strong enough opinion for the both of them, if not the entire group. He introduced himself as a local representative of the Albian Banking Advancement Conglomerate, and that his role was to enforce Arterran compliance with ABAC's right to business. Interestingly, he didn't mention anything about ensuring his own branch's adherence to local law. It either wasn't worthy of mention, or, even more likely, he simply didn't care about legality.

"The Albian Banking Advancement Conglomerate has expressed its desire for my presence on your voyage," he announced. "Ah, *pilgrimage*—forgive me for my incorrect terminology. You're not offended, are you?" He looked concerned.

"Not at all," the captain assured him. "Though I have to ask you, and with all due respect: What business do you have with a religious rite you won't be participating in?"

Mr. Green laughed but seemed annoyed that the captain would dare to question ABAC's desires. He not-so-subtly reminded the party that ABAC's interests were Telluria's interests. "And, as you must understand, there are things that our corporate management knows that *you* do not and *will* not. My presence on your ship is *confidential*, as is my business. But I promise you that you won't even know I'm there." He cracked a rotting smile. "And when we reach Earth, you won't have to see me again."

The Gebaliyans who accompanied Mickel Green didn't say much, let alone engage in the paranoia-driven interrogation that Silviano had inaccurately predicted. Ultimately, they didn't ask a single question, and simply stood behind the ABAC representative with frustrated looks on their faces. There was a palpable tension in the air, rooted no doubt in the Gebaliyans' distrust of ABAC, or any group aligned with its policies. The fact that the Conglomerate was an unwavering supporter of any and all things Shatarin wasn't conducive to a warm welcome, either.

While ABAC and Gebaliya may have had conflicting interests, Gebaliya and the Tellurian Imperium both shared a common bond of a long, violent history with the Shatarin Empire. The Gebaliyans may have found their own world after their forced exile at the Shatarins' hands, and consequently found peace, but the Tellurians' Holy Vendetta was still being waged, and neither Telluria, nor the Shatarins, seemed willing to be the first to call for a ceasefire. Livia's people had plunged into the religious war for generations, and she was raised in a culture of conflict and martial duty against its enemies. Even in her own mind, she was at war, fighting a battle between spiritual honor and terrible shame. And like her people and the barbarians who hoped to slaughter them, she had little hope for lasting peace.

4

"In the full lexicon of Millennial Anglic, there are over three dozen synonyms of 'responsibility,' each carrying its own specific nuance. Interestingly, there is no true concept of 'entitlement.'"
—The Zgl'jan Language Group Linguistic Report, 2851 Æx.

IT DIDN'T TAKE LONG for Natharis to pass through the Arelim Deferment Facility, through which all visitors to the Tartarus system passed as their first security checkpoint. The procedure was simple enough, mainly because of his status as a well-decorated investigative marshal. Natharis presented his badge and identification, stated his business and duration of stay, and was sent on his way. Most people around him were relatives of workers in Tartarus, whose immediate families lived in the seaside paradise of Port Seraphine. The Tartarus personnel worked a three- or four-day shift, then returned to their loved ones for the remainder of the week, replacing the crushing gravity of Hades and the deadly cold of Jotunheim with sun and clear skies. Natharis's brother

Sebasteon was one such worker, whose husband and newborn twins faithfully awaited his return each week.

The shuttle ride revealed a jewel set in the shadow of a deep blue gas giant. It glimmered in the sunlight like an opal, and the soft curve of its atmosphere was a brilliant but delicate shield. The paradisal moon was painted with white-tipped strokes of mountains, patches of sea foam and aquamarine, and smears of emerald forests. As the shuttle began the last phase of its descent, the city of Port Seraphine emerged through the clouds, a bright crescent clinging to the shores of a warm, tropical bay. It was Seraphine's only settlement, and it wasn't a city that boasted towering skyscrapers of unrivaled stature or bustling six-lane boulevards. Its buildings were short, at most five or six stories tall, and they were made of white stone, not glass or chrome. Palm trees and orchids lined the streets, not streetlamps and awestruck tourists. The city certainly lived up to its reputation as a paradise in the inferno. Natharis wasn't disappointed.

He donned his sunglasses the moment he stepped out onto the street, baggage in hand, with his unnecessary jacket draped over his shoulder. The roads were designed for bicyclists, paved with two bicycle lanes for each auto lane, though there wasn't much traffic. The beach was just across the street. The sand was a dazzling white, a soft blanket beneath children drying off after a swim, and a bed for their young mothers who worked effortlessly at achieving the perfect tan. Natharis thought he could hear music in the distance, but it might have been the hollow clatter of wooden wind chimes rustling in the soothing ocean breeze.

He didn't know how his brother meant to grab his attention upon arrival; all he knew was that Sebasteon was supposed to have been there a good ten minutes ago. He stood on the sidewalk, looking from side to side, upset with himself for not having dressed appropriately for Port Seraphine weather. A jogger passed uncomfortably close behind him. The man stood running his place, his shorts swishing up and down at his knees. In the heat, he was exercising with a shirt left in his closet. The hard muscles of his chest bounced under his skin as he maintained his raised heart rate. His body was accustomed to the Seraphine sun and his skin had darkened to a healthy bronze, enhancing the icy blue of his eyes that marked him as a Ruke. He exhaled strongly and spoke before fully catching his breath.

"What? Expecting a Wessex convertible?" he asked. Sebasteon bent down, hands on his knees, then wiped the sweat from his brow. Mostly recovered, he straightened his back. "Missed my run this morning. Besides, I figured you of all people wouldn't mind a short walk."

The irony was that Sebasteon, the Tartarus Judicial Complex's most experienced criminal psychologist, could probably afford himself a Wessex auto meticulously crafted in the factories of the Kingdom of Windsor Britannia. In fact, he could likely afford one several times over, but Natharis questioned if Sebasteon or his husband owned an auto at all, as he'd never seen one during any of his visits to the Ruke-Wilhelms family's coastal, sunny-skied home. But with the recent birth of their twins Cadren and Johannes, the new fathers would soon be in the market for a more family-oriented vehicle, since infants weren't well fit for jogging.

Natharis adjusted his shirt, which was beginning to cling to his back, gradually growing damp with sweat in the hot sun. He smiled and outstretched his arms as if to hug his brother, but Sebasteon waved him away, reminding him of just how disheveled he was after his run. The ensuing conversation was effortless and adamant. It'd been too long since Natharis last saw him, and they had much to catch up on.

"Tobias's hotel has been ranked number one in the latest travel reviews," Sebasteon declared proudly; "We finally got our best lead yet in hunting down Qorbanin Vashtaan," Natharis revealed without mentioning his integral involvement. Sebasteon looked at him as though he knew there was more to the story, but he didn't say it. Surely, he'd seen the news reports and assumed that the dedicated marshal could have been none other than his overachieving little brother.

Sebasteon must have been equally aware of the disappointment surrounding Natharis's failed engagement. Natharis wasn't even sure if he'd told his brother about Kerinne and all that had befallen their relationship, but there was no doubt that their mother would have been quick to inform him. Sebasteon didn't mention it, though he made subtle hints, using his skills as a psychologist in an attempt to pry out the truth. It irritated Natharis that he was being treated like one of the interrogated criminals of Tartarus, whose lies and truths were discerned by the expert mind of Sebasteon Ruke-Wilhelms. When asked how his love life was going—*He knows,* thought Natharis—he replied that he'd chased a couple fugitives at work. It was a deflection, but one that revealed just a bit too much of reality.

Tobias was waiting in the parlor when they returned, rocking one infant in his arms while feeding the other a spoonful of puréed squash. The instant the babies laid eyes on Sebasteon in the doorway, they burst into a crying frenzy, to which Tobias could only groan in frustration. He handed off one child to his husband and rushed to tend to the screaming baby in his highchair, whose face was wet with spilt food. Sebasteon forced a smile at Natharis—"Sorry for the mess," he apologized—and worked to calm Cadren, who whined incessantly in his arms. But Johannes, like his grandfather of the same name, quieted down as easily as he was irritated, most easily in the arms of Tobias, rather than Sebasteon with his reddened face.

The warm sea breeze carried away the last squeals of unhappy infants as it wafted through the open windows and rustled the ethereal, white curtains. The house became quiet and Sebasteon sighed, exhausted. Tobias whispered to his husband and the two tiptoed to the twins' room, each with an infant clutched to his chest, as silently as possible, out of a fear of waking them. They disappeared into the hall and came back empty handed, the twins in their cradles, rocked away by the sound of the waves just a short walk away.

"Once again, everything was going *fine* until Sebasteon came along," Tobias complained, but rubbed his husband's shoulder to lessen the blow of his grievances. "If there's anyone who needs a vacation here, it's us. Don't get me wrong, I love them to death—but honestly, for ten thousand Talents each, you'd think they'd be a little quieter." He laughed to himself. "I should have watched our surrogate a little more closely. Who knows what the bitch was eating behind our backs?"

He hugged Natharis and welcomed him to their home, which, he explained over and over again, would have been immaculately clean if Sebasteon had given him ample time to prepare—"He clearly just wants to embarrass me," he stated, playfully shoving Sebasteon in the shoulder. Tobias presented the place as if Natharis had never seen it before, but Natharis allowed him his lapse of memory, and pretended not to recognize the stone-top island, the state-of-the-art media center, and the wine cellar stocked with bottles from the Tellurian Imperium and the iconic vineyards of Romaea.

He showed Natharis the guest room and offered to prepare any dinner of his choice—"Or we could dine out, if that suits you," he reluctantly added, eager to amaze him with his culinary prowess. Natharis obliged him and proceeded to politely mention how he didn't often have the opportunity to eat a home-cooked meal. And, just like any of his other relatives would have done, Tobias replied, "Maybe that's because you work too much."

––––––––

The conference room in the Convergent Capitol was far too small for comfort, and at the crowded table, Desh Maru felt stifled, constricted by the number of chairs beside him. The twenty-one seats of the Executive Council ran down the length of the heavy table. He resented the briefing the

Congressional leaders were forced to suffer before the Parliamentary session. He even more deeply resented his placement beside Parliamentarian Panzi Illoszia of Bahía Brumosa, the newly declared Lord of Parliament, whose mere presence gave him a sour stomach and an unshakable headache. The dialog exhausted time and time again would also contribute to the rapid onset of his migraine.

The woman had been in politics longer than anyone could remember, her age the butt of endless jokes told among Colonial commentators. Her face revealed years of botched plastic surgeries in the crowded, unruly hospitals of the Commune, all in the pursuit of a delusional beauty and twisted semblance of youth. Rumors circulated throughout the Interstellar Convergency that she'd kept herself alive for centuries with the blood of children slaughtered viciously by Shatarins. The lack of discernible wrinkles also lent to a lack of discernible emotions, kept hidden by the tight, unmoving flesh of her brow and eyes. She had a poker face that even the unfeeling Procyon Executive couldn't match—she couldn't be read, except through the shrieking tone of her voice, and the flecks of saliva that sprayed from her mouth upon uttering the words "taxation" and "greater good."

Desh endured her madness for the sake of his people; they'd fairly elected him, without ever having seen his face—in a blind election, as they called it. It was only after they'd been swayed by his words alone that they had the chance to look upon their new executive councilman, whose handsome looks were a pleasant surprise.

He found it shocking that a woman as physically repugnant as Panzi Illoszia could have been elected after having a single photo released, though she *was* one of the Communals, and their outlandish culture never ceased to puzzle him. Even their language was bizarre: a degraded, bastardized Anglic, a tongue fit for a babbling troglodyte. The simplicity of Unispeak grammar, or oftentimes lack thereof, was particularly fitting in Desh's mind, because he imagined the

Communals were so nonproductive that they'd never bother to master the complexities of the Colonies' Millennial Anglic. Panzi, along with the other Communal parliamentarians, senators and executives, always masked her meaningless utterances by imitating the better educated, but there were times when, in her characteristic tantrums, she'd slip into Unispeak and thoroughly amuse the eloquent Arterrans.

While the Colonial media and Telluria's Sol Radiofónica portrayed Panzi as some kind of hysterical, overopinionated clown, Desh knew firsthand that she wasn't a woman to be underestimated. Telluria's famous news anchor Claudia Aiola found endless entertainment in the unbelievable Illoszia, as did the Colonial pundits, but their honest humor had gone from harmless to dangerous. Maybe Panzi had limited pockets of intelligence, but what she lacked in intellect was made up for in instability. Her rhetoric was beyond predictable, but her actions were another matter entirely, as she'd managed to conquer Parliament with frightful words and unwavering support from her personal hero, Executive Brock Dunham.

ABAC's executive hadn't arrived yet, and his seat was empty at the center of the table, flanked by loyal disciples at their teacher's last supper before the session. They were the representatives of the Convergency's most powerful corporations and private entities, who, in Desh's opinion, ought to have had no place in government. There was Giles Bronson of the Academic Truth and Eliminating Dissent Organization, with his droopy eyes and sloppy hair, who fought for the authority to censor history for the sake of the rightful loser. Armando Marcotti of the Convergency Ameliorated Legal Union spat lies about Arterran civil rights violations with his massive mouth and its rows of baby teeth. Cross-eyed Sanders Flick of the Communal Entitlement Recipients' Organization sat beside him, grumbling about how Arterra should finance the Commune's inalienable right to endless reproduction. The sniveling Nahar Wali-Mutalbin, a Shatarin convert born Eliezer Crowne, represented CISRA, the Council for Interstellar Shatarin-Related Affairs, and repeatedly insisted that the Shatarins were the inexplicably indigenous population to nearly every planet in the known galaxy. And then there was the Politically Correct Broadcasting Company's executive, Reon Harlequin, who had fake blond hair and a block-shaped head filled only with future lies to tell in his farcical newspaper, *The Harlequin Post.* But even with each other for support, the corporate fat cats were nothing without Brock Dunham, who might have been too brazen to attend the briefing at all.

Panzi spoke of him as if he were there, or even as if he were everywhere, an omniscient, omnipresent force. She described conversation with him as a sort of divine communion and addressed him in ways meant more for a god than a sharp-speaking but mortal man. Desh remembered hearing at least one story on the news about small cults cropping up across the Commune; apparently, some people felt that Dunham was an incarnate deity worthy of worship and praise. He'd read that new laws were being drafted that would make the desecration of any image of Brock Dunham a punishable crime, but it could have easily been a rumor, a joke, or just an outright lie. The line between truth and lies, however, was blurred when drawn by a Communal.

"He's just so generous," Panzi said with a smitten sigh. "So selfless. So noble. So—"

"—behind schedule?" Sir Byron Clay interjected. Panzi glared.

Sir Byron, the elected executive of the Kingdom of Windsor Britannia, always had something snide to say, with his perfectly coiffed hair and handlebar mustache lending to his Britannic charm. Both he and Executive Oksana Molotova of the Tsardom of Romanov Muscovia found it hard to keep quiet in the presence of Panzi Illoszia or her savior. The platinum blond Oksana was famous for the way her eccentric makeup enhanced the red of her face when she suppressed her opinions. She was one of two female representatives for Arterra on the Council, the other being Mireille Leveque of the Federated Republic of Gallia, who groaned with a typical Gallic demurral at Panzi's verbal defecation. Desh always appreciated their presence. The four made up the whole of Arterran representation on the Executive Council—a number that Lord of Parliament Illoszia and Executive Dunham found to be heinously unfair. While waiting for Dunham's appearance, Panzi must have felt heavily outnumbered.

She didn't even have the Shatarin executive to rely on, though their political relationship was particularly one-sided to begin with. As the *Ghourad* of the Shatarin Empire, Sawal Pezh-Lekaah was responsible for all secular diplomacy between the devout theocracy and the rest of the nonbelieving universe. He, like many Shatarin executives before him, was quickly declared persona non grata amid dozens of controversies, most often involving the molestation of young children and the killing of religious minorities for sport. Before he was barred from participation in Congressional sessions, he refused to attend any catered function—*One intelligent decision on his part,* thought Desh— because the establishment didn't serve food appropriate for a Shatarin believer. Even when he was told that they could prepare a special menu for him out of respect, he still defiantly skipped the events and argued that he'd only come if everyone were forced to eat in adherence to Shatarin dietary laws. Panzi always supported his demand and advocated for the obligatory Shatarin-friendly meals, but curiously never ordered such dishes herself.

Had the Shatarin executive set aside his irrationality, the Tellurian Praetor and Executive Domínico de la Réina would have been thrown into a particularly uncomfortable situation, even more unpleasant than Panzi Illoszia staring back at the Arterrans in disgust. Desh could only imagine what a civilized leader like De la Réina would do if forced to sit and dine with a barbarian warlord whose goal was to exterminate him and his people. *And all in the name of God,* he thought.

He was just as thankful as the Tellurian for Sawal Pezh-Lekaah's absence. Like many Colonials, Desh followed the Mithneshi teachings; the Shatarins, however, viewed them as abominations in the eyes of God. And even though Panzi never showed any disapproval toward the most basic of Shatarin policies—the unapologetic, ever-justified use of genocide—she herself hadn't decided to convert to the Shatarin religion, despite her claim that its doctrines could only be described as "perfectly peaceful."

If anything was for certain, it was that the coming Parliamentary session was to be far from peaceful. The deadliest, cruelest weapons of war were put aside, and the hateful opposition would fight with carefully crafted words. And just as a modern leader no longer fought on the battlefield with his soldiers, neither did most representatives, waging war with speeches written by nameless, faceless individuals. Desh wasn't about to be used as a speaker for someone else's scripts, so he'd written his own repertoire for what was to come, and acknowledged the possibility that he could, with enough provocation, be driven to throw away the pages and speak freely in the present. He was the Colonies' strongest weapon in the Congress of the Interstellar Convergency, and his eloquence, unrivaled among his peers, could easily prove more powerful than the heaviest of aetherium bombs. Panzi Illoszia and her peons had a daunting fight ahead of them. Desh smiled, knowing they had no idea.

––––––––––

The skies over the farms of outer Hudson were always clear and bright in Natharis's mind; the dreamy sunlight eclipsed the memories of rains long prayed for and the wet, black soil that followed. He remembered how the midday sun made shirts an example of summertime oppression and the sweat on his ruddy back a mark of hard, dedicated labor. His tan was a badge of honor boasting the work ethic Dienne and Johannes Ruke had instilled in him. But now, lying in the sun on a Port Seraphine shore, the bronze he'd soon call his complexion would not be the result of hours spent in the fields of corn and wheat. Instead, it'd reveal the rare repose Natharis finally had the chance to enjoy. He couldn't shake the feeling, though, that he'd taken this break too late.

He chose to lay his back upon the blanket of soft, white sand, and left the beach chair unoccupied behind him, serving only as a place to put his well-loved Old Earth literature. With closed eyes he took in the sounds around him. The carefree Colonials playing in the summer heat were like his father's workers shouting to one another from across the fields. The youthful girls in their bathing suits, bordering on risqué, but not quite, were like his sister Sayra's friends waving at him from the shade of his mother's front porch. He preferred the farm girls, but he didn't reject his present admirers and their flirtatious giggles. He was no longer one to be so cavalier, but there was no harm in letting them look. Amused, he cracked a subtle smile and casually slipped on his aviators.

Seraphine certainly must have been a relief to all those who called themselves Tartarus personnel. The infamous prison complex, spread among planets and moons throughout the Tartarus system, was a place of crushing gravity and biting, mortal cold. To come back to a family on a paradisal world, Natharis imagined, warmed the body and the spirit, and made the execution of judicial duties in the bleak hell of Tartarus considerably more bearable. He wondered how Sebasteon fared in his work, and if he really did find joy in picking through the minds of convicted criminals, and more so, the very worst of them. Did their twisted thoughts ever follow him home, haunting his dreams? And did knowledge of their heinous crimes—rape, pedophilia, murder, genocide—ever leave him with a dwindling faith in the world? Natharis was reluctant to ask him. Besides, he'd certainly cover the truth.

Back in Chesapeake, his friends probably wouldn't have believed that Natharis had spent a good deal of time on the beach, and they would have been even less likely to accept a story involving a fully unproductive Natharis Ruke. But perhaps easing his mind, which was more exhausted than he'd realized, could be considered productive. He certainly deserved his tropical retreat, he told himself. And there wasn't a single person who thought otherwise.

————

A set of piercing eyes slid open to reveal only blackness. They were like mirrors, reflecting ghosts of the world around them for the boy to see. Stars sparkled in the night sky as a cold wind cascaded over his naked torso. He saw the sky in the eyes' haunting gaze, but then the stars flooded from them until comets, moons and planets spilled out in every direction. Selas drifted among them, caught in the currents of shimmering stardust and the tidal seas of glowing nebulae. They carried him through the darkness with no sense of time, but then came to a stop before a spectacular phenomenon like nothing he'd ever seen.

It was as though the Creator Himself tore the universe in two, unleashing the fires of a mythical underworld. The glowing wound pulsed with crimson and deep blue, and the colors seemed to be caught in an endless battle, overtaking the other only to be overtaken. A lifeless ring of icy mountains and debris rotated around the unknowable anomaly, which churned and warped, shifting shape, and began to shrink inward, until the glorious colors merged into a molten gold. The frozen stones gathered together one by one, and soon assembled into a formidable planet, across which spread swaths of metallic cities, orbited by sprawling facilities high above the hazy atmosphere. Selas raced closer past the unanchored iron islands that drifted up in the sky, and he looked upon the massive city on the surface. Its skyscrapers dwarfed even the tallest in the Convergency, but as he rushed over their peaks, they became smaller and older, like he was looking upon stages of civilization stretching far into the past. At the edge of the city, there were no buildings. There was only an elegant sphere, crafted of gold and silver lacework.

The web of metal beams retracted to reveal a robed figure at the heart of the sphere. Selas couldn't see its face—there was no face, only shadow. The being hunched over what the boy thought was an altar but was in fact some sort of computer. It laid its hands upon the device's surface, and the object burst with light. The planet beneath it roared, and shook with a terrible force, and millions of voices cried out in anguish. The screams didn't echo with a physical pain; it was deeper than that, a spiritual defeat, as though uncountable souls were stripped of their divine essence. The boy couldn't understand their words, as they spoke not in words. He wasn't even sure if he heard their wailing out loud. It all seemed to be inside his head.

An unspeakable power tore the planet asunder and hurled burning debris out into the void. The explosion glimmered with reds and blues, and the cleaved stones became a halo around the terrible scar upon the universe. At its center stood the hooded figure, its shadowy face directly ahead of Selas. Hands pulled back the cloak and revealed its identity. Selas clenched his eyes shut and tried to look away, but he still saw them. There was no body attached to them. There were only the two black mirrors gazing back at him, and in them he saw his reflection. He screamed but heard nothing in the silent vacuum. He saw his face, and his eyes were that same chilling black, and in horror he clawed at them and sank his fingernails into them until he could see no more. He was blind to the nightmare. When he awoke, he remembered nothing else.

———

The call came when Natharis had just finished showering, and he was standing before the bathroom mirror with a bottle of Lutetian cologne raised to his chest. It was Sebasteon who answered it, though by the sounds, Natharis recognized it as his own timepiece, not his brother's. He addressed himself as speaking on Natharis's behalf, then fell silent; his footsteps grew loud and quick as he approached the door, opened it without a knock and presented the device to its rightful owner. Natharis raised his eyebrow and took it from Sebasteon's hand.

"Marshal?" the caller asked.

"Speaking," Natharis replied. The caller's accent was a common one in Chesapeake, and Natharis didn't have to check the screen to know that he'd failed in avoiding his superiors and their requests. The tone in his voice had a concern that was unusual for the normally worry-free citizens of Acadica; whatever was about to be said wasn't going to be lighthearted.

"I'm correct in saying you're staying in Port Seraphine at the moment?" the higher-ranking marshal inquired, and, when Natharis confirmed the speculation, continued, "We're sorry to have to intrude on your time off, but the Judiciary needs you." He paused, regretful, though he seemed to have his hands tied. "And as of now, there isn't a single marshal of your merit in the Badlands. We have no choice, I'm afraid."

Natharis braced himself for somber news of a tragedy in the farthest regions of Arterran space—the Badlands, in which he currently found himself taking repose.

"There's been a breakout."

"In Tartarus?" Natharis asked in disbelief. "That's impossible. A breakout's completely unprecedented. There isn't a single force in the Convergency with enough resources to pull it off."

"We suspect there may have been involvement from the inside."

Treason? A true Colonial would never consider committing such an act of betrayal. Their questioning of authority, done in the name of liberty and the power of the people, didn't lead to stabbing the greatest civilization the galaxy had ever seen in the back. The prisoners of Tartarus—of the prison installations of Hades and the even more nightmarish Jotunheim—were too closely guarded and too weak to escape. Even the Interstellar Convergency's highest security prison, Gaas Greed, looked pathetically vulnerable to sabotage in comparison to the strictly controlled Tartarus. The absurdity of the situation only served to darken the conversation.

"From what facility?"

"You may not believe it, but Jotunheim."

Sebasteon overheard the news, and his expression turned from curious to horrified. Natharis saw the change in him and motioned toward the kitchen, advising him to fetch himself a glass of water. When his brother had left the room, Natharis resumed the dialog.

"So, what do you need?"

"We've scheduled you a flight to Jotunheim, leaving in three hours," his superior announced. "A little presumptuous on our part, but we felt it'd be unlike you to refuse." Natharis wasn't sure if he should take the statement as a compliment or a subtle criticism. "I apologize for how vague all of this might be, but we'll discuss the details when you arrive. There's a team of corrections agents at the Jotunheim facility waiting to brief you in person."

"Send me the flight information, and I'll be there."

Natharis worried he'd soon regret his compliance. Sebasteon heard his response and came back to the bathroom door; the steamy clouds had dissipated, and the foggy mirror shone clear. Natharis saw him and his visible disappointment and felt a brotherly guilt he hadn't wanted. It'd only been two days in paradise before he'd been forced to give it all up for the sake of professional obligation—of patriotic duty in defense of his nation. He wasn't ashamed of his decision. In fact, he was proud of it, as he always was when it came to his work. But the look on Sebasteon's face made Natharis cover his pride, and he ended the call without words, eyes slightly lowered like a dog with his tail between his legs. He'd seen that look before. He'd hoped to never see it again, but it seemed to be the only face he saw those days.

5

"Each time the Arterran executives block our efforts to stimulate the economy, they destroy hundreds of trillions of jobs each passing day."
—Parliamentarian Panzi Illoszia of Bahía Brumosa
(When the reporter's response included the Convergency's census data of a total population of 4.2 trillion, the parliamentarian responded with accusations of racism and intolerance.)

THE ANCHOR RESTED ALONE, inactive in the vacuum of space. There was a coldness to it, a remoteness, but it was far from malignant. According to the sensor relays, it was the only manmade object within fifteen light-years, but the scientists who observed it planned to change that. With the keystrokes of an encrypted password and the flip of a switch, the device began to glow, no longer lifeless. In a blinding burst of color and light, an unmanned spacecraft flashed into view. It appeared out of nowhere, sliding out of the unseen tachyon vein that bled out into free space for only an instant.

The prolonged testing phase had come to an end, and the anchor was finally active. Under average circumstances the moving craft's voyage would have required the precise navigation of the invisible tachyon veins that ran between the deep gravity wells of the galaxy's myriad stars. Their paths were curved, spiraled, and indirect. Such travel between distant stars could take several days, maybe weeks if the veins were particularly meandering. But the anchor, one of dozens strewn far from the molecular highways, had broken this previously unchallenged law of physics. The arrival of the ship in a total of two and three-quarter minutes was proof of the scientists' success. The view from the vessel's bridge was awe-inspiring—the result of years of scientific testing funded exclusively by the Albian Banking Advancement Conglomerate.

Pentakiya Curicon smiled as the data trickled across the screen before her. She subtly adjusted the instruments— flipped a switch, turned a dial—while the ABAC crew scurried about the bridge, undertaking both its routine maintenance and the vigilant observation of its new rush of uploaded information. Pentakiya turned her head to address the captain who stood behind her. She took a deep breath before saying the words she'd been dying to say for years.

"The anchor's ready for active testing, Captain. The self-diagnostic phase is complete."

The captain grinned and pointed at the two men in charge of communications. They nodded, and one eagerly entered a command code on a silent keyboard. The confirmation signal was dispatched. It was to jump between the transmission buoys that followed the path of the ship like a trail of chirping breadcrumbs from an Old Earth children's story. The signal would eventually reach the officially sanctioned communication buoys that circled the Interstellar Convergency's web of tachyon veins. The network facilitated instant communication across the Convergency's cut of the galaxy. And the final order of confirmation would come down from Executive Brock Dunham himself.

With the commencement of the completed project, it was inevitable that the people of the Convergency would abandon Desh Maru's political movement and accept the sensibilities of Executive Dunham's ideological camp. ABAC had convinced the local governments to do so; it was only a matter of time before others followed in the more progressive states' footsteps. The people would see through Maru's false promotions of liberty and come to realize that he'd been playing them all along.

The ABAC vessel received Executive Dunham's confirmation order within minutes of the original transmission. It took several seconds to decode it. Had he sent the order without proper encryptions, the Colonials—the self-appointed "moral" authority of the Convergency—would, without a doubt, intercept it and attempt to thwart ABAC's new means of promoting much-needed galactic altruism.

Damn them, thought Pentakiya. *Those "do-gooder" Colonials. "Moral" my ass.*

Only the Colonials and their brainwashed allies could oppose ABAC's efforts so zealously. How could they not grasp the concept that providing for the needs of the greater community was of the utmost importance? The Colonials' bizarre emphasis on putting the individual first was selfish and self-destructive. Desh Maru's delusional call for individualism was just a façade for his desire to benefit himself and his people, and no one else. ABAC, on the other hand, was honest, its intentions pure. But it was sadly characteristic of the Colonials to fuss about an issue that would benefit the galactic community. And somehow, they'd swayed others into buying into their self-serving system.

It was no surprise that the Colonials would strictly enforce their policy of closed borders, barring ABAC and its research teams from accessing the defunct technology in the depths of their territory. The anchors were a network of navigational correction stations abandoned by the Procyon long ago, and so far as Pentakiya knew, the Colonials were completely unaware of their existence. Space was an unfathomably expansive place, and even with all their advanced technology and self-proclaimed awareness, the Colonials fully overlooked them. It was by a stroke of luck that ABAC managed to find them while exploring the uncharted regions of Colonial space for the sake of the greater good. Yes, it was illegal under Colonial and Convergent law for ABAC to engage in operations within sovereign borders, and they were legally restricted from utilizing, or even studying, the secret anchors. But Executive Dunham, in his political and moral sharpness, had managed to work around it. Altruism was above the law. And ABAC *was* the law.

A golden moon hung in the night sky over Bhalenjar as a delicate ornament. Small, twinkling particles shimmered and shone around it, like strings of silvery holiday lights. The metallic sphere the dazzling debris surrounded was the only naked remnant of a larger body's once molten core, now frozen and turned to solid metal, and the rings that turned about it were all that remained of its rocky surface. It was an image of an almost beautiful destruction, the decimation of a planetary body thought like all others to be long lasting. Its death came at the Procyon's hands. It was fatefully reminiscent of the murder of their own homeworld, the root of their spacefaring existence.

The vista was crisp and clear even through the thick shell of the pyrgopolis's residential bubbles, but its majesty was more captivating in the highest domes that overlooked the entirety of the Tower of Bhalenjar and the planet's surface below. The heart of the Interstellar Convergency was the final symbolic atom atop the spiraled, gleaming molecule; within its protective sphere, the Congressional complex, the Capitol of the Convergency, stood as a grandiose seat of power, a structure both regal and menacing in its magnitude. Most officials authorized to enter ignored the spectacular sights they could have beheld, if only they'd raised their gaze for just a moment. They'd become preoccupied with artificial feuds, the rejection of compromise, and circular rhetoric. They had no time for the wonders of the natural universe. They were too busy for its beauty.

Instead, they engaged in useless banter and cutting whispers just a bit too loud to be called private, praising one faction and condemning others. An amethyst-eyed Caspian exchanged arguments with an aging Communal; the Caspian asserted that Arterran policies were the only hope for preserving the Convergency. His opponent groaned, but predicted that the sun would set on Arterra's cultural and ideological dominance. Desh fought the urge to interject. He picked up his pace and ascended the mezzanine steps, his thoughts kept to himself.

The inner chamber of Congress was even larger than the edifice led one to believe. It was an immense, open circle with the air of an arena stained with the blood of the moderate and soft-spoken. Long, chestnut-colored rings of desks and leather seats covered the floor of the chamber, meant for the lower house of the Convergent Parliament and its outspoken, out-of-their-minds representatives. Extensive balconies jutted from the walls above and circled the chamber like a perch for vultures: those senators sitting cynically in the Convergent Senate. Staircases, the spokes of a great wheel, led from the Senate level to the floor in intervals, giving the higher politicians access to the lone podium that stood in the very center of the chamber, atop a raised, round platform reserved for the highest Congressional body, the Executive Council, of which Desh found himself a part.

The seats of the Council were arranged in a horseshoe pattern, with its gap aligned with the steps that led to the central podium from the floor of Parliament. The Council was present for every Congressional session, whether

Parliamentary or Senatorial; that day, the senators were absent, and the upper levels of the chamber were left empty and unused, veiled by a royal blue curtain. The parliamentarians, however, were beginning to take their seats, scrambling through the aisles like termites in the tunnels of a subterranean hive, with brains just as primitive and with an equal lack of foresight. The chatter that echoed throughout the chamber bordered on deafening. Before any session, there was a lack of order and decorum. It was even worse when the sessions began.

ABAC Executive Brock Dunham was unfailingly the last to arrive at every political event, consistently citing his "busy schedule" as the cause of his tardiness or complete absence, though his schedule was filled almost exclusively with re-election rallies. His puppet, Panzi Illoszia, was exceptionally punctual and had already taken her spot on an island-like platform set before the Council—she was, after all, the Lord of Parliament, and its most prominent and influential speaker, and she deserved an auspicious place from which to spew her verbal refuse. She sat, staring directly at Desh with a hateful glare. She lowered her eyes and scrolled through her notes, preparing herself for an unfair battle of wits that she managed to convince herself she'd already won.

The corporatist collectivists—the faction that so furiously opposed Desh and all that he and his nation stood for—looked helpless without their god-king. The minarchist individualists, who found a strong, faithful leader in Desh and his fellow Arterran executives, had already taken their seats and settled in, prepared for the coming debate. The Shatarins, a part of no faction or shared ideology, were, as usual, up to no good, harassing female representatives with the misfortune to be sitting next to them. But soon enough, the misogynistic laughter of lascivious Shatarin men and the spiteful insults uttered by collectivists gave way to a hushed silence, and Brock Dunham himself entered the chamber. The sound of his footsteps up the stairs was immediately drowned out by the clamor of his cheering followers. He waved at his disciples and motioned for them to sit down in quiet reverence. He took his seat and made it a papal throne.

Dunham was a man of tall stature but with a gangly sort of figure, like his arms were just slightly too long and his body far too thin. His hair was combed carefully to the side, with a slicked crest at the front, and he always presented himself clean shaven. He was a decently handsome man, Desh had to admit, though his appearance in person was far less grand than that in his thousands of campaign ads littered throughout the Convergency. In the photos, they'd strengthened his chin, broadened his shoulders, and brushed away the fine wrinkles beside his eyes that stress and anger had given him. Panzi Illoszia would have swooned for him even if he'd been as hideous as her, however. She was incapable of wiping away her smitten grin.

Panzi leaned forward over her podium and took one last look at her holotab. She wasted no time in beginning the session, foregoing most introductory formalities, with her sights set immediately on Desh and his three Arterran allies.

"Sentients of Parliament, and the honorable Executive Council, we meet during the darkest days of the Interstellar Convergency, and we have little time to waste." She spoke with her usual urgency, as if the process of legislation could possibly be hastened in such a bureaucratic monstrosity as the Convergency. "We must take this opportunity to present and pass as *many* laws as time allows, though we do not have the luxury of full, *in-depth* analysis of these laws. Parliament hasn't the time or resources." She looked to Brock Dunham. "But the good people of the Council do *indeed* have the wisdom and dedication required to judge each law *fairly*, or, at least, *some* of the Council, as others seem unwilling to participate in saving the *beautiful* political system we've created and kept alive through progressivism and hope."

Desh, Sir Byron, Oksana Molotova and Mireille Leveque chose to shrug off her insults, and waited for the opportune moment to respond, which was not then. Panzi continued her meticulously crafted speech, never failing to glance down every few seconds at her holotab, without which she was powerless, lost for words. "Like-minded parliamentarians and I have full trust in the leadership abilities of *Executive Dunham*, who has consistently displayed a faithful, *unwavering* devotion to the wellbeing of not just the Commune, but the Convergency as a *whole*, and, one day, the entire population of this glorious galaxy." She stopped for a second to scroll through her notes until she found the one-liner she'd been desperate for. "The only obstacle in his way is *this* man sitting right here—Executive Maru, as well as his *blind* following, and the bloodthirsty, *selfish* people of the sickeningly self-serving League of Arterra.

"If it weren't for Arterran *stubbornness* and their pathetic obsession with the past and its *delusional* virtues, Executive Dunham would be free to ensure the prosperity of the Convergency. He would be free to promote and defend the *greater good*. Those of us in Congress who understand this, who live and breathe the desire for *universal wellbeing*, and who are *proud* to call ourselves corporatist collectivists, find ourselves suffering in the utmost frustration at Executive Maru's unwillingness to compromise his own twisted ideals for the sake of the less fortunate.

"The Arterran executives have served *one* good purpose, however—they've proven to us that Executive Dunham is patient and kind, and just the sort of leader this Convergency needs. Instead of removing Executives Maru, Clay, Molotova and Leveque from the Council, which he, in his *well-deserved* authority, could easily do, he chose to *embrace* their presence and engage in a dialog that, one day, might open the eyes of Arterra to the common sense of *all* collectivist policies."

"I've never known Executive Maru to be so quiet," Dunham noted smugly. Desh scowled and accepted the implicit challenge. The Colonial stood up from his seat at the Council table and put his hands on its surface, the muscles of his arms stretching the sleeves of his gray, fitted suit. The white of his flawless smile contrasted the dark tone of his skin, a shade the love-struck news anchor Claudia Aiola once described as being "like the richest of Tresorian chocolates." The executive unfailingly caught the attention of all those around him each time he spoke. Even the asexual Crystalline seemed to notice.

"Thank you, Parliamentarian Illoszia, for the passionate speech we've heard so many times before," he said, smiling condescendingly at the Lord of Parliament, who had expected Brock Dunham to immediately jump to her defense; much to her disappointment, he did no such thing. "I'm well aware that you mean to insult us, calling us 'selfish' and 'an obstacle' in the path toward a fictitious utopia, but I find your attacks to be rather flattering." He looked to Sir Byron, who gave him a subtle thumbs-up, and Oksana, who crossed her arms in anticipation of Desh's coming argument, while Mireille casually examined her meticulously painted fingernails, characteristically apathetic. "If you ask me, being the sole deterrent to a terrible future is praiseworthy.

"The corporatist collectivists can call us what they will, but it's well established by now that the League of Arterra and her allies have proudly disrupted Executive Dunham's efforts, and, in doing so, have saved your ungrateful people from an otherwise inevitable doom. You can label me a hateful tyrant; you can accuse Executive Molotova of imaginary war crimes; you can condemn Executive Clay and all that he, and our people together, believe in and hold sacred; and you can scream in ridiculous defense of the Shatarins each time Executive Leveque deports them from Gallia. The reason for your holding office is simply to drain the Convergency of all its wealth, and all its freedom, until you in your incompetence control every single planet, every single trade route in the known galaxy. Who exactly do you people think you are?"

Sir Byron joined the debate as Desh lowered his voice. "I think the collectivists, in their awestruck, faithful devotion, have completely overlooked Executive Dunham's blatant lack of credibility," he added. "He's even more detached from reality if he truly expects us to believe that the presence of these other corporations on the Council is not a conflict of interest for ABAC."

Desh continued. "You, sir," he said with a finger pointed directly at Dunham, "are a charlatan and a liar, and one day, whether you are prepared for it or not, your little secret will be exposed for all of Congress—all of the *Convergency*—to see. You might think you can cover up your ties to ATEDO, the CALU, the PCBC and CERO, but the fact is, Executive, that the more you try to hide them, the more obvious it becomes." Parliament stirred, whispers spreading across the floor. "If you were willing to release your tax records to the good people of Parliament and the Council, I suspect we'd see that ABAC owns the majority shares in these private entities, and that you personally have benefitted from such business, because you've manipulated these impressionable pushovers into obeying your every decree."

"Corporate involvement in modern politics is disturbing," said Executive Molotova, who clicked her colorful fingernails against the desk before standing. "With Executive Dunham directing his obedient puppets, ABAC has tried to seize control of Congress. Its meddling in others' affairs cannot be tolerated. Tsardom of Romanov Muscovia will collapse before suffering reign of Brock Dunham."

"The *only* reason you people so vehemently *despise* ABAC is because it is the complete antithesis of your *disgusting*, individual-based ideology," snapped Panzi. The corporatist collectivists cheered from the floor, and she grinned with a delusional confidence. "How can you have the *arrogance* to refute ABAC's demonstrated *devotion* to the financial support of the Convergency? If it were as deceptive as you *claim* it to be, then why would so many eparchies approach *ABAC* for loans, which they are given without question or expectation? The money that ABAC has so *generously* given to our people is the Convergency's lifeline, and with our *rightfully* acquired wealth, we have managed to secure an eternally stable, sustainable economic system—one that the known galaxy has never before seen. The other eparchies trust ABAC. Why can't *you*?"

Desh returned to the spotlight and looked toward Brock Dunham, who was smiling like a child given an undue amount of attention, and then to the floor of Parliament, wild and restless and hopelessly divided. The individualists waited anxiously for him to back Panzi and her idol into a corner, to completely dismantle their argument and turn the debate against them. The collectivists were nervous, which they tried to cover up with shouts of disapproval and derogatory heckling.

"The United Colonies of Acadia—and the League of Arterra—cannot and will not place their trust in an institution that has done nothing but clandestinely weaken the foundations of the galactic economy," he declared. "Parliamentarian Illoszia, your claims that ABAC's handouts are unconditional and without self-interest are not only baseless, but outright dangerous. The sole reason for the uncomfortably high number of eparchies looking to ABAC for loans is not because of the Conglomerate's honor or merit, but because these states have no other choice, as they were driven to turn to ABAC because of ABAC's own destructive policies.

"ABAC's power and influence exist only because of the wide consumer base of the Commune, which itself is the result of its unfathomably large population. And ABAC uses the size of the Commune's consumer base to strong-arm eparchies with the threat of excessive, suffocating tariffs, to the point where to reject its collectivist policies would be to exile oneself from the galactic economy. Because these smaller states have no choice but to comply with ABAC's demands, they've opened themselves up to waves upon waves of undocumented, unwanted migrants from the Commune and the Shatarin Empire. And with their new, unsustainable welfare states, set up by ABAC to accommodate the incoming hordes of non-producing consumers, these states are required to take out immense loans from ABAC. So no, Parliamentarian Illoszia, these eparchies don't approach ABAC out of a deep sense of trust—they come to ABAC for money to prevent the risk of collapse that, had the Conglomerate minded its own business, wouldn't even exist.

"But it doesn't stop there, proud members of Parliament. The Albian Banking Advancement Conglomerate actively promotes the immigration problem with the full knowledge that the people of the Commune and the Shatarin Empire— these so-called 'Children of the Dole'—would never dare to vote against their own interests and vote for anything other than collectivist candidates. Their growing numbers, encouraged by ABAC, serve to only further indebt the states to the Conglomerate. They've become slaves to ABAC's agenda, supporting collectivist legislation simply to receive more loans, and more loan extensions, at higher and higher interest rates."

Brock Dunham couldn't hold his tongue. He shouted, with Panzi falling into a trancelike state, repeating everything he said like a mantra. "I have yet to see the League of Arterra, or any of the individualist systems, offer an alternative to our current financial system," he noted. "If you, Executive Maru, really believe what you preach, then perhaps the League should start handing out loans to those who need them. But, as of now, you've proven unwilling to offer anything to anyone other than your own selfish people." He smirked. "So, until the day Arterra decides to share its undeserved wealth, the Convergency will have no choice but to look to ABAC for the support it so desperately needs."

Panzi rejoined the debate with a bleeding heart. "What is it about the concept of *altruism* that scares you so much? Is the idea of providing for the good of the *whole* so terrifying that you can't *possibly* stand to approve it? Have you no *shame?*"

Desh straightened his thin tie and puffed out his strong chest. "The only shame here is your complete arrogance toward an inevitable collapse of your own making."

"Everything we do is for the greater good," Dunham contended with a smile. Oksana laughed and covered her mouth with a flamboyantly manicured hand; the individualists found equal humor in his assertions. The executive glared at her. "You people think only in the short term. It was *ABAC* that bought the Tellurian Imperium's debt, and now its people have prospered, fostering a renaissance of culture and creativity—one that, I expect, the League has hidden from its citizens. The genius of our economic system is self-evident, Executives. You can't hope to go on denying it for much longer. Eventually, your people will come to see that they've been in bondage all along, and not living the lives of liberty you profess to provide them. The individualists, too, will realize that their entire identity has been built upon a terrible lie."

The collectivists voiced their thunderous support. Dunham continued: "It is becoming clearer than ever that the League of Arterra opposes ABAC out of a morbid jealousy of what it cannot provide: a sense of security, a sense of *hope*. Hope and ideals are all we need, Sentients of Parliament. With them, we can ascend higher than any of our predecessors, and build a Convergency more perfect than any civilization before us. With me, under the flag of collectivism, you can achieve a better tomorrow—a tomorrow the League of Arterra would keep from you while waving it in your faces." He focused his gaze on the Arterrans. "Go with them, and you will find yourselves anchored to the ground, restrained by words like 'responsibility' and 'realism.' But go with me, and you will see just how glorious this galaxy could one day become."

Even though Desh represented the nation with the most powerful weapons, the most formidable fleets and the most loyal citizens, he felt powerless in the face of the overwhelming, spiritual devotion the collectivists held toward Brock Dunham. No matter how convincing his rhetoric was, and no matter how much support he gathered from the rest of Congress, he was helpless to turn the collectivist mob away from their idealistic madness. Neither Sir Byron with his irreverent wit, nor Oksana and her unapologetic temper, nor Mireille with her patronizing sighs, could do any better. Dunham had a hold on Congress that no other figure could hope to rival.

Desh knew that the citizens of the Colonies held him in high esteem and looked to him as a noble, honorable figure. But his status as a role model was nothing near the divine position held by Executive Dunham, who sat upon a desk chair turned to a gilded throne. The enjoyment he took in suppressing dissent was repulsive, reprehensible, and there seemed to be nothing Desh could do to stop it. After all, how could any man hope to defy the will of a god and not suffer his wrath?

———

The tempestuous clouds of the gas giant Gehenna were plumes of black smoke and brimstone carried on an infernal wind. The storms, the color of blood and ash, tore across the planet at fatal speeds evident even from thousands of miles away. From behind the crimson arc emerged a darkened moon, passing through the shadow of Gehenna but never quite reaching sunlight, caught fatefully in an eternal night with no hope of a coming sunrise.

The frozen hell of Jotunheim was within reach. It was an unforgiving child of Gehenna, swept by cutting gusts of frigid wind and torrents of hail and shards of ice. The howling of the storm was deafening as Natharis stepped off the grounded shuttle, protected from the deadly elements in a black spacesuit lined with thick layers of insulation and radiation shielding. The dark color of the suit, and the green and red lights upon his shoulders he could activate during times of distress, were meant to make his figure more noticeable through the white walls of icy wind. But with such low visibility, and with no chance of ever hearing a single cry for help from a distance, the shade of the suit seemed to be a false reassurance for a traveler who'd never seen such a hateful winter.

The snows Natharis recalled from his childhood were powdery, soft, produced and delivered each year on children's beloved Jack Frost Day. He'd romped in the white blankets within the comfortable climate control complexes that never let the temperature fall below thirty degrees—a winter cold that felt like sweltering summer heat when compared to the abysmal chill of Jotunheim. The sheets of ice stretching across the moon's landscape couldn't allow for holiday traditions; no child could stand the wind's blades across his face while building the most complex and artful sculptures of the wintry mischief maker, crafted with snow miraculously grown with simple water reformers. The gentle precipitation of a Hudson winter was a sign of a heat wave on Jotunheim. A night without a fatal blizzard was unheard of.

Through the white haze emerged the complex, a vague, artificial blur from twenty feet away, and invisible from any farther. High-mounted spotlights glowed in the mist, the soft spheres of yellowish light too dim to fully illuminate his path. Natharis struggled his way toward the building, fighting the mighty push of the wind that tried so angrily to keep him away. He heard the hiss and thud of Militiamen, the mighty, mechanized warriors that scoured the surface of Jotunheim, destroying anyone found vainly wandering beyond the prison's threshold. The Militiamen and their pilots had no concern for their targets' identities; it was a worker's own fault if he were too careless to be caught blind in the storms. He'd find himself torn in two by metal beasts, with the bloody disc of Gehenna watching over his demise, its bands of black clouds a cruel, sinister smile in the face of death.

Two thousand years of legends surrounded Tartarus, with whispered stories of monsters and demons spread throughout the Outer Rim long before the Militiamen roamed the desolate worlds. Those who adhered to the mystic faith of the Mithneshi Coven found comfort in the belief that the spiritual order had sealed the ancient evil within the system's borders, with the spirits of chaos bound eternally to the cursed wastelands of Hades and Jotunheim. They could never escape the Creator's infinite Emanation— the neighboring systems were safe from infestation. But in the minds of the superstitious people of the Outer Rim, the prisoners suffering in the hopelessness of Tartarus were fated to roam the landscape after death, searching for a way out until heaven and earth passed away. The prison that stood before Natharis was the mouth of hell itself, insatiable in its hunger for lost souls.

Natharis stood before a massive, armored door; a beam, narrow at first, then broad, shot out and scanned the length of his body, ultimately confirming his identity. The door slowly slid open, and as he passed through it, he discovered its incredible defenses: it was a barrier ten feet thick. He entered the airlock and thanked the Creator for the much-needed shelter, though the air in the complex was still frigid, and the parka he wore under his suit let in the chills. He peeled off the suit and draped it over a rack already lined with others' protective effects. The chamber was otherwise empty, containing only a lone, metal dome rising from the floor in the center of the room.

A tickling feeling spread down Natharis's body, like a hundred soft brushes were running over his skin, as the dome emitted a rainbow of colored light. A digital voice resounded through the room without a clear source. Like an interrogation, it asked Natharis a series of security questions—*"What is your name?"*; *"What is your identification number?"*; *"What is your business here?"* It accepted his input. With the hum of machinery the dome opened, its interlocked components sliding down into the floor. It had concealed a circular lift, just wide enough for a single man's shoulders, and

Natharis stepped within its boundaries. Sensing his weight, the access lift began to descend, taking him down a vertical passage illuminated by strips of black lights that left the white of his parka glowing eerily in the dark.

The lift settled gently on the floor of a subterranean passageway, one that stretched for only a few feet before coming to a stop at a heavy door with its edges marked by bright, red lights. After surrendering to a fingerprint and retina scan, and after answering yet another series of individualized security questions, Natharis didn't know whether to be annoyed or impressed by the Jotunheim facility's ultra-secure protocols. The idea of someone escaping the prison was unthinkable and deeply disquieting. And most troubling of all, the prison's best security measure—that is, being thousands of feet below ground—had failed for the first time in its history.

His answers were satisfactory; the door opened. He heard the hiss of sliding metal and looked ahead, and found his gaze met by that of a uniformed corrections agent, who stood safely behind the small window.

"We request your identification, sir."

"Natharis Ruke." He handed his ID to the agent.

"Your weight?"

"One hundred and eighty-one pounds."

"Height?"

"Six feet, one and a half inches."

"Your place of birth?"

"Hudson, Acadica."

"Who is your employer?"

"The City of Chesapeake, Mariska District Precinct."

"What is your position?"

"Investigative Marshal."

"What is your rank?"

"The highest for my position."

"What is your business here?"

"I've been called to assist in a criminal investigation."

The corrections agent returned his identification card. "Welcome to Jotunheim, Mr. Ruke."

The window closed and the booth commenced its descent, a controlled fall that drew on for five minutes or so, fostering the accurate assumption that the heart of the prison was miles below ground. *It'd be impossible to get out of here,* he thought, *so how the hell did they do it?* He couldn't clear the question from his mind. A dangerous criminal was on the loose in the League of Arterra. And most unsettling of all, the Colonies, and maybe the League altogether, were no longer invincible against the sinister plots of those who wished them dead.

6

*"Colonial scientists are baffled by the Xaztechuan quagmire.
The Xaztechuans have completely exhausted all natural
resources, but their population of five-hundred billion
continues to grow with a fertility rate of no less than twenty-
five. And when they fear that their entitlements may not be
sufficient, their youth often engage in welfare immigration to
the industrial worlds. However, while collectivist worlds
would give citizenship to the twenty-five children simply
because they were born on collectivist soil, the Xaztechuans
will find no such luxury here. We do not have a concept of
birthright citizenship in the Colonies, nor in the League of
Arterra."*

—Colonial Executive Desh Maru, in response
to Sugar Pastures' criticism of Colonial
citizenship laws.

PENTAKIYA REVELED IN THE SOUND of her own pulse in her
ears—a throbbing, excited heartbeat that rumbled from her
chest and drowned out the voices around her. She suspected
there were few people that would understand her pride, if
any, as she had accomplished something no one had ever

done. And at that moment, she was at history's doorway, with every intention of stepping through.

She had long waited for the opportunity to enter the holy grail of access codes. She'd memorized it months, maybe years, prior. When the holoscreens lit up with the electric glow of incoming data, she knew it was finally time to use it. With the entry of the ten-keystroke code, she and ABAC were about to make history. The physical structure of the universe would never be the same.

She had a colleague, once—Rocky was his name—who would have stood beside her in triumphant joy. He was a scientist of the same rank, with the same unwavering dedication to the cause, who'd contributed directly to their success with his expertise in physics and engineering. Pentakiya missed him dearly; she wished he could have been there to share the experience of watching one's work bear magnificent fruit. But he'd been taken from her by the Colonials. It'd been months since she'd heard anything about him or his safety. She feared the worst, and it made her success even that much more important. She wouldn't allow him to have been wrongfully detained in vain. His work was not forgotten.

A lever emerged from the computer interface and Pentakiya pulled it without hesitation. Prompted to provide biometric authorization, she laid a finger on a small, black pad, and the lever retracted back into the mainframe. Suspended in the frozen dark, the orb before the ship began to flash and glow in a more uniform sequence. Had sound traveled, Pentakiya imagined a distant crescendo of energetic humming. Rather, she watched her project commence in silence.

The navigation officer burst out into excited laugher. "We've detected a viable tachyon vein!" he declared, whipping his gaze away from the relay. The crew erupted into applause. Pentakiya stayed quiet but smiled widely. She—and the other scientists, of course—had done it. They'd managed to accomplish exactly what Brock Dunham was hoping for.

He'll be so proud of us for what we've done!

The captain, with his normally emotionless expression turned to one of satisfaction, ordered the navigator to set a course for Albion. The crew took their seats and listened as great masts emerged from the ship like a sailboat on Old Earth. The masts spread wide with shimmering, metallic sails. Their wind would be the rivers of tachyon particles flowing through the Aether far beyond the speed of light. From the bowels of the sailship the aetherium core rumbled, hummed, and a blinding burst of light enveloped the vessel. The vein was open, unnaturally accessible.

The path they were to follow to Albion was no longer the route they'd known just hours prior. It was straight, direct. The anchor, rivaling the influence stars had on the mutable Aether, was like a dam that forced the veins into a different course. The twisting, lengthy river that used to zigzag from star to star was now a rerouted shortcut. It was history in the making.

Pentakiya was overjoyed but exhausted. She hugged the crew and the scientists who'd contributed to their success, but she felt a tinge of sadness knowing that Rocky wasn't there to see it, but he was with them in spirit. A young engineer drew a bottle of champagne from the galley and poured glasses for the group. With the celebration dying down, Pentakiya chose to retire for the time being. She headed to her quarters and drifted off.

Her sleep was cut short. A startling jolt brought her back to consciousness. The sailship had exited the tachyon vein— *But so quickly?* She must have been dreaming. *Was it all a dream? The anchor, too?*

She snatched her holotab off the table and smiled. The dream was real, turned to life. Her success wasn't just a hopeful delusion. They'd arrived at Albion, the throne of Brock Dunham's righteous kingdom. And soon her dream would come to its climax when she stood before the Executive himself and heard his string of praises. It was time to pack up her belongings and descend to the city of Dearborn, her Promised Land. Brock Dunham was waiting for her with open arms.

————

Selas woke up in the middle of the night shivering in the cold air of his family's quarters. He must have pushed the blankets off his bed, as they lay in a pile on the floor with just one side draped from the corner of the mattress. With goose bumps all over his body, he realized he was naked, though he had most definitely been dressed when he slipped under the covers just a few hours earlier. It was odd, but he shrugged it off as something he'd done in his sleep. He searched around in the dark for his clothes but couldn't find them; that was even stranger. He closed his eyes and tried to recall what he'd last done before falling asleep. He remembered nothing, but when he looked out into the shadows, something sparked his memory, and stirred up images of dismaying illusions he would have otherwise forgotten.

It was a vague dream, and he couldn't recall his surroundings, but he had the sensation of a metal floor beneath his knees. He was alone in the black landscape, with a single, bright light right above him that made him feel like he was trapped in an illuminated cage. His calls for help were useless, as no one listened, if there was anyone there at all. He outstretched his arm to pass out of the column of light, but recoiled once the darkness swallowed his fingertips, as if some force kept him bound within the glowing boundaries of his silent prison. All he could do was wait for someone, or something, to enter the room and acknowledge his presence. He lost all sense of time; he couldn't discern if he'd been there for minutes, hours or days.

Then they came for him. The hands emerged from the shadows, dozens of them, cold and skeletal, and grasped at every inch of his body. He tried to scream but couldn't let out any breath; he wanted to kick free of their grip but couldn't even move his toes. His back hit the ground hard when he fell down, stiff as a board. The floor slid against him as the hands dragged him out of the light, and it stung his skin when the beings tore away his shirt in pieces. Blades sliced his pants and the hands shook them from his legs. They stripped him and left him crying while chilling, black eyes gazed down upon him without pity or remorse. He desperately wanted to cover himself, but their stare kept him pinned to the ground, and hands spread his arms and legs and needles plunged into his flesh and pierced his organs with the most excruciating pain he'd ever felt in his life. He writhed in agony, submitting helplessly to the will of the phantasms that invaded his body and tortured away his innocence. A morbid scream escaped his lips, and in a flash, he was awake and naked in his bed with an inescapable dread pressing upon his chest.

The bolt of light shot across the sky and slipped into the clouds that blanketed the horizon. For that brief moment, it lit up the grassy plain beneath it, and reflected its brilliant flash off the formidable rail that split the fields in two. The mass driver rail stretched a great distance across the flat terrain. The metal stream came to a head in the shadow of a cliff that sheltered an unnatural octagon, a facility with a tower that curved upward. The structure echoed with mechanical clatter and raised voices as the next cargo load was prepared for its sling into orbit.

While most would have fortified their offices with sound-proof glass, Tageron Dagonari chose to leave the windows wide open. There was something gratifying about hearing one's own creation brought to life from its roots in thoughts and on paper. From the top floor of the skyscraper, he enjoyed the sight of the synchronized orbital launches and the glow of the cargo pods as they scorched through the clouds. To his left, in the southeast, were the arcs of light; to his right, in the northwest, the city of Tarem bustled in the day and sparkled at night. It was the largest transport and distribution center on the Caspian world of Hatal-Om, and the perfect home for a shipping company and its strong-willed father, who dispatched his clients' goods across the Convergency and even into the deepest regions of the Sorn.

The coming sunset made the launches that much more spectacular. As the sky darkened and the burning orbs shone more brightly, Tageron's reflection in the window became clearer. He'd aged well over the years. His skin was the same light bronze it had been in his youth, and his hair was still metallic gold without a hint of gray. He was admittedly typical of his Caspian division; like the others, his eyes were a striking shade of glasslike emerald, a trait his son and daughter inherited, as would their future children. His posture had begun to weaken slightly in his early forties, so Tageron made sure to stand as upright as possible. He was proud of his appearance, striking and professional; it certainly gave him the upper hand in business. He adjusted his tie and smiled at himself in the window.

An attention klaxon set off from his desk, but Tageron didn't turn away from the glass. He uttered a command for the desk-integrated computer to answer the call. His secretary's voice filled the room and informed him that a new client had just arrived for her meeting. Tageron glanced at his calendar to see the dossier on the potential client, though he'd already researched her thoroughly. He would likely have to converse in Anglic, as he was far from proficient in H'jani, and he doubted that the businesswoman from T'jan had any knowledge of Scythian. Most outside of the Inner Rim had little knowledge of Caspian culture at all.

The new business deal wasn't high-profile enough to result in a great increase in profits, but Tageron was set on acquiring as many new accounts as he could in as little time possible. Recent events in politics had driven him and other concerned business owners into a panic that he tried to keep quiet. The last thing he wanted was for his employees to see him worry.

But there was little he could do to calm his mind in the face of the rising cost of business. The corporatist collectivists had suggested new, choking taxes that Hatal-Om had foolishly implemented, and Tageron and his colleagues were to suffer the consequences. The Albian Banking Advancement Conglomerate was offering the planet a loan in exchange for its economic obedience. Hatal-Om's leaders had found the deal far too tempting to refuse.

The self-destructive state Hatal-Om fostered in recent years was expensive and unsustainable. There was a time when the planet's standard of living was among the highest in the Inner Rim, but that was long ago, and just a faded memory as far as Tageron was concerned. The decline began when ABAC and its collectivist allies sought to spread their influence with imaginary wealth and empty promises. One Caspian conversion led to another until the Inner Rim had become infested with ABAC's viral ideology. Hatal-Om was one of the last to submit, and even it proved vulnerable to the looming contagion of the Commune.

It was ABAC that convinced the planet that to address legitimate concerns was a blatant act of ignorance, and that to act upon those concerns was not only fascist, but racist. Hatal-Om, ashamed of its inadvertent bigotry, chose to turn a blind eye to the waves of Children of the Dole that arrived like locusts to ravage the harvest. Tageron always wondered how they managed to find their way so close to the galactic center, flocking from the shadows of the Outer Rim in search of a new home to plunder and illegitimately claim as their own. By caving in to the collectivists' demands in exchange for a paltry loan dwarfed by mounting debt, Hatal-Om had dug its own grave.

Tageron shook his head and brought himself back to his office, with its inspiring view of the Tarem skyline. He had business to attend to, and he wouldn't allow his frustrations to show through his professional façade, much less his growing fears. It was getting difficult to find new clients willing to strike a deal with any companies based out of the inner regions of the Convergency. He wasn't about to lose this one's trust, and he would fight tooth and nail to ensure her confidence in his company's ability to endure coming political changes. But beneath his salesman exterior, Tageron feared the future.

———

Natharis didn't know what the rehabilitation officers were about to tell him, or where they would take him. They stood before him in a crisp, modern lobby, unexpected given the simplicity of the surface station above. Neither did he expect their pleasantries, which were a welcome relief from the uncomfortably professional curtness of the previous computers and security personnel.

"Thank you for coming, Marshal. Having someone of your merit here will be a great asset."

It was the officer on the left who addressed Natharis and slipped in a bit of grateful flattery. He shook Natharis's hand, revealing a metallic security bracelet that clung to his wrist; his partner had one as well, and Natharis immediately recognized them as biological keys. They both twisted the metal rings and a double door slid open across the lobby. With their genes authorizing otherwise restricted access, they'd opened the gates of hell. The officers had no fear of passing through, as they'd witnessed its horrors many times before. Natharis convinced himself that he, too, was fearless in the face of such unthinkable darkness, and that he was immune to the monstrous words and deeds of all those who found themselves in rightful bondage. But he couldn't shake his racing thoughts of what crimes they could have possibly committed, or whom they might have raped or murdered, or to what world's demise they hoped to contribute. He couldn't suppress his morbid speculation with reason or rationale.

The doors shut behind them—Natharis realized there was no going back. One of the officers brushed his fingers over the keys of the holoboard that emerged from the wall, the square letters of its surface outlined in soft, blue light. The small antechamber they stood in began to groan, and it crept forward, acting like a rail car in some sort of massive coal mine, leaving Natharis and the other two passengers with nothing left to watch but the dim lights of the tunnel passing overhead. They came to a sudden stop; further verification was requested, and promptly given. Satisfied, the artificial will of the security system opened a cruciform doorway to the back of the car, the triangular panes of its gate retracting into the walls. Just beyond the threshold was the heart of the complex itself—the belly of the beast called Jotunheim, which pounded with the sound of inmates' fists against the frozen walls.

The cell block was a bleak canyon lined with heavy metal doors, five rows high. Armed guards climbed stairwells and traversed catwalks in grave silence, their rifles resting against their shoulders, handguns tucked into holsters at their sides. He'd expected to hear untamed cries and obscenities echoing from the cells, but he heard nothing; the cells were sound-proof, adding to the prisoners' interminable agony, left only to their perverse thoughts. But when a guard placed a tray of defrosted food into one cell's access port, the sound of a furious criminal shot from the opening and pierced Natharis's ears. It wasn't the brutish, male voice he'd imagined. He almost pictured a cat on the other side of the door, writhing on the ground in the pangs of heat, crying out in shrieking, feline moans to draw in fiendish male suitors. The woman screamed and groaned, but not in a pain that came from torture, but one that sounded more like the agonizing signs of drug withdrawal.

"Some Shatarin woman, caught out in New Wellington," the corrections agent explained, having noticed Natharis's obvious curiosity while leading him toward the site of the breakout. "No idea how she made ground fall, seeing as it isn't right on the border. But this here's what you get when you deny a reproductive colonist her fertility hormones."

Both he and his partner laughed as they promptly shut the window. The demographic terrorist disappeared into silent isolation like she'd never even existed.

Two men were waiting at the failed cell, one of them with a holotab in his hand, its flat surface glowing with an electric haze. They stood solemnly as they watched Natharis and his guides approach the impenetrable door. One wore the uniform of a decorated marshal, in deep blue and black, and the other was dressed in a manner typical of a Colonial administrator, with a flat, rugged cap and a light military jacket. The marshal presented his badge, revealing his name to be Erixen Dade. He looked more youthful than most who worked in the depths of the Jotunheim complex, a job generally reserved for more seasoned officers. He was a heavily muscled young man of average height, shorter than Natharis, but not profoundly so; his shoulders were so bulky that they seemed to slope directly into his strong, chiseled jaw. Short-cropped brown hair framed an almost contradictorily delicate face, one better described as pretty rather than handsome. His eyes, however, were hardened and intense, and the deep brown of his irises seemed as cold as his rosy ears.

The administrator outstretched his hand and greeted Natharis, introducing himself as Tomas Stone, the prison warden and highest-ranking official in Tartarus. "So, here we are," he said, and pointed a thumb behind him toward the cell door. "Never thought I'd live to see something like this. Let's just pray the media don't find out about it too quickly. We don't need to be dealing with reporters while undergoing the most urgent investigation in Colonial history."

The marshal beside him nodded and expressed to Natharis the need for the utmost discretion. The warden then stepped forward and handed Natharis the holotab. He'd been presented with a surveillance video of the cell block; two men guided hovering computers down the corridor, stopping at each cell to scan and examine its alignment with Convergent regulations.

"Just under twenty-four hours ago, two Convergent officials decided to pay us a surprise visit," he explained. "Told us they were inspectors acting on behalf of the bureaucracy. You know, the usual bullshit—looking for evidence of Sentient rights abuses, unsafe living conditions, legitimate enforcement of Arterran law, the works."

"Coincidence?" Natharis asked.

"I doubt it, but we can't quite figure out what the Convergency would want with a run-of-the-mill serial killer," Tomas replied.

"They caught the Crystalline in Kensington," Erixen added, "after he butchered five women in an alleyway, and one teenage boy walking in the wrong neighborhood."

The warden approached the security panel next to the cell. "As far as we can tell, the prisoner had no traceable ties to the Convergency or to any other political authority, and he had no criminal record prior to the murders. He's a nobody, really. About to be dispatched. No one would have even remembered his name."

He ran his ID card through its scanner, placed a thumb on the panel's fingerprint analyzer and entered a long string of numbers on the keypad. A digital voice asked him to confirm his intentions of opening the cell. He responded affirmatively in a strong, clear voice; the security system verified the warden's identity by his pitch and cadence. The overlapping doors slid open like blades, retracting into the frame around them with a sharp, slicing hiss.

The cell was cramped and suffocating. The walls were bare, crafted with thick plates of aging, dull steel, and only a small lamp set in the ceiling above provided light, albeit very little. Four hidden spotlights, tucked secretly in the corners, suddenly activated, synchronized with the opening of the cell door. The contents of the space became more visible: a shaky cot stood along the far wall, low to the ground and cold, the sheets torn off and tossed across the floor. And there was a gaping hole in the wall beside it, like part of the cell had been blown out with explosives. An oxygen mask dangled from the ceiling by its thin hose. It swayed in the frigid breeze that passed through.

The warden of Jotunheim explained that the Convergent inspectors had already left the complex by the time the breakout occurred. "The automated systems detected a dangerously high level of flammable gases in the cell," he said, pointing to a tiny pipe protruding from the broken wall. The system had initiated a toxic release protocol—"An emergency atmosphere extraction," Tomas clarified. "Hence the respirator, not that a Crystalline has much need for one, anyway."

Natharis inspected the damages and looked back toward the warden. "Based on the pipes, I'm assuming this is where the latrine would have been." The warden nodded, and Natharis knelt down to take a closer look. "Do you think the inspectors' computers could've been a Trojan horse?" He stood up. "A small canister of hydrogen or acetylene is probably enough to set off the alarm."

"Even so, there's no signs of an explosion," Tomas stated. "No burns, no residue, nothing. We did find a gas pressure conductor—well, what's left of one, anyway." A heap of metal parts, the twisted remains of what looked like a metal cube with loose, rubber hoses, lay scattered on the floor. "The prisoner rerouted the atmosphere transfer through the sewage lines."

Natharis raised an eyebrow. "Maybe he managed to turn the septic pipe into a vacuum, but there's no way anyone could fit through there." He pointed at the exposed line and its opening, which was less than a foot wide.

"Don't forget: The prisoner was a Crystalline, not a Sapien," Erixen noted. "They collapse and reassemble their molecular structure the same way we move our legs to walk.

He easily could have slipped through that pipe as a pile of gravel."

"Okay, so then what?" Natharis asked. "He's just stuck wandering on the surface?"

The warden pointed to the holotab that Natharis still held in his hand; Natharis resumed the digital briefing, which had shifted from a surveillance video to air traffic data overlaid with satellite imagery. Tomas elaborated, "The inspectors' craft experienced some noticeable engine trouble upon liftoff. With these storms and those run-down Convergency drives, there's no way something like that was going to get into orbit without some sort of technical failure.

"They barely managed to get off the ground, and even touched down for about ten seconds." He drew Natharis's attention to the large, solid object present on the sensor readout, and how its sluggish movement ceased for a moment. "Right where the sewage ducts feed out onto the surface. Convenient, isn't it?"

He took the holotab from Natharis and swiped his finger across the display. He returned it, the screen presenting a plain-text list of recorded coordinates. "As per standard protocol, we downloaded the craft's flight logs the second they touched the landing pad. The thing is, though, that they weren't encrypted in typical Convergency code. The inspectors looked like Convergency officials, they talked like them, but they sure as hell weren't."

"We're thinking they're working for a third party," Erixen added. "A private entity, but as of now, we have no suspects and no obvious motive."

Natharis looked up. "What'd you learn from the flight logs? Where'd they come from?"

The warden took the holotab for the last time and exited the cell. Erixen followed, motioning for Natharis to cross the threshold; he spoke as they activated the unbreakable lock. "This is the best lead we have yet, Mr. Ruke."

"They came from Gaas Skaago," the warden stated firmly. "The only city left standing after the nuclear war—the last city left on Earth. And that's where we're gonna start looking."

The Tellurian ship deployed its rows of bladelike sails as it entered the tachyon vein. Glimmering and metallic, they caught the flow of superluminal particles rushing through the Aether. The current carried the ship down the quantum stream at speeds that made light seem heavy and sluggish, though there was no sound of rushing wind or waves—only the gentle hum of the aetherium drive, like a rudder guiding the sailship through that invisible pocket of reality.

Upon boarding the ship, Livia had expected a reverent silence, not the unbearable chatter of the uninvited ABAC representative Mickel Green, who'd so presumptuously imposed himself on their most sacred pilgrimage. She didn't know much about ABAC or its interests in any field of business or politics, but with the interminable narrative uttered by Mr. Green, she was easily able to fill in the gaps in her knowledge. The consitor Silviano was considerably more aware of the Convergency's political and military climate, educated in the study of war and diplomacy since he'd first set foot in the Imperial Temple as a boy. He engaged in conversation with greater fervor than his Neptunian counterpart, though Livia, not wanting to appear disinterested, offered a quick interjection whenever she felt she could fit in the words. Mr. Green, however, spoke enough for the three of them.

"Ever since I was a boy, I've held the Tellurian Imperium in the *highest* regard—along with all the *other* states, of course, because I'm not prejudiced. Maybe they're not *all* perfect, but they've got cultures—*real* cultures—and a history of struggle the League of Arterra couldn't ever understand. *Hardships*—that's it, they had *hardships*. And now that they're starting to climb out of the hole the Arterrans dug for them, the *oppressors* can't stand to allow it."

"Actually, the Imperium has a cultural connection to some Italic systems in the League, though you don't seem willing to admit it," Silviano argued. "We're both descended from the same Roman population thousands of years ago."

"What, *Romaea*? Perhaps you share a common ancestor, but *you* are the Sapiens among apes. They're still swinging from their trees of selfishness and greed—yes, *greed*—while Telluria flourishes in a spectacular golden age—and how *glorious* it is! They might be the unmet sons of your forefathers, but they're just a mob of bigots who happen to speak a Romance language—though not as beautiful as *yours*, of course. Indeed, I find Tellurian to be the most *sophisticated* idiom of the Inner Rim, no offense to your neighboring linguistic groups. Is that offensive?" Mr. Green talked as though he were out of breath after his first word, and when his cheeks flushed and his hands trembled, a lone bead of sweat slid down across his brow. "I don't think it is. My intentions were the best, of course.

"ABAC's intentions are the best as *well*, I'll have you know. We're *always* looking out for the greater good—yes, the *greater good*, quite unlike the Arterrans, who only care about the rights of *one man*—one *person*, I mean. Or one *Sentient*. Not all species have gender, of course. Forgive my brief lapse in political correctness. But ultimately, the Imperium's economic boom is, in part, due to *ABAC's* willingness to provide it with the most generous of loans—oh, and of course, the *Imperium's* willingness to approach ABAC for such needs. How *sensible* your leadership is! Who in their right mind would turn down one of our generous, one hundred fifty percent loans?" He began to laugh uncontrollably. "Well, other than the Arterrans and their pitiful five percent, which, as we *all* know, demolishes *any* chance of living a life free of toil and oppression, falsely labeled as '*productivity*,' as the Arterrans so deceitfully say!"

Mr. Green took a moment to calm himself and catch his breath. He wiped away the shit-eating grin that stretched his skin and tightened his eyelids. Livia, desperate to change the course of conversation, mentioned the first thing she laid eyes on. "I've been looking out the window for hours now," she said, "but I haven't seen a single ship pass by. We can't be the only ones in this vein, right?" She was embarrassed to have to bring up a topic that the two men likely considered common knowledge. Mr. Green opened his mouth wide and inhaled, about to offer an infuriatingly verbose answer. Fortunately, Silviano cut him off before he could give them all an earful.

"Right now, we're sailing through a river of tachyon particles," he replied with a gentle smile. He was far from patronizing, but she speculated that he might, in fact, have been trying to impress her. "Tachyons move faster than light—a lot faster. But you don't see them much in free space, so you go into the Aether to find them. The sails carry us along the current faster than physics allow in free space. We're passing other ships, but they're flashing by too quickly for your eyes to register. Unless you come to a full stop, you're effectively invisible, going light-years in just a few hours. The tachyon veins are as important to the Convergency as your own veins are to you.

"You know, the Mithneshi Coven teaches that the whole galaxy's a sacred body—a living organism, and its core is a spiritual heart that beats for eternity," he explained. He met eyes with Livia, his gaze more captivating than the shimmering Aether he described. "And the tachyon veins carry its power throughout the galaxy, bringing life to every world with the Mithneshi divine energy, the Emanation. The veins let us travel immense distances in the blink of an eye, but the Coven would say that they do so much more than that. They carry the vibrations of our actions throughout the universe." He leaned in toward Livia; she didn't recoil. "They say that love travels faster than hate, and even light. And I'm inclined to agree." He smiled, shifted in his seat, and clenched the muscles of his chest as he put his hands on his knees. "As for the rest, I'm not so sure."

Mr. Green immediately leapt into the conversation and took it in an entirely irrelevant but predictable direction. "Don't be a *fool* and think the Mithneshi have *any* grasp on the truth," he snapped, addressing Livia. "They practice a bastard religion and preach only ignorance, stupidity and *intolerance*—but what could you expect from such an *uneducated* order?" He tried to catch his breath, closing his eyes, but couldn't quite settle down. "And even worse, they are unquestionably the worst propagators of *hate*, especially toward the Shatarins—yes, the *peaceful Shatarins!* As if they deserve such terrible treatment!"

His statement drew death glares from the Tellurians. The anger in Silviano's eyes was so intense that Livia imagined Mr. Green's clothes catching fire. She, too, harbored resentment toward Green's sympathy for the very group that had terrorized the Tellurian Imperium for centuries. Mr. Green quickly realized his grave mistake; he tried to pull his foot from his mouth by apologizing for diving into the uncomfortable topic of religion. He finally stopped talking, much to the Tellurians' relief. He turned in his seat and pulled a book from his belongings. Livia and Silviano looked to each other; Silviano shrugged, then shut his eyes as if for sleep.

Livia, too, found herself drifting away from the cold quiet of the cabin and the sound of labored breathing that croaked from Mr. Green's seat. She gazed into the infinite blue of the tachyon vein that rushed past the ship, inlaid with impossible shades that shone with a vibrancy unseen in the heaviness of free space. She lost herself in the swirling colors that carried her light-years away from the Imperial Temple, the place she'd been forced to call home. Her true home was even deeper into the galaxy, where the stars grew close together and clustered in the sky. She found a small comfort in knowing that its energy may well have been carrying her to Earth at that moment, radiating outward into the darkness. And if what the Mithneshi Coven said was true, then she may have been swimming in the lost love of her mother and father.

7

"The welfare queen reigns supreme in the tax-heavy Albian scene."
—Traditional Colonial proverb

THE AIR IN DEARBORN WAS STALE, almost choking. Pentakiya felt as though she were breathing thin air at the top of a mountain; Desh Maru once referred to it as "shallow breathing in an ivory tower." It was a noisy city, cacophonic with shouting in the streets, piercing car horns and blaring sirens. She heard the cries of beggars on the sidewalk jingling loose change in a plastic bag, and the whimsical laughter of recently manicured women and their impressively large broods of children.

The view from above was much more spectacular, a sight inspiring an eventual disappointment with such disorder in the streets. Descending in the space elevator from orbit revealed a sprawling, white city, with skyscrapers clustered to the south and a maze of low-rise apartment complexes stretching on for miles in the opposite direction. It was huge, dwarfing even the greatest of Arterran cities. The common Arterran accusations of laziness and sloth were clearly propaganda. There were people everywhere, going about their business and cluttering the sidewalks.

The exoport was equally packed. Albion had only a single orbital bridge—a fact that Pentakiya had learned after much impatience and frustration. It was just another shame that Pentakiya felt could ultimately be traced to Brock Dunham's opposition. If the Arterrans would take a second out of their busy, "productive" lives, they would see that planets like Albion—booming with life, but hindered by their technological backwater—were all too common. But from that one, lonely station, high above the planet's surface, Albion appeared peaceful, free of worries or wants.

It didn't look like the photos Pentakiya had seen of Colonial cities begrudgingly included in her elementary school textbooks. The landscape surrounding Dearborn was barren, the topsoil long since stripped away, and there was little vegetation. City planning, or lack of it, had disrupted the local ecology. Even within the city limits, there were few green parks to be found; the Albians built outward, not upward as the Colonials did, and with so many people to accommodate, open spaces were a luxury Dearborn could hardly afford.

There was no relief from the crowding in downtown Dearborn. In the several minutes Pentakiya had stood on the sidewalk in the hope of hailing a cab, she'd been nearly trampled by throngs of gossipy, young girls wearing clothes eight years too mature for them. A homeless man came close to knocking her over when tugging on her purse, asking for one lira after another. And she'd almost broken a heel dodging out of a speeding motor scooter's path, piloted by a grotesquely shapeless woman gasping loudly through her oxygen mask. Dearborn wasn't what it used to be. But Pentakiya was certain that Executive Dunham couldn't possibly be to blame. He was working as hard as he could to make things right. Faith in her leader was key.

She stumbled backward in the wake of a reckless motorcyclist. But before she hit the pavement, someone caught her, slipping an arm beneath hers to prevent an embarrassing fall.

"First time to Albion?"

Pentakiya composed herself and hastily fixed her hair. "No," she replied. "I actually live here, believe it or not." She finally looked up at her rescuer. "Are you from Dearborn?"

The woman laughed. "No, I'm Caspian," she said smiling, pointing to her eyes. "Can't you tell?"

Her eyes were a rare, unnatural shade of amethyst. They caught the hazy sunlight and sparkled like gemstones. Her skin was a soft copper, and her hair was a river of molten gold. She looked young, but Caspians always did age well. In her low-cut blouse and provocatively short skirt, the woman was captivating, enveloped in an instinctual sense of the erotic.

"From a planet you've probably never heard of," the Caspian added. "So, where are you going? Maybe we could share a cab."

Pentakiya couldn't resist the woman's offer. Something drew Pentakiya to her. It'd been weeks since she felt herself clinging to another warm body. She wondered if the Caspian wanted the same hedonistic encounter.

"To the ABAC Headquarters," Pentakiya replied. "I'll be meeting Executive Dunham. I have to admit, I'm a little nervous." She waved her hand in the air to catch a taxi driver's attention. "I just want to make a good impression."

A cab came to a violent stop at the curbside. The driver, who looked as though he considered bathing out of fashion, yelled from the taxi for the two women to get in or get lost. They crawled into the back seat and slammed the door shut. Pentakiya told the driver to take her to the ABAC Headquarters, and the Caspian requested a stop in the residential Ferris District. He slapped the time clock and slipped back into the flow of traffic.

"At this time of day, I'd say we have a good two hours together," the Caspian predicted. "I'm sure you've experienced your share of Dearborn traffic."

Pentakiya slumped her head back and sighed. Dearborn was notorious for its gridlock, which, on most days, could drag on for hours, and there were some stories circulating of traffic jams lasting for several days. The congestion grew and dispersed like tides, ebbing and flowing with a chaotic mess of outdated cars and exhaust fumes, coming in cycles aligned with the phases of the moon and the first of the month. Had the Arterrans chosen a life of altruism, every citizen in Dearborn would enjoy a personal, airworthy shuttle. Always giving an excuse, they said that even the highest of Arterran officials didn't have their own tax-funded transports. Again, she was inconvenienced by their selfishness!

The Caspian crossed her legs and leaned closer to Pentakiya. She placed her hand on the peeling, faux leather seat between them. "I have to ask: Are you single?"

The upfront question and the frankness in her voice caught Pentakiya by surprise. She wasn't sure how to answer, brought to a moral crossroads. "I'm married," she sighed. She waved her ringed finger in the air. "But right now, I can't even remember her name."

The stranger exhaled softly and slid her hand down the length of Pentakiya's thigh. The taxi driver looked back in his rear-view mirror, his eyes revealing an appalling curiosity; the Caspian noticed, glared at him, and pressed a button on the interface before her to roll up the partition. In thankful privacy, the Caspian worked her fingers inside Pentakiya, and she moaned, unable to contain herself. She knew what she was doing was wrong, but after such a long, frustrating period of forced abstinence, morality was barely a thought in her mind.

Pentakiya's blouse gave little resistance when the Caspian tore it open. She freed her full, supple breasts from their tight brassier and kissed her way down from Pentakiya's neck. The cab rocked as Pentakiya leapt up and threw the Caspian down on the seat, pulling open her legs to lap her tongue between them. With every stroke of Pentakiya's brush along the Caspian's rosy canvas, the woman's moans grew louder, until they filled the cab and shook its tinted windows.

As waves of pleasure crested through the Caspian's body, driving her to shudder and curl her toes, Pentakiya worked her tongue faster, until the woman was begging for her to stop. She looked deep into the stranger's hypnotic, violet eyes and leaned in to kiss her, letting her lips linger upon the Caspian's. The woman pulled away. They both began to laugh, smiling widely.

"I'll never understand people whose marriages left their sex lives in ruin."

The Caspian gripped Pentakiya's arm and hugged her. She pulled her wedding band out of her clutch and slid it back onto her finger. Pentakiya never failed to enjoy their creative role-playing. She considered it a genius tradition, one that always kept their fire burning. It made marriage not just being accustomed to another person, but always wanting more of her.

"Kids change things sometimes, but we don't have that problem," her wife Artimpasa explained. "By the way, I'm going to your mother's house, and she's still pestering me about our plans for motherhood." Pentakiya's mother lived in the famous Ferris District—the only ritzy neighborhood in Dearborn, a suburban paradise with three-story homes and a badminton court at every corner. The collectivist elite claimed possession of the enclave, each house embowering a politician or a union representative, and sometimes simple friends of the exorbitantly wealthy.

They caught up on work and family life, the goings-on in Dearborn and the groundbreaking discoveries made in deep space. Artimpasa described a particularly comical dinner experience with her relatives, and how her nephew Arax was now famous in the family for his chicken nugget–eating abilities. And an hour later, after fits of laugher and constant embraces, they'd finally arrived in Ferris. Pentakiya's mother's house was tall and thin, with long, marble columns flanking the front door and its elaborate glass design. Her nieces and nephews peeked through the windows, giggling with excitement. She'd see them soon, after her meeting with Executive Dunham. And as her wife exited the cab, she smiled, knowing that she not only had the woman she loved, but her personal hero as well, whom she'd adored since the very first time she read his name on the ballot.

The Gameer caravan had entered the tachyon vein just hours before Selas and his sisters settled down in the dining hall. They'd decided to eat away from their mother and father, who hadn't had time to themselves in months, maybe years, though privacy was something largely unheard of among the Gameer. Their situation was hardly unique.

The brother and sisters left their family's tight quarters and sat among the noisy adults who frequented the dining hall simply for its bootleg liquor. The smell of long-frozen food and cheap cigarettes filled the air, mixed with the lingering stench of burnt meals and toxic alcohol. The prominent Burton family distilled the Gameer's liquor from any kind of grain they could get their hands on; when a planet they'd worked didn't have wheat fields, they'd collect what plant matter they could find, and let it rot in drums on their ship, the *Esyevim*, until the odor became unbearable. Even when drained and filtered, it still stank of decay.

Selas and the girls filled their cups with stale-tasting water, melted on the tanker *Sohaias* from icy particles caught in finely woven moisture nets draped along the hull. They drank slowly, savoring the water rations that too often went dry. The caramel-colored liquor, however, was always plentiful, and the men and women around them downed the poison from tiny glasses that clattered when slammed upon the table. Selas pushed his food around on his tray, unlikely to finish it; Ileya, his voracious little sister, eyed it eagerly.

"You know, I had a dream about you last night."

Evua looked up, intrigued by her brother's statement. It was the first thing either of them had said since entering the dining hall. Over the past week, Selas had grown quiet, disinterested, and had little to say to those around him. His mind felt hazy, like he was wandering in some foggy swamp. Perhaps it was too little sleep, or dreams too strange to grasp, but the cause of his social recoil was ultimately unknown and went unquestioned by his family. He was young, they said, and prone to that sort of behavior.

"I don't usually remember my dreams," Ileya interjected. "But I had one about a horse once."

"Well, I do," said Selas, pushing his tray away. He wondered if his little sister would scavenge what remained of his meal; she didn't touch it. He turned back to Evua. "We were in this dark room—I've had dreams there before, but I'm always alone. Except this time, you were there."

Ileya picked up her fork and began to guide it toward Selas's plate. She set the fork down quickly, hoping her brother wouldn't notice her lapse of self-control. "What was she doing?"

"Nothing. She wasn't doing anything."

"That's boring."

"Sure is," Evua sighed.

"You weren't doing anything because you couldn't move."

"And why couldn't I move?" she asked.

"I don't know. I couldn't, either."

"So, what happened, then? We just sat there in the dark, not moving?"

"You were on the far side of the room, just standing up straight, like you were strapped to a board or something. I was standing the same way, but I couldn't talk, even though I wanted to scream out for help. And I figured you were trying to do the same thing—in the dream, I mean."

She paused with a sardonic grin. "You had a dream someone strapped me to a board?"

"*No*, not to a board. You were being held down."

"By who?"

"I told you: I don't know, or at least I don't remember."

"So, we're being held down. Then what?"

"There were eyes watching us."

"Eyes?"

"Eyes."

"What color eyes?" Ileya asked with a mouth full of food.

"Just eyes? No bodies, just a bunch of eyes floating in the air?"

"I couldn't see the bodies, if they even had any. It was too dark."

"But you could see the eyes."

"Yeah, I could see the eyes. And I could feel them seeing *me*."

"Okay, so you're having dreams about us being held down, with a bunch of disembodied eyes staring at us." Evua held back her laughter. "What kind of broadcasts are we picking up out here in the middle of nowhere that *this* is the kind of thing you come up with?"

Selas groaned, and Evua let loose her laugh. She pulled his tray away from a frowning Ileya and pushed it toward him, picked up his fork and stabbed it into the defrosted food. "C'mon, finish your plate," she insisted, stirring the whipped potatoes into a spiraled peak. "It's getting cold, and it's foul enough to begin with."

The boy wasn't sure why he bothered to mention the dream, knowing that his sister, like anyone else, would simply dismiss it as the ramblings of a restless teenager. Maybe he, too, should have brushed it off, but he found himself incapable of doing so. While it wasn't every night that he had to gaze into the eternal blackness of the phantom eyes, Selas still went to bed with the fear that he might have to endure the horrors of his subconscious mind. He didn't remember having such nightmares on the Hindostani planet they left behind. He prayed that they might stop when they reached their next planetary campsite, but he could only hope.

———

Over the years, Tageron Dagonari had developed a penchant for small talk. The pleasantries exchanged upon the H'jani businesswoman's arrival at his office were tried and true, used countless times with other clients. The woman didn't complain of her travel fatigue as Tageron's last client had, despite T'jan's greater distance from Hatal-Om than Shang's, the world from which the previous Mei Zhi entrepreneur had hailed. Tageron concluded that her patience was a product of her non-humanity. Sapiens were far more likely to lament something at any given time.

In many ways, she looked Sapien—her figure was feminine, and she had a pretty face, with long, dark hair with a bluish undertone. Her skin, though, was pale, laced with fine veins just beneath the surface. When she spoke, a strange air sac bulged at the base of her throat, almost like a frog's. She didn't croak, however, and pronounced her Scythian carefully, with an exotic accent unique to the H'jan. Whenever she reached for a word but couldn't quite recall it, she waved her hand upward from her lap. She'd painted her nails a bold pink, though they were more like claws, and her fingers were subtly webbed.

The woman introduced herself as Taktkh'mii G'vaqr, and Tageron immediately abandoned any hope of pronouncing her name correctly. He opted to refer to her solely by titles like "Miss"—she didn't seem to mind, probably accustomed to the unintentional butchering of her name. Taktkh'mii quickly turned the subject of conversation to business, much to Tageron's relief. He might have been good at making superficial conversation, but it was something that he by no means enjoyed. She went straight to the point.

The H'jani stated that she represented a company that produced a portable, simple-to-use water condenser. Her company was set on expanding into the economic frontier of Arterran space and was particularly interested in marketing to newly settled Colonial worlds. The product she'd developed would allow for colonists to generate individual rations of water; the condenser, small enough to carry in a handbag, took just under a minute to produce a cup of water from atmospheric vapor. Every family settling the new, untouched planets would no longer have to concern themselves with obtaining water rations from their leadership. Tageron thought the concept had exceptional potential. However, he, a realist, waited for the catch.

"The problem is: the quickest route between T'jan and Arterra's Outer Rim frontier is through Shatarin space," Taktkh'mii explained with a hint of regret. "And we all know how much the Shatarins love to disrupt trade."

Tageron understood her frustration. Shatarin ambushes of trade caravans and their unlawful seizure of commodities in transit were subjects that the Convergency—or, more specifically, ABAC and the Commune—had declared taboo. Tageron seethed at the thought that it was considered hate speech to even suggest that Shatarin space was more dangerous than other galactic regions. It was racist and shamelessly uneducated to address the all-too-common capture of shipping personnel at the hands of Shatarin corsairs. It was even more bigoted to include the unfortunate fact that Shatarin prisoners of war were consistently and unapologetically murdered or enslaved. Oddly enough, the only ones making excuses for the Shatarins were non-Shatarins.

Tageron commented on his client's legitimate concerns, citing facts to relieve her anxiety. "I've spent a lot of money building up this fleet," he said, "and after a long, expensive process of acquiring the best ships money can buy, I can now proudly say that your cargo will be virtually untouchable."

He elaborated, explaining that his ships could outrun any Shatarin vessel in free space. And with the defensive countermeasures newly developed on Aldebaran-Zion, his cargo ships could push through any Shatarin blockade with ease. "As long as we're not dealing with a corsair battle fleet, we're good to go," he concluded. "And lucky for you and me, the corsairs have never organized to stop a solo cargo ship, at least to my knowledge."

Taktkh'mii looked relieved. After discussing the specifics of their business deal, the two came to an agreement, despite the woman's shock at the recent price hike that Tageron had no choice but to implement. "I'm embarrassed to have to offer my company's services at such an unprecedented rate," he lamented, genuinely apologetic. "But there've been a number of tax increases in these parts, and I've got to offset them somehow. And I'm sorry to say that this seems like the only way to do it."

The H'jani seemed to understand his plight and accepted the inflated prices. Tageron had lucked out. The new taxes limited his ability to turn a profit and hire new employees; worst of all, they scared away potential clients, but he tried his best to put it all out of his mind. Worrying about the suffocating policies the collectivists used to choke the life out of capitalist dreamers would only make him that much more uncomfortable during a new business deal. The establishment had its sights on stealing what he and his workers had rightfully earned, but Tageron wasn't about to give up. All men went through a period of trial and tribulation. He had every intention of beating the odds and, ultimately, coming out on top.

"Now, they've already got a head start on us," the warden of Jotunheim stated with a frustrated urgency in his voice, one he couldn't hide. "But you'll be on their tail in the fastest inceptor we've got here in Tartarus. Marshal Dade will accompany you—you'll need someone familiar with this sort of business. I can't imagine Chesapeake seeing too many serial murders. I expect you're used to less violent crimes."

"You'll need someone to guide you on the street level," said Erixen. "We're not dealing with a lone criminal anymore. He's gone to the worst hotbed of lawless trash the Mid Rim has ever seen." He pulled a firearm off the rack along the office wall and tucked it into a holster strapped to his thigh. "It's not the same Earth as the one in the history books."

"You should know," Stone continued, "that the breakout wasn't even the most unnerving part of this whole ordeal." He pulled up a map on his holotab, and with the tap of a finger, the image projected onto a larger screen on the wall. He didn't explain what Natharis was viewing, but it was self-evident; the map showed Jotunheim, Gehenna and Hades, as well as the various moons and gravity-anchored stations scattered throughout the outer parts of the Tartarus system. A moving blip detected by orbital sensors moved rapidly across the field of vision toward the system's outskirts, pursued by a larger swarm of flickering dots—no doubt a small squadron of Tartarus security forces. And, inexplicably, the hunted suddenly vanished from the screen.

Stone enlightened a perplexed Natharis. "Our interceptors were right on their tail, and then, nothing." He swiped his finger to another virtual page and the map shifted to an invisible tachyon vein illuminated in blue, detected by subtle energy sensors. The communication buoys that traveled along the routes were perpetually gathering data, marking the points of entry and exit of any ships rushing along the vein's energetic currents. Stone pointed to the screen.

"The only vein that runs through Tartarus is the Frontier Trail—and believe me, it's heavily monitored. No one gets through it without us knowing. The problem is: the Convergency ship, or whoever it was, didn't escape through the Frontier Trail."

"Where'd they go, then?" Natharis asked. "There aren't any other veins for light-years."

"Watch," Stone instructed. A thin blue line swept across the full width of the map, lashing through the boundaries of the screen like an energetic whip, and flashed by the security vessels with no visible effect on their movement or position. But when the line struck the blip Natharis knew to be the Convergency craft, the dot was carried away along its length, fleeing the system as quickly as it came. Natharis looked to the warden, then Erixen, for an explanation.

"It's a tachyon vein anomaly unlike anything we've ever seen," Stone said. "That vein doesn't naturally run through Tartarus. In fact, it doesn't run anywhere near here. It's as though something pulled it from its usual course—rerouted it, even." He noticed the concerned look on Natharis's face and deactivated the holotab; the image on the wall flickered off. The warden placed the device on his desk and took a seat. He motioned for Natharis and Erixen to do the same, though neither obliged him. "The Convergency doesn't have the technological capabilities necessary for this type of operation."

"No one does," Erixen added. He put his hands on the back of the seat he'd been invited to sit in, clenching his fingers around the false leather backing.

"But lucky for us, the shift in currents didn't affect our communication buoys," Stone continued. "We're still tracking the bastards, and by our monitors' calculations, we figure you'll be able to reach Earth right after they do. The interceptor's ready and waiting." He stood from his desk and outstretched his arm toward the door. "Don't worry, Marshal. Your new partner will give you the full briefing in transit. I have no plans on sending you in blind. But right now, we don't have a whole lot of time to spare. Duty isn't something that can wait."

———

Massive mountains of stone floated silently through space, following an eternal path around the lifeless planet in hopeless silence. They were the frozen remnants of a prosperous past long since faded away. The face of the Moon was broken, pummeled by mankind's most terrible weapons in the distant past. There was a time when the debris smoldered and burned, glowing with fire in the night sky. But now it was dead, dark—as was the Earth below it.

Where once there was a soft blue haze that swaddled the planet, there were only black clouds, swirls of soot that swept across the skies. The gaps in the choking smoke revealed a barren surface that had turned from vibrant green to lifeless gray; deserts stretched across continents that flourished as grassy plains in ancient times, and great lakes had boiled away into parched steppes. The atmosphere, decimated by the Sapiens of old, was no longer a shield against the sun's merciless radiation. The plants of the earth had suffered the consequences, and, unprotected from the unforgiving fire above, their brown leaves crumbled upon the ground.

Seas of blood rose and swallowed thousands of miles of coastline. The oceans were bringers of death, not life, and the beaches were littered with the bones of whales and fish, suffocated by the blankets of red algae that floated on the water's surface. With the planet's ecological balance irreversibly ruined, the crimson blooms spread rapidly and left the oceans sanguine. The waves were hateful, raging with the force of a vengeful tempest bent on drowning the very species that let its planet die with so little dignity.

The military vessels remained in orbit as per custom, suspended over the shameful vista that exemplified the most terrible of Sapien capabilities. The civilian sailship that carried Livia began its descent through the clouds of black pollution, and the sight of the hell below became clearer, more disturbing, with the knowledge that it had once been a paradise and the birthplace of the earliest Sapien civilizations. It was frightening but heart-wrenching, like looking upon the desecrated grave of a loved one. The swirls of ash and acid rain came to a head in the heart of the continental American desert. They circled and spread from a cluster of dark needles—the derelict buildings of the one city left standing on Earth, Gaas Skaago.

Built upon the ruins of one of the many perished cities of ancient America, it was a home to thousands of wanted criminals, and criminals who were soon to be wanted, ranging from the petty smuggler to the dangerously influential crime bosses of underground mafias. They slipped in and out of the Drom Graat Exoport without any risk of surveillance or arrest; it was part of the Commune, with open borders for any interstellar felon to cross. Earth had plunged into lawlessness and violence. Murder in the streets was not only commonplace but expected, and forced prostitution was a fact of life.

Rome couldn't look like this, Livia thought—prayed.

Rome was beautiful, she'd been taught. It was the one place the sun still shone. The cypress trees stood tall in the afternoon breeze, and the marble pillars of ancient temples reached toward the sky in reverent hope. Green grasses poked through the spaces between the cobblestones, and birds sang as the pilgrims processed down the Appian Way. But from orbit, she saw nothing like the legends. The whole planet couldn't be like Gaas Skaago.

It just couldn't be.

8

"Any person who watches and believes The Patriot Hour is undeniably uneducated and misinformed. That despicable news outlet is only a propagator of ignorance and Colonial lies, slandering the good nature and respected name of ABAC and all that it stands for. To support The Patriot Hour is to deny the plight of all those in need of our financial support to ease the burden of their economic hardships in their choice to live a life free of employment."
—ABAC Executive Brock Dunham

PENTAKIYA HAD BEEN TO THE ABAC HEADQUARTERS before, but she didn't remember it being so ominous. Its massive arch was a gaping, hellish mouth sculpted into the cement facing; it enveloped the main doors, which were formidable themselves, at least three or four times Pentakiya's height. It was like a cold palace made of concrete in place of whitewashed marble. But upon reaching the doors, Pentakiya realized that the entire gate wouldn't be swinging open for her like royalty welcomed back into her kingdom. The actual doors were tiny and disappointing, hidden at the inner

ical rodent the offensive Colonials depicted him as. She
ntly realized the stupidity of the thought. *Of course, he'll be
some! What was I thinking?*
ntakiya was living a fantasy she'd always hoped to realize,
she didn't know how to contain herself or calm her
g thoughts. Her heart pounded in her chest, and she
ed more rapidly, trying to fight the glistening tears that
ed up in her eyes. She felt as though she was dreaming,
ing each second that she wasn't about to wake up. But the
passed, and her meeting crept closer and closer, and
n she pinched herself five minutes before her
eduled appointment, she realized she wasn't just
entarily lucid, but fully conscious. It wasn't a delusion.
really was about to meet Brock Dunham. And he'd praise
he same way she'd praised him for so many years.

---

aris felt a flash of energy rock through his body, though
hip around him wasn't affected; he didn't need to look at
screens to know they'd left the tachyon vein. The Sun
e from behind them, casting light on the soft, hazy
ds of Venus, which rapidly grew closer ahead of them.
nd Erixen had made use of the incision point that saw
most traffic in the Sol system—the one place within the
ndaries of the asteroid belt that gave access to the rest of
known galaxy. The tachyon vein that ran between the
s of Venus and Mercury was a smugglers' highway; it
ght forth the most villainous of outlaws and carried
n back to the darkest regions of the Outer Rim, their
ness on Earth complete, for the time being.
blue light blinked in the cockpit, announcing the
tion of a communications transmission, which Natharis
med had its origins on Earth. The Commune was
pletely inundated with radio waves and television
dcasts, but the sensors were advanced enough to filter
even the most classless of Communal programming—

corners of the greater mock gates. No one opened the door for her, either.

The brutalist lobby was large enough to turn voices to echoes; the walls were concrete as well, but striped with tall, vertical mirrors every few feet that reflected the light of cold, spherical lamps suspended from the ceiling. The cables that held them were thin, almost like thread, and could have quite possibly been bare wires dangling from above. The lights looked cumbersome—too heavy for the tiny power lines to support. Pentakiya could too easily picture the lamps, the only source of light in an otherwise windowless room, crashing to the floor in a spectacular burst of sparks.

One particularly large light, above the lone reception desk at the far end of the lobby, was set into the ceiling in such a way that it resembled a skylight, though it emitted a glow too unnatural to be cast by the sun. It left an artificial highlight on the hair and shoulders of the silent receptionist. She didn't greet Pentakiya upon her entry into the lobby, nor did she when Pentakiya approached the desk. Instead, she acted as though Pentakiya had interrupted something important, though she didn't seem to be doing anything at all.

The receptionist wore a cynical look on her face, which left creases between her eyebrows that appeared darker from her excessive makeup. Pentakiya was surprised to see a woman who'd chosen skin-lightening powder over a near-orange bronzer, but based on her flamboyant, work-inappropriate manner of dress, she was likely Bahía Brumosan. She had a face that, ten or fifteen years prior, might have been considered pretty; now, aged and perceivably unhappy about it, the woman looked like a past beauty vainly struggling against time. However, her attempts at maintaining a youthful appearance were as pointless as her attempt to blend her pale makeup with the much ruddier tone of her slightly sagging neck.

She didn't look up; she clicked away at her mobile with long talons for fingernails that made typing a nuisance, her thoughts elsewhere. Pentakiya coughed to catch her attention. The receptionist looked up and scowled. "Can I *help* you?"

"Yes, I'm here to see Executive Dunham." Pentakiya swooned as she said the words, but she did her best to keep herself from using his first name, as if she knew him personally. She looked up at the massive painting of the executive—an icon, almost—that hung on the wall behind the desk.

"He's very busy, you know."

Pentakiya paused. "I do have an appointment, miss."

The woman sighed and checked the schedule she'd left idle on the holoscreen before her. She scrolled downward, shaking her head. "He won't be seeing you for another three hours." She pulled her hands away from the keyboard and checked a chip in her obnoxiously bright nail polish. "So, I guess you'll have to wait."

"The appointment was for ten minutes from now," Pentakiya replied.

"Well, looks like you've been pushed back," the woman snapped. "Executive Dunham works on *his* schedule, not yours."

Pentakiya looked about the lobby. "That's alright. Is there anywhere to sit?"

The receptionist rolled her eyes. "Over there. Don't know how you could miss it." She pointed to a small, hard-looking bench set against a wall, hidden between two faux ferns. Pentakiya's heels clicked as she walked over to the seat and sat down.

Under normal circumstances, in a room as quiet and lifeless as the ABAC lobby, Pentakiya would have worried about dozing off. The bench, though, was far too uncomfortable to allow for sleep, and the way it pressed into the underside of Pentakiya's thighs was enough to keep her eyes wide open. The only sound to be heard was that of the receptionist's fingers striking her mobile. Pentakiya hadn't brought a single something the Sapien brain couldn't possibly do. Natharis looked to Erixen before accepting the transmission.

Erixen nodded and motioned for Natharis to press the necessary button. "The warden told me we might get a call on our way," he mentioned. "He had reason to believe there's a Muscovian operative undercover in Gaas Skaago, working some ZGB case. Looks like he might've been right."

The transmission began to play; it wasn't a voice, but a superficially meaningless series of beeps and pings. Erixen smiled with a pleasant nostalgia. "Classic encryption," he laughed, "from a long time ago. The first Colonists used it." He paused and listened, then began to repeat the words spelled out by the chirps of the speakers, the sentences broken and disjointed. Natharis, both sympathetic to and frustrated by his partner's attempts at cracking an ancient code, flipped a switch beside the alert light; the audio code was replaced by a digital voice, converting the sounds into words quickly and easily, while rearranging and artificially editing the otherwise short and efficiently simple messages. Erixen stopped interpreting, disappointed.

"Operative can confirm arrival of Convergency inspectors at Drom Graat. You Colonials certainly took your time. More information will be provided at your landing."

Natharis didn't know how they were expected to contact the Muscovian operative, let alone recognize him, but he was sure the agent would manage to find their sailship upon landing. Earth's air traffic was disorganized and unpredictable, but with Muscovian technology and natural wit, the agent could track their arrival as easily as he had the Convergency ship. The only catch he could see in getting help from a Muscovite was the strong chance they'd be drawn into a fight that could have otherwise been avoided. The Tsardom had little tolerance for threats, no matter how small—and its people were known to fight fire with nuclear weapons.

————

The daylight turned to darkness when the Tellurian sailship began its descent through the pitch-black clouds. Livia no longer needed to shield her eyes from the sun's unfiltered rays, so she looked through the window and watched as the noxious wisps of lingering smoke overtook the field of vision, until all she could see was the hateful storm that cloaked the ship in shadows. When they broke through the lowest clouds, the Tellurians coasted over the barren plains, littered with irradiated stones and trees that had caught fire long ago, never to turn green again.

A massive cable stretched across the plain, winding like a rattlesnake between the former Atlantic and Pacific. The soil buckled beneath it and jutted up on either side. Earth's first space elevator had fallen to the surface within weeks of its beginning construction and was promptly abandoned, remembered only as the skeleton of a mighty serpent that fought bravely against gravity and lost the battle. Mickel Green didn't hesitate to pin the blame on the League of Arterra, arguing that the space elevator project would have been successful if the Arterrans' ancestors had chosen to remain on Earth, instead of venturing elsewhere in the pursuit of selfishness. He blamed them for the polluted atmosphere, the death of the grassy plains, and the toxic, crimson seas. Any problem he laid eyes on was inevitably the Arterrans' fault. The Commune and its ancestors, then and now, were innocent.

The derelict city of Gaas Skaago stood at the edge of what Livia at first thought to be a crater, the hollowed-out remains of a terrible impact, but she soon realized it was all that was left of a great lake. It had boiled away in the blinding light of the global nuclear war waged millennia ago. The decaying skyscrapers teetered along the cliff so precariously that it seemed as if a strong gust of wind—and it was a particularly windy plain—might toss the buildings over the edge. They looked sharp, like pointed, jagged spires, some made of corners of the greater mock gates. No one opened the door for her, either.

The brutalist lobby was large enough to turn voices to echoes; the walls were concrete as well, but striped with tall, vertical mirrors every few feet that reflected the light of cold, spherical lamps suspended from the ceiling. The cables that held them were thin, almost like thread, and could have quite possibly been bare wires dangling from above. The lights looked cumbersome—too heavy for the tiny power lines to support. Pentakiya could too easily picture the lamps, the only source of light in an otherwise windowless room, crashing to the floor in a spectacular burst of sparks.

One particularly large light, above the lone reception desk at the far end of the lobby, was set into the ceiling in such a way that it resembled a skylight, though it emitted a glow too unnatural to be cast by the sun. It left an artificial highlight on the hair and shoulders of the silent receptionist. She didn't greet Pentakiya upon her entry into the lobby, nor did she when Pentakiya approached the desk. Instead, she acted as though Pentakiya had interrupted something important, though she didn't seem to be doing anything at all.

The receptionist wore a cynical look on her face, which left creases between her eyebrows that appeared darker from her excessive makeup. Pentakiya was surprised to see a woman who'd chosen skin-lightening powder over a near-orange bronzer, but based on her flamboyant, work-inappropriate manner of dress, she was likely Bahía Brumosan. She had a face that, ten or fifteen years prior, might have been considered pretty; now, aged and perceivably unhappy about it, the woman looked like a past beauty vainly struggling against time. However, her attempts at maintaining a youthful appearance were as pointless as her attempt to blend her pale makeup with the much ruddier tone of her slightly sagging neck.

She didn't look up; she clicked away at her mobile with long talons for fingernails that made typing a nuisance, her thoughts elsewhere. Pentakiya coughed to catch her attention. The receptionist looked up and scowled. "Can I *help* you?"

"Yes, I'm here to see Executive Dunham." Pentakiya swooned as she said the words, but she did her best to keep herself from using his first name, as if she knew him personally. She looked up at the massive painting of the executive—an icon, almost—that hung on the wall behind the desk.

"He's very busy, you know."

Pentakiya paused. "I do have an appointment, miss."

The woman sighed and checked the schedule she'd left idle on the holoscreen before her. She scrolled downward, shaking her head. "He won't be seeing you for another three hours." She pulled her hands away from the keyboard and checked a chip in her obnoxiously bright nail polish. "So, I guess you'll have to wait."

"The appointment was for ten minutes from now," Pentakiya replied.

"Well, looks like you've been pushed back," the woman snapped. "Executive Dunham works on *his* schedule, not yours."

Pentakiya looked about the lobby. "That's alright. Is there anywhere to sit?"

The receptionist rolled her eyes. "Over there. Don't know how you could miss it." She pointed to a small, hard-looking bench set against a wall, hidden between two faux ferns. Pentakiya's heels clicked as she walked over to the seat and sat down.

Under normal circumstances, in a room as quiet and lifeless as the ABAC lobby, Pentakiya would have worried about dozing off. The bench, though, was far too uncomfortable to allow for sleep, and the way it pressed into the underside of Pentakiya's thighs was enough to keep her eyes wide open. The only sound to be heard was that of the receptionist's fingers striking her mobile. Pentakiya hadn't brought a single thing to fill her time with, having expected to see Brock Dunham within minutes of arrival. *No matter*, she thought. *It's worth the wait. The man must be exceptionally busy—keeping the Convergency together, and all.*

It was simply ridiculous of her to expect that she'd be able to see him so quickly. After all, to consider oneself entitled to his sole attention was nothing but selfish, self-centered—just plain wrong. She was sure that the executive rarely had a break from his work, unable to enjoy the daily repose that most Communals considered essential to good health. He was probably preoccupied with counteracting Desh Maru's ruthless tactics, preserving the good of the Convergency against the blight known as Arterran individualism. To wait a few hours was well worth it. The suspense was killing her, but it was such sweet suffering.

If her wife had been there waiting with her, she would have offered at least fifteen complaints and criticisms over the course of the next three hours. She would have cited Desh Maru's willingness to provide a personal interview at any given time, because apparently, he had nothing to hide and was a friend of the media, not a bully who tried to coerce them into overlooking his faults; Artimpasa said Executive Dunham had myriad faults, though Pentakiya strongly disagreed. Her wife was a political and historical writer with an unwavering sympathy for the individualist Arterrans, and while the two women often clashed in terms of opinion, Pentakiya found the conflict a consistent turn-on. She loved her wife despite her misguided convictions. Even when she found magazines turned over on their coffee table simply because Brock Dunham's face graced the covers, she still wanted no one else but her. At that moment, however, she had only the executive in mind.

So soon! I've been waiting for this ever since I first saw his face on television! She wondered if he'd look as handsome as he did in the bold photos on the front page of every issue of Dearborn's *The Harlequin Post*, or if he'd look more like the comical rodent the offensive Colonials depicted him as. She instantly realized the stupidity of the thought. *Of course, he'll be handsome! What was I thinking?*

Pentakiya was living a fantasy she'd always hoped to realize, and she didn't know how to contain herself or calm her racing thoughts. Her heart pounded in her chest, and she blinked more rapidly, trying to fight the glistening tears that welled up in her eyes. She felt as though she was dreaming, praying each second that she wasn't about to wake up. But the time passed, and her meeting crept closer and closer, and when she pinched herself five minutes before her rescheduled appointment, she realized she wasn't just momentarily lucid, but fully conscious. It wasn't a delusion. She really was about to meet Brock Dunham. And he'd praise her the same way she'd praised him for so many years.

———

Natharis felt a flash of energy rock through his body, though the ship around him wasn't affected; he didn't need to look at the screens to know they'd left the tachyon vein. The Sun shone from behind them, casting light on the soft, hazy clouds of Venus, which rapidly grew closer ahead of them. He and Erixen had made use of the incision point that saw the most traffic in the Sol system—the one place within the boundaries of the asteroid belt that gave access to the rest of the known galaxy. The tachyon vein that ran between the orbits of Venus and Mercury was a smugglers' highway; it brought forth the most villainous of outlaws and carried them back to the darkest regions of the Outer Rim, their business on Earth complete, for the time being.

A blue light blinked in the cockpit, announcing the reception of a communications transmission, which Natharis assumed had its origins on Earth. The Commune was completely inundated with radio waves and television broadcasts, but the sensors were advanced enough to filter out even the most classless of Communal programming—

something the Sapien brain couldn't possibly do. Natharis looked to Erixen before accepting the transmission.

Erixen nodded and motioned for Natharis to press the necessary button. "The warden told me we might get a call on our way," he mentioned. "He had reason to believe there's a Muscovian operative undercover in Gaas Skaago, working some ZGB case. Looks like he might've been right."

The transmission began to play; it wasn't a voice, but a superficially meaningless series of beeps and pings. Erixen smiled with a pleasant nostalgia. "Classic encryption," he laughed, "from a long time ago. The first Colonists used it." He paused and listened, then began to repeat the words spelled out by the chirps of the speakers, the sentences broken and disjointed. Natharis, both sympathetic to and frustrated by his partner's attempts at cracking an ancient code, flipped a switch beside the alert light; the audio code was replaced by a digital voice, converting the sounds into words quickly and easily, while rearranging and artificially editing the otherwise short and efficiently simple messages. Erixen stopped interpreting, disappointed.

"Operative can confirm arrival of Convergency inspectors at Drom Graat. You Colonials certainly took your time. More information will be provided at your landing."

Natharis didn't know how they were expected to contact the Muscovian operative, let alone recognize him, but he was sure the agent would manage to find their sailship upon landing. Earth's air traffic was disorganized and unpredictable, but with Muscovian technology and natural wit, the agent could track their arrival as easily as he had the Convergency ship. The only catch he could see in getting help from a Muscovite was the strong chance they'd be drawn into a fight that could have otherwise been avoided. The Tsardom had little tolerance for threats, no matter how small—and its people were known to fight fire with nuclear weapons.

————

The daylight turned to darkness when the Tellurian sailship began its descent through the pitch-black clouds. Livia no longer needed to shield her eyes from the sun's unfiltered rays, so she looked through the window and watched as the noxious wisps of lingering smoke overtook the field of vision, until all she could see was the hateful storm that cloaked the ship in shadows. When they broke through the lowest clouds, the Tellurians coasted over the barren plains, littered with irradiated stones and trees that had caught fire long ago, never to turn green again.

A massive cable stretched across the plain, winding like a rattlesnake between the former Atlantic and Pacific. The soil buckled beneath it and jutted up on either side. Earth's first space elevator had fallen to the surface within weeks of its beginning construction and was promptly abandoned, remembered only as the skeleton of a mighty serpent that fought bravely against gravity and lost the battle. Mickel Green didn't hesitate to pin the blame on the League of Arterra, arguing that the space elevator project would have been successful if the Arterrans' ancestors had chosen to remain on Earth, instead of venturing elsewhere in the pursuit of selfishness. He blamed them for the polluted atmosphere, the death of the grassy plains, and the toxic, crimson seas. Any problem he laid eyes on was inevitably the Arterrans' fault. The Commune and its ancestors, then and now, were innocent.

The derelict city of Gaas Skaago stood at the edge of what Livia at first thought to be a crater, the hollowed-out remains of a terrible impact, but she soon realized it was all that was left of a great lake. It had boiled away in the blinding light of the global nuclear war waged millennia ago. The decaying skyscrapers teetered along the cliff so precariously that it seemed as if a strong gust of wind—and it was a particularly windy plain—might toss the buildings over the edge. They looked sharp, like pointed, jagged spires, some made of rusted metal, and others from cracked cement turned dark gray with soot from caustic dust storms.

The exoport of Drom Graat was a short distance outside the city limits. It was dangerously crowded and notorious for aerial collisions, having no noticeable guidance lanes; air traffic control simply assigned a docking bay number, and nothing more. The captain eased the sailship lower until it touched down on the dusty landing pad with a thud and a quick recoil. The hiss of hydraulics marked the opening of the cabin doors.

Air traffic control had given them the largest available docking bay, though not on account of the sailship's size, which was, in fact, much too small to warrant such space. Their cultural prominence—and lack of ties to the League of Arterra—inspired the city of Gaas Skaago to bestow upon them a sprawling courtyard of a landing pad. The smooth but dusty ground stretched across a third of the exoport itself, flanked by short, cement walls and cut-out walkways. The size of the bay allowed for the initial traditions of the Tellurian pilgrimage; upon landing, the sailship's religious cargo was unloaded and set up meticulously around the vessel and the ground upon which it settled. Livia, too, would become a feature of the first rites.

It was too cold for the palms and ferns they'd nestled in the cargo hold, but the party placed them outside regardless, intent on lending a natural, calming air to their sacred space, in stark contrast to the lifeless environment of urban Gaas Skaago. The sheer silk drapery, in lavish shades of purple and gold, billowed in the wind overhead, having been drawn between the sailship and the docking bay's outer walls. Livia saw the ritual bath she'd immerse herself in for a purification of body and spirit that would only be reversed soon after. It was set above a raised platform for all the onlookers to see, and Livia would bathe with their eyes running over her skin like unwelcome hands, as her body was theirs to touch and behold.

The festival wasn't set to start until full darkness had consumed Gaas Skaago, but Livia had seen the dwindling light of day on Earth and knew that the nights would be cold and dangerous. She had a few hours to spare before she took her place in the sacred rituals of her people, however reluctantly, and wandered away from the docking bay on the tired tram that ran between Drom Graat and downtown Gaas Skaago on a rickety, old track. She'd wanted to go alone, and take in the abhorrent sights of the city, but had no such luck. The other pilgrims insisted that she stay, concerned for the safety of an important member of the religious rite, but she ignored their discouraging words. Mr. Green imposed himself on her sightseeing, insisting that she'd understand more if he were there to explain it eloquently, as an ABAC representative was meant to do.

"Furthermore, Earth can be dangerous—no more dangerous than any *other* planet, mind you, and keep in mind that Colonial claims of near-zero crime rates are almost *certainly* exaggerated—so you'll be thankful later that you had a… well, *man* with you—but not in a *sexist* sense, I promise."

There were no words in Tellurian, Unispeak or any language of the Convergency that could have possibly deterred Mr. Green from joining her, so Livia tacitly accepted his presence but tried her best to ignore it entirely. She looked back at the sailship as she stepped toward the docking bay exit, and saw Silviano, not surprisingly, surrounded by Earthling women. Livia wished he'd notice Green's imposition, and at least impose himself as well. He'd be more willing to carry on a repetitive, circular conversation than Livia, who prayed her god would sew Green's mouth shut with fate's golden thread.

Two men entered the festival space, as unfamiliar as the women who'd so frustratingly caught Silviano's attention. They pushed a large crate down the corridor, toward the sailship; it looked incredibly heavy, but it moved with ease as it hovered above the ground. Mr. Green, always eager to act the part of know-it-all, said, "Artifacts, from the ancient Roman Empire of your ancestors. It's a gift, from the Albian Banking Advancement Conglomerate, for your executive, Domínico de la Réina. What better way is there to honor his sensibility in taking out such a *generous* loan for his Imperium?" He smirked. "The Convergency will forever remember *ABAC* as always protecting the *greater good*."

Green's self-declared topic of conversation carried on through the duration of the shuttle ride and well into their walk through the outermost streets of downtown Gaas Skaago. He was hell-bent on enlightening Livia to Earth's tragic history, as if she had any real interest, though the unbreakable zeal behind his words clearly convinced him that he could sway any person into agreement, no matter how apathetic. "I don't think it's nearly as bad as *some* people say," he remarked while Livia stared at the run-down city block. "I'm sure *Chesapeake* has neighborhoods like this. But, you know, Earth wasn't *always* like this. *No*—there was a time when Earth *prospered* under ancient leadership that would have *fully* supported modern icons like the inspiring Brock Dunham, and the people lived wonderful lives, free of the *oppression* of work and lifelong struggle.

"Of course, even the Arterrans' *ancestors* couldn't handle the thought of the less fortunate acquiring what was *rightfully theirs!* They couldn't stomach the thought of giving up their unfair wages—they were *too high*, too much for such undeserving, *ignorant* people!—so they got in their ships and left. They *left!* They *abandoned* the people they had a moral duty to support! Where's the righteousness in *that?* Where's the famous Colonial *morality* in digging an economic grave for the needy and *throwing* them right in?"

Gaas Skaago certainly did look like it'd been buried in a financial graveyard. But Livia, knowing just how twisted Mr. Green's words most likely were, deduced that the Earthlings did little to help themselves. The homeless and the beggars reached out and grabbed her by the loose ends of her clothes, imploring her to take pity on them; when she offered one the small amount of lira she had on her person, he had the audacity to demand more. Mr. Green chastised her for not surrendering more money to the needy, ignoring her assertions that she didn't have any more to give. He blamed her for not carrying enough, as she should have expected to support at least one person along the way.

"I don't mean to *offend*, of course," he said, "but your behavior at the moment is *very* Arterran. You're a *Tellurian*, and you'd do well to act like one—*conscientious*, I mean, of others' *needs*, unlike the *Arterrans*, who shamelessly couldn't care less."

But she really didn't have enough to give to the poor, and she did her best to look away from each beggar who approached her expecting a handout. She wanted to tell Mr. Green that if she were to give away all her money to the ungrateful vagrants of Earth's streets, she'd end up just like them—a fate she had no intention of ever seeing realized. And though she had no money to spare, she entered a smoky marketplace that stretched the length of a narrow side street, walking far ahead of Mr. Green, who, with his uneven, graceless gait and bad knees, trailed behind. Livia couldn't tell if the sounds of puffing air were from street vents ejecting choking fumes or Mr. Green pointlessly trying to catch his breath. Regardless of their source, she didn't look back.

Between a neon-lit brothel and a bar with broken windows stretched a narrow alley, lit by strings of tiny, white lights that flickered and swayed on their web of naked wires. The alleyway housed a busy market, cramped, with little room for walking, and wood and tin booths lined the smoke-stained walls behind them. Livia heard the unintelligible chatter of Earthlings speaking a diverse mix of languages. The shop owners, dressed in rags and old clothes they'd found on ancient skeletons, looked terrified of the mob that insisted on lower and lower prices, to the point where they'd be giving away their products for free. When denied a consumer handout, the infuriated, offended Earthlings stormed away, barreling through the crowd like children who'd had their candy taken away. Livia detected the stench of entitlement wafting through the air, but her curiosity got the best of her. She wandered into the market, intrigued by what the Earthlings could possibly be selling. Mr. Green fiercely objected.

"*So*, you can afford to buy *yourself* something unnecessary, but you won't give one more lira to the *poor* and *homeless?* These downtrodden people are the *Children of the Dole*, the *wrongfully* oppressed victims of Arterran *self-absorption*, and to *not* support them is undeniable proof of *bigotry*, whether conscious or not. This is *greedy*, *selfish* and *ignorant*." He paused as he attempted to catch up to her. "I do apologize if you're offended, however. I never had any intention of offending a *Tellurian*, of all people. And quite a *beautiful, cultured* Tellurian, I must admit. But *not* in a sexist way, of course."

Livia ignored the useless banter she'd suffered for hours. Green didn't seem to enjoy being dismissed, but neither did his fellow Communals. He tagged along uninvited like a barking dog following its master, and while Livia examined the worthless products on display, Green was more interested in watching her every move, scanning her figure invasively with his eyes. Communal consumerism kept Livia distracted and she avoided his unspoken advances. She noticed one vendor who was selling Old Earth artifacts—as if the Children of the Dole had any interest in Sapien history. The man behind the booth negotiating with the occasional academic was straggly looking and tired, his thin, gray hair reaching his shoulders like a dirty mop. The lines on his face were caked with dust, and his fingers were unusually long, spindly, like pale tarantulas scurrying across the table.

The display was cluttered with old, rusty trinkets and costume jewelry from a golden age in the distant past, when plastic was considered not only trendy, but beautiful. But one object in particular caught her eye: a tiny, bronze medal, hanging from a purple ribbon, shaped like a star. What intrigued her was the image engraved upon it, however dull and faded. The profile of a majestic eagle branded the medal, the likeness of a species long since wiped out by Sapien small-mindedness. It resembled the emblem the Colonials were deeply and proudly fond of. It may have even belonged to their ancestors.

She picked up the medal and slipped away from the world around her. It all became a blur, a ghost of reality, visible but too far to touch. Livia looked to the sky and watched in awe as an eagle, painted in gold and pearl white, descended from the clouds and perched itself atop the vendor's booth. It leaned down toward her and stared. Its eyes were an icy blue, so bright as to almost light up the inner world she'd entered, and she felt as though she'd seen the eagle before—not just on the front of the antique medal, but perhaps in the lost days of her childhood.

She didn't want the vision to end. She'd seen the sun peek through the clouds for the first time in what seemed like months, and felt the frigid, desert air of Gaas Skaago turn to a warm ocean breeze. The ethereal beauty of her subconscious reality was her only release from a world she had no desire to experience. And the eagle, with its wintry eyes and calming rustling of feathers, was an imaginary friend in a lonely city, one she planned to keep in her memory even after she plunged back into the universe, forced to bathe in a pool of shame for all to see.

———

The news studio was bustling with people; audio technicians diligently adjusted the acoustics, film crews prepped the cameras, and makeup artists made final touchups. The standing spotlights turned to face the stage, as did those above the lone, glass desk set in the center of attention, behind which sat Misha Matsumoto, the Vega 1 News Network's most respected anchor.

She hadn't requested an interview with the Politically Correct Broadcasting Company's star pundit, Sugar Pastures. The exorbitantly wealthy Communal corporation had insisted on her being there to represent the mainstream media outside Arterran borders, and to shamelessly promote her own show, *Good Evening, Royals*. The interview was sure to be monotonous and repetitive; Misha suspected that Sugar Pastures didn't have a single opinion of her own, but only spewed the twisted views of collectivist leadership and their ultimate font of knowledge, the Albian Banking Advancement Conglomerate.

A studio worker brought over a second chair—a much wider chair than Misha's—and placed it to the left of the desk. They were finally prepared for Sugar's arrival, ending with the accommodating seat, and beginning with a ten-foot table decorated with a spread of donuts and processed desserts imported from the Commune. The sight of Sugar devouring frosted cupcakes was nothing less than nauseating. Misha hoped that she would remember to wipe away the powdered sugar from her face before coming on stage.

Misha was surprised she didn't hear Sugar Pastures coming, having pictured her approach as announced by thunderous, ground-shaking footsteps, perhaps even spreading ripples through the glass of water set in front of her. The woman slipped out of the shadows of the backstage and slumped onto her seat, her breath heavy and strained, as though a twenty-foot walk was a grueling task. Misha shuddered as she looked upon the PCBC's most outspoken—and hideously obese—media figure. She was a brunette who'd decided to highlight her hair by herself, turning what was already dull into a flat, thin mess of pale browns and dirty gold. She'd cut it at her shoulders, but straight across, without a single hint of blending or other hairdressers' tricks. Her beady eyes were the color of tar, set in a permanent squint from the mounting pressure of her swollen cheeks. Misha speculated she'd also dabbled in plastic surgery, because the pasty skin of her face and neck was stretched back so tightly as to leave lines where it'd suffered too much tension. Her appearance alone was enough to make most viewers change the channel. Misha wished she could do the same, but she had no television remote to save her—only a penchant for debate and a much more tasteful ensemble.

She heard the countdown to going live, stood up straight and set her hands on the desk before her. Sugar Pastures shifted in her seat to find a comfortable position but failed in doing so. Misha didn't give her a chance to compose herself. She began before Sugar even looked up.

"Good evening, sons and daughters of Liberty. This is Misha Matsumoto for Vega 1 News, and you're watching *The Patriot Hour*. We're joined today by the Politically Correct Broadcasting Company's leading anchor, Sugar Pastures." She held out her hand for a half-hearted handshake. "Thank you for coming today, Sugar. We Colonials are always interested in hearing your interesting views on current issues."

"I appreciate your being polite, but let's not lie to ourselves here," Sugar groaned.

Misha paused, taken aback. "I'm not sure I understand, Sugar."

"The entire Convergency is aware of the unfortunate fact that your people have *no* concern for the views of others, and absolutely *no* desire to hear them speak their minds—that is, unless they *agree* with you, in which case you'd have them shout their opinions from the rooftops."

"Colonial society is built on freedom of speech. It's an indisputable fact."

"If that were true, then why hasn't the League of Arterra implemented a single *Commune*-suggested policy? It's as though they're trying to silence the opposition."

"Arterra and the United Colonies fully respect the right of the people of the Commune to say what they will and believe what they will. We just have no desire to see their failed policies at work within our borders. It's our right to govern ourselves how we see fit, as it is your right to govern yourselves."

"*Failed* policies? Clearly, the Colonies haven't been paying much attention. Perhaps if you'd simply *listen* for once instead of *haranguing* and *patronizing* the good people of the Convergency, you'd all come to see that it's the *Commune* that has a firm grasp on reality." Her voice turned froglike after consuming can after can of sugary soft drinks before the show; she loudly cleared her throat. "And the reality here is that the *League's* policies are failing, but your media—no, *you*, Misha—have been covering it up."

"The only Colonial failures are my own attempts at grasping your logic."

"You and your leadership are shamelessly *lying* to your own people, and to the rest of the Convergency that, for whatever reason, humors your pathetically *ignorant* worldview. You sit there on your high horses demanding that the people of the League, and eventually the entire Convergency, toil day after day in stressful, interminable affairs, while calling it *'freedom'* or *'liberty'* or whatever other classical buzzword you've currently chosen to adopt. And then you *shun* those who only wish to experience all that life *really* has to offer, *truly free* of financial degradation, and call them *'lazy'* and *'unproductive!'* The Children of the Dole are no such thing!"

"These luxuries you're promoting all sound fine and good, but you're ignoring the sobering fact that they are at the expense of others' hard work. It's one thing to ask for help in a time of need—it's another to *demand* it for the sake of laziness."

"Your emphasis on the 'rights of the *individual*' is *selfish* and *uneducated*. It's even more *disgusting* that you have no guilt toward having caused billions of Sentients to starve, all because you're *so* convinced that the needy should have to fend for *themselves* in such a financially hostile galaxy. We collectivists believe in the *greater good*—the good of the *whole*, which is something you'll never understand. But perhaps the *real* greater good would be for the League of Arterra to finally *shut up* and *leave* the Convergency it seems to despise. The Commune and the *rest* of the known galaxy would be better off without the Arterrans and their *backward* ideals."

"I suppose professionalism was too much to ask of you," Misha snapped. "Only a Communal would have the audacity to disrespect her host on live television."

"What you're saying is *bigoted* and *racist!*"

"I do thank you, though, for giving us a reason to cut this interview short, as I'm sure we can both agree that it would have otherwise gone nowhere, as it has proven to time and time again. But let me be clear, Ms. Pastures," Misha said with her eyes set firmly on Sugar, "that my reluctance to engage in a useless debate is *not* a journalistic white flag. Our ratings are probably plummeting because of your very presence, and if there's one thing I won't do, it's sacrifice the success of this company for someone who'd love to see it fall apart.

"Yes, I was born in the League, and yes, I was raised with a sense of patriotism, but my unwavering belief that Arterra is the only beacon of hope left in the Convergency is *not* the product of brainwashing. I've seen the systems outside our borders and spoken with their peoples, and all I've seen is corporate greed and *barbarism*, with no sense of respect for Sentient life or the rights of an individual to better her own life. You and the society you represent seem to have a deep hatred for the middle class, for the poor man who worked his way to wealth, or for the woman who works hard to live how she wants to live. Your poor are poor because of the naïvely idealistic policies you've endorsed, and your rich are rich from the exploitation of others' hard work. One day people will come to their senses, but it won't be in 'finally' condemning the League. They'll ultimately see the Commune and its allies quarantined from the rest of the Convergency like a deadly contagion, and, if the Creator so wills, removed forever."

———

The young brother and sister went to work early that morning. They stood among the other hydroponic technicians with the crust of sleep in their glossy eyes and hair just slightly matted in the back. Evua had hers pulled back in a ponytail, but her brow still glistened with perspiration; Selas's hair dripped with sweat and clung to the sides of his face. The humidity in the farm hall was stifling, and it left their clothes damp and irritating. Some of the men labored bare chested, but Selas was too modest for that. Evua was envious that they could find a slight relief from the heat when she couldn't.

The crops grew in rows, each a hundred yards long. They spanned the length of the hangar-like room, but there were other farm halls on the *Massyulan*, which was one of the larger vessels in the Gameer caravan. Theirs was devoted to the cultivation of protein-rich vegetables and roots, while others specialized in sugary fruits and produce heavy in complex carbohydrates. The plants grew from the ground and the roof in rows of troughs filled with a gelatinous, pinkish substance. It stuck to the inside edges of the troughs like thick putty, playing the role of an artificial soil that retained water thoroughly and could be easily injected with liquid cocktails of plant nutrients. Bean plants rose up out of the rubbery earth toward hanging lines of hot, bright lights strung over the rows, and from up above dangled other vegetables like a mirror. All the workers wore protective goggles because of the blinding lamps. When they left for the day, their eyes felt perfectly fine, but their fingers stuck together because of the glutinous dirt they spread around new plantings.

They assigned Selas and Evua to harvesting that day. He'd filled up two crates with vegetables, while his sister was half a crate behind, much to her frustration. To be fair, her patch was unusually rotten, and their overseers quickly instructed her to pull out the plants by their roots and discard them to prevent the spread of blight. The brother and sister would be well under their quota by the time their shift was over, but their family wouldn't have seen the literal fruits of their labor directly, anyway. Their produce went straight to the Harrison family that protected the agrarian *Massyulan* against less benevolent clans.

The Harrisons weren't tyrannical in their guardianship of the agricultural vessel, and generally kept to themselves, but this was to be expected from a family whose namesake was the control of food rations and the unmatched size of their waistlines. Most Gameer were thin from labor and scarcity. The Harrisons, however, never went a night without a luxurious dinner, which made them all the fatter, and undermined their assertions that they had the ability to protect the people of the *Massyulan* against the other families of the fleet.

They were just one of four great houses, all of whom exercised influence over divisions of the caravan. Their power wasn't derived from monetary wealth; the Gameer had no real currency among themselves. Instead, they allocated resources to the population, who had to depend on each for their most basic needs. On the tanker *Sohaias*, the obnoxiously pretentious Webbs horded the caravan's water supply, collecting it from microscopic shards of ice and the recycling of biological wastes, no matter how unpleasant the thought. Then there were the Crawfords, who called the defensive *Vorasai* their home, and who had in their possession the only weapons the Gameer managed to get their hands on. Their vessel boasted ten defense batteries and a stockpile of firearms that they continuously threatened to keep for themselves in the event of a Shatarin raid—unless the lesser families paid them their proper tribute. Extortion was their specialty, even when they claimed their niche was armament.

There were other influential families, but they provided less essential commodities, like the Burtons of the *Esyevim*. The Burtons ran the makeshift distilleries and produced a constant flow of putrid alcohol, which they themselves didn't drink, as they considered it low class. They offered up two liters of brownish liquor to the Crawfords for each liter they sold to the common folk, because they were terrified of the Crawfords, who often blamed the family for disorderly conduct around the caravan. The Burtons were famous for their shameless appeasement of the stronger family, and rumors abounded that they'd even outcast some of their own children for offending the Crawfords and dishonoring the family name. A few weeks of heartache was nothing compared to the fear of living on an undefended ship.

But at the top of the familial food chain were the far-reaching Livingstones, who lived aboard the *Inaida*, and to whom even the arrogant Crawfords paid their tithes. They were the kings and queens of the fleet, the loftiest patricians among the poorest of plebeians, for they had in their possession the entirety of the aetherium reserves, and without them, the caravan would be stranded in the darkness of space. The *Inaida* was a tiny freighter, and while there were much larger carriers in the fleet, it was the only one suitable for the transport and storage of the unstable material. It was fully unarmed, without a single turret, torpedo shaft or even a stock of guns, but it needed no weapons to exert dominance over every vessel around it. Despite their total control, the Livingstones were curiously laissez-faire, and even more strangely benevolent. Of all the feudal families, the Livingstones were the most likely to keep their promises. And for those who didn't keep their promises to the Livingstones, they would soon find their aetherium crucibles running empty, though so far as Selas knew, nothing like that had ever come to pass.

He wished he could be part of a family with more influence than his own, but he was a Smyth, and the Smyths were just like the Archers, and the Taylors, and the Whites and the Carletons and all the other families whose men and women labored endlessly in the farm halls of the *Massyulan*. He wanted to wear soft clothes like theirs, and not the rough woolen shirts he had to pull over his head every morning. He imagined himself with hand-crafted glasses to frame his turquoise eyes and help him read words that looked like blurry scribbles from afar. He and his family could afford none of the luxuries that the greater Convergency took for granted. The only comfort he found was in knowing that the great families were just as homeless as his own. They too were fated to wander the stars for time immemorial. They, like Selas, had no future.

———

The interceptor settled down on the desert plain that encircled the decaying city of Gaas Skaago, locked forever in a nuclear winter that left the land scorched and barren, preserved in its horror by the chill of a man-made ice age. The dust kicked up from beneath the ship, sparkling in the dwindling daylight with the shimmer of frozen particles. The gentle bounce of the interceptor touching the earth was followed by the groan of the cargo bay doors, opening to deploy their surface transports.

Their speeders, like hovering, ancient motorcycles without wheels or thunderous engines, floated above the ground, anchored in place magnetically to combat the planet's vicious winds. Natharis and Erixen stepped out of the interceptor and set foot on a world the Arterrans swore to never return to. The earth crackled and crunched beneath their feet. The goggles they wore to protect their eyes from the sun's blinding radiation masked the dull sepia of the landscape, and when they mounted their speeders and raced across the plain to the west, Natharis was thankful to be wearing them. The sun set over the crumbling towers of Gaas Skaago and turned the skyline to a shadowy pincushion on the horizon that brought only a sense of dread.

"After all these years, the planet's still devastated," Natharis observed with a wistful sigh, his emotions readable even through the fluctuating reception of the com-link.

"We have only our ancestors to blame," Erixen said disdainfully. "They knew what they were doing, but didn't care, and because of their negligence, the climate collapsed."

"*Our* ancestors?" Natharis asked, confused by Erixen's strange take on history. "No, they left before this all happened. The need for cheap consumer goods, cheap energy, and even cheaper food caused this, all because of overpopulation."

"Well, that's part of the problem, isn't it? Our ancestors just fled!"

"Now you're sounding like ATEDO," Natharis sneered. "Listen: the ancient collectivists encouraged the original Children of the Dole to reproduce as a means of securing an unjustified income to support work-free lives. Then they stole the fruits of the productive population's labor—our *ancestors'* labor—and drove them to escape. Over-industrialization was the natural consequence of the Children of the Dole's need for cheap *everything*, leading to the collapse of the climate. Our ancestors realized this system wasn't sustainable and would lead to an environmental catastrophe, so they abandoned Earth in self-defense. And for all we know, we're the first of our kind to come back home."

The wind whipped against Natharis's skin, cold and bone dry; it rustled the scarf he'd tied over his nose and mouth to block the gusts of dusty earth they parted like seas in the myths of Old Earth. The marshals set their course for Drom Graat, the exoport that, from a distance, was an impenetrable wall protecting the city from dust storms and avalanches of irradiated ash. The Muscovian operative was waiting for them, ready to provide further detail.

"Picking up any transmissions?" Natharis shouted into the com-link.

"I'm getting a hell of a lot of trash TV, but nothing important yet."

"I'll scan the channels—you do the same. Hopefully we'll pick up more than just *The Real Welfare Queens of Albion*."

Natharis cycled through the available frequencies as they cut across the desert, and in the lower range of channels, he caught the same ancient code they'd heard in the distant emptiness of the inner solar system. He activated a response signal and announced their contact to Erixen, who readied himself for the briefing. The operative switched codes, and the beeps of the classical encryption gave way to a Sapien voice, deep, almost croaking.

"He's masking his voice," Natharis noted.

"Still can't cover up that accent."

"Target touched down at 16:24; it seems Tellurian pilgrimage is under way, as well—landing just twenty minutes prior. Your 'inspectors' made contact with Tellurians and transported supply crate to Tellurian docking bay. It had bio-signature of silicon-based life form. Looks like we may have found your Crystalline."

The transmission cut out and Natharis accelerated, leading Erixen to do the same as the coarse pebbles clattered beneath them. "Ever been to a Tellurian party before?"

"Can't say I have. Don't know if I could keep up."

"If two Convergency inspectors can just walk in without a hitch, then there's no reason we can't. Just be quiet about it, and no one will notice. The Tellurians probably won't remember a thing in the morning, anyway."

"You don't think two Colonials racing around in the Commune will turn some heads?"

"We'll leave the speeders at the door, then."

In a matter of minutes, the Muscovian operative had transmitted the coordinates of both the Tellurian pilgrims and what was once thought to be an administrative vessel of the Convergency. The outer barricade of Drom Graat grew closer, a mighty wall jutting out of the dusty plain with a series of niche-like passageways lining its base. Natharis felt a heaviness in the pit of his stomach as he hit the brakes, and the drag of the wind on his jacket left his skin tingling and numb. He looked about the area until he was certain they were out of the range of any cameras, though he didn't notice even a single one, and pinned the lack of security on the Commune's curious—and dangerous—policy of open borders. He felt strange slipping into an exoport unnoticed, the idea evoking images of Shatarins and Xaztechuans attempting to infiltrate the outer worlds of Arterra. Except unlike them, he wasn't about to get caught and swiftly deported.

Erixen tended to the speeders and insisted that Natharis scout out their route through Drom Graat. Natharis stepped into the dim corridor and saw movement up ahead at an intersection of passageways; a narrow skylight made visible the crowd that scurried along like rats in a sewer. He waited for Erixen, and the adrenaline that rushed through his body primed him for action, raising his heartrate and leaving his impatient muscles twitching in anticipation. They were within reach of their target, and though the Crystalline was unarmed, Natharis was wary of the men who posed as Convergency inspectors, who could have easily been carrying weapons at the ready. His chase hadn't ended with Geoffrey Mikain. It had carried on in the back of his mind, even on the beaches of Port Seraphine. He had a new outlaw to catch. But this time, the outlaw wasn't working alone.

9

"When you have subdued the nonbelievers and exercised Lekaah's will upon them, may they remember that they are below the ranks of the believers, and may you limit them in number by the sword or by law; but preserve some, such that they may offer their resources unto you and be reminded of their submission."
—The Eternal Mutalbin

NIGHT HAD FALLEN ON GAAS SKAAGO, and the lone exoport of Drom Graat saw the coming and going of travelers in shadow, their business cloaked in darkness far away from the prying eyes of the Convergency and the righteous hand of Colonial justice. The Tellurians' docking bay flickered with firelight, and the orange and yellow glow of torches danced on the hair and shoulders of the pilgrims that tended to the ritual. A trio of traditional musicians plucked at antique lyres and beat upon leather drums. The stage was set; all that remained was the entry of Livia Nettunaya, altaria of Neptune, the final player in a sacred theater.

Many of the pilgrims dined as they conversed and gazed upon the dancers, and they took from platters carried by servant boys and girls, savoring the rich tastes of Tellurian cuisine—roasted pork, sweet figs and purple olives, the likes of which Livia couldn't enjoy, as she was to retain her ritual purity and remove herself from the world of the mundane. She looked to the bathing pool where she would wash away her impurities. Silviano had just finished his ablution, and he stepped out of the pool, his hard body dripping with holy water, the firelight sparkling over the crests of his muscles. He took a towel from a servant boy and wrapped it loosely around his waist, then approached Livia barefooted and just shy of naked, with a distinctly Tellurian shamelessness.

"It's your turn, *altaria.*" He used the title smugly, sporting a cocky grin.

"It *seems* it is," Mickel Green interrupted, approaching from behind Livia's back. She hadn't noticed his presence; she assumed he'd be busy harassing the servants for more food. "A *shame*, really, as it means you'll be playing your *role* soon enough, and you'll be outside the reach of conversation, which, I must say, has been *quite* engaging. Oh, how I wish *I* were a Tellurian right now! I would love *nothing* more than to make *my* offering to your gods."

Silviano glared; Livia looked away. Eager to silence Mr. Green, Silviano interjected. "But you're not, and, in the end, you're just a Shatarin sympathizer who'd love to see us all killed. So, I think it's time for you to either mind your own damned business, or find another culture to fetishize." He pulled the towel from his waist and shoved it into Green's arms, and left him holding the wet cloth as he walked naked and irritated toward a servant holding his ritual garb. Green was seething in anger, clenching his fists with Silviano's bathwater at his feet, and Livia slipped away from the scene. He didn't notice her absence, his vision too obscured by his Communal vulnerability to being offended.

She climbed the steps to the bathing pool, slid the slippers from her feet and let the drapery of her dress fall over her shoulders and down her body. It lay in a bunch around her ankles, the only skin left concealed. The air was cold, and as the breeze caressed her skin, it left her with waves of goose bumps rushing across her back and breasts; she hugged herself to stay warm, though her hands, too, were cold. She dipped her foot into the pool, and the warm water soothed her aching toes. She didn't know if the water was truly holy or not, but at that moment, it could have easily been blessed by Neptune himself, giving her life in the death of winter. For the first time in ages, she was thankful.

The water reached her waist and she cupped her hands, drawing some up to wet her hair. She let it run over her face and mask her skin with steam in the cold Gaas Skaago air. She kept her eyes shut, but she knew the pilgrims were watching her. She knew their stares were fueled by the knowledge that what they saw would soon be tangible, ready for the taking, for all who desired to profess their faith. She was their altaria, both their savior and their slave, and it was through her that men experienced the divine. She saw the Matra Altaria in her mind, a mirage, standing at the edge of the bathing pool. The sacred Whore-Mother told her to be strong in her faith, to forget her earthly cares and think only of the sublime ecstasy of the god she so faithfully served.

"Let the waters wash away your fear, my daughter," her ghost said. *"Nothing can hurt you when the soul is pure. And forget not, dear girl: You are doing the gods' work."*

———

The exotic music echoed down the corridor in a steady crescendo. It led to an exhilarating release upon entrance into the Tellurian ritual space. Dancers, twirling in a whirlwind of silky ribbons, glided around the sailship in an ecstatic trance, their bodies locked into the pounding heartbeat of the ancient drums. Chanting in a foreign language Natharis didn't speak, the dancers began to spin faster and faster, their arms raised to the darkened heavens and heads cocked back in rapture. The spectacle drew in more passers-by, and the entranced travelers of Drom Graat stood at the gaping doorways to the docking bay with eyes fixated on the strange rites of the Tellurian state religion they'd certainly never seen before.

"The ZGB operative could be here, and we wouldn't even know it," Natharis noted.

"Even if he were, we couldn't expect him to break his cover just to help us out with some low-level criminal. It's just a murderer of no importance to the ZGB," Erixen replied, his eyes fixed on the sight ahead.

"We're on our own, then."

"Sounds about right."

Natharis took the first step into the festival and Erixen followed suit. The leading marshal made sure his weapon was properly concealed—the Tellurian soldiers eyed the plainly dressed Colonials with suspicion, but said nothing, their stares glazed over by wine. A blond-haired dancer in a silken loincloth twirled past Erixen, sliding a pastel ribbon around his neck with a mischievous smile before taking his revelry elsewhere. Natharis frowned and leaned in toward his partner.

"Flirting with dancers isn't protocol."

Erixen smirked. "A minor distraction."

Natharis pulled him forward and they passed into the crowd. "All we've got to do is make it to the ship."

"And get inside. And smuggle a Crystalline prisoner past all these people. Posing as tourists."

"I'm sure if we wait a little longer, these Tellurians will be too drunk to notice a—"

Natharis stopped, his words stolen from him by a fair-skinned woman bathing naked in the torchlight. She stood at the edge of a pool, steam rising from its surface, her clothes having fallen to the ground. Her descent into the water was slow, seductive—paralyzing in its numinous beauty. She drew water with her hands and let it cascade over her dark hair. Natharis took a step closer. As if she felt his stare, she turned and looked to him, arms crossed to conceal her nakedness. They met eyes, two curious stares merged into one, and Natharis froze in the face of her otherworldly perfection.

Who are you?

His sense of time vanished, washed away by a waking dream, and he didn't notice Erixen's absence, who'd gotten lost in the crowd. Natharis's world was miles from reality, and he felt as though he saw eternity in the woman's eyes, lost in their limitless cerulean. But he was torn away from his trance by Erixen, who'd found his way back and gripped his arm urgently, pulling him toward their target. Natharis shook his head and brought himself back to the present, to the life crossed with limits and boundaries, devoid of the sapphire seas of her eyes.

Erixen broke the silence. "The ship's access port probably won't have a biometric lock like ours," he speculated. "From what I know about Tellurian sailship design, they'll be using a standard passcode. Just give me a few minutes, and I'll have the door wide open." He withdrew a codebreaker from his belt and activated it; the handheld device lit up with a flurry of small, blue and white lights, and when they reached the sailship's tightly sealed boarding ramp, he set it against the metal hull and left it mounted there. It remotely scanned the access system for the necessary passcode. "Three minutes, at most."

"Cc'istán! Subo la nabícula!"

A Tellurian soldier pointed toward them and shouted for support. Three others emerged from the crowd, raising their weapons. And then, rushing out of each darkened entryway was a battalion sworn to another flag—the badges on their arms revealed they had their guns pointed in service of the Albian Banking Advancement Conglomerate. Natharis looked straight into the barrels of their rifles, flanked by the Tellurian automatics, and put his hand on his gun. Erixen slowly raised his hands, but glanced at Natharis with a smirk contorting his face. He had a plan of some kind, but Natharis was reluctant to trust it. He'd seen too many trigger-happy soldiers before. But Erixen was a Colonial, and no matter what he was planning to do, it would surely be for the sake of duty. And it was a goal Natharis had no choice but to support.

Brock Dunham had insisted on meeting Pentakiya on the ABAC Headquarters' terrace, or so said his personal assistant, who led her up from the lobby to the sprawling courtyard atop the concrete spire. It was an oasis of greenery surrounded by the artificial dinginess of Dearborn. Despite the smog that crept overhead, the air smelled fresh.

Flowering plants lined the edges of two shimmering surface pools that danced with snaking streams of fountain water. Benches branded with bronze memorial plaques to ancient leaders stood set against the terrace walls. It was a garden fit for a man like Dunham, who deserved a tranquil place to think and take repose from his eternal struggle against Arterran greed and self-interest. In Pentakiya's mind, he paced across the terrace with racing thoughts. She wished she could know what went through his head. But he was a genius, of course, and she couldn't possibly hope to understand a genius's thoughts, and it was heretical to suggest otherwise.

The rooftop door opened, and her heart skipped a beat. But instead of her cherished executive stepping out onto the terrace, it was a group of eight men and women, all of whom Pentakiya recognized—they were her top scientists, who'd helped her in the pursuit of Brock Dunham's dreams. She smiled widely, happy to share the auspicious meeting with them, though a part of her wanted the executive's attention all to herself. Dunham's personal assistant, bearing a serving tray of champagne glasses, ushered them out in a line toward the pool to Pentakiya's back. She embraced her team and proposed a toast as they held up their glasses, anxious for the executive's arrival and official recognition of their dedicated efforts.

"To us, to the Commune, and, most importantly, to Executive Dunham!"

Pentakiya heard a lone pair of hands clap slowly and appreciatively behind the group. The realization of Dunham's arrival stole her breath. She and her team turned to face him, and tried their best to suppress their desire to run to him and ambush him with a fury of hugs and handshakes that lasted just a little too long. He smiled, and the fine lines that spread from the corners of his eyes, which Pentakiya hadn't expected, became more visible. He was handsome, she couldn't ever deny, but the more she compared his real-life appearance to those all over the Albian news networks and *The Harlequin Post*, the more she realized that he'd improved himself in his photos—*Just a little, of course*, she thought, *and no more than any other politician.* She regretted ever having considered the word "misleading" appropriate.

"My dear followers," Dunham began. *Yes! Followers!* thought Pentakiya. *We aren't just fans, or supporters—we're followers! And damned proud of it!*

"I've gathered you here today to recognize the scientific innovations I've brought to the Commune, and the unprecedented success I am so incredibly proud to have achieved. Even so, I couldn't have done it without you or your team, Dr. Curicon."

"Pentakiya, sir. I would be honored if you'd call me Pentakiya."

"Of course. Pentakiya it is." Brock Dunham smiled. Pentakiya felt her legs turn to jelly.

He continued, "With this technological breakthrough, perhaps the time will finally come when the whole of the Convergency fully realizes my political genius, which, as of late, only the educated and tolerant have come to recognize. I have never been more confident in my abilities to overcome the League of Arterra politically, economically—militaristically. The development of tachyon anchor capabilities is more important than you could possibly imagine.

"But these are dangerous times, loyal collectivists, and we cannot delude ourselves into believing that trust can be distributed as easily as wealth. The Arterrans have eyes and ears around every corner, both man and machine, and a prolific figure such as myself, with so much to lose, cannot afford the luxury of trust. Knowledge can be dangerous, dear followers—it can even be fatal. And sadly, I'm afraid you've accumulated the latter kind."

Four armed guards, brandishing military-grade rifles, stepped out onto the rooftop. And behind them followed none other than the Lord of Parliament Panzi Illoszia, saying nothing, only watching with a satisfied grin. The guards stood two by two on either side of the executive, who spoke, declaring, "Worry not, my children, for you have done me a great service, and I, in my mercy, have given you rest."

The torrent of bullets unleashed a furious thunder, and Pentakiya froze, awaiting the shot that would end her life, but felt nothing. She was untouched, unharmed. The ringing in her ears drowned out the screams of her scientists who fell to the ground bathed in blood, crying out for help, and begging Executive Dunham to spare them, to take pity upon them. He nearly shouted over their desperate pleas as he turned to Pentakiya and looked into the eyes that were quickly filling with tears.

"But you, Dr. Curicon," he said, "are a woman in whom I've solely placed my trust, and I believe that you will not disappoint me. I've heard of your loyalty to the Commune, your unwavering adherence to collectivism, and your fanatical hatred of the League of Arterra. These are all qualities I expect of my followers, and you have them, Dr. Curicon, even when those closest to you don't. You will continue your work, and I will provide you with the necessary means. I think

I can make a *powerful* example of you. The people of the Commune could learn much from someone who *surely* would follow my decrees in spite of more personal loyalties."

He smiled with a hidden knowledge in his eyes. "The worst is over, Pentakiya. All that remains is my glory."

He motioned to his guards, and they escorted him off the rooftop, to a flight set for the capital of Bhalenjar. Pentakiya was left to stand alone, gazing upon the desecrated bodies of those who'd dedicated their lives to the pursuit of Dunham's utopia. They'd lived for the cause, bled for the cause, and died for it. At that moment, she didn't understand why—and couldn't possibly understand why. She'd been told that Brock Dunham was the noblest man the Convergency had ever seen. Was this nobility? Was it mercy?

She tried to come to her senses. *He knows more than I do,* she thought, *and the risk of betrayal was too high.* Executive Dunham had the utmost foresight. She cursed herself for forgetting it. He'd charged her with the task of continuing his mission, of bringing the Commune to the forefront of Congress, and one day, the galaxy. She'd carry on her team's legacy, even when their faces were replaced with others unknown, whose names might be just as easily forgotten by history.

They didn't die in vain, she told herself, wiping away tears from her eyes. *They died for the greater good.*

The plasma bolts lit up the docking bay like fireworks, flashing across Livia's field of vision in a blaze of shooting stars, and her heart pounded to the sound of their crackling thuds against the sailship's hull. She climbed hurriedly out of the bathing pool and snatched a towel off the ground, dropped by a frightened servant who'd since fled the festival. She wrapped it around her body and ran to her handmaid, who cowered against the docking bay wall, cloaked in shadow and crying softly. Livia slipped into her clothes and put her arm around the young girl, assuring her she was safe, though in reality, she didn't know of any way to protect her.

"Thank *goodness*!" shouted Mickel Green, who ran desperately toward Livia and her servant. His breath was strained and shallow, and the fat of his gut swayed with his unsteady gait. "You're *safe*! And if you *weren't*, you certainly are *now*! I *am*, after all, an *ABAC* representative." He smiled slyly. "And *I'm* granting you immunity." He winked. "You *need* it—there aren't any *soldiers* to save you."

Green put his hand on the handmaid's shoulder and shoved her away. "Run along now, girl," he commanded, pointing his finger toward the passageway. "You're not safe here. But don't worry, with *this* pretty one right here, I've got *everything* under control."

Livia tried to stand up, but Green pushed her down on her knees. "We wouldn't want someone to *see* you now, would we?" He grinned and put his hand on her chest, pinning her down. "Hiding is best done in the *dark*, you little Tellurian whore."

"There's too many of them!"

The sound of energetic gunfire covered Erixen's shouts, but Natharis didn't take his eyes off his targets, who unleashed a barrage of plasma bolts shot with the accuracy of a Communal who'd slept his way through military academy. The Tellurians had better aim—a bullet grazed Natharis's arm, and he recoiled, the sting of hot metal still seething on his skin. With one hand covering his wound he continued to fire upon his enemy, aiming more intently at the ABAC forces, whose presence he had a deeper reason to fear. The Tellurian troops had limited backup on Earth; ABAC had an infinite army of blind, zealous soldiers ready and waiting to die for their god-king.

"I thought you had a plan!" Natharis yelled through the fray.

"What gave you THAT idea?!"

Erixen scanned his surroundings for an exit and ran, but Natharis didn't look back to see him retreat. He scowled as he dodged the onslaught of bullets and returned fire, taken aback by Erixen's spinelessness. He wondered how he managed to become a marshal in the first place; abandoning his partner was a renouncement of the Judicial oath he took in his naïve youth. He left Natharis even more vulnerable, and the combined ABAC and Tellurian forces encroached on his position in a shrinking circle. The boarding ramp still hadn't opened, and there was nowhere to hide.

He shut his eyes and prepared for the single inevitable shot that would bring his mission to an abrupt, ignoble end. But just as he began to clench his teeth and wince in fearful anticipation, he heard one of the soldiers scream out for help; they opened fire, but away from Natharis. He opened his eyes and saw the chaff of ABAC's war machine collapse to the ground, and the torches turned spilt blood to the color of fire. And in their flickering light soared a darkened silhouette with the likeness of a woman.

The figure spun head over heels in the air, and she ended her graceful backflip with a breathtaking landing on towering stilettos, her dual pistols blazing and decimating the horde of troops encircling her. A siren sounded and heavy spotlights drowned the docking bay in light, and Natharis's unexpected savior was revealed. The woman was stunning in her furious beauty, with the way her straight, black hair tossed about her as she fired upon the enemy, and the distinct, Muscovian green of her eyes seemed to glow, shining brightly beneath eyelids painted blue and over deep crimson lips. The atomic bombshell, with skin as white as phosphorous and a stance as fearsome as a Muscovian carpet bombing, took the entire crowd by surprise, but most especially Natharis Ruke, who'd not only been unaware of her presence, but who'd ultimately expected a man.

The soldiers' jaws dropped, and with her dagger-like heels, she broke the very jaws she'd caused to hang open, awestruck. She pegged Natharis with another handgun strapped to her thigh. "Keep your back to mine, Colonial!" she shouted with a heavy Muscovian accent. "We will pave our trail with corpses!"

The sound of her gunshots was like the spectacular percussion of the most glorious of Tchaikovsky suites, to which Natharis added his part, the rolling field drums of Colonial marches. They pushed their way through the security forces toward the Tellurian sailship at the heart of the docking bay, the position Natharis had abandoned upon the Muscovite's dramatic entrance. He finally caught sight of Erixen—he was hiding to the side, having crept back toward the ship once the situation appeared less hopeless, and Natharis caught him by the arm and dragged him along toward the access port. The ZGB operative trailed behind, her stiletto lodged in the mouth of an ABAC soldier. She pulled it from his lifeless body and stomped on the ground to shake off his slimy gray matter.

The marshals reached the sailship and Natharis rushed to see the codebreaker's progress. "Just over forty seconds left!" he yelled. "But I think we'll have to take the ship with us!"

————

"This is a religious pilgrimage!" Livia cried. *"What have you gotten us into?"* She flailed her arms and kicked her legs to push Mickel Green off of her, but his weight kept her pinned to the ground. The putrid heat of his breath touched her face; she cringed, and tried to look away, but he grabbed her by the neck and forced her to look him in the eye.

"Shut up, you worthless, little bitch," he snapped. "You and your ignorant people will all be speaking *Shatarin* by the time you see what we've set in motion." He tore open her delicate robe and began to lap between her breasts; Livia felt as though she might vomit as his thick saliva dripped over her chest. She begged him to stop, but Green dismissed her cries for mercy, asserting, "You're a Tellurian sacred whore. It's your *duty* to want this."

She thrust her knee between his legs and he howled, rolling over in pain. Livia desperately tried to crawl away, heading deeper into the docking bay to cross into the spotlights. Just as she reached her arm out of the shadows, Green reappeared, and dropped his foot onto the small of her back. He knelt down and stroked her hair. "They *won't* save you. After all, you'll just be doing what you were *born* to do." Tears streamed down her face when she heard him unzip his pants and push them down his shapeless thighs. She begged her god to save her. She begged the whole of the Pantheon.

But it wasn't Neptune's trident or Jupiter's thunderbolt that struck Mickel Green down. The icy blue eyes revealed the man who'd haunted her visions, and whom she saw, if only for an instant, while naked in the ritual bath. His face was chiseled like the statues of Apollo, his arms as strong as those of Atlas, his muscles swelling as he swung his fists straight into Green's face. He beat him until blood ran from his nose and mouth, and each blow rattled with the crunch of broken bones. The blue-eyed man didn't stop until every fat-cushioned rib was broken. He stood, and Green, sobbing and spitting blood, tried pathetically to escape his assailant. The beaten ABAC representative writhed upon the ground like a bloated worm. The victor stepped away.

He came for Livia and helped her to her feet. His eyes locked her in a trance, and she felt his hand on her shoulder as an eagle's wing, tucking her in his feathers for a spectacular escape. But the sound of Green's gargling screams broke his stare, and he looked behind him to the ground, as did Livia. The consitor Silviano was running toward Livia and her rescuer, and he tore a soldier's knife from its sheath without warning. He lunged for Green, and thrust the blade deep into the wounded man's back. He withdrew it violently with two hands, and the man's body went limp, his terrified eyes held lifeless in their hopeless stare. Silviano looked down upon him and smiled. He kicked his corpse in its side and spat on it.

———————

"Get to the ship!" Natharis commanded. He wrapped his arm firmly around the Tellurian girl as he guided her toward the center of the docking bay, the focus of the festival. The backstabbing bodybuilder followed, his eyes fixed solely on the girl, whose own gaze was cast unwaveringly upon Natharis's face. They ran across the platform past the few soldiers still standing; Erixen and the Muscovite were waiting anxiously at the sailship's access port. To Natharis's relief, it was wide open, and when he heard the shouts of approaching reinforcements, he urged the Tellurians to run faster.

The Muscovite stood her ground until they reached the ship, and after firing one last fatal shot, she dodged up the access ramp and immediately began her search for the crate delivered in ABAC's name. The Tellurian stayed at the base of the ramp, ushering in his female counterpart, who looked back to Natharis in desperation. The man pushed her up into the sailship, where she watched their escape from the passenger windows. And Erixen, refusing to engage in a fight he found unfair, made a run for the back of the passenger bay, abandoning his assumed post on the ground. He thrust his weapon into the Tellurian man's hands—"It's all yours," he panted—and took cover inside the ship.

With the Tellurian at his side, Natharis held off the oncoming troops. While thankful nonetheless, he was taken aback by his foreign partner's willingness to open fire, though he did focus his attention on ABAC's incompetent troops and not his own people. The soldiers began to target the ship itself, and plasma bolts pummeled the cockpit; the ZGB operative, sitting in the passenger seat, shouted and cursed silently behind the windows. But the shower of bullets came to an end when a distant rumbling drove the soldiers to drop their weapons. They ran, screaming to one another to organize a place to regroup, and Natharis and the Tellurian stood with their guns still raised.

The Muscovite pounded on the cockpit window to catch Natharis's attention. She motioned urgently for him and the

Tellurian to retreat into the sailship. Natharis cupped his hands around his mouth and yelled, "I know—I see them!"

Opening the hatch and poking her head out into the open, the operative addressed the Tellurian, saying, "We'll be borrowing your little church van." The crashes in the distance grew louder and she snapped closed the hatch. Natharis and the foreigner rushed into the ship, but before shutting the access port, Natharis took one last look at the coming enemy.

The Tellurian Legionnaires lurched forward over the desert plain to the west, and the earth shook beneath their mechanized limbs, like giants decimating their way across the world. He didn't wait to see the blinding flash of their weapons; he smacked the switch and the ramp withdrew. The door slid shut, muting the thunderous footsteps of the Tellurian forces, who'd descended from their orbital fleet to turn one of their own ships into a pile of smoldering debris. The Tellurian man looked to Natharis for an explanation as he passed into the passenger hold, asking, or shouting, "Why the hell are they firing on their own ship?"

"At this point, I think ABAC's pulling the Imperial strings."

The ship's atmospheric engines roared, and it rose into the air high above the encroaching column of Legionnaires. When its Muscovian pilot steered it toward the battalion, Natharis instantly objected. "What in God's name do you think you're doing?" he barked.

"It is fastest way out. Don't worry, Colonial," she assured him. "I've flown before."

She hit the accelerator and the sailship rocketed across the sky over the shadowy desert. The Legionnaires charged their cannons and opened fire, targeting the ship with heavy plasma bolts and rocketry, and though the repurposed pilgrimage vessel raced ahead of the metal beasts, it wasn't beyond their reach. Its passengers struggled to keep their balance inside of the shaking cabin rocked by artillery fire. Natharis knew they'd soon go down in flames if he didn't act.

He leapt into a gun turret suspended from the belly of the sailship and took the handles in his hands, gripping them tightly as he spun the light automatic until mechanized soldiers were at the very tip of its barrel. He shouted at the Tellurian, who jumped up at attention. "You take the other gun!" he commanded. The cranking thud of machine gunfire reverberated throughout the ship as he engaged the ruthless giants, crashing to the sound of the upper turret's deadly drumroll.

"You know, we could have just taken our speeders and avoided this whole mess!" Natharis yelled from the turret at the Muscovian operative, who darted her eyes back just for a second to acknowledge him, her attention fixed firmly on her evasive maneuvers.

"You mean burning wrecks I saw outside exoport?" she laughed. "Very strange, to be caught so easily by such incompetent soldiers. You must have had terrible hiding spot." She lowered her voice when they passed out of weapons range. The entire party seemed to sigh in unison, and for the moment, they were relieved, until they heard the breathy screech of a nearby aircraft. The ZGB operative ordered them to sit and shouted, "Your Imperium doesn't give up, does it?"

Two Tellurian fighters were right on their tail as they flashed over the barren wasteland, and the enemy gunfire rapidly began to deplete the sailship's shield barriers, such that the ship itself shook and groaned, tilting left and right like it was balancing on a tightrope track. The damage was mounting, and the sailship was growing tired, cumbersome, unwilling to respond to the Muscovite's aerial demands. Natharis aimed and fired at their pursuers, but the Tellurian hesitated, his face revealing his shock. Natharis sympathized with the man. He'd been doing a service to his nation, only to be stabbed in the back by those meant to protect him, all in the name of a corrupt corporation.

"This thing won't hold together!" Erixen screamed. He hugged the crate that hovered just a bit off the floor, ABAC's coveted property, and tried his best not to look at the massive canyon stretching out below them.

The Muscovite stood up from the pilot's seat and pointed to the back of the passenger cabin. "Take stolen property with you," she instructed. "We're going to have to jump ship." She spoke nonchalantly about the idea of plummeting to their deaths instead of burning away in the sky. "Everyone to cabin!"

"Are you crazy?!" Erixen shrieked.

"You're welcome to stay onboard," the Muscovite replied. "It will be old-fashioned Colonial barbecue when Tellurians blow you out of sky."

She didn't bother to warn the passengers before she pulled the emergency jettison switch, nor did she draw attention to the limited set of parachutes behind them. Erixen was the first to scream out. The operative smiled.

"Bombs away."

The cabin floor collapsed. Its metal surface ejected down toward the seemingly bottomless canyon, tumbling in the wind until it disappeared into the shadows. And right behind it fell the passengers, kicking and screaming and flailing their arms and legs in the cold rush of air, down into the gaping mouth of the canyon that threatened to swallow them whole.

10

"There has never been a greater threat to galactic prosperity than the cancerous demographic of Xaztechua and Bahía Brumosa. Under my tenure, the streets of Chesapeake will never hear the boasts of migrant Children of the Dole glorifying their own theft of Colonials' rightly earned income to support their seemingly limitless reproductive capabilities."
—Colonial Executive Desh Maru

THE SHEER, BLUE CURTAINS billowed in the warm breeze that brushed through the open window, and the rising sun over Bhalenjar glowed golden through the delicate silk drapery. The radiance of the sunrise began its ascent at the base of the bedroom walls and climbed higher, creeping up until it'd reached the ceiling like a spotlight. The executive's wife turned over at the edge of sleep, adjusting her naked body to face away from the window, and the sunlight revealed the snow white of her skin and the gentle curve of her back. Her breathing was soft and gentle, spreading over her husband's chest like the wind that caressed him beside her. Desh cherished the peaceful morning, thanked Heaven for its beauty, and pushed back the thought of Congress's next session, to be commenced in just a few hours' time.

He placed a hand gently on her shoulder and whispered in her ear. "Chloé," he sighed, then kissed her cheek. She stirred, turned to face him, and she smiled with newly opened eyes. Her husband touched his lips to hers. He kissed her, and breathed deeply as he settled beside her.

In that moment he recalled their first night together, when he'd kissed her just as deeply, and felt a love for her that was new and exciting, which over the years became the most unshakable commitment. They'd met in law school on the Gallic capital of La Seine, in a serendipitous encounter at a café. Desh went there to meet someone else, but that girl stood him up; he no longer remembered her name. Seeing a sullen young man sitting alone with two cups of coffee, Chloé, a complete stranger, sat down to join him.

"Excuse-moi, cette place est-elle prise?" she'd asked with a charming smile, pointing to the untaken seat across from him. *"Tu as deux cafés, mais je ne vois pas ton rancard."*

Within hours, they were holding hands on an evening stroll by the riverside, and found a quaint hotel for the night, with open windows overlooking the twinkling city of Lutetia in place of the university mall. It was a night he'd wanted to last forever, just like the morning he was currently spending in bed beside her.

Soon there'd be no more joyful sighs or excited smiles, and there'd be no relief from the unpleasant reality of his presence on Bhalenjar for one purpose only: to recite the same words over and over again to no effect before a mob of screaming, irrational extremists. He was glad his wife wanted nothing to do with his politics. She'd insisted on staying out of the spotlight, not out of a fear of eclipsing her husband or out of a traditional obedience, but because the very thought of interacting publicly with collectivists was inherently repulsive. Desh had to agree on just how sickening the Congressional sessions truly were. He just wished he had the luxury of turning a blind eye to them, like he turned a blind eye to the alarm clock beside him, waiting only for his wife's next breath.

———

The Crystallines weren't known to be particularly vocal in the legislature, even with their representation on the Executive Council. While they were an economic power and a leader in mining and distribution, they didn't often find themselves in a situation warranting a public complaint. When they did, they always had the Arterrans for support. And when the Crystalline lobbyist group presented their testimony before the Council that day, Desh knew he'd soon be compelled to defend them. Brock Dunham, though a vocal critic of what he consistently termed "racism," was fiercely racist against the Crystallines, who, having no societal concept of money among themselves, were useless in his game of relentless, systematic theft.

Their bodies flickered with bursts of internal electricity, but the entirety of Congress was unable to decipher their binary language, and instead relied on a well-programmed computer to relay their electrical impulses in audible words. The translations were often monotonous, though not in their cadence or intonation, but in their subject matter, as they addressed a topic exhausted time and time again by numerous races throughout the Convergency.

They, like many others, complained of the Shatarins' consistent disruption of their trade routes and shameless disregard for the Crystallines' border policies. The lobbyists demanded the legal right to patrol the tachyon veins running between their systems to prevent the illegal settlement of Shatarins and Xaztechuans alike—the former considered an immediate danger in terms of safety and demographics, and the latter a serious economic threat. Evidently, the Sapien invaders had little concern for the Crystalline planets' inhospitable environments. The Crystallines' physical need for solar radiation and atmospheric gases poisonous to

Sapiens made their worlds unsuitable for organic life. And naturally, the collectivists condemned the Crystallines as a species of racists and xenophobes, who were too bigoted to give undue shelter to the Children of the Dole.

The lobbyists begged for Desh's support, saying that collectivist pressure on their civilization was now leaving them little choice but to expend resources on providing safe and adequate housing for individuals who had no right to be there in the first place, let alone demand a single provision. Their internal economy, known for its strength and low-risk business, would crumble and break apart just as the Convergency's as a whole.

Executive Dunham had heard enough. "What your little lobbyist group has proven is that there is not a single Crystalline in the galaxy with even a basic education," he stated bluntly, addressing Executive Feldspar, who represented the fearful Crystallines. "If you'd stop wasting your money on industry and infrastructure and actually put it toward something culturally productive, you wouldn't be having this problem. But you seem to be set in your ways, so for your people, bigotry it'll have to be."

Desh let out a sigh of boredom. Executive Dunham noticed but dismissed it. "ABAC, the Commune and the other collectivists unanimously agree that the Crystallines should be compelled to engage in a program of wide-scale terraformation. The idea that innocent immigrants should be incinerated by gamma rays or suffocated by atmospheric cyanide is completely unacceptable. And should the Crystallines reject our call for Sentient rights despite our mounting pressure, then we will force them to comply by whatever means necessary."

"Do you plan to tax them out of existence?" Executive Molotova chuckled. A stir of quiet laughter spread through the individualist groups in the balconies of the Convergent Senate.

"If their nonexistence is the only way to provide a proper home for a poor family, then yes, I suppose I do," Dunham replied. He looked to the collectivist senators for support, which they readily gave in the form of cheers and shouts of votive admiration.

"Is that a threat?" Desh asked. "A sensible leader would watch his tongue. Genocide is a crime you can't hide from."

Dunham smirked. "A *sensible* leader speaks out against *injustice.*"

"Indeed, he does. Which is why you must know that any attempt to forcibly terraform a Crystalline planet, or any enabling of foreign, demographic conquest, will result only in the immediate arrival of Colonial fleets at those systems in question. And in the defense of the Crystallines, we will consider no weapon off-limits."

"Executive Maru, it is only a matter of time before you and your beloved Arterra finally accept that the only sustainable system is one in which the people's financial doubt is eradicated," Dunham asserted. "And when the day comes that you choose to put aside your self-serving worldview and truly consider the plight of others, the name 'Arterra' will be forgotten. You'll just be another part of the Convergency—the one that was *meant* to be, not the one stifled by your constant vetoes and cries of opposition. Each new law we pass will drive the League of Arterra's ideology deeper and deeper into the ground."

Mireille Leveque of Gallia was visibly disgusted. "Our ideology is the reason we are still standing. Your policy of open borders is a farcical solution to economic problems. What good is bringing in an additional workforce when you have no jobs for your *own* population? Do you really think that adding *more* to your dole will nurture prosperity?" She laughed at the thought, and with each dismissive wave of her hand, her sapphire bracelets glittered. "In *La République Fédérée de la Gaule*, we simply deport those who wish to take advantage of our hospitality, and we have prospered for it.

Every illegal Shatarin we send away is just another dollar left in a working man's pocket."

Brock Dunham refused to allow such racism to go unpunished. "We will *never* stop supporting the right of the less fortunate to live within your borders, whether with your permission or not. They, too, have a right to happiness and prosperity, and if they deem Arterra to be their best option—for whatever reason—then we will fight with all our might for their freedom to do so. The League of Arterra has shamelessly stolen their livelihood by dominating the economic arena of this Convergency, and these immigrants, documented or not, simply want to take what is rightfully theirs, and what should have been given to them from the very beginning with no questions asked or conditions imposed. And when you find your cities bustling with diversity and chattering with the sound of a thousand languages, you'll know you've been defeated. For with your quaint, little democratic system will come your downfall. When there are three Shatarins, or Xaztechuans, or Bahía Brumosans for every native Arterran, it is inevitable that you and your camp will be voted out of power.

"All around you, civilizations are coming to their senses. Those with open eyes have recognized that to be truly progressive is to redistribute the very root of all our problems: money. But when all citizens of the Convergency have equal wealth and equal savings, money will no longer be the greatest issue. The only problem that will remain will be the League of Arterra itself, standing alone in the face of more civilized, more evolved societies that proudly identify as collectivists.

"The Arterrans lived for centuries in the hollowed-out ruins of the decadent Procyon, and, in due time, will collapse into the graveyard of Procyon civilization that the League was built upon. The childish and archaic concepts of 'individualism,' 'self-fulfillment' and 'productivity' are virtues that only a culture cradled in Conestoga wagons would cherish. But I do believe that the Arterran problem will solve itself with each release of a Convergent census. Its only resolution will be when the League of Arterra submits to Convergent policy and begins to consider itself part of the whole—the greater whole that is the Interstellar Convergency, and not just a collection of backwater planets claiming to be eternal havens of prosperity and righteousness."

Desh had grown immune to the collectivists' unending insults, their criticisms offered without evidence or proof to validate them, and their quickness to resort to ad hominem attacks in place of a legitimate, constructive debate. But he still found himself unable to truly understand the delusional logic that governed all their words and decisions, especially those of Executive Dunham, who seemed perfectly content to live in a fantasy world in which there was no middle class, but two extremes. He wanted a massive support base of poverty-stricken voters who voted to perpetuate their own poverty over the generations, and an elite group of the super-wealthy who profited off the suffering of others. The corporatist collectivists wanted to see the death of the middle class, the eradication of self-earned wealth and independence from government meddling. And the people of the League of Arterra were that same middle class who suffocated under the reign of the Albian Banking Advancement Conglomerate, its flock of sheep followers, and its most infallible pontiff, Executive Dunham.

———

The stage lights glared brightly over the news studio, but they were dim in comparison to the blinding platinum blond of the episode's guest contributor. Misha shielded her eyes to protect herself. It was like staring directly into the sun, hence the name of the woman's newest line of salon-inspired products, *Solar Flare Your Dark Hair*. Rumor had it that leading scientists declared the dye to be particularly dangerous, as when it caught the sunlight in just the right way, it had the potential to cause a loss of vision. She couldn't imagine that her guest would deliberately try to burn the retinas of innocent onlookers, though she likely hoped to blind the hordes of paparazzi that followed her from interview to interview. Her name was Valeria Estrada, the leader of the pack on the less-than-tasteful serial, *The Schnazzy Wives of Vizcayami*, and Misha meant to interview her that day—that is, if she could just find herself a suitable pair of sunglasses.

Valeria was a beautiful woman, Misha had to admit, and it was no surprise that she'd ascended the ranks of celebrities until she came out on top. It wasn't long before she started to give her opinions on politics and social issues, and while Misha would have normally dismissed a celebrity's input as useless and uninformed, Valeria was, in fact, quite intelligent. When she wasn't lunging over ritzy restaurant tables to slap her rivals across the face, she was writing editorials about immigration, demographics and gun control. No one expected to, but everyone respected her, despite her serial's reputation for being a guilty pleasure that few admitted to following. Misha herself had never really kept up with the series, but she knew its premise, and consequently had little desire to learn more. She was, however, interested in what the Vizcayamian socialite had to say as the cameras went live.

The renowned journalist began with her usual introduction, addressing the sons and daughters of Liberty directly, as though she knew each of them personally. She announced that Valeria would be discussing her always interesting views on immigration, and that it would be an especially fascinating subject, given that critics of her serial too often compared Vizcayami to the socially tasteless Xaztechua in the heart of the Commune. Misha began, "The latest reports from Bhalenjar recount Executive Dunham's promotion of illegal immigration into the League of Arterra. Tell us, Valeria: Is this something we should be worried about?"

"Unfortunately, yes, it is. But Brock Dunham doesn't have to do a thing about it, because people were already pouring out of the Commune long before he started telling them to. The Shatarins have always had a religious policy of engaging in demographic warfare, and the Xaztechuans are notorious for their ability to fill up an entire neighborhood of tenements in less than two or three days, which Arterran scientists haven't been able to fully explain."

Misha nodded, equally confused by the seemingly impossible data. "No one can argue that the League of Arterra is the most prosperous alliance of eparchies in the Convergency, so it's logical to assume that refugees would be inclined to come here. But there's an abundance of uncharted planets out there, which they could easily and legally claim as their own, instead of deciding to infiltrate other states' borders."

"They're nonproductive," Valeria argued with a roll of her eyes. "They're not going to build something for themselves. They just need to take what others already have, until there's nothing left to steal."

"I can't speak for the whole League, but I can tell you that Colonials are by no means xenophobic, nor do we have any moral objection to immigration. We welcome people who express a desire to contribute to our society or have talents we might have a shortage of. But the Communals who flood our tachyon lenses don't fit either of those categories."

"The only particular talent Xaztechuans have is in repeating the same mistakes over and over again, and never considering that they themselves might be the problem," Valeria quipped.

"And what mistakes are you referring to?"

"Look at the Xaztechuans and their dictator. President Chamorro has been voted into power time and time again, regardless of his destructive policies. Then the Xaztechuans run from their collapsing society and come to more developed ones seeking political asylum. And *then* they vote for the same policies that drove them to run in the first place. They've got no foresight, and when their elected leaders fail them like they always do, then the Communals claim it's because of racism, which we all know isn't the real problem.

"The fact is that people need to take a good look at themselves and really question if the system of thought they were raised in is beneficial or destructive. It doesn't do anyone any good to accept something just because you grew up believing it's true. That's how you collapse a society. And that's how you turn your citizens into slaves."

Pentakiya had always taken pride in her unwavering beliefs. She wasn't one to change her position, and she never apologized for her loyalties. She'd been born and raised with a collectivist mindset, and as far as she was concerned, there was little reason to question her upbringing and the ideology it had nurtured in her. The defense of the greater good was the noblest pursuit for a woman like her, and Executive Dunham, a champion of righteousness in the face of selfishness and bigotry, became her personal role model. He was just and fair, and no one could challenge the steps he took to exalt the wrongfully oppressed Children of the Dole. The ends undeniably justified the means; it was frustrating that anyone would dare think otherwise. But for the first time in her life, she wondered if different steps could have been taken to achieve the same moral goal.

The guilt was unfathomable. She knew that he must have had a greater reason for the massacre, for watering the rooftop garden with the blood of his followers. They'd done everything he asked of them, and they did it all for his glory, not theirs. Yet he still felt they deserved to die. Perhaps they did—perhaps she did as well. She certainly felt like a traitor, and she began to doubt that she could be trusted, let alone trust herself. Brock Dunham was a man of limitless wisdom, surpassing even a celebrated scientist in knowledge, and he knew more than Pentakiya did about her own project. There must have been a grave threat at hand, one of which she was unaware. He never would have slaughtered innocent people so casually, though they may not have been truly innocent to begin with.

Rocky was innocent, and even that wasn't enough to save him from the despicable Colonials. Pentakiya missed him every day, but for once was glad he hadn't been with her at the Headquarters. He, too, could have been chastised with bullets; tragically, the punishments he would endure under Colonial law were even crueler. She had no doubt that he was far away in the frozen prison of Jotunheim, never to be seen again. Everyone knew about the icy moon's nightmarish reputation, that it was the final resting place of what the Colonials thought unforgiveable. She might as well forget his name. The Colonials would erase him from memory, miles beneath a darkened tundra.

He was detained under curious circumstances, and even Pentakiya had to admit that there was something strange about his disappearance. Colonial authorities caught him within their borders and immediately took him into custody, but never sent a subsequent search party to look for their detainee's partners. He was aboard a short-range shuttle; they must have known that he couldn't have come from very far. As ruthless as the Colonials were, they were more inclined to deport undocumented migrants in their territory, especially when they were innocent of violent crimes. She would have expected them to send Rocky back to the Commune with a nasty bruise on the wrist, but he never returned. For some reason, they kept him. There was more to the story—she was sure of it.

As an experienced researcher, she always lived her life in pursuit of the elusive answers. This time, though, she didn't want to solve the morbid riddles of Brock Dunham's choices or Rocky's disappearance. She wasn't sure if she could handle the reality behind them. After all, she understood that lies were nothing more than the truth in masquerade. And the faces behind the masks might prove too hideous to look upon.

————

Tageron gazed out his office window over the open plain. Temporary fences marked its borders, a sign of imminent construction. He'd recently bought the land with the intention of laying another mass driver rail. Shipping capabilities would be greatly expanded, as would his profits, and the whole endeavor would create hundreds of jobs, many permanent. With that new rail, stretching across the grassy plain with the sun caught on its edge, he'd not only benefit his own company, but the city of Tarem as a whole, at whose border the site's fences stood.

His hopes for the future brought the same smile he'd worn while signing the deal. He'd suffered a number of setbacks over the past several years, and a successful project was a welcome relief from the difficulties of keeping a business afloat in the raging sea of collectivist politics. Good things were coming—he could feel it. After the storm he'd see the brilliant light of ambition and accomplishment, just as he had so many years ago as a poor boy living in the slums of Tarem. Like then, he had an idea, nurtured it, and found a way to make a living off of it, as did those whom he very fairly employed. He even planned to raise their wages with the increased revenue. Everybody won.

The businessman heard someone quietly push open the office door. He didn't need to look back to know who'd entered unannounced. The shallow, hurried breathing and the curiously loud clack of his shoes on the floor gave away his identity. His lawyer had arrived—without an appointment.

"What do you want, Alit?"

He turned around to face the briefcase-toting attorney and sighed. He had the same mousy face as he did ten years prior, just with more wrinkles on his brow and at the corners of his bright eyes. Though he often looked worried, Alit arrived that day with a gray aura of nervousness, one that made the thinning hair on his head seem to stand on end. He hurried to the chair set before Tageron's desk and put down his effects, then rummaged through them until he found a single sheet of holopaper that he thrust into his client's hands. Tageron glanced at it briefly but only noticed the gleaming sigil at the top of the page, representing the government of the City of Tarem. Whatever the notice was, it was sure to be frustrating, if not completely infuriating. He looked to Alit for an explanation before sitting down and reading the contents of the letter in full.

"They're seizing your land," the lawyer announced. Tageron slammed his fist on the desk.

"The new construction site? I've already purchased it. It's a done deal—finalized, irrevocable."

"The city government is under a lot of pressure, as I'm sure you already know," Alit continued. "The corporatist collectivists are pushing for an expansion of government-funded housing for Tarem's low-income population."

"You mean the influx of Shatarins and Xaztechuans who've graced us with their bloodsucking presence?"

"Well, I suppose that's one way of putting it. But like it or not, these people are here, and they're here to stay." Alit closed his briefcase and settled down. "Maybe canceling the deal is an inconvenience, but it's better than having hundreds of impoverished migrants starving in the streets."

Tageron stared in disbelief. He'd hired his lawyer years earlier, back when Hatal-Om boasted a free-market economy and an ideology that fostered the rapid growth of small businesses; at that time, the planet's standard of living was the highest in its sector. And, back then, Alit had a different attitude toward those sorts of issues. He always did have a habit of abruptly switching clients according to changing trends in thought, but he proved fairly consistent with Tageron, who started to believe the attorney had finally given up on his past flakiness. But it seemed that nowadays he held another opinion, one bordering on sympathetic to the collectivists' meddling in Caspian affairs, and that he really hadn't changed much at all.

"An inconvenience? No. It's an outrage, and completely unacceptable. I'll fight this—I promise you." Rubbing his temples, he fought a coming headache. "I'll have my assistant contact the proper authorities and sort this whole mess out."

"It's pointless, Tageron. The city has already made up its mind. The government housing will be built over the next few weeks, and you'll have a bird's-eye view of its construction."

"So, I'll spend the coming months watching as the government mocks me each passing day."

"They're not *mocking* you, Tageron. If anything, it's a reminder of the plight of others, and our shared responsibility to provide for their wellbeing."

"Then house them somewhere else. I bought that property. It's mine."

"What does 'mine' mean, anyway? In this day and age, there's no room for such selfish rhetoric."

"Selfish?" Tageron barked, dumbfounded. "Is it *selfish* to want to keep what I've rightfully earned? Why should I be forced to give up the very project that could increase profits and allow me to hire new employees, and pay my current employees even higher wages?"

"The poor in question don't have jobs, and I doubt you have any intention of hiring *them*."

"I doubt they have any intention of working," Tageron snapped.

"It's thinking like that that put these people in this situation to begin with," Alit said. "You expect they'll pass up an opportunity, so you deny them that very opportunity before they've even had a chance to decide."

"Trends across the Convergency show that they do have a tendency to choose a sedentary lifestyle over one of productivity."

"Well, maybe *these* people won't."

"Maybe they will."

Alit paused, unsure of how to respond, and withdrew another notice from his briefcase. He slid it onto Tageron's desk.

"And what is this, exactly?"

"It's a declaration of the city's approved taxation plan for the coming fiscal year," the lawyer explained. "It goes into effect in less than a month."

"Just say it, Alit."

"To fund the housing project, the City of Tarem plans to implement a forty-eight percent raise in corporate taxes. And sadly, you fall under that category of 'corporation.'"

Tageron ran his finger along the printed lines and scowled. "So, not only are they seizing my rightly purchased land, but now they're raising my taxes to support the same project that drove them to steal from my company in the first place?" He laughed in disbelief. "It's bad enough that we won't be generating the revenue we'd projected from the new rail, but now we'll be *losing* money."

"Somebody has to pay for the housing, Tageron."

"It's no one's place to force me to do so."

"The City of Tarem—"

"The City of Tarem thinks that it can hold a gun to a business owner's head and force him to support the undeserved livelihood of people who shouldn't even be here," Tageron argued. "The city's rewarding the subversion of immigration law and punishing those who've built legitimate lives for themselves—*independent* lives."

"You know as well as I do that they didn't come to break the law, but to escape persecution on their own homeworlds."

"What persecution? The Shatarin Empire probably paid for them to settle here."

"Even if that were true, it doesn't mean they don't still need help."

"You're saying that people who traveled to our planet with the sole purpose of outbreeding the native population need help from *us* in doing so?"

"Would you prefer that they die of hunger or exposure?"

"No, I'd prefer that they leave."

"They have nowhere else to go. They won't leave."

"Then deport them."

"You know we can't."

"Why not? The Arterrans deport them every day."

"We're not the Arterrans."

"Well, maybe that's the problem, then, isn't it?"

Tageron crumpled up the tax notice and tossed it into the wastebasket under his desk. And just when he thought the infuriating conversation was over, Alit presented one last letter.

"There's more, Tageron. Your property taxes are going up as well."

"By how much?"

"Thirty-five percent."

"*All* property taxes, or just mine?"

"Just yours."

"And why is that?"

"The notice states that your proximity to the new housing project is grounds for higher taxation. The Children of the Dole are going to be forced to look at your shiny, luxury office every day, and it's going to upset them knowing that they aren't getting any share of your pay, since you have so much, and they have so little. Your success is offensive."

"Offensive?"

"It makes others feel bad about their own, less grandiose, accomplishments."

"So, I make them feel bad that they've chosen not to do a damned thing with their lives?"

"It's important to keep their feelings in mind, Tageron."

"There's more to this than their 'feelings,' I guarantee it," Tageron grumbled. "They're trying to force me off my property so they can seize this land as well. They think that if they suffocate me with enough taxes and prevent me from expanding my enterprise, they'll force me to move elsewhere."

"I doubt they want you off the planet."

"I suppose you're right. Without people like me and my employees, they'd have no one to support the financial grave they're calling 'government housing.'"

"The only grave that's being dug is your own, since you refuse to change your ideology to align more with the collectivists'. Arterran thinking is delusional and obsolete."

"So, Alit, you come here to tell me three pieces of incredibly bad news, and now you stand before me in my own office *insulting* the way I run my business? And *belittling* my opinions?"

"It's all for the greater good."

"I'll tell you what I'll do to promote the 'greater good.' I'm letting you go."

"What?" Alit gasped, shocked.

"Looks like *your* grave is ready, and your career is falling right into it. I don't need someone like you as a legal advocate."

"I've been *nothing* but loyal, Tageron!"

"Loyalty means nothing when pledged by a collectivist, Alit."

"We have a *loyalty* to the poor and suffering of the known galaxy!"

"You have a loyalty to your twisted and perverted leadership."

"Executive Dunham is a great man," Alit asserted.

"I suppose in my 'selfishness' I must be incapable of recognizing true greatness."

"I never said that."

"Even so, you've said enough."

Alit snatched his briefcase off the floor and marched toward the door. "You'll regret this," he sneered. "Good luck finding an attorney more like yourself. Most have come to their senses already." He stormed out of the office and slammed the door shut. Tageron pulled open his desk drawer and withdrew a small bottle of imported Arterran whiskey. He poured himself a glass and took a sip, exhaled slowly, and let the sweet sting of the drink linger.

He felt a crushing blend of anger, disappointment and betrayal, and it left him suffocated under the weight of his worries. He'd planned so much, with such unwavering belief in his inevitable success, but his dreams were taken from him—by the greedy, meddlesome hands of the faction that sought to see his company's demise and the collapse of all those like it. He'd even announced his intention to raise wages after the project's completion. Now he'd have to tell the men and women who'd expected an even better standard of living for their families that the City of Tarem gave him no choice but to break his promise. He wished he didn't have to, but without the new rail, to raise salaries would only end in the company's financial collapse and the loss of everyone's jobs. And now the government expected him—and ultimately, his workers—to pay for the building of free housing for migrants who never had any desire to contribute to society in return.

The taxes were piling up, and Tageron was just starting to feel the worst of their consequences. It'd been hard enough keeping a business afloat in a collectivist city. But now, the full weight of his financial burdens finally proved it might just pull him under.

———

The screech of old brakes and the impatient honking of car horns echoed between the high-rise apartments on busy Leftway Avenue, their blare softened but still distracting through the bedroom window. It was a hot night, and the sticky humidity left a ghostly fog on the glass, glowing softly with the halos of streetlights below. Pentakiya lay in bed, the thin sheets wrapped around her naked body, and while her wife slept next to her beautifully uncovered and undisturbed, Pentakiya kept her eyes wide open, sleep evading her.

The squeal-crunch-honk-swearing of a car accident woke Artimpasa, and she stirred, grazing her leg against her wife's. Pentakiya rolled over to face her and ran her fingers through her hair. Artimpasa smiled and asked, "It's not the noise that's keeping you up, is it?"

Pentakiya sighed and shut her eyes, but Artimpasa was persistent. "There's something bothering you—I saw it in your eyes all evening. Sadness." She touched Pentakiya's cheek. "Maybe fear."

Pentakiya couldn't help but hesitate—she knew how Artimpasa, with her unwavering pride in her individualist beliefs, would react to Pentakiya's doubts, or so she thought she knew. More than anything, she dreaded an "I told you so" that she couldn't realistically deny.

"I'm not sure what to think anymore."

"About what?"

"I don't know. About everything I thought I believed in."

"These are strange times. Sometimes we just don't know what to believe when there's so many loud people telling us they're right."

"Except I know who's right."

"Then you're worrying for nothing."

"Maybe."

She grew quiet, saying nothing, but only waited for her wife's response, which came too late for comfort. "Tell me what this is all about," Artimpasa implored. "I don't like seeing you like this."

"I saw something terrible. And I keep telling myself it was for the greater good."

"You're a good judge. It must have been."

"I was told it was."

"Do you trust them?"

"I did."

"You don't anymore?"

"I don't know."

"If you have any doubts, then no, you don't trust them."

"I can't. I have to trust him."

"Why?"

"He's the best thing that's ever happened to us."

"How do you know?"

"He says so."

Artimpasa embraced Pentakiya and wrapped her legs around hers. She let the warmth of her breath spread across her wife's neck. Pentakiya sighed. "He needs me, though. For the greater good." She pulled herself away from Artimpasa. "What scares me is that I'm not even sure what he plans to do with my work."

Her wife smiled. "I'm sure whatever he has in mind will only make me prouder of what you've done. You're strong. You're noble. And most of all, you're loyal. You have something you have to do, Pentakiya," Artimpasa encouraged. "You have a mission in life when most people don't. Don't let fear, or doubt, or whatever else you might be feeling get in the way of that."

She kissed Pentakiya softly. "So, go to sleep. Pretty soon, your dreams will be reality. And it'll be you who made them happen."

But that night, Pentakiya had nightmares.

———

The clatter of forks and knives against old plates was dreamy, like Selas never really woke up that day, much like the day before it, and the one before that. He felt a step away from the world around him, even with calls for more grog barked in the background. Each day was plagued with an unshakable fatigue, and he spent his nights tossing in bed, thrashing beneath the sheets until he woke up half-naked and dripping with sweat. And for that brief hour or so when he managed to fall asleep, he dreamt of hideous, black eyes, and begged them to go away. They were relentless and wouldn't leave, and he found himself alone, so unsure of his own sanity that he was terrified to think of his sisters', his parents', or anyone else's reaction. They'd call him crazy—he knew it.

"Get a move on it, kid. I'm starvin'."

The smoky voice pulled Selas to the present with a startled jerk, and he grabbed his tray like more of a flinch than a conscious effort. He kept his gaze low and moved forward in line; he took a helping of rehydrated corn slop and a piece of stale bread. The man behind him stood uncomfortably close, and in the corner of his eye, Selas could tell he was being watched.

The boy knew who he was. He was a man with the sort of reputation Selas dreaded he'd one day have—a reputation for being a crazy old man. His name was Ssmid Burton, or just Burton, "because Ssmid sounds too weaselly," he'd complain. He was probably in his sixties, but most Gameer didn't keep count, and he looked older than his age, anyway. Thin, straggly hair hung from his scalp to his shoulders like gray string, and his face bore the years of hardship that eventually wore down all Gameer. He looked like he hadn't shaved in over a week, and the rough, salt-and-pepper stubble on his face lined a mouth filled with curiously white, straight teeth. His full smile alone was enough to lead others to speculate about his upbringing; many assumed that he might have been, in fact, an ostracized member of the powerful Burton family, though he himself insisted that the shared surname was nothing more than a coincidence. If he legitimately was a part of the wealthy family, then they must have cast him out in suspicion of what foreign psychologists referred to as Gradual Onset Deep-Space Psychosis, popularly called the Rakes among space travelers.

The meaningless ramblings of a hermit in a crowded room were the cause of his social exile among the commoners. People were afraid of him and kept their children away from him. They whispered about the Rakes turning to mass panic. Rumor had it that he was patient zero in a pandemic of paranoia and, ultimately, violence. It was the Black Death of interstellar travel, and they'd seen it before. They quarantined him socially to combat a devastating plague of the mind.

"Look at you. You're half asleep."

Selas groaned and moved along without acknowledging Burton's uninvited observations. He took a small cup of freeze-dried fruit and a chalky milk substitute distributed for its heavy protein content, as meat was in short supply. Selas wasn't hungry but took his food automatically, the routine beaten into his mind like a repetitive, unchanging hammer. Evua and Ileya weren't even waiting for him at the table. He'd gone to the hall alone, and it was late at night, although day and night were marked only by the brightness of the fluorescent lighting.

"You're not here 'cause you can't sleep. You're here 'cause you're *avoidin'* it."

"I'm fine. Stop talking."

Burton wasn't satisfied. He followed Selas to the table, and the boy glared at him angrily. Selas sat down and started to eat—carefully, like eating at a picnic with a bee buzzing around his hand. Burton started up again. "I—"

"*You* are just a crazy, old bastard," Selas snapped.

"So they say."

"And I'm saying I want to eat alone."

"I know about the dreams, kid."

Selas froze. There was no way he could have known—the only people Selas had told were his own sisters, and they weren't mingling with the likes of Ssmid Burton, and certainly weren't giggling with him behind their brother's back. The boy's immediate reaction was to run from the situation, to hide from the one man who could maybe—just maybe—understand him. But he stayed, curious for, but also dreading, Burton's elaboration on his night terrors.

"Don't bother keepin' it to yourself anymore. You ain't the only one bein' watched."

Selas already had no appetite, but after Burton's assertion that he, too, suffered at the invisible hands of disembodied dream-eyes, he felt sick, and the thought of food disgusted him. He pushed his tray away and the fork fell off the plate, clattering against the rest of the utensils set beside the dish. He nearly knocked over his cup, but caught it just before the protein supplement spilled across the table and right into his lap. He made eye contact with Burton for the first time. And when he felt a connection, a sort of shared experience that came through his tiny, round spectacles, he regretted it.

He scrambled to assemble his untouched food and rushed to the garbage to throw it all away in a wasteful frenzy. He heard objections from the others who sat close enough to notice, but he didn't care that he was disposing of perfectly good rations, and made his way toward the door to flee the dining hall and the disquieting dialog. Selas took one last look at the hermit as he stood in the doorway, where the vents above him blew warm air onto his hair and shoulders, rustling his rough, woolen shirt. Burton shouted across the room. The diners did their best to ignore him, as they always did.

"They ain't gonna stop, kid," he warned. "Doesn't matter what you try and do about it. They're comin' for you for a reason, and there ain't nothin' you can do to keep 'em away. They always get what they want. And what they want is you."

11

"Working is a choice, just as abstinence from working is a choice. Should you make the choice to work, then you must respect the choice of those who have chosen not to work by contributing more of what you earn to them."
—Parliamentarian Panzi Illoszia of Bahía Brumosa

NATHARIS HIT THE SURFACE HARD, but he didn't hear the crack of shattered bones or feel the warmth of blood pooling beneath his head. He'd fallen onto another ship, its metal hull softened by a shallow, energetic field that kept him suspended an inch above its surface after the initial jolt that penetrated the shield. The Tellurians, the Muscovite and Erixen all hit the ship with a muffled thud, unharmed but with their bodies strangely contorted, and then came the stolen crate, still levitating in the air, which settled down gently on the top of the craft.

The marshal couldn't see the ship directly, but it distorted the image of the canyon below, giving away its shape simply because he was close enough to notice. It was masterfully cloaked, concealed by Muscovian stealth technology. The tingling cushion that broke their fall was a safety net the ZGB operative had deployed just seconds before their potentially devastating impact. She deactivated the field and remotely opened a hatch, just large enough to accommodate the size of the crate, and the group scrambled into the cabin, eager to put their feet on something less precarious.

"Don't touch anything," she commanded. She eyed Erixen with suspicion. "Colonial," she said, addressing Natharis, "you come to cockpit with me. Rest, stay here and keep quiet."

He sat down beside her in the copilot's seat and examined the controls around him, all of which were labeled in Cyrillic, which he couldn't read. The Muscovite ordered him to activate the shields, but he couldn't carry out her commands, and only stared blankly at the cryptic screens and their unintelligible buttons. She sighed and shouted in Muscovian—*"Angliyskiy!"*—and the displays changed to the Latin alphabet of Millennial Anglic. He saw the correct button and tapped it. The hum of the shield generator shook the cockpit while it primed and projected the defensive field around the ship. The flashing of warning lights caught his attention, and he announced the alert to the operative. "They're jamming our transmissions," he shouted as she began their ascent, accelerating violently into the sky. "They don't want us calling for help."

"Help?" she laughed, guiding the ship into a bold, vertical spiral. "Who do they think I am?"

She hit the gas and the skies faded into black, and the stars became brilliant, unmasked beyond the clouds of dust and ash. Natharis looked about but didn't see any enemy craft, and assumed the cloaking mechanism had allowed a clean escape. But their communications were still jammed, their sensors deactivated, but they seemed to have reached a safe spot where they could gather their thoughts and plan their next move. They were lucky.

"Ninotchka Voronova," the Muscovite said, holding out her hand. "ZGB, naturally."

Natharis shook her hand and introduced himself. "Natharis Ruke. Colonial Investigative Marshal."

"Well, at least one of you behaves like marshal. Your partner is useless."

"I think he's new."

The ship rumbled violently. Ninotchka groaned. "We're not invisible, after all. Tellurian warships. Right above us."

The Tellurian fleet assembled miles above them and drifted in front of the brilliant sun, leaving Natharis and Ninotchka in its shadow, gazing upon triremes with golden halos. She cut the power to the cloaking device and rerouted it to the top shields, preparing for the incoming bombardment. Natharis wasn't new to dogfights; he'd joined the Colonial Navy just before his nineteenth birthday and had seen his fair share in his defense of the outer protectorates. But he'd never seen a fight on such a scale, with such a disparity in strength and numbers. He wanted to enter the fray with the youthful bravery he'd felt years ago, when, as a teenage boy, he was invincible. He felt differently now. He took his place as copilot and waited for Ninotchka, who nodded, grinning arrogantly. He primed their engines and waited for her signal. She counted down just as the projectiles began their approach. She winked.

———

"I would like to begin by thanking Executive Dunham for his *generous* funding of a new government fleet," began Lord of Parliament Panzi Illoszia, standing behind a lone podium before the two Houses and the ever-watching eyes of the Executive Council. "I have *long* been calling for the Convergency to provide each and every representative with her own personal warship."

The Lord of Parliament had argued on numerous occasions that the adequate defense of the known galaxy's highest-ranking figures was integral to the survival of the

Convergency and its monstrous bureaucracy. But Desh Maru and the other Arterran executives, as well as the minarchist individualists of Parliament and the Senate, were wary of her calls for taxpayer-funded armies whose sole purpose was to defend the indefensible. The corporatist collectivists, once again, proved they were perfectly willing to use unfairly amassed tax revenue to increase their own power—now militaristically, surpassing their previous pursuit of political and economic dominance.

Panzi's sharp voice echoed throughout the chamber as frothing, verbal vomit gushed from her oversized mouth. She glared at Desh as she testified. "In addition to Executive Dunham's *inspiring* efforts to protect us, the rest of the Commune was *heavily* involved in this program as well," she proclaimed. A prideful smile spread across her face. "We've *always* argued that a slight increase in Convergency-wide taxation would allow for freer government spending, and now, our assertions have *evidently* been proven valid. Every citizen of the Convergency has a *duty* to those who represent him, as *we*, too, require personal protection. And since *real* citizens are fully willing to contribute—" she said, eyeing the four Arterran executives, "—there's no guilt on *us*. But there are *some* who clearly hope to *assassinate* us in the name of a *backward* ideology."

Executive Leveque chuckled at the thought. "So, you're finally admitting that the Shatarins are dangerous?" she quipped.

Panzi fumed. "*Never.* I was referring to *individualists*—the greatest *traitors* to the integrity of our perfect government."

Executive Molotova smashed her fist on her desk and clenched her hand so tightly that her skin began to pale, contrasting the angry red of her face. Desh leaned forward and spoke. "Parliamentarian Illoszia," he said, "do not for a second mistake the League of Arterra's reluctance to fund your personal army as a sign of some sort of Convergency-wide mutiny. The fact of the matter is that no man is innately required to give up his earnings to individuals who would gladly see him starved for their own undeserved benefit."

"If your beloved League is so *prosperous*, your citizens should have no trouble with giving a *generous* portion of their income to the preservation of the *greater good*," Panzi retorted. She looked around her to the other collectivists, who stood up on cue and applauded her perceived bravery and wit in the face of a self-serving, merciless enemy. "You and your people are *narcissists*, living in a fantasy world where selfishness is called '*rationality*.'" She addressed her support base, turning away from the executives. "Even as we speak, innocent Bahía Brumosans are unable to feed their families because of thinking like Desh Maru's."

"Maybe it is my ignorance of your strange, Outer-Rim dialect," Oksana Molotova interrupted, standing, "but you seem to have contradicted yourself at least three times." Her accent left her words rounded but staccato, as if she were swallowing while spitting up in her nausea. "Is your economic system successful, or are your citizens starving?"

Panzi's sense of decorum vanished. "Parliament and the more *sensible* executives don't have time for Muscovian fact twisting, and especially not blatant Arterran *lies*, if that's what you're about to suffocate us with. I think I can speak for *all* of Parliament in saying that we are sick and tired of your *unwillingness* to concede that your policies *don't work*."

"The only thing *not* working in the Convergency is your own electorate," Sir Byron sneered. Panzi grew furious and threw her holotab on the floor. Byron took a sip of water from the glass before him. "Parliamentarian Illoszia has clearly reached the limit of her already meager rationality. I invite Executive Dunham to speak on her behalf."

Panzi panted and sat down, beseeching Brock Dunham for support. Her prophet obliged. "ABAC has always questioned as to why the League of Arterra—if it truly is such a bastion of freedom—consistently refuses to come to the aid of those who are far less blessed."

"The Creator gave us freedom. Our individualist ideology gave us prosperity," Desh interjected. "Our success isn't the result of a divine blessing or predestination. Your belief that our economic strength is just a cosmic mistake is dangerous and naïve."

"Whatever the cause, it's undeniable that you in your *bigotry* would enjoy nothing more than to see the Commune fade into the dark." Dunham's accusations drove the collectivists into a frenzy, who responded with shouts of praise and gratitude. Their opposition grumbled among themselves. They waited impatiently for Desh's rebuttal.

"If criticism of theft is bigotry, then consider me the worst of bigots."

His support base went wild, cheering and laughing hysterically at the infuriated looks shot by the collectivist representatives and their allies. Desh, however, maintained his composure and presented himself professionally, masking his inner satisfaction. He saw the Procyon executive in the corner of his eye, watching, observing the scene around it, and envied its neutrality and adherence to an unwavering isolationism. The Procyon's haunting black eyes never reflected approval or disapproval, morality or immorality. Its race held the most advantageous position in the Interstellar Convergency—one where they were impervious to the sinister interests of others. They'd never suffer the group psychosis of the Sapiens.

"And here I thought you people could stoop no lower," Dunham murmured. He rose from his seat and attacked the Arterrans as a group. "Your culture is so imbued with racism and ignorance that you consider it *noble* to publicly announce it!"

"To us, it's noble to denounce evil when it flaunts itself as righteousness," Desh replied. "The League of Arterra holds nothing more sacred than the civil liberties of her people, and of the people of the entire Convergency—except your own, who seem not only willing but *excited* to toss their freedoms aside for the sake of a lifelong retirement."

The Conglomerate's executive was far from satisfied. "I find it deplorable that the Colonials and the rest of the degenerate League place these so-called 'civil rights' above the rights of the poor. It's truly despicable." Dunham looked over at Oksana, who sat with arms crossed. "But from what I understand, the term 'civil rights' is unheard of in the Tsardom. I suspect the word 'charity' is similarly absent."

"We know its meaning," Oksana snapped, "but we are unfamiliar with concept of charity at gunpoint. It appears to be unique to your planets."

"On *our* planets," Dunham declared, "we have written selflessness into law."

Desh couldn't shy away from the confrontation. "What your law dictates would be considered treasonous in the Colonies," he said, smoothing a previously unnoticed wrinkle in his suit.

"Or at least in remarkably bad taste," Sir Byron added. "Seizing another's property is still a crime, is it not?"

"Not in Commune. There, it is apparently praiseworthy," Oksana scoffed.

"The Commune has low unemployment because it considers theft a legitimate profession," Mireille concluded.

She, Desh, Sir Byron and Oksana waited for Dunham to respond to their four-way counterargument. Without a teleprompter, the man appeared powerless, unsure of his words. The Muscovian executive filled the silence for him. "In Tsardom of Romanov Muscovia, criminals are given prison sentence. In Commune, they are given reward."

Dunham's tone grew even more resentful. "Only Arterran *racists* would label innocent, needy people 'criminals.' And we *reward* them only with what is rightfully theirs: the wealth historically snatched directly out of their hands by the rich— the kind that compel Executive Maru to support policies that favor the *wealthy*, and only the wealthy."

Mireille chuckled. "Yes, because collectivist leadership is so terribly impoverished."

Desh rejoined the debate. "When these allegedly 'entitled' individuals decide to generate their *own* wealth and improve their *own* lives—"

"Unlikely," Sir Byron muttered in the background.

"—then the Commune, and maybe the Convergency as a whole, might finally prosper. But until that time, we'll just have to sit back and witness the decline that you are so proud to have facilitated."

"The Commune will survive any collapse of the sort," Dunham boasted. "Our people are accustomed to hardship—a life's struggle imposed by *you*."

Desh sighed. "Pass the blame as much as you want, Executive. When your planets fall apart, your people revolt and you come groveling to us for help, you'll find that we have turned a blind eye to your unfortunate 'struggle.' And that will be the day you realize just how destructive your infectious ideals really are."

———

The Tellurian fleet stood in the ship's way of the tachyon vein. The warships' massive silhouettes passed in front of the blinding light of Sol and eclipsed the sprawling framework of the heavily trafficked tachyon lenses. Ninotchka Voronova's ship didn't need a lens to pass into the invisible current; its crucible, not yet activated but waiting in a cold slumber, would cut open the fabric of space and time to allow their escape at a speed that left light lagging behind.

She grinned and cackled madly as she hit the accelerator. The ship rocketed toward the fleet, barreling through the shower of plasma bolts that rained down upon them from the cannons lining the sides of the furious triremes. Their sails shimmered in the sunlight and burned a shadow into Natharis's vision, whose eyes were unshielded from the glare—unlike Ninotchka's, which she hid behind dark sunglasses with lenses so large as to make her look like a deadly insect. The ship rattled with each impact and Natharis heard the screams of the passengers just outside the cockpit door. He gripped his seat and shouted to Ninotchka, who was focused intently on making her way through the gaps in the fleet. *"Don't go between them!"* he yelled. She didn't take his advice.

"Don't underestimate me, Mr. Ruke," she warned him sternly. "I was born during carpet bombing."

She winked at him and aimed for the command deck of the largest warship she saw. They streaked through the fleet, spiraling between battleships and dodging heavy fire, until the bridge was just a few hundred yards ahead. Natharis glared nervously at Ninotchka—she only smiled. They didn't have the firepower to penetrate the shield scaffolding, even with a direct hit at such close range, so Ninotchka, a typical Muscovite, fired one shot just for laughs. She tilted the ship upward and flashed past the Tellurian warships. She was right: Natharis had underestimated her. She took a breath and slowly turned the ship around.

"Tachyon lenses are right over there." She nodded toward the complex. "Nice, clear shot. Let them waste time thinking they can track us through lens traffic recorder."

"And then what?"

"Head for the Outer Rim," Erixen said from behind them. He coolly slipped into the cockpit, eager to participate now that the coast was clear. "They won't follow us there."

"Yes, why don't we just go straight to Albion?" Ninotchka scoffed.

"She's right. Toward the Core's our best bet," Natharis concluded.

"You'd take us straight to the Imperium!" Erixen barked. *"They're* the ones shooting at us!"

"Telluria might be firing weapons, but ABAC is giving orders," the Muscovite argued.

"Deep Core it is, then."

"Couldn't agree more," Ninotchka said, tapping her finger on the throttle in anticipation. "I make it quick." The Tellurian battleships slowly shifted their course to face the lone ship, and an auspicious window in their formation opened. Ninotchka seized the opportunity and fired the engines. But as they rocketed toward the closing door, the ship suddenly began to shake under a surprise assault, though the Tellurians hadn't opened fire. From behind the mammoth warships emerged a squadron of lightning-fast fighters, branded with ABAC's black and red and its ominous icon across their hulls. Ninotchka cursed under her breath in Muscovian.

"Get in turret," Ninotchka commanded. "Take Tellurian with you."

Natharis jumped up and dragged Erixen out of the cockpit, ordering him to keep calm and monitor the damage control relays. He rushed to the gun turret with the Tellurian right behind him, who took the adjacent weapon. They swiveled their seats to aim precisely at ABAC's fighters, each taking them down with relative ease, though some were simply too fast to catch. Like a swarm of biting flies, the fighters followed the craft as it flashed through the columns of Tellurian triremes and approached the tachyon lens complex. Natharis shouted to Ninotchka through the open cockpit door. "Are communications still down?"

The Tellurian raised his voice and added, "Those fighters can't jam our transmissions—and we're out of the fleet's range! Maybe it's the ship!"

"No time to fix it now!" Ninotchka yelled over the rumble of the siege. "We're still in weapons range." She paused. "And look, they target us." The screens in the cockpit flashed red and urged preparation for an imminent attack. "*No one* targets Muscovite without at least buying her vodka first."

From the look on her face, Ninotchka really wanted to double back and fire everything they had at the command decks, in hopes of taking down at least one Tellurian admiral.

She leaned over the controls and pounded a switch with her full fist, and the hum of the aetherium engines filled the cabin. The tachyon lens complex was right ahead of them—and so was the invisible vein. Red lights flashed, the alerts sounding a coming bombardment, this time from the heavy Tellurian cannons. But Ninotchka, in control of the ship and the fate of its crew, affirmed that it was not their day to die. She fired up the crucible and they disappeared into the shimmering blue just beyond the physical universe, the Tellurian warships far behind, and Earth vanishing into the distance light-years away.

The breeze was soft and gentle as it made its way up from the tiny village in the distance. It carried the scent of home-cooked meals that Selenia Santiago de Sonora hadn't tasted in months. It had been too long since she'd dwelt among loving families, dining together and sharing good company. Having spent her time in service among the forgotten children of Earth, who wandered from star to star in search of a home, she'd become accustomed to life in stale confinement, but what it lacked in connection to nature it made up for with friends and family. She missed their cooking, however simple, and as she relished the fragrance of spiced rice from open-windowed kitchens in the village ahead, her hunger steadily grew. But the pungent scent of moist soil was the most nourishing, as it was food for her soul, which longed for the sensual beauty of nature while she tended to the needs of the Gameer. She was on a backwater planet reminiscent of Sonora, the place of her birth, and she had work to do.

Families on such remote and nameless worlds told their children to behave, or the Witch of the Deep in the woods would come looking for them. It was a story that most, when fully grown, came to dismiss as parental lies whispered before bedtime to frighten sons and daughters into fearful obedience. But Selenia Santiago knew better. It was one of those stories that many believed to be fiction, and only fiction. She sensed, however, that it was rooted in truth, as did the other Mithneshi seers. The lone witch did prowl in the shadows of the forest. She was an ancient enemy of the Mithneshi Coven, and her days were numbered. It was Selenia's solemn duty to vanquish her.

The warm rain fell upon her skin. The sparkling droplets were a memory of the celestial flower petals sprinkled by the Creator to replenish barren worlds, as her father had once told her. He used to wake at the early hours of dawn to gaze upon the morning rains in springtime. The sound of the door often woke young Selenia, and, in her restlessness, she would peek through her window to watch her father stand alone in the rain. He kept his arms outstretched, hands open, taking in the beauty and power of the life-giving rains. While he thanked the skies for their mercy, Selenia looked upon her father with equal gratitude. He, like the rains, had given her life.

On those days when the light raindrops fell as torrents and walls of water, her father would draw his knives—one dulled, for his daughter—and train in the fog. Neither Selenia nor her father were able to see into the dense clouds that formed along the ground; the mist concealed the target. Over the years, Selenia grew accustomed to blind combat. When she threw the knives into the billowing haze, all she would hear was the muffled sound of metal striking wood. And when she made her way to it, she'd find the knife lodged straight in the center of the target. Her experience shaped her into an adept fighter and a dangerous opponent. The witch had a futile fight ahead of her. Selenia had never tasted defeat.

Her mind returned to the present as the rains faded into a veil of mist. It was only a matter of time before the coming sun parched the softened soil. She trod silently into the woods. The leaves and fallen twigs beneath her feet were soggy from the morning downpour, and would remain so well into the daylight, sheltered from the sun in the cool shade of the trees. Selenia passed between the gnarled trunks with the grace of a fawn and the focus of an experienced hunter; her movements reflected the spirit of both the stalker and the prey. Evil would find itself in her crosshairs. The hunt was on.

Hastened heartbeats pounded in her ears, pulsing in unison with the soft clinking of her Breathtaker. She had the Mithneshi ritual weapon tucked into a belt strapped across her chest. Before she'd returned to the region of Alvira to cleanse it of its evils, it had been months—years, even—since she'd had to draw it in combat. Her mission among the spacefaring Gameer was for the sake of healing the sick and tending to the needs of the neglected, and she had little use for her weapon. But the feeling of its smooth grips in her hands would always be familiar and fresh in her mind. The red of her last target's eyes still haunted her, as did the sharp crack of his neck when she pulled the Breathtaker's chain tight around his throat.

The smell of smoke filled the air. A black plume rose into the canopy ahead of her; it carried with it the stench of malice, an ancient evil clouded with flies and stinking maggots. The witch was unaware of Selenia's approach. Had she known, she would have extinguished the fire burning in her makeshift shelter. Embers spiraled upward through the opening in the thatched rooftop. While the hut looked like any other in a small, agrarian village, it still carried with it a sense of heaviness, a darkness that left the unprepared gripped with fear. Selenia suffered no such reaction. Her thoughts were clear, and her soul, strengthened by the Creator's Emanation, was immune to the spiritual corruptions of the Witches of the Deep. Her reflexes were loyal, and her training never betrayed her. Her faith blocked every poison word, her strength, any blow. But that day, she found herself caught off guard.

The strike came from the side. Selenia stumbled and fell to the ground with dirt caked under her fingernails. The witch, draped in rags as sheer as cobwebs, was just a blur in the corner of her eye. It was as if she'd flown through the air on black wings. She pressed her foot down on Selenia's neck.

"So, the Coven sends a little Alviran whore to do away with me, does it?"

Selenia tried to turn her head to look up at her assailant, but the witch kept the pressure on her throat. She coughed, dust and soil choking her breath.

"I expected more from the Mithneshi."

The witch ate her words when Selenia's knife sunk deep into her leg. She howled, pulled back, and Selenia finally looked upon her. She was pale, almost gray, with cadaverous, blue lips and shadows beneath her sunken eyes. What remained of her teeth was filed down into needles that stuck from black, swollen gums. And when she bent back to pull the blade from her flesh, Selenia caught sight of a deep, festering gash stretching across her chest. The skin at its edges was frayed and decaying. Her body could no longer heal itself, and yet she still survived. Her flesh was necrotic, just as her soul had long since rotted away.

Selenia leapt up from the ground and drew her Breathtaker. She pulled its chain taut and lunged toward her attacker. In a flash the witch darted around her, but Selenia reached behind and grabbed the knife being jabbed toward her back. The warm blood still dripping from its blade left her hand slick. She cracked the witch's arm backward and heard her wrist snap.

The struggle endured, and the sounds of the forest grew louder, as if the animals hiding in the shadows were shouting in support of good's triumph over evil. The leaves rustled overhead like the brush of the witch's robes against Selenia's skin. Knives slashed. Chains rattled. The hot wind surged with them; it carried away the witch's last breath. Her gasps grew strained as Selenia bound her throat with the unforgiving Breathtaker. She fell silent and slumped to the ground. The chains unraveled and hung from Selenia's hand.

Selenia knelt over the corpse and bowed her head in prayer, seeking forgiveness for the shedding of blood, however justified its spilling. Her highest mission was to save the lives of the innocent, but she was torn between two paths that led there. She could help heal them and bring them spiritual comfort while they wandered blind in the dark. But she could also vanquish those who threatened them, and who would claim them as victims of their ancient evil. To her Coven, free will was the highest ideal; it was inalienable, untouchable. And when one sought to suppress it, he would be met with her Breathtaker. And yet, it wasn't something to take pleasure in.

The seer was faced with a choice, as she was each time she took a life—one that would end in salvation, or inner damnation. She could serve the Creator's children through peace and redeem her own spirit. Or she could protect them through bloodshed, and risk becoming numb to the gravity of death. After all, when one fought to preserve life, death wasn't something to be taken lightly.

12

"Brock Dunham could drown a litter of kittens in a televised Parliamentary session, and the media would find a way to criminalize the kittens."
—Misha Matsumoto, for Vega 1 News.

LEFTWAY AVENUE WAS A BUSY STREET with four lanes on each side of its double yellow lines. The decades-old cars and lethal taxi cabs were never separated by more than two inches, so crossing at street level was impossible, unless one wanted to jump over stalled vehicles in the middle of an intersection. Pentakiya Curicon wasn't on the right side of the avenue. She'd been looking for the nearest metro station to reach the exoport, but with a lack of planning typical of any public works in Dearborn, the stairwell that descended into the depths of the City of Entitlement was only accessible from the north side of Leftway. She'd have to walk farther until she found a crossing bridge, which would be just as jam-packed as the streets, but with lethargic, foul-mouthed people.

Such hours-long disruptions in traffic flow were commonplace, usually without a foreseeable cause, as the term "rush hour" was absent in the colloquial language of the Commune. But that day, Hybris Street, a usual tributary of cars to and from Leftway Avenue, was closed off with portable barriers and recently erected flagpoles. Pentakiya smiled when she saw the first preparations for what was meant to be an annual event in Dearborn. The city's most prominent lobbyist groups had drawn inspiration from Bahía Brumosa's famous Fair at Mongers' Row, a cultural festival celebrating the sexual liberation of Communal society, unapologetic and unafraid of judgment or consequence. She wondered just to what extent her city would mimic the unique sights of Mongers' Row. Surely, they'd engage in open-air orgies like their Bahía Brumosan neighbors, but the fair would draw in more than just men and women bent on expressing their most hedonistic, and natural, desires. It was a family event, all in the name of open-mindedness. If it was anything like the Fair at Mongers' Row, then it was the perfect place for a family outing. Younger children would benefit from exposure to such sexual spectacles. After all, what better way was there to learn the values of tolerance except through immersion, wide-eyed beneath the waving banners of pluralism and understanding?

Massive billboards lined the buildings, displaying videos of the endearingly classless pop singer, E.B. Teen, the Commune's cultural pride and joy. The scantily clad trash, her provocative dance more like drug-driven writhing and thrashing, blew kisses at the camera and promoted her new single, "I'll Never Pay A Dime." Pentakiya supported the inspiring messages E.B. Teen conveyed in her poorly edited music, but she understood that she wasn't the best social role model. Even E.B. Teen admitted that the real role model was Brock Dunham himself.

She was quite public about her close friendship with the executive, calling him on a regular basis, as did many well-known Communal celebrities, both singers and actors alike. The executive never failed to find an ally in the media, and his heartwarming friendship with music, cinema and the news generated some of the finest cultural achievements the Commune had ever seen. E.B. Teen had written an ode to Brock Dunham that she hoped would one day become the Commune's anthem, if not the entire Convergency's. It hadn't caught on politically, but Dearborn's elementary schools consistently included it in their children's choral repertoires. Albion, at least, made sure that its youth grew up with an effective motivator and object of devotion: a man who was living proof that anyone could achieve greatness through taking what was rightfully his.

She was wrong for doubting him. She knew he was the man her future children and everyone else's children should idolize. It wasn't too late—even she could one day become like Executive Dunham. He'd already recognized her accomplishments. She had more in store for him.

She was bound for a research station operating just outside the Veil of Bhalenjar to continue her work for the man she'd been shamefully beginning to doubt. His emissaries had sent her a notice informing her of her next, and hopefully final, scientific task. She was to find a way to quickly transport the anchors she and her team had modified and successfully activated. He wanted the system spread out, expanded to span distances he'd kept secret from even his top scientists. She hated the idea of leaving her wife just as quickly, for the sake of completing a project she didn't fully understand.

Pentakiya knew she'd accomplish what she was told to do—she wasn't worried about her success, which she viewed as inevitable, but she found herself caring less about the fate of her work. The view from the space elevator wouldn't inspire awe or wonder, and neither would the sight of the Veil of Bhalenjar in the perpetual night of interstellar space. She would only remember Artimpasa's face, her naked breasts pressed against her body, and the smile that reassured her that fear was meant to be conquered. She'd wavered. But it was time to destroy her doubt by doing what she'd been trained to do.

———

Selas could never really be certain of their whereabouts while they were drifting in interstellar space. The caravan's movements were guided more by the search for a faint, meaningful signal than by maps. He knew they'd been wandering somewhere in the Outer Rim for quite some time, but with each slip back into free space from the limitless rush of the tachyon veins, the stars seemed just a little bit denser, closer together, indicative of a slow approach toward the middle band of the known galaxy. The Mid Rim was home to the League of Arterra, whose territory spread far and wide and whose culture dominated the region as if it'd always been there. With the Mid Rim and Arterra came the hope of a run-in with the Mithneshi. Selas couldn't help but pray that, by some chance, he might meet Selenia Santiago again when they arrived at their next cosmic pitstop.

The Ssimvomai Center for the Lost was still far away, but Selas smiled at the thought of taking refuge among the Coven, who tended to the vagrants and vagabonds that sought sanctuary at the beacon in the endless dark. At the Ssimvomai Center, they took into their care the thousands of migrant children from the Outer Rim, some of whom were not much younger than Selas, but the Mithneshi gave shelter to any who came to their door, not just helpless youth. The nomadic Gameer hoped to perform any number of jobs the Mithneshi might offer, as was their way, in exchange for even the most meager pay, which the Mithneshi provided from their Convergency-wide donations. They felt that employing the needy was integral to their wellbeing, but sacrifice was always necessary for growth. They'd work for their livelihood and improve their own lives, with just a little bit of help.

The boy was never excited about the prospect of toiling for money he'd never directly see, but he was a teenager, and was susceptible to youthful laziness. He did, however, find great comfort in knowing he'd soon get to stretch his legs and see a new group of people he'd never had to look at every day of his life. And meeting a Mithneshi was always a profound experience. He hadn't seen a member of the Coven since Selenia left the caravan years ago, and it left him with a sense of emptiness. There were scars on his spirit that couldn't heal so long as the eyes stared him down each night. His own willpower wasn't enough to stop them. He convinced himself that the Mithneshi would provide a chance for redemption. After all, the dreams only began after Selenia had moved on.

Their healing arts could finally bring him sleep and ease his worried mind. Sadly, it would be some time before the caravan reached the Ssimvomai Center, which meant he'd suffer more nights without anyone to watch over him. The boy was tired—more tired than he'd ever felt before. He was taught since before he could walk that the Creator's power, through the eternal Emanation, could heal all wounds. But these were wounds he couldn't see, nor could anyone else hope to see. They were gashes in his psyche that wouldn't close. Every night brought a fear that opened them again, and the wounds remained. Without sleep, without an escape from his paranoid reality, they'd never fade.

Ssmid Burton never seemed to sleep, and when Selas caught him dozing off, he always appeared to be faking it. He, too, must have been fearful of what lay in his subconscious, of what might resurface if he were to plunge into the oblivion of sleep. The boy hated to admit it, but the lunatic was the only one who might understand him; coming to that conclusion made him feel equally insane. But delusional or not, he felt he needed to find him. He was probably wandering the corridors or talking to himself in the bowels of the ship, sitting with his back to the wall on a metal catwalk over the reactors. He could be anywhere, but he would be found only when he wanted to be, and Selas had an eerie feeling that it was Burton who'd be approaching him, not the other way around. The crazy old man's words had resonated with him ever since their encounter, and Selas feared that he was right, and that the dreams weren't about to stop—at least on their own. Maybe he could force them to stop. And maybe Burton knew just how to do it.

————

The ship sailed gracefully through the energetic currents of the tachyon vein, its passengers relieved to sit in the tranquil silence that accompanied such travel. They crossed the invisible planes of reality at speeds once thought impossible, but the walls didn't shake or vibrate, and the hull of the ship didn't tear away under the stress of surpassing the speed of light by hundreds, if not thousands, of times. The only indicators of motion were the shimmering streaks of particle streams that flashed by just outside the windows. The rush of the Aether was inaudible, if it even made a sound at all.

Natharis Ruke sat among the mismatched crew with the ship's autopilot engaged. He was the first to address the subject of their destination; their only established condition was that they set their sights on the galactic center, the Deep Core, where their chances of finding sanctuary were higher among the tightly clustered stars. "If we go any farther, we'll be outside of Arterra," he warned. "It'll be our last chance to go to the proper authorities." He noticed that the Muscovite was ready to speak her mind. "I think it'd be best to turn back, even if we don't go far."

"I'd be inclined to agree," Ninotchka said, "but don't forget: I was in undercover operation before you two came and blew it." She glared at Erixen, who was quick to deny any fault, then continued: "This ship is under guise of high-profile smuggler. We fly as wanted men. Any civilized system wouldn't hesitate to shoot us out of sky."

Erixen finally offered some input. "Our communications are down, anyway. Even if the Arterrans *didn't* open fire on us, we still couldn't contact them. If we're *really* going to be mistaken for criminals, let's at least do it in the Outer Rim. No one's going to question us there."

Ninotchka groaned at his lack of foresight. "We're not flying into lion's den. I guarantee ABAC is regrouping."

"The Tellurians are probably waiting, too," Erixen grumbled, "and you want us to go right to them."

"Not to them—*through* them," Natharis corrected. "We'll pass right by without ever going back into free space. They won't even know we're there."

Erixen lowered his eyes, demoralized. But he hung his head low for only a second, and he shot his gaze back up, grinning widely, like he'd just had an epiphany that could save their lives from an otherwise inevitable doom. "I have contacts on Kojv," he announced. "In the Occupied Territories."

"Rosc have big guns," Ninotchka scoffed. "Are you sure you're not afraid of them, too?"

Erixen scowled but shrugged off her sarcasm. "They can get us another ship. I'm sure they'd be willing to dismantle ours for parts. They're always in the market for industrial equipment. Hell, they practically *own* the market."

Natharis scanned through the digital cartographs glowing on the holotab he held in his hand. He traced his finger along a highlighted tachyon vein superimposed over free space. A blinking dot caught his attention. "There's a Mithneshi facility near Kojv," he stated, "called the Othonas Shrine of Genuine Charity—in orbit around a small Crystalline planet, right outside the Occupied Territories. The veins are a little indirect in that area, but we could get there in less than two days from Kojv, at most."

"Waste of time," Ninotchka judged. "What good would Mithneshi do us?"

"We could contact the Judiciary—and get the Coven's blessing. We could probably use one right about now."

"I never thought *you'd* be so superstitious," Erixen sneered. "I'm sure we could survive without their pointless incantations."

"What blessings could we need when we have Tellurian consitor with us?" Ninotchka cooed with a sly smile, her eyes locked on the rugged man. She glanced at his female counterpart. "And sacred whore." The operative sighed, rolling her eyes. "But I suppose we could humor innocent Colonial delusion."

Natharis hadn't expected much respect from the Muscovite, whose lack of concern for religion revealed her people's interest in more pragmatic issues, or, more specifically, their faith in a strong army, not God. He'd hoped Erixen, a fellow Colonial, would have at least had his back. While Natharis, like all Colonials, had no intention of pushing his religion on others, he still thought that crossing paths with the Coven might open at least one person's eyes. Maybe Ninotchka would put down her guns for a minute to clear her head; maybe Erixen would find a sort of inner bravery he'd yet to reveal. The Tellurians, however, were likely set in their ways, but that was their business, not his.

He looked over at the two, who sat in silence beside each other, neglecting to offer a single suggestion. He thought they'd be excited to be so close to their Imperium, but neither seemed interested in returning to their pagan home. The virile man paid more attention to his partner, who was just as quiet, but whose focus was on Natharis's words alone. The marshal looked to her and smiled; she returned the gesture. The consitor, without a frown but with a tangible defensiveness, put his thickly muscled arm around her. At first, she recoiled, but eventually accepted his protective invitation. She laid her head on his chest but kept her eyes on Natharis, feigning sleep for her presumptuously physical consitor. She smiled subtly to the Colonial and set his heart aglow. But he reminded himself that they were on a mission, and he couldn't afford such whimsical distractions. And the altaria and consitor, though innocent of their countrymen's crimes, were Tellurians, and ultimately slaves to ABAC. They shouldn't be befriended so rashly. And they certainly shouldn't be trusted.

The smuggler's ship, or one under the guise of such, glided through the swirling sea of colors with its course set and its mechanical mind at the wheel. It was no longer in the skilled hands of Ninotchka Voronova, who was stubborn in setting aside her own pride for the sake of a machine. She didn't fully trust an artificial navigator, so she stayed in the cockpit. Ultimately, she stayed not to keep watch over the monitors, but to shamelessly force a minute alone with Silviano, whom she'd coerced into joining her.

Livia doubted Silviano would cave in to the Muscovite's unapologetic desires; the look on his face as he heeded her heavily accented call was one of both intrigue and hesitation. He followed nervously, as if even he, an experienced—very experienced—consitor, couldn't possibly perform up to the dominant Arterran's expectations. Livia imagined a kind of erotic dread inside him, a fear that the woman would leave him stripped of his strongest resource, his masculinity, just like any other Muscovian slash-and-burn campaign.

She had no doubt that Ninotchka was a black-leather widow in terrifyingly high heels who viewed men as disposable objects meant only for a single brief and likely less-than-satisfying use. She'd take advantage of a man's sex, then condemn him to one of two fates: social emasculation, or a bullet to the head. Admittedly, she had no real proof of the sultry agent's sexual tyranny. Perhaps she, as a woman, simply felt threatened by another beautiful female. It was biological, innate. It'd take her a while to trust a stunning off-worlder with her own life. The Arterran wasn't Tellurian. And everyone knew the Tellurians were exceptional among Sapiens. Culturally, they had no equal.

Silviano himself was a model of Tellurian aesthetics, sculpture-like in his ideal, classical form. Like Mars himself made hardened flesh, looking down on weaker men with even weaker frames, the consitor had, so far, spoken to Livia with a divine confidence, a numinous, pagan charm. His heavy whispers and the feel of his strong chest pressed against her cheek had left her with a warmth she'd neither expected nor intended.

As powerless as he seemed around Ninotchka, the god's living spear had no fear before Livia, who, like him, served a higher power in the arms of the faithful. But he must have known as well as she did that such a transgression of her vows would result only in expulsion from the Imperial Cult. She'd be cast out into the slums without a single lira to her name, forced to live out her life in poverty. She would no longer be regarded as a pristine vessel of the Pantheon, but a broken, forgotten bridge between the worlds of the flesh and the formless. Silviano could have had his way with the Muscovite, or the Muscovite her way with him, and be considered faultless, still loyal in the eyes of his god. But Livia, her god's most sacred altar for the worship of men, could only offer the rites of her body to those who came to the Temple in prayer. For her, there'd be no casual encounters, and certainly no love.

She was left alone anyway, with Silviano locked in the cockpit with the captivating predator, while she watched as the other Arterran—Erixen, she'd overheard—demonstrated a complete lack of practical knowledge. He knelt on the ground before an open computer panel, examining the central electrical hub for the ship's communications. He'd been working on it for hours but seemed to be making little progress. His incompetence was surprising; she might have expected little from a Communal, but a Colonial? They always seemed more sensible than most. His partner, however, validated her idea of a Colonial's classic demeanor.

He was at the peak of physical fitness that the Colonials held as ideal, a goal to always aspire to achieve through labor and evening runs after a hard day's work. He was handsome, the kind of handsome that was so thorough and pervasive that it could only exist in Livia's most fantastic dreams, like the classic heartthrobs of ancient cinema, whom men respected and women desired so many centuries ago. The firearm tucked firmly at his waist clicked against his belt as he approached her, making each step he took into a field march leading the Colonials' musket-armed ancestors to battle. But Livia wouldn't put up a fight. She couldn't, not with the icy blue eyes looking into the very depths of her mind, body and soul. They were eyes she'd seen before. They were eyes that she, somehow, had always known.

"Are you okay?" he asked, his voice gentle but assertive, unafraid of a stranger's response. "You haven't said a word since we left Earth."

She smiled weakly, appreciative of his concern, and spoke in his native Anglic with more fluency than he might have expected. "I'm fine. I can handle more than you'd think."

"I figure this must be pretty different from what you're used to."

"What I'm used to," Livia said, sitting up straight, "is praying for an escape every day."

"An escape from what?"

Livia didn't answer; she only sighed, embarrassed to have even addressed the subject of her past, her present, and her unavoidable future.

"When we get to Othonas, we won't have to run anymore." He sat down beside her but held himself back, just enough for comfort and respect for a woman's space. Livia countered his courtesy and shifted her knees to graze his thigh—*By accident, of course*, she thought, though she was surprised at her own boldness, no matter how subtle. She wasn't about to challenge Ninotchka's role as the alpha female in a pack of weak-minded men—but not this man. Not the mindful Colonial, who sat with his strong arms kept modestly to his sides, hands far from her legs. He was no Silviano. He was reserved, collected. He must have had the most basic drive that all men had, but he seemed in control of it, his conscience the ruler of his actions, not his masculinity.

He continued to insist on a coming relief. "With the Coven's blessing, we'll have nothing to worry about."

"I've given my share of blessings," Livia murmured, "all in the god's bed. And all that time, laying hands on all those men, I never felt his presence."

"They come to you to know God, don't they? It sounds to me like they honor you."

"They only come to know him *through* me. At the end of the day, I'm just a means to an end, and nothing more. A bridge to heaven still gets stepped on."

She didn't know why she'd delved into her past so honestly in front of a stranger. It was like he, just by glancing at her with his wintry eyes, sieged the walls of her discretion and heroically tore them down to rubble. As a Colonial marshal his life was devoted to judgment. But at that moment, she saw no judgment in his eyes. Nothing had changed in him. Nothing that she could see.

"What's your name?" he asked curiously, as if she'd never said a word at all.

"Livia," she answered. "Nettunaya—of the god Neptune."

"Well, Livia Nettunaya, it's never too late to start over."

What she did in service of the Imperial Cult was something she thought a Colonial would condemn outright, without sympathy or concern for anything but the most objective moral principles. Maybe she'd been wrong about them. Maybe their priority wasn't an institutionalized set of ethics or worship of the law. Maybe it was freedom—freedom from the tyranny of others, and from the dominion of one's own past. The story of her hidden shame could be rewritten, he claimed, so long as she made the decision to help herself. At that moment, as they looked at one another in silence, not one of awkwardness, but of potential, she understood what the Colonials had been testifying to all along.

"Natharis Ruke, by the way," he concluded with a confident grin. "Pleased to make your acquaintance."

———

The silence that pervaded the Procyon executive quarters was chilling. It lent to a tomb-like atmosphere, evoking a sense of terrible reverence before a being that thought itself wiser than God. Shadows cloaked the chamber, the spiraled, spine-like columns flanking the walkway visible only from the cold luminescence of black lights at their base. The temple pillars led a visitor's eyes to the focal structure of the executive quarters. A greenish glow radiated from the floor in rings, encircling three tall, broad tanks, the glass of their curved walls lit by the pale light. The fluid that filled the tanks was cloudy but translucent, and caught the light in such a way as to give a sense of thickness. And in those three tanks were suspended three ghostly figures, tall and skeletal, their heads covered by gray, sack-like masks. Their faces were turned away from the door behind their death shrouds. The macabre silhouettes didn't move or react to Desh's entrance. They only hanged.

Before the center and foremost being sat a single *emist*, bound to the medical apparatus that curved behind him and lifted him above the floor. He sat with his body twisted and contorted, held up by atrophied muscles and fluid-filled cables that ran directly into his veins. His thin hair grew in patches, and his skin was tired, lifeless. Desh heard only the interpreter's labored breaths as he looked about the chamber, anxious to be acknowledged, but the chemically crippled young man sat with his head low. But then the breathing stopped. The suspended creatures' masks were pulled away. Their leader slowly turned to face him. Desh was frozen before its black, lidless gaze.

"We know why you have come."

The emist's voice creaked from his cold, pale lips like the sound of old wood beneath heavy feet. It crept from his vocal cords, pushed from shallow lungs refilled by a sharp, agonizing gasp. He groaned his words slowly, weakly, as if every sound uttered would never be again, carried out on a dying breath. He raised his eyes—bloodshot, with pupils so dilated that his glance revealed only black—and gazed straight at Desh. There was little consciousness behind them, and they were cloudy with drugs and hopelessness, but for just one fleeting moment, the executive saw a hint of what humanity still remained. The emist's fading mind stared out desperately. His deadened eyes begged for his freedom.

Desh looked away and left the emist vague in the lowest part of his vision, keeping his attention fully on the Procyon who spoke through the pitiful vestiges of what was once a man. He addressed the alien executive with forced confidence, his comfort since eroded by the silent cries of a Sapien robbed of his freedom, stripped of his ability to speak and reason, all while convinced of his own liberty with chemicals and years of mental servitude.

"Then you must know that a serious threat is looming on the horizon."

"We come to understand that you are referring to *your* ideological enemies."

"Don't fool yourselves into thinking that you're untouchable. Maybe the Hive Mind can't be manipulated, but there are other means of eradicating your race. You can't underestimate them, Executive. Every system that has done so has found itself in bondage. The collectivists will destroy everything the Procyon have created. Arterra is not the only defender of the Convergency. Our people are, after all, its co-creators."

"We acknowledge that the faction you speak of supports policies that are ultimately detrimental to Sapien livelihood as you define it. We additionally concede that we have not fully come to understand this faction's unending pursuit of its own destruction. What your state and history call an 'economic collapse,' your enemies call 'progress.' But whether collapse or progress, the Procyon will see neither benefit nor detriment."

"While it's true that the value of money doesn't mean a thing to you, the outbreak of war just might. Is that something your social scientists have predicted?"

"It is a small possibility with even smaller consequences."

"ABAC would have no problem exterminating your species, and its collectivist supporters wouldn't shed a tear over your demise."

"ABAC would only ensure its own annihilation through military action."

"But you've forgotten the Tellurian Imperium. With the Imperial Armada behind him, Executive Dunham is even more of a force to be reckoned with. And then you've got the Shatarins, who are more than willing to slaughter anyone who hasn't sworn himself to their god, which I suspect you haven't. Your *Aitar* and *sonas* might even be converted to flying Xaztechuan tenements one day if you keep ignoring the problem."

"Our calculations prove that their combined forces would find even a single sona indestructible. They would only line Communal space with their own corpses. As such, we have no concern for their belligerence."

"You should be grateful your kind has no concept of fear."

"We know only curiosity and aversion. And fear, as we have observed it, is a curious thing. It is when you are afraid that the Sapiens' intrinsic unpredictability reveals itself. However, in your species' inalienable, self-destructive impulsiveness, you are paradoxically consistent. Your fear of the 'other' and terror in the face of the unfamiliar is natural, however unfortunate, and your reaction of violence and suppression is quite possibly instinctual. Even so, we admit that we had not accurately predicted the Arterrans' behavior in response to the growing collectivist influence in this Convergency. And our foresight is not often disproven." The emist paused, twisted his head. He revealed a jagged, broken smile. "Bravo."

Desh was taken aback by the Procyon's attempt at an expression of almost snide respect, as if it could ever possibly hope to understand respect, let alone offer it. He held himself from raising an eyebrow. "We've always made sure to avoid war, when possible."

"Even more curious is that despite the denial of your Sapien instinct to eliminate the 'other,' you have still managed to survive as a society. Our observations conclude that, until your fascinating case, your species succumbed to only two possible, self-imposed outcomes in confronting the unfamiliar: aggression toward it, or destruction by it. A creature that does nothing to rid itself of the worms inside it is eventually killed by the parasites. And your opposition, like worms, has no concern for its own existence while it slowly destroys its host." The emist leaned his head in ever so slightly to examine Desh, and from behind the glass of the feeding tank, the Procyon's black eyes, though unmoving, seemed to scan the Colonial's face. "Yet your civilization appears immune." The emist pulled his head back to its slumped position against the apparatus. "Remarkably uncommon among your species."

"We kept them from entering. We didn't have to cure ourselves of them."

"An enlightened and resilient policy. With closed doors, you have found violence unnecessary. Few Sapien societies have displayed such foresight."

"We've learned from our ancestors' mistakes."

"And how thoroughly you have. But your self-awareness is unique. The Tellurians' ancestors—your 'Romans'—found their civilization in ruin for many reasons. But one cause stands out among the others in light of your species' more recent developments: a pervasive mentality of entitlement bankrupted their society. A once small but rapidly expanding group of unbalanced consumers successfully outbred the dwindling productive population."

"They demanded more and more and refused to earn it themselves."

"Precisely. Your own ancestors did the same. The only notable difference is that, by the advent of your ancestors' civilization, half the population possessed an innovative thought system and a respect for your Sapien concept of 'freedom.' Without them, your ancestors could never have pioneered their way across the void of space to establish your thriving 'City on a Hill.' Your modern concern for history has allowed you to keep it standing."

"If things continue as they are, then the memory of the past as we know it will be abandoned. Past mistakes will be forgotten, erased from the history books by the collectivists." Desh inhaled deeply and introduced the topic he'd come to discuss. "They're unstoppable when their main target is Sapien youth. I've come to you to ask for your support in rejecting their coming proposal. I'm sure you're aware of it."

"Changes to Convergent standards of Sapien education are irrelevant to the Procyon."

"They'll revise our history. Does the shameless murder of knowledge mean nothing to your historians anymore?"

"The full span of your species' history has passed only in the blink of an eye."

"But when they've turned the past into a lie, the future can be no different."

"We predicted your future long ago."

"Arterra has proven you wrong before."

The emist paused; its Procyon master didn't quickly respond. Desh knew he hadn't outsmarted it—he couldn't have, as no Sapien ever could. The Procyon was silently calculating, but with no emotion behind its eyes, it was unreadable. The lack of insight into the being's secret thoughts was disquieting. The silence was broken by the sound of draining liquid, and the central tank steadily emptied its nutrient-rich reserves and set the Procyon's feet upon the floor. The executive stepped down from its platform when the glass had withdrawn. It gazed at the Colonial with haunting eyes no longer clouded by the organic substance it'd fed upon. Unintimidated, Desh spoke.

"Without your vote, the individualists are outnumbered. The collectivist propositions at hand will be passed, no matter how vocal their opponents. We know how the five neutrals plan to vote. You're the last third party—and the most critical."

"We intend to abstain."

"Your refusal to vote has brought us too many losses and too many stalemates already. The Procyon have abstained from nearly every vote since this Convergency was founded." Desh was growing tired of the Procyon's unshakable apathy. It was outright maddening. Without a concept of right or wrong, morality or immorality, the Procyon cared little for the suffering of Sapien groups that only wanted to preserve their own livelihood. "When Arterra and the Procyon created this Convergency, this was not the outcome they'd hoped for. Everything they stood for will be forgotten."

"Sometimes in the game of creation there are unintended consequences."

"These consequences could have been stopped, and still can be."

"It is a risk that must be taken to bring forth new creations. Our geneticists were successful in engineering the H'jan and altering the Caspian Sapiens. Our social scientists, however, did not foresee the negative effects of nurturing what would become the Shatarin civilization." The Procyon raised a long, spindly arm and pointed a single finger toward the chamber door. Its attending *Ssimfar* flanked Desh and stood silently to his sides, staring coldly at him. He was no longer welcome.

Desh seethed with frustration. "We will all come to regret your neutrality."

"Time will tell—more observations are needed. We do not act on impulse. To intervene at this moment will not necessarily provide the benefit you seek." The Procyon put its hand on its emist's shoulder and slowly rapped its fingers on his protruding bones. "One's creation can easily become terrors in the night. And one may find himself forever haunted by it, even in the face of his own perceived immortality."

The diminutive Ssimfar reached for Desh's wrists with their long, slender fingers, but he shook them away with little resistance. He didn't need to be escorted out like a peasant before a king. He walked on his own with thoughts kept to himself. He resented that the patronizing Procyon was likely predicting what he was thinking at that very moment. He even more deeply resented that the Procyon would probably be right. As the leader of the free galaxy, he should have been less predictable, though no man could have hoped to do better. He was a Sapien. And the Procyon were far above Sapiens.

———

Time seemed to stop in the endless darkness of space, because without a single object to help her perceive her own speed, Selenia felt like she wasn't moving at all. She couldn't recall if she'd spent hours or only minutes drifting in the lifeless void; she'd long since put her tiny ship on autopilot. She sat in the one-woman cockpit reclined in her seat, eyes closed. She had passed through the Arterran directorate of her birth, the Alvira Confederacy, and found brief rest on its bustling capital of Cundinamarca. It was a tropical Acadica, one she was reluctant to leave behind, but her spiritual work was not for the successful, but for the suffering and poor. She'd slipped away into the Aether, but its shimmering blue flashed by her what felt like days ago. She knew she was close to her destination. It'd emerge from the shadows like a dim drop in an infinite ocean, so small that she'd do well to keep a close eye on her surroundings, but her eyelids were heavy, and without the earth beneath her feet, she felt drained.

There it was—an asteroid, dusty and gray, tumbling in the vacuum before her. As she decelerated upon her approach, a crude structure came into view. It clung to the surface of the asteroid like a mysterious parasite, the one that Selenia had been searching for. Her orders were clear, and she, having vanquished the last of the known witches who'd infested Alvira, was to report to her priestly overseer and announce her full cleansing of the Arterran region. Selenia had fulfilled her duty to the innocents. It was time for her to declare her belief once again, her spirit strengthened by the Emanation that flowed through her and guided her work.

She descended into a shallow, square indentation in the asteroid's surface, and when her ship's landing gear touched down on the landing pad, the open roof above her slid closed, and spotlights instantly illuminated the chamber. The hiss of the air ducts pumping atmosphere into the docking bay ushered Selenia out of the craft and through a second airlock, leading into a subterranean tunnel. At the end of the passage stood the Mithneshi archpriest, Hadrián Montoya, his silhouette looming on the far side of the gauntlet. Floor lights flickered on; she followed their lead.

He was dressed humbly, in rough, woolen clothes and worn-down boots just barely adequate for walking. His scalp was bare, but two long, thick locks of silver hair hung from a crescent above his temples. Selenia suspected he was in his late forties, but he might have been older, as it was said that the spiritually advanced retained their youth well into old age. For whatever age he was, he was in good physical condition, keeping his body as strong as his spirit, as was the Mithneshi way. His Breathtaker peeked out from the folds of his clothes.

Selenia wasn't the archpriest's only acolyte, and she didn't know if any of the others had completed their spiritual missions as well. She was alone on the asteroid with her overseer, Archbrother Hadrián. That day—or night, as she couldn't tell—he'd address her, and her only.

"Sister, have you cleansed Alvira of its evil, and brought light into the darkness?"

"I have, Archbrother."

"Then your journey is complete. I'm sure the Creator is smiling upon you."

He broke his religious decorum when Selenia stepped out into the light. He embraced her and kissed her on the forehead. "Nine Witches of the Deep. That's impressive."

"Thank you, Hadrián. But I'm just doing my duty to those who can't protect themselves."

"There aren't many who could take on such evil and come out unscathed."

"I have a few bruises," Selenia laughed.

"Negligible, at best. But spiritually, not even the strongest of us are invincible. You've seen violence—you've seen death, brought at your own hands, even if for the sake of good. And though those who've perished by your Breathtaker were enemies of the innocent, anger and the pursuit of revenge will always tarnish the spirit." He led her to the small altar at which he prayed each day, from which rose a thin, ethereal column of smoke, spiraling upward from a smoldering stick of incense. "But don't let that scare you, Selenia, for the Creator is merciful. It would be wise for you to go to Bhalenjar. The Ziggurat is calling you, as it calls all of us in need of spiritual rest."

Selenia bowed her head. He said he advised her, that it was just a suggestion, but she knew it was an order, given in an attempt at polite subtlety. He asked her to raise her head, because bowing should only be done before God. "The Othonas Shrine of Genuine Charity is only a short distance away, just outside the Rosc Occupied Territories." He referred to the Mithneshi station anchored in the depths of interstellar space—a major hub of pilgrim traffic, where she'd certainly be able to find a means of reaching the Veil of Bhalenjar. "Be mindful of your vow of poverty, Selenia."

The pilgrimage to the Great Ziggurat was the most sacred of undertakings, and though she was permitted to travel short distances in her own private transport, she would have to reach the galactic core through the generosity of others. There was a reason for the Mithneshi's reputation throughout the Commune as a group of cosmic hitchhikers, but it was for the sake of modesty and trust in others. Selenia would spend her flight to Othonas praying for a compassionate believer to cross her path. She'd met many among the lost

Gameer, and she wished for their company again. She hoped to find a soul like the one young Smyth boy who stood out in her memory, who believed so desperately, and whose face she saw on every frightened child facing his greatest fears.

———

The stale air in the caravan was always chilly, and it brushed the boy's nose with an icy tickle and a musty, dry scent. He crossed the bathroom in a hurry, tiptoeing barefoot over the synthetic tile floor, and stripped off his clothes while stepping beneath the showerhead. The pipes lurched and rattled, and the water came first as a tired trickle, then a slow downpour with little pressure and even less warmth. The steam that rose seemed to mock him, present only from the tiny contrast in temperature that the boy couldn't even perceive. It was all cold to him, a pervasive cold, the kind that would slip its way beneath his clothes when he redressed himself, and linger upon his once naked skin as he exited the shower hall.

He'd come to shower in the early hours of the morning, but with no sunrise or sunset to discern the time of day or night, morning was just a number, an idea, an abstraction based on the cycles of an ancient world he'd never been to. His dreams had cut sleep short, leaving him feeling restless and defiled; the nightmares were a blight on his spirit. So, he crossed his darkened bedroom, passed through his family's main quarters and slipped out into the empty, sterile corridor. He was happy to be able to bathe in peace, regardless of how unsatisfying that bathing turned out to be. There were no clusters of naked men and women chattering as they briskly washed away their sweat. There were no glances cast his way. There were no eyes watching him—especially not those in his nightmares.

The hazy blanket of fog wrapped itself around his shaking body and shrouded his chattering teeth and ice-cold lips; he imagined only the redness of his nose and cheeks being visible through the chilling cloud. His shower lasted as long as his last night's sleep—not long enough, though unlike much-needed rest, he didn't long for a more extended experience beneath the arctic cascade. The timer sounded abruptly when he'd expended his rations. The flow of water stopped with the same weak trickle he'd first welcomed then cursed. He stepped away from the showerhead. The simple mirrors along the wall were still fogless and clear, except for the rust stains that crept inward from their thin, metal frames.

Looking at himself, he understood that the racial ambiguity characteristic of his people was one of many causes for the majority's lack of interest in Gameer affairs. Among Sapiens, they were similar in many ways to the diverse groups throughout the Convergency, but, at the same time, looked like none of them. It was unfortunately instinctive for the numerous communities to either ignore them or exploit them. Their light brown skin and turquoise eyes were just enough to separate them ethnically, and, as such, the majority related poorly to their narrative. Selas imagined the Gameer's ancestors as a diverse mix of men and women of all races and ethnicities from the almost mythical Old Earth. Over the generations, their children began to look like Selas, ambiguous and, to some, exotic. But unlike most boys his age, he was smaller in stature, of an otherwise average height and a lithe, though not quite scrawny, build. He scanned his body while standing in the mirror, leaning forward to see his stomach, cropped from the reflection.

He ran his hand over his side to scratch an itch; the sensation of fingernails against his skin wasn't a relief, but stung, even burned. He raised his arm to get a closer look at his irritated skin, examining the redness that spread across the crest of his hip. Maybe it was the cold air—*It's freezing in here, and now I'm getting frostbite!* he told himself—or maybe he just needed to start clipping his nails instead of chewing them down to jagged stumps. He touched the blotchy, red patch and watched it pale with pressure. It seemed to be creeping to his back, stretching beneath his shoulder blade. Turning to look further, his eyes widened. Twisting his arm back, he felt bumps, ridges. Scars.

He hadn't the slightest idea of where they could have come from; manual labor sometimes left him with a bruise or two, but he hadn't been working such jobs, not for some time. The cuts were precise, almost surgical—they couldn't have been an accident. There was intent behind them, an intelligence. An anonymous intelligence—uninvited, and unprovoked.

In a panic, the boy began to franticly search his body for more marks, more evidence that he wasn't, in fact, going crazy. The nightmares couldn't have been just nightmares. A hard, unprecedented bump at the base of his spine convinced him. It felt like there was something under his skin, slipped in during the night while he slept, or was led to believe that he slept. He pressed his fingers into it and breathed deeply, trying to shift it, but it seemed embedded, locked in place. It was as immobile as he felt at that moment.

The cold of the room no longer froze him. It was fear that paralyzed him, backing him into a mental corner, where he was forced to look upon the face of what he once thought was madness, but proved to be a horrifying reality.

13

*"Devotion to the truth is the hallmark of morality; there is
no greater, nobler, more heroic form of devotion than the act
of a man who assumes the responsibility of thinking."*
—Old Earth philosopher, Ayn Rand.

A SMILE CROSSED TAGERON'S FACE as he waited for the lift
to arrive at the ground floor. He stood before the brassy
doors and watched the numbers count down one by one,
slowly to someone as excited as him. It was a countdown to
something he'd been anticipating for weeks.

He'd come to a deal with a new metal supplier based out
of the Occupied Territories, operating on one of hundreds of
ore-rich planets controversially claimed by the Rosc. His
proximity to their strip-mining outposts proved beneficial in
lowering the cost of the newly developed materials. It was a
bit of a risk, tempting the wrath of the Convergency by using
untested, unregulated metal. In the far-reaching bureaucracy
of "safety" and "inspection," any departure from the
accepted norm was viewed as apostasy from the
unquestionable doctrines of collectivism. But he'd signed the
deal regardless. Without a doubt, his decision would increase

efficiency, lower costs, and improve the reliability of his mass drivers. With that satisfaction, he awaited the only other meeting he considered more important.

In his tireless work ensuring the livelihood of his enterprise, he found himself intruding on time he'd otherwise want to spend with his family. His wife Isseda had passed tragically, and now all he had left were his children, Koshann and Leveda. The brother and sister with their mother's smile and their father's stature were sitting in his office dozens of floors above him. To everyone's joy, Leveda had also inherited her father's ambition. Her older brother, Koshann, however, didn't receive such dedicated genes.

It was something that Tageron had come to resent, no matter how guilty that resentment made him feel as a parent. He was a father who had to regretfully admit that he was disappointed in his son, and not just for a single act of foolishness or irresponsibility, but for the very way he chose to live his life. He didn't have any desire to dictate his children's lives or tell them how they should lead them, but he'd hoped for much more for his eldest than he'd chosen to build for himself. No matter how unproductive his son chose to be, his sister Leveda never failed to provide solace for an otherwise disenchanted father. The only thing keeping him from her—and, begrudgingly, his son—was the excruciatingly sluggish elevator. But the doors opened in time, and he relished the smooth but exhilarating sensation of ascending to the skies in elegant silence.

His secretary nodded with a smile as he passed through and informed him that his children were waiting, though he already knew. He stepped through the open doors, already overjoyed without even having laid eyes on them. It was a father's instinct, no matter how biased his opinion of one or the other. And there they were, their age always a shock to him, as he pictured the two as imaginary toddlers, stuck in an eternal youth in their father's mind even into their late twenties. His daughter, with her catlike, emerald eyes glowing happily, rose from her seat to embrace Tageron and kiss him on the cheek. Koshann stayed seated, not quite pouting, but almost, and did little to acknowledge his father's arrival. Tageron congratulated Leveda for her rising to the company's Board of Directors; her elder brother said nothing, but only scowled like a child. With him, Tageron's memories of their childhood hadn't much changed through the present.

Leveda carried herself with an intellectual confidence, having excelled in her fields of study, carrying three Masters of Science in Business, Finance and Mathematics, respectively, earned through years of hard work at Acadica's prestigious Ayn Rand University. Her brother, on the other hand, had failed out of Tarem City College after only a few days of attendance, all in a very short-lived pursuit of a Liberal Arts degree that would have served him little purpose anyway. Leveda graduated with full honors; Koshann dropped out and brought an unspoken shame to the family. Despite his never having completed his studies and barely having begun them, he still felt his opinions on matters of business and economics held some delusional value. Tageron suspected his son was on the edge of falling into the collectivists' ideological trap. But like all the collectivists' acts of intellectual imperialism, there was little that could be done, other than to watch the willing victims crushed under the monstrous weight of their own proudly built system.

Luckily, it was Leveda who'd chosen to become involved in the family business, and who, after only six years of work, had risen from the mess of the mailrooms to holding a seat on the Board of Directors. She'd applied for her first job in the lowest company ranks under a pseudonym, outright refusing any sort of special treatment or favoritism. Like her father, she found the very concept of nepotism abhorrent and inherently unfair. If she were to prove herself, it'd be because of her work ethic, not because of her family name. Tageron made sure he didn't involve himself in her career; he didn't pressure her into entering the business. It was fully her decision, and he would have been just as proud of her success if it'd been attained at another establishment. Her brother, however, was another story. Tageron only wished he'd do something productive—or anything at all.

Koshann had no desire to generate his own livelihood, and instead viewed the company as a means to an end and his father as a personal ATM. His reckless spending and lust for luxury had led him into trouble time and time again, and Tageron had no choice, up until recently, but to bail him out of every messy situation he'd run into, whether financially or with the law. He finally cut his son off after the very incident that'd haunted the family ever since, and that remained unspoken of since the entire travesty was settled legally.

Koshann, a shameless libertine, had called in the city's most beautiful and expensive escorts to attend a party thrown at his unwitting father's expense. In a drunken rage, he set their family penthouse ablaze, destroying their property beyond repair and ending three whores' lives with it. He lit their lingerie on fire as they lay in a drug-induced coma on his living room floor, vomit on their faces and eyes rolled back in their heads. The blaze nearly took down the entire building, and Koshann, always the pointless risk taker, thought his only way out was to jump forty stories off the balcony. He survived the fall, having landed in an ornate fountain pool just outside the lobby doors, but the water from that height was like pavement and broke almost every bone in his body. The medical bills he accumulated were devastating, as were the punitive legal fees and lawsuits at the hands of the city's sexual labor unions. And to make it all worse, the very party itself was paid for on the corporate credit card.

"Oh, yes, *congratulate* her," Koshann groaned. "That's all she ever gets: *praise.*"

Tageron raised an eyebrow. "She gets it because she deserves it—earned it." He patted Leveda on the back, who, if she'd been a child again, would have certainly stuck her tongue out at her jealous brother. "If anyone should be heir to the family business, it's your little sister."

"I'm your *eldest* son!" Koshann snapped. "It's *my* right."

"You can beat this dead horse all you want, Koshann," Tageron said firmly, "but there's nothing you can say or do to change my mind. You had your chance to prove yourself, but you've disappointed me more times than I can count, and I'm tired of you expecting me to solve all your problems." His son looked shocked that he'd been so bluntly confronted, but Tageron continued his criticism. "To be quite frank, you've done nothing but hurt this family and this company. I'm *still* paying off fees from your little debacle, and you haven't shown even an ounce of gratitude—or *remorse*, for that matter." He looked to his daughter after a brief but terribly tense pause. "This isn't up for debate. Your sister's my heir, and this will not be discussed again."

Koshann glared, his emerald eyes burning with a visible hatred, made even angrier with the feline slits his pupils had retracted into. "I suppose I should be *thanking* you, dad," he sneered. "This means I'll never end up like one of your corporate wagemongers. I'd rather inherit *nothing* than become a capitalist tyrant. You know—the kind *you* and your petty *Board of Directors* applaud."

Leveda was in no mood to tolerate her brother's cynical drabble. "You know damned well that every director here only wants to see the company succeed. And you know who makes up that company? Our employees. I started at the bottom and made my way all the way to the top, and not because I got any help, but because I worked for it—worked *hard* for it—and didn't take a single handout along the way, which is more than *you* can say. Do you really have the nerve to call dad greedy or even *stingy* when all he's ever done is get you out of all the disasters *you* made?"

"You'll end up just like the rest of them," her brother prophesied. "You'll spew the same demoralizing *garbage* this company's leadership has been calling *'encouragement.'* I bet you'll change your mind about taking that position when the *labor unions* come knocking at your office door."

"What's that supposed to mean?"

"It *means* that it's only a matter of time before these employees and their rightfully powerful unions get tired of being subjected to the excessive demands your leadership puts on its workers."

"What excessive demands? You have no idea what you're talking about."

"You expect your employees to work *much* harder than they have to. What you expect of them is practically indentured servitude, if not complete *slavery*."

"What we expect from them is a hundred percent of their ability," Leveda argued. "It doesn't do anybody any good for our workers to operate at half capacity simply because they don't value their employment enough to excel in it. If an employee does a half-assed job inspecting the mass drivers, then not only will he put the other workers in physical danger because of his negligence, but he'll also slash our profits with rail failures and emergency repairs. And then, the *rest* of the workforce suffers when we can't afford to maintain their fair pay and the whole company comes crashing to the ground." She sat down across from him on a matching lounge chair. "If they don't want to work, then fine, we'll let them go. There's plenty of unwillingly unemployed people on this planet, and I'm sure *they'd* be willing to take a job and do it right—and be grateful for it, too."

"You're making your underachieving employees look bad by rewarding those who work *more* than the labor unions mandate as the maximum."

"It's no one's place to tell a man how much he can work. If he decides to work extra hours to provide even better for his family or for whatever other personal responsibilities he might have, then it is fully his right to do so, and I'll be dead before I see a single employee of ours stripped of his right to work. You can't expect us to sit here and hold our less productive employees at the same level of esteem as those who've proven themselves reliable and hard-working. What you're proposing is communism—an even more insidious kind of slavery."

"What you call *'quality employees,'* the labor unions call *'brainwashed drones.'* Your concept of any form of work ethic beyond the most minimal necessity is oppression at its worst. And I can tell you without a doubt that the unions won't be turning a blind eye to your tyrannical management. If they're not satisfied with your leadership, then your workforce won't be, either. And they have the reach and influence to depose any one of you financial despots. It's up to the *workers* to decide when they've been pushed to their limit, *not* the directors. You can't quantify their capabilities."

"But we *can* quantify our profits, and believe me, if they go down any more than they already have because of your collectivist friends' policies, then our employees will suffer— not because of anything we'd *want* to do, but because our hands were tied by the rope of your laziness and sick fetish for regulations."

"No, sister. It's the *Board* that will suffer."

Tageron was silent throughout the entire exchange, but at that moment, he wanted to jump into the fray to defend his daughter from the poisonous beliefs of her misguided brother. He couldn't quite tell if Koshann was threatening his sister, or if he was just puffing his feathers, as someone of his ideological camp so often did. There was a lingering dread that accompanied the mere mention of the labor unions and their unimaginable power over the course of a business's development. He wanted to believe that his son, though an unapologetic disappointment, wasn't vindictive enough to set the union dogs loose on Leveda and her colleagues. But when the union leaders were hungry, they always found someone to devour. And if his son was right, the unions would be having themselves a feeding frenzy in the boardroom.

————

The moments before the start of an Executive assembly were tamer than those suffered before Parliament or the Senate. The uncomfortably silent prelude left the air even tenser. An anxiousness pervaded the crescent chamber, stronger than that created by parliamentarians at each other's throats. The scene of their verbal brawls and battles of witlessness lay just beyond a grand curtain, its royal blue pleats, woven from the finest of Mei Zhi silks, drawn across the greater Congressional chamber. The seats were empty, Desh knew, but he could picture Panzi Illoszia, the Lord of Parliament herself, shivering in a lone chair to the sound of Brock Dunham's voice.

ABAC's executive representative didn't waste any time in introducing his political protégé, Giles Bronson, or his modest proposal. He represented the Academic Truth and Eliminating Dissent Organization—the recently but controversially founded political entity that fed on dead scholars and burnt books. Dunham was wild about Bronson, an Arterran-born academic with an unexplained hatred for his homeland. He was young—too young for politics, Desh judged—and talked with the air of a recent college graduate convinced of his own intellectual superiority while having little to prove it. The only person wiser and more learned than him was, in his own deluded mind, Brock Dunham.

"My fellow Executives," he began, flashing a smile in Bronson's direction. "This is the moment I've long been waiting for. Today is the day we can finally and *legally* establish that individualism is an illogical and dangerous ideology. It is the day when the *oppressed* finally get the protection they so rightfully deserve. It's the day we can say that collectivism triumphed in the face of selfish tyranny."

Bronson stood and straightened his tie, puffing out his chest to convey the kind of confidence a slight-shouldered, lanky young man could only hope to muster up. He pushed back his ratty brown hair, bangs slick with nervous perspiration he attributed to his excitement, not hidden insecurity. "You have before you a new proposal, drafted by ATEDO and, of course, Executive Dunham." He glanced at his mentor with love-struck gratitude. "I introduce to the members of the Executive Council the *Banning Criticism of Shatarin and Collectivism Act*. Its contents are summarized as follows:

"*Provision One:* All resources concerning the historicity of all alleged genocides as committed by Shatarins shall henceforth be purged;

"*Provision Two:* All history resources concerning criticisms of and crimes allegedly committed by the following groups shall henceforth be purged: communism and communists, fascism and fascists, socialism and socialists, social democracy and social democrats, and anti-clericalism and anti-clericals. Anti-clericalism is hereby defined as any and all opposition to the influence of religious groups in politics *other than* the Shatarin religion, which henceforth shall be legally protected from undue criticism and intolerance.

"The Academic Truth and Eliminating Dissent Organization argues that this reformation of Convergent standards of education will result in an immediate and permanent tolerance for all groups, beliefs and ideologies other than the evil Arterrans and their sinister policies. Peace will prevail when our youth is protected from their selfish rhetoric and hatred toward the less fortunate. We can have a Convergency free of altruism's shameless enemies."

Dunham clapped his hands and chuckled. "So, shall we?"

The individualists all looked to Desh. He'd been waiting impatiently to speak his mind, furious at Dunham and Bronson's call for history's demise. He began just as Dunham inhaled to continue.

"Executives Dunham and Bronson," he said, driving Dunham to frown and Bronson to huff like a frustrated teenager. "What you're proposing is the death of knowledge."

"It's the death of knowing that an *abominable* system like yours even *exists*," snapped Sanders Flick of the Communal

Entitlement Recipients' Organization. A vein in his neck bulged dangerously as he spat his criticisms. "We're *saving* our children from *deceit* and from *ever* making the same mistakes as their *bigoted* neighbors."

Desh shot back, "The only mistakes they'll be forgetting are those of their ancestors—the ones that drove this Convergency into the ground and laughed the whole way down. You'll breed us a generation of robots and drones."

Armando Marcotti of the Convergency Ameliorated Legal Union gasped in shock and horror. "So now you're racist against the *biologically challenged*. Does your bigotry have no limits?" The other collectivists chortled among themselves while Desh breathed deeply, remaining perfectly calm. Flick's pitiful attack wasn't over. "Of *course* the 'freedom-loving' League of Arterra would oppose a law like this. It'd keep the Convergency's children from thinking that the Shatarins could *ever* commit genocide. They'd have a lie-free childhood!"

"For the sake of our Convergency's children, the truth *must* prevail," Dunham preached. He clenched his fists with conviction. "The children of this galaxy do not belong to their parents, or even to their nations, but to the interstellar community. An upbringing of lies and hateful propaganda will only lead to a violent future, much like the divisive, dangerous environment of our present day. The poisoning of young minds with your *bigoted* 'historical facts' will add fuel to the fire we ourselves must dampen."

"The chaos we've seen in our lifetimes is not the result of 'Arterran intolerance,' but because of the Shatarins themselves," Desh countered. "Their presence breeds violence and civil unrest. And the collectivists, all in the name of 'tolerance,' turn a blind eye to their crimes. Your 'tolerance' gives them carte blanche to rape, murder and exterminate."

Gaping-mouthed Armando Marcotti of the CALU immediately tried to refute Desh's irrefutable argument.

"Even if a significant act of violence *had* been committed by Shatarins, it should *surely* be considered permissible, given that such an act would be *acceptable* in their culture. Punishing or even drawing attention to *any* Shatarin act of violence would inhibit their religious freedom and their innate right to express their beautiful and ancient culture!"

Nahar Wali-Mutalbin, the rat-faced, bespectacled mastermind behind the Council for Interstellar Shatarin-Related Affairs, barked back in his yappy voice, like a privileged, spoiled brat caught in a lie. "Each time a Shatarin man is denied his right to lay hands on his wife, you are *violating* the freedoms of *all* Shatarins. In fact, it is offensive to even *mention* it, because he should be allowed to do *anything* his religion says is permissible, *without* our acknowledgment."

"An improved curriculum will teach children how tolerant and accepting the Shatarin religion is," Bronson reiterated. "It is a moral fact that the consideration of others' feelings in the publication of academic material is more important than the factuality of what is being published. It is, after all—"

"For the greater good." Dunham smiled.

Sir Byron Clay relieved Desh of his role as sole speaker for the individualist coalition. "I'll be *damned* before I see a single Arterran child sing a hymn to Lekaah in the classroom!" he shouted.

Mireille Leveque wholeheartedly agreed. "It will be a cold day in hell when students are given foreign pen pals who want to behead them."

CISRA's executive threw his stylus at her. "Are Gallic children taught to be so *racist* that they can't handle a harmless cross-cultural exchange?"

Muscovia's Executive Molotova voiced her agreement. "Your new curriculum will only foster generation of terrorist sympathizers," she barked. Like a verbal stampede, the collectivists began to scream about the Muscovite's bigotry. In unison, they condemned her as an enemy of progress and a traitor to goodwill.

Executive Dunham calmed his zealous lot with a downward wave of his hands; they complied like a shrieking, tone-deaf orchestra bent on pleasing their mad conductor. "Sentients of the Council, we could spend weeks—*months*, even—trying to enlighten the individualists to the myriad errors of their ways, but it would be only a waste of fairly taxed citizens' money. It's our *duty* to them to deliver a standard of education fit for a civilized Convergency. I suggest we vote—sooner, rather than later, I might add. The longer we wait, the more *indoctrinated* our children become."

Giles Bronson stood to lead the vote. "The Academic Truth and Eliminating Dissent Organization, naturally, votes to approve this bill."

"As does the Albian Banking Advancement Conglomerate," proclaimed Brock Dunham.

"The Communal Entitlement Recipients' Organization votes in favor of the bill."

"The Convergency Ameliorated Legal Union approves."

"The Council for Interstellar Shatarin-Related Affairs voices its support."

"The Politically Correct Broadcasting Company votes yes as well."

A pause ensued as they reached the Shatarin vote; Bronson drew attention to the empty seat and spoke on the absent executive's behalf. "As we all know, the Shatarin Empire's executive councilman, Sawal Pezh-Lekaah, has *wrongfully* been declared persona non grata, as was his predecessor, and his before him. Thankfully, this bill will prevent the individualists from *ever* hurling such a political insult again, and we will see Executive Pezh-Lekaah's return to the Council soon enough. The Shatarins have voiced their intention to approve the bill."

Domínico de la Réina of the Tellurian Imperium hesitated to announce his vote when his turn came. He was always one to be quiet, passive beneath the thunderous words of his not-so-secret master, Brock Dunham. He was powerless before ABAC, which owned his administration politically, and which held the Imperium's economy hostage, with the bank's loan-loaded gun held right to De la Réina's head. The Praetor must have been painfully conflicted; his Imperium had been at war with the Shatarins for generations, and now, ABAC expected him to defend his enemy's right to slaughter his people. Desh pitied him in a way, though at the same time, he was disgusted by his weakness and willingness to cave in to the Conglomerate's every desire. The executive's hands were tied. No one but Brock Dunham could loosen his bonds, but freedom was a currency ABAC only collected. The Conglomerate was not in the business of distributing rights.

"The Tellurian Imperium votes yes in this matter," he murmured without passion or conviction. He was lying, reciting a script prepared by Dunham with his iron pen. The Tellurian reluctantly elaborated, explaining that war could only be won through compassion and understanding, more to convince himself that he was right in doing so than to enlighten the individualists, who knew better.

Mireille seized the chance to criticize his hypocrisy. "You claim to represent your people, but the polls have suggested that most of the Tellurian population supports your ongoing 'Holy Vendetta' against the Shatarins—admittedly the best Imperial policy since colonization. You cannot reeducate them in a single generation. You will have riots on your hands when you try to implement these academic measures."

"It is our children's birthright to receive an unbiased, truthful education. The Imperium votes yes, for them." He took a deep breath and surrendered. "And for the greater good."

Executive Dunham smiled with an unbridled satisfaction, a prideful approval of the Imperium's adherence to his will. Telluria and its leadership bowed to him, to the golden calf of collectivism, prostrating themselves before the self-anointed messiah of the Commune and the Convergency itself. But the faction's spiritual leader turned his eyes away from the Tellurian executive and passed the baton of allegiance to the next acolyte, who'd repeat his words like a creed. Domínico de la Réina sat back, dismissed as quickly as he was summoned. It was Gottia's turn to publicly submit to the man who'd bound them in chains and called it "freedom." Executive Leipox Aparin testified.

"Gottia, with the purest regard for the wellbeing of her people, votes in favor of the bill. Our dedication to the collectivist ideology will raise us above the backwardness of all other Caspians." He cursed the governments of Bhalenjar and Khiteziya, condemning them as traitors to the greater good. In his view—or Dunham's view, ultimately—Bhalenjar had engaged in the unforgiveable by aligning itself with Arterra. And Khiteziya, with its insistence on neutrality, was just as guilty. Aparin quoted the Lord of Parliament Panzi Illoszia, repeating her assertions that the neutral parties effectively gave the individualists an extra vote, and that, through their unwillingness to participate in the battle of good and evil, they cost the people of the Convergency trillions of jobs each passing day.

The executive even drew attention to the other Caspians' "suspiciously foreign" eyes, justifying hatred with ethnic divisiveness that existed only on the part of the collectivists. The Caspians had been mostly unified once in the distant past. But when Communal academics began classifying Caspians not by planet, ideology or moral code, but by their varying physical features, in order to manipulate a previously untapped voter bloc, the Caspians ceased to be Caspians. Others might call them Caspians, of course. But to them, there were only Gottians, Khitezi and Bhalenjari. Such division was in the Commune's best interest.

Remy Vlotoscu Dostjya II, the Rosc executive with a mouthful of a name, took to the pulpit. He, nor his people, had given much attention to the growing presence of collectivism in the Convergency. They were busy strip-mining contested planets and selling weapons to opposing forces. As such, Executive Dostjya abstained from most votes, except those that would affect his state's arms trade, but Desh could see in the executive's eyes that day that he had no intention of staying uninvolved. There was something different about his rhetoric, like it was driven by a hope for some sort of revenge. And Desh knew exactly what he was avenging.

"The Rosc vote yes," he announced, drawing whispers from the executives who hadn't foreseen his decision. "Perhaps it's for the best that Rosc children forget who the Arterrans are." He had no problem insulting the League, which he'd once viewed as an invaluable trade partner. But ever since the Colonials began to crack down on dirty banking in the Rosc financial center of Hosc Rejtz, placed heavy sanctions on them for their unlawful occupation of resource-rich planets, and closed the Rosc consulate in Chesapeake, Executive Dostjya had an axe to grind. Desh doubted the Rosc would even implement the curriculum changes in their territory. If they did, they'd be sacrificing their children's futures for the sake of affronting the League of Arterra.

The H'jan came to Arterra's defense. Sel'zhiiq Zatsh shouted at the stone-faced Rosc: "Rewriting history for the sake of the loser can only lead to more loss. The H'jan vote against this proposal. It is just another collectivist attempt at mind control."

"Khiteziya rejects the bill," Executive Zaran Bvelet stated, supporting a cause that he would have otherwise removed himself from. "Khitezi children cannot and will not be taught to believe that *Gottia* is a bastion of economic progress and prosperity. Khiteziya will *not* suffer their same fate."

"Nor will Bhalenjar," added Executive Gokol Kodraku. "May we never live to read a textbook in which the *Shatarins* built the spiral Tower of Bhalenjar."

"If Sapien children grow into adults thinking that the Shatarins have a claim to Crystalline worlds, then our civilization is over as we know it," said Executive Feldspar of the Crystallines. The digital

voice of the translator didn't quite carry the force a natural voice could have, but he expanded his argument, eclipsing the monotony of his mechanical cadence. *"Our system will collapse under the strain of illegal immigrants claiming to be 'indigenous' to our Sapien-hostile planets, and with inevitable sympathy from indoctrinated Sapien youth, we will have no choice but to hand over our worlds and fade quietly into the dark."*

"Tsardom of Romanov Muscovia finds proposal pathetic and worthy only of use as toilet paper," Oksana scoffed. "We would sooner vote for *no* education than support collectivist domination of learning and academia."

"The Kingdom of Windsor Britannia already pays enough in Convergent taxes. We don't need our own children thinking they're not giving their fair share to a group of 'oppressed' pedophile rapists, even when, by the time they're grown, they'll practically be giving up their entire income to the Convergency," Sir Byron said.

"One can only dream," Dunham interjected wistfully.

Sir Byron scowled. "Britannia rejects the bill."

Mireille yawned, "The Federated Republic of Gallia votes no, of course."

"The Red Kingdom also votes no," announced I-Lin Xai of the Mei Zhi, her atypical involvement taking some by surprise. "Sapien children throughout the Convergency will *not* forget that the history of the Mei Zhi stretches even further into the past than that of the Tellurian Imperium. And we will *not* give up our portion of the luxury goods market, simply because spoiled, entitled Communals are taught that the Red Kingdom is 'insensitive' to the poor by not showering them with Shang pearls and Ta-Gang silks."

A computerized voice spoke up, similar to that of the Crystalline's artificial translator, but breathier with the hiss of static. Executive Gh'vuur of the Vehisipen had chosen to speak, extending two of its nineteen tendrils outward upon the desk. The slit-like mouths that stretched across its crescent body screeched and growled, in a pattern no Sapien could possibly understand. Its three red eyes peered outward from behind its many tendrils, examining the Sapiens' reactions through the invisible spectrum of infrared light. *"The Vehisipen will abstain. The way in which Sapiens choose to raise their offspring has no bearing on our society. It is not our place to involve ourselves in your affairs, if, as you claim, there is so much at stake."*

"You'll regret your lack of action when the Shatarins come to exterminate your species," Desh warned. His powerful voice commanded the entire Council's attention, even Dunham's. The mad king was helpless to overpower him, in rhetoric or good looks. "From what I learned through a legitimate education, I'd say that since the Shatarins couldn't rape a Vehisipen, they'd settle to just slaughter and eat you instead."

"How *dare* you insult the honor of this Council by spitting your *racist* lies!" screamed Bronson, his face red with outrage and his words a pitiful defense of his idol.

"Be calm, Giles," Dunham urged soothingly. His ideological progeny sat down obediently, his head hung low in embarrassment. "There's still one vote left."

The Council looked to the Procyon. Desh knew the individualists couldn't outright defeat the proposal. The best he and the rest of the right-minded Convergency could hope for was a stalemate, if only to delay the inevitable just a bit longer. But even that hinged on the Procyon's decision to either abstain, as it'd led Desh to believe, or to reject the bill on behalf of Arterra. He still held hope that the Procyon might honor its historical pledge of allegiance with the Colonials' ancestors, in spite of what it'd said. Maybe it'd find some logic in aligning with the individualists. Some part of the Hive Mind must have had a desire to defend its specimens.

Tension filled the air as anticipation mounted, and even Desh held his breath for a second. He couldn't see a hint of intent behind the void of the gray creature's eyes. It alone had the power to destroy the most valuable knowledge, something it'd always professed to preserve in its entirety, or delay its censorship until more opposition could be rallied. Its emist spoke the fateful words:

"We abstain."

"Explain yourself!" Desh shouted in furious desperation over the sound of the collectivists' excited banter. "You're betraying *everything* you hold sacred."

"There is no 'sacred,' or 'unholy.' There is only the useful, and the worthless."

"In condemning Sapiens to a future of ignorance, you've deemed *all* truth worthless."

"Your truths *are* worthless. Reality is something only grasped by the Procyon."

"Your reality, then, will be extinction."

"Our reality is entirely our own. And no Sapien could ever hope to comprehend it."

The Procyon stood, finished with the discussion, and turned its back on the Council. It left the chamber without another chilling word from its emist's mouth. Desh clenched his fists in anger, his heavily muscled arms threatening to tear his fitted suit at the seams. The collectivists had gotten what they wanted all along: to poison young minds with their ideological perversions, and to rear a new generation of statists and slaves to the cult of Dunham's personality. The truths the League of Arterra upheld would be even less credible in the minds of foreigners, who would have been raised to despise individualism, if they even knew of it at all.

But the consequences of the collectivists' support of the education reform ran even deeper than a simple act of brainwashing. The Academic Truth and Eliminating Dissent Organization, led by Bronson and his patron and mentor, Brock Dunham, could make any opposition to their revisionist history a crime, if not a blatant act of treason, punishable by death. The Convergency's children would have no choice but to repeat the mistakes of their predecessors, whose destructive beliefs would be promoted as righteous and effective. And those among them that learned the truth would one day find themselves buried in unmarked graves in the shadow of the ABAC Tower, the sun setting on the Convergency they once knew.

14

"Religious belief must not be written into law."
—Second Catechism of the Mithneshi Coven

WAITING IN THE SECURITY LINE at Dearborn's only exoport was a painful experience, the kind that only a masochist would welcome. It was excruciating in its endless immobility, and the roar of its crowds was deafening. The ropes marking the course of the lines served as a toy for undisciplined children to hang from or tug on. Toddlers and their countless siblings darted between the demarcated aisles and knocked into strangers' luggage; one little boy had kicked Pentakiya's belongings onto the ground without so much as an apology. When she went to voice her disapproval, the boy's mother only glared at her, and blamed Pentakiya for putting her luggage in his way. It wasn't her son's fault. In Dearborn, there was always someone else to blame.

A security agent made an announcement over the loudspeaker. *"Due to new Convergency-wide regulations, all Arterran literature and publications must be disposed of prior to entry. Any written or recorded materials found among a traveler's belongings, including videos, photos and artwork, will be confiscated at the security checkpoint. It is for the greater good."* Pentakiya wasn't carrying anything of the sort, and shrugged off the message. She wasn't doing anything wrong and had nothing to hide. Why should she care?

The security procedures were thorough and invasive, lasting for what seemed like hours, and no person was spared the process. Pentakiya knew it was necessary, and that Colonial nationalists could otherwise slip through undetected and spread their propaganda to Albion's youth. She waited, and waited, until she reached the body scanners. A security agent snatched her luggage from her hands and tore it open, rummaging through her belongings until he was sure she wasn't carrying Arterran paraphernalia. He tossed the bag aside and motioned for her to step forward.

Following the necessary protocol, she stripped down in front of the crowd as she stood in the examination booth. She waited in only her underwear, which she thought would be sufficient, but the security agents weren't satisfied, and demanded that she completely expose herself. Always obedient toward the law, Pentakiya did as she was told, though she did hesitate. She cringed while the rhythmic banging of magnetic scanners echoed through the booth. When it finished, an agent forced her to bend over and touch her toes, while he pried open her genitals to rule out any internal smuggling. After forcing two gloved fingers into her and concluding that she wasn't, in fact, carrying explosives deep inside her body, the agent cleared her for entry. After letting her go, he laughed to his coworkers that she was considerably tighter than the other female travelers who were getting dressed in tears.

An agent dragged a young woman away in handcuffs, taking with him the individualist materials he'd found tucked into one of her sweaters. She protested, insisting that she'd throw it away, but he didn't pay her any attention. He smiled as two mask-clad Shatarins walked straight to the front of the security line and, with a quick acknowledgment of the exoport personnel, stepped through without even being scanned. The detainee screamed that they'd bypassed security. The agent who pulled her along told her he wouldn't stand for her bigotry. When she urged him to let her go, he beat her until she fell silent.

She deserved it, Pentakiya told herself. *Spare the rod, spoil the racist.*

The exoport staff was much friendlier beyond the threshold between what was considered safe and unsafe. Pentakiya found herself greeted with a much-needed smile by the boarding attendant, and, relieved to see such a simple act of kindness, smiled back. She presented her boarding pass, which the young woman—*Hazel*, her nametag read—was happy to run through the system. But the attendant's cheerful grin soon faded.

"I'm sorry, Dr. Curicon, but you're not authorized to board this flight."

"Excuse me?"

"Your boarding pass was canceled."

"*Canceled?*" Pentakiya gasped. "They were paid for by *the* Executive Dunham himself!"

"Well, he must have changed his mind."

"That's impossible."

Hazel sighed, and shot a glance at two security guards standing by the gate. They didn't leave their posts, but from that moment on, Pentakiya could feel them staring at her, even with her own eyes fixed solely on Hazel and her suddenly somber tone. "Either way, you're on the list."

On the list! Pentakiya shouted joyfully in her mind. *That explains it! He's putting me on a luxury charter flight!* She praised his good judgment and thought eagerly of first class.

"The VIP list?"

"No, the *no-fly* list."

Pentakiya was at a loss for words, choking on what basic words she could recall. She refused to believe that Brock Dunham—*the* Brock Dunham, the wisest and noblest man to have ever walked the face of Albion—would take her off the project as if her work had meant nothing. It couldn't have meant nothing to him. She thought it was *everything* to him. Her hard work, her ambition, her *devotion*—was it all worthless? Certainly, the project's success teetered on her shoulders, and she doubted she had any real rivals qualified enough to claim her scientific throne. Growing more convinced that Hazel had made a major error, Pentakiya fought what she was told.

"There must be some mistake," she insisted. "Check my bags again. I'm innocent of whatever imaginary crimes your computer says I committed."

"Dr. Curicon, I have no way of knowing what 'crimes' you committed. All I can tell you is that there's no way you're getting on this flight."

"But I *have* to. I have work to do. For *Executive Dunham*." She tried to appeal to the love for the executive that she assumed all Communals harbored. Hazel must have idolized him as well, but it seemed that, in her strange dedication to a job many Children of the Dole would have passed over, she wasn't willing to cave in to her own emotions.

"Doctor, if you don't step away from the line, I'll be forced to call security."

"*Security?*"

"Guards—"

Pentakiya scowled and snatched her luggage from the ground. "That won't be necessary," she snapped as the two hulking officers began their approach. "You'll be hearing about this when I contact your management and tell them their boarding attendants don't know how to read a background report. And I expect Executive Dunham to be fully reimbursed for the *inconvenience* you've caused him." Hazel didn't answer; Pentakiya pointed an accusatory finger at her. "*You*, Hazel, have insulted our noble leader."

"Clearly, *you* insulted him somehow. Guards, if you will…"

"*No*," Pentakiya barked. "I'll show myself out."

As she stepped away with the security guards no longer flanking her, Pentakiya couldn't help but succumb to her racing thoughts, worrying about what she'd done wrong, and speculating as to how her punishment was justified. If the attendant really hadn't made a mistake, then Pentakiya had brought it upon herself. She was sure of it, because she knew that Brock Dunham had the most impeccable judgment, the fairest and the swiftest. But with her myriad accomplishments in tachyon dynamics and in the field of Aetherial manipulation, she had no idea where she'd gone wrong. He must have appreciated all she'd done, even if she didn't fully understand how he planned to use it.

It was useless to question his motives. His only goal was to ensure the preservation of the greater good. The steps he took along the way were beyond criticism, as one couldn't possibly hope to question what transcended the ignorance of the average person. She was being irreverent in her desperate search for a cause. No matter what it was that she'd done to offend Executive Dunham, she knew she had to make it right. She'd repent. Her executive was merciful.

It'd been some time since Selas had prayed. He'd seen miracles worked by the Mithneshi in the Creator's name, said their prayers for peace, and held a deep respect for His servants, but in his teenage years, his faith had begun to wane. He had more practical matters to worry about than the Supreme Being who whispered to the world through ripples in His Emanation. But with the fear of God struck in him as he rushed from the bath hall into the quiet corridor, he instinctively prayed to that Creator in desperation. His doubts were gone. Hell was real; he'd seen its marks upon his body.

He wanted to hear recitations from sacred scripture and cries of joy echoing to the heavens, but the din of an overhead alert broke the reverent silence. The wailing tone blared louder and softer in waves, piercing Selas's eardrums then pulling away only to stab him again. He figured he was one of only a handful of people who'd gotten out of bed so early in the morning. The alert instantly changed that statistic.

The speaker's tone was familiar and casual, his voice muffled a bit by static, but his lightheartedness fully conveyed. *"To adjust your sleep cycles to Ssimvomai Center local time, get up and go about your day, ladies and gents. Sorry, but what we were calling 04:00 hours is now mid-day, and by evening we'll be starting docking procedures. Next alert will be around 18:00."*

Selas had dealt with unpredictable time changes before, at least once a year for as long as he could remember. No one was about to get up and face the day after having enjoyed only a few hours of sleep. After their initial anger at being woken up by an unwelcome message, the Gameer would just fall back asleep and wake up to the deafening evening alert. He suspected, though, that Burton might just be awake, probably wandering about without a destination or reason for his frantic search of something he couldn't quite name. He was the only one Selas could go to. He was the only one who'd believe him.

The boy raced down the hallway past the narrowly fitted doorframes and the sleeping families that tossed and turned behind them. He ran, faster than he'd ever really had to run, the patter of his bare feet on the metal floor thumping with each step. He'd forgotten his boots but didn't have the time or concern to go back and find them. He'd hurried out before even putting on a shirt, though he kept it tucked into his belt, dangling from his side like a cleaner's overused rag. He knew the scars were visible, and that, if he were to be seen in his panic, rumors would fly of self-harm, and ultimately, a brewing outbreak of the Rakes. But he wanted Burton to see them. There was no way the old man would accuse him of having lost his mind. Burton himself had been accused of such insanity many times. He wouldn't say the same to someone else.

Selas had no idea where the outcast's quarters were, and even if he did, he had no way of knowing if he'd be there. It didn't seem like he slept in his own bed. The boy and many others had stumbled upon him sleeping while slumped on the floor or propped up against the wall, not in his own bedroom, but in the corridors or the engine rooms. Brave children would see who could creep up to him the closest without waking him. Selas suspected he wasn't asleep at all. One could always see just a sliver of white in his eyes, his eyelids not fully closed behind his circular, tinted spectacles. And drowning in the roar of the matter-antimatter reactors, no man could ever hope to sleep. At least not any man with a shred of sanity.

But the engine room was locked; the security procedures for docking made sure of it. Selas dashed past the shadowy dining hall without its usual sound of clatter and hoarse laughter. He shouted into every restroom he could find, but he began to lose hope, and his run down the corridor became a tired jog. He paused to catch his breath, then reached for the scars on his body he'd hoped to explain. He prepared to head back to his family's quarters, but he stopped when he heard the faint sound of static coming from an open doorway ahead. Someone was watching a video in the next room. At that hour, it couldn't have been anyone but the outcast he'd been chasing.

Selas entered the room and recognized it as the musty library no one used. Only a few shelves' worth of crumbling books and archaic compact discs remained, all having been salvaged from the remains of Old Earth before the Gameer's exodus long ago. The spacefarers had acquired just a handful of newer books since that time, but an author or a filmmaker hadn't walked among them in over three millennia. Instead, the caravan's residents had no choice but to skim through tasteless pulp fiction and less-than-stimulating Classical Anglic dictionaries. But some opted for film and television, like the unconscious hermit who lay slumped over a crude, wooden table with a mostly empty bottle of liquor. He snored violently, loud enough to cover the haunting whistle of an ancient TV program's title sequence. Selas had found him. He pounded his fist on the table to wake him with a jolt.

Burton shouted out something unintelligible. He shook his head and scratched at his scalp. "Gimme a minute to wake up before you start houndin' me with questions," he groaned, slurring his words. He sat upright and exhaled, looking up. "Where's your shirt?"

"What the *hell* is this?" Selas barked, twisting his torso to reveal the unexplained marks on his body. Burton smiled; Selas fumed, clenching his fists with teenage aggression.

"You're askin' questions you might not want answers to."

"Not knowing is what's killing me," Selas confessed. He raised his arm to let the hermit more closely examine the scars. He leaned in and pulled back the skin to exaggerate the marks, making them more visible. Selas cringed. The wounds burned like a brand.

"They don't usually leave marks like these," Burton noted, puzzled. "Least not in such an obvious spot." He sat back up. "You fought pretty hard, though. I almost thought you'd get away for a second. Must've gotten cut doin' it."

"*What was I fighting?*" Selas shouted.

"If I help you remember, you won't be able to forget it again."

"I have to remember."

"You'll want to forget."

Selas paused, surrendering to the tightness in the pit of his stomach. He thought of the eyes, how vulnerable and disturbed he felt in their gaze. If all he could remember was just a small glimpse of horror, then how terrifying was the entirety of the scene? How grotesque were the faces with the piercing black eyes? Were they something he really wanted to remember?

"What are they?" the boy asked. He'd made his decision—he couldn't live in ignorance. "And what do they want?"

"Let's have a closer look at their handiwork," the old man said, pointing to the red cuts running across his side. "Then you can tell me."

———

Thoughts of the god flooded Livia's dreams, but his presence was like an emptiness, not a fullness added to the candlelit chamber. She could see him, not just in his marble statues with their powerful stance, but even in the air, in the beams of light that shone through the stained-glass windows and the fragrant smoke of incense. The god had no body or solid form, but Livia could feel his weight upon her and a breeze, like breath, upon her neck. She stirred beneath him, arms pinned at her sides by unseen shackles, and her sense of curious wonder at the god's manifestation turned to panic. She felt him invade her body, piercing the very depths of her soul, until she could bear no more and surrendered to his eternal hunger.

Then a holy light flooded the chamber. It burst so brightly through the stained glass that its color was no longer visible, but drowned out only in white, the most brilliant white she'd ever seen. It was blinding but soft, overwhelming but gentle, radiating with the most infinite power and endless beneficence. The shadowy ghost of the sea god disappeared in its glow, chased away into the dark by the glorious cry of an eagle, perched upon the tallest statue with angelic wings outstretched. With its talons it tore away the marble face of the god's image and threw the broken pieces upon the floor, where they crumbled into dust. It baptized her in the crystal blue of its eyes, washing away the stains of idolatry upon her spirit. She felt a pureness she hadn't experienced in years. She felt as she did before she'd been taken to the Imperial Temple in her youth. She thought she'd forgotten that feeling. She thought she'd lost it forever.

"The girl sure is pretty," said a disembodied voice, echoing through the chamber. The divine light faded away; the eagle disappeared. The voice was familiar, but Livia couldn't quite place it. She listened. "Too bad every other guy's said the same thing."

She woke from her dream, disgusted. The voice was the other Colonial's, not Natharis's—certainly not his. She listened to them talk across the cabin, letting them believe she was still asleep and unaware of their commentary. Erixen sighed, shifting in his seat. "Sad, really. I'd say you should go for her if everyone else hadn't already."

"You know, her own people don't look down on her," Natharis replied. "If anything, they'd call her devoted to their religion."

"Just because the Tellurians say she's godly doesn't mean she is. The Shatarins would have a real good time with her. Bet she'd love it until they stoned her to death."

"Say whatever you want," Natharis sighed, "but she's as faithful to her own beliefs as any good Deist is to theirs. Honestly, I can respect that."

"You'd be okay with fucking a whore?" Erixen scoffed. "A *real* whore, not just some easy foreign girl?"

"People can change," Natharis said. "I don't hold someone's past against them. You'll get nowhere in life holding on to what's been. You just have to look to what can be." He stopped, as if he wasn't just letting the words settle in Erixen's head, but his own.

Livia smiled and clutched the thin pillow closer to her cheek. She found solace in the Colonial's lack of judgment, though he, as a marshal, devoted his life to it. He'd sworn his life to civil law, as she'd sworn hers to higher law, to the heavenly judges who demanded that her body be their temple. Natharis was right in saying her people respected her. But she didn't feel respected as a human being. They respected her as one would respect the majesty of a great cathedral or feel reverent before an altar. Though beheld with wonder, she was still just an object to be adored, not a person to be treated with dignity. She was merely a means to an end, a stepping stone for the feet of others on the path to salvation. Natharis must have known that. And if he didn't, he'd surely come to learn the shameful truth. She was no celestial beauty. She was just a candle flickering in an empty chamber, and when the flame of her youth burned out, she'd simply be tossed aside like the others that'd burned before her.

————

Natharis was no stranger to beautiful women. He'd won the hearts of many back in the days of his youth on his family's farm; he drew glances from girls at his regular gym and even onlookers at the scenes of criminal investigations. While he didn't often make the time to get to know them any further than what their stares gave away, it wasn't that he didn't have the desire to. He'd learned a great deal about himself since Kerinne left, and if there was one thing he'd been forced to admit, it was that work didn't often permit the pursuit of a woman's company beyond a casual night out.

Kerinne had taught him that lesson the hard way. It was unexpected, though all the signs were there, and if he'd just taken a moment to look at what their life had become, he might have noticed. He'd chipped away at their relationship with every extra hour he worked at the precinct; every phone call saying he'd be home late was another nail in their coffin. When the Judiciary asked him to pick up a shift, he never said no. He didn't do it for the money—he was paid quite well already—but for the thrill of the chase. Unfortunately, he'd stopped chasing Kerinne, whom he thought he'd already caught: the ring on her finger was proof of it. When she left one morning without so much as a goodbye, it was clear that she'd been slipping away with each canceled dinner. He'd taken her for granted. When he read her regretful letter and held her diamond ring, shedding tears he swore never to shed again, he couldn't blame her. The fault was his, and his alone. He'd spent his life in pursuit of the guilty on the streets of Chesapeake. Now, for the first time, he only had to look in a mirror.

He knew he needed to move on, and he'd told himself that he had, for the most part. His friends thought otherwise, but they were always ones to delve too deep into his problems. To them, the easiest means of putting the relationship behind him was to go out, meet a girl—either while waiting for the bartender, or on the dance floor—and take her home that night, or one not long after. But he wasn't one to chase a pretty face as fiercely as he pursued a wanted criminal. He held little interest in women whose only goal in life was to look good, to please the eyes of the men they passed on the street and in the office. But he laid eyes on the Tellurian girl and couldn't help but lose himself in her beauty. For once, he took repose in it.

Livia, he thought with a smile, *Nettunaya, of the sea god.* She truly looked like a servant to the ocean's majestic power, a nymph bathing in its holy waters, bringing sorrow to those men who looked on with no hope of touching her. Her soft breath was like a song sung by an otherworldly siren, beckoning him to come closer, just close enough to feel the warmth of her skin, though Natharis saw no danger in following her. She didn't swim in the blood of men crushed on the rocks of her love. She couldn't. In her serenity, she was captivating. Despite her actions for the sake of men's faith, she was pure.

The Tellurian consitor had taken notice as well. Natharis observed the way he stared at Livia's vulnerable body, her soft, fair skin and the curve of her hips. His eyes were focused so intensely on the sleeping girl that his gaze was almost tangible, like a red-hot poker or a molten blade. There was hunger in that stare, and though he probably knew Natharis was looking at him, he refused to turn away from admiring, or coveting, Livia's body. Something about the look in Silviano's eye left Natharis feeling defensive, almost jealous, and he was surprised by his own instinctual desire to cover her from the other man's invasive stare. He had little reason to be so protective, as she wasn't his to protect, and, if anything, she should fall into Silviano's arms, not his. She and the consitor shared an experience that Natharis couldn't understand, at least at that moment, but he desperately wanted to, and hoped that he could.

He wondered how it must have felt for the two to be torn from their people and their pilgrimage, caught up in a mess that had little to do with them. He was even more curious about their roles in that pilgrimage. It'd been a long time since he'd taken a course on Tellurian history, culture or language. He saw and read in the news the standard references to the Imperium's ties, or bondage, to ABAC, and he'd regrettably come to witness it firsthand. He knew about their polytheism, their basic rituals and beliefs—enough to have a decent understanding of Livia's situation and to defend it from undue criticism.

Natharis couldn't relate to their experiences, to their roles as sexual conduits for communion with the divine. He considered the consitor and how perfectly satisfied he must have been in the part he played in their pagan Divine Comedy. He hoped Livia felt the same. While he himself didn't want a part in it, he held to his firm Colonial belief that if one was to do a job, one should excel in it. If she wanted to live her life as the god's carnal altar, then he hoped she'd find fulfillment in it.

As a follower of Mithneshi Deism, like many Colonials, Natharis's beliefs conflicted with some aspects of the Imperial Cult, like their denial of the oneness of God. But he followed his faith and held back his judgment. He did what any good Deist would do and remained humble instead of claiming to know the Creator's will. And as he sat back and exhaled, he looked upon Livia and thought to himself that nothing so beautiful could ever be wrong in the eyes of God.

On most days, the bright atmosphere in Pentakiya's apartment provided her with a quiet relief from the cacophonic mess of public Dearborn. The tall windows let in the warm sunlight and made the white of the walls and furniture even whiter, and painted them gold when the sun began to set. Their classical Gallic décor was conducive to illumination, and Pentakiya loved the contrast of long shadows along the floorboards against the pearl upholstery. And when she walked through the front door, she saw her wife sitting on one of two couches, her copper skin like the golden sunlight that spread over the room. She had a holotab in her hands; she tapped away at its screen, obviously writing. She looked up to acknowledge Pentakiya and smiled.

"So," she began, standing up to greet her wife. She embraced her and gave her a kiss. "You decided to stay with me instead? And to think, I made the bed and everything."

Pentakiya would have laughed, but her mind was preoccupied with thoughts of shame, not sex. She smiled weakly and caught Artimpasa's attention with her half-hearted attempts at normalcy. "What's the matter?" Artimpasa asked, her hand on Pentakiya's shoulder. Pentakiya shook her head. She wasn't quite sure how to explain what had happened. She herself didn't even really know how or why it'd happened. All she could do was speculate.

"They turned me away."

"Turned you away?"

"At the gate. Right when I was about to board the flight."

"What, did leadership decide you'd be better off working from home?"

"If that's the case, they didn't bother to tell me about it."

"Maybe they didn't have time to."

"Maybe I did something wrong."

"What could you have possibly done wrong? You're loyal—to a fault, sometimes."

"Well, whatever it is, it's keeping me here."

"You act like that's a bad thing."

"It *is* a bad thing. The last thing I'd want to do is upset Executive Dunham."

"Haven't you done enough work for him?"

"I don't think there's such a thing as 'enough' when you're trying to reshape the Convergency. And here I thought I was his favorite scientist." Pentakiya sighed. "Guess I was being childish."

"You've never been childish. Maybe a little too trusting, but not childish."

Pentakiya didn't know what to say—her overwhelming worry consumed her thoughts, made worse by Artimpasa's assertion that she had too much faith in others. Her faith, though, was limited to only three near-spiritual entities in her life: her wife, corporatist collectivism, and, of course, Executive Dunham, the leader of the free worlds and champion of the greater good. And while in the past she'd never faltered in her belief, it seemed that, as of late, it was beginning to wane. She told herself it was her pride that compromised her once unshakable faith. She cursed her own hubris in thinking she could accomplish *anything* that could satisfy a man whose only satisfaction would come from liberating the universe from Arterran selfishness. She never should have held herself in such high regard. It wasn't right to be so proud of one's accomplishments. Maybe she'd achieved too much for one person. Others must have been left dead in the tracks of her ambition. With success always came casualties—collateral damage.

"You know, you're not the only one who's had a deal broken," Artimpasa said as she sat down on the couch, motioning for her wife to join her. "Got a call from my publisher today. They've changed their minds about my new book."

"They've never done that before," Pentakiya answered, now with her legs pressed warmly against her wife's. "Your other books were even *more* inflammatory."

"And that's why they're discontinuing those, too."

"You're kidding."

"Nope. Looks like they're booting me out of history. Ironic, given I've devoted my life to *preserving* history. Funny how things work out."

Artimpasa was well known in Dearborn and throughout the Commune, but because of the unfamiliar slant she put on her recollection of the past, she was considerably more popular in the League of Arterra. Her strange tales of Shatarin violence appealed more to an Arterran audience than that of the Commune, who called her a hack and a charlatan, shameless in her perversion of history. Pentakiya had to admit that even she questioned her wife's research sometimes. It was inevitable that she'd find a completely different version of the past when citing Arterran and Tellurian sources. They were references fueled by an ancient bigotry. Though she supported her wife's right to disagree with the common view, she did have concerns that, one day, Artimpasa would end up like one of her quoted historians. For all her hard work, history might remember her as nothing more than a petty racist.

She knew her wife was no such bigot, but if they'd met under different circumstances, she might have easily dismissed her as one. Pentakiya had fallen in love before Artimpasa ever had a chance to reveal that she was, in fact, the enemy Pentakiya had been raised to revile. They'd met at an anti-war protest in their senior year; it was the one place where both their sides could come together in agreement, if only for one rowdy afternoon. Student groups from across the Commune were flocking to Albion to march before the planetary capitol, and both their universities had sent representation. When Pentakiya first saw Artimpasa, she didn't know she had just finished a semester abroad in Britannia, or that her alma mater was the infamously individualist Revere University, which she'd seen described in the news as a domestic terrorist training camp. All she knew was that she was the most beautiful Caspian woman she'd ever seen, whose amethyst eyes were the only ones she ever wanted to gaze into again.

Two months passed before Artimpasa broke the news to Pentakiya: she was an individualist and would not change, and she understood if Pentakiya wanted to walk away. At that moment, part of her did; to share a bed with a bigot was bad enough, but to publicly declare her love for one was social suicide. It took her a day to make up her mind, pacing back and forth in her dorm room for hours. She knew Artimpasa wasn't like the rest of them. She accepted that her friends would likely disown her, and that she might even be cast out of her own home. But Artimpasa was worth it. Pentakiya might have doubted her future wife's beliefs, but never her love. Unfortunately, years later, it seemed her wife's publisher had lost faith in her and cut ties just as quickly.

"Don't you have a contract with them? Can they really just change their minds like that?" Pentakiya asked.

"They can when the collectivists tell them to." Artimpasa handed Pentakiya her holotab, upon which was displayed a news article published in *The Harlequin Post*, the most reliable and rightfully opinionated news source in the Commune. She read the article quickly, skimming most of it, and looked only for the most essential key words. The major player in the political scenario appeared to be ATEDO, the Academic Truth and Eliminating Dissent Organization, which had Brock Dunham's full approval and, consequently, Pentakiya's. They'd passed a new law, it seemed. It clearly had some relevance to her wife.

"My work is illegal now," Artimpasa explained. "Apparently, they've decided it endangers the minds of young readers—as if university students can be called 'young readers.'"

"What, history as told by Arterrans?"

"No, history as it really was. From now on, the Shatarins are only 'peaceful farmers.'" Artimpasa made a living on accusing the Shatarins of all sorts of atrocities. Pentakiya was upset that Artimpasa had worked so hard for nothing, but, on some level, she was glad she'd been forced to learn that her research might not have been so accurate after all.

"It's okay, though," Artimpasa said. "Maybe it's illegal to publish me on Albion, but there are plenty of foreign publishers. I'll just find a new one, preferably in the League. They *never* go back on a promise. They value them more than we do." She took the holotab from her wife and set it on the coffee table. "I planned on contacting a few today. I'll fix this whole mess by the time we go to bed." She smiled and put her hand on Pentakiya's thigh, caressing it softly. "Maybe we could lie down for a bit right now." She kissed Pentakiya on the neck. "We both could use it."

Pentakiya felt as if she'd been brought to an emotional crossroads, with one way led by ideology and the other paved in romance. For the most part, she'd been willing to accept the thought that the two of them would be able to coexist with their disagreements, no matter how serious or opposing, and up until that point, they did. Pentakiya, while she was put off by Artimpasa's stances on matters of politics, still found her wife's ambition and passion to be some of her most provocative traits. But it seemed she might have to make a choice between her higher thoughts and the primal warmth her wife had come to put her hands upon. Her belief in collectivism was at odds with the woman she'd always called the love of her life. Artimpasa claimed to tolerate Pentakiya's ideas. But if her wife was so eager and willing to put their freedom on the line by publishing anti-collectivist ideas, then what did she *really* think of Pentakiya's beliefs?

15

"Coexistence? How can the Shatarin religion peacefully coexist with other belief systems when its adherents have denied every genocide they've carried out throughout history, all with the smug endorsement of collectivist 'academics?' Can one really coexist with a faith that rose to power through genocide since its inception? The Shatarins have not lost their way from peaceful beginnings; their ideology has always been rooted in violence. The only foreseeable way to achieve coexistence with them is through separation."

—Colonial Executive Desh Maru, addressing Parliament in response to claims of Shatarinphobia in the Colonies.

THE LONE PLANET OF KOJV was nascent in the distance, just a small, grayish dot as the ship reentered free space. With a lurch that made Natharis feel like his body had been pulled in two directions, they slipped out of the tachyon vein just as easily as they'd entered it light-years away. Natharis had chosen not to sleep during their last stretch of transit to the isolated, Rosc-claimed world. He'd relished the chance to catch his breath and clear his mind, but the coming rendezvous with Erixen's contacts kept him alert. He didn't want to let his guard down. The Tellurians had turned on their own people without any hesitation. He didn't know much about the Rosc, but he assumed they'd betray their own just as quickly. The marshal made sure to keep his rifle strapped to his back. He thought of an ancient cliché: *Better safe than sorry.*

Erixen, on the other hand, didn't seem concerned at all. When Natharis reminded him that ABAC had far-reaching ties, Erixen eased his fears by citing his long relationship with the Rosc they'd be meeting. "And besides," he continued, tucking only a single handgun into his belt, "they wouldn't want to draw any unnecessary attention to their 'questionable' operations here on Kojv, or on any of their occupied planets, for that matter. They don't want the Convergency involved—and *especially* not the Colonials." He mentioned that the Rosc had been under fire in the political sphere because of their contested claims to Inner Rim planets, none of which had any significant settlements or permanent populations. The Rosc altered the planets' atmospheres just enough to allow for Sapien habitation, though not nearly enough to be sustainable, but it was argument enough for them in Congress to defend their strip-mining operations as "ecological conditioning."

Erixen stood up and addressed Ninotchka. "Agent Voronova, power up communications. Hopefully, I didn't get all these burns on my hands for nothing." He sat down in the copilot's seat and withdrew a small chip from his jacket, then slid it into a data slot on the transmissions panel. Ninotchka flipped a switch, and the interface began to glow. Erixen applauded his own efforts.

"Better send your entry code quick," Ninotchka suggested, pointing a finger at a series of orbital defense batteries that lined their path to the surface like castle guards.

"Don't worry—trust me." He pressed a button and the computer confirmed the transmission's successful delivery.

They waited anxiously for clearance. The barrels of the intimidating battery cannons stared them down. Their ship glided past the sentinel with everyone but Erixen holding his breath. To their relief, they passed by without a problem. Though the lack of formal confirmation of their clearance left Natharis feeling uneasy, he managed to relax when the ship's sensors informed them that they'd entered the upper atmosphere, the vacuum of space just miles behind them.

The effects of the ore extraction operations became evident as they began their descent. What Natharis would have otherwise thought to be craters, scattered in clusters over the surface of the planet, were gaping quarries cut into the terrain, some fresh, some decades old. Plumes of dust rose high into orbit, spewed from smokestacks littering the rocky landscape: the powdery, caustic debris produced from aetherium mining. The Rosc were scouring the Inner Rim for planets rich in the priceless mineral, all for the sake of their booming arms development industry, and to secure their strong position in the weapons market. They'd pull the plain-looking rocks from their quarries, crush, sift and refine them, until they had cargo loads of the substance to send off to the central worlds. Unlike Colonial mining procedures, Rosc protocol had no concern for future occupation once peak aetherium had been reached. They'd abandon the planet and take its meager population with them, leaving behind a devastated world.

Their landing was rough, even with the Muscovite's exceptional flight skills, because of the deep potholes and cracked pavement beneath the ship. The sheer weight of cargo freighters, carrying thousands of tons of equipment and machinery, must have been too much for the hastily constructed runway to handle. The landing gear scraped against the buckled cement along the web-like fissures, and the seat upon which Natharis sat shook with each light impact, until they completed their descent and came to rest in a landing slot marked by dim, yellow beacons.

"How do you expect them to know it's you?" Natharis asked his unfazed partner. "All we did was transmit an access code."

"And obviously that was enough. They'll put down their guns as soon as they see me. It'll be a nice, little reunion."

"Let's hope you didn't lose favor with these contacts of yours," Ninotchka sneered. She assembled her gear, slipping her firearms beneath a white fur coat that reached down to her ankles. Accentuating her Muscovian ensemble, she pulled a black hat, also lined with furs, over the crown of her head. "It's cold out there," she explained while Erixen criticized her choice in attire. "I always come prepared. It's like winter walk on Petrograd."

"We don't need spacesuits?" Livia asked. Natharis assumed she'd never been to any planet not comprehensively terraformed. He read the atmospheric analysis and relayed the information to the inexperienced traveler.

"Around eighty-four percent nitrogen, sixteen percent oxygen," Natharis replied. "A little thin, but perfectly breathable. It's cold out there, but nothing terrible." He drew a smile from Livia, who then followed Silviano to the door. Ninotchka stroked a finger against the control panel; the door snapped open with a sharp hiss. Livia mentioned the Crystalline, asking what they were to do with it while they were gone.

"Leave him," Erixen advised. "He's not going anywhere."

They descended the ramp onto the landing pad, and Livia, upon reaching the ground, began to cough, as did Silviano, then ultimately Natharis. The air was thick with a chalky dust, and the sunlight cast hazy beams through it while its smoky particles danced overhead. Natharis took off his jacket and held it to Livia's face. Silviano, having noticed, swooped in to guide her under his arm. Natharis backed away, struggling to see with his eyes irritated and tearing up from the pollution.

From beyond the ground-level cloud emerged a single Rosc, his long, black leather coat billowing in the wind as he approached. Even with smears of soot on his face, the fairness of his skin was evident; his dark hair, falling over his brow, matched the color of the sky above him. On his face he'd placed a gas mask, and he shielded his eyes with workers' goggles. His heavy boots crunched the crumbling pavement beneath his feet.

The man motioned for two others to hurry over, each carrying a small crate. They opened the containers and produced a collection of additional gas masks for the party to wear, as well as much-needed goggles. Livia returned Natharis's jacket as soon as she'd found technological refuge from the choking air, and though he couldn't see her mouth from beneath the mask, he imagined that she was smiling—he could see it in her eyes. But she quickly looked away from him as the Rosc greeter began to speak.

The gas mask muffled his voice, leaving it breathy and hoarse. He addressed Erixen first. *"Jazej bizkozy tusc dvu hol roscj premmos?"* he asked in the Rosc language, which Natharis didn't understand, and he assumed that the Tellurians and the Muscovite were equally confused. Erixen smiled, as if he understood, or was feigning understanding.

"Anglic would be better. My friends here don't speak Rosc."

The Rosc examined the visitors, then spoke in Natharis's native tongue with a heavy accent, though with impressive fluency. "So, Erixen, you've brought a Colonial, two Tellurians, and, based on how she's dressed, a Muscovite," he observed. Ninotchka glared, insulted by his tone. "What are you doing on Rosc territory, expecting me to speak your silly language?"

"It's been a long time, Tuscar," Erixen replied, "and this is how you greet me?"

"You're lucky we didn't greet you with artillery fire. Entering an occupied system in a notorious smuggler's ship displays either exceptional bravery, or baffling stupidity." The Rosc stepped forward to shake Erixen's hand. Erixen expected a friendly embrace, clearly forgetting the Rosc's stoic demeanor, which they were universally known for.

"Well, we're in the market for a new ship, now that you mention it."

"I see. Perhaps we could work something out."

"That's the idea."

Tuscar began to walk, motioning for Erixen and the group to do the same. The bustling quarry lay ahead of them, and the roar of machinery blared in Natharis's ears. The sight of the cliffside, obscured by the dust ascending into the air, was framed by the rows of shanties that lined the street. Natharis caught his foot on one of many tracks on the rocky dirt road, but prevented a clumsy fall by dragging his hand on the side of a building. Its cheap polymer siding shook and buckled beneath his weight.

Erixen struck a private conversation with Tuscar in Rosc; Natharis was unaware of Erixen's fluency. Natharis himself had learned non-Colonial Arterran languages in his childhood and high school career, and he'd held on to some knowledge into his adulthood, still able to speak Latigón and a handful of phrases in Gaulois. But it wasn't common for Colonials to learn truly foreign languages, and if a Colonial were to speak one, it would likely be Tellurian, only because of their prominent media. The Rosc weren't a common topic of interest in the Colonies. Natharis was impressed that Erixen had studied, and clearly mastered, such a complex and unfamiliar language.

"Lutzaj scimuz vulistaj kvistalj, vuslavip sje kil vlotoscol. Zaj mos flasco lutzpremsca djun lupot an luscjom pry lidj." Erixen pointed back toward the ship in the distance.

"Dy zej lufilliz ky dostol?"

"Murnjya lutzpremsca. Brijtjya lundj lutzaj slavar." Erixen smiled.

"Ja slavka."

Erixen turned to the group and summarized his unintelligible dialog. "Looks like we've got ourselves a ship," he announced with a smile. "We just need to sign some exchange-of-ownership papers, then we're good to go."

"What's the catch?" asked Natharis, unconvinced it could be so easy.

"We give them the old ship—and half its aetherium reserves."

"So, they want us to run out of fuel in the middle of a tachyon vein? We'd be better off risking it as smugglers."

"We're not going far. And besides, we're seeing your Mithneshi friends, remember?" He seemed disdainful upon mentioning the Coven, but Natharis, though bordering on annoyed, stayed calm. He didn't want to make waves in front of the Rosc who'd been open enough to strike a deal with a group he barely knew, all except for Erixen. And while he wasn't sure how willing the Mithneshi would be to fill their aetherium reserves, if at all, he knew they were safer in a Rosc-manufactured ship than one with a deadly mark on its record. Their newly acquired transport would also have heavier weapons than the smuggler's ship, having been built by a state obsessed with advanced military technology. They wouldn't have to worry about being shot down in a burning wreckage. Instead, those around them would have a reason to be concerned, because only the Rosc would bring a planet cracker to a knife fight.

––––––––

There was something about lying on a table with nothing behind his back that left Selas feeling uneasy and vulnerable. He had vague memories of being outstretched on a metal surface before, the cold slab pressing against his bare skin. He lay on his side, as Burton had instructed, and he heard the old man rummaging through drawers, making a clatter with the random odds and ends he'd stored away with little purpose. The boy breathed deeply, unsure of what was to follow. Maybe he wanted to look at the scars again. Or maybe there was something more to it, something he didn't expect.

"I don't think you got those cuts from any standard procedure of theirs," Burton stated, approaching the table behind the boy's back. "But there's one thing they definitely gave you. Classic trick of theirs. They hide it in a spot where you probably won't look." He put his finger to the lower curve of Selas's back and tapped the slight bulge of his vertebrae between the two dimples of his muscles. "Let's get this thing outta you."

"Get *what* out of me?" Selas asked. He saw a shiny object in his peripheral vision, held in Burton's other hand. "And what the hell is that for?"

Burton grazed the razor against the boy's skin, tracing a circle around the spot he'd drawn attention to, not hard enough to break the skin. The tingle of the blade gave Selas chills. Burton donned a pair of tiny goggles in lieu of his darkened spectacles, the lenses like magnifying glasses, before leaning in closer to his body. He pulled his skin taut. "There's a reason you don't remember anything, kid. They don't *want* you to remember. If you did, you'd tell the whole world what's really goin' on, and that'd blow their whole plan to pieces. Lucky for them and shitty for you, no one's gonna believe you when you do remember."

Selas winced as he felt the razor sink into his back, sliding across to make one small incision. Burton kept talking to keep him distracted. "The first time they took you, they tagged you," he explained, "just like they tag everyone else. And I'm takin' that tag outta you."

"Can they find me without it?"

"Of course they can. But without the neural implant, they won't be able to leave you paralyzed when caught off guard. And you'll be lucid through the whole damned thing. Once you remember, you can't forget."

"Won't they just put another one in?"

Burton pried at a tiny foreign body Selas could feel pressing against his spine. "Your body's used to it now, especially your neurons. They won't be able to take control of you again. But listen to me when I tell you that this ain't gonna keep 'em away." The object popped out from the lips of the boy's split skin, and Burton pinched it between his fingers, withdrawing it from Selas's flesh. "There it is. Got it."

He put a bandage over the wound and invited Selas to put on his shirt. The boy set his feet on the ground and turned to face Burton, leaning over the table to look at the object he held in the palm of his hand. It was small, cylindrical with rounded ends, and dark in color—not shiny like metal, but with a matte finish that made it look more mineral. At its tips were frayed wires with a gel-like coating, which Burton described as neural conductors.

"I still don't remember a thing," Selas sighed, having expected an instant epiphany.

"Give it a little bit," Burton instructed. "Your brain needs to warm up to the repressed memories. When you go to sleep tonight, it'll all come out." He took off his goggles and set them on the table. He dropped the device into an empty glass. "And then you can tell me if this was the biggest mistake you ever made."

———

The makeshift storehouses and dormitories were primitive compared to what Livia was used to. She lived in the majestic Imperial Temple that stood at the center of the Imperium's ancient and thriving capital. Roma Ceisora boasted palaces lush with greenery and towers built of whitewashed stone, but the bare-bones settlement on Kojv was simply a collection of worn polymer shacks at the lips of the gaping mouth of the earth. Any man careless enough to leave his gas mask behind would perish with burnt lungs, singed by the caustic dust of his exploits. She saw no life there, and what life there once was or could have been, she saw being raped by the greed of mankind.

But as she looked down one of many alleyways, something caught her eye. A tree, with fresh leaves shimmering in the wind, stood peacefully in the distance. She tried to continue walking with the rest of the group, but couldn't find the willpower to do so. Her curiosity got the best of her, but it was more than just curiosity. She felt a connection to it, to that one untouched part of nature, and it drew her in, a spiritual fascination guiding her steps. She departed from the group's march to the quarry with no concern for anyone's reaction to her absence. She'd find her way back. It'd just take a minute.

The tree rose from the ground in the center of the narrow street. It had shed its springtime flowers onto the rocky earth beneath it, and a ring of pink petals encircled its base. In its branches were birds' nests swaddling eggs and newborn chicks, tended to by colorful songbirds chirping from behind a curtain of bright green leaves. Livia felt a warmth in the air as she approached the unexpected scene, like she'd walked into a glimpse of summer on a planet that knew only dusty winters. The pale light in the Kojv sky turned to gold. The roar of machinery behind her faded into silence. Amid an otherwise distressing situation, she felt at peace, and savored it as long as she could.

There came a humming in the distance, not the mechanical whir of mining equipment, but like the buzzing of cicadas on a hot summer day. The sunlight dimmed until she saw only shadow, and she looked to the sky, where black clouds gathered above her. They twisted and swirled in the wind as if they were living, breathing creatures, and their hum turned to a roar. Livia stepped back slowly as she realized she wasn't looking at clouds—it was a swarm of locusts, piercing her ears with the sound of millions of beating wings.

The horde spiraled downward and overtook the tree from its roots to its highest branches, and its leaves fell one by one, until torrents of green poured upon the ground and turned to dust. Eggs fell from their nests and cracked on the rocks below, and the birds took to the skies to escape the insatiable swarm, their only home ravaged by the greedy, mindless insects, whose existence was governed by compulsion and desire, not reason or morality. Livia heard wood splitting under its own weight, and branches fell from the tree. The swarm's thunderous din swelled louder, and the horde abandoned its feeding ground, leaving only a gnarled, dead trunk surrounded by decay. Again, she heard only silence.

Then the tree's tragic remains vanished. Livia stared at where it once stood and tried to understand it all. Her daydreams—her visions—were starting to get the best of her. She shook her head to return to reality and looked about, turning to look down the alley from the direction she'd come. The group was well ahead of her, far out of sight on a perpendicular street. If she walked fast enough, she could catch up. But as she took her first step back toward the quarry, she didn't see the man approaching from behind, or the heavy wrench he wielded like a club. He swung the wrench; she had no chance to evade it. She fell to the ground, her head throbbing with pain. She touched her hair, and blood trickled through her fingers. The gray skies faded to black. She once again fell silent.

———

Selas had no idea what time it was when he returned to his family's quarters, but he knew he'd been gone long enough for his parents and sisters to have woken up and prepared themselves for the day. If they were up and about, they surely would have noticed that he'd disappeared, though if the docking procedures hadn't commenced, they wouldn't have much reason to be upset. But the overhead announcements declared the protocol to be in effect, and Selas was violating one of their basic codes by wandering the halls. He was supposed to be in his room biding his time before they successfully docked at the Ssimvomai Center for the Lost. He was lucky they didn't have security guards to enforce the rules, or else he'd be in even more trouble.

He slipped through the doorway in hopes that his parents might not see or hear him, no matter how slim the chances. He'd hoped in vain; his mother was standing right inside. She demanded to know where he'd been, to which he had no response. He couldn't tell her he'd been with a crazy old man prying implants out of his skin, or even about the scars that had started it all. As far as she was concerned, Ssmid Burton was a dangerous loner raving with the Rakes, and consequently could not be trusted, especially with the safety of a teenage boy. If she knew, she'd go on about how he could have been held there and tortured, molested, raped or killed, or any number of other tragic fates he could have met if he hadn't been so lucky as to escape. Selas knew he couldn't get away with lying. Not answering was best.

"I just don't understand what's been going on with you lately," his mother sighed. She cited his admittedly strange behavior as evidence of some internal torment he'd neglected to share with her, mentioning his screaming in the middle of the night, of which he was unaware, and his lack of participation in family conversation, or any conversation, for that matter. He tried his best not to look her in the eye, because the longer she went on about his mood and his recent changes in attitude, the closer she brought herself to tears. He didn't want to see his mother cry, especially not over his problems, which she only saw a glimpse of. He wasn't about to apologize, because what he'd been doing was out of his control, as he'd come to learn, but he still felt guilty for upsetting her.

"You were gone for so long, I thought something might have happened. Only the crazies would be out of their rooms right now."

"You've never noticed me missing before," he muttered. His mother didn't understand his statement and insisted on knowing what he'd meant by it. He didn't bother to elaborate, regretting ever having said it.

"You don't have to tell me what's wrong, Selas, but just know that things will be better once we're with the Mithneshi. Their blessing will do you some good—I promise. You seemed so much less worried when Selenia was with us." She saw the sad look in his eye and knew she'd accidentally hit a nerve. "You know, whenever you had nightmares as a kid, I'd remind you that the Creator and His Emanation would keep you safe. Even when you were crying about how the 'big white bugs' were going to take you away, that thought would always calm you down. And it's still true now, even with you all grown up."

Selas had no recollection of the childhood fears his mother had mentioned, but the term she'd used—*he'd* used, as a child—resonated with him, and evoked a feeling of fear he couldn't place. He started to think he'd met the eyes before, that they'd stared into his mind even when he was young and helpless. Maybe they'd been there all along. And if Burton was right, and the device under his skin really had been keeping him in the dark, he'd be meeting the big white bugs again. There was no going back. He might be able to control his screaming in the night, but as for the rest of the scenario he had yet to recall, it seemed there was little he'd be able to do to stop it. He was a child again, with a child's paralyzing dread, and now he felt as though the promise of a fulfilled adulthood had been stolen from him, left mutilated on an exam table somewhere in the darkness of space.

The dusty gravel Livia lay on dug into her back, but she couldn't gather the strength to crawl up off the ground. Her head throbbed in pain, and her hair was damp with blood. In her hazy confusion she kept still, her eyes only half open, and the sounds around her echoed distantly under the ringing in her ears. She couldn't remember how she'd gotten there, lying helplessly in the middle of the darkened alleyway, but she heard two voices above her, both male, and both excited to take a closer look at her. She felt rough, gloved hands pinching at her clothes and grasping at her arms and legs. She winced and tried to hide her return to consciousness. She chose to surrender and let them have their way with her, rather than die for seeing them do it.

A third voice joined the conversation, not from right above her, but off in the background. The two men stopped talking and took their hands off her; she squinted to see what was happening without giving herself away. Ninotchka sat on a crate behind the two men, spread-eagle, with her legs high in the air. Her heels stuck up from her upturned shoes like pikes meant to impale a criminal. She smiled and cooed at Livia's attackers.

"Dead-fish is no fun. At least I *pretend* to fight back." She spread her legs wider to draw the two men closer, their attention torn away from their helpless prey and now set on the sultry predator. Ninotchka smiled, knowing the men took the bait.

"There's no place like home, boys." She clicked her heels together and grinned. Livia heard the crack of a fired projectile; Ninotchka's stiletto heels shot like arrows straight into the men's necks. The fatter of the two fell to the ground grasping at his throat, while the other, with a severed jugular, sprayed torrents of blood from his wound. He collapsed, exsanguinated. Ninotchka laughed in the spirit of victory and replaced her heels with knife-like spikes she'd kept tucked in her clothes. She pulled Livia from the ground and dragged her by the wrist.

"They tracked us down. ABAC is more competent than I thought," she grumbled. She rushed Livia down the alley, who was still clutching her head and stumbling as she tried to keep up. "We're being set up. There's no reason for these *mudaki* to be here." She reminded Livia that Kojv was just one of hundreds of low-key strip-mining operations that would have been of little interest to ABAC. "Back to my ship," Ninotchka decided. "Prisoner has to be secured before ABAC finds it, if they haven't already."

"What about Silviano? And the Colonials?"

"They'll be fine. Mr. Ruke can take care of himself. His partner, not so much, but we'll pick up boys after we steal back my ship."

Much to Livia's relief, the Muscovite's undercover transport was right where they'd left it, and still in one piece, instead of the twisted metal skeleton she'd been expecting. There was a new ship adjacent on the landing pad, its engines still hot and spreading ripples through the air. She didn't see any other ABAC troops, though the entry ramp on Ninotchka's ship was still deployed, with its access hatch wide open. She caught a glimpse of a figure in the cockpit window, and alerted Ninotchka to the enemy presence, prompting the two of them to scramble for cover behind a large shipping crate at the edge of the runway.

"We march through front door and take back what's mine." Ninotchka cocked her first weapon and slipped a fresh magazine into the other. "Keep close—don't let them see you."

The two women tiptoed across the landing pad and up the entry ramp; Ninotchka drew her guns to the patter of their footsteps up the thin metal board. She slipped her head in to make sure they weren't walking straight into an ambush, and when she was certain the coast was clear, she signaled for Livia to enter the ship behind her. The chatter of excited voices stopped Livia in her tracks, and Ninotchka stood still as well. Two soldiers bickered in the back of the cabin, crouching over the hovering crate that held the Crystalline prisoner. They clearly weren't sure what to do with it, and debated over their course of action.

"C'mon, open it. It's been in there so long—what's he gonna do?"

"They broke him out of Jotunheim. He's gotta be dangerous."

"Then hold your gun out when I open it, if it makes you feel any better."

"I'd feel better if we'd just get it off the ship."

"Just cover me. I'm opening it up."

The more reluctant soldier stood upright and pointed the barrel of his gun at the crate while his partner began to fiddle with the lock panel. He cursed as he entered an endless number of incorrect codes, and smashed his thumb onto the biometric scanner as if he could fool it. He sighed and kicked the crate. "We might have to blast it open."

"Not with broken skull, you won't." Ninotchka whipped her pistol against the back of the soldier's head, who stumbled over the crate onto the floor, unconscious and bleeding; she shot his partner in the chest with perfect accuracy. Without saying a word, she dragged their bodies to the access port and kicked them down the ramp. They tumbled down to the landing pad with holes in their uniforms, pierced by Ninotchka's lethal heels. She hit a button on the control panel and the ramp retracted. The port snapped closed.

"Grab guns from rack," Ninotchka commanded. "Big ones. Colonials have probably run into ABAC already."

"I've never fired a weapon before," Livia confessed. Ninotchka rolled her eyes.

"Not *you*. Guns are for me. I learned to shoot well before learning ballet." She pointed to the cockpit door after deciding to get the firearms herself. "Start up engines. We're going."

"I don't know how to—"

"You don't know much, do you? If ship were man, you'd do fine, I'm sure," she scoffed. "Stay by cargo doors. Open them when I say so. Think you can handle it?"

Livia nodded, insulted, degraded by a woman she thought more beautiful than herself and more stunning and sexual than any she'd ever met. She stayed near the larger of the access ports, covered by a retractable section of the ship's hull; when opened, much of the side of the cabin would be exposed. She gripped its inner edge when she heard the roar of the engines. The ship rose from the decrepit surface of the landing pad.

"We still look like smugglers!" Livia yelled. "We should have taken one of the Rosc ships, or even one of ABAC's!"

She wasn't sure if the Muscovite could hear her from the cockpit. "This whole thing was pointless, then!"

"And be tracked everywhere we go? Stick to what you know, Tellurian. You do job of fucking and blessing. I'll do mine of fucking and killing."

The ship rocked as Ninotchka hit the accelerator, and they raced over the shanties with just a few yards between the hull and their rooftops. The quarry grew larger as they approached, like a gaping mouth ready to swallow them, and Ninotchka dipped the craft down over its rocky lip in a single graceful maneuver. Through the windows Livia saw a tall, thin tower, embedded into the wall of the quarry, each floor exposed to the open air with just a small railing at its edge. Suspended platforms, like open-air elevators, rose and fell along the length of the structure. Silviano and the Colonials had been headed in that direction. Ninotchka must have predicted they'd be in the mining tower, walking right into a trap.

"Open cargo bay!" Ninotchka barked. She ran out of the cockpit to ready her guns. The ship, with the artificial smoothness of autopilot, began to rotate until the cargo bay doors faced the tower. Livia hesitated, but just as Ninotchka, eyes rolling wildly, went to hit the button herself, she complied. The door retracted at a steady pace to reveal a blazing firefight.

Natharis took single shots at their adversaries, and one by one the ABAC troops dropped to the ground. Silviano had a rifle pressed firmly into his shoulder and provided Natharis with backup, because Erixen was standing with his back against the wall, darting his eyes about the scene like he couldn't quite figure out what to do next. Ninotchka shoved Livia out of the way and knelt at the cargo bay's edge, drew a sniper from the holster on her back and lined her eye with the scope. She pointed her finger at a rusty rock grinder several floors beneath the balcony and told Livia to pay attention and learn something.

"Pick one," she demanded. Livia wasn't sure what she meant. "One of ABAC's."

Livia chose a soldier who'd just entered the fight, figuring him to be an easy target. Ninotchka grinned and turned the barrel of her sniper toward him, quickly pulled the trigger and shot him in the arm. The crack of the shot reverberated off the rocky walls of the quarry and drove Livia to cover her ears impulsively. The soldier, gripping his wound and stumbling forward, looked up in horror as Ninotchka shot him a second time. A splatter of blood burst from his leg, and he fell over, hitting his stomach on the frail railing at the balcony's edge. He screamed as he tumbled over the barrier and fell toward the rock grinder below. Livia cringed when she heard the sound of cracking bones and the final cries of a misguided crusader.

Ninotchka ordered Livia to grab some rope from the utility storage bin set into the wall beside her. Livia rummaged through it and found a sturdy, carbon-fiber rope. Ninotchka set down her rifle and took the cable, unwound it and slung it out the cargo bay door to the balcony beside it. She secured the close end of the rope to a metal hook protruding from the floor, then ran to the cockpit; Livia saw the balcony across from her begin to sink lower in her vision, and as Ninotchka guided the ship upward, the cable dangled beneath them. Livia shouted out to Natharis and Silviano, begging them to grab hold of the rope. Erixen ran to it first, shoving the other two men aside.

He might have been an unreliable opportunist, but Erixen had surprising strength, climbing his way up the rope with ease. Silviano, with his sculpted muscles flexing impressively, came second, and winked at Livia when he pulled himself up into the cargo bay, as if she were to swoon at his impeccable fitness. But when Natharis reached the top, Livia knelt to grab his hand, though she was sure he could have crawled inside perfectly well on his own. He smiled after clasping his hand with hers. She knew she hadn't saved him from certain death, but he thanked her as though she had.

She didn't notice the feeling of the cold wind whipping back her hair, or the sound of the cargo bay door sliding shut. She didn't care about the transition of dusty clouds into the black emptiness of space. The threat of bombardment didn't concern her, nor did Ninotchka's shouted commands. Even the flashes of light outside the ship, the energetic bursts of artillery fire, didn't leave her paralyzed with fear. She kept her eyes only on Natharis, her ears focused solely on the sound of his voice, her attention only on his actions. Fear was nothing to her, because at that moment, she saw her eagle rescuer, not in a dream, but standing right before her. Her protector was fearless—as was she.

16

"In a perfect world, we would prefer a form of individualist anarchism, with no state at all to dictate affairs. But we recognize the practical necessity of a minimal state to prevent individuals from infringing on other individuals' rights— legitimate, innate rights, such as freedom of expression, and not glorified 'wants,' as the Commune would define them. Sapien nature prevents the creation of the utopia of a stateless society. Minarchist individualism is the closest functional semblance of this individualist anarchism that history has ever known; indeed, it is its direct descendant."
—Colonial High Juris Consul Shivani Prashad, in her inaugural address.

WHEN TAGERON FIRST ESTABLISHED his company, he'd made a promise to himself that he would never allow the infamous labor unions of the Inner Rim to weasel their way in. It wasn't out of a reluctance to pay his workers fair wages, or some fear of a workers' strike, because he knew he was a generous employer, and that his staff's loyalty was unwavering. After all, why would they turn against the company that treated them so well, paying them at a rate unheard of on even some of the more developed worlds? The unions weren't necessary. He wasn't running a sweatshop, and he wasn't in any mood to deal with their pointless meddling.

But then came the collectivists to Hatal-Om, and where there were collectivists, there was always a powerful union close behind. The political faction, with its fanatical support base, made it a point to criminalize all union-free businesses on Hatal-Om. Had Tageron not caved in to their demands for a union presence in his company, he would have found himself out on the street, his enterprise in ruin and his reputation decimated. Their legal influence was far-reaching and outright unsettling. He knew they had friends in high places, probably reaching all the way up to the Convergency's Executive Council. Brock Dunham was a proud proponent of the virtues of organized labor, and his mindless cronies couldn't have agreed more. They despised people like Tageron. Business owners were dangerous. Innovators were traitors.

The union representative sitting in Tageron's office that day was there for that same purpose: to admonish those who employed the efficient and not the lazy. He was slumped in the chair across from Tageron's desk, his bloated, shapeless body limp in the seat like a giant, horrifying larva. The man's light bronze skin was pinched together in deep wrinkles caused by fat, swollen flesh smashed against another blubbery layer, two doughy tectonic plates colliding and sinking beneath the surface of his face. The puffiness of his cheeks left his eyes squinting and beady, the emerald color of his irises only vaguely visible, like a light peeking over a soft, blob-like hill. He'd smugly introduced himself as Quba Vaski, one of the city's top representatives of the planetary labor union. Tageron didn't offer the enthusiastic welcome the man had anticipated, much to his resentment.

Tageron wasn't sure how the man had managed to find a designer suit large enough to accommodate his titanic girth, or even a tailor with unrivaled skill in the art of squeezing the obese into expensive formalwear. The man's sausage fingers were tightly adorned with rings of gold and silver, some sparkling with diamonds and other precious stones, and his love of dazzling displays of wealth extended even to his cufflinks and tie clip, both of which were studded in spectacular, light-catching gems. When he smiled, Tageron half expected his teeth to be made of pure gold, but much to his surprise, they were tiny and rotted, sparsely protruding from reddish, infected gums. Each time he spoke, his lips would slide over them with the sound of sloshing saliva, and flecks of spittle shot from his mouth. Tageron thanked Heaven for the desk between them.

"Mr. Dagonari, the union has *concerns*," Quba began, folding his hands together on the bulbous crest of his gut. "Specifically, about the quality of your *management*."

Tageron knew exactly whom the fat-cat union representative was referring to. While he was sure that the union had a problem with any form of management, no matter how fair, Tageron waited for Quba's specific reference to one of his most valued directors, Magas Ingir. He was the head of the Rail Safety and Maintenance department, the company wing in charge of ensuring the efficiency and reliability of the mass driver rails that provided their revenue and, ultimately, the workers' pay. Magas had worked his way up from a low-level technician to the department director, all through hard work and dedication to his role, holding the admirable belief that even the most basic of positions should be valued and respected, as honest work was honest work, no matter how unglamorous. And, naturally, a hard-working man only had to hold a position of influence for a few weeks before the labor unions began to voice their complaints.

"The subject of an employee's lunch break might not seem particularly *important* to you, Mr. Dagonari, but I *assure* you that the workers are beginning to feel the weight of the *odious* burden your management is placing on them."

"They get an hour's break, as well as a number of shorter ones throughout their shift. Our policy is perfectly reasonable."

"Your *employees* think otherwise, as does the union."

"You mean the *union* thinks otherwise, and therefore, the employees."

Quba dodged the accusation and continued with a scowl. "Over the last four weeks, the union has *repeatedly* demanded that your management *revise* your policies and extend the workers' breaks from one hour to four."

"That's unacceptable. Magas was right to deny your request."

"It's not a *request*, Mr. Dagonari. It is your employees' *right*."

"The policy stands."

Quba Vaski was outraged by Tageron's stubbornness. He argued that any civilized employer would conform to Communal standards, and that four hours was actually shorter than lunch breaks in the Commune, and therefore, Tageron should have been thankful for their generous compromise. But he was wasting his breath, as Tageron had no intention of ever acquiescing to such ridiculous demands, which would decrease productivity for the sake of a fully unnecessary repose from already fair duties.

"The union also wants to address the *atrocities* committed against two *victimized* employees of yours: Mr. Heso Nyereg, and Ms. Khati Tenger," the union representative added, because one unjustified complaint was never enough for a man of his rank.

"What about them?"

"They were *wrongfully* and *abusively* written up by none other than your favorite Magas Ingir, all because they didn't attend work that day."

"We don't tolerate no-call, no-shows in this company, Mr. Vaski. They're lucky he didn't fire them."

"It's nothing short of a *travesty* that you, *nor* your management, respect the right of an employee to *choose* whether to go to work on any given day. What you are doing is restricting their freedom of *choice*, Mr. Dagonari. It is a *violation* of Sentient rights that cannot and *will* not be tolerated—not by this labor union, nor by the collectivists.

"I find it even more disturbing and abominable that you *yourself* decided to promote Mr. Ingir to the position of director, *despite* his lack of seniority over your *other* candidate, Mr. Bemul Narax," Quba growled. He reminded Tageron that Bemul, easily one of the laziest employees Tageron had ever had the foolishness to employ, had been in the department just a few weeks longer than Magas, and thus, according to the union contract, should have been handed the higher position automatically, without question or evaluation of merit.

"I run a meritocracy here, Mr. Vaski. Nobody benefits from promoting or even *keeping* an unproductive employee, whether entry-level or upper management. Against my better judgment, I kept that useless Bemul around, but just long enough to get the tenure he needed to keep his job. Now, all because of *you* people, I can't get rid of him, no matter how often he fails to show up for work, or how many times he half-asses his rail inspections, or even if his pitiful performance results in the loss of lives, all because of his negligence. If I can't fire him, I sure as hell won't have him running a department."

"You hired Mr. Narax *exactly* three weeks *prior* to hiring Mr. Ingir. And, according to the contract *you yourself* signed with the labor union, any *new* managerial position to open up is reserved for the department employee who holds the *longest* tenure, regardless of his or her *performance* record. In promoting Mr. Ingir instead of the rightful candidate, Mr. Narax, you have violated the union contract."

"Bemul Narax isn't worth the pay I give him. If I had my way, he'd be looking for another job right now. If anything, you should be thanking me for keeping someone as incompetent as him around."

"Call him what you want. You're *still* in breach of your contract."

"There won't be a new director. Your 'oppressed' employee will keep his current position, and Mr. Ingir will keep his as director."

The union representative squirmed in his seat like a colicky infant, grunting and sputtering as he mustered up the strength to move his morbidly obese body. "You're making a *terrible* mistake, Mr. Dagonari. If you do not comply, the union will be obligated to take *legal* action against you, and the consequences will be *severe*, I promise you."

"Are you threatening my company?"

Quba shrugged and feigned ignorance like a child. "I've heard of quite a few businesses these days who've been *shut down* overnight by the courts. When you don't treat your employees *fairly*, it's only a matter of time before they get *tired* of it." He rested the hanging rolls of fat from beneath his arms onto the sides of the chair. "*Never* underestimate the power of an organized workforce, Mr. Dagonari. Remember: *You* are the one percent."

Tageron paused to think. Quba Vaski was right—legally, he had his hands tied. The fines the courts would impose on him would be more than punitive, and with the collectivists' taxes already choking the life out of his business, Tageron couldn't possibly afford to pay them. The only option, for the sake of the company, was to comply.

"What am I supposed to do, then?" he asked, praying for a light punishment.

Quba smiled and flashed the few teeth he had left, overjoyed that he'd succeeded in getting an honorable businessman to violate his principles and surrender. "Under *normal* circumstances, the labor union would demand that you simply *exchange* their positions—*promote* Mr. Narax, and *demote* Mr. Ingir." Tageron wasn't happy about the idea, but took a small bit of comfort in knowing that he wouldn't be forced to deny Magas an income. But the union representative wasn't finished, adding the catch to their arrangement. "*However*, due to Mr. Ingir's record of *grievances* against him, including, but not *limited* to, his *denial* of extended, *fairer* breaks, and the *punishment* of employees who'd chosen a day of relaxation over one of *toil*, the union demands that you terminate his employment."

"*Terminate* him?" Tageron shouted. "That's completely out of the question. His wife just had a child—he's been celebrating it all week. And now you want me to *fire* him when he didn't do a single goddamned thing to deserve it?" He stood up and pointed to the door. "Your union is a joke. Get the hell out of my office."

"We will *not* take no for an answer," Quba said without a hint of sympathy. "He is just as guilty as *you* are. If he had *any* concern for his fellow worker, he would have turned *down* the position you unlawfully offered him. Both of you must pay the price for thinking of the *individual* over the needs of *others* who deserve an equal opportunity."

"Equal opportunity does *not* mean equal outcome. They all had a fair shot, and Magas proved the most worthy."

Tageron refused to respond to the man's unwillingness to compromise, and the silence drove the union representative into an irate frenzy of labored huffing and puffing. He attempted to push himself out of the chair, but the width of his hips kept him bound to the seat, stuck between the wooden arms that were just slightly too close together for comfort. Tageron didn't help the vile beast escape his sedentary trap. After a minute or two of struggle, Quba slipped gracelessly out of the furniture vice and waddled his way toward the door.

"You have forty-eight hours to change your mind," he snarled as he just barely passed through the door. "Wait any longer than that, and you'll be hearing from our lawyers. That is, if another government agency doesn't get to you first."

Tageron tried his best to ignore the man's cryptic threats, but couldn't help but wonder what he could have possibly meant by his ultimatum. He'd already come under fire with his higher taxes and his new identity as a target of individual tax hikes. He couldn't imagine any other force at work on Hatal-Om that could possibly do any more damage than he'd already been dealt. It was a lost cause, promoting a system of labor based in merit and responsibility, not handouts and arbitrary privileges, in an environment where the lazy sought only to justify their own laziness. It was a society in which employees chose their management, and not vice versa, and the thought was disquieting. If the labor union didn't like someone who tried his best to improve the quality of the company, he could lose his job. No one was safe—not even Tageron himself. He'd created and nurtured his company like a child. And now, a greedy, jealous parent with no child of her own was seeking to seize it from him.

He would find Magas another job despite his personal distaste for nepotism, as he had a number of business connections throughout the Inner Rim, but there was no way to spare him the humiliation of being laid off, even if he were to consciously understand the reasons behind it. Tageron dreaded the meeting he had no choice but to schedule. If Tageron was lucky, Magas wouldn't blame him for the unfortunate outcome of his promotion, but he couldn't imagine that anyone, even someone as familiar as Magas, would be able or willing to be objective in such a situation. He knew the news would devastate the new father. What he had to do was wrong, but after it was said and done, he'd do whatever it took to make it right.

The cashier at the grocery store offered Pentakiya Curicon the choice of either traditional paper or polymer shopping bags. When the lackluster employee uttered the word "polymer," she had a foul tone in her voice that made her disgust toward synthetics clear as day. She was especially offended when Pentakiya chose not to purchase a reusable shopping bag, as she'd already bought two, but consistently forgot to bring them with her to the supermarket. According to the woman's judgmental glare, Pentakiya was an environmental offender, a callous, self-centered Sapien who had little concern for the wellbeing of the planet. The awkwardness that ensued and the tiny bead of sweat that slipped down the side of her brow drove Pentakiya to choose the antiquated paper bags. She wasn't engaging in ecocide. She was a good Communal, and she always bought environmentally friendly products, no matter how expensive or frivolous.

She carried her groceries home in the noisy, oversized bags that crunched with each step she took toward the door of her apartment building. No one offered to hold the door for her as she struggled to open it wide enough to slip in with her cumbersome burden. While she normally would have taken the stairs, she couldn't bear the thought of climbing all the way up to her floor with bulky, astoundingly heavy shopping bags clutched painfully in her hands. She chose to take the elevator, happy to put down the groceries for a minute as she waited.

Pentakiya had planned an elegant dinner for her wife that evening. Knowing that Artimpasa was still struggling to find another source of income, Pentakiya felt that a date night would be the best thing to take her mind off her stress. Artimpasa had recently received several notices discouraging her from seeking a publisher outside the Commune, threatening to silence her with a prison sentence if she didn't stop her pursuit of a voice. Despite the government ultimatums that Pentakiya could neither support nor reject, Artimpasa wouldn't be home for another four hours or so, having decided to give a historical lecture that day at the local library. Artimpasa wouldn't stay quiet for anybody, not even Pentakiya.

The elevator doors opened; Pentakiya stepped inside and pressed the button to take her to her floor. She made sure not to drop the expensive bottles of imported wine as the elevator ascended with a jolt. She'd cook dinner, light some candles and set an exquisite table, all before Artimpasa got home from her lecture. If she'd suffered any harassment at her event, the romantic gesture would surely ease her mind. The city despised women like her, but Pentakiya would make sure she'd always have a loving home. The least she could do was make dinner. It was just what she—what they—needed.

But when she stepped out onto her floor, she couldn't believe her eyes. Her apartment door was open, just slightly, but enough to notice from a distance. She knew she'd locked it before she left to go shopping, and Artimpasa wasn't supposed to get back for another few hours. Even if it was her wife, she couldn't imagine Artimpasa being reckless enough to leave a door ajar in Dearborn—she was more safety-conscious than that. So Pentakiya approached her apartment slowly, carefully, then nudged the door with her shoulder, having left the bulging bags of groceries sitting in the hallway. She didn't hear any movement inside the apartment. Thinking the intruders must have already left, she worked up the courage to enter her home, and found herself in shock at what she saw.

Bookshelves were overturned, toppled over upon the floor, some broken and others still intact. The hundreds of ancient books she and Artimpasa had collected over the years of their marriage were reduced to only a dozen, scattered irreverently across the floor. Her wife's holotab was no longer sitting on the coffee table where she'd left it; it was nowhere to be found. Pentakiya's, too, had vanished, and she frantically rummaged through the careless piles of torn and crumpled documents that littered the room, but couldn't find it. The filing cabinets had been left gaping open with their contents strewn around them, some folders untouched, and others empty. Whoever broke into their apartment had searched through all their personal records, everything she and her wife would have preferred to keep private. And all of Artimpasa's work was gone. It'd been stolen from her by a force Pentakiya couldn't bear to identify.

She knew deep down that she'd been robbed by the Commune's most powerful agencies. It was something she didn't want to admit, as to admit it would be to violate her most sacred belief: the government was a parent to be trusted—wasn't it? Their leadership *always* had the greater good in mind. They never could have broken into her apartment and stolen her property, and if they had, then they must have had a reason for it, even if that reason was beyond the knowledge of a single woman. If the Academic Truth and Eliminating Dissent Organization really had ransacked her home, then it meant Executive Dunham likely knew about it. He'd kept her from finishing her work for him, and now he was letting his agents terrorize her, all within the limits of the law.

At that moment, Pentakiya wondered if Artimpasa could have been right all along. The thought was overwhelming. It was too much for her to handle, and she stumbled through the apartment, catching her feet on all their belongings that lay broken upon the ground. She made her way to their bedroom, intent on finding the one thing she didn't want anyone, not even her wife, to find. If it was gone, her life was over.

She'd kept a copy of all her research data on a small disc secretly tucked behind an old, unpowered electrical socket. It was hidden by the nightstand on her side of the bed, which didn't seem to have been moved. She pulled it away from the wall and popped open the metal plate covering the outlet. It clattered upon the wooden floorboards. Pentakiya sighed in relief. The disc was where she'd left it; her work was still safe.

Her past partner Rocky had insisted on making copies of the data, for reasons that weren't entirely clear. Then he vanished. She kept hers hidden out of fear, and tried to convince herself to destroy it, but the memories held her back. It was technically ABAC property, and by keeping a copy of it, she was stealing. But the data was important to her, and the last thing she planned to do was lose it. She'd keep it safe, just in case—not for the sake of blackmail, or the potential for treason against her government, but because it represented a close friend who'd been taken from her.

Her wife, though, wasn't so fortunate in preserving her property. All her academic achievements, all her hard work and research had been taken, as if it'd never even been accomplished at all. The hours Artimpasa had spent scouring old history books and primary sources, all the days and nights she'd slaved over her papers, essays and books—they were all wasted. Pentakiya might have kept the fruits of her labor, albeit only by a stroke of good luck, but she couldn't say the same for her wife, and she wept for Artimpasa's loss, who didn't even know of it yet.

Pentakiya calculated how long it would take her to straighten up the ravaged apartment; she was sure she could finish by the time Artimpasa got home, but she knew that no matter how clean or organized she made the house, there was no way to retrieve the stolen books. There was no excuse she could possibly offer for their absence. There was nothing she could do to bring them back. Their seizure was beyond Pentakiya's control. It was beyond the control of any one woman, because the thief who'd taken them could never be brought to justice. The burglar's hands were the hands of the law, and so long as those laws remained, no one's property was safe. A woman who'd unwittingly angered her cherished leader could lose everything she'd ever called her own—and what was taken would never be returned.

Livia was tired but she couldn't sleep. The droning of the aetherium drives was beginning to make her stomach churn, like a sickeningly low bass tone that resonated deep inside her. Silviano didn't have much trouble ignoring it, and he slept soundly in his seat, grunting unconsciously every few minutes in a way that made Livia speculate as to what he could have possibly been dreaming about. Natharis, though, was wide awake. He was playing a film clip over and over again on his timepiece. Livia didn't see what it was, but she heard the voices of an older man and woman. They sounded happy. She envied them.

"This is my first time off Telluria since I was a child, and I'm already getting tired of space travel," Livia remarked, catching Natharis's attention. He silenced the timepiece and sat beside her, listening. "At first, I was in awe of the Aether. Now I'm just bored."

"Can't say I disagree," Natharis replied. "Nothing like solid ground beneath your feet."

"You must be homesick for Chesapeake. I would be."

"A little. But I'm fonder of the countryside outside Hudson," he sighed. "I grew up out there. That's home—not those high-rises and skyscrapers. They're spectacular, sure, and no one's seen anything like them, but the Colonies are built on farms like my family's."

"A farm boy, then." She smiled, finding the image endearing.

"So they say." He recalled the horse he had when he was a boy—"A whole barn full of them, actually," since his father was a rancher. He used to ride past his father's workers while they kept the farm running smoothly, heading for the orbital bridge on the horizon, but it was always too far away. And his mother, being a florist, always made sure to have a fresh bouquet of flowers arranged on the kitchen table. It sounded like a good childhood, one that would nurture a young boy into becoming an honest, decent man. Then he asked her of her own past. She wasn't sure where to start.

"I wasn't born on Telluria," she confessed, as if it were something she should apologize for. "I grew up on Dea Vena, not far from Telluria, but much simpler." It was strange to say the name so many years after being taken away. She recounted her childhood in the small town of Vadessa, where her father the orchard keeper grew his livelihood, in a landscape much like the one where a young Natharis played.

"Why did you leave?" Natharis asked. "It sounds like you loved it."

"They never gave me a choice. The priests took me away when I was young—only me, and no one else." She painfully described the broken look on her parents' faces when the acolytes of the Imperial Cult claimed custody of the teenage Livia Delreza, whose surname was to be Nettunaya, for the god they meant for her to serve. It was all because of the color of her eyes and the dark waves of her hair. She was a beautiful girl—so beautiful that only gods were fit to look upon her, and they dismissed any talents she may have had, or interests or desires, because her fate was to please the Pantheon, and this was a great honor. She'd been the smartest in her class, but they cared little for her intellect. They kidnapped the only daughter of Faravia and Guelio, the only sister of the handsome Feliszo, and she never saw them again.

"When this is all over, you could go back," Natharis suggested with a hopefulness she didn't share. "What's the rush in getting back to Telluria, anyway? Take your time and enjoy the ride, even when that damned Aether starts driving you crazy."

It was a touching thought, but Livia couldn't bring herself to put her trust in it. For better or worse, she had a new mother now, and the Matra Altaria had a greater hold over her than her own mother ever had. The Imperial Temple was her home, with its marble walls and ever-watching statues. There were no apple trees there, nor men carrying baskets of fruit out of the orchards. And there was no one like Natharis there. With him, she was starting to feel at home. She didn't need to return to Dea Vena to find that comfort. It was light-years away, but he was right beside her. She fell asleep with his arm around her shoulder, and rested soundly knowing he wasn't going anywhere.

———

Selas turned off the lights in his bedroom and slipped beneath the coarse, woolen covers of his bed. The apprehension that smothered him, however, was heavier than any crudely woven blanket, and left him even more uncomfortable, damp with nervous sweat. It was then that he fully understood that there was no going back. He'd made the decision to remember, to dig up buried memories, and it was a choice he'd have to live with, for better or worse. But the thought of not knowing was more agonizing than his nightmares becoming lucid. He could conquer his fears, if only he knew the root of them. He couldn't fight an enemy he couldn't see, let alone recall.

The boy waited and waited, but nothing came to him. He didn't know what to expect, but he held a number of scenarios in his mind as to how he would come to remember his nocturnal oppressors. Maybe it'd come to him in a vision, or in short flashes of consciousness, or even a hallucination projected onto the room around him. Maybe he'd hear sounds in his head, echoes of the past, or become overwhelmed by the emotions kept hidden against his will. Or maybe Burton was wrong the whole time. Maybe Selas himself had been wrong. The crazy old man could have simply been a lunatic, albeit a convincing one, at least to a vulnerable youth.

He wasn't sure how long he'd been lying there, with his awareness focused solely on the progression of his own thoughts, but he couldn't fight the inevitability of sleep. He drifted off, teetering on the tightrope that stretched over the dark pit of unconsciousness. The world around him faded away into the distance like tunnel vision, though with his eyes closed, he would have described it more as tunnel hearing, if there was such a thing. The low, droning hum of the caravan's engines, a sound he'd learned to tune out over the course of his life, tapered off into silence, as did the static crackling of the television in the adjacent room. He succumbed willingly to the death of consciousness, to the silence in his own mind he'd been longing for, but the peace that sleep brought him was short-lived.

He knew he was asleep, but he could feel the scratchiness of the blanket on his skin and his own weight upon the thin mattress, both of which were sensations too clear for a dream. There was something different about the series of images that flashed before him. They weren't just collections of random thoughts throughout his day; they were an experience in themselves, lingering from the past, though they struck the boy as new and unfamiliar. He knew he'd seen these images before, perhaps just a hint of them. But in that strange, realer-than-real dream, it was as though he was laying eyes upon them for the first time with a full understanding of their meaning.

There it was—a brilliant white light shining in the thin outline of the bedroom doorframe. It enveloped the whole room, until the details of the boy's surroundings became white, and only white. He looked down at his hands, and his body was perfectly in focus, as was the door itself. The door handle began to turn. It clicked as the door slowly swung open, with intent. Shadows stretched across the illuminated floor as long, dark lines cast by spindly arms and legs. Three of them stood in the doorway, all silhouettes, like thin, sickly apparitions manifesting from the realm of the bizarre and unknown.

The sensations came in bursts of awareness, each skipping closer to the present. He felt cold, bony hands gripping his wrists and ankles, pulling him across the floor, though he didn't perceive himself fighting back or struggling to get away. He didn't try to tear his limbs loose from their callous grip, or even open his mouth to shout out. They'd subdued him—how, he had no idea, but he remembered the sharp pain of an electrical shock at the base of his spine, and then he felt nothing. His legs went limp; his will to fight was extinguished. He was helpless before his captors. They took him easily.

The gritty tiles of the floor became a metal table, its hard, sterile surface sending shivers up Selas's spine. He wasn't alone. He counted four of them, all small, shorter than him, but for such frail beings, their presence was terrifyingly powerful. It was their eyes—black, lidless… pervasive. He felt the creatures gazing deep into the very core of his being, like they knew him better than he knew himself—like they'd known him all along, or maybe, like he'd known them. Seeing his own reflection in the darkened, emotionless mirrors around him, he saw himself as a small child, growing through the first stages of puberty up until his present young adulthood, all before the creatures' eyes. They looked at him as would a cruel, heartless parent. They expressed dominion over him. They expressed possession, like otherworldly slave owners with hatchets held over his ankles and wrists.

But there was one more of them—taller, towering over the rest, and it appeared to be guiding the others to do its bidding. They paced around the table preparing tools for their overseer's use, none of which Selas was able to identify, until he saw the knives, like surgical scalpels, cutting away his clothes; they stripped them from his body and tossed them in a shredded pile on the ground. They pinned him down and muffled his weakened, tired screams with their hands. The tallest of them took an instrument from a subservient being's hand, and when Selas laid eyes upon it, he was stricken with a primal, paralyzing fear. He didn't know what the creature planned to do with the needle. He didn't want to know. It was more than twice the length of his arm, shining in the examination lights pointed directly at his face. The needle sank below his field of vision; he couldn't tell what they intended to do next. Tears streamed down his face, and in his head, he begged for mercy, but found none.

He felt the sharp tip of the needle grazing against the small of his back, at the hard ridge of his tailbone. It plunged into his flesh, piercing through tissue and bone, and the excruciating pain spread inside him and through him all the way up the length of his back. The natural curve of his spine straightened into a crippling, rigid line, and his body, now numb with shock, lay like a board before the grotesque, gray sadists. He felt a pressure at the base of his skull, like the needle had worked its way up into his brainstem, or perhaps even deeper. He clenched his fists and curled his toes, for a moment breaking his paralysis, but the beings held him down, leaving his lean muscles flexing in vain, struggling beneath the shocking strength of the skeletal figures.

They procured another menacing needle; it sank into the boy's stomach, and its bearer twisted it, driving it deeper through his abdomen. They stifled his cries with a long, flexible hose forced down his throat, and blinded him with bright, glaring lights. The high-pitched whirring of delicate drills filled his ears. But then he heard something else. The screams from beside him weren't the sounds of equipment or spinning instruments of torture. They were familiar. They were a child's cries for help, for her mother—for her brother.

He could move his eyes just far enough to see his baby sister, Ileya, fighting hopelessly to escape the beings that held her upon another operating table. She screamed for Selas to help her, to protect her from the ones who were hurting her. He cried along with her, and gave up his struggle against the black-eyed monsters, knowing that there was nothing he could do to save his four-year-old sister from her pain. He couldn't even save himself. He surrendered to his captors' will, and endured every endless moment of their violating him and his body, but suffered the worst agony from a child's desperate pleas. As he lay bound to the shape of the pithing needle, he couldn't be the big brother she needed.

Then he woke up. He awoke violently, jumping up from his bed with his heart pounding. The door was closed, his clothes, still on, and not torn to rags. His spine wasn't cracked and reshaped, and he saw no stab wounds on his stomach. The greatest relief of all was not hearing heart-wrenching screams echoing from his sister's bedroom. He wiped the sweat from his brow and crept out of his room to stand in Ileya's doorway. She was sleeping soundly, and Selas thanked the Creator for waking him from his nightmare. It was, after all, another nightmare—but the implications were now much more crippling.

He wouldn't be able to hide anymore, and the cruel beings that tormented him wouldn't be able to make him forget. From that point on, his memories wouldn't be masked in the guise of unpleasant dreams. And it was all his choice. He'd made the decision to remember. He began to worry that he'd only done so because he expected memories to remain memories and not turn to a present reality. Deep down, he viewed it as a glimpse into the past, but he came to a grave realization as he watched Ileya sleep innocently, sheltered from their painful experiences. He'd been given a chance to relive the past, but not as a conclusion to an ending problem. His memories resurfaced to prophesy the future. And he was fated to repeat them.

Prefaced by the flash of violet lightning and shimmering waves of pulsing cerulean, the dark emptiness of space came into view. For just a few seconds, Livia saw two silver ladders, parallel to one another on each side of the cockpit. The scaffolding lined their straight path from the Aether into free space, stretching hundreds of miles outward from a massive, colored shell, like the back of a turtle floating in the frigid vacuum. It shone with bright lights and bursts of radiant color as other spacecraft exited the invisible tachyon vein. They'd escaped through an incision point cut by man's sheer will.

The path of the lens structure led straight toward a hazy, beige sphere in the distance. Natharis, relaying a readout on Ninotchka's holotab, announced it as a Crystalline planet, the Shard of Diamonds. According to his quick and superficial research, it'd been colonized for the purpose of becoming the Crystallines' regional center of culture and trade. They'd planned it as an economic paradise, rich in natural resources and potential for lucrative industry. But to Livia, it looked barren, and she likened the lifeless vista to the one seen by Earth's ancient pioneers stumbling into the orbit of Mars. No matter how devoid of life, the Shard of Diamonds was not the crew's destination. What they were searching for rose from behind the planet's edge, catching the sunlight like a lighthouse beckoning the wayward wanderers to shore.

The Othonas Shrine of Genuine Charity was the pinnacle of an ornate monument built many thousands of years ago. It was suspended and anchored over concentric rectangular frames, laid one inside the other, built of immense, metal blocks fashioned in the appearance of black stone. The step pyramid gleaming over the ancient ruins, sparkling with white lights from windows and docking bays, was the symbolic heart of Othonas; Natharis told Livia it likely enclosed a smaller ziggurat, in which the Coven performed its most sacred rites. She pictured a crystal pool shimmering under celestial lights. She imagined herself as the center of the ritual, one that she'd never seen, and yet seemed so familiar. Natharis hadn't told her much about it, if anything, but her imagination ran wild with thoughts of an exotic faith.

The station's traffic control didn't request any identification, nor did they inquire as to the purpose of their arrival. There was no mandatory upload of travel logs or tracking data. It seemed the Mithneshi had no concern for their visitors' pasts, their identities or intentions. They maintained a haven for the lost and the hunted. Livia marveled at Natharis's assertions that such stations were scattered across the Convergency, and that an unconditional sanctuary always lay just off the beaten path. He offered a number of enticing and mysterious names—the Adhatas Shelter of Divine Mercy, the Ssimvomai Center for the Lost—and told her she'd be seeing refugees from all walks of life. The outposts brought in all sorts of travelers, of whom Livia and the mismatched group certainly weren't the strangest, but Livia suspected they were in more dire circumstances than most who sought refuge at the foot of the ziggurat.

"We'll sort this whole thing out. We've just got to clear our heads first," Natharis suggested. He promised it'd be easy, even with the threat of ABAC finding them looming over their heads. Livia begged her Pantheon to make it true. She needed a sense of clarity.

Two strangers approached the craft after the docking procedures, a man and woman, both Sapien with youthful faces framed by straight, white hair. Their clothes, too, were white, form-fitting and tailored to the lithe shapes of their bodies, as the Mithneshi were mindful of the soundness of both body and spirit. Their suits were sewn from bolts of fine cotton, wrapped tightly around their limbs and torsos like bandages concealing the skin beneath. At their belts dangled a weapon, one for each of them—a metal chain, curled up to hide its length, tipped at each end with a bladed handle. The curved knives crowning the fearsome chains shone like mirrors in the bright lights of the docking bay. They clinked together as the two seers came closer.

"All life makes ripples in the Emanation," preached the man. "But yours are especially strong—stronger than most, and far-reaching. From even light-years away, we felt your presence."

"Such echoes in the Emanation precede only the most virtuous, or the most deceptive," the woman elaborated. "But both may find sanctuary here. The Coven turns no wanderer away."

Ninotchka scoffed and did little to hide her lack of respect. Erixen, too, looked smug before the two members of the Coven, and Livia found it strange, having come to understand that most Colonials were like Natharis, who listened carefully to every word spoken by the Mithneshi. She could tell by the look in his eyes that he'd found something familiar there, something comforting. She saw that he felt the kind of security and reverence she wished she'd felt in the Imperial Temple all those years, but never experienced. She bowed her head to do as he did.

"We're honored to find shelter with true servants of the Creator," Natharis said respectfully. The seers smiled, pleased by his piety, but they seemed more focused on the less faithful travelers, eyeing Ninotchka and especially Erixen. The nonbelieving Colonial looked uncomfortable under the scrutinizing stare of the Mithneshi.

"We'll take you to habitation," the woman replied. "If you intend to stay a while, you may bring your belongings with you." She motioned to the ship and its open entry ramp.

"About that…" Ninotchka interjected. "We prefer to leave them here—with no questions asked."

"We need to contact the Judiciary," Natharis explained. "We've got cargo they're looking for."

The seers responded to Natharis's statement with looks of curiosity and suspicion. Livia felt as though they knew something they otherwise had no way of knowing. Their stares reflected knowledge, a cognizance of events in the remoteness of space. Perhaps they had visions like her own. She, herself, always seemed to know what was coming, or what once came.

The woman spoke with a distant, removed tone. "There are others looking for it as well."

Her partner clarified, speaking in the same voice, like his mind was an onlooker just beyond the boundary of reality and eternity. "You bring grave danger to this Shrine."

"And we'd like to make our stay short and sweet," Ninotchka snapped. "Then you won't have to deal with mess. Send transmission to Colonials, then we leave."

The Mithneshi weren't as compliant as the fiery Muscovite had hoped, and Livia found herself a spectator in a coming verbal dual, if Ninotchka had her way. The man addressed her demands. "The Mithneshi Coven upholds the universal laws. Just as the Creator distances Himself from His creation, we have vowed never to intervene in the affairs of those who seek refuge here. We will tend to your needs and give you rest, but we will not fight your battles, no matter how just your cause."

Ninotchka countered with a series of subtle threats that progressively lost their subtlety, and Natharis, a hundred times more respectful, tried to negotiate divine law. Livia knew the Mithneshi wouldn't change their position. She took some solace in knowing that, for at least a short while, she and her companions would be safe; she'd listened to Natharis saying ABAC wouldn't dare strike a Mithneshi station for fear of Arterran military reprimands. But they couldn't stay there forever, and when they left, they'd still be carrying the prisoner and the threat of capture. For the time being, all she could do was ignore the inevitable. It was something she'd tried most of her life to do, but always with little success.

17

"Believers come to the aid of those willing to aid themselves."
—Eighth Catechism of the Mithneshi Coven

THE STREETLIGHTS IN LUTETIA glowed yellow from below the hotel balcony and shone subtly through the deep burgundy curtains. The windows were wide open, and Desh felt a soft tingling as the breeze caressed his naked body. Even with the sun already set, he still heard the voices of men and women chatting in open-air cafés, and the sound of gentle music floating up from the street below. La Seine was one of his favorite places to vacation, and a few days' repose in its capital city always helped him relax after enduring Congress's exhausting politics. He and Chloé frequented coffee shops and small family restaurants, visited museums and art galleries without the need for bodyguards, and took strolls along the banks of the river that shimmered under the city lights. They drank fine Gallic wine and laughed all the way back to their favorite hotel, *La Bonne Fuite.*

Desh had insisted on leaving the lights on, just as he did every time. He didn't want to cloak his wife in shadow, to mask her soft, bare skin with a blanket of darkness. He wanted to see all of her as she lay naked beneath him, her shapely, supple breasts that he cupped in his hands, and the way her hair cascaded over her shoulders in black rivulets. He wanted to see the look in her eyes as he leaned in to kiss her neck, and her face as he pushed inside her.

But then he heard footsteps just outside the bedroom. He leapt up from the bed and snatched his sidearm from the nightstand; Chloé covered her body with the sheets and knelt down in the corner behind the bed. Desh stood with his gun drawn and pointed straight at the door. He didn't shout any warning at the intruder. He simply waited for him to enter, and then, once he had a clear shot, he'd punish the intrusion without mercy.

The doorknob began to turn. He stood his ground, waiting to face the assassin. And when the culprit revealed himself, he threw his hands up in the air staring into the barrel of Desh's gun, and begged the executive not to shoot. He was wearing a suit, as were the man and woman behind him, with the flag of the United Colonies branded on their shoulders. Desh lowered his sidearm and tossed it onto the bed. Seeing that he'd been standing naked with his weapon drawn, the men looked away out of respect. The one woman, however, didn't seem to have the same concern for propriety. She smiled and winked as he slipped on his clothes.

He demanded to know why they'd entered uninvited and unannounced, but with a tone much calmer than they'd expected, more composed. Chloé dressed as the two strange men averted their eyes, heads turned. They identified themselves as officials at the local Colonial consulate. They understood that he'd turned off his mobile for the night; he'd been hoping to avoid politics, but they found him anyway, as they had little choice.

The primary speaker apologized profusely for their intrusion, and implored the executive to forgive their inappropriate and unorthodox means of making contact, but he assured Desh that their motives were of grave importance.

"Again, I'm sorry, sir, but there's a ship ready for you," he stammered. "We just got a notice from Bhalenjar. They need you right away."

The executive groaned and sat down on the edge of the bed. "The next Congressional session isn't for another week. I'm declining their invitation. I have more important business to attend to right here."

"The Lord of Parliament sent the ship herself, sir. She says it's urgent. There's something she says she wants you to 'hear for yourself.' I'm not sure if she has this authority or not, but she's also threatening to hold you in contempt of Congress if you don't comply."

Desh clenched his fists in disdain. He couldn't imagine why Panzi Illoszia would ever willingly invite him into her presence, given her public hatred of him. He outwitted her in every fight, eviscerated her faulty logic in every debate, and proved to the civilized regions of the Convergency that she and her cohorts were nothing more than thugs and liars. And yet she *still* wanted him present for the impromptu convention?

He agreed to terminate his vacation early, but only after getting permission from Chloé, who was visibly disappointed. Not only had Panzi managed to ruin every aspect of his political, social and economic life, she was also wreaking havoc on his marriage, like some kind of cruel, delusional mistress who offered pain and suffering in place of sex. He kissed his wife after the officials had left and assured her they'd make time for another getaway soon enough. She smiled and said she believed him. He wasn't sure he believed himself.

———

The Coven provided Natharis and Erixen with comfortable living quarters—not grand, but with all the amenities two exhausted men would hope for. Erixen helped himself to a hot shower that filled the room with clouds of steam floating through the bathroom door. Natharis took no notice of the television and chose not to read any number of classical books at his disposal. Instead, he sat at the edge of his cot with his guns disassembled, their parts strewn about him, and wiped each clean with a soft rag. He wasn't looking to relax with such material things. He'd advocated their detour for spiritual reasons, as he was battle-weary, and sought nothing more than to clear his soul of all the senseless violence he'd been dragged into. When he wiped away the residue from the barrel of his sidearm, he imagined that he was polishing away his fears and regrets.

Erixen stood at the mirror with a face full of shaving cream and a razor held to his jaw. He was a muscular man, as was to be expected of an active marshal, with a stocky build that made his neck seem rather short. A tattoo of an unfamiliar planetary flag bulged on his shoulder as he raised his arm to make another pass of the razor over his chin. He splashed it into the running water a few times before he decided to strike up a conversation, speaking carefully, as to not nick himself while shaving.

"Really haven't spoken Rosc in a while," he confessed. "I gotta say, I was worried for a minute during my little negotiation. Thought maybe I'd slip up and get us killed."

Natharis rolled his eyes. *You might as well have. Some friends you've got.*

"Learned it in school, actually. Never used it much after that."

"What school?" Natharis asked, thinking of his own language studies at Ayn Rand University, though he didn't remember seeing many classes on the tongue-twisting intricacies of the Rosc language.

"Out in the backwater parts of the Colonies, on the border. You wouldn't know it, and knowing you, you probably wouldn't want to. Most of the subjects focused on foreign cultures—Rosc, Tellurians, you know—and I'm sure you're used to things closer to home." Erixen put down the razor and wiped away the last of the shaving cream with his hands.

"Actually, I really didn't know much about our own history until the Academy. Or at least their version of it."

Hope you didn't pay much for that education, then. Natharis clicked the final piece of his gun into place and set it carefully upon the table. "So, what's your take on the Tellurians?" he inquired. Erixen must have known more than he did about their culture, and Natharis was growing more curious about them by the day. "Interesting religion, from what I can tell."

"This is about that *girl*, isn't it?" Erixen groaned. He pulled a gray shirt over his head and sprayed a bit of cologne he'd bought at the station bazaar. "Don't bother getting to know her. She's just a prostitute, and we've got plenty of those in the League."

"I'm not sure they have the same take on it."

"And besides, you've got a job to do, and I'm not about to get shot just because you're too distracted to do it right. Just find an escort to fuck on the side and leave it at that. It's not like it's illegal, and we all love the law, don't we?"

There it was again—someone who barely knew him, psychoanalyzing him and drawing attention to his inability to balance work and play. But it wasn't play Natharis was interested in, because he'd had his fair share of that. "She's not an escort—she's an *altaria*, and maybe I don't know what that really translates to, but I can say for sure that they almost treat her like royalty."

"If that were true, then why isn't she ordering us around like one? She's no princess. She does what we tell her to do because that's what she's always done, for every lucky son-of-a-bitch who walks through that temple door."

"It's more than that. She's like a prophet for them."

"A prophet with a cock in her mouth, not the word of God. Face it, Nate: You're setting the bar a little low here."

"Just make yourself useful and help clean those rifles."

Natharis was in no mood to listen to Erixen's insults, especially not with Livia right in the next room. His defensiveness was uncharacteristic, and he was surprised by his own reaction. Erixen had been right to judge him as married to his work, but Natharis sensed that something in him was changing. No matter what Erixen, Sebasteon or Isarion said, in the end, Natharis wouldn't be forced to make a choice. He wasn't dedicating himself to his work in place of a woman; instead, he strove to make his duties *for* her. The mission with which the Judiciary charged him had more gravity than anyone had expected, as ABAC had taken an intense interest in them. Completing that mission might just help the Colonies rid themselves of ABAC once and for all, in some way or another. And defeating the Conglomerate meant liberating the Tellurians, who'd been sold into bondage by their own leaders. They would all be free. Livia, too, would be.

Selas's father and mother left their family quarters early that morning, leaving a note that charged him with the duty of watching Ileya. His older sister went off to shower and ready herself for the day, while Selas, having decided to take the day off, sat at the kitchen table with Ileya and ate what was left of their breakfast. They'd managed to earn enough over the last few days to buy luxury foods they weren't used to eating. The butter was so savory that Selas came to find it nauseating, and he'd eaten one too many pieces of crisp, salty bacon, leaving his stomach heavy and sour.

Despite his aching cramps, he didn't mind the consequences of overeating. For too long he'd survived on bland, less-than-satisfying meals that did just enough to keep him alive. He couldn't even really call it food—it was simply sustenance. It fulfilled his biological requirements, but not his spiritual need for a good, delicious breakfast. Neither the butter nor the bacon was fresh, of course. Both had been kept frozen in storage for weeks, as there were no cows or pigs on the caravan, but the family didn't mind at all, and especially not the children.

Ileya put down an incredible amount of food for a child so small, dominating her older brother in their informal eating contest. She was particularly enticed by the scrambled eggs, which were a fresh, vibrant yellow, and not the grayish white they were all used to gagging over. Selas watched her finish her plate and obliged her when she asked him to fix her another. She eventually slowed down and stopped eating. By the time she decided she was full, Selas suspected she'd consumed more than twice her body weight. She deserved the opportunity to do so.

He wished he could have shared her enthusiasm, but he'd spent the past nights waiting for the inevitable, a horrifying eventuality he only partially understood. He'd avoided seeing the old man who'd helped him remember it all, afraid there might be more he didn't know. He no longer wanted to know. The memories were enough, but he tossed and turned during the night with the threat of capture looming over his head. His sleep hadn't improved; he hadn't found any comfort. It seemed that ignorance had truly been bliss, and he'd let it slip away because of his own morbid curiosity. He supposed it was because he was young. Had he been less brazen, he might have heeded Burton's warning.

It was no short of a blessing from God that Ileya didn't have any recollection of the events that plagued her brother. He knew she didn't remember it and that she couldn't, because he suspected that she, too, had a device wired to her spine, just as he once did. He wasn't willing to do anything to remove it, let alone draw attention to it. She was unaware of the gift of her own ignorance, and he wasn't going to take it from her.

He did feel that he needed to address it somehow, in a way she might not understand, but that would lift the feeling of guilt off his chest. The look in her eyes as she lay on the operating table still haunted him, more painfully than any of the torment the creatures put him through. It killed him inside to know that there was nothing he could do to stop them from hurting her. He would have gladly sacrificed his own safety for hers, his own comfort, his own autonomy, but the creatures were intent on taking them both, and they would do so again and again, with no concern for their victims' pleas for mercy.

"You know we all love you, right?" he asked her. She nodded without saying a word. "And you know *I* love you, don't you?"

She bobbed her head up and down again. Selas smiled and prayed she was really listening to him.

"You know, there's some bad people out there in the world," he explained, trying his best to enlighten her to the possibility of danger, but not enough to scare her. "And I just want you to know that no matter what happens, I'm always gonna be here to protect you. I'll be here, Evua will be here, and so will mom and dad. I promise no one's ever gonna hurt you when your big brother's around."

He knew it was a promise he couldn't keep, but he needed to tell her. If words were the only comfort he could give her, then he'd offer words. Ileya wouldn't wake up to remember that he couldn't stand by them. She didn't even know why he swore his loyalty in the first place. She simply smiled and wandered away from the kitchen, intent on watching some lighthearted children's broadcasts from the Colonies.

He wished he could hide away in that world of innocence again, but he wasn't a child anymore. A real childhood was something a Gameer couldn't afford to enjoy for long, because work was always just a short trip ahead. And any shred of childlike naïveté that remained in him had been stripped away on the operating table, leaving scars he knew would never fully heal, and never fade away.

———

"I say we open the box."

Natharis spoke frankly with Erixen with full knowledge that he would react cautiously. He wasn't one to take unnecessary risks, eager only to join those fights he knew he'd survive. "Yes, let's let a wanted *murderer* free. Free to kill any of us—you know, the *first one* it sees," Erixen groaned. "Keep it there. Let it rot till somebody takes it back to Jotunheim. Or even Albion. I don't give a damn."

"The prisoner will be weak. It's not dangerous. I just want to see if we can get it to talk. Don't you want to know *why* ABAC wants it back so bad, they'd be willing to kill for it?"

"That's *their* business," Erixen snapped. "Not ours—not *mine*."

Erixen announced that he'd be at the nearest lounge, and that Natharis had better not come looking for him. He left their quarters in pursuit of either the chance to mingle with interesting strangers, or alcohol, whichever was easier. Natharis was relieved and seized the opportunity to open the box without opposition.

He brought Ninotchka to the hangar to board the ship and get their hands on it. She finished her vodka in one shot upon his invitation, having been sipping it on ice while forcing Silviano to bathe in front of her at gunpoint. He wasn't afraid of exhibitionism—he was a Tellurian consitor, after all—but must have been terrified to know that Ninotchka was waiting with blades on her heels, ready to crack his skull.

She insisted on opening the box herself, saying she was the first to find it, so the honor was hers. Natharis didn't resist, choosing instead to let her do as she pleased, because he, too, found himself intimidated. Ninotchka placed a codebreaker over the biometric lock; the crate's four seals withdrew, clicking open with the hiss of escaping gases. She pulled the lid away.

"Let's see what they're so afraid of."

They both leaned in to peer into the open crate. Natharis suddenly worried that he'd see a crystal hand reach out to grab their throats, but he lowered his gaze, and no harm came to them. The prisoner wasn't about to attack anyone. It lay at the bottom of the crate as a pile of large, glassy pieces, like dull but translucent stones dumped into a pit. It pulsed with a dying light, just a weak flicker through foggy crystal crisscrossed with fissures and tiny cracks. Natharis pitied the creature. He thought he'd feel disgust, aversion. But he couldn't help but wonder if being a criminal to ABAC made one a hero to Arterra.

"Good luck making it talk," Ninotchka scoffed. "I expected execution."

"Maybe it's not too late. The Mithneshi could stabilize it."

"Mithneshi, *Mithneshi*. You put too much faith in superstitious *khuynya*."

"Trust me."

Ninotchka groaned but humored him, put the lid back on the box and pushed it down the entry ramp and across the docking bay. Natharis walked with the hovering crate in front of him, hoping that no one would notice the nervous look on his face, nor the frustrated, judgmental scowl Ninotchka sported. As they entered the main corridor, as wide as an avenue in Chesapeake, Natharis looked for a small panel on the far wall and tapped his fingers against the touch screen to hail a medical team to their location. A flashing red light on the panel confirmed that help was on the way. He was embarrassed that they'd rush to assist them and find two perfectly healthy Sapien adults. He drafted his explanation in his head while they waited.

Sure enough, the medical team arrived quickly but calmly, carrying themselves with an air of optimism and serenity. They were members of the Coven, a trio of doctor-healers, dressed in standard Mithneshi garb, but with smooth white gloves and red strips of cloth bound around their right shoulder. Without a word, they beckoned Natharis and Ninotchka to follow, and they took the crate from them, hurrying the group toward the closest medical center.

"We take it the patient is non-Sapien?" Whether prophets or good guessers, the healers weren't wrong.

"It's a Crystalline. In a pretty bad state," Natharis answered.

"Their species thrives on radiation. We have such devices, but we confess that the levels of radiation we can produce will not be enough to restore the patient entirely."

"Will it be able to communicate?"

"We expect we can bring it to consciousness, yes. Our digital translators will be sufficient."

The medics concluded that the container that carried the prisoner was highly resistant to radiation, and that it'd been deprived of life-giving energy just long enough to carry it to the brink of death. They attributed their timing to cosmic ripples in the Emanation, merging currents and the manifestation of subconscious will. Ninotchka laughed at the idea. Natharis silently acknowledged it.

They weren't permitted to stand in the radiation therapy room, but watched from windows in an adjacent area, staring at the lifeless pile of rubble that lay reassembled as best as possible. The lenses of the radiation emitters rotated around the table like three spokes of a wheel; the glassy shards began to glow brighter and brighter, and the broken fragments gradually fused together. The technicians deactivated the device and entered the room to observe the results. They looked down upon the Crystalline and smiled.

"It is stabilized." They placed a translator bolt on one wide face of the crystal creature and stepped away when it chirped to confirm a connection, but if the prisoner was speaking, Natharis couldn't understand. The words, short and sporadic, crackled from the translator in bursts of static and meaningless noise, fading in and out until it finally fell silent. Ninotchka scoffed at Natharis and reminded him that she'd told him so. He rolled his eyes and asked the seers what could be done.

"Crystalline medical technology is highly sophisticated. Sapiens have not done the necessary research to adequately treat Crystalline injury and disease."

"That's fine, then. We'll just go down to the planet and do it."

"You will not be welcome there," the Mithneshi warned. "The Crystallines can no longer call the planet their own. A new population has settled and expanded there. You will find a civilization blighted by the greed and gluttony of the Children of the Dole. There is little development left—and there are few hospitals remaining that can provide what you need."

"This rocky scum isn't worth our time," Ninotchka groaned. "It is pointless endeavor."

Natharis grew angry. "If it dies, the Judiciary won't take it lightly. Our mission was to find the prisoner and bring it back to Tartarus. I will *not* have a mark of failure on my record. Even if we have to storm the capital ourselves, we *will* keep that thing alive."

"I do not have same obligation. Tsardom cares little about fate of prisoner. My mission is to keep ABAC from taking it. Nothing more."

"I'm going to the surface, with or without you. I'm sure Silviano would be willing to join me. We'll take a ship and get this whole thing over with."

The seers shook their heads. There was fear in their eyes. "They will open fire and take down your craft. Air traffic is no longer permitted on the Shard of Diamonds."

"Then we'll find another way."

"What, you want to jump to planet?" Ninotchka sneered.

"That's exactly what we're going to do. I'll get the suits ready. You go find Erixen." He laughed like even he thought the plan was crazy. "Just don't tell him the odds."

———

It was a cloudy afternoon in Dearborn, certainly not the kind that would inspire any average person to dine al fresco, but Artimpasa had insisted on it anyway. They closed up the red umbrella on their café table. It'd served no purpose, with no sunlight to shield them from, though it looked like it might rain, and Pentakiya worried they'd be forced to open it up again. The noise from the street didn't do much to create a romantic atmosphere, either. Their lunch date was a far cry from sitting in a quiet Lutetian coffee shop, sipping espressos and snacking on buttery, chocolate croissants.

It didn't bother Pentakiya. She enjoyed her new opportunity to see her wife every day. Her months in the depths of space toiling over the Conglomerate's secret projects kept her away from Artimpasa for too long, and it was about time that she lived a normal life. She only wished a "normal life" didn't have to involve such consistent invasions of privacy. But they were, after all, for the greater good, but for the good of whom, Pentakiya was no longer sure.

"I guess I'll just have to consider this an early retirement," Artimpasa sighed, lamenting her lack of work. "Not that I had any choice in the matter. Same goes for you, beautiful. We're just two brilliant female minds, wasted and thrown away by cowardly men."

Pentakiya wasn't sure how to respond. She wasn't particularly happy that Artimpasa brought up such a sore subject. Pentakiya wasn't in the mood to talk about the limbo her professional life had become. Artimpasa noticed the look on her face and kept chatting, but her talkative mood only revealed an inner nervousness. She laughed to herself. "What am I going to do with myself? It's not like I have any *books* to read."

It was enough to make Pentakiya smile, even if the humor was expressed a little too soon for comfort. Artimpasa's reaction to finding her personal library stolen from her was burned into Pentakiya's memory, probably forever. She still thought about how painful it'd been to watch her wife cry, mourning the loss of her life's work, and weeping for what she was referring to as the death of knowledge. She felt Artimpasa's anguish as her own, even if she couldn't fully understand what it was her wife had been crying over. Pentakiya hadn't ever read the books Artimpasa had collected over the years, written by old colleagues and like-minded intellectuals. She'd even gone so far as to judge them as trash, fiction published as history. She wouldn't get the opportunity to see if she'd been right or wrong.

"So," Artimpasa said, redirecting the flow of conversation. "I've got a lecture planned for Thursday night. I'd really like it if you'd come." She threw Pentakiya off guard; as Pentakiya had understood it, Artimpasa wouldn't be lecturing anymore.

"You've never asked me to come before." She smiled, flattered that Artimpasa had opened up an opportunity she'd made a point to keep closed. "Of course I'll go. Where's it going to be?"

"Well, it took a whole night's worth of scouring the city and a dozen cups of coffee for me to find the place. No academic establishment is willing to let people like me speak out anymore, so it looks like I'm going to be speaking at the Enlightened Church of the Nazarene on the other side of town."

"I didn't even know there was one. Nobody's religious in Dearborn."

"I'm not expecting much of a crowd."

Pentakiya pictured herself sitting in an empty church pew, with little old ladies, probably racists of Romaean ancestry with gray shawls that covered their hair, chattering behind her as her wife lectured. The church couldn't have been very big, and neither could its congregation; Dearborn wasn't a city with a pious reputation. Pentakiya had learned from a young age that anything God could do, the government could do better. She knew it was more logical to trust in an entity that she could see, touch and hear, instead of an invisible Supreme Being she couldn't understand. Religious law was subject to interpretation. Civil law wasn't up for debate, as it well shouldn't.

"I'm going to call it *The Silent Genocide: Shatarin Immigration and the Subtle Warfare of Demographics*." She held her hands out wide, like the title was displayed in bright, sparkling lights on a theater marquee. "What do you think? Catchy? Edgy? A little bit of both?"

"I think the title alone might get you arrested."

Artimpasa giggled at the thought, laughing off an issue about which Pentakiya was growing progressively concerned. "No one ever got anywhere in academics by tiptoeing around peoples' feelings. The truth isn't something people want to hear anymore, but that doesn't mean I don't have a God-given right to preach it."

"ATEDO says otherwise, you know. What you're doing is treason."

"They can call me a traitor to my country, but I will *never* be called a traitor to reason." She touched Pentakiya's hand from across the table. "You more than anyone should know that my loyalties are to you, and to freedom." She pushed a hastily folded newspaper across the table. "And this—this isn't freedom."

"Public Book Burnings a Popular Success," read the headline of *The Harlequin Post.* But it was the second article that left her concerned. The bold title declared, *"Prominent Professor Detained for Vile, Bigoted Sedition."* Pentakiya pushed it aside and looked away. "Why would you risk this? Is it really worth it?"

"If I end up a martyr for the truth, so be it. You know I've got a thing for literary endings, especially my own."

"I don't know what I'd do if I lost you."

Artimpasa leaned across the table and put her hand on Pentakiya's. "It's just one last speech," she insisted with a smile. "Then we can go back and try to build a quieter, safer life—trust me. And besides, I doubt anyone's even going to show up." She kissed Pentakiya on the cheek. "Nothing to worry about."

Nothing she could have said would have rid Pentakiya of the uneasiness she felt deep in the pit of her stomach. She knew Artimpasa was right, that her presentation was so low-key that she wasn't likely to draw a large crowd, and therefore, much public attention. She supposed she owed it to her wife to allow her one last goodbye to her field, after having seen all that she'd gone through to have her voice heard. Part of her, though, wished she'd turned down the invitation to come watch her speak. It wasn't out of shame, jealousy, or any other petty emotion. It was out of fear—fear for her own safety. If speaking out was treason, then being a willing listener made one an accessory to treason. She'd been punished enough, shrugged off by her cherished leader, Executive Dunham. She didn't want to offend him even further. As of late, she was already a sinner in the hands of an angry god.

The view of the Shard of Diamonds from the airlock chamber was one that evoked a feeling of emptiness. Its surface appeared barren, with miles of desert steppe stretching to the horizon, and an endless mountain range rose out from the planet like a mighty spine. Hidden in the shadows of those mountains was a glassy dome, a solid bubble that caught the sun. It was the Crystalline city since fallen to the endless whims and desires of the Children of the Dole. It was where Natharis intended to fall, in a leap of faith through darkness and clouds.

When Natharis said he was making an orbital jump, Livia thought he was joking. She couldn't imagine a more dangerous way to get to the surface, so unsafe that the very idea was worthy only of a good laugh. He said that with a good spacesuit, there'd be nothing to worry about. Ninotchka was equally nonchalant, and groaned impatiently as Erixen hesitated to go along, insisting that they simply get it over with.

"So far, we've been outnumbered a hundred to one, *shot* at—on the ground, *and* in orbit—and almost incinerated more times than I can count, and now you want us to *jump* through the atmosphere and *definitely* be incinerated?" Erixen rambled in a panic.

Natharis tried to calm his fears. "We've dealt with ABAC plenty of times, and I don't think we've got much to worry about. Their troops are more of a danger to themselves than to us."

Ninotchka couldn't have agreed more. "They didn't send army to this planet. We fight Children of Dole down there. Fat and unarmed. Easy targets with no one to help them."

The thought of an unfair fight seemed enough to sway Erixen. He especially liked the idea that they would be too small of a target for the surface-to-air batteries, and that they wouldn't be hitting any defense barriers other than the bloated stomachs of the gluttonous Children of the Dole. Knowing that the planet had no real communications with other worlds, and that there'd be no witnesses and no one to stop him from killing any target of his choosing, was what ultimately changed his mind. The eager look in his eye made it seem like it was the chance he'd been waiting for all along. They just hoped he wouldn't do anything stupid.

They stood in the emergency repair exit, a chamber with the feel of a garage or docking bay but lined with tall, wide windows that offered a bird's-eye view of the planet below. Warning signs posted on every side of the room advised that all personnel wear protective gear to combat the frigid vacuum of space and the deadly radiation that rippled through it. They acquired only three spacesuits, two male, one female, meant for the two Colonials and the ever-fierce Muscovite.

The three stripped down and slipped into the form-fitting suits, shielding their fragile bodies from the endless hazards just outside the station's hull. The body suits were fashioned from lightweight, synthetic materials, black, leathery and almost plastic-like, with thick, grayish plates covering the chest and stomach. On their backs protruded oval-shaped backpacks, which they stocked with ammunition and sleek reconnaissance equipment courtesy of the Tsardom. They certainly looked prepared for an orbital jump. Livia worried that their preparedness was simply a tragic illusion.

Ninotchka picked up on Livia's silent concerns, grabbed Natharis's shoulder and sensually ran her finger down his bicep. "Don't worry, *malyshka*," she sneered, putting a hand on the edge of Natharis's chest. "Mr. Ruke will be safe with *real* woman around." She smirked upon seeing Livia's resentful scowl, and insisted that she and her male counterpart leave the airlock chamber. She offered a snide farewell, pointing toward the door.

Livia looked to Natharis and caught eyes with him. She wanted to approach him, to embrace him or kiss him on the cheek. She didn't want to let him go without showing some kind of acknowledgment. As far as she was concerned, it could easily be the last time she ever saw him, and though she'd only just started to know the enigmatic Colonial, she didn't want to give him up so quickly. She felt she might be falling for him, as fast as he'd soon be falling from the sky.

"Don't worry," Natharis insisted. He touched Livia's shoulder and smiled reassuringly. "I'll be fine. And not because of her." Ninotchka stood behind him, rolling her eyes.

"We'll be waiting," replied Livia. "I'll be."

She believed him when he said everything would be alright, enough for her to leave the chamber without a fight. But something festered in the back of her mind, an instinctual, primal fear, grown from a tiny seed of doubt.

Within her, voices whispered of deception, of betrayal. Through her inner eyes she saw two eagles locked in a fearsome battle, slashing each other with razor-sharp talons far up in the sky above. She watched in horror and awe, frozen with the knowledge that there was nothing she could do to end the struggle. One bird of prey would fall to earth, defeated. The other would soar away into the setting sun. She prayed she'd see icy blue eyes sparkling in the sunlight, and not find them dull and lifeless upon the cold, hard ground.

18

WITH THE SLEEK HELMET SECURED over his head, Natharis couldn't hear anything but the sound of blood pumping in his ears. The airlock had closed and sealed behind him, and with stage one of the jettison procedure complete, red alert lights flashed along the walls of the chamber. He, Erixen and Ninotchka climbed into a curved, metal sled that rested upon thin tracks on the floor, pulling themselves in with hands clenched firmly on overhead handlebars. Ninotchka initiated stage two; sensors relayed the depletion of the chamber's atmosphere, ejected out into space like cloudy geysers, and the air around them became a vacuum. Natharis began the countdown, speaking through the com-link in his helmet as Ninotchka reached for the final switch.

"Here goes nothing," he said. "Hit it."

"Thought you'd never ask."

Vibrations shook through Natharis's body as the sled rocketed forward on the tracks and down the open exit tube. And as the end of the tunnel rushed closer and closer from up ahead, Natharis whispered an old Mithneshi prayer to himself. He didn't care if Erixen or Ninotchka heard him. He saw the light ahead of him, and right at its threshold, the sled stopped; their momentum jettisoned the three jumpers out into the emptiness of space. They streaked toward the planet like arrows shot from a mighty bow, plummeting to earth in formation. There was no air resistance, no rush of wind past their faces. Their fall was silent, their speed, unfathomable.

It wasn't until his heat shield deployed that Natharis felt the rough whip of the atmosphere. An orange glow rippled across the front of his body, a hazy aura blazing just inches from his skin; he still felt the heat, but his body wasn't set ablaze. They fell farther into the upper atmosphere, through the vague boundary between a jaundiced sky and the silent, black void. Ninotchka bathed in the fiery light of her shield alongside Natharis, laughing through the com-link, and Natharis admitted it was a spectacular rush. He looked upward toward Erixen's position in their triangular formation—he was nowhere in sight. Ninotchka ordered him to relay his position, barking through the com-link in harshly hissed Muscovian military jargon. He didn't answer.

His suit could have been pierced, choking the life from him in the endless vacuum, turning his skin to ice. His heat shield could have failed, with the burning air engulfing him in flames, turning him to a living, breathing meteor in the sky. He could have deployed his chute too soon, by accident or through thoughtless error, locked high up at the edge of space with his oxygen supply steadily depleting. There were a hundred ways for him to die, and each was equally horrific.

Ninotchka announced it was hopeless, that he was lost for good. She admitted she was glad to be rid of him—death was of little consequence to her, as it was a natural part of life that arrived early for those caught in her crosshairs. But Natharis fell silent; he took a moment to let the thought set in that Erixen might have perished for the sake of duty, something he'd so far been unwilling to risk. He felt a tinge of guilt for it. He'd asked an unprepared man to jump to his death. He was responsible.

"Shit!"

Natharis was blown out of formation by a rogue plasma bolt shot from high above him. A piercing siren blared in his ear, indicating damage to his heat shield, and he forced himself to breathe calmly in the face of panic. He heard another gunshot, then many; Ninotchka opened fire into the sky with a fearsome war cry. Her bullets grazed past a vague shape falling above them, coming to overtake them. It was Erixen, with his heavy rifle drawn, aiming straight for Natharis.

A radiant shower of charged bullets streaked through the sky like divine thunderbolts. Natharis and Ninotchka lit up the clouds with their gunfire, answering each of Erixen's shots with two. They were locked in combat falling to earth, caught in a fierce war of the heavens, themselves angels vanquishing the most deceitful of devils. But evil had the upper hand with the blinding sun to his back. They struggled to lock him in their crosshairs while keeping in formation to their landing site.

"Get on top of me!" Ninotchka ordered, a sexual tone to her command. She streamlined her body to slip beneath him and pressed herself closely against his chest. He grinned, knowing what she was planning. Erixen cackled through the com-link and focused his fire on Natharis, the only visible target. Ninotchka nudged Natharis with her elbow to get his attention.

"Brake to your right!"

They separated from their aerial leg lock and shot off in opposite directions. Erixen spun in a circle to keep his bullets spraying at both of them, but they were out of range. With the deafening blast of air jets Ninotchka shot upward, activating the thrusters hidden in her breastplate. She glided toward Erixen in a graceful backflip, rushing through the air straight at him. Two plumes of exhaust spiraled from her chest as she accelerated, faster and faster, and just as she was about to overcome Erixen, he struck her with a projectile from the top of his gun. He nicked her in her stilettos, finally proving to be too dangerous for wear, and sent her spinning off hundreds of yards away.

Natharis had no chance with Ninotchka thrown out of the way; his heat shield was depleted to dangerously low levels, and he attempted to keep his fire locked on Erixen, but he was fighting a losing battle. The alerts ringing in his ears were becoming painful, both to his eardrums and his morale, and as he fell with Erixen's glowing gunshots streaking past him, he knew he might not make it. One pummeled him directly in the chest, knocking the wind out of him. It'd only take one more shot to finish him, to irreparably destroy his only means of protection from the burning of the resistant wind against his body. He held his gun upward toward Erixen and closed his eyes, no longer looking at his target, but simply hoping that the Creator might guide his hand. Erixen's figure above grew larger, fell closer, as did the barrel of his gun, pointed directly at Natharis's head.

"So, you like to play rough, *sobaka?*"

A feminine silhouette descended upon Erixen, the sun shining behind her. He turned to face his attacker; she simply mocked him through the com-link in a fit of laughter, and cursed at him in Muscovian before finally overcoming him. "Let's see how you like *this!*"

Her stiletto slammed straight into Erixen's hand, drawing a desperate, weaselly scream from his shaking lips, and his firearm slipped from his fingers and flew off into the distance. He made an attempt to grab at her arms and pin her in a vulnerable position, but he only made her guffaw even louder. They fell closer to earth with Erixen struggling to break free from Ninotchka's powerful grip, but she had no intention of letting him go. She swung her legs over his shoulders and clenched his head between them like a vice. She curled her body over him and looked straight into his eyes.

"From Muscovia with love, Colonial."

She snapped his neck without another word. His body went limp; his screams cut to silence. And with the crackling of static through the com-link, Erixen's body dropped from Ninotchka's grip, free-falling without kicking or protest. Ninotchka deployed her chute, and Natharis did the same. While they floated gracefully downward, their fight over, their breath, slower, Erixen plummeted beneath them, until his lifeless corpse hit the ground below, twisted and broken upon the rocky surface of the unforgiving Shard of Diamonds.

Natharis said nothing, and for once, neither did Ninotchka. They settled down in silence, Natharis's wordlessness out of reverence, Ninotchka's out of fatigue. Their chutes billowed and slipped across the ground when they touched their feet upon it, and Natharis's fell over Erixen's contorted body like a shroud. It covered his face from the harsh sunlight and hid him from view, lending a sense of dignity to a man fallen, but who deserved little respect or memory. Natharis had witnessed betrayal. And Ninotchka had punished it without mercy or regret.

———

The audit notice was waiting on Tageron's office desk when he walked in. He almost didn't notice it, as his secretary had failed to mention its delivery, and placed it inconspicuously atop a pile of holodocs yet to be filed away. It wasn't until the furniture began to cast long shadows in the golden light of sunset that he saw it, illuminated by a hazy beam through the tall windows of his office. It was like a heavenly sign, drawing his attention to the mysterious envelope left unannounced for him to discover. And the second he saw the sender's name and agency address, he knew he'd soon be plunging into a frustrating struggle with the planetary government.

He reluctantly opened the envelope and unfolded the letter it carried. The ornate, glowing seal of Hatal-Om's Planetary Revenue Service stood boldly, even arrogantly, at the top of the page. The sight of it was enough to drive him to pour himself a glass of whiskey, and he took one large sip of the lukewarm drink before beginning to read.

It started out cordially enough, following a set format for all outgoing correspondences, and it greeted him with a line meant to sound amicable and unintimidating. It quickly declared his audit with little introduction, much more to the point than he'd expected. The collectivist-dominated government agencies rarely made such unpalatable facts clear and obvious, opting to bury the truth within pages and pages of useless filler. But the declaration didn't surprise him. He read on, morbidly curious to know the reasoning behind it, if there was any reasoning at all.

According to the notice, his accounts with the Arterran-based Liberty Bank made him subject to more intense scrutiny. *"Citizens entrusting their capital to foreign banking institutions are often in violation of the tax law, whether knowingly or unknowingly,"* it read. But he'd never considered his bank to be foreign—neither had anyone else. He'd filed his taxes the same every year since opening those accounts and never run into problems before. Now, he was under the government's magnifying lens; he thanked God he'd emptied his closets of skeletons long ago. He didn't have any extra wealth hidden away, immune to the collectivists' insatiable lust for crushing taxes. It was a mess he thought would be simple to sort out, however inconvenient. They'd left a number toward the end of the letter. He just had to give them a call.

Tageron reached for the phone and begrudgingly dialed the number. He leaned back in his seat and sighed as it rang aloud, the volume unintentionally high. It rang thirty-five times before a digital voice announced he'd have to be put on hold for lack of available phone representatives; he waited on hold for ten minutes or so, though it could have been longer. Tageron leapt up when he heard the voice of a living person.

"Planetary Revenue Service. What do you need." It was a statement, not a question, and certainly not a very welcoming one.

"I'd like to discuss an audit notice I just received—"

"One moment."

The light, mediocre lounge music began to play, and Tageron knew he'd been put on hold again. He scribbled on the letter with a pen while he waited.

"Tax Audit Department. What's your problem." Again, another statement, but by a different speaker with a rough, smoky voice, and an attitude just as irritated as her lungs.

"I received an audit notice in the mail today. I'd like to—"

"What's your name."

"Tageron Dagonari."

"Convergent Identification Number."

"092-46-135N."

He heard the sound of lethargic typing. The representative pulled up his tax files and cynically asked Tageron to explain his probably pointless problem.

"The letter stated that my accounts with Liberty Bank are under suspicion. Apparently, you're now claiming it's a foreign bank, even though I've been banking with them for over a decade now, and I've never had an issue before. I can only assume that there's been some kind of mistake."

"We don't make mistakes, Mr. Dagonari."

"Then offer me another explanation."

"Please hold."

The elevator music played again, and Tageron pounded his fist on his desk in frustration. Another representative came on the line, this time with a friendlier sounding voice, like that of a nice, new and optimistic employee. He could tell by her tone that she was a recent hire—they always sounded the same, speaking with the fresh enthusiasm they'd soon lose over the coming months. He wasn't sure why he'd worked his way through transfer after transfer and ended up talking with a rookie. Perhaps it was for the best.

"Thank you for waiting. What seems to be the problem, Mr. Dagonari?"

"As I told your associate, I received an audit notice today, which cited my accounts with Liberty Bank as the cause."

"Oh no," she said with a nervous giggle. "That's not the red flag listed on your file."

"So, it is a mistake, then."

"Unfortunately no, sir. It looks like you're suspected of disturbing the peace. It mentions hateful, anti-collectivist propaganda, specifically." She paused for a second, as though she'd just come to some sobering realization. "You know, I really shouldn't be telling you this."

"Do I not have a right to know why I'm being singled out?"

"Well…"

"And for the record," Tageron snapped, "I've never spread any anti-collectivist propaganda to the public, as you claim. I'm by no means 'disturbing the peace.'"

"We have a list of instances in which you *criticized, insulted or incited unjustified hatred against*' the collectivist ideology in private correspondences, sir."

"If you've been screening my calls or emails, then they're no longer 'private.'"

"For example, sir, just three days ago, you referred to the Commune as 'an irrational inconvenience that the Arterrans will eventually remove from the playing field.'"

"Did you even have a warrant?"

"Warrants are no longer necessary, sir."

"This is illegal," Tageron hissed through his teeth, trying to remain calm. "You have no right to invade my privacy like this. I've done nothing wrong. The only lawbreaker here is your director."

"The informants listed insist otherwise."

"Tell me who they are. I have a right to know the names of my accusers—and a right to confront them."

"Sir, I would be in breach of protocol."

Tageron's thoughts rushed through his mind as he struggled to identify his accusers. He'd been in business for a long time, and he'd liked to think he hadn't made very many enemies. But lately he'd been drawn into the kinds of conflict he tried his best to avoid, and he could have easily had thousands of indoctrinated union lobbyists plotting his demise at that very moment. He began to speculate out loud and barked names at the representative.

"Is a Bemul Narax on your list?"

"No, sir, and even if he was—"

"Quba Vaski?"

"No, I don't—"

Tageron paused. Another name came to mind, and of all the people he'd conjured up in his head as lying, deceitful rats, he was the worst. He lowered his voice and spoke it calmly.

"Is it Alit Pashe?"

The representative stopped for a moment—Tageron had hit a nerve by mentioning his sniveling ex-lawyer—but then replied, "Mr. Dagonari, you know I can't divulge this kind of information to you, and certainly not over the phone. It is our duty to protect the identities of the victims here."

"*I'm* the one being harassed by government thugs, here, and let's not forget it. I have victimized *no one*."

"New laws passed by Congress—"

"You mean Brock Dunham."

"Executive Dunham is a good man, Mr. Dagonari, and let's not forget *that*. If he says your sort of behavior is dangerous to society and more importantly to *him*, then we have no choice but to suspect you of criminal activity, because he is a wise and perfect judge."

"Your executive is not my god, and I do not bend at his command. My fate doesn't rest in his hands."

"No, Mr. Dagonari. It really does."

"Audit me. I have nothing to hide." He hung up the phone. He gulped his whiskey.

Tageron knew he'd have to be more careful. The phones had to go. How he'd replace them, he wasn't sure, but so long as he was talking through those same lines, Big Brother would be listening, watching. Waiting.

He had no idea what the bureaucracy's deity wanted, but he knew that at any moment, the collectivists might show up at his door and demand their tribute. They'd already stomped out his ability to expand the company. They'd buried him in taxes and stripped him of his ability to lead and manage his own employees. He dreaded what they might demand next of him. If his tax records came up clean and he kept himself out of prison, they'd need something else. Alit had been right—the law no longer protected people like him. The laws of man had been replaced by higher laws, those dictated verbatim from the mouth of God's messenger. Brock Dunham hated his kind; this false god was not merciful. And his wrath always superseded what little mercy he possessed.

———

The windswept planet glared boldly through the window as if to mock Livia, playing with her thoughts and worries. She gazed upon the arc of the horizon and thought of Natharis, who was too far away to see, but whose image was burned permanently in her mind. She saw flashes of lightning, followed not by thunder, but gunfire. The eagles would turn on each other, their talons buried in each other's flesh, raining blood and feathers upon the earth below. She willed the visions to disappear. She looked away from the window.

Her fears clung to her like dirt, a spiritual filth that dampened the light of her soul. She needed to cleanse herself of it. A long shower and a short prayer would ease her troubled mind and purify her unclean spirit. She stripped off her clothes as she crossed the room, tossed them softly upon the bed, and stepped into the shower. The glass door closed behind her with a gentle hiss. She turned on the water; the steam began to rise.

The hot water cascaded over her body and washed her secret worries away. She closed her eyes and lost herself beneath it. She felt it trickle off her dark hair, leaving the skin of her breasts glistening in the gentle light. The man she saw in her mind was no longer wounded, and his blood had been swept away by the waters. She imagined his naked body bathed in a sacred pool, rippling just barely over the muscles of his chest, and saw him smile. Her skin flushed from the thought, even more than from the scalding water running down her back. She grazed her fingers down her stomach and slipped them delicately between her legs. She gasped lightly, pressed her shoulder to the wall and whispered Natharis's name. She'd never felt such compulsion before—such desire. Such hunger.

She almost didn't question the touch of a hand upon her waist. It seemed so natural, so fitting to the theme of her fantasy. But the voice didn't belong to Natharis. Livia jumped, and abruptly turned to confront the intruder who'd stolen her vision from her. She glared; Silviano laughed playfully, though Livia didn't find it amusing.

He touched her face and apologized, then pushed her aside to step beneath the falling water. She frowned and reached for the door, saying, "I wanted to be alone. You should go."

"What, am I distracting you?" he scoffed. "Go back to thinking about the Colonial. I won't interrupt, I promise." He smirked. The sound of the last trickle of water caught his attention; Livia shut off the shower without a warning. He shivered in the cool air.

She left him there and wrapped a white towel around her body, tucking one end into a fold to keep it snug. It still didn't deter Silviano, who stood in the shower door with beads of moisture dripping over his hard muscles. He couldn't bear to give her the silence she'd asked for, nor the privacy.

"Don't be embarrassed. You're not the only one who stays in the shower just a little too long. But while you're there moaning his name, I'm thinking of you—and what we could do together with no one to stop us." He looked deep into her eyes. "I hope he satisfies you. You know I could do so much better."

"It's more than that. It's not just his body that'd satisfy me. It's a shame you can't see me for anything else."

"We're not children anymore, so it's time to stop thinking like one. The Imperium never gave us that luxury. With a past like ours, you should know that sex and love are one and the same. All emotions have their root in the most primal desires. Those butterflies in your stomach aren't proof of love—it's the warmth between your legs."

The towel that covered Livia's body didn't help to hide her nakedness. She pulled another from the rack and handed it to Silviano. He looked disappointed, then draped it over his shoulder. She bet he thought he was clever, finding a way to keep himself boasted. She couldn't help but glance down, having fought the temptation for the length of their conversation until she could no longer. Even soft, he looked as thick as her wrist, but the more she looked, the more he seemed to enjoy it, until his manhood slumped over to one side, swelling up just a little with a noticeable twitch.

"So, which makes him more worthy: his thoughts, or that hungry look in his eye?" Silviano asked. He finally pulled the towel around his waist and shut the glass door behind him. "You know the answer, even if you can't bring yourself to say it."

"It's not even his thoughts. It's something deeper. Something spiritual."

"There's a spiritual connection every time we satisfy a believer under the statue of the god, and they love us for it. They always come back for more. They can call it prayer, or faith, and say that they came to make their offering, but that's not the reason. One day, the gods are going to strike us down out of jealousy."

"They didn't come there for us. They came for the experience, and that's what you don't understand. They don't get to pick who to lie with; they get who they get, and that's it. Maybe they really are happy while you're pushing yourself inside them, and maybe they *are* becoming one with the god, but any consitor could do that for them—not just you. They don't love you, Silviano. Like me, you're just a means to an end." Her ability to satisfy the pilgrims, to make them climax and think they experienced god, did nothing to strengthen her self-worth. It didn't empower her, and it wasn't a skill she'd asked to learn. "It feels good for everyone—the pilgrims, and us—but I always wanted something more. And I feel that now. I think Natharis does, too."

She felt a tingling on her skin as Silviano moved closer. The electric sense of his body just inches away from hers sent shivers up her spine, not out of fear, but a guilty anticipation she only halfheartedly tried to fight. He put his mouth to her ear and exhaled deeply; his hot breath brushed teasingly over her skin.

"Tell me you've never felt that connection with me," he whispered. He pressed his body against hers and grazed his lips against her neck. She sighed when he ran his hand down her arm and the curve of her body. The sink behind her kept her buckling knees from giving in. She gripped its edge firmly to keep from falling to Silviano's feet in sensual submission. She closed her eyes, listening to the words he groaned roughly under his breath.

"If I meant nothing to you," he murmured with a fiery look in his eye, "you wouldn't be so wet."

He slid his hand up her thigh, under the towel; the trail his fingers followed tingled and tensed. She gasped when she felt his fingers kneading between her legs, slick with her wetness, each stroke against her bringing her closer to crying out in pleasure. She gave in to his desires, but for only a moment.

She came to her senses and grabbed his wrist, pushing his arm away.

"You need to go." She tried to catch her breath. Silviano could tell she was feigning her discomfort, her nervousness—it'd felt good, and they both knew it. The waters of regret threatened to swallow Livia; the only regret Silviano held was allowing her to reject him. He stepped away and gave her space, all with an angry glare that revealed she might have actually hurt him. He wasn't just frustrated, thinking she was playing hard to get. He reacted too personally to the rejection. Perhaps it was because he'd never been rejected before.

"You're making a mistake, falling for a foreigner," he warned. His heavy breathing was no longer out of sexual hunger, but out of indignation, anger—crushing disappointment. Knowing he wasn't about to leave her, Livia took the first step toward the door. He wasn't finished. "The more you tell yourself he might one day love you, the more devastated you'll be when he throws you away. Anyone would. Anyone but a Tellurian, and I'm all you've got.

"I know where you come from, and I know how you think. Like it or not, I'm the only man who can relate to you, or understand what you've gone through. Your past isn't something most people can swallow. It'll push any foreign man away, and Ruke won't be any different. You're lying to yourself if you really think he'll look beyond it, or even be able to. He'll call you a whore, just like everyone else. And he'll be right."

The Colonial marshal and the ruthless ZGB operative crossed the dusty steppe with their helmets still on, defending themselves against an atmosphere not fit for Sapien lungs. Far behind them lay the body of Erixen Dade, denied a proper burial much to Natharis's discomfort. They'd left the twisted corpse beneath its shroud without a word or eulogy. Their silence was irreverent, not a moment for reflection and respect, but for curses muttered too low to hear. Natharis tried to put his regrets behind him. It would have been impossible to take him alive and hold him hostage, bound in handcuffs. Their freefall hadn't allowed it. Still, Natharis wished it had.

The dome ahead emerged from behind a craggy ridge, and the silhouette of the jagged rocks lined the base of the shining, translucent structure. Its architecture had no hint of Crystalline influence, and its purpose was just as alien. The Children of the Dole who dwelt beneath the life-giving canopy found great comfort in it, breathing air transformed specifically for them. The mammoth terraforming devices, like towering buffalo migrating across a barren field, proved the inhabitants didn't want to live in confinement for long. The whole of the planet would be their home one day, and the Crystallines would be pushed farther beneath the ground.

The traipse was draining, the gravity stronger than Natharis was used to. He relished the opportunity to stop to catch his breath for a moment when they reached the top of a daunting cliff. It overlooked a deep gash in the earth, one of many, a shadowy spider web that crisscrossed toward the city. It became clear that they'd built the structure like a roof over the largest canyon, allowing the unwelcome residents to infest the ancient riverbed below. But hundreds of feet down, at the base of the cliff upon which Natharis stood, he saw no Children of the Dole. There were only Crystallines, abandoned at the edge of their once proud city.

They lived pitiful lives in cramped, tired quarters, their cliffside niches dug clumsily in hurried desperation. Those that had slipped into the shallow compartments had little sunlight to bathe in; *They thrive on radiation*, thought Natharis, though it looked like they had none. Sparks flew and machines whirred in the dark, evidence of industrial work carried out by Crystallines. Ninotchka speculated that they were bound to the collectivists' demands, forced into indentured servitude and the production of consumer goods. She had no proof, but the idea wasn't far-fetched. It was a standard narrative in the development of a collectivist dystopia. Had the Crystallines been working for themselves, Natharis would have certainly seen bustling mines, radiation harvesting, or even artistically curious sculptures. Instead, he only saw hulking trucks carrying off the fruits of their labor, headed straight toward the parasitic hive.

He was sure the slaves below would notice them scaling the cliffside, but he heard no protest or alarm while he kicked off the rough wall. They rappelled downward until they stood among the Crystallines, many of whom ignored them, but some seemed to take notice. Ninotchka produced a translator bolt from her belt—"Gift, from your favorite Coven," she said—and held it out toward a Crystalline, who stood before them, unable to communicate. With no way of knowing if the creature approved, Ninotchka carefully approached it and gently pressed the device against a flat plane of its glasslike body. A series of beeps and chirps confirmed a connection. They waited for it to function properly.

"Don't expect Tolstoy," Ninotchka joked.

The device projected a digital voice, deep, almost croaking. *"You should leave."* The Crystalline shifted its mutable shape to appear more humanoid. *"You are not Communals. They will kill you on sight."*

"They don't know we're here," Natharis explained.

"They will. There is nowhere to hide."

"We need access to your medical facilities. We've got one of your own up there on the station, and it's in bad shape. It doesn't have a chance if we don't get in there."

"We have no medicine; our hospitals have been shut down by the Communals. Many of us are dying. We cannot help you."

"Minor setback," Ninotchka declared. "We operate medical equipment ourselves."

"No one will notice us if we're in an abandoned hospital."

"Sapiens cannot operate our technology. You have little understanding of Crystallines. You will harm the patient without knowing it."

"If we can't use it, then we'll take one of you with us. Just one can't draw too much attention. The Children of the Dole are usually distracted by pointless bullshit, anyway."

"Crystallines cannot enter the city. We must stay at the border. We have no other option."

"Don't underestimate me," Ninotchka growled. "This isn't my first act of espionage."

"We can smuggle one of you in," Natharis reiterated. "It'll be simple. Get in undetected, break into a defunct facility and get our hands on some equipment. Once we've got it, we'll bring the prisoner—the *patient*—down from the station."

"If a Crystalline is caught trespassing, the punishment is death."

"We won't get caught, then."

"We are forced to work as slaves outside the city boundary. The false royalty inside have ensured our servitude through the capture of our leadership. If even our strongest are not safe, then you most surely are not."

"Would you agree to it if we brought your leaders back? If that's the price, we'll pay it. We're no strangers to prison breaks."

"We do not know where they are imprisoned."

"If there's one thing I'm good at, it's extracting information," Ninotchka boasted. "Especially from dumb, lazy targets. Give me minute, and they'll be screaming their secrets."

"We'll track them down and get them out. Then you'll hold up your end of the deal."

"We will agree to your terms. We will show you how to enter the city, and follow you for your own sake. If you are identified, you will not escape."

Natharis wasn't afraid of whatever threats lay beyond the city wall, having learned full well that Communals, and even ABAC's own tactical forces, were pathetically incompetent. But he was never happy about walking into a blind fight. He liked to be prepared, to know what he was up against, and to not have to rely on his own suspicions. For all he knew, the innately entitled could be wielding weapons paid for by the hardworking Crystallines' unfortunate tithes. They could have gotten up off their couches and readied themselves for a violent defense of their undeserved lifestyle. They wouldn't give up their handouts so easily. They were, after all, an inalienable right. And they'd fight to the death to preserve them.

19

*"Aetherium drives our economy; it powers our ships.
Aetherspace connects our worlds. It is all one Aetherverse."*
—Misha Matsumoto, for Vega 1 News.

"LET ME MAKE THIS CLEAR: The corporatist collectivists are committed to action, and move to *change* the present when others simply *criticize* it and offer no solutions. We exercise our will when it is necessary, and I have called this emergency Congressional session to demonstrate it."

Panzi Illoszia expected an enthusiastic response from her faction. They applauded her, but shouts of disapproval and disdain covered up the sound. Panzi's face turned from a prideful smile to one of seething indignation, with each *"Boo!"* cried from the floor of Congress driving the knife deeper into her bleeding heart. Desh found it more than amusing. The individualists guffawed and accused the Lord of Parliament of simply wanting to boast about her myriad failures. The session was pointless, they insisted. Desh was inclined to agree. According to Panzi, that made them all uneducated, ignorant racists.

"Enough," Brock Dunham commanded. "I will *not* stand for this kind of vilification. The Lord of Parliament, like the Children of the Dole, is a *victim*—a victim I intend to empower. While the League of Arterra would have her silenced and starving in the streets, I, as her protector and loyal guardian, will raise her up above them."

Panzi praised his mercy, humbling herself before her false prophet with the support of her fellow cultists. When Dunham had first appeared on the political scene, he was arrogant, but not as egomaniacal as he one day became. He seemed to thrive on the obedience of others he thought below him, almost drunk on the zealous attention and unwavering support of his every decree. It was a self-absorption any Colonial would have condemned. For Dunham, the "greater good" was just a reflection of his own will.

God's vicar drew attention to the bound stacks of holopaper set before each member of Congress. Most wouldn't bother to read it, choosing instead to take Dunham's word on blind faith. He began: "You have in front of you an Executive order I have officially signed into action. The contents of the order are as follows: *(1)* The Executive Council decrees that the Commune and its peoples shall receive twenty-five percent of the Interstellar Convergency's aetherium weapons reserves."

A thunderous roar of disapprobation rose up from the floor of Congress, rumbling in the individualist storm that furiously reviled Dunham's unlawful actions. He grinned and ignored his opposition, relying on his followers to pester the individualists into silence. "*(2)* The arms exchange shall be implemented immediately, and the cost of preparation and delivery shall be financed by raising the Convergent sales tax by no less than two percent; *(3)* Any act of aggression or sabotage intended to interrupt, delay or cease the exchange shall be punishable by severe economic sanctions, and, if necessary, military intervention."

Desh calculated the result of the exchange, and swiftly interjected, "Twenty-five percent of the Convergency's arsenal is three thousand aetherium warheads. This kind of high-security arms exchange can only be approved by a majority vote in the Executive Council. Your Executive order is illegal and a sickening subversion of democracy."

"Your backward principles will get you nowhere when you're already outnumbered in this Council," Dunham sneered. "The collectivists have the majority. A vote would have been just an obsolete formality."

"The democratic process is not 'obsolete.' It's the timeless foundation of a free society."

"Most on the Council don't subscribe to your childish ideals, Executive Maru," Dunham asserted. He noted that the collectivists had finally won the Vehisipens' support, citing the Shatarin Empire as the praiseworthy cause of their coming to their senses. "After the Vehisipens were paid a 'diplomatic visit' by the noble Shatarins, their once ignorant people felt compelled to support Shatarin rights and the collectivists who so selflessly fight for them." He praised the Shatarins for their tolerance of those who submitted to them and converted to their medieval faith.

Panzi screeched, "Yes, Executive Maru, the collectivists are *proud* to defend the Shatarins' right to subject others to their every demand. To not do so would be to reject an innocent culture that *must* remain immune to criticism. But while we support the Shatarin Empire, we also must protect *ourselves*— from ignorant *bigots* like yourselves. The Commune *needs* an aetherium arsenal to defend itself against Arterran aggression."

Sir Byron couldn't stand to listen to Panzi's blatant lies. Desh was equally infuriated, as he was sure the collectivists believed her every word. Sir Byron spoke for the both of them, cutting off the Lord of Parliament's incoherent rambling. "The League of Arterra has never given any indication of plans to pursue a military option. We'll deal with the collectivist problem soon enough, but we would never declare war until all other options have been exhausted."

Desh argued, "In the entire history of this Convergency, we've never seen a single eparchy drop an aetherium bomb for anything other than scientific research. The United Colonies of Acadia have no plans to change history in that manner. And if we've proven anything so far, it's that the Colonies, and the entire League, are more than willing to choke the life out of your pathetic economy with an endless number of trade sanctions. Watching the Commune plunge into bankruptcy is satisfying enough. Senseless killing isn't necessary or deserved."

Panzi wasn't about to be refuted so easily, though all her arguments were easily refuted. "It's only a matter of time before hateful Arterran rhetoric is put into action. The Commune *needs* to be prepared for it, but it can't ready itself without help. Executive Dunham was *generous* enough to provide for the poor and their wellbeing. Their defense is, without a doubt, the *greater good*. The fact of the matter is that the League of Arterra simply can't swallow the idea of having a level playing field in the Convergency."

Executive Molotova, her fair skin now burning red, slammed her fist on the table and stood up, glaring directly into Panzi's watering eyes. "I will intercept any weapons shipment *myself*," she threatened. Panzi gasped at the thought, and Oksana fed off her fear and beat her further into the ground. "And I promise you that Executive Maru will *not* try to stop me." She turned to Desh and smiled; he nodded, tacitly agreeing to her terms.

"I must say, Executive Molotova, that in my entire history of knowing you, I've never heard you be so upfront about your *racism*!" Panzi hissed. "Only Muscovian *bigots* would fight to strip the innocent poor of their right to defend themselves against capitalist war dogs."

Mireille Leveque entered the debate, asking, "Your personal army just wasn't enough for you, was it, Panzi?" A wave of hushed laughter spread among the individualists on the floor of Congress. "You're a fool if you think you can boost your reputation by force."

"No matter how many warheads you get your thieving hands on, you'll never change the laughable fact that your own planets will destroy themselves before anyone else does." Desh mocked the Lord of Parliament until he thought he saw steam rise from her ears. "Collectivist policies are more dangerous than any aetherium weapon." Panzi looked as though she was about to cry, as she'd probably expended the last of her weak arguments and was backed into a corner. She begged Brock Dunham to intercede.

He spoke over Panzi, who shrieked and cried about Arterran injustice; she stopped once she finally heard his voice. He folded his hands. "Executives of the League of Arterra, your days are coming to an undeniable end. The more you try to deny that you are fading out of history, the harder the blow will be when you're forced to accept it. Your people are not prepared for the truth—you've shielded them from it for far too long. You tell them the collectivists are evil and deluded, that the Shatarins are genocidal murderers, and that the Commune isn't sustainable. These are all lies, Executives—lies you've concocted systematically.

"Executive Molotova, I *dare* you to try to stop the shipments. If the Tsardom makes even a single pass at the convoys, I will make sure that Petrograd suffers dearly. ABAC's entire army will rain warheads upon your cities, and the Tellurian Armada will reduce your navy to smoldering wrecks.

"And you, Sir Byron—*you* are a despot who hates to see the underdog succeed. Your sniveling people have been raised from birth to value accountability over the natural lack of it for certain special groups. They deny that the Shatarins, the Xaztechuans and the other Children of the Dole have an innate entitlement to their tolerance and the fruits of their labor. They're brainwashed into believing that the less fortunate don't deserve our help. And worst of all, they don't believe that those who reject the greater good must be stopped by any means necessary.

"And then there's the detestably smug Executive Leveque, who has an obscene fetish for deporting innocent Shatarin immigrants from the Republic of Gallia. Every time you send a helpless Shatarin back out into the dark, it is a violation of her innate, biological right to settle on your planets with or without your permission and outbreed the native population for her own gain. It is offensive and intolerant for you to suggest that her presence is a demographic threat or a threat to public safety. If there is ever a suicide bombing in Lutetia, you must admit that it is because of some fault of your own, and that your society most certainly deserved it. The only victims here are those of your own foolish provocations, not your dead citizens.

"Finally, Executive Maru," Brock Dunham concluded with a sly look in his eye. "The United Colonies would do well to watch their back. You can go on telling yourselves that you're the dominant power in this Convergency, and that you always will be. Your irrationality is baffling when you say you'll never have a worthy rival. But a new power is rising, Executive. It is a potent force, like none you've ever seen. It is more than a civilization—it is an idea, a belief, that spreads like wildfire through those open to the truth and consumes those who reject it in their ignorance. The sun is setting on the Colonies and the League, Executive. And it is rising over the coming hegemon that refuses to stand beneath the individualist flag."

———

The sun was setting behind the shadowy Dearborn skyline. It painted a ruddy sky, leaving a bloody halo encircling the formidable ABAC Headquarters. The dust and smog that loomed in a choking cloud over the city led to stunning sunsets that always caught Pentakiya's eye, even when the screeches rose from the busy streets to distract her. It was one of the very few connections to nature that remained on

Albion, other than the potted plants in Pentakiya's apartment and the simian roar of Albians demanding their monthly handouts. But the sunset itself was silent, the twilight, peaceful and nonintrusive. It didn't keep her up at night partying at others' expense. It didn't raise treasonous questions in her mind.

The cacophony rose in a deafening crescendo as Pentakiya encroached on the ever-crowded Holder Boulevard. Named after a historic judge who always defended the rights of the oppressed, it was, as usual, sectioned off from auto traffic in favor of a brutal pedestrian gridlock, for one of a seemingly limitless number of events targeting the most loyal of collectivist supporters. That day, it was the Biannual Wel-Fair. The fair marked two days a year when overcrowding could very possibly lead to suffocation or being trampled beneath a voracious, stampeding throng. The attendees were notorious for rushing at the vendors' stalls with no concern for the safety or lives of their fellow misers. Pentakiya valued her existence too much to traverse the unruly horde. She stayed off the main roads and kept to herself on the side streets.

Dusk fell and the streetlights flickered on, sluggishly at first, like the bulbs were well past their prime or the power just wasn't strong enough to fuel them. Their yellowish glow seeped along the pavement only a few feet into the alleyway, but Pentakiya chose to take her shortcut, regardless of how poorly lit it might have been. She made sure to take smaller steps, as to avoid stumbling on a stray beer bottle or being stabbed in the foot by a well-loved hypodermic needle. She enjoyed how quiet it was in the narrow street, the sound effectively blocked by the tall cement walls flanking her on either side. Nobody would bother her there, and no noises would blare out her thoughts. She'd walk peacefully to the next block, make a quick right, and her apartment would be just a few doors down. It'd be a pleasant stroll, one long overdue for a woman with a troubled mind and a wife in danger.

Pentakiya's footsteps grew louder, strangely loud, and she blamed the narrow corridor and its concrete walls, thinking it was just an echo. But when she heard the clatter of an empty tin can being knocked across the pavement, she knew it couldn't have been her. She turned her head to glance behind her for just a second; the shadowy figure in the distance had the heavy footsteps she'd heard. It wasn't uncommon to see the homeless wandering the streets with outstretched hands, but Pentakiya picked up her pace, the outlet of the alley not far ahead. She could make it without ever having to drop a dime in a deranged man's hat. But then she was stopped dead in her tracks.

"Most people know better than to walk alone after dark," a second man said, emerging from behind a dumpster. He stopped Pentakiya with his hand against her chest. She saw the badge hanging from his neck catch what little light penetrated the alleyway. He brandished a city police badge, but his uniform wasn't standard at all. He was dressed in a dark suit covered by a long, black coat, and she could discern little about him. Without identifying himself or the other man, he continued: "You should have stayed with the crowd."

"I was just cutting through. I don't live far."

The man checked his mobile, scrolling down the screen with his middle finger. He nodded his head to his partner, who'd caught up, standing ominously behind Pentakiya's back. "That's right," the man before her said, as if she needed him to confirm her own address. "Curicon residence: 102-07 Leftway Avenue, Apartment 8B." He paused and checked his records again. "Looks like your wife's waiting for you. She called and said so, didn't she?"

"That's none of your business," Pentakiya snapped. She was surprised at her own defiance. Too shocked and offended to keep quiet, she demanded to know how they'd found out about the time and subject of her private calls. She accused the men of screening them without her knowledge, as it was the only explanation she could think of.

"Your wife's been a very bad girl," the man snickered with a sly smile. "You're lucky we even let her talk at all. A lot of people have been rightfully silenced lately. Sooner or later, someone will find a way to shut her up, too."

"Bet a man-hating traitor like her wouldn't be so talkative with our cocks in her mouth," the man behind her sneered. She whipped her head around and glared, reproaching his vile perversions with her eyes. She was horrified at the thought.

"Or maybe a gang of Shatarin men could show her what she's missing," his partner growled. "That bitch will forget all about you when she begs for more, just like the pig-whore she really is."

The other man grabbed Pentakiya's arm and forced her to face him. "If you don't stop her, we will," he threatened. "You'll regret your treasonous inaction when you come home to your wife getting fucked by a hundred Shatarins." He laughed with no concern for Pentakiya's disgust. "And I guarantee you they won't be gentle with her. They never are."

"Go tell your wife we've got our eyes on her. And if you're *really* loyal to Executive Dunham, you'll find a way to stop her. Then maybe—just maybe—we won't gag her into silence ourselves, no matter how hard the thought gets me."

And then, without another word, they let her go. She didn't question it or give in to her mistrust. She ran and didn't look back, though she could feel their perverted glares searing her back. She succumbed to her natural temptation to glance behind her once she escaped the confines of the alley. The two agents were nowhere to be found, like they'd never even been there. Certainly no one would have believed her had she cried for help. And if they had, they would have condemned her, not them.

Pentakiya stopped to catch her breath, put her hands on her knees and tried to compose herself. Her heart was racing at an unstoppable rate; the lump in her throat was suffocating, choking the breath out of her. Hot tears welled up in her eyes but didn't fall. She was too angry, too afraid, to allow herself to cry. She had to be strong. Artimpasa would need that strength, or so she told herself. Artimpasa had always been the brave one—dangerously brave. But it seemed that her courage to speak out might finally prove to be too dangerous. The consequences were something Pentakiya didn't have the stomach to consider.

———

The heart of Tarem was inundated with hordes of emerald-eyed Caspians. They strolled leisurely, with no appointments to attend or job to be worked, and made it hard for Tageron to walk at a reasonable pace. He wished he didn't have to pass through the central square, but his former employee Magas had a favorite Tellurian restaurant nearby, where he'd be meeting him for lunch. He raved about the pork-wrapped figs and vintage wines, claiming it was well worth the struggle through the crushing crowds.

With a metro blocked by beggars and streets too dangerous to drive on, Tageron had no choice but to go on foot. He'd stopped giving out spare change years ago, and when he looked upon the faces of people who demanded he surrender more than what he had on him, he remembered why he'd lost his sympathy. His wallet fit snugly in his front pocket, but he kept his hand on it just to be safe. Crime ran rampant in the city of Tarem those days. There was a time when people had no reason to resort to theft, but that was long ago, and the collectivists made sure everyone forgot about it.

Tageron first came to realize that Tarem truly was in shambles when he heard pathetic stories of "space dragons" circulating among the people of Hatal-Om, spreading to even the other, less delusional Caspian worlds. Even on that day, he saw graffiti depicting all sorts of mythical beasts, invented by the plebs as a distraction from the nonsense spilling out of the Convergent Congress onto Tarem's doorstep.

Sometimes on the news, pundits blamed the disappearance of cargo ships on these gargantuan monsters, but Tageron was in the business of shipping, and he himself had never heard of such a thing. Some media figures took his side: Claudia Aiola of Sol Radiofónica bluntly stated that she'd never seen an interstellar leviathan, and that the only space dragon she'd ever want to see was the one in Executive Desh Maru's trousers. He watched that interview briefly on the street, but kept on walking, shaking his head at her humor, which both amused and irritated him.

People taped signs with misspelled headlines onto the security camera poles at every street corner; they advertised closet-sized apartments for obscenely high prices, and beseeched the crowds to return a lost bag of syringes and spoons while offering no reward. But one caught Tageron's eye, not because it had a flashy title or a boldly printed image, but because it'd been torn down and hatefully trampled beneath the foot of a collectivist with dog shit on his shoe. Somebody had written *"traitors"* in red ink across the crumpled paper instead of simply throwing it in the trash, because it was the job of garbage men to dispose of trash, and not the pedestrians who scattered and trod through it every day. Tageron didn't want to pick the sign up without rubber gloves, so he stood over it with his head low, trying to read the runny ink.

IYRKARIM, it declared in loud letters, A SAFE HAVEN FOR THE WORKING MAN.

Safe haven, Tageron thought. *That's exactly what someone like me needs.* But he kept on walking and dismissed the vague message that had obviously offended quite a few people.

But he saw it again, this time, painted onto the side of a building like graffiti. IYRKARIM, the artist-vandal sprayed across the crumbling brick, BUILD YOUR HOME AND KEEP IT. Whoever designed the image chose to skillfully depict a planet, semi-terraformed but habitable, with a line of men, women and children in middle-class clothes marching toward it with Arterran flags waving proudly. Most of the banners had been defaced by passers-by who held a deep-rooted contempt for all things individualist, and at least one had taken a hammer to the wall and broke away the cement where a second descriptive line was once written. Tageron wished he knew what it'd said before the collectivists censored it by force. He supposed he'd never know, but he imagined it as a promise for a better life, one where theft wasn't lauded as noble, and where laziness wasn't promoted as an entitlement.

"Safe haven," he muttered under his breath. "There is no such thing."

———

There was a time when Selas liked the silence, but that was a long time ago, before it became a reminder of bedtime, of the inevitability of sleep and the nightmares that ensued. He could only hear the sound of his own breath echoing in his helmet, like a warm, humid wind through a glass cave. Space was a lonely void that begged for a voice to resound through it, but with nothing through which to travel, there would be no sound. All that carried thought across space and time was the Emanation, as the Mithneshi would say. Their words brought him comfort, as did their generosity. Before the dark days he found himself waking to, Selenia Santiago had brought him both.

He drifted with his hands grazing the metal framework hundreds of yards from the main hub of the Ssimvomai Center for the Lost. The caravan slept in the distance while smaller craft came and left in tiny flocks. The Mithneshi Coven tended to their needs, gave them food and water and more updated technology, when available. In exchange, the Gameer assumed the responsibilities of the station's maintenance and repair; the men often found themselves floating in the vacuum of space, while women and children worked more domestic tasks within the shelter of the station. His mother and sisters were working inside; Selas and his father shared the men's responsibilities. He examined the scaffolding for any damage caused by orbital debris, and when he found a small breach (there were many), he marked it with a simple beacon. It was tedious but easy work. The only problem was the feeling of isolation that haunted him every time without fail, something he'd be forced to endure for hours.

He believed the Mithneshi were capable of great things, either by their own power or the Creator's, and he prayed that he'd be safe from his captors with the Coven present. He had to believe that sanctuary with the Mithneshi made one immune to the will of a cruel and unfeeling race. They had Selas bent to their every whim without ever telling him why. He wished he could hear them speak, just once, to explain the reasons behind his suffering. If he were to hate them, he should at least have some understanding of them. He was sure Burton could give him further insight, but he hadn't mustered up the strength to go seek him out. He didn't want to admit that he regretted his decision. He knew he wouldn't be able to hide it.

The best he could do was hope and pray that his wishes would ripple through the Emanation up to the Creator, and that He would have mercy on him. In some ways, Selas felt as though God had forsaken him. He knew he should fear no evil, but he did. He saw Hell in his hopelessness; he'd chosen to enter it by digging up dead memories. He'd descended deeper and deeper through the circles of ignorance until he reached the truth. He became bound to that truth, forever frozen in it. There was no escape—not from his frigid prison, nor from those who threw him down from heaven into its depths.

———

Livia's tears had dried by the time she reached the station bazaar. She'd spent too much time wanting to be alone. She told herself that the chatter of the marketplace would cover the echoes of guilt that resonated in her head, but even in the jumbled speech of the small crowd, she heard Silviano's words. The farther she walked, the more she hoped she could put them behind her. She couldn't walk fast enough.

Shops lined the street, selling all kinds of commodities, ranging from preserved foods to beautiful jewelry crafted from rare and captivating gems. Some booths displayed luxurious silk clothes in the traditional Mei Zhi style, while others sold personal electronics and other high-tech toys. She noticed a convenience store with its front door congested with pedestrian traffic. People entered in a hurry and left with digital magazines and bottled drinks in hand. Some bought cigarettes. Others left with water pipes and Colonial sativa.

She pulled a serial off the rack and handed the vendor a few lira in exchange. She'd never seen a holozine, though she'd heard of them; Tellurians preferred traditional newsprint, as they cherished all things classical. It was thin, only a few pages thick, but it wasn't fashioned out of paper, but a sheer, shiny plastic that felt strange between her fingertips. The text was printed in Millennial Anglic—it must have been published in the Colonies.

Livia tapped a photo on the front page. She smiled when the still image suddenly became animate, brought to life at her command. Within its frame she saw a whirlwind of lights flashing in brilliant neon colors—pinks, blues and greens, all glowing like rainbow lanterns visible even beneath the hot rays of the equatorial sun. A superimposed label identified the planet as Vizcayami, somewhere in the League of Arterra, and the colorful lights were shining along the central boulevard of the planet's infamously ostentatious capital, Coral Grove. The premier sun-soaked neighborhood boasted Art Deco skyscrapers and luxury apartments along bustling seaside avenues. It was a display of affluence that Livia never had in her childhood. She wondered if all Arterrans lived that way.

The newest Wessex Falcon 920 convertible raced down the magnetic motorway past high-end boutiques. Electronica with a hint of Old Earth salsa blared as the sunlight gleamed off the diamond-white paint. The auto recklessly swerved into a parking space; the reserved hologram flickered off when sensors recognized the vehicle's registration. The driver side door retracted downward; an open-laced shoe, supported by an eight-inch stiletto heel, slid out from the car and clicked gracefully onto the amber-lined pavement.

The driver emerged smoothly, with impeccably coiffed and blow-dried hair dyed a blinding shade of platinum blond. Her perfectly feminine silhouette exited the convertible, meticulously constructed by Zionese surgeons and dressed in the newest and finest haute couture from Mediolanum. She slipped on her feline sunglasses and pulled her designer handbag from the auto's leather interior. Her name was Valeria Estrada, and she was the leader of the classless pack in the weekly serial, *The Schnazzy Wives of Vizcayami*.

It was that exact gossip column that Livia held in her hands, bedazzled with holographic photos that supplemented the less-than-tasteful written content. The video came to a close, but it was just one of several clips demonstrating the "busy" and "difficult" lives of wealthy, bored housewives, all considered opulent by Colonial standards. While she was mildly disgusted by the housewives' behavior, she couldn't take her eyes off the page. Two Caspian girls giggled at her from the side; a cute, golden-haired boy shot her a glance that seemed to call out her ignorance of pop culture. They'd clearly noticed Livia's fixation on a cultural phenomenon she'd never seen before, though it was all-too familiar to those around her. All three held a copy of the serial in their hands but made sure not to be too obvious about it. The weekly publication was something of a guilty pleasure for the contently reserved population of the League, a shameful but widely popular source of entertainment that never failed to deliver its promised drama, no matter how scripted.

The girls paused at the paragraphs and holophotos printed in the fashion sections; the boy had his eyes firmly locked on the animated depictions of the housewives' risqué beachwear and their low-class behavior at high-class discotheques. Livia couldn't help but compare herself to the images she saw before her, to these unnaturally beautiful women, and lamented the simplicity of her life next to the lives of the rich and famous. Her romance was hopeless. If this was the kind of woman a Colonial man aspired to be with, she had no chance with Natharis.

She sighed in emotional defeat, but then an auspicious quote caught her eye, attributed to Valeria Estrada herself: "My husband—and all men, for that matter—aren't hopelessly attracted to me because of my flawlessly sculpted body, sexy style or exorbitant wealth," the text read. "They chase after me because of my confidence and the attitude of self-reliance that no man could possibly resist or disrespect. It might take a long time for a woman to overcome her insecurity these days, but it's worth it—it's the most important thing. Without it, she'll be a doormat for men, a piece of trash just to be used and thrown aside. She might desperately chase men who show no interest in her, or disrespect herself by giving herself up to any man who walks by. She's got to have confidence. Without it, she has nothing."

———

A breeze tussled Livia's hair as she passed out of the far end of the bazaar. She thought it was odd; the caress of the wind was unknown on a station like Othonas. It reminded her of her childhood home, and the warmth of the summer breeze rustling the silvery leaves of the olive trees. It carried the scent of jasmine in the warm months, apples in the fall, wafting from the orchards in the distance, through which she'd run and pick the lowest fruit in her youth. Livia was unable to ignore the feeling, nor the memory. She wandered off her path to follow the wind and find its source. She wanted to know what had caused her memories to resurface, memories she'd been trying for years to forget, because to remember them was to open an old, stubborn wound.

Elaborate inscriptions in an alphabet she couldn't read stretched down the length of the corridor she'd come to; she couldn't understand it, let alone read it aloud, but she felt it conveyed a solemn, sacred message. She cautiously walked down the length of the corridor toward the light at its end. She felt as though she was traveling down a passageway into the deepest parts of her mind, reaching further into her memories with the truth at the tunnel's end. Her breath turned shallow, quick and apprehensive. She stepped into the light, and what it had hidden stopped her in her tracks, awestruck.

The central ziggurat, like the great stone heart of the station, stood regally in the open courtyard. It loomed over Livia as an ancient holy of holies, inspiring fantastic thoughts of the Coven's most sacred rites in the sanctuary of the temple. She didn't know the exact nature of their ceremonies or even the tenets of their faith, but the religion intrigued her. The ziggurat beckoned her to come closer, to investigate and discover its secrets, esoteric and elusive.

Its darkened entryway had no doors, no great seal of wood or stone to keep wanderers from entering the inner sanctum. Artificial lights, glowing like fire, lit the path from small niches cut into the wall, each with curtains of green ivy hanging over its lip. The living drapery dangled along the wall and brushed the stone floor beneath; it slithered down the tunnel along the base of the wall. Livia ran her hand over the smooth, waxy leaves and relished the sight of plant life, which was something she'd almost forgotten, having spent an unpleasant amount of time in the most inhospitable wastelands she could imagine. Even the presence of a single ivy plant made Othonas more beautiful than Earth's remains could have ever hoped to be.

What the ziggurat concealed was even more numinous. The stone floor turned to grass, soft and lush, with a reddish tinge that Livia had never seen before. Tall, slender trees—five, she counted—lined the border of a clearing in the grass, where the ground once again became stone. In that auspicious place stood an altar, and a single lantern with a white candle flickered upon the polished granite. It was a tranquil sanctuary, lit by starlight from a circular opening at the peak of the domed ceiling. Livia breathed in the cool air, fresher than she'd expected. She felt the breeze that had guided her to the temple.

She heard the blurred echoes of projectiles in the distance. Looking through the veil of sacred trees, she saw a woman surrounded by a dangerous cluster of combat drones. They encircled her, hovering at eye level like a spinning wheel, threatening to pummel her body with their glowing, lethal bolts. Livia knew she couldn't help her. All she could do was watch.

The woman tore out a weapon from beneath her white, form-fitting body suit. She gripped its two handles and pulled them apart, revealing a thick, metal chain that stretched between them. The hooked blades at the end of each handle caught the silvery starlight, shimmering as the woman swung the chain over her head and whipped the drones onto the ground. She disabled each device without sustaining so much as a scratch. She tucked her weapon back into her belt and noticed Livia. She smiled, and motioned for her to come closer.

"Come, pray with me, sister," the woman invited. She must have taken Livia for a Deist.

"I really don't know how, at least how you would," Livia admitted.

"You don't have to speak. Just listen to my words and meditate on them." She knelt down and put her hands on her knees, cupping them with her palms upward, as if to receive an unseen gift. Livia followed her lead and did the same. She closed her eyes and let her thoughts drift away. The woman's gentle but confident voice was all she heard.

"Infinite Creator, Prime Mover of Heaven and Earth, we take refuge in Your eternal peace. Through the great sea of

Your Emanation, may the ripples of Your mercy and the waves of Your wisdom wash away our iniquities, our weaknesses and our fears, so that we may come to know You with all our heart, all our mind, and all our spirit."

They opened their eyes; the woman saw that Livia looked confused, knowing little about the nature of the Mithneshi Creator. "You came here because you were curious. Was this your first prayer?" the woman asked. She insisted that if there was anything Livia wanted to know, all she had to do was ask.

"No, but I've never heard one like it. All I've ever known is the Pantheon—the classical Tellurian gods."

"Then you already know the supernatural."

"Not your concept of it. I'm not even sure I know mine."

The woman asked for Livia's view on beings greater than herself. Livia replied that she found her own gods petty and uncaring, and that, if the priestesses were right, they only cared about sex and sacrifice. She asked if the Mithneshi believed in a self-serving, anthropomorphic god. The woman smiled and told her that the Creator was nothing like the flawed deities of the Pantheon.

Livia was intrigued. She'd started to doubt if her own gods even existed, as she'd never felt their presence in her candlelit chapel before, let alone in other walks of life. She confessed to the woman that she found it difficult to believe in anything at all. "The god is never pleased. And I've been forced to pretend he is."

"Every faith is a river, but they do not all lead to God's great ocean, the endless waters of His Emanation. Everyone drinks from a different stream. But if your stream turns stagnant with disbelief, dries up from doubt or runs black with the worms of hate or violence, then you need to stop drinking from it. Don't try to make it flow again, because it never will. Find another stream. It's as simple as that."

"Your God wouldn't want me."

"He turns away no one. And if you're afraid to turn to Him simply because you feel unclean, don't be. He redeems anyone who asks for His redemption—redemption from sin, and redemption from your own fears. When you realize your connection to Him, you will know no fear."

She looked at Livia as though she could see into her soul, beholding Livia's past, present and future. "You already have a strong connection to the Emanation. You must have faith in yourself. When you acknowledge and embrace that connection, you will find yourself seeing visions, healing others with your words, and you will channel God's strength. Without faith, however, you will have none of these. You need only an open heart to become the bridge between Heaven and Earth."

"I've seen visions, but I haven't told anyone. I can't help but feel like I'm going crazy. Or maybe I'm just a fool."

"The only fool is she who hears God's Word in her heart and dismisses it as madness."

"Even if these visions are real, and I'm as connected to this Emanation as you say, I still can't get others to look beyond my past. They won't view me as anything other than a temple prostitute. I can't escape that identity, no matter how hard I try to leave it behind."

"Are you concerned that *no one* will respect you, or is there a single man in mind?"

She hesitated, then confessed, "One man."

"The soul cannot grow if it's busy looking outward. You can't let yourself fall into the trap of thinking that your self-worth is derived only from the respect of others. Until you embrace yourself, you'll never find the true strength or wisdom to love another."

"But I see all these beautiful women," Livia sighed. She envied Ninotchka's stunning beauty, her sexual confidence and fearlessness, but could only come to admit it in her jealousy. She even thought of Valeria Estrada, who she assumed was considered elegant by Colonial standards. She looked like neither of those women, and she felt as though she'd fade into the background in their presence. "I just wish

I'd been born different. In a different society. Into a different life. This isn't something I asked for or wanted."

"It's never too late to change it. You control the course of your life, and no one else. Even the Creator Himself allows things to run their course. Free will is a gift He has given each of us, and it's one that cannot be taken from you. Remember the prayer we said together, sister. Find strength in powers greater than you, and let yourself be a vessel for divine wisdom. These are the tools you need to shape your life, and nothing more. Faith is the most powerful force this universe has ever known, and it takes only a single thought to shape reality. Go back to your life outside this sanctuary and carry that knowledge with you. With it, the universe will bend to your slightest will."

The seer's words resonated deep in Livia's soul, and she felt as though her eyes had been opened for the first time. Maybe she was stronger than she'd given herself credit for. She might not have been an experienced pilot or gunfighter, but she had a different kind of strength, rooted in devotion and faith, not bloodlust. She could redeem herself—the Mithneshi Creator, if real, could redeem her. And if that God could uplift her and cleanse her of her past, then perhaps Natharis, in his belief in that God, could look beyond it, too. Silviano had been speaking only selfish lies for his equally selfish gods. The Coven and its followers preached and practiced forgiveness; they didn't judge the lives of others. It was more than she could say for the most faithful of Tellurians. The Mithneshi God was benevolent and eternal. Her own were petty and inconsequential. It was time to leave them behind. She just hoped they weren't spiteful enough to strike her down for it.

———

"You can't be serious," Natharis groaned when the Crystallines led him and Ninotchka to a ditch by the city wall. At the bottom of the rocky pit lay two fresh corpses, a man and woman, the area around their heads littered with hatefully thrown stones. Having been found guilty of adultery by the unlawful Shatarin courts, the couple had been sentenced to death by stoning without the dignity of a proper burial. They hadn't yet begun to decompose, but the sight of spilt blood and shattered skulls was just as unpleasant as the stench of rotting meat. The Crystallines brought them to the couple's remains not to show them the cruelty of the Children of the Dole, but to strip the dead of the clothes they no longer needed. Natharis hesitated to accept his new, morbid ensemble, but he knew it was their best chance at deceiving the enemy.

Natharis struggled to pull the man's clothes off his body, as the dead weight of his abdomen and arms made it difficult. Ninotchka removed the woman's Shatarin face mask and strapped it over her nose and mouth; it left her voice muffled and hissing as she spoke. "You are not fat enough to pass for Communal," she remarked while Natharis stripped down to his trunks in the shade of a rocky outcropping, his oxygen mask still covering his face. The clothing he'd acquired was far too small for the bulky cadaver it came from, but it hung loosely over Natharis's well-sculpted body. Ninotchka was right—his physique would certainly stand out in the crowd, but he had little choice, as the gaping holes in the sack-like shirt where the sleeves should have been hung open down his sides to reveal a chiseled core and biceps too strong for the lazy to bulk up. The Shatarin clothes fit Ninotchka well, as the executed woman was considerably thinner than most of her nonproductive sisters. The black cloth of her form-fitting robe clung to the tight curves of her body, revealing only the skin of her neck and wrists.

The innately entitled Children of the Dole didn't seem to know much about the settlement they'd invaded. Natharis and Ninotchka's guides led them to a small opening in the ground. It was just large enough for Natharis to fit through, though he had to crouch low to do it, while Ninotchka had little trouble slipping in. According to the Crystallines, there were many such passages, hollowed out for emergency evacuations upon a foreign invasion. The unwelcome migrants had stumbled upon some but not all of the tunnels, and a few were left unguarded. They were creeping through one of the unsecured passages, stumbling along its unlit path deep beneath the boundaries of the city dome into the heart of the earth.

The sun was dim when they emerged from behind a rocky crag, to the back of a building clearly designed by amateur architects with little concern for appearance or functionality. Natharis was relieved to see the light again, but a dusty film on the otherwise transparent dome blocked wide cuts of the sky. What subtle light remained sparkled on the treads of impressive, mechanical carriages that passed in the street. One carried a slew of Communal women boasting their freshly painted nails, while others brought litters of obese children to the candy stores across the city. The barges' wheels seemed to be made of pure diamond, catching the sunlight and bursting with a rainbow of colors. But as Natharis and Ninotchka stepped forward to cross the road, it became clear that there were no wheels of precious stones. Crystallines endured the weight of the barges on their backs like slaves carrying a queen. Natharis knew the Children of the Dole were greedy and shameless, but he hadn't expected an act as despicable as their use of Crystallines for their lazy enjoyment. He shuddered to think that his own homeworld could be just as vulnerable. The collectivists were smart, and found subtler forms of slavery to force their fellow Sapiens into bondage, calling it "charity" and "compassion" to deceive those who were too blind or unwilling to open their eyes to the sinister reality.

"Crystallines have no concept of money," Ninotchka noted as she pretended to lead their alien partner as a bondservant. "This is Crystallines paying their 'fair share of labor.' Now welfare royals can live oppression-free lives." She pointed to flashing billboards overhead that displayed all kinds of messages meant to motivate their Crystalline slaves to work harder for the sake of the elusive "greater good," preaching the message that forced labor was actually compassion, and that servitude was generous freedom. They depicted the enslavement of native populations and flaunted charts indicating the benefits of punitive taxation and institutionalized theft, both of which were necessary for the protection of the less fortunate. Ninotchka laughed and said it conveniently provided extra profits for ABAC and its corporate allies. The nefarious Brock Dunham smirked on the screens, his baleful eyes staring down at Natharis. The omnipresent executive reminded the people of the city that only through him could they find economic salvation.

His voice echoed down the streets like the Word of God, past the makeshift storefronts and tenement buildings. They passed a bar with no name beside the illegible Shatarin graffiti across its door; Natharis couldn't read or speak their language, but the vandalized signs and broken windows led him to conclude that it'd been consistently defaced by the religious zealots. It wasn't abandoned, however, and the boisterous voices of drunks caught Natharis's attention. He saw the glitter of a Crystalline's glassy body behind the bar. A Child of the Dole shouted and shook his fist at the helpless slave. He threatened and harassed the bartender, and tried to grab at the Crystalline but failed, as his arms were too short and blubbery. Natharis approached the window.

"Give me my goddamned *drink!*" the man barked. He waved his empty glass in the air.

"I have given you seven for free," the Crystalline said through its translator.

"Brock Dunham said you *have* to give me what I want!"

Natharis couldn't stand to listen to his sickening demands. He swung open the front door and marched toward the flustered and insulted man, who was too busy berating the Crystalline to notice his approach. Natharis grabbed the man by his shirt collar and pulled him away from the bar, knocking his shoulder to spin him around to face him. He commanded the Communal to shut his mouth, get out of the bar and stumble back home. The man was both too drunk and too brazen to listen.

"It's my *right!* A right *Brock Dunham* gave *all* of us! Our will is *their command!*"

Natharis silenced the irascible, ungrateful degenerate with a fist to his jaw; he dropped onto the floor with a satisfying thud. The Colonial never kicked a man while he was down, so he simply watched as the Communal struggled to crawl toward the door on all fours, dragging the immense weight of his grub-like body across the rough floor. The other drunkards in the bar didn't bother to stand up to help him, as they themselves were too bloated to handle the task. They laughed but still gave Natharis a dirty look. Ninotchka entered the bar and pulled out her handgun, then waved it at the drinkers. They barely squeezed through the door when they scrambled to escape a potential flurry of bullets.

"So much for keeping a low profile," Natharis muttered as Ninotchka slipped her gun back under her clothes.

"You decided to beat shit out of Communal. I just followed your lead."

"Let's just hope no one noticed."

The Crystalline worker's body began to flicker with an inner glow. The pulses of electrical light carried a meaning that only its translator could decipher.

"You are not Communals," the worker noted in its digital voice. Their foreignness was obvious enough, at least to a Crystalline who'd never been defended by a Sapien before. *"I am unable to repay you."*

"We're trying to track down your leaders. The other Crystallines outside the city lost contact with them. They don't even know if they're alive."

"They are alive, in a secure location."

"Where are they?"

"The repurposed district police station. There are multiple guards. It is dangerous."

"I didn't dress as Shatarin whore just to turn back now," said Ninotchka. "Collectivist guards are like fat children with guns. No danger at all, except to themselves."

Natharis had to agree based on his experience with the consistently incompetent soldiers ABAC sent to do its dirty work. But while he once thought them to be only a mild threat, one easily disarmed, he was starting to see that ABAC's strongest and most insidious force wasn't its throngs of inexperienced troops, but the ideology it so zealously promoted. It wasn't ABAC's army that captured the city and enslaved its natives—it'd been the Children of the Dole themselves. In spite of their infamous laziness, they were quick to violent action when it meant fighting for their rights and entitlements, which, as of late, were anything they could think of. It was a twisted world where madness was considered sanity, where stealing was considered laudable and oppression was called compassion. And if even the Crystallines, who had no concept of money, could fall at the hands of the endlessly avaricious royals, then the Colonies, with their bountiful wealth, could fall just as quickly.

20

"The signs of a growing corporatist system have been consistent throughout history. First, a large corporation can't compete for consumers, so it sends lobbyists to sway the government into regulating its industry. Second, the government creates a monstrously expensive set of rules; because the large corporation pushed for them, it is already able to plan for them and afford them, while many of its competitors cannot. Third, as the players in the corporate field drop like flies, the large corporation can develop into a mega-corporation, and buy out what few competitors remain. Fourth, the consumers grow suspicious of the mega-corporation's near-monopoly, and they call for yet more government regulations as the solution. Fifth, a society is free to repeat these previous mistakes until its inevitable collapse."
—Colonial Executive Desh Maru

IT'D BEEN A LONG TIME since Tageron set foot in Tarem City's Kaloxa District. He'd grown up there in the slums, playing in the littered streets as a child, and struggled to make ends meet as a teenager working full-time after school. His mother worked multiple jobs, too many for one poor woman.

She was the sole inspiration behind his deep respect for hard, honest labor. It wasn't the money or the lavish lifestyle that could come of it that drove him to succeed. It was the memory of a woman who took jobs most thought were below them, all so her son could have a better life, even if she didn't.

She worked her nineteen-hour days with the goal of securing their escape from the dangerous and degenerate neighborhood, full of social parasites with no desire to do the same through their own efforts. She managed to provide for him until, one day, she died. He left the ghetto and never looked back. She'd never been given the chance. Even into his adulthood, Tageron mourned the woman who'd done so much for her son and so little for herself.

Few of the storefronts had been there decades ago, and those that had were now long since abandoned, their windows cracked and electric signs displaying names that hadn't been heard in years. The barbershop where Tageron got his first haircut was barely recognizable, boarded up and a home for the unwelcome homeless. He wondered why his son-in-law would have invited him to lunch in such a bad area. Working in Tarem's metropolitan Justice Department, Sharsir was probably used to the sounds of car alarms and gunshots that characterized the Kaloxa District. But his wife Leveda, Tageron's only daughter, wouldn't be so familiar or comfortable with abject poverty. It wasn't the best location for a quick lunch with family, especially when that family walked in shoes worth more than the property value of the entire neighborhood.

Tageron checked his mobile to make sure he was at the right address. Sharsir had asked him to meet at the Et-Tu Café, before which Tageron uncomfortably stood. It was a dingy hole-in-the-wall that used the word "café" to mask its low-class atmosphere and equally low-class clientele. One small, round table sat outside the bulletproof glass doors, accompanied by a broken chair and a moldy umbrella that looked like it hadn't been opened in decades. The beggar that lay sprawled out by the doormat demanded a handful of change. Despite his usual reluctance and often outright refusal, Tageron reached into his pocket and gave what he could; the beggar reacted indignantly and called his benefactor cheap for not giving more. It took considerable willpower for Tageron to keep from snatching the undeserved handout right out of the man's tin cup. He ignored the ungrateful insults and pushed open the café doors. The last word he heard was, not atypically, "racist," though their skin was the same shade of bronze.

The peeling yellow paint on the walls, like the jaundiced eyes of an old, sickly hag, did little to increase his appetite, and neither did the cockroach that scurried across his path. Sharsir, one of only three patrons in the establishment, sat with his hands folded and eyes forward, purposely turned away from the spill stains and pests on the floor. Leveda wasn't sitting at the booth with him. Tageron sat and shook his hand, greeting him as the successful son he'd always wanted. He had no problem admitting that he felt his own biological son didn't deserve the title. At least his daughter had proved to be a true source of pride.

"Where's Leveda?" Tageron asked. A waitress interrupted to bring a cup of coffee, which he reluctantly accepted, even after noticing its mud-like consistency, and a smell even worse than decaying sludge.

"She's at home," Sharsir replied, stirring four packs of sugar into his coffee in an attempt to mask its foulness. "I'd rather keep things quiet at the moment. I wanted you to be the first one to know what's under way." He spat his coffee back into the chipped cup.

"I'm not sure what you mean," Tageron said. He looked about his surroundings and grimaced. "You know, we could have met at the office for lunch, if you'd wanted to."

"I have reasons to believe your office isn't a safe place for conversation anymore. There's a strong chance it's bugged. A chance too strong to risk."

"Unless we're talking about treason, I have nothing to hide."

"You're not supposed to know what I'm about to tell you. I'm breaking the law by even meeting with you."

"It's illegal to meet with your father-in-law for lunch now?"

"No, but it *is* illegal to alert a criminal of an impending raid and arrest."

Tageron was at a loss for words; perhaps he just had too many words to choose from. He fell silent from the implications of Sharsir's statement. He knew the government considered him a borderline criminal, right at the edge of violating their pointless and unfair laws, but he thought they had no real ability to press charges. There was no evidence of criminal activity—not because he'd hidden it, but because there was none to begin with.

"There's a plan in the works to nationalize the company. My colleagues in the Justice Department informed me of it. There's only a handful of right-minded people left in this city, and thank God I work with them."

Tageron took a huge gulp of the stinking coffee to rinse the even fouler taste of Sharsir's news from his mouth. It was exactly what he'd been fearing for some time. The collectivist government, jealous of and angry at his success, would inevitably decide that he didn't deserve it. They'd already tried to choke the life out of him in punitive taxes, but their plans proved unsuccessful. This was a last-ditch effort on their part, and an extremely dramatic one—an unjust, outrageous one, one that he couldn't possibly allow.

"Their own laws require them to make at least one offer of compensation before taking action. So, unless my secretary has stopped doing her job, they've made no effort to contact or inform me. There's a complete lack of due process," Tageron argued. He might not have been a lawyer, but he was knowledgeable enough to deem their plot illegal.

"New laws have been passed, all of which have been ignored by the collectivist media. And from what I've heard, the legislature didn't even read the bill. Apparently, they were told by the Lord of Parliament Panzi Illoszia herself that they had to pass it to find out what's in it.

"With the bill signed into law, the City of Tarem can seize any property and nationalize any company if they deem the business or property owner to be in 'dangerous and treasonous opposition' to collectivism. I assume the law was inspired by Brock Dunham's calls for an end to private companies altogether, all for the preservation of the 'greater good.'

"In a matter of days, they'll be coming for you. They've already set aside twenty officers to execute the plan, but I wouldn't be surprised if they send more of them. They'll 'acquire' the property with or without your consent. I'm sorry I don't know more of the details, but I'll keep my ears open, I promise you."

"Don't apologize. At least I know I should be prepared. You're a loyal son-in-law, Sharsir. I always knew my daughter had good judgment. Wish I could say my son had the same."

"What are you going to do?"

Tageron sighed and pushed his coffee away. "I don't know yet. But there's no way in hell I'm handing over the company without a fight. This business is *mine*, and their beloved 'greater good' means nothing to me. So, let them show up at my door. I'll be waiting."

———

"Where are you headed, sister?"

The Mithneshi seer walked alongside the Tellurian polytheist as she wandered down the main corridor. After having learned her name—Selenia Santiago de Sonora—Livia insisted that she follow her. Signs for the medical wing were visible up ahead. It was there that she was planning to go, but she couldn't rationally say why. She had an intuitive sense that she was meant to stand beside the Crystalline prisoner on the operating table. She could have gone alone, but she felt compelled to ask for Selenia's company. She knew it was strange, but even after a short while, she had come to trust her.

"The medical wing. I'm sorry if I'm pulling you from your duties."

"My only duty is to tend to the needs of the innocent, and you're one of them."

"I'm not sure how, but you've given me a kind of confidence I never had. Maybe it's what you're teaching me, or maybe I just need a friend, but it feels like I've known you for years."

"When you truly feel a connection with God's Emanation, time is meaningless. Time is a trivial fact of the physical world, but in the world beyond our sight, it is irrelevant. When a person realizes this, the past, present and future all become one."

Livia wished that time had no meaning for the Crystalline, but she knew it was running out, and that they didn't have the comfort of eternity before them. She walked with urgent intent, and Selenia followed without question. They had little company in the prisoner's section of the medical facilities, and although there was no clear night or day in that area, it felt like they'd arrived in the cover of darkness. There were no visitors, no family members wandering between beds, and the lights were dimmed for sleep. The silence wasn't tranquil, but distressing. Selenia seemed unaffected, at peace.

The sight of the dying Crystalline was heart-wrenching. It lay upon an examination table separate from the patient beds, alone beneath a single white light. There was barely a hint of life; she feared Natharis might have been too late. Selenia approached her and put her hand on her shoulder. She looked upon the Crystalline with a dignified smile.

"Open yourself to the Emanation, Livia. You'll find that death is nothing to be feared. It is just a rite of passage, one of many innate to the Sentient experience. But this one has not yet crossed that threshold. There is still time."

Livia took a deep breath. She knew in her heart that Natharis was in danger, and that he might make that grave step through death's door, along with the Crystalline he hoped to save. She knew if she were down on the planet's surface with him, there was little she could have done to protect him from harm, but she found herself wishing she'd gone with him. It was an intense emotion she couldn't dismiss, as much as her rationality told her otherwise. The idea of Natharis being stolen from her by fate scared her too deeply for rational thought. She couldn't bear the feeling, and stumbled forward, lightheaded, her balance compromised by fear. She placed her hand on the Crystalline by accident to catch herself.

A jolt of electricity passed through her fingers and she pulled her hand away. The Crystalline's body flickered with pulsing light; Livia's eyes opened wide, as did Selenia's, and the two gazed awestruck upon the prisoner. The crumbling pieces of its glassy body drew closer together and began to join, until the Crystalline was almost whole, surrounded by a ring of unhealed stone. The digital translator crackled with static. A voice murmured from it, a monotonous representation of the otherwise inaudible speaker.

"The god comes for me. I cannot be saved."

Its body crumbled apart, and the translator shut down. As quickly as it'd been awakened, the prisoner fell back into a lifeless silence. Livia was stunned. "What god? I don't understand."

"The 'god' it speaks of is no god at all. He is a false god—a man, mortal, like you or me. He is collectivism made flesh. And he is anything but merciful."

Executive Dunham. He's looking for the Crystalline personally.

"Be careful, Livia, because a new cult is growing. And when it declares dominion over the Convergency, it will march with such hatred that the Shatarin religion will seem peaceful. There are those who will tell you that Brock Dunham is worthy of worship, the kind reserved only for the Creator, and they will stop at nothing until every man, woman and child in the Convergency bows down before their idol. The golden calf of collectivism will be paraded through the streets of every capital, and parents will offer up their children to the Moloch that commands the Commune and calls itself the 'greater good.'

"Hold on to the emotions that woke the Crystalline. Your thoughts at that moment were a source of great strength, so do not forget them. Your faith will protect you, and your loving thoughts will be a shield against evil. When you focus on them, you open yourself fully to the Emanation, and your intent will ripple to the farthest reaches of the universe. It is love, Livia, that can make mountains bow, and the seas part before you. Never allow yourself to hate. Hatred consumes us like wildfires and swallows us up like a violent tide, and once it has been unleashed, it cannot be tamed."

———

The police station was inconspicuous, as it didn't have a single sign to identify it as more than a rocky mound. It looked like a hill covered in a shell of jagged stones, and there was only one entrance: a small, round portal blocked by a gate of primitive iron bars. The station must have been repurposed, as though the city's rapacious invaders had claimed an old cave to use as a center for law enforcement. What laws they meant to uphold, Natharis hadn't a clue, and he could only assume that Communal police simply served to beat the natives into compliance when they objected to their indentured servitude. The building was far less secure than the precincts Natharis was used to. There wasn't even a lock to secure the front gate from wandering drunks or rebellious Crystallines.

They stood before the station and Ninotchka drew attention to the circular opening at the mound's apex, which could only be noticed from the rippling heat distortion in the air above it. Apparently, what was now the police station was once a place for Crystallines to rest and absorb the solar radiation they needed to survive, hence the simple skylight at the structure's peak. There'd be, or there would have been, niches in the inner walls spiraling up toward the pinnacle, each of which a Crystalline claimed as its own. Those with greater prominence in society, with a greater productive value, took the highest niches. Those with less influence took the lower ones. With no concept of money, interpersonal exchanges were facilitated only by reputation. Unfortunately, reputation meant little to the Children of the Dole, who couldn't possibly steal it, or use it frivolously as a God-given entitlement.

Ninotchka swung open the gate with no resistance. Natharis drew his firearm, but the Muscovite pushed hers into his free hand. She peeled away her Shatarin garb to reveal a far less modest ensemble, and Natharis had to admit it didn't surprise him. Proving once again that she was perfectly willing to use her sex as a weapon—an incredibly dangerous one—the top of a red corset peeked out from beneath her oppressive cloak, barely able to accommodate her. She stood tall on her deadly stilettos and took back her gun. She fixed her hair with a shake of her head.

"You're always underdressed." Natharis pulled back the other side of the gate.

"Fighting is like fucking, Mr. Ruke. Clothes just get in way."

She was the first to step into the building, strolling forward with a sultry sway of her hips. Her garter became a gun holster and the rocky floor turned to a catwalk. And when the five liquor-guzzling Communals looked up with a glazed but fixated look in their eyes, Natharis knew his partner had already won. The self-appointed officers, likely overpaid with taxpayer money, had no desire to question her identity, and didn't even notice how foreign she looked with her tiny waist. They sat slumped in their chairs, beer bottles in their hands, listening to tasteless music from a rusted radio hidden behind a mountain of junk food wrappers. They watched as the prowling lioness came closer, until even the one female officer couldn't help but wheeze with excitement. One man slipped off his chair and fell to the floor. Ninotchka stepped over him on her ten-inch daggers like he wasn't even there.

Natharis never involved himself in anything other than a clean fight, and what he saw was far from clean. But there was an obvious effectiveness to Ninotchka's erotic strategy, as it had yet to fail her, and it seemed that Communals were especially vulnerable to her sexual hypnosis. A Colonial marshal would never have succumbed so quickly to an admittedly captivating distraction, but they weren't dealing with Colonials.

The male Communal pushed himself up in his seat with thick, sausage-like arms and leaned as far forward as his stomach would allow, which was not particularly far. Ninotchka placed a light kiss on his cheek, then moved on to his two comrades. They ogled her with bright lipstick prints on their faces, and even as Natharis encroached on their positions, they didn't reach for their weapons. The vile woman on her buckling chair was even less eager to defend herself from what any sensible officer would have recognized as an immediate threat.

The Communal let out a delighted squeal, laughing to her fellow officers that the raise in taxes must have allowed the precinct to hire two foreign strippers, and that the two were a reward for the exhaustingly hard work they claimed to engage in. Natharis couldn't be completely certain of the meaning of their bastard utterances, but in the context of the rotund woman's visible enjoyment, he assumed he and Ninotchka had nothing to worry about. The Communals' self-absorption led them to believe that they, once again, were the center of attention, and the receivers of tax-funded eye candy.

The hideous woman commanded Natharis to strip down. Instead, he pulled out his pistol and knocked her out with a blow to the head.

The other Communals screamed, but not because of the assault on their partner. They grasped at their faces and then, one by one, slumped back in their chairs. When their hands fell down to their sides, Natharis saw burns on their cheeks in the shape of Ninotchka's lips. She laughed and praised her venomous lipstick, withdrew her gun from her garter and shot the farcically appointed officer that writhed in fear on the ground.

"Giving him his 'fair share,'" Ninotchka said to justify the unnecessary shot.

They found the captured Crystallines in a cell in the back of the building. Of a group of a dozen or so of their kind, five appeared larger, more grown, with colorful mineral veins glowing through their glassy bodies. They flashed with electricity and tried to communicate. Natharis's Crystalline guide entered the room and made itself useful as an interpreter.

"*You are strangely dressed,*" their guide translated. Ninotchka thanked it for the compliment.

Natharis toyed with the cell lock, which was more sophisticated than the antiquated station gate. He randomly tapped numbers on the holoscreen, but came to accept that they'd stand there for hours without a codebreaker. Ninotchka shot the panel. The powerful magnetic field binding the cell dissipated, and its hum turned to silence. The bullet hole two inches from his hand left him slightly shaken.

"We can't just walk down the road with them," Natharis insisted. "We've drawn enough attention already, and this is one we really can't hide from."

"*The canyon walls behind us are thin, and easily breached.*"

"Maybe if we had explosives."

Ninotchka frowned. "For once, I should have worn coat. I always keep some in pockets."

"*The Crystallines are excellent diggers.*"

The canyon wall wasn't far behind the station, and Natharis understood there was no other option. Time was running out to save the Crystalline orbiting the planet thousands of miles above them, and Natharis couldn't waste it worrying about an impulsive plan of action. They hurried the Crystallines out of the building through the front gate. Many of them made sure to trample the Communals that lay lifelessly on the floor.

Natharis stayed to the back of the group with his gun drawn but held low. The Children of the Dole passed by on the street in the distance, but they were too far to notice the evacuees. He raised his thumb up to Ninotchka to confirm their safety. A half circle of craggy stones concealed the base of the cliffside, and the Crystallines rushed to hide behind it. Natharis heard the sound of tumbling rocks and thought one hadn't caught up, but it became clear that he was hearing footsteps, and he looked back to see a Communal struggling to climb the hill. The oppressed miser tried to grab Natharis's leg and pull him down.

"You can't *leave*! *You* need to work for the *greater good*! The law says so!" the man shouted desperately. Natharis picked up a stone that fit snugly in his palm and brought it down upon the man's head. He immediately ceased his demands.

The Crystallines had already begun to dig their way through the wall, and the two Sapiens simply stood and watched them work. They were a species of miners, and they knew what they were doing. The stone crumbled and turned to sand as they ground their bodies against the face of the cliff. Sharp protrusions from their crystal faces stabbed at the wall until it was crisscrossed with cracks and fissures. They'd only dug a few feet into the cliffside when they burst into a subterranean chamber, one of many tunnels hidden from sight.

Natharis turned to their Crystalline guide. "We held up our end of the deal." He withdrew a com-link he'd tucked into what was left of his clothes and clipped it to his ear. "So don't get too comfortable. I'll confirm with our partners on Othonas that it's safe to send the patient down to the surface, and then we're going back in."

"We will fulfill our promise as well," one of the leaders said through their interpreter. *"After we take back our city."*

"Revolt?" Ninotchka laughed, until she realized the proposal was serious. "At least wait until we get what we need. What we *don't* need is slave uprising getting in our way."

"Look, you have our sympathy, but we don't have time for a rebellion. Give us two or three hours, then you'll be free to do whatever you think is necessary. Overthrowing your enemies could take days."

"The environmental dome is fragile. Its demolition will be simple."

Ninotchka rolled her eyes. "Again, I should have worn fur coat."

"Without the dome, there will be no obstacles. Our medicine will be yours."

She considered the Crystalline's proposal for a moment. Her green eyes lit up with excitement when she realized that they'd be sentencing thousands of criminals to die. It was a distinctly Muscovian passion for carnage that drove her to support the plan—but only because her targets were undeniably guilty. Natharis voiced his disappointment that they couldn't simply deport the invaders, as would have been the Colonial way of doing things. He had no choice but to agree with them, however unpleasant the consequences. They had to land their prisoner by any means necessary, because its death would mean the death of an incredible secret. Natharis, most of all, wanted to know what it knew. It had knowledge of something that clearly terrified ABAC, and Natharis vowed to uncover the truth, even if it took a rebellion to do it.

———

The pungent smell of sautéed garlic woke Selas up from a much-needed nap. It wafted from the kitchen into his bedroom, accompanied by the sound of his mother moving saucepans from the burner to the metal countertop beside it. He had no idea what she was cooking for dinner, but he knew his appetite was stronger than it'd been in months. For once, they had real food—not dehydrated, freeze-dried slop, but real, satisfying food. The Mithneshi made sure of it, as they always treated those who came to them for refuge better than they treated themselves. An ascetic lifestyle was reserved for the Coven. Their wards lived comfortably, if only for a fleeting moment.

He wished he could say the scent of spices and herbs reminded him of his childhood, of an ethnic grandmother or grandfather, but he had no such childhood memories for the smells to evoke. A good meal was something reserved only for the present, not lingering in the past like the symbol of a lost golden age. He was thankful for the luxury, despite the brevity of his enjoyment. He'd learned to be grateful for it— his mother and father had made sure of it. They didn't want him to grow up spoiled, though such an upbringing was difficult to achieve as a Gameer, few of whom boasted the required wealth.

"It isn't much," his mother said as Selas took a seat at the table. "But your father and I felt we've made enough these past few days to justify it."

Selas stretched his arms high above his head and rubbed the sleep from his eyes, then accepted the bowl of vibrantly green vegetables from his older sister. He tore a piece from the loaf of bread and put it on his plate, along with a ground meat he couldn't identify, though it smelled delicious regardless. He plunged his fork into the greens and took a large bite. The savory taste of garlic and oil flooded his senses; the flavor was almost too much for his stomach to handle, as he'd become accustomed to bland, tasteless food over the past months. His sisters didn't have the same problem, and helped themselves to seconds before Selas had even finished his plate.

"Thank God for the Coven," Evua sighed in relief. Their father cited the Mithneshi love of nature, and therefore, natural farming, as the reason behind the quality of their meal. The Gameer might have grown their own food on the

Massyulan, but the produce they tore from the artificial soil was genetically modified and consequently dissatisfying; even the sweetest fruits from the farm halls left a bitter aftertaste. The family hadn't been charged with the task of farming aboard the Ssimvomai Center for the Lost, as it was something they were quite tired of, but Ileya wished that her older brother had been.

"I don't think space is safe," she told him with legitimate concern in her tiny voice. "You'll fall away and I won't see you again." She pouted, and Selas thought she might even cry from the thought. He felt the need to reassure her once again that he wasn't going anywhere.

"You don't have to worry about that, because I won't let it happen." He lightly wrapped his fingers around her wrist and shook it, trying to elicit a smile. "I'll tell you what: How about if you're ever scared, just wave to me out the window. I promise I'll wave back so you know I'm okay. Does that sound good?" Ileya smiled and started picking at her food again. To Selas's satisfaction, she looked much less afraid.

"You know, I hope you consider yourself lucky that *you* get to put on a suit and get off the station," Evua groaned. "God knows *I'd* enjoy the open space. I'm getting cabin fever stuck in a room packed with smelly homeless people. I swear, I'm going to suffocate to death in that kitchen. Even a spacesuit has fresher air."

Their mother wasn't about to allow her daughter to be so brazen. "It's for a good cause. Nobody's forcing us to be charitable, Evie, since we came here by choice—and that's how it's supposed to be. You're doing your part in improving the lives of others, which is exactly what the Creator would want. And besides, it means we get to have a nice family dinner to ourselves. We don't get to have that very often."

"So don't ruin it," their father added. "No complaining at the table."

Ileya jumped in, having come to a soon-to-be-explained realization. "We didn't give thanks. Can't we say it so it's not ruined, too?"

Their parents, proud of their little girl's innocent faith, let her say the short prayer of thanksgiving. She didn't say it verbatim, but it was to be expected from such a young girl. She simplified it, changing the words to those of a wide-eyed, genuine child. They had a purity that transcended their simplicity. She was a child who kept her family's hope alive with one short prayer.

Selas looked upon a little girl who managed to still have unshakable faith, even having been through hell. Though she didn't remember it, it was more than anyone should have had to endure, especially a child. If she could suffer through it with hope as her shield, then certainly he could as well. It was time for him to stop fearing the dark, to stop letting his dread keep him awake at night. He was no longer a child, a scared little boy. He was a man now—and he needed to face his fears as one.

———

The window overlooking Leftway Avenue was still open, a violation of Pentakiya's nightly ritual of securely locking it and pulling closed the curtains. The sound of sirens and shameless partiers enjoying themselves at others' expense normally would have driven her crazy, but she was happy for once to be kept awake. The noise drowned out her thoughts, or so she hoped it would. She didn't want to lie in silence with her worries screaming in her head. She'd rather it be barely legal girls shouting obnoxiously in the street, or the distant pops of gunshots in a drug deal gone bad. Anything was better than the deafening echo of her own thoughts.

Artimpasa lay with her head softly pressed against Pentakiya's breasts, her sleeping breath light, almost inaudible. She hadn't had trouble at all falling asleep that night, a luxury Pentakiya envied greatly. But then, Artimpasa had no reason to toss and turn with worries growing more numerous each passing day. Even her direct confrontations with the law hadn't seemed to bother her much as of late. She despised their attempts to keep her from speaking, writing or teaching, but considered them more of a nuisance or inconvenience than a force to be truly feared. Pentakiya knew better. She'd been told by them firsthand that they didn't take her wife's disobedience lightly, and against her better judgment, she hadn't said a thing about it since.

She regretted not telling her wife about the consequences she might face. She felt guilty knowing that she'd done nothing to protect Artimpasa from a fate she could easily bring upon herself. But Pentakiya expected she wouldn't listen to her anyway, thinking her warnings were too outrageous, too unbelievable to be heeded. Her wife was too proud a woman to cave in to her enemies' demands. Her convictions were far too strong for it, and for better or worse, Pentakiya felt her only option was to stay quiet. The last thing she wanted was a fight between them. There had been enough conflict already.

Thankfully, the fights between the two wives never led to violence, to laying hands on each other in any way other than a pleasurable one. But Artimpasa's high-ranking adversaries weren't nearly as pacifistic or respectful. Pentakiya had seen her colleagues slaughtered like cattle right before her eyes; she'd seen her once idolized leaders turn on their supporters, even ones as loyal as she'd been. There was a time when she feared the Colonials more than any other group in the Convergency, but lately they seemed like just an afterthought. It was the collectivist faction that now struck terror in her heart. It was Executive Dunham.

Painful memories resurfaced, rising from the depths of her psyche like ghosts from the underworld. She remembered the anger she'd felt when the Colonials took her partner Rocky away without warning. She recalled the hatred, the anguish, and worst of all, the grave terror that shook her to her core. Knowing they'd detained him simply for his opposition was the root of her personal vendetta against Colonial selfishness. At that moment, however, as she lay with the tickle of her wife's warm breath on her chest, she wished they were living in the Colonies. Artimpasa would be safer there. It was a realization that left her more uneasy than any had before. Her most hated enemies were the only ones who'd allow the love of her life to voice her opinion without the risk of imprisonment, or worse, execution. Pentakiya's own trusted government had turned its back on her and was now thirsty for her wife's passionate blood. They wanted her silenced at any cost. For the first time in her life, Pentakiya cursed Brock Dunham.

"God damn you," she whispered in the dark, the executive's face boasting a sinister grin in her mind. *"She's mine. And you won't take her from me."*

The rebellion began to the thunderous drums of detonations, rhythmic explosions in the distance. The terraformation devices burst into flames of all colors, tinged with the greenish blue of hydrogen fuel and the pitch-black smoke of burning organics. Even through the oxygen mask of his suit, Natharis could smell the noxious fumes that crept across the steppe. He knew it wouldn't take long for the Communal colonists to notice the strike on their means of survival, but there was always the chance that they were simply too immobile to defend themselves.

Ninotchka imposed herself as supervisor of the dome sabotage operation, and she took well to the role, barking orders at the Crystallines by means of their translators. As they climbed higher above Natharis and Ninotchka, they were too out of range to pick up the sound of her distant voice, but she commanded them anyway, just for her personal satisfaction. The Crystallines ascended the black stone spires encircling the city; their protean bodies turned to puddles of diamond pebbles that crept up the face of the crags. Slipping up the surface like pools of shimmering mercury, they came to the base of the dusty dome. Natharis heard the sound of knives on glass as the Crystallines turned to sparkling urchins and smashed their sharpened bodies into the dome. Ninotchka grinned when the first web of cracks began to appear. Natharis held his breath.

A deep fissure slithered over the crest of the dome and divided it in two. The Crystallines leapt from their positions down to the ground, reassembling their bodies upon landing from a pile of rubble into recognizable figures. The closest hemisphere began to slip, and it lurched downward with a deafening screech. Natharis heard screams. Ninotchka laughed to the sound of terror and panic. She nudged him in the shoulder and told him to watch justice at work.

The Crystallines marched through the tunnels leading into the city, and their Sapien allies followed close behind, because a Muscovite would never pass up the opportunity to watch a good, old-fashioned riot. Natharis, on the other hand, wasn't comfortable with the idea of thousands of people burning and suffocating to death, even if they were part of a group he wasn't particularly fond of. He braced himself for a scene no Colonial would ever hope to see. If he'd had his way, they'd simply deport the Communals. Death was rarely a necessity, most of all among civilians, no matter how parasitic.

The Children of the Dole scrambled through the streets with their hands over their eyes. They screamed in pain as terrible burns spread over their skin, smoldering with the stench of burnt flesh. Parents abandoned their children and left them to die beneath the lethal rays of the sun. Then he saw a woman with eyes like Livia's, the color of the deepest oceans, and realized the tragic mistake they'd all made. He couldn't stand to watch the horrors; he ran into the road and grabbed two crying children by their shirts and pulled them indoors. He knew he couldn't save them all, and he knew Ninotchka would be insulted if he asked her to help a Communal. He shouted to the Crystallines, who were crushing the innately entitled under their weight, impaling them on their glassy shards.

"Stop this! Round them up! We don't have to do this!"

He pushed a bovine Child of the Dole through the front door of her house and commanded three others to follow her; in their desperation, they complied. The Crystallines paused and considered Natharis's strategy, then accepted it. They collapsed their bodies into piles of rubble and swept the invaders off their feet and into the makeshift buildings. Ninotchka pouted in her disappointment.

"You Colonials ruin everything with your pacifism."

"Non-interventionism. And when there's a nonviolent option, you should always choose it."

"It is far less satisfying. I like to see justice served."

"So do I. But this isn't justice."

Without control collars to disable their slaves, the Communals were outnumbered a hundred to one by the Crystalline exiles. They found themselves forced indoors, but they didn't fight the Crystallines who tossed them gracelessly through doors and open windows. Natharis and Ninotchka, in their radiation-shielded suits, simply stood and watched as the unwelcome colonizers were rounded up in preparation for their deportation. They'd managed to remove an obstacle without too many casualties. It was safe to continue their operation.

Natharis pressed a button on his com-link and spoke into the earpiece, the channel set to communicate with Silviano miles overhead. "Send down the prisoner. The landing site's been secured." He transmitted their coordinates to Othonas and shut off the com-link. He didn't need a response—he was sure they'd received his transmission. He confirmed with Ninotchka that they were ready to proceed as planned. She still didn't seem satisfied with the way their mission had panned out.

The Muscovite had hoped for blood, just as many Muscovites would have. They had a love of swift, undeniable justice that was foreign to the Colonial mindset. While the Tsardom was only contented when it'd fully erased a target from history, either under the falling warheads of a carpet bombing or clouds of white phosphorous, the United Colonies preferred isolation over war. There was no reason to destroy an opponent when he'd been cut off from all contact. The Colonials let their enemies wither and die outside their borders. They didn't feel a need to exterminate them.

He had to admit that, deep down, he'd found the sight of harsh retribution to be just as gratifying as Ninotchka did. But it was a dark pleasure that no Colonial should ever succumb to. It was best kept secret, as the logic he'd been instilled with since childhood would no doubt overpower it. Only Communals caved in to their most despicable desires so shamelessly, and he was not one of them. Rationality always triumphed over a lust for primal vengeance, at least for a civilized person. And Natharis knew that the Commune's lack of it, and lack of shame, would not go unpunished, either by the Colonies, or by the eager hand of Ninotchka Voronova.

21

"Speak softly, and carry a big stick."
—An ancient leader, revered by Acadia.

EXECUTIVE OKSANA MOLOTOVA piloted her personal strike craft toward the tachyon vein marked on her navigation screen. She was flanked by a squadron of Muscovian fighter pilots who were just as eager to shoot down any collectivist in their way. Oksana had a strict, personal policy when it came to the prospect of war: she would not send her men to die for the Tsardom if she herself were not willing to die for it as well. She knew the exchange of aetherium weapons had to be stopped, and as she'd promised in the Congressional session, she'd stop it herself. Even her critics would have to acknowledge the courage it took to personally intercept the shipment. But in Oksana's mind, it wasn't courage. It was obligation.

She sat in the cockpit and blew a kiss into the flight recorder's camera lens. Her heavy makeup was plainly visible, even when partially covered by her luxury fur hat and salon-crafted blond hair. Lutetian silver and diamonds glittered around her neck. She'd slipped a single, though massive, ring over her leather cocktail gloves, and its cumbersome stone caught the lights inside the hangar bay. Oksana confirmed her launch verifications with the larger warship's docking control. Just as she was cleared for launch, she told the dispatcher to wait a moment. She slipped on a pair of Padanian designer sunglasses and inserted a Colonial cigarette into her cigarette holder. Glorious music filled the cockpit when the computer responded to her command: Tchaikovsky's *Swan Lake*, Act II: No. 14 Scène: Moderato.

She activated the launch light and the fighter was propelled toward the hangar doors. With a flick of her fingers she produced a flame from her white gold lighter, encrusted with jewels in the shape of the Romanov family crest, and lit her cigarette. The smoke muffled her voice slightly as she called the other fighters into formation; she exhaled a wispy cloud, and they confirmed her orders one by one. Oksana addressed the command deck of the warship miles behind her.

"Target tachyon vein exit point. Destroy any ship that exits." She then ordered her wingmen to enter the tachyon vein—"Force *sobaki* into free space. They'll have planet cracker waiting for them." The glow of a tachyon crucible flared up behind her, radiating energy from the heart of the massive warship, and the forward camera recorded the spectacular sight of a controlled vein incision. A tear in reality opened wide for Oksana's skilled squadron, a gash revealing the shimmering Aether. Without warning, Oksana accelerated toward the rabbit hole and laughed. She tapped ash from the end of her cigarette and clutched the joystick before her with her other hand.

She crossed the energetic threshold with little concern for what was ahead of her. She took a crystal liquor glass from a wood-paneled compartment and filled it with fine vodka from a bottle she'd kept grappled between her thighs. She took a sip and examined the mixed fleet ahead of her, a mess of cargo ships and military escorts bearing the flags of Albion, Bahía Brumosa and, of course, the Albian Banking

Advancement Conglomerate. Commanding the computer to scan the enemy ships for aetherium weapons, she put out her dying cigarette and lit another. When the scan confirmed that the fleet was, in fact, engaging in an exchange of weapons of mass destruction, she gulped down the rest of her drink. She ordered her wingmen into attack position.

"Drop out of tachyon vein, and prepare to be boarded," Oksana barked in a heavily accented Anglic transmission to the transport fleet. "Tsardom of Romanov Muscovia is cancelling your rendezvous."

After a moment of tense silence, the enemy answered her call. *"You have no jurisdiction here—the veins are international territory. Your own government hasn't even sanctioned your illegal activities. You have no business being here."*

"I took some initiative."

She was counting on the enemy ship's inevitable warning shot; she greeted it with a devious grin. With the bright burst of energetic gunfire, Oksana knew it was the perfect time to strike. "Good. You fired first. Terrible mistake."

She switched back to her own channel and gave her fighters their orders. "Destroy *sobaka's* tachyon sails! Let planet cracker finish them off in free space!" She screamed at the computer, "Repeat, full sound!" and rocketed full-throttle toward the ABAC command ship. Her words were almost inaudible with the Moderato blaring in her ears. She snatched up her crystal liquor glass and studied it for just a second before tossing it behind her with a crash. She gripped the vodka bottle by its slender neck and finished it off in one aggressive gulp, then threw it behind her as well. With her vodka all gone and her fighters in formation, she fired a round of shield-piercing torpedoes toward the enemy fleet.

Her comrades rushed at the command ship and broke their formation. As they pulled away from their target and accelerated vertically to engage the smaller cruisers, objects fell from the underbellies of the Muscovian strike craft. They'd deployed their Cossacks to demolish the ships' tachyon sails. The mechanized warriors, with a stature dwarfing a man's and metal limbs with a lethal grip, tore off the sails one by one. They leapt from battleship to battleship with pulses of energy from their backs and disabled the fleet. Their host fighters fended off the bombers, which had no choice but to keep their fire off the Cossacks, for fear of damaging their own cruisers. Oksana congratulated her squadron, but noticed one smaller ship fleeing the battle. She wasn't about to let it get away.

"Push transports into free space. Their escorts won't give us trouble anymore," she ordered through the com-link. "There's one more. I've got him."

A projectile pierced her fighter's shield and shook the cockpit; Oksana glared upon learning her shields were down to eighty-five percent. As she took a puff from her thirty-first cigarette of the battle, she concluded it was time for a new strategy. She told her flight computer to engage her signature Ballet Extravaganza maneuver. She took her hands off the controls and stood up.

The fighter accelerated toward the escaping ship. Oksana slipped into a leathery, protective spacesuit and pulled off her fur hat. She covered her long, platinum blond hair with a sleek helmet and stood over the jettison hatch. Her ship raced closer and closer to her target, just seconds away from a lethal collision. The hatch blasted open beneath her; she launched from her ship at full speed, her head up and arms kept folded over her chest. Her fighter sped off on its course, straight toward the enemy ship's main tachyon sails. Its devastating impact damaged the sails beyond repair, but the kamikaze maneuver equally crippled the shield generator. It burst into a flurry of bluish sparks and the ship's radiant shields flickered off.

The hull was fully exposed. Oksana landed on the sabotaged vessel and clicked her towering heels on its metal surface. She recalled her past career as a universally praised ballerina in the Petrograd Theatre Ballet, and danced in a perfect circle on the unshielded hull. Laser cutters from the tip of her heels burned through the metal beneath her and sliced open an entry point. She lightly tapped her foot and pushed the detached cut of the hull into the ship and slipped in right behind it. She beamed in prideful victory as she had after crushing her opponent in her first election, winning by three hundred million votes in her run for Executive office. She boarded the ABAC ship just as easily.

A blast of air rushed past her as the pressurized atmosphere was sucked out into the vacuum of space. Flashing red lights and blaring alarms erased all hope of a clean entrance. Oksana made her way into a still-pressurized corridor and quickly shut the airlock behind her.

"The Muscovish zore! Tomer 'er! She b'a kappler d'Ethad-Arter!"

Two bloated ticks in ABAC uniforms barked in barbarian Unispeak to Oksana's right. She whipped her head to the side and strafed to her left. The bumbling man and woman waddled toward her with their short arms outstretched. Oksana swung her heel and kicked the man square in his pendulous stomach; her laser heels sliced through his abdomen and blasted his blubber onto the wall behind him. The hulking woman tried desperately to smother Oksana under her weight, but the Muscovite quickly snatched a broken beam that dangled from the ceiling and bludgeoned her in the back of the head. The ABAC crewwoman collapsed to the ground, and Oksana, in a typical Muscovian act of excess violence, coolly walked by and fired a single shot between the eyes.

She turned a corner toward the ship's bridge. Four soldiers stood as a bulging barrier in a line across the corridor. One pointed a sausage-like finger at her and screamed, *"She'll destroy the taire 'nd tomer the cumbles witter! Wackiff 'er!"*

They opened fire but soon began to slow their shots. They hesitated, too fixated on their sultry target, who subtly pulled down the collar of her spacesuit as she approached delicately on her heels. But when she'd pulled it so low that the degenerate soldiers were drooling like hounds, she revealed not an exquisite bust, but two disc-shaped explosives. She threw the mines like shuriken at her opponents; two of them exploded into a shower of fatty tissue and blood.

Oksana somersaulted over the falling entrails and plunged thin knives hidden at her wrists into the two rear soldiers' throats; she backflipped over them and landed gracefully on her feet with a pile of twitching, bovine carcasses behind her. They hadn't stood a chance.

The command crew on the ship's bridge was equally unprepared. The Muscovite beauty barged through the door with a pistol in each hand. Only one crewman worked up the courage to confront her, and he stumbled closer to grab her throat. Oksana effortlessly grabbed him by his hair and kicked him onto the ground. She stepped on his face until he stopped screaming.

"You will enter free space now," she instructed, "and Tsardom will take weapons off your hands." The crew protested but didn't do anything to stop her. They chattered in their bastard language until she shouted more commands. "You will also testify against ABAC in Convergency court. Do you understand and agree to Tsardom's demands?"

The crew stayed silent—their years of brainwashing had rendered them unbreakable, and made an act of betrayal against ABAC unthinkable. "So be it," Oksana concluded. She approached the holding bay controls and deployed the cargo with a smile. The crew gasped in horror. Just one energetic burst from a tachyon vein incision would be enough to detonate the hundreds of aetherium warheads being carried in the belly of the ship. She shot the control panel and left the cargo hold vulnerable and irreparable.

One of the ABAC officers muttered something in Unispeak and the entire group rushed toward Oksana. For once, she'd been caught off guard. They grabbed her by her ankles and wrists and carried her out of the command deck and toward the closest airlock. One of the men made sure to grasp at her breasts before they threw her in. She was disgusted by his perversions and swore to herself that he'd be the first to die. She just had to get out of their greasy clutches first.

She hit the floor in the airlock with a sore thud and groaned as the door locked behind her. The Communals were planning on exposing her to the frigid vacuum just outside the thin hull, but she slipped her helmet back on, and ruined their hope of asphyxiating her. She could make out some of their words through the transparent plastic of the door, and they figured that if they couldn't choke the life out of her, they would take her down with the ship. Even they understood that there was no hope of escape from the coming detonation. Their fear distracted them from the transmission she sent to hail her military escorts.

The fighter came swiftly. The outer hatch of the airlock tore open and jettisoned out into the shimmering void of the tachyon vein. Oksana sprinted toward the opening and leapt from the ship. She landed on the strike craft with feline grace and pulled herself inside through the hatch on its underbelly. In the silence of the Aether, she couldn't hear the detonation of the aetherium weapons to her back. But when she looked behind her to see the explosion shrinking into the distance, she found it to be the most terribly beautiful thing she'd ever seen. The fluorescent glow of destructive power arced from the cargo bay and filled the vein with a blinding burst of energy. The crew didn't even have time to cry out. They were incinerated by their own brazen greed, and their lust for a power they didn't deserve. It was justice served just how a Muscovite preferred it.

———

Lights flashed through the halls of the Congressional complex as throngs of reporters began their assault on high-ranking figures, snapping pictures from every angle. Misha had no doubt that the collectivists would doctor their photos before publishing them, erasing the myriad imperfections permanently plastered on their leaders' aging faces, though there wasn't a single digital artist skilled enough to airbrush away gravity's unfortunate influence on Panzi Illoszia's skin.

Misha, an honest reporter, had no desire to alter reality in any way, unlike her rivals at the Politically Correct Broadcasting Company, who not only sought to make the subjects of their interviews appear younger, but appear sane as well, perhaps even competent. A Communal audience would fall for their tricks, but not a single Colonial would have ever believed even the smallest of stretched truths. Colonials were informed, and interested only in facts, not appearances; Communals, on the other hand, were perfectly placated by glamour, glitter and fame, especially when fully undeserved.

The bustling corridors echoed with talk of Executive Molotova's historic disruption of Brock Dunham's unlawful aetherium weapon exchange. Her flight recorder's video feed had been broadcast across the Tsardom within hours of her successful operation; the Colonials learned of it soon after, witnessing her heroic act with their channels tuned to Vega 1 News, which had been the first domestic news outlet to get its hands on the footage. The network's other programs all invited political scientists, military officials and public figures to speak on what was to come, though even the most oblivious of viewers would have been able to predict that the imminent Congressional session would be a full-on ideological brawl. But while many of her colleagues were reporting from the safety of their studios, Misha took it upon herself to travel to Bhalenjar with her crew to document the political reaction firsthand. She'd caught barely any sleep, though coffee and nerves kept her alert. She looked through the crowd to find a suitable subject for a brief interview. It didn't take long before she found a prime, and pathetically brainless, target.

A bulbous globe of a head rose above the brown-nosed horde of reporters, topped with a poorly colored hairstyle that could only be called matronly. It was indicative of the graying politician's age, which the PCBC fought so hard to conceal and defend against undue criticism. She was Diannary Rodton, the long-time protégée of Panzi Illoszia, who had shamefully lost her bid for the office of ABAC executive to Brock Dunham. Since her crushing electoral defeat, she'd declared herself one of Brock Dunham's most loyal followers, obeying his every decree, and executing every illogical, unlawful order in the defense of collectivism. In the same breath, Misha suspected that Diannary viewed her willful servitude as merely temporary, and all part of a clandestine plan to one day take the office she felt she rightly deserved, though she'd never publicly admit it. Like her deified overseer, she was the type to shirk all forms of media transparency, unless the media were on her side. In the Commune, she always found a pundit to flatter her with sugar-coated, irrelevant questions; journalists in the League, however, never let her off so easy, and it was for this reason that she scurried away from Misha with a disdainful scowl, marching brusquely into the cover of the crowd.

Misha grabbed her cameraman by the shirt collar and pulled him in determined pursuit of her journalistic prey. Diannary glanced back and gasped, her eyes wide with surprise and disgust, and picked up her pace, her horribly tailored pantsuit clinging repulsively to her square, bloated behind. Misha called out her name, but the horrified woman crashed into the shoulders of two close-standing men in suits, who cursed loudly when they stumbled back unexpectedly. Misha, with the skill of an experienced military leader, directed her crew to flank Diannary and cut her off; her cameraman stood beside her, while the sound team dodged oblivious public figures and jumped out to block Diannary's escape. The seething weasel demanded that they let her past, declaring that she would never speak to any reporter who has not been approved by her campaign management team, and especially not a Colonial, who would no doubt twist her words into blatant lies, regardless of how little substance her words contained in the first place.

"Why the hurry, Mrs. Rodton?" Misha inquired smugly, producing a microphone and holding it uncomfortably close to Diannary's sagging face. "Are you off to some hideous pantsuit convention?"

"I'll have you know," Diannary snapped, glaring into the camera for a split second, breaking a television taboo, "that I am late for a peace conference—something I'm sure you've never bothered to cover on your racist program."

"You'll miss the Congressional session," Misha lamented with an insulting pout. "How unfortunate. What will your superiors think when you abandon them in their time of need?"

"I came to support my mentor before her participation in the debate. I've said my words of encouragement already, and now I must be going." She snatched her slender briefcase from the floor, filled with coveted files that she'd recently come under fire for accumulating and distributing through unofficial channels, and which she'd refused to disclose to the courts, despite their constant calls for a formal investigation.

"I have no intention of sabotaging your famed punctuality," Misha sneered, "but I'd like to ask you a few questions. It's been months since you've allowed a single non-Communal journalist within even a few feet of you, and I'm sure you'd relish the opportunity to dispel any foreign rumors of secrecy and subversion."

"I will take no such questions at this time—not without my team's consent. They've already put together a nonnegotiable list of approved media contacts, and unluckily for you, you are not one of them. If anything, I'm doing you a favor by even telling you this. I'm sure your greedy company will pay you dearly simply for recording a few words." She clutched the briefcase tightly under her arm, as if defensive of something hidden and ultimately indefensible. "But if you must know, the peace conference concerns a tragic and offensive legal case against a group of innocent, peaceful Shatarins wrongfully accused of fictitious crimes against the Zionese. I think it's safe to assume that you've either never heard of it, or that you, in your bigotry, have taken the side of the Zionese oppressors."

"I'm familiar with it," Misha countered, "and I sincerely doubt that a convention defending the rights of the Shatarins to murder and cook children could ever be considered a 'peace conference,' even by your detestable standards. Perhaps a seasoned and sautéed infant is the Shatarins' finest cultural delicacy, but this is multiculturalism at its ugliest."

"I can't say I'm surprised by your ignorance," Diannary sighed. "But I really must be going. I am to be the keynote speaker, and I refuse to keep my audience waiting. Surely you'd do the same on your program, except I will be promoting tolerance, and not placating the backward and uneducated, as is your way and your unfortunate prerogative." An armed bodyguard in a black suit and dark sunglasses approached the politician and whispered in her ear, drawing attention to a white-haired man standing along the far wall, who smiled with the slyness of a pervert who'd managed to get away with his groping and still be considered a moral advocate for women.

"Ah, my husband is here to escort me to our freighter," Diannary announced proudly, just in time. "Good luck, Ms. Matsumoto. Do your best to emulate the PCBC. Hounding me with any further questions would be blatantly offensive and deserving of censorship by the authorities. Your public interrogations are improper and unethical."

"But I haven't asked you a single—"

"Good day, Misha. This interview is over. Do not attempt to contact me again, or I shall be forced to press charges."

Misha fumed as Diannary rushed over to her husband, Wilferson Rodton, who didn't bother to embrace her or even show a shred of affection, until collectivist cameras panned across them. Mr. Rodton had arrogantly served as ABAC's executive decades in the past; ever since his tenure came to a quick and fortunate end, he'd engaged in the business of paid speeches and made millions over the years, though both he and his wife pompously claimed to be both impoverished and staunch defenders of the poor. After dozens of book deals and years devoid of any pro bono events or work, Mr. and Mrs. Rodton had ascended the ranks of the wealthy until they rivaled Brock Dunham in the size of their untaxed bank accounts. Like his wife, Wilferson rejected all calls for an explanation as to how a man so poor could afford such consistent luxuries, such as the private freighter he and his homely spouse were about to board. He dodged all questions, no matter how minor, unless they were meant to paint him in a favorable light, in which case he'd speak all day long—for a "meager" fee, of course.

The elite couple offered a cursory greeting to a Caspian representative, uttering their halfhearted words in a regional accent with which they hadn't spoken just seconds prior. They were masters of adjusting their manners of speech to align with those who listened, no matter what region they hailed from. Coached by professional linguists, Mr. and Mrs. Rodton had sweet-talked their way through community after community, presenting themselves as natives to any planet, city or system they visited, just as their Shatarin friends were wont to do. That week, Diannary was born and raised on Gottia, though she'd referenced an upbringing on Pontchartrain the week before; Wilferson, however, had never been to Pontchartrain (though his birth records insisted otherwise), but was a city boy who grew up in the derelict slums of Xaztechua.

There wasn't a single Colonial who believed their lies, but the Communals ate their self-righteous shit with a spoon. It was an eagerness to chew and swallow steaming piles of verbal feces that marked the Children of the Dole as pitifully impressionable and incapable of free thought. And in the Congressional session that was just about to commence, the collectivists would be holding an equally repulsive banquet, partaking in a feast of filth where the courses had no end, and the vomitoria were overflowing.

———

Executive Molotova sat at her desk on the Executive Council with a glass of vodka set before her. The ice clinked in her glass as she held it to her lips and took a small sip; her other hand was empty, free of the numerous cigarettes she'd smoke throughout the day. She looked particularly calm in spite of the withdrawal she was suffering, but the clear liquor took the edge off, both of her headache and Panzi Illoszia's tiresome rampage. In the face of Panzi's hateful tirade, even a non-smoker like Desh would have been itching for a cigarette. But Oksana took the Lord of Parliament's angry rhetoric without lashing back or hurling an endless number of potential insults at the hideous politician. She allowed the creature to spew her illogical rubbish, and waited for the prime opportunity to respond—with the dignity and poise expected of her in her black cocktail dress.

"It is an *outrage* that not a single person in the League of Arterra has a moral issue with Executive Molotova's *unlawful* disruption of the Commune's aetherium arms exchange. The Tsardom's complete disregard for the sovereignty of other nations, and for Convergent *law*, can *no longer be tolerated.*" She turned to Desh and pointed a gnarled finger. "And *you*, Executive Maru—you should be *ashamed* of yourself for allowing such a *blatant* subversion of the law. Isn't this the exact kind of injustice you claim to *despise?*"

"The arms exchange itself was a subversion of the law that never should have taken place to begin with. It was a decision the Council, and Congress as a whole, never even had a chance to vote on, all because Executive Dunham seems to think that democracy is just a useless and archaic inconvenience. Executive Molotova only did what was necessary, and nothing more."

"The corporatist collectivists of this legislature will *also* do what is necessary, Executive Maru. We will pass more and *more* legislation to raise this Convergency's pitifully low taxes. We *cannot* sit back and allow your incessant vetoes any longer. With each bill you slash down, you are *denying* the Convergent government the revenue it needs to *survive*."

"Thirty-five percent increase in income tax is criminal, at best," Oksana snapped.

"Our now fairly taxed citizens can afford the increase, and *yours*, most of all," Panzi argued. "Now that *all* private loans will be financed by the Albian Banking Advancement Conglomerate, the people of this Convergency will have the resources to pay for the costs of our brilliant policies."

"*All* loans?" asked Sir Byron. "What, to avoid their new debt-structured lives?"

"Because we can't possibly rely on *you* people to support the needs of others, ABAC will be the *sole* lender in the greater Convergency—that is, the *sensible* regions outside your borders," Panzi sneered.

Desh had no intention of humoring the madwoman. "This 'sensibility' you boast of is nothing more than the delusions of tyrants. You, along with your collectivist friends and Executive Dunham, are only implementing a system of unlawful seizure and red tape. You and your ideological faction have done nothing but use the power of legislation—and now, the *neglect* of legislation—to promote the tyranny of your insatiable majority. And with that unchallenged authority you illegally gave yourselves, you take the fruits of a man's labor straight from his family's dinner table, all in the name of some sort of pseudo-moral guilt. You then have the audacity to not only waste his wealth on your own personal arsenals, but on those who produce *nothing*, demanding more and always more—more money, more entitlements, more preferential treatment. The corporatist collectivists have redefined the word 'wants' to mean 'needs,' all as part of their core ideology of illogical, altruistic theft."

Both Panzi and Dunham made an attempt to interrupt the Colonial's harangue, but he gave them no chance. He spoke over the first outbreak of personal attacks. "If I may," he said, raising a hand to silence the pair. "I'll tell you what your problem is: Parliamentarian Illoszia, you have absolutely no legitimacy, and you are well aware of it. You hold an unelected position handed to you by Executive Dunham using ABAC's money, and you've allowed yourself to become his loyal lapdog with no willpower of your own. Your accusations of brainwashing within the Colonies is pathetic, seeing as you yourself are fully incapable of forming a single thought or opinion of your own. And now that you've convinced yourself that you hold some special place in Brock Dunham's heart, you're trying to make a name for yourself in the worst ways possible. But what you don't realize is that once you are no longer of any use to him, he will abandon you without a second thought, just as he has everyone else.

"And as for you, Executive Dunham—you are an egomaniac and a narcissist with absurd delusions of grandeur. It's no secret that you think you're equal to God, if not God Himself. You've actively promoted this disturbing cult of personality growing around you. You think that by putting on an air of divinity you can distract people from your mental simplicity, but the people of the League of Arterra have known the truth for some time. Your hubris will be your downfall, Executive. It's only a matter of time before your own followers realize they've followed you not to paradise, but to the edge of a financial cliff, and that you've been shamelessly misleading them all along. You'll find yourself betrayed by your own fanatical voters when your unsustainable system fails and you can no longer provide for their endless needs."

Dunham merely chuckled, throwing Desh off guard, as he'd expected a frenzied response. ABAC's executive replied, "I can't say I'm surprised that a man with a detestable ideology would accuse me of such fanciful crimes of character. You simply hold an inexplicable hatred for *any* society founded on the premise of the *greater good.* Your own society is based only on ridiculous, selfish philosophies. It's no wonder why you have yet to foster any sensibility within your borders."

"There is an undeniable truth behind our philosophies, and consequently, our policies. You yourself have validated the tenets of individualism and the foundations of Arterran society. If there's one thing we've learned, it's that the approach you've taken toward central banking is a fatal one. The Convergent lira is a failure. Your policy of printing an infinite supply of worthless coin has led to a Convergency-wide recession; at this point, a single Colonial Talent is worth more than a life's savings in Convergent lira. The very concept of a galactic currency was a failure before it'd even been implemented, but since you've taken office, Executive Dunham, you've managed to devalue it by more than ninety percent, and numbers are not racist. But I suppose that's the natural consequence of printing money without any valuable resource to back it.

"Your beloved economic experiment has led to nothing but the death of prosperity. So, because the lira has virtually no value at all, I have submitted this petition to the Supreme Court of the United Colonies." Desh opened the file that sat before him and revealed a printed notice, complete with his signature. "Should the Judiciary accept this proposal, the UCA will officially devalue all currencies bought with Convergency debt. The devaluation will be no less than ninety-nine and nine-tenths percent." He passed the notice to Brock Dunham with a satisfied smile.

"You have no right," Dunham growled, seething.

"We have *every* right. We are a sovereign entity, as is every man, woman and child ever born into the Creator's vision. You have no discernible concept of freedom, except for the freedom to exploit one's fellow man. The lira is worthless.

The Colonies will simply be recognizing the truth you've tried so hard to hide."

Panzi nearly fell from her podium. "This is illegal! This is *treason*!" she screamed. She begged Dunham to do something to stop the individualist monsters, but even he didn't seem to know how to respond. In his anger, he gripped the paper until it crumpled between his fingers. "If your Judiciary goes through with this, your actions will collapse every market outside the League!" Panzi barked. "The Children of the Dole will have to spend a year's worth of government checks just to buy a piece of Colonial bread!"

Giles Bronson of the Academic Truth and Eliminating Dissent Organization extended Panzi's list of consequences. "The price of aetherium will skyrocket and *every* non-Arterran shipping company will go *bankrupt*! Billions will *die* when foreign hospitals cannot afford updated medical technology from Aldebaran-Zion! Even more will *starve* when Colonial food exports are too *expensive* to even bring into a foreign port!" he cried, tears of frustration welling in the corners of his eyes. Like all collectivists, his emotions got the best of him in the face of a logical argument.

Sir Byron was the first to comment on his contradictions. "It's amusingly ironic that the collectivists have continuously asserted that the Convergency would be far better off *without* the Colonies and the League of Arterra, but the second they're faced with the exact scenario they've been hoping for, they admit they can't survive without them. So, which is it? Is the League of Arterra a detriment, or the only force keeping your system alive, however begrudgingly?"

Desh agreed. "God willing, the Judiciary will vote on the petition, and, if it does, I'm sure it will approve it. There is no hope whatsoever for the Convergency if it maintains the status quo. But, should the Convergency actually care for its own preservation, the law may be repealed under the following conditions." He addressed Brock Dunham personally and wagged his finger. "Pay attention, Executive

Dunham, because this is the only way you will be able to save your precious government.

"First, the Convergency must sever all central banking ties to the Albian Banking Advancement Conglomerate. It can no longer buy Convergent lira from ABAC in exchange for Convergency debt bonds. The current system is a cancer that must be removed from this Convergency to ensure its survival.

"Second, Congress—including the Executive Council—must be reformed to exclude voting representatives from private and academic entities. ABAC, ATEDO, the CALU and the rest of these corporate whores must be removed from office immediately, as we have been saying for years. They are not sovereign states with an autonomous population, and have no place in this legislature.

"Third, all representatives must henceforth be elected by the constituency; no representative may be appointed to higher positions without a vote by the respective legislature. As such, we deem Panzi Illoszia to be in an illegitimate position, and we call for the reversal of her unlawful role as Lord of Parliament. For true freedom and democracy to prevail, Panzi Illoszia must be deposed, along with Brock Dunham and his cronies. There is no other option."

"I *am* the Lord of Parliament!" Panzi screeched. She outstretched her arms like a crucified deity. "This seat is *mine*! Given to me by *Brock Dunham*! There is no greater legitimacy than *his approval*!" She threw her glass of water and it shattered at Desh's feet. He kicked it aside with only a single drop landing on his Romaean designer shoes. When Panzi ran out of projectiles to hurl at her opponents, she gripped the edges of her desk until her knuckles turned white. "You only want to see me *fall* because you're a *racist*! The *only* reason you're trying to depose us is because of your *bigotry*!"

"And not because of your incompetence, of course," Oksana added.

"I will not give up my seat!"

Desh smiled at Panzi and concluded, "Then the Convergency will collapse, all because of your pride."

Dunham interceded on Panzi's behalf. "No, Executive, the Convergency will *not* fall to pieces," he promised, "because you will not go through with this little plan of yours."

"It is already in the works."

"Your Judiciary won't approve it."

"Popular support will."

There was a look in Dunham's eye, like he knew something Desh didn't. It was an unfamiliar feeling for the Colonial executive, who was used to being a dozen steps ahead of his dim-witted collectivist nemeses. Dunham and Panzi looked to each other as though they were mutual mind readers, coming to some conclusion that was fully lost on their opponent. Dunham fixed his tie and folded his hands on the desk. "If you *do* manage to pass this law, I promise you, it will be a terrible mistake."

"Is that a threat?"

"It might prove to be, if you continue to undermine ABAC's ability to strengthen the Convergent economy. A law like the one you're suggesting will tear this glorious system apart. But *I* have the support of this entire Convergency, Mr. Maru. You might be a role model for your people, but for *mine*, I am the *only* one worthy of adoration. Their belief in me will keep this Convergency alive, and their hatred for my enemies will render you powerless. My word is *law*, for I am their leader. And it is their most urgent command, for *I am their god*."

Panzi glared at Desh with a deceptive grin. "And for his enemies, there will be *no* mercy. You *can't* hope to save yourself, Executive, because you've led your people to *destruction*. Pray to your God all you want, but salvation will *not* be Arterra's when that glorious day comes, because only by submitting yourself to *collectivism* will you be redeemed."

———

Livia knew that Silviano wasn't going to be open to having Selenia in their company. He wasn't one to humor deep thoughts of the supernatural—for him, the Imperial Cult served only to boost him onto a pedestal of social respect. He embraced the role of the god's living spear, and even more zealously pierced the bodies of faithful women and submissive men with downward-turned faces. If his own pleasure truly was a sign of divine communion, then Silviano had most certainly achieved oneness with his god. And if it was nothing more than a natural flood of his essence and ecstasy, he was satisfied nonetheless. Men were easily satisfied, as Livia had come to learn, time and time again.

"He's perfectly content with his religion," Livia said to Selenia as they encroached on the group's sleeping quarters. "Women and men make their pilgrimage to him, and he makes his own pilgrimage into their bodies. Everyone's happy—him, most of all, I'd expect. He's had no shortage of visitors."

"His god must be particularly fond of him for his devotion."

"Maybe so, but I think Silviano's more fond of himself than the god he serves. I'm surprised he hasn't lost his mind yet. The last time he 'gave the god's blessing' was on Telluria."

"Perhaps he's been worshiping in private, with the lights dim behind closed doors? A 'personal rite,' maybe."

"His hand must be very blessed."

Livia welcomed the lighthearted moment, however brief, as humor was something she hadn't had the opportunity to enjoy in quite some time. Her life in the Imperial Temple was solemn, and the pilgrimage was a grave affair, one cut short by even graver circumstances. But she had to admit that she much preferred the chase and the dodging of gunfire to the fate she would have otherwise suffered, had the sacred journey progressed as planned. She'd only narrowly avoided feeling the weight of dozens of pilgrims, one after the other, pressing upon her body. ABAC couldn't have chosen a more perfect time to open fire. She'd rather have felt her flesh pierced by bullets than men.

Selenia told her it wasn't a coincidence. "The Creator allows all things to run their course," she explained, saying that free will was God's only unbreakable law. "Your own intent—your own will—echoed through the Emanation, and it responded, as it always does. You drew yourself into those circumstances, though you were unaware. There can be no coincidences when all events are sparked from the depths of your mind."

It was the union of many wills and many intentions that swept Livia away from the pilgrimage. The ripples through the Emanation brought her to Natharis and into Selenia's company. Their paths crossed at auspicious times, not by chance, nor by divine intervention, but through the strength of their own consciousness. "Never underestimate the power of thought, Livia," Selenia advised. "It is a force that shapes realities and brings great change. Always be mindful, and never let your mind be empty, even in meditation and rest. The most pitiful of men are those who'd prefer to let others do the thinking."

And when Livia heard the sound of skin slapping skin through the dormitory door, she was reminded that Silviano was a man who preferred to let his manhood do the thinking.

"It seems we were wrong about his deprivation," Selenia remarked.

Livia hesitated to open the door. She didn't want to know what, or whom, Silviano had gotten himself into, though the uninhibited squeals that escaped the mouth of the submissive left little to the imagination. She lightly tapped her finger on the biometric scanner and the door slid open without a sound. It opened so quietly that Silviano didn't notice. He kept his eyes locked on the obedient young man whose waist he gripped firmly, who rocked back and forth upon the bed on his hands and knees. Livia's jaw dropped in disbelief;

Selenia shook her head in silent disapproval. Silviano finally saw them. He looked over, and merely grinned. He seemed to have no intention of stopping until he was satisfied.

"Enough!" Livia snapped. She couldn't stand to see Silviano take advantage of a runaway slave. With his olive skin, sandy blond hair and arms decorated with gilded bracelets, she recognized him as a sex slave of the Shatarins. She was disgusted.

Silviano scowled, then pushed the fugitive off the bed and toward the door. "Get out," he groaned. "We're done here." He tossed a handful of lira at the young man's feet for his services. He frantically picked them up off the floor and hurried out into the corridor, slipping his loose-fitting crimson tunic back over his slender body. He kept his gaze low, but for just one moment, he looked up at Livia and caught eyes with her. There were no tears, and his dark eyeliner wasn't running down his cheeks as she'd expected.

The look behind his eyes was all-too familiar to the altaria. It was a numbness that only someone robbed of youth could understand. She wondered how long he'd been forced to endure the shame that she, too, suffered every day. She felt sick knowing that he'd likely been passed around many rooms full of rich Shatarins like an object meant only for their gratification. It was a story she'd heard before. In a way, it made her appreciate her sacred status. She was a whore, and she'd always felt like one, despite what the believers said of her. When they were finished with her, they felt closer to the divine. But when the Shatarins were finished with their harlots, they were immediately forgotten. Silviano had used him just as carelessly, and sent him away without a second thought.

"This is a refugee station," Livia hissed. "That runaway's probably trying to leave that life behind—trying to *forget* it. How could you?"

Silviano pulled his pants back on and made his way across the room. "It's all he knows. It's all *I* know. So, I did it, and so did he. He's never lived any life but this one. I just made him feel at home."

He raised an eyebrow upon noticing Selenia and smiled. "Silviano Martizo," he announced as his introduction. He took Selenia's hand and lightly kissed it—*He just can't help himself, can he?* thought Livia.

"Selenia Santiago de Sonora."

"I wasn't expecting a Mithneshi in my bedroom."

"Put your clothes on," Livia commanded. "Not everyone here is Tellurian." Silviano looked down at his bare torso and shrugged, not seeing any issue with his half-nakedness.

"What? Would the Coven rather me deny my nature? Don't tell me their 'Creator' didn't create sex, too."

"On the contrary," Selenia countered. She stepped into the room and put a hand on Livia's shoulder to keep her from protesting Silviano's state of undress even further. "We believe that it is one of the most powerful ways to connect with His Emanation, and, indirectly, with the Creator Himself." She picked up Silviano's shirt from the floor and handed it to him. "It's a belief familiar to you. But it must be consensual. Nothing in service of God can be compulsory or against one's will."

"And *he* didn't consent, I'm sure," Livia said.

"Well, he didn't complain. Not that anyone ever does," Silviano laughed. Livia wasn't amused, but Selenia didn't bother to acknowledge his arrogance. After he'd pulled his shirt back over his head and made himself mostly presentable, Livia got to the point.

"Get your head out of the gutter and pull yourself together. We're not staying long, and we don't have time for you to go screwing everyone on this station. Pretty soon we'll be on our way to Bhalenjar." Silviano looked surprised at Livia's sudden assertiveness. "And Selenia will be joining us."

"And why is that? Is she as big of a Tellurophile as Mickel Green?"

"You won't get her to obsess over you, if that's what you mean. She's going to Bhalenjar for her own reasons."

"I'm on a pilgrimage of my own," Selenia explained. "But I can't reach the Great Ziggurat of Bhalenjar without your help. I've taken a vow of poverty, and it's something I have to uphold. I can only make the pilgrimage through the charity of others."

"We're not Deists," Silviano reminded her. "Shouldn't you find some *real* believers to tag along with?"

"Natharis is," Livia said.

"Oh, of course—*Natharis* is."

"A 'real' believer isn't marked by his religion, but by his actions," Selenia said. "Charity and goodwill aren't limited to Mithneshi Deists."

"We don't need any more women on the ship. One bleeding-heart altaria and one Muscovian nymphomaniac are enough, if you ask me." With Livia's rejections and Ninotchka's lethal sex drive, Silviano was at his wit's end. Livia knew that while he was secretly terrified of the Muscovite and her advances, he was even more uncomfortable knowing that Livia was the one woman who didn't surrender herself to him at the sound of his voice. Perhaps he didn't want to risk rejection by one more woman.

Selenia wasn't deterred. "Two powerful women are invaluable," she argued, "although acknowledging it might not be something that you're used to. I'd be willing to guess that they've come to your rescue before. Am I wrong?"

Livia smirked at Silviano, who, being forced to recall the ambush at Kojv, was at a loss for words. Selenia continued, "With three women to save you, you'll have absolutely nothing to worry about. Wouldn't you enjoy some peace of mind for a change?"

"I'll have some peace of mind when Livia and I get to Rome and leave all this shit behind us," he replied, as if Livia agreed with him. "I won't keep you from coming with us. But don't be surprised if you get dragged into the same mess we're in."

Even after all of Livia's expressions of doubt, all her blatant opposition and protests, Silviano still thought that she'd return to her sacred duties. How could he have been so blind? Didn't she make it clear enough that her life as an altaria wasn't the life she wanted, or was even meant to live? Earth and its sacred city were as far away in her mind as they were in the universe, light-years away in the darkness of space, just an invisible speck among billions of stars. To her, it was just as irrelevant, just as meaningless, both spiritually and mentally. But for Silviano, it was all he could hope for. He was incapable of seeing any semblance of a larger picture. He had his eyes set strictly on his religious goal of serving not the gods, but himself. Livia wanted no part in it. The pilgrims who used her were selfish, as was he.

But Selenia Santiago encouraged her expanded vision of the world, of her own life and purpose. She understood her, even when Livia thought she never could. The Mithneshi Coven made her feel more at home than the attentive priests of the Temple ever did. She felt more reverence at the base of the station's ziggurat than she ever had at the foot of the god's statue, watching over her—not like a guardian, but an uninvited observer peering through an invisible window. The lifeless, stone eyes conveyed no compassion, despite what she was taught. She didn't want her eyes to become just as dead. She had to fight that future—and Selenia was a strong ally.

———

The Crystalline hospital was a sprawling network of caverns beneath the ruined city. Unlike any medical facility Natharis Ruke had ever been to, it boasted walls of naked rock glistening with droplets of cool water. Any doctor on Aldebaran-Zion would have been horrified by its lack of sterility, the stone floors and the coarse sand upon them. For a Sapien, it would have been unsuitable for any sort of healing. But for the Crystallines, whose bodies were formed from energetic minerals, it was a nurturing environment.

Bright lamps emitted ultraviolet rays into the tunnels, set in niches in the walls. Without the light, the Crystallines would succumb to a fatal fatigue, unable to maintain the integrity of their molecular structures—just as the prisoner had. Natharis prayed that Livia and Silviano would make a quick descent to the planet's surface. They carried the prisoner with them in their shuttle, and until they arrived, all Natharis and Ninotchka could do was wait. As the minutes passed, Natharis worried more for the Crystalline's life.

"That Livia will fuck something up," Ninotchka muttered. "Never trust timid women."

"She's more competent than you give her credit for. She's just not as used to killing as you are."

"With man with her, I suppose you're right, Colonial. Even if Silviano *is* timid in bedroom. I expected more of Tellurian consitor."

"She's made it this far without much help from him."

"She is useless," Ninotchka concluded as she adjusted her leather bustier. "Just like Silviano." Sunlight appeared at the end of the entry tunnel. "Speak of devil."

The roar of the shuttle's engines reverberated through the cavern, and a hot wind rushed past Natharis's face. The handgun at his waist swayed back and forth in its holster. In the entryway, he saw three silhouettes, but had only expected two. The crate carrying the Crystalline hovered in front of them; Silviano pushed it, his identity obvious from the size of his shadowy arms. Livia walked beside him, the light behind her like a halo or a captivating eclipse of the sun. But who was the third figure with the Breathtaker dangling from her hand?

"You are bigger idiot than I thought," Ninotchka snarled. She drew her gun from her side and aimed for the third shadow's head. "Who did you bring with you?"

The stranger stepped into the light. She wore the white, form-fitting garb of a Mithneshi seer. Even with a pistol pointed straight at her, she looked calm, though she clinked the Breathtaker's metal blades together with a flick of her finger. Dark hair fell past her shoulders, and her skin was a deep bronze. She spoke with a slight accent that identified her as a native speaker of Latigón.

"My name is Selenia Santiago de Sonora, seer of the Mithneshi Coven, and I am making my sacred voyage to the Great Ziggurat of Bhalenjar." She turned to address Natharis, clearly recognizing him as a Colonial, and thus, likely a believer. "Your Tellurian friends were generous enough to take me in as a passenger."

"*She* did," Silviano frantically explained, fearful of the burning glare Ninotchka shot his way. He pointed an accusatory finger at Livia.

"You can stifle your jealousy for one more day, can't you?" Livia asked Ninotchka.

The Muscovite squeezed her handgun so tight that her knuckles turned white. "Watch your tongue, sacred slut. There's more than one bullet in this gun."

"Enough," Natharis ordered. In spite of herself, Ninotchka complied, and sighed as she lowered her sidearm. Natharis smiled and stepped forward to shake Selenia's hand. "There's room for one more without Erixen to slow us down."

"We don't know her," Ninotchka argued. "Your blind trust will get us all killed. It almost did before, until I took care of it."

Natharis couldn't say no to Selenia's presence for two reasons: his innate trust of the Coven, and Livia's obvious enthusiasm for her being there. Just making a quick stop at Othonas was enough to satisfy his spiritual needs; bringing a Mithneshi seer along with them to Bhalenjar was an even greater blessing. And Livia, though she practiced a foreign religion and worshiped strange gods, seemed to be particularly enthralled by Selenia—she looked at her the way a student looks upon a respected teacher in awe. He couldn't bear to disappoint her, to take someone away from her who uplifted her as quickly as she'd appeared. He might not have known this Selenia Santiago, but if Livia felt safe around her, then he did as well.

Three Crystallines took away the crate and carried it toward the surgical suite. Natharis approached Livia to caress her shoulders, and asked if she was alright. She slipped her arms around his neck; Ninotchka rolled her eyes at their embrace. Silviano flinched, as though Ninotchka were about to hug him, then stab him in the back.

"Wait—what happened to Erixen?" Livia asked, confused. There was genuine concern in her voice. Natharis touched her hand and explained what had transpired. Neither she nor Silviano expected that he'd even been capable of such calculated betrayal.

"He destroyed our speeders back at Gaas Skaago. He sabotaged the com-systems on our ship, and led us straight into that ambush on Kojv. And then he opened fire on us during the orbital jump. We almost didn't make it."

"He's lucky to have me," Ninotchka boasted, eyeing Livia while slapping Natharis on the shoulder.

"I'm sure he was involved in the prisoner's escape from Jotunheim," Natharis explained. "It was an inside job. And he's just been trying to get it back to ABAC ever since we left Earth."

"Traitor proved incompetent, as usual," Ninotchka scoffed. "I left his body out in desert. Let him rot."

The hum of medical equipment caused the cavern walls to vibrate, making the pebbles on the ground shake and hop. The group looked to the surgical suite; a brilliant light shone through the cracks in the door, and even though they could only see slight slivers of it, they covered their eyes. The Crystallines had activated the technology the dying prisoner so desperately needed. Natharis wished he could have witnessed it, but the two Crystallines at the door kept him and the others from entering—*"A Sapien could never survive in there,"* they warned. *"Be patient. The procedure will be completed soon."*

They waited until the door opened and the Crystallines ushered them in. At the center of the room was a silvery dome, just slightly shorter than Natharis. Its apex was made of a transparent material, not metal, unlike its base. It looked like a nest, meant to cradle a vulnerable creature. The once blinding lights were now just a faint glow emitted from hundreds of tiny diodes on the inner surface of the dome.

"The device produces more ultraviolet radiation than two hundred G-type main-sequence stars," the Crystalline technicians explained, *"so intense that some collectivists have tried to classify it as dangerous 'military technology,' simply because they cannot use it themselves."*

The clear peak of the dome split in two and retracted, exposing the prisoner inside. One technician applied a translator bolt, and the other opened a hidden hatch on the side of the device. The prisoner inside didn't move. The technicians assured Natharis that it'd be a few minutes before it was fully conscious. They were wrong.

"You should have let me die," the prisoner insisted. *"ABAC will stop at nothing to find me. And they will kill anyone who gets in their way."* It still didn't move. *"You have no concept of what they will do to me when they track me down."*

"And you think Jotunheim is comfortable alternative?" Ninotchka asked.

"Look, even *it* says we shouldn't have saved it," Silviano said with arms crossed. "It's a murderer. We should have just let it die. Everyone would have been better off."

"I regret my actions, but I had no choice," the prisoner confessed. *"Jotunheim was the only place where I believed the Conglomerate could not reach me. Ultimately, I was wrong."*

Natharis couldn't understand why anyone would voluntarily sentence himself to the harshest punishments under Arterran law. Jotunheim was where the very worst of society lived out its final days. For someone to actually *want* to go there, and to murder multiple victims to *ensure* his sentencing, there must have been a dire reason, but Natharis couldn't possibly think of one.

"What were you so afraid of? What do they want with you?"

The Crystalline hesitated to respond. A palpable tension filled the air. And just as Natharis thought their questioning would get them nowhere, the prisoner finally chose to answer him. It rose up from its place in the radiation device and stepped out of the metallic nest. Its protean body cracked and popped as it anthropomorphized itself. Natharis stood his ground but grew concerned. He made sure that Livia was outside the Crystalline's line of sight, just in case.

"I will explain myself soon enough," it promised. *"But first, I need to make a call."*

————

The Shard of Diamonds shrank away into the distance, until it was just an indiscernible, hazy dot. Ninotchka piloted the craft into the tachyon vein, and in a shimmering burst of color and energy, the planet disappeared completely, left behind in the openness of free space. She was an undeniably skilled pilot, but she was more adept at operating an ABAC ship than Natharis had expected. Even he had a difficult time interpreting the meanings of some of the words on the displays, which were written in clumsy Unispeak, but they had no choice but to quickly adapt to the foreign—and somewhat backward—technology, given to them by the Crystallines as an act of goodwill. It was the perfect cover. Much to their relief, they anticipated a clean pass through the Veil of Bhalenjar.

The Crystalline, however, wasn't so optimistic. *"It is suicide to bring me to Bhalenjar,"* it asserted, voicing a concern not just for its own safety, but for theirs. *"You might as well call Executive Dunham right now and let him know I am coming."*

"We don't have a choice," Natharis replied. "We've exhausted every possible option. We thought the Rosc might help us, and they stabbed us in the back. The Mithneshi won't get involved because of their vow of neutrality. And we'll never get back into the League flying an ABAC ship, or the ship we had before this one. The Colonial consulate on Bhalenjar is our best bet." He looked up as Ninotchka exited the cockpit, having activated the autopilot. She sat down across from him and listened to their conversation.

"Who'd you plan on calling for help, anyway?" Natharis asked.

"*A past colleague, whom I have not seen or heard from since before my arrest. With any luck, she still lives on Albion.*"

"With any luck?" Ninotchka scoffed. "We need *reliability*, not luck. What good is ex-colleague of yours if you don't even know how to contact her?"

"*I cannot know for certain, but we were quite close. She was my confidante, and I was hers. She would do anything for me, as I would for her. We worked together for years. You see, before my arrest, I was a high-ranking scientist working for the Albian Banking Advancement Conglomerate.*"

"Murderer *and* ABAC pawn?" Ninotchka barked. "We should have let him die!" Natharis kept her from drawing her weapon; he pushed her foot down when she tried to aim her stilettos at the Crystalline instead.

"*I never would have worked for them had I known the true purpose behind my research,*" the Crystalline confessed. "*The project was top secret—most of the Conglomerate's research department did not even know it existed. At first, I did not question the secrecy. After all, we were told that only Executive Dunham himself was entitled to such knowledge. Even the most loyal of supporters could never be fully trusted. But it was only a matter of time before the secret was revealed. And I was the first to learn it.*

"*She stood by the project, unaware of its true purpose; I, however, could not. So, I defected from the Conglomerate and fled to the League of Arterra. My colleagues were under the impression that the Arterrans wrongfully detained me—a misconception that I regret, as it only strengthened their hatred of your people. It was then that I committed my unforgivable crimes. In my desperation, I saw no other option, though I am ashamed to admit it.*

"Even in the League, I was not safe from ABAC. I was an apostate to collectivism, and therefore, good as dead. Brock Dunham is not a forgiving man, and there was no hope of escape, no matter how far I ran. But Jotunheim… The stories about its impregnability, its inescapable horrors, all led me to believe I would be safe there. Arterran interrogations would be a summer's stroll compared to what Dunham would have had them do to me.

"Those women did not deserve what I did to them, nor did the one boy. No person deserves that. But I knew your laws, and I knew your punishments. Any less of a crime and I would have continued to be within ABAC's reach, even in prison. I needed maximum security. If I were to carry such guilt within me, I should have at least been safe from capture. But even miles below the frozen surface of Jotunheim, they found me.

"Ironically, it was the same technology that I researched that they used to seize me."

"What technology?" Natharis asked. "In the entire history of the Judiciary, no one has ever successfully orchestrated an escape from Tartarus. We had evidence of some sort of tachyon vein anomaly, but the science required for that kind of vein manipulation is hundreds of years away—and that's being optimistic."

"ABAC has been working on that very science for years. Of course, I knew the immediate purpose of my work: to covertly develop the technological capability to manipulate and reroute natural tachyon veins. Though to a layperson it might not sound so easy, the task was simple enough. I worked with a brilliant team, but I must admit that we stood on the shoulders of geniuses to achieve our goals.

"The Procyon developed the technology in the distant past. They constructed a small collection of devices that we have labeled 'tachyon anchors' for our purposes. We do not fully understand their intended use, as there were too few of them to be of any real consequence. But for reasons unknown, the Procyon abandoned their project. Like many Procyon artifacts, the anchors were located in Arterran space, as the Procyon

homeworld was once located within those boundaries. But the Colonials were completely unaware of their existence, and it was by mere luck that ABAC stumbled upon them while unlawfully trespassing on foreign territory.

"Clearly, ABAC had no legal right to the tachyon anchor technology, and no right to cross the borders in the first place. But Executive Dunham is a clever man and a shrewd politician. He is well versed in subverting the law, believing himself to actually be the law.

"My team and I reverse-engineered the technology and created dozens of new tachyon anchors. We asserted that they should not be deployed until the final testing phases were complete, but Dunham insisted on it. ABAC placed them at various strategic coordinates between major tachyon veins. I had originally thought that they had meant our research to be solely for the purpose of gaining knowledge—to glorify ABAC's name and create a legacy not only of social progress, but scientific innovation. But once they began to construct additional anchors, I realized their true purpose. I fled hoping that my absence might hinder their progress. Evidently, they proved successful nonetheless."

Ninotchka looked unimpressed. "So what? They wanted faster travel?" she asked. "Maybe creating more direct routes is convenient, but it is not particularly sinister."

Natharis, however, suspected it had a different purpose. His eyes lit up when he came to a disquieting conclusion. "They don't want to travel faster. They want to control transit."

"Precisely. Imagine what ABAC could do if it could cut off a system from its natural vein. It could force every planet in the Convergency to comply with its policies by threatening to remove them from interstellar trade. It is a fate that no society would ever choose to suffer. ABAC policies are destructive in themselves, but an even graver demise would come from complete isolation.

"ABAC uses its position as the Convergency's central bank to acquire what it needs to construct its anchor network; it then uses its unwarranted political power to keep quiet those who would hinder the project or expose it. Very few even know of its existence. I suspect that

my research team will be threatened into silence, if not executed at Brock Dunham's command. It is only a matter of time.

"This is why it is imperative that I contact my colleague. The network will ultimately be activated from Bhalenjar—at the new central banking tower, if I am not mistaken, as the planet is the primary hub to and from which the majority of tachyon veins run. She alone has the access codes to both activate it, and deactivate it. For the sake of the greater Convergency, the codes must be given to the higher authorities. You have expressed your desire to reach the Colonial consulate. Should my colleague agree to transmit the access codes, I will not hesitate to give them to you, such that you might hand them over to the Colonials."

"How do you know she isn't dead yet?" Ninotchka asked coldly.

"I do not, but she is my only chance at rectifying the problem I helped to create. We both made copies of the classified data, without ABAC's knowledge—I proposed the idea, but only to keep it safe, and not to use for our own gain. I stored the data as all Crystallines would, coded into my molecular structure. She kept hers on a disc, which I hope she still has in her possession. Unfortunately, because of the damage I sustained and the subsequent, intense revival procedure, the data I have stored within me is incomplete. Fragmented access codes are useless. I need her."

For a moment, nobody spoke. Natharis's mind raced with the same thoughts of duty that he'd held since his first days at the Judicial Academy. He couldn't sit back and allow such a plot to unfold. He'd known the Crystalline was important to ABAC, but not in the way he'd come to learn. He hadn't, however, expected that the prisoner would be even more significant to the greater picture of the Convergency. It wasn't just a matter of getting back to the League anymore. It was a matter of saving it.

"We'll inform the consulate. If we get the codes, then great. If not, we won't need them if the Judiciary sends in troops to disable the system."

"Perfect way to start war," Ninotchka interjected. "This 'colleague' is probably dead by now. We need to be more subtle. We will storm tower ourselves."

"First time I've ever heard a Muscovite advocate subtlety," Natharis muttered. Ninotchka glared back without a response. She stroked the gun strapped to her thigh out of habit.

"I would have expected prisoner to *want* to avoid Colonial authorities. He'll be detained once we walk through front door."

"I have accepted my fate," the Crystalline stated. *"I have brought this punishment upon myself, and I will not try to escape it. Surrendering the codes will be my final act. I will atone for my crimes and I will die without guilt. My colleague cannot say no. It will be my dying wish."*

––––––––––

The last thing Livia remembered was staring out into the pulsing blue light of the tachyon vein. She recalled Selenia's voice, asking her why she was so entranced by the sight just beyond the sailship's windows. She felt like she'd been posed the question in the distant past, and the memory felt hazy and remote. She understood that it had happened, but it seemed too dreamlike to be real. She knew she told Selenia that she'd thought she would never see anything outside the Imperial Temple. And she was aware that the new world she found herself standing in was truly a dream, but it seemed realer than reality.

She was running through an ancient forest, though she had no idea how she'd gotten there, or where she was going. She felt rich, damp earth beneath her bare feet, cool and fertile between her toes. The air was fragrant and fresh, and shafts of light shone through the warm mist that floated beneath the canopy. She danced in the golden sunlight, beneath the primeval trees that surrounded a tranquil clearing like temple columns, and she reveled in the wonders of an untouched world.

The noble screech of a mighty bird broke the forest's silence, and Livia looked up to the sky to see a beautiful eagle soaring above her. She was drawn to it, knowing what it'd symbolized so many times before—surely it was another vision of Natharis. She followed its lead as it glided through the trees until she reached another circular clearing in the woods. There was a single tree standing at the center of the grove, massive, with a laced trunk like a spiral reaching up to the sky. Silvery moss crept up the sides of the tree, shining with gold highlights in the sun. The eagle made the tree its perch, landing among its crystal leaves.

Livia stepped toward the tree to get a closer look at the eagle. It was majestic, more regal than any she'd ever seen, and realized that it wasn't the same bird of prey that had soared through her past visions. Its brown feathers were tipped with gold; it didn't have the white face she was used to seeing. *Who could it be?*

The tranquility of the scene was short-lived. On the far side of the tree, the green grass began to wither, and the blight spread across the clearing until the greenery faded and died. The earth turned to stinking mud, bubbling with murky water. Livia gasped in horror as a figure emerged from beneath the swampy ground; a head rose through the mud, set atop a twisted, spindly body. Wiry, disheveled hair fell over bony shoulders, and the creature was only vaguely feminine. She, or it, panted wildly and foamed at the mouth. Her mud-slick fingers were wrapped tightly around a hunting rifle pulled from the earth. Livia recoiled in fear.

The hideous woman grinned, flashing a broken set of sharp, yellow teeth; she pointed the rifle up at the golden eagle. Livia tried to scream, to stop the grotesque hunter, but she was frozen in place. She wanted to look away but was incapable. The crack of the gunshot echoed through the forest. Livia cried out in despair.

"No!"

As quickly as she'd appeared, the heartless killer vanished, and the forest was still once again. And upon the ground lay a man, encircled by a halo of gilded feathers. She recognized him immediately. The Colonial executive's body, naked, but not covered in blood, was motionless upon the bed of feathers, his eyes open but lifeless. His arm was outstretched, his finger pointing toward the horizon. She looked into the distance. Over the trees rose the Great Ziggurat of Bhalenjar, with a brilliant light shining from its apex. She stared into the blinding beacon; a ringing in her ears overtook her. Then she awoke with a startled gasp, the forest revealed to be only a fantasy, and the galaxy's greatest leader still alive somewhere far away.

Restless and shaken, she tried to bring her mind back to the present. The others on the ship slept soundly. But Natharis, still awake, came to her. She found comfort in his arms, and drifted back to sleep, without dreams or visions. She slept with a stillness she hadn't felt in ages. It was a forgetfulness she welcomed with all her heart, a surrender to unconsciousness she needed more than anything. The strength of Natharis's embrace was all she held in her mind, and all she needed to remember. It was her only thought, her first and her last.

22

"May no society come to witness the horrors of aetherium as a tool of war. Though that rare element once breathed life into the embryo of galactic civilization, it may well prove to be its swift destroyer."
—H'jani President Stel'zhii M'jal, after the development of aetherium weapons on T'jan.

SELAS HADN'T GOTTEN A GOOD LOOK at the Ssimvomai Center for the Lost when the caravan first arrived, but now that he could view it at a distance, he realized that it was quite an impressive structure. The refugee station shined like its own twinkling, starry sky, with thousands of windows glowing white and cyan in the darkness of space. There were hundreds of domed habitation pods, each a mile or more in diameter, floating in concentric rings around the center of the complex. The heart of the Ssimvomai Center was crafted in the form of a massive ziggurat, the Mithneshi's sacred symbol; it looked ancient and weathered, as if it'd seen the passing of millennia and the whole of the history of the Convergency.

The station saw transients from all walks of life, but the Coven devoted most of its resources to children, who made up the majority of refugees. They were sent away by their parents in the Commune, who saved up what little money they had just to give their young sons and daughters a chance at a better life. The heartbreaking stories were all too common, and more often than not, the mothers and fathers stayed behind, left to labor for the rest of their lives for the sake of the avaricious Children of the Dole. The Mithneshi gave the children the opportunity to grow up in a compassionate environment and become adults who had an endless number of open doors to choose from. The Gameer had a similar life experience as orphans from the fallen Earth, but had never found a stable place to mature as a people.

Some of the caravan's cruisers were still moored at the station in the distance. Selas, however, was aboard one of the few that'd been isolated for engine maintenance. There were four such ships: three cargo freighters and the agrarian *Massyulan*, all of which required intensive repairs. The inspection and repair of the aetherium drives were time-consuming and dangerous tasks, which Selas wasn't at all qualified to carry out. Only the most experienced engineers were able to contribute, as one small error could quickly result in an unspeakable disaster. Instead, Selas took part in patching small breaches in the passenger carrier's hull. With welding gear in one hand and a slack length of tether in the other, he glided along the side of the ship toward the next gash, marked by a bright violet flare.

He'd been doing such work for the past few years, trained by his father and other grown men around him. It wasn't difficult or particularly risky, but even though he knew the tether was as close to unbreakable as possible, he still clutched it as tightly as he did when he was an amateur. He pulled himself over to the first ragged hole; he'd seen impact damage like that many times before, most of which wasn't any more than a few inches across. He pulled down the reflective visor on his helmet and switched on the welding torch. It sparked and burst with blinding light as he touched it to the metal hull. In the vacuum he heard nothing, but imagined it hissing and crackling. Space walks were always a less sensory experience than imagined.

His older sister Evua was jealous of his role as the family spacewalker, but he was sure she would have found it fairly boring. There was no sound other than that of his own breathing and the thoughts in his head. His whole family was still on the station, some probably worrying about him, others unconcerned. Women weren't generally permitted to do such work, out of a collective concern for their reproductive health, as exposure to cosmic rays too often left them barren. As for his father, he had a nasty ear infection that affected his balance, and when even healthy people had trouble orienting themselves in microgravity, his condition kept him inside on a solid floor. Selas thought of his little sister and turned to face the Ssimvomai Center. He waved to her, even though he was too far for her to see. For a moment, he wished she could enjoy the view with him.

But Selas wasn't alone. There were some other men working on the hull a few dozen yards away, chatting through their com-links. Their conversation about unfamiliar women didn't interest him. He was just about to shut off his radio when he received an unexpected transmission.

"Who you wavin' to?"

Arkos kicked himself off the scaffolding below and drifted upward toward Selas, who wasn't in much of a mood for talking. Arkos was tolerable in small doses but had the irritating tendency to treat Selas as if he were a decade younger, instead of the two years younger that he really was. He also had a penchant for asking invasive questions, unable to mind his own business and equally unable to understand how his questions could even be considered intrusive. Selas couldn't blame him that day, though. Most of the men floating outside the ship had little else to do but engage in idle conversation. He, however, had no desire to be one of them.

"No one's gonna see you out here, y'know."

"I'm not an idiot. I know that."

"Then why bother?"

"Made a promise, that's all. And I'm not saying any more about it."

"And I promise you that there ain't no one to save you if you let go of that there tether. Mithneshi's blessin' or not, you'd best hold on tight."

Selas pointed over his shoulder to his back, to where the tether connected to his suit, right between his shoulder blades. Arkos shrugged, knowing he'd been caught exaggerating. There wasn't much for the boy to worry about. The one in the most danger was Arkos. One shove and he'd be floating away with little hope of return. Selas smiled at the thought.

"You ain't doin' it right," Arkos critiqued, pulling himself closer to the ship's hull. He circled a finger around a tiny gash in the metal that Selas had missed. He pulled out his own welding torch and with one quick burst of light, he sealed the hairline fracture shut.

"I know what I'm doing," the boy replied. "I wasn't finished yet." He was lying.

"With half-assed work like that, the ship's gonna run out of air. You really wanna be stuck on this station even longer while they clean up your mess?"

"I don't mind it here, but apparently you do."

"Listen, I ain't a believer, and I ain't never gonna be one. You can listen to all that self-righteous Mithneshi bullshit all you want, but no matter what they say, this ain't a magical world and there ain't no Creator behind it. If there was, we wouldn't be wanderin' around from planet to planet with nowhere to go. He ain't answering your prayers, or anyone's."

Selas wanted to argue to the contrary, but was dismayed when he realized that there wasn't a thing he could say to convince Arkos otherwise. He was right—they'd been wandering for generations, with no end to their exile in the foreseeable future. Their faith hadn't manifested a planet for them to call their own, and it hadn't brought them any sympathy, or even recognition, from the greater Convergency. It didn't protect them from exploitation or deliver them from those who'd wish to use them and abandon them. All it did was help Selas sleep at night. Or at least it once did.

Arkos couldn't move on from the subject, even with Selas's silence indicating his discomfort. "I've seen a lot of shit in my day," he said—*"My day," like he's so fucking old,* thought Selas— "but I can tell you there ain't no God, there ain't no Emanation, and you ain't got no guardian angels flyin' over you to keep you safe." He paused, and looked upward. "Ha! Look at that!"

Three small ships blazed overhead in formation; their thrusters glowed bright with plasma, as brilliant as the welding torches. They rushed past them in such a blur that Selas couldn't get a clear look at them, but he knew by their size and speed that they couldn't have come from the caravan. "Those aren't ours," he murmured. He let go of the tether and drifted several feet from the hull, too curious to continue his work. Arkos only laughed, and asked if he, in his superstition, thought they might be heavenly beings descending right on cue.

"With drives like that, they've got to be strike craft," Selas speculated.

"Whatever they are, they're headed for the station. They'd better slow down or the Coven's gonna have some nasty repairs on their hands." But the ships didn't decelerate. They didn't plan to dock.

"What the—"

The squadron split in three directions and sped off away from the station; a flare shot from the lead ship straight toward the central ziggurat. Selas quickly realized it wasn't a flare. Arkos grabbed him and forced him to look away, shoving him against the hull.

"Cover your eyes!"

He heard nothing. He felt the dull pain of his brow striking the inside of his helmet as he crashed into the ship, and the pressure of Arkos's hand against his shoulder. The skin of his back burned in a way he'd never felt before, like he was being seared by flames deep into his body, even through the thick padding of his spacesuit. He saw a flash of light in the corner of his eye; he tried to turn around, but Arkos kept him pinned, unable to look back. He knocked the other boy in the side and whipped his head around.

The sphere of light was immense, and it glowed an icy blue from its core, exploding outward so rapidly that it filled Selas's field of vision. It looked like a supernova detonated not by nature or time, but by the destructive will of man. It consumed every structure that surrounded the station, immolating them in its fiery wake; Selas braced himself for a certain death. But when he closed his eyes and prayed to his God, the blast stopped, and shrunk inward, imploding on itself until it was just a tiny point of light. He would have sighed in relief, but he couldn't exhale. He kept his breath locked in his lungs. It wasn't over yet.

The ring of plasma and burning debris came without warning. It opened like the terrifying eyes in his dreams, out of the blackness, shining with nameless colors. Selas saw the wall of shrapnel rushing outward; he tried to warn Arkos, but the radiation had killed his com-link. He scrambled up the side of the cruiser to find refuge behind the shield scaffolding. He looked downward toward the other boy. His tether was caught—he couldn't untangle it.

The furious wave crashed upon him. The initial shock kept him pinned to the ship's surface; Selas averted his eyes in horror as the deluge of metal shards pummeled Arkos's body. One severed the tether; the rest slashed holes in his suit. The fatal blade that came last slammed into his stomach, and surrounded by weightless spheres of blood, Arkos drifted upward, lifeless and still. Selas peeked over the scaffolding and screamed as the boy's ravaged torso floated before him. He met eyes with the dead and felt sick to his stomach. He tasted bile but swallowed it down.

The ship lurched beneath him, and he almost lost his grip on the scaffolding. He slipped backward and his tether snagged on a sharp sensor array protruding from the hull. The antenna sliced through the cable and Selas sailed freely through space, scraping his gloved hands along the surface to keep himself close. Plumes of pressurized atmosphere escaped through the breaches in the hull, geyser after geyser erupting from each impact of white-hot debris. He pulled himself along the surface until he'd reached the underbelly of the cruiser, shielded from the lethal bombardment. He frantically searched for the airlock, though he knew the cruiser wouldn't be habitable for long. He needed to find help. He didn't know what the Gameer might do to escape, and he didn't want to be caught outside when—or if—they did.

He fiddled with his com-link but could do nothing to fix it. He tried not to panic, but he had no cable to follow back to the airlock. Without his life-giving umbilical, he had no extra oxygen, no winding trail of breadcrumbs to lead him back to safety. Instinctively, he prayed to the Creator, whispering the words he'd recited since childhood.

"Infinite Creator, Prime Mover of Heaven and Earth, we take refuge in your eternal peace…"

He gasped when he felt someone grip his ankle. He opened his eyes and kicked without thinking, but the man in the spacesuit beneath him waved his hand gently, attempting to calm him down. He knew he was safe, but didn't care. In his brief moment of security the gravity of what he'd witnessed finally struck him. He screamed but the man couldn't hear him. He fought as his rescuer pulled him toward the hidden airlock, trying to get one last look at the radiant nebula that was once called the Ssimvomai Center for the Lost.

He hadn't heard their voices cry out in terror or despair, if they even had a chance to. All he heard was his own screams, as inaudible to those around him as the final cries of the immolated dead. It had to have been a dream. The horrors he'd seen were always locked away in his nightmares. But this one was unfamiliar and utterly devastating. He willed himself to consciousness, back to the waking world where his mother was cooking and his sisters were in the next room sleeping. He cried out when he realized his eyes were already open, filled with tears.

———

The great silk curtains were drawn back, and the spotlights on the Executive Council intensified. The Congressional chamber was titanic, with a vaulted ceiling that lent to a sense of grave emptiness. Like an ancient arena awaiting a gladiator fight, the chamber encircled the Council's raised platform with concentric rings of slowly occupied seats. The members of both the Convergent Parliament and Senate took their places. Colonial Executive Desh Maru sat at his desk, completely surrounded by those who hated him and wished him dead, and those who held him in the highest regard. He took a deep breath. The room's aura of tension made the air seem thin, his breathing shallow.

Mireille tapped her desk to catch her fellow executives' attention. "Something's not right," she speculated, looking around the Congressional chamber. "The collectivists are quiet for once."

"There are rumors," Oksana added, "that their leadership has some 'dramatic announcement' to make."

Sir Byron shook his head. "Look at those animals down there. Always up to no good."

All four executives heard an arrogant chuckle to their right. Brock Dunham had arrived. His followers saluted their pontiff with boisterous applause, as was their routine act of devotion. For once, he didn't acknowledge his flock. He grinned at the Arterrans and took his seat.

"What's *that* shit-eating grin for?" Sir Byron scoffed.

"You look quite happy for man with endless record of failures," Oksana sneered.

Dunham merely folded his hands on his desk and smiled. "Just sit back and watch the show, Executives. It's going to be a good one—I promise you."

Then entered the brazen Lord of Parliament. Panzi Illoszia marched smugly down the center aisle like an illegitimate queen in her royal procession, but she was greeted not by the brassy blare of trumpets or the beating of war drums, but by a cacophony of screams and cries that seemed to support something that Desh couldn't identify. Had she accomplished something he had no knowledge of? What could she have possibly done? The only success she'd had since taking her position as Lord of Parliament was in destroying the very foundations of the galactic economy with her lust for punitive taxes. She and her beloved teacher had done it together. And for reasons Desh didn't understand, Dunham rose from his seat to salute his loyal follower. It was the first time he'd ever seen the executive show a sign of respect to anyone but himself. She must have done something truly great in the service of collectivism. To the few sensible representatives left, it must have been something abominable.

Oksana couldn't contain her laughter. Dunham shook his head in disgust; Panzi didn't even acknowledge Oksana's heckling. It was another action that Desh had never seen or anticipated. For once, Panzi didn't lash out, fiercely defensive. She didn't scream obscenities at Oksana, insult her for her individualist beliefs, or call her a selfish, ignorant war criminal. She stayed cool and collected, and ascended to her podium. She cleared her throat. Desh braced himself for the worst.

"Look around you, dear members of Congress. You sit here today among the three great houses; senators, parliamentarians and executives alike have gathered here to witness a profound change in the course of history. What do you see, loyal collectivists? Are you still outnumbered? Are you still a voiceless minority in this Convergency? A quiet but desperate voice, unheard and overlooked?" She looked about, pointing into the crowd. "*No!* Not any longer!" she shouted with conviction. "I have *seen* collectivism grow and transform, from a grassroots movement among the oppressed and forgotten, to a force that *no* power in this galaxy can stop. Each day, more foolish individualists come to their senses and realize that the greater good *cannot* and *will not* be defeated. Their battle is lost, and soon, their war as well. Arterra *is* on the decline. We *will* see its collapse within our lifetime. A civilization *cannot* hope to survive when it so pointlessly opposes the will of the people. *The greater good prevails!*"

Desh had to shout over the thunderous applause to counter Panzi's baseless argument. "Offer us proof, then, Parliamentarian Illoszia. I do believe the people of this Congress—and of this Convergency—deserve to know the facts and numbers before they're forced to make such an important judgment for themselves. Your talking points serve little purpose other than to placate your followers and irritate your enemies. If you truly want to win this war of yours, then explain yourself. You've gone in verbal circles for years and said nothing of consequence. You *do* have evidence to support your argument, don't you?" He didn't give the Lord of Parliament a chance to respond. "No, of course you don't. Because only a delusional, washed-up, repugnant Lord of Parliament would convince herself that Arterra's days are coming to an end. You profess your victory while the facts unanimously indicate that you are suffering a shameful and devastating defeat. Admit it, Lord of Parliament: You have lost your war."

Panzi smirked. "No, Executive. This Congress will *no longer* humor your ignorance. You and your cronies are lucky that we've even tolerated you for this long. But I'm afraid your *selfish*, *hateful* rhetoric is becoming quite the bore. You can keep beating your dead horse all you want, but while its carcass rots and crumbles into dust, the Commune is *thriving* on the horizon. Soon enough, you'll be *forced* to make a choice: either submit to the greater good, or be cast out into the cold wasteland of history."

"You, nor your children, nor your children's children, will ever see the day when Arterra submits to the will of those who wish to destroy her. Say what you want, but you don't have the influence you need to preserve your 'greater good.' Your position is irrelevant. You have no real power."

He heard the hiss of doors sliding open and the crack of their weight as they retracted violently into the walls. Every executive looked up; Desh took his eyes off the Lord of Parliament and clenched his fists at what he saw. Soldiers emerged from every side of the Congressional chamber, automatic weapons in their hands, the flag of Bahía Brumosa and ABAC branded on their chests. With a shouted command from a masked squad leader, they raised their firearms, pointing them into the crowd. The red dot of a laser sight glowed below Desh's ribs. Oksana had one on her chest, as did her allies.

"What the hell is the meaning of this?" Desh barked.

"This is the *last* time you underestimate me, Executive. Your denial of the Commune's strength was your biggest mistake—your *deadliest* mistake.

"You've *lied* to us for long enough. So, as we speak, your symbol of *'freedom'* and *'free will'* is finally getting the retribution it deserves. The Mithneshi's day of reckoning has arrived, Mr. Maru, and they have been devoted to *destruction*. I have personally ordered the demolition of a Mithneshi refugee station, using the aetherium weapons the Convergency has given us, launched by ships granted to the

Commune with taxpayer money. This is an act of *justice*, Mr. Maru—and you *love* justice, don't you? *You* brought this punishment upon them, Executive, for your *stubbornness* and *ignorance*. Think of the children *screaming!* Think of them crying out for their mothers as they wait for death, unable to escape the missiles raining down upon them! *And your selfishness pulled the trigger!*

"*No longer* can the League of Arterra deny the strength and influence of the Commune in this Convergency. We *are* a superpower, Mr. Maru. *We* are the rival your people thought they'd never see. *We* are the truly prosperous—the *truly righteous! We are the protectors of the greater good!*"

"*This is an act of war!*" shouted Sir Byron.

"One aetherium warhead is *nothing* in face of full Muscovian arsenal," Oksana threatened. "Your cities will *burn.* You accuse Tsardom of war crimes? Now you will see them, and weep at loss of your pathetic, backward worlds."

"You will regret this," Desh growled, "as will your supporters."

"Oh, *no*, Executive," Panzi replied. "My supporters outnumber yours, and their numbers continue to grow. And with the Commune's strength more undeniable than ever, *nothing can stop me.*

"I am *no longer* the Lord of Parliament, Executive. I am the *Supreme Doge* of this Interstellar Convergency! *I* have ascended to the throne at the right hand of Brock Dunham, and *you*, Executive, lie defeated beneath my feet! Your precious '*liberty*' is in *my* hands now, Mr. Maru! *You will follow my commands, or it will perish!*"

"Liberty is an *idea*—a *principle*," Desh countered, his tone unshaken. "And even you, with your imaginary position of power, cannot destroy the indestructible."

"And that's where you're *wrong*, Executive. *Your* power is fictitious, not mine. Any and every proposal is subject to my veto; laws will be passed *at my will.* Your vote means nothing, Mr. Maru, and mine means *everything. I* am more powerful than the entire Council, and there is *nothing* you can do to take that power from me, for *Brock Dunham supports it*, and his will is the expression of higher law."

"Now you will be an even bigger puppet for Dunham. He's the one calling the shots. And no matter what you say, you will always be a mindless pawn in his political game. He doesn't love you. He uses you, like he uses everyone for his own gain. You are living a dangerous lie."

"*I am his most cherished disciple! I am a true believer!*" Panzi insisted, tears welling up at the corners of her eyes. "*And your heresy will no longer go unpunished.* Goodbye, Mr. Maru. Hell is waiting for you on the other side."

Mireille cried out; Sir Byron jumped up from his desk. Gasps and screams resounded from the individualists on the floor of Congress. But the loudest sound was the crack of a single gunshot, fired at the Supreme Doge's command. Without another word, Desh covered the wound in his stomach, and blood trickled through his fingers. He fell to the floor. No one rushed to help him, as all were paralyzed with fear. And the collectivists cackled like hyenas over a kill.

––––––––––

Tageron set down his pen and sat back in his chair. He took a deep breath and sighed in relief. The deal was done: he was the owner of a new, massive plot of land. It wasn't on his own planet, as the government would never have allowed such a purchase. It was on an alien world, tens of light-years away from the economic bondage of Hatal-Om.

He found the planet Iyrkarim on a registry of newly terraformed worlds. He gave it little thought after reading its name on a trampled flyer, assuming it was too good to be true. But since that day, he heard its name more often, whispered by honest business owners and the financially oppressed. After doing his research, he learned that the planet was indeed the home of an exodus of economic and political refugees—*Productive, hard workers*, he thought, *the wrongfully punished.* He considered himself one of them, as well as his employees. Iyrkarim was to be their new home, and his new place of business, where they'd all be safe from the clutches of collectivism.

He financed the purchase of a hundred square kilometers with his own savings and with help from the few right-minded businesspeople left on Hatal-Om. They made the joint decision to construct a new city, one that would surpass Tarem in every way imaginable, and would be a safe haven for entrepreneurs and average people who wanted to enjoy the fruit of their labor instead of having it stolen from them. They were to name the city Tarem-Sai—"Tarem's Lineage," so their children, and their children's children, would never forget the tragic history that led to their exile.

His fellow colonists worked diligently on the ground; he watched from his office window, overlooking their operations with a smile. They started in the early morning after the transports had arrived. Tageron made sure to arrange for the cargo ships as quietly as possible, and filed the necessary paperwork with the planetary government to permit the landing. He had no choice but to lie on his applications and state that their purpose was to deliver a shipment of pure gold bars as a gift for the city's union bosses. He was surprised they bought it.

In reality, the transports were to be loaded with his company's precious mass drivers—the key to his business and the remarkable success he and his employees had once enjoyed. That day, he gave the brainwashed unionized employees "the day off," just to get them out of the way. Naturally, they celebrated their mandated lack of work. Without the union presence, efficiency increased a hundredfold. Those who remained were the workers who still held a desire to earn a livelihood through their own hard work, rather than sucking the blood of others. Once their work was complete, they and their families would be on their way to Iyrkarim, and they wouldn't look back. But Tageron had one more invitation to offer.

He searched for Magas Ingir's mobile number among his contacts and selected it; he poured himself a drink while the ringtone sounded. From what Tageron had heard, Magas was out of work again. Tageron had found him a job within hours of letting him go, but it seemed that the unions followed him even to his new place of employment and crucified him a second time. People like the union boss Quba Vaski knew no limits. They would follow a man to the ends of the earth to punish him for violating the union's right to mediocrity.

"Hello? Tageron?" Magas answered, a shakiness in his voice. He sounded fearful.

"Magas, if I were to offer you a way out of this hellhole, would you take it?"

"I'd do anything to get out of here. You know that."

"Splendid. Then I have a proposal for you."

Tageron explained his situation, starting from the very beginning. While Magas already knew why he had no choice but to fire him, Tageron felt the need to reiterate his regret. He told him about the government's constant tax hikes targeting him specifically and the union's relentless vendetta against him. But Tageron wasn't the only one having union trouble. Magas was having problems of his own.

"My family can't even feel safe in our own home," Magas grieved. "Mr. Vaski made sure to send my name, my number and address to every union employee. They've vandalized my auto, smashed my windows and sent constant threats to me and my wife. We even had a break-in last week." He sounded like he might lose his composure. "They're barbarians, Tageron. All of them."

"I'm well aware, and that's why I'm leaving. I'm taking every last hard-working person in this city with me, and I'd like you to come as well. There's no future left in Tarem for you or your family. It's about time you seized a better opportunity."

Magas was at a loss for words. Tageron smiled. "Gather your belongings and bring your wife and kids to my office at sundown. We're leaving at dawn. The others are prepping the transports as we speak."

"Is this really happening?" Magas wondered, overwhelmed with hope. "Tageron, I don't know how I can repay you. I already owe you my life—twice over, now."

Tageron chuckled. "You can repay me by making sure you never utter the word 'collectivist' again once we've left this god-forsaken rock. We're starting over, Magas, and the parasites won't follow us this time. We won't let the bastards steal our livelihood any longer." He looked out the window at the transports and grinned. "The future is ours, Magas. And they will have no part in it."

———

Pentakiya's hands were shaking when she hung up the phone. At first, she didn't recognize the voice on the other line. It was digital—fluent, but recognizably artificial—so she thought it might have been just an automated junk call. But when she asked for the caller's name and heard *"Rocky"* as a response, she froze. It was the last name she expected to hear. She hadn't heard it spoken in months, except in her own head. In truth, she never expected to hear it again.

She'd always wondered how she'd react if he simply reappeared in her life, but her hypothetical reaction was nowhere near as complex as reality. Excitement, disbelief, anger—she couldn't decide which, as it was a painful mix of all three, and an overall feeling that she couldn't fully comprehend or stomach. Her nerves led to nausea, then a loss for words. She stuttered. She had too few words to say; at the same time, she had too many.

But how else should she have reacted? After such a long time of not knowing where he was, or if he was even alive, what was she supposed to say? A wave of euphoria overtook her, a rush of pure excitement and joy. Then she learned what had happened. Her mood immediately soured; her belief turned to disbelief. The true story was nothing like what she'd been told. It wasn't at all what she wanted to believe, all to fit her own worldview.

The Colonials had indeed detained him—that much she already knew. But it wasn't because of a Colonial fetish for harsh justice or corruption within their Judiciary, or any other number of fictitious, prejudiced reasons. Rocky was a murderer. A *murderer!* How could he have done it? *Why* had he done it? He *wanted* to go to Jotunheim? He thought he'd be *safe* there? Safe from what? *From his own people?* Didn't he trust them? Didn't he trust *her?*

He'd lied to her—he'd lied to all of them, the entire team, to all his colleagues who'd known him and loved him as a partner for so long. He left them willingly and didn't even bother to explain himself. He led them to believe he was innocent. But he wasn't innocent. And now he was coming out of his silence to ask her for a favor—a favor, like he *deserved* one after what he'd done!

She was surprised at her anger, at the way she snapped back without thinking. "How *dare* you ask me that?" she'd hissed. She had a wife to live for, a life to salvage. She couldn't do what Rocky had asked of her. It was far too dangerous, and she was in enough danger already. The government had probably been listening to her phone call from the second she answered it. She had to lie. She had no choice.

She told him she'd destroyed the data. He didn't believe her—she was a terrible liar—but she couldn't admit the truth. Her wife's unshakable ideology had put them on Brock Dunham's blacklist; if Pentakiya were to transmit the access codes that she wasn't supposed to have to begin with, let alone share, then she would have sealed their fates. She and Artimpasa would die behind the chemical sheds. She'd seen the firing squads before. Their crosshairs could just as easily be set on her. A treasonous act of that magnitude would neither go unnoticed nor unpunished.

When Rocky told her that her inaction would lead to ABAC's ultimate defeat of liberty, she couldn't deny that he was right. Her silence secured the Conglomerate's victory; Dunham and his cronies would get away with the evils they'd committed. Rocky didn't call her a coward, but she knew he must have thought her one. When she calmed herself down and let go of her anger, she felt guilty that she couldn't help him when he clearly needed her. But her hands were tied. There was nothing she could do for him.

Really, there was little she could do for herself. It was a hopeless fight, and in her mind, she'd already been defeated. The best she could hope to do was survive. Her freedom had been taken from her. Her sense of security had been taken from her. All she had left was Artimpasa and her own life, and she had no intention of giving up either of them, even in her old friend's most desperate hour. It hurt her to admit it, but he was dead either way. She, however, had a shot at survival. She wouldn't waste it. With a clear conscience, she couldn't.

———

The acquired ship sailed through the Veil of Bhalenjar like a kite through shimmering clouds. Masked by the billowing colors of the nebula, its crew thought they were alone. The Veil's inner glow grew brighter as they passed farther into its hidden heart, and the faint flicker of distant stars became clearer. Natharis soon realized that he wasn't gazing at stars at all, but at the lights of hundreds of other vessels with their sights set on the planet of Bhalenjar. Hundreds turned to thousands, thousands to numbers uncountable; the traffic converged in the shadow of the golden tower ahead.

"Looks like we're surrounded again," Natharis joked, "but at least this time no one's trying to kill us." Their cover as just one of many ABAC passenger ships kept them safe for the time being, but Natharis knew their sense of comfort wouldn't last long. They didn't have any ABAC uniforms to hide them once they stepped off the ship.

"None of us is ever truly surrounded, with no means of escape," Selenia said calmly. "There's always a way out. The door's in your mind, and you need only ask for it to open. Some of you already know this."

"Spare us Mithneshi proverbs for once," Ninotchka growled. "I'm sure we would all do just fine without your life lessons. Besides, isn't contemplation best done in *silence?*"

Livia grew defensive while Selenia merely smiled acceptingly. "Aren't you Arterran?"

"I am from Tsardom of Romanov Muscovia, first and foremost," Ninotchka replied with a scowl. "Only higher power I need is this one right here." She patted the gun she kept strapped to her bare thigh. No one dared to question her faith in her trusted firearms.

Bhalenjari traffic control contacted the crew, but their exchange was short and to the point, much simpler than any of them had braced themselves for. *"Vessel classification?"* an anonymous voice asked; Natharis confirmed them as a passenger ship, carrying six individuals. Ninotchka jabbed him in the arm for admitting Rocky's presence, but he insisted that they wouldn't be asked to personally identify themselves, neither by name nor by species. When instructed to describe the nature of their trip, he kept his answer vague, to placate the Muscovite. "Civilian business in the surface district," he declared. Traffic control seemed satisfied; they didn't mention the sailship's registration as an official ABAC vehicle. There must have been so many traveling to and from Bhalenjar that even traffic control didn't bother to keep track of them. It was an irresponsibility that baffled the Colonial, but which he was thankful for. *Maybe ABAC doesn't want them to know where they're going, or how many,* he speculated. They received their docking bay designation and continued their approach.

He tried his best to act as though he'd laid eyes upon the spiraled Tower of Bhalenjar before. He didn't want his awe to be so visible, or for it to be evident that it was his first time seeing it firsthand. He had looked at pictures of it in textbooks in school and many times on the news screens all over Acadica, but the images couldn't capture its true grandeur. Even from thousands of miles away, it was immense, and its size made him feel insignificant, irrelevant in the grand scheme of galactic history. The pyrgopolis twisted out into space farther than Natharis ever thought was possible: it looked as though it might even scrape the broken moon that hung over the Bhalenjari sky. The miles-wide residential spheres caught the sun's light, nestled in the spiral structure of the tower to form a string of massive atoms on a strand of ancient, immutable DNA. He wondered if the Procyon had designed it in the image of their own genetic markers. Or perhaps it was Sapien—the answer eluded him. He knew he could never answer it, anyway.

"Oh my god," Livia gasped as she stood with her nose to the window. "It's beautiful." She turned around with a childlike smile and looked at Natharis. "I had no idea."

He wanted to tell her that it was nothing compared to her, that her beauty was more captivating than the sunlight on the golden tower and more ethereal than the incomparable colors of the Veil. He wanted to say how he'd love nothing more than to look down on the planet below from the tower's peak, to hold her and feel the embrace of the starlight surrounding them, to see every sunrise over Bhalenjar like each was their first. But he couldn't. He had to be the Colonial marshal who was unaffected by the unfamiliar; he had to maintain his air of unshakable composure and professionalism. It was how he'd always lived his life. Really, it was all he knew.

He approached Livia, but Silviano cut in front of him and stood next to her with his chest against her shoulder and a hand near her waist. *Another man set in his ways,* thought Natharis. Livia pushed his hand away but let him stand close—too close, in Natharis's opinion—but she didn't look very comfortable with his advances. Natharis cursed himself for moving too slowly.

"I'll admit, it's impressive," Silviano sighed. "But do you really want to give the Procyon so much credit? You're from

Roma Ceisora. We've got plenty of monuments of our own, and we built them from the ground up, without the Procyon's ruins as their foundations. I doubt the Colonials could say the same." He talked so nonchalantly about the tower that Natharis knew he must have been feigning disinterest. If anything, he probably thought *he* was their most impressive monument. Silviano touched Livia's hair; she acted like he hadn't. "And if you ask me, the beauty of our *people* is what we should be most famous for."

"Ever been to Acadica?" Natharis asked. He stepped to the other side of Livia. She looked relieved. "Maybe we inherited some technology from the Procyon you hate so much, but our cities are so much more than any of these 'alien roots' you've invented."

"This is not time for dick-measuring," Ninotchka groaned. "We're landing." She pointed at Livia as the two men stepped away. "And you—stop doing your job and sit down, sacred slut. I have better things to do than watch you take it twice."

———

Livia took Natharis by the wrist and he followed her into the open air. The hangar was tiny but had no roof; the golden tower spiraled into the sky and faded away as it stretched higher into the atmosphere. Even from a thousand miles away it was the most obvious sight, but Natharis's eyes soon wandered off to the east, where a brilliant light shone on the horizon. He didn't need to see it to know what it was: a glimpse of the pilgrims' lamp atop the Great Ziggurat. Pointing upward, he opened his mouth to tell Livia. Ninotchka's arrogant voice cut him off.

"Your friend is useless," she shouted back at the Crystalline, who stood at the top of the exit ramp, reluctant to set foot on a world visited so frequently by Brock Dunham.

"There's still time," Natharis said. "Let her think on it. For all we know, she might change her mind."

Silviano scoffed, "People don't change. You're wasting your time."

"I know her well, and the Tellurian is right, I am afraid. She is not likely to change her position. I expect that she is still loyal to her leadership. I had hoped she might have come to her senses by now."

Ninotchka sealed the hatch and set the lock. "So, she is idiot as well."

"It is not entirely her fault. Many others have fallen prey to the collectivists' hunger for complete control. They are raised from their earliest years to believe that individuals like Brock Dunham are a model for perfect behavior and rationality. When one spends her childhood putting naïve faith in an ideology like his, she will retain that loyalty her whole life. Collectivism is a curious and dangerous thing. Of all types of brainwashing, it is the most irreversible. It is a religion more dogmatic and oppressive than any this galaxy has ever seen, and this galaxy has seen many evil religions already."

The corridor just outside the hangar opened into a narrow catwalk, and it didn't take long for the group to make it out into the city. They walked along its path a hundred or so feet above the ground-level streets, surrounded by the light-and-dark checkered windows of countless skyscrapers and industrial complexes. From their vantage point, Natharis saw that the urban landscape continued on for miles: it spanned the entire land area of that continent. The only glimpse of the natural world came in the form of a lush, green ring encircling the golden tower at the center of the city, far away. Bridges arched over nature's final refuge to allow for unhindered traffic flow. While Natharis thought such a sprawling park was necessary for the health of a settlement, the collectivists seemed to view it as some kind of inconvenience, as there were no such parks in Communal cities. Nature was a reminder of the before-times, when the pinnacle of Sapien achievement was a chipped rock just sharp enough to cut animal skins. It was a symbol of a primitive past they hoped to leave far behind them.

Natharis himself considered the light atop the Great Ziggurat to be a memorial to the greatest of Sapien achievements—the greatest that any sentient species could hope to attain. It represented the liberty that he and his people respected and cherished so dearly. It was a symbol of the free will that all living beings had a God-given right to express. Even behind the bright lights of the city skyline, he could see its radiance piercing the heavens. It was both soft and blinding, a numinous light guiding the spiritually lost to the Mithneshi Holy of Holies.

"That's it, isn't it?" Livia asked. "That's where you're going?"

Selenia nodded affirmatively. "Yes—that's the Great Ziggurat. My journey ends there. For others, it is only the beginning."

"All this talk of collectivist cults and we still humor your delusions," Ninotchka groaned. "Your own cult isn't much better than Dunham's. Like every other mankind has ever pointlessly followed, it is worthless superstition. The sooner you get out of our hair, the better."

Ninotchka rejected the proposal that they all go to the Great Ziggurat; she asserted that Selenia, if she really were so independent, should simply go there on her own and leave the rest of them in peace. Silviano appeared to agree, much to Natharis's chagrin, who argued on Livia's behalf. He must have had little interest in letting Livia explore new systems of thought, as the only peace he wanted her to have was in the afterglow beneath his sheets.

Ninotchka decided to leave the rest of them behind for what she declared to be more pressing matters. She knew of a ZGB safe house not far from their location. She lamented that she wouldn't likely find any operatives waiting for her, but insisted that there would be a formidable supply of ammunition there, and possibly a communications transmitter to call for backup, if necessary. As she saw it, there was little point in expecting the Mithneshi to provide the necessary equipment, because not only did they take a vow of foolish neutrality, but also preferred archaic weaponry that had no place in a civilized fight.

Selenia didn't try to force her, but wasn't about to let her judge so hastily. "Have you ever been to the Ziggurat? Seen it? Marveled at its grandeur?"

"I don't need to."

"Don't be so quick to judge, then. It holds secrets that might surprise you. So, until you look upon it with your own eyes and see all the wonders it holds, you are living in the dark. I might not convince you and maybe nobody can, but trust me. You won't have so many words to say when you're standing before it. No one ever does."

23

*"Only a willing spirit touched by love will be healed, so release
your love upon the Emanation, and know no boundaries."*
—Fifth Catechism of the Mithneshi Coven

THE FAMILY SUITE NEVER FELT SO EMPTY. Selas was sitting
in a tomb, but there was no memorial to those he'd lost, only
unwashed dishes sitting in the sink and half-drunk glasses of
water in his sister's bedroom. His little sister's stuffed animals
had been knocked onto the floor after the blast. It seemed
only right to put them back in their place. He did so carefully,
making sure to arrange them in the exact way he remembered
them, though he couldn't be sure that he was right. She wasn't
there to correct him. She wouldn't know, anyway. She no
longer could. None of them could.

The hum of the aetherium drives haunted him like a ghost
whispering in his ears, and in the droning noise he thought
he heard voices, groaning and wailing in the dark. What
remained of the caravan escaped into the tachyon vein and
disappeared, leaving the ruins of the Ssimvomai Center for
the Lost far behind. They had no destination. They fled
without any concern for what was to come. They only knew

that slipping into the Aether was their only chance at survival. To stay in free space was to welcome another strike. They didn't know if the bombers would return, and quite frankly, they didn't care. It was a risk they were willing to take. Selas, however, wished they would. He would have preferred immolation by fire than by his own despair.

He lay in his bed with his face in his hands. He once hated the dark and all the terrible possibilities it contained, but he kept the lights off and wept in the shadows. The nightmares that crept forth out of the blackness didn't tie his stomach into knots. The terrors in the night were welcome after all he'd seen. The worst horrors of all weren't reflected in the haunting black eyes of his abductors, but in the faces of those who perished at unnamed hands. He hadn't even seen their faces with his own eyes, but he saw them nonetheless. He saw them in his mind's eye, burned into his memory forever like the charred bodies that drifted out into the emptiness. He clawed at his temples in agony, overwhelmed by the screams he imagined against his will.

But then the screaming turned to a dead silence when he heard a knock at the door.

Who could it have been? Selas didn't even know the number of survivors. He had no idea how many of them were left on the untouched *Massyulan*, or which of them would have any interest in seeking him out. He couldn't handle any more bad news, if that was what the visitor was intent on offering. He didn't want to hear it.

The boy clutched the pillow and pressed it firmly against his ear, muffling the sounds from the door, and it provided him a brief, modest repose from the unwelcome messenger just outside the suite. But the pounding on the door grew louder, until it rivaled the violent thud of debris against the cruiser's hull. He couldn't ignore it, no matter how hard he tried. Selas crawled out of bed and tiptoed toward it. He took a deep breath and swung open the door.

"You've been crying. I don't blame you."

Selas wiped the tears from his reddened eyes. Burton stood in the doorway with a cloudy bottle of liquor tucked conspicuously into his coat pocket. Ruddy, circular burns covered half of his face, a trail of cracked patches of skin from his jawline to just above his left ear. It reminded the boy of the radiation burns he himself had sustained. He touched his back and felt the rough ridges that crisscrossed his skin. Burton asked if he could come inside. When Selas didn't answer, he invited himself in and set the bottle upon the kitchen table.

"I'm sorry for what happened." He removed the cap and offered the liquor to the boy, who only stared at him. "This is the best I can do to help." When Selas didn't accept, Burton simply took a swig from the bottle himself.

"I don't need your pity, and don't bother saying you're 'sorry.' It doesn't do shit for me, and it won't do shit for them. They're gone now."

"There's nothin' you could have done to stop it, if it means anything."

"It doesn't. It doesn't mean a fucking thing."

"Sorry. I shouldn't have said nothin'." He took another sip from the bottle.

"You know what?" Selas snapped, snatching the bottle out of Burton's hands. He gulped down a swig of stinging liquor, just a bit too much to swallow at once. "If you're gonna be sorry, then be sorry for destroying my goddamned life. You never should have let me remember. I didn't know any better, but *you* did."

"You asked me to. I hate to remind you, but you *wanted* your memories back."

"If I knew what they were, I never would have."

"I told you it'd be hard."

"What's *hard* is watching my baby sister being *tortured* and screaming for me to help her. And I couldn't, just like I couldn't this time. Now she's gone."

"She's safe from them, now."

"She's *dead.* That's not the kind of safety I wanted." Selas slumped down onto the chair and stomached another drink from the bottle. "I wish I could be with her. I wouldn't have to deal with the bullshit you put me through."

"I didn't put you through it. *They* did."

"At least they don't lie about their intentions," Selas barked. "Get out."

"You shouldn't be alone now, kid."

"Get the fuck out of here."

He put his hands on Burton's chest and shoved him back, but the old man didn't fight him, and didn't protest when Selas slammed the door in his face. He didn't hear footsteps at first—Burton wasn't leaving. But once the boy broke down and fell with his back against the door, sliding down until he was cowering on the floor, Burton complied. Selas heard him walk away, but he didn't care. He buried his face in his hands and surrendered. He thought of his abductors and spoke to them in his mind. He knew they could hear him. They were always listening.

"Just take me," he pleaded, looking up toward an imaginary sky. Tears fell as he admitted his hopelessness. "I have nothing left to fight for."

———

Livia stood before the towering wall that encircled the Great Ziggurat of Bhalenjar. She stopped in her tracks where the expanse of skyscrapers ended and greenery began; she saw the light atop the pyramid shining just a few hundred feet away, though eclipsed by the silhouette of trees that served as a fortress wall. The ancient redwoods rose high into the air, growing in a perfect ring that enclosed the Mithneshi Holy of Holies, the beating heart of Livia's dreams. Glass spheres hung from the tree branches, lit by an inner fire that glowed not from the burning wicks of candles, but with a delicate light that made the lamps look like bottled stars. An arch of the purest white ivory marked the threshold between the mundane and the ethereal. Livia stepped through it with apprehension, excitement. Ribbons of green ivy brushed her shoulders and billowed in the warm breeze.

The living barrier gave way to walls of another sort: concentric rings of makeshift tents, whose diverse drapery swayed in the wind. She saw some made of stitched patches of gray rags, others, white linens. Each was large enough for a single occupant. A hand emerged from the loose lips of a tent opening, and a Mithneshi seer parted the drapes to examine the mismatched group of visitors. Like Selenia, he wore the white, form-fitting robe of the Coven; he smiled and withdrew into his tent. Others peered out as well, all with looks of peaceful contentment on their faces. They didn't seem to mind sleeping on the bare earth beneath flimsy, crudely pitched tents.

"Even till the very end of our pilgrimage, we maintain our sacred vow of poverty," Selenia explained.

"Another reason not to be religious," Ninotchka remarked. "You make believers travel light-years to get here, then you make them sleep like Xaztechuans."

"Laypeople can stay outside the boundaries in any luxury hotel they want. Faith isn't meant to be difficult, and we expect no one to be an ascetic. But we do expect it of the Coven. Poverty and modesty are our burdens, and no one else's."

Polished stone lined the path that led Livia forward to a destiny she'd only just come to realize. Cypress trees and crimson rose bushes served as columns supporting only the sky above them. Ninotchka rudely tore off a rose and slipped it into her pocket for the sake of wanton deviance. Livia grazed her hand against a velvety, delicate flower, but pricked her finger on a thorn. She couldn't imagine that a place of such beauty would have thorns, but it did. Pain was something that had always been present in her life. Even standing before God, it persisted. Perhaps that was simply part of being mortal. It was natural, maybe even something to be embraced. She sucked the tiny drop of blood from her finger and looked away toward something greater than herself.

The very sight of the Great Ziggurat was enough to steal her breath. Its seductive light had already taken hold of her thoughts, woven a spell around her heart and soul, but to lay eyes upon the structure that wore the lamp like a crown was overwhelming. Her eyes grew wide, her heart beat faster, and she grabbed Natharis's wrist instinctively, in need of something, or someone, to keep her from falling to her knees. She gazed higher into the heavens, following the stairway that stretched from the solid ground up to the very top of the Ziggurat, to the lamp that guided the faithful to the place where the celestial and the earthly became one. There was an open doorway set at the base of the stairs, splitting the path of religious procession in two; she saw the flicker of firelight from within. She wanted to know what secrets it embowered. She needed to know.

"I've seen enough," Ninotchka snapped, breaking the reverent silence. "I think it's time for Ms. Santiago to go." She motioned for Selenia to keep walking. "Let's get out of here. We have work to do."

"As quickly as they crossed, our paths must diverge," Selenia concluded with a hint of sadness in her voice. "She's right. My journey is complete—but yours isn't yet."

"I won't leave. Not now," Livia declared.

"Fine. Stay here," Ninotchka laughed. "We're better off without you consistently ruining our plans. Now we have *two* less liabilities. Move along, little girl. I have conspiracy to expose."

For once, Livia was happy to oblige her. She continued her procession toward the sacred pyramid without looking back; the shadow that followed her along the shining stone path could be none other than Selenia's. Livia kept her eyes fixed on the gateway ahead but paid attention to the feeling of being watched. A tension grew as she began to worry that Natharis might not follow her, but then the skin on the back of her neck tickled with goose bumps, and she knew he was right behind her. He caught up and walked by her side. He smiled, and she returned the gesture with quiet affection. She needed no other company than his.

She surrendered to her curiosity and turned back to see who else might rebel against Ninotchka's ironclad will. Silviano looked torn, caught in a dilemma that had no safe outcome. He didn't want to anger Ninotchka, whose temper was as volatile as a Molotov cocktail, but wouldn't want to be alone with her either, as he'd made perfectly clear in his constant avoidance of her sexual predation. He grimaced; his near-rapist glared. Just as Livia thought he'd surrender to the Muscovite, he sprinted toward the Ziggurat with a single bead of sweat falling from his brow. Ninotchka groaned in the distance, clenching her fists. She was left alone with the Crystalline. With no choice but to follow, Ninotchka rolled her eyes and sighed.

"We're wasting time. You know that."

"We can wait a little longer," Natharis said. "There's still a chance we might get our hands on those access codes."

"She's not sending them."

"Your partner is correct. That is no longer an option."

"Then let's get it over with," Ninotchka decided. "Save your pointless worship for later."

"If you really plan on storming the ABAC Tower, you should probably wait till nightfall," Livia suggested. "Do you really think you can pull this off in broad daylight?"

Natharis nodded. "She's right, you know."

Ninotchka couldn't allow for competition. "She has been dead weight so far. Now you think she has valid opinion?" She must have known she'd been beaten.

"So, now it's just a waiting game," Silviano added. He pointed toward the horizon, to the spiraled Tower of Bhalenjar that loomed in the distance. "It's got to be a thousand miles from here, at least. We'll need to find a transport. It's a big city—they've got to have shuttles."

"I don't suppose Mithneshi could help us out with that?" Ninotchka sneered. "Or would that be violation of their inconvenient 'vow of neutrality?'"

They all looked to Selenia for an answer. The seer bit her lip and shut her eyes, like she was searching her memory for some way to justify an unprecedented intervention. She took a deep breath and nodded her head. "Without your help, I never would have made it to Bhalenjar," she said. "A true servant of God would do well to express her gratitude. Sometimes vows must be broken in order to repay our debts." She stepped forward to shake Ninotchka's hand. "Yes. I'll help you."

Ninotchka eyed Selenia with suspicion but reluctantly accepted her handshake. "Let's just hope you've got something useful for us. It'd better not be prayer."

"There are tunnels beneath the city, up in orbit," Selenia began.

"Metro?" Ninotchka laughed. "I will *not* ride on subway with Caspian plebs."

"No, not the metro. Ancient pathways, like a web, even deeper than the train tunnels. We believe them to be catacombs, left by the Procyon thousands of years ago, when they controlled this planet for their own research. Our suspicions are that the bones that line the walls are the remains of genetic engineering projects, but we can't be sure. You'll be the only ones down there, with no one to stand in your way. If you truly want to reach the Tower, I will show you the untraveled path."

———

The sound of the ticking clock on Tageron's desk sounded out through the darkened office. It was a priceless antique from an age long ago, when slowly spinning gears drove time forward, not circuits and glowing numbers. The clock had been in his family for generations; it was the one possession of value that his mother once called her own. He hadn't learned how valuable it was until much later in life, when he no longer needed the money. But if his mother had known, he was sure she still wouldn't have sold it. It was a reminder that the passing of time was variable. It seemed to tick slower when he was concerned for the future. The digital clocks never changed their pace. That night, the hands on the old clock's face barely moved.

He turned away from the clock and gazed out through his window. He looked to the horizon; the black of the eastern sky was lightening to a deep blue, soon to become even brighter, with the pale yellows of a fateful sunrise. His men on the ground kept watch for the coming strike team, but he wanted to see it himself. He imagined bloodthirsty termites pouring through the fences to devour his life and property and chew away the very foundations of his accomplishments like old wood. Sharsir had mentioned that they'd have to fend off twenty or so officers. Tageron feared that they'd be meeting more than twenty. Until the sun rose, he could see little from the building.

The transports were close to ready, and the refugees' children had already been safely boarded. The mass drivers were dismantled and loaded into the cargo holds. Food rations, water and medical supplies were packed and accounted for. *There's nothing to be afraid of,* Tageron told himself. *We're ready.*

Sharsir arrived earlier with three heavy crates branded with the Justice Department's seal. He revealed a stock of firearms and an excess of ammunition, which he freely distributed among the refugees. When asked where he'd gotten the illegal weapons, he explained that they were smuggled out of the Justice Department's stockpile of confiscated guns, all taken from the citizens of Tarem. Tageron groaned when he was reminded of the government's strict gun control laws. Apparently, after an off-world Shatarin broke into a small family's home and made an attempt at raping the young daughter, the parents pulled out their household gun and shot him dead. According to the collectivist government, it was the parents who were at fault, as only racists would dare open fire on a Shatarin, no matter what his crime. Laws were immediately passed that made the ownership of any weapon a criminal offense. The citizens were then left completely defenseless.

Tageron held a rifle in his lap and polished the barrel with a soft cloth. He was ready to use it when the time came, though he wished there could have been a more peaceful solution. As the sky grew brighter, and the edge of the sun's disc peeked over the horizon, he loaded the gun and set it down on his desk. He took a deep breath, glancing over at the clock that shone in the morning light. Time had never been on his side. And now, in his anticipation, it threatened to stop altogether.

———

The world passed by like a dream, hazy and vague, flashing before Desh's eyes as he stared upward into the sky. Above him he saw stars, a bright sun far away, and though he saw whitewashed walls flanking his field of vision, the light of the heavens pierced through them. The spectral figures around him might not have seen the light, but he did. Whether natural or supernatural, the caress of the starlight left him with a feeling of deep peace. He tried to ignore the sensation of his back pressed against a solid surface beneath him—was it a bed? A stretcher, or a gurney? The answer evaded him, as did the identities of those whose distant voices echoed around him, their shouts more like whispers, and their fears tangible in a way he'd never felt before.

The executive searched his memory for an explanation, but he found himself without much recollection of anything. All he saw was his childhood home on Catskills-Atlantic; he smelled the earthy scent that pervaded the ancient forests and felt cool soil between his toes. He closed his unfocused eyes tightly, and then he remembered: a sharp pain in his stomach, like a knife thrust into him, but hotter, searing. He couldn't move his arms or touch the wound he knew was there. A warmth spread down his sides in an unseen cascade—blood, maybe? The thought of his life draining from his body filled his vision with a deep crimson cloud. He remembered ruddy moons setting on the horizon from his family's old home. The memory brought him an unexpected comfort.

"Where the hell can we bring him?" shouted a faraway voice. Bring him where? Why the rush?

"No hospitals. They've all been shut down." Hospitals? What for?

"So, he's fucked, then." Why?

"Not just him. All of us." All of whom? Why such despair? Why such hopelessness?

Memories of his childhood resurfaced; he'd heard his parents cry for him too many times when he was a young boy. He remembered the hospitals, the constant fatigue and the cold sweats he had to suffer through every night. He recalled the tightness in his chest, and how breathing wasn't always easy. The distant voices merged with those of his mother and father, who spent their days praying for their son to grow stronger, and their nights wiping his brow with cool washcloths. Their lives were centered around an unshakable dread, one that his mother one day came to leave behind, but his father never lived long enough to see relieved. The men around him were living the same nightmare.

Desh didn't share their feelings, their sense of fear. He felt no fear—only acceptance. He didn't know what was happening to him, but he knew there was nothing he could do, and while the thought brought the others anger and frustration, he found it comforting. For the first time, he didn't fight the reality he'd been thrown into. He didn't struggle against the specter that overpowered him. He felt compelled to pray—not in desperation, but gratitude. He recited ancient words in his mind, and basked in the light of his God, wrapped in the warm, loving blanket of His Emanation.

And then he saw it: a brilliant light, like a lighthouse, atop a mighty memorial to the unseen world and its glorious

Creator. He heard incantations but no mouths to recite them. He'd seen and heard it all before, but he couldn't recall how or why. He felt a tingling on his tongue, an anxiousness, like he meant to say something, but couldn't compose the words. He surrendered to his dream; the words flowed through him like a stream of inspired consciousness. Whether it was in his head or aloud, he wasn't sure, but the words echoed around him and lifted him up from the world that knew only pain and suffering.

"Listen! He's saying something."

"What? The Ziggurat? Give me a break."

"It's the only chance we've got."

"He's got."

"No, we've got."

Yes, the Ziggurat! Its blinding light beckoned him closer. It drew him in not as a lighthouse guiding him to the next world, but as a beacon of hope, for a chance at life anew. He stood at the boundary between worlds, but the light pulled him back to the world of men, not angels. It was not yet his time. And though he did not know it, he smiled. It brought hope to those who carried him toward salvation, and for a moment, he saw them not as men of flesh and blood, but as beings of light, ushering him back into a world he'd almost left behind.

Pentakiya leapt up from a deep sleep with a panicked gasp and a tightness in the pit of her stomach. Her heart raced as though she'd just awoken from a terrible nightmare, but she had no memory of a nocturnal terror. The sense of dread overwhelmed her. Had it been a nightmare, she would have shrugged off her anxiety as the result of an unfortunate delusion. But she knew it wasn't that. The source of her fear was elusive, not in the past, but in the present—perhaps the future.

She tried to catch her breath as she sat upright in bed. The room was dark; it was silent except for the sound of her own breathing and her wife stirring gently in her sleep. She was happy she hadn't woken up Artimpasa. She deserved a good night's sleep after all the stress she'd been put through. Pentakiya watched her and wished her good dreams. Her breathing deepened, and her heartbeat slowed back to normal. Without her thunderous pulse pounding in her ears, the room was peaceful. There wasn't a single sound to disturb Artimpasa from her sleep.

But then she heard footsteps.

They came from outside the apartment, heavy and determined, like men's boots making the wooden floors creak painfully in the otherwise silent building. She thought she heard voices, but she couldn't be sure. She slipped out of bed and tiptoed across the room; she pulled the first clothes she could find out of her wardrobe and put them on in a hurry. With her breath held, she put her ear against the bedroom door. She heard nothing.

She cursed herself under her breath for being so paranoid. She might have still been dreaming. Maybe that's why she couldn't remember the nightmare—because she was still in it. Convinced that the only way to wake up was, ironically, to go back to sleep, she crawled back into bed and put her head on the pillow. It felt too real to be a dream, but she told herself not to care. She'd had a few glasses of wine before bed, and now she was paying the price with bizarre and twisted dreams. She shut her eyes and willed herself back to consciousness. She smiled at the thought that, for once, she had nothing to worry about, except for the delusional fears of her own unconscious mind.

Then with a crash her bedroom door burst open and slammed against the wall. Pentakiya jumped up screaming, waking her wife. Three men dressed all in black stormed into the room, weapons drawn, pointed straight at the bed. The harsh glare of powerful flashlights blinded her; Artimpasa covered her eyes and pulled the blankets closer, as though they would protect her from gunfire. Pentakiya knew that she herself couldn't protect her wife, and the thought killed her inside. She could barely see the intruders behind the stinging lights. She saw heavy bulletproof vests, helmets with tinted visors, but nothing to identify them or whom they worked for. But she knew who they were. They barked for her to get on the ground. She did so without protest. She peered up from the floor to make sure her wife had complied. But Artimpasa was gone. The armed men were carrying her away.

"*Stop!*" Pentakiya cried, scrambling off the ground to chase them. "Don't take her! *You can't!*"

The men didn't listen. She ran out of the bedroom and watched as her wife, naked and screaming, was rushed out of the apartment. Pentakiya managed to grab her hand, but she slipped away. She looked into her wife's eyes and saw only hopelessness. Tears fell down her cheeks.

"*I won't let you take her!*"

She clenched her fists and aimed for the back of the last man's neck, but he heard her coming. He smashed the butt of his rifle into the back of her head. She fell to the ground, no longer screaming. The men disappeared; Artimpasa vanished with them. The apartment fell silent once again, as if none of them had ever been there.

Her vision blurred, and her thoughts were just a stranger's whispers. A pool of blood spread over the floor beneath her, but she didn't care, and didn't try to stop it. She wept. It was more dreamlike than ever. She felt like an onlooker, an observer, crying for those she watched out of empathy, not out of direct involvement in a tragedy. Hallucinations overtook her; she saw and felt rain on her skin. Then she realized it was tears—her tears. They were real. And there was no hope of waking to the soft light of dawn.

The sun was setting lower on the horizon, casting shadows on the walls of the Ziggurat's inner chambers. A single beam of golden light broke through a small shaft in the stone structure and bathed an intricate carving on the wall in its radiance. Words in a forgotten language narrated the scene, and from the looks of it, the artist seemed to depict an ancient battle between good and evil. It was a battle Livia felt was ongoing, without end.

Tension was high as they waited. Ninotchka had left to raid her agency's safe house of all its guns and ammunition, and Natharis was nowhere to be found. He'd wandered deeper into the heart of the Ziggurat, and made clear that he wanted to go alone. Livia understood the drive to isolate oneself in the face of coming danger, but until then, the greatest danger she'd ever dreaded was the look in the next pilgrim's eye after she'd sanctified the one before him.

"He's gone to pray for guidance," Selenia said, scouring over old cartographs. She shuffled through the crumbling parchment and studied a second map. "And protection, I'd expect. You have quite a struggle ahead of you, but don't be afraid. Trust me: You have a connection to the Eternal."

"I wish I'd gone with him. I'm not ready to die."

"Neither is he." Selenia pointed to the others. "And neither is Ninotchka, no matter what she says. No one ever is, Livia, and even though death is just another rite of passage, it's still difficult to face. But you can stand prepared for it. Natharis knows this, and so do you."

"I want to face it with a clean spirit. It seems like the best way to cross over."

"Do you feel unclean?"

"I have for most of my life, even if my people say I'm not."

"Then wash it all away. Even a lifetime of spiritual dirt can be swept away with one simple act of faith."

"I don't know how."

"Go to the Holy of Holies. Bathe in the sacred pool and pledge your spirit to the Light, if that's truly what you believe and wish to do." She pointed down the torch-lit corridor. "Natharis may already be there. The chamber echoes with his prayers. And soon, yours will resonate with his in perfect harmony."

Livia walked away in a trance without another word. She wandered down the hall, following the torches on the walls. It reminded her of the Imperial Temple, but she saw no graven images of divine beings or beds upon which sacred, living vessels lay with the devout. She had no way of knowing what she would find up ahead. As the torches became fewer and more distantly mounted, she ventured into darkness. In her heart, she knew that the night always fell before the day could break, and that shadow always preceded the light. She fell into the darkened depths of her consciousness and embraced her anxiousness. She didn't know what to expect. The feeling left her both nervous and excited. She was on the path to salvation, walking through the valley of the shadows, with green pastures in her mind ahead.

Then what she saw took her breath away.

The darkness gave way to a brilliant radiance, to colors she couldn't name. The chamber was massive, and the dome of its roof was sparkling with crystalline stars and constellations. Nebulae shimmered up in the living, breathing sky as clouds of blues, violets and indigos, spreading like wisps of subtle paints across the dark canopy of space. The lights twinkled upon a lake that stretched across the Holy of Holies. Its waters were perfectly still, pristine, such that the sacred pool seemed to be made of flawless glass. In the distance, there was a tiny island that peeked just above the surface of the water, upon which stood a polished stone altar. A single lamp sat on the ritual table, and the firelight flickered on the columns of an ivory ciborium above it. The starlight cast subtle shadows from a gnarled but elegant tree beside the altar. White petals covered the grass like a blanket of soft feathers.

The crystal mirror of the water was no longer still; delicate ripples drifted outward in shining rings, like one crescent moon after another. Livia knew she wasn't alone. She looked to the source, hidden behind a natural wall of mossy stones at the water's edge. She heard a light splashing, a deep breath.

And out from behind the rocks and tall grass emerged Natharis Ruke.

He didn't turn around or even notice her. He stood waist-deep in the water, naked and unafraid. The muscles of his back tightened as he cupped the water in his hands and poured it over his head; the light of the sky above him glistened on his skin, and his hardened body glowed with starlight. He didn't whisper prayers. He only breathed deeply, letting his mind find peace, away from the prying eyes he didn't know were watching him. The caress of cool water calmed his once racing thoughts; it brought him a comfort he so desperately needed. And Livia, looking down upon him from the grassy shore, wanted to console him with the brush of her fingers.

She stepped softly through the grass. Without a word, she dipped her feet into the water, and chills rushed up her spine. She made her own ripples in the lake, and they drifted outward, lapping against Natharis's back. He felt the gentle disturbance and looked back—then he saw her. She said nothing; she only let her white robe slide over her shoulders and fall behind her. The chamber was warm, the water, cool. There was an energy in the air, an electricity, and it sent waves of goose bumps over her skin, driving her to want more. She felt a warmth between her legs, a primal aching.

"Livia—"

She smiled, and waded deeper into the water. Natharis didn't know what to think. It was a moment he'd been waiting for, longing for, since he saw her bathing in the ritual pool on Earth. He was speechless. His eyes were fixed on the dark cascade of her hair over smooth, fair skin, and the way it fell so delicately over her chest. She pushed her hair behind her shoulders, revealing her supple breasts. Natharis moved closer. Their bodies were just inches from touching. They could feel the heat of each other's skin. They felt the tension of two young bodies that longed for perfect union.

"You don't have to—"

"—I know," Livia whispered, grazing her hand against his cheek. "But I'm here because I want to be. It's my choice."

"I know, but—"

She put a finger to his mouth, and hushed him into silence. "I came here to find salvation," she said. Natharis closed his eyes. "And I found it." She leaned in farther; their lips were so close that Natharis could barely hold himself back. She whispered as their brows met, "You've saved me before, Natharis. Now let me save you."

Natharis put his hands on her shoulders and pulled her close. He kissed her deeply, more passionately than he'd ever kissed a woman before. He took her in his arms; she ran her hands over his strong chest as he pressed himself firmly against her. He eased her head to one side and kissed her neck, drawing a soft whisper from the woman who'd wanted him so badly for so long. She dipped her hand beneath the water and wrapped her fingers around his thick manhood; he groaned and gripped her tightly, his body burning with desire. She stroked him gently, sliding her fingers down his length until his breath rushed past her ears. With a coy smile, she pulled away, beckoning him to follow her to the water's edge. She saw a wildfire in his eyes as he followed her lead. He was consumed by it, and she wanted her body to burn with his.

He took her by the small of her back and laid her down upon the grass. She tangled his hair in her fingers as he kissed his way down her body, and arched her back when his tongue brushed between her legs. She squeezed her thighs tightly around his neck; he reached up to cup her breasts in his hands, and swirled his tongue hungrily until she bucked her hips and cried out in pleasure. Her legs quivered; her toes curled. She could barely breathe.

She put her hands on his chest and pushed him back upon his knees. Natharis gripped her waist as she straddled him. They looked into each other's eyes and felt an unbreakable connection, one they'd both felt since the moment they'd first set eyes upon each other. As she looked down at him, losing herself in the icy blue eyes she saw in her dreams, she felt as though she was looking into the face of a god. And Natharis, even without a word from his woman, knew she'd been dreaming of him all along. Somehow, he'd always known that his soul visited hers when her eyes closed and she drifted away. His body would finally become one with hers as well—two souls, one body, with one aching desire.

Livia held his face to her breasts as she slid down upon him, and gasped when she felt him open her. He kissed her, rocking her gently in his lap, restraining himself from tearing her apart with no concern for her pain, only his own pleasure. He didn't want to hurt her. All he wanted was for her to lose herself in the ecstasy that only he could give.

The feeling was incredible; Livia had never felt so whole. Natharis lost himself when he entered her, and felt no separation between them, no sense of ego. Her soft lips against his, the sensation of her body grinding against his—it all took him far away. They lived and breathed a dream, each thrust deep inside her wakening them to a reality even more beautiful than their surrender. She slipped her arms around his neck and pulled him close. In her embrace, he sank deeper inside her.

"Natharis…" Livia moaned in his ear. "I want it… Please, give it to me… Claim me. I want to be yours, and only yours…"

He wanted so desperately to feel release deep inside her, and she wanted it just as badly. He was her man, and he wanted to please her. He wanted nothing more than to satisfy her every desire until her body burned. Natharis gripped her and pushed himself deeper, until he couldn't give her any more of himself. He felt her muscles tighten as a tension built between her legs. She trembled with an overwhelming energy that grew stronger with each breath. Natharis shouted out, groaning so loud that his voice echoed through the chamber. He was close—Livia could see it in his crystal blue eyes, no longer icy, but hot with azure flame.

Livia's heart beat faster, harder. Her blood pounded in her ears, coursing through her body; Natharis's pulse quickened to match hers, and the rhythmic throbbing of his manhood revealed that he'd reached the edge of losing control. He pulled her down in one last thrust, and her toes curled, and his muscles tightened. She cried out, and with the feeling of him filling her, she lost herself entirely. Waves of pleasure crashed over her, flowing through her veins, through every inch of her body and soul. She arched her back with no control over her muscles or movements. She dug her fingernails into his back. Her thighs quivered. Silvery embers flashed and burned away before her eyes.

"Livia, I love you—"

"I—"

And then the dome of the sky exploded with colors unknown to the eyes of men. The stars burst with a blinding light, lost in a sea of ecstatic nebulae, until there was no division between earth and sky. Vibrations rippled through the air and surrounded Livia and her man, showering them in chills that spread over their hot, flushed skin. The world opened up to them, and they knew no limits. Livia's consciousness extended to the ends of the universe. Together, they shared one heartbeat, and their thoughts raced as one. All memories surfaced in the light, and in that utmost union, Natharis and his woman were boundless, harmonized with each other and the world around them. They looked upon the face of the Divine and came to know the madness that was the purest love. They gazed upon it for eternity. They had no fear of the threat of death that loomed over them, for the future was theirs, and theirs alone.

———

Selenia couldn't help but smile as Livia headed off for the Holy of Holies. The look of hope on the girl's face brought Selenia her own sense of optimism. It was the hope that the lost might all be found. There was a certain satisfaction—spiritual, not selfish—that came with turning the doubtful to the truth. Livia had come to her willingly, and her interest was clear. Her curiosity was the seed of the mighty oak of her growing faith, and in guiding her, Selenia had strengthened her own faith, for which she was inexpressibly grateful. She savored the peace she felt in that moment. She closed her eyes and drank of it.

"Clear the way! We've got an injured man over here!"

Selenia snapped open her eyes and stood. Shouting in a panic, uniformed men rushed closer, their frenzied breaths echoing off the stone walls. The mindless groans of a dying man were just barely audible beneath their clamor.

She pointed to a small shrine to the back of the chamber. "Lay him out," she instructed, trying to keep herself calm; she knew she had to be the one source of composure in the room. The men scrambled to the candlelit altar and lowered the stretcher to the ground. It was then that she got a good look at what she was dealing with—or whom she was dealing with. She'd seen his universally recognized good looks before, displayed throughout the Convergency on news screens and in the papers. She'd heard his voice on the radio, recorded in heated Congressional sessions and in tamer news studios. She knew who he was. He was Desh Maru, the Colonial executive, and she now found him in her care. She had to admit that she wasn't at all prepared for it.

She knelt over him and whispered ancient words to relax him. She could only hope that he was a believer. His shirt was drenched in blood; she couldn't see the wound beneath it. With trembling hands she began to unbutton it, but one of his escorts produced a combat knife and cut the shirt open. With just a single glance, she could tell the wound was fatal. A wave of discouragement washed over her, but with the men looking to her as their last and only hope, she couldn't express it. She took a deep breath and cleared her mind. She told them to do the same, however difficult. They fell to their knees beside her. One of them wept.

———

The world was slipping away, but Desh didn't mourn its loss. Darkness overtook him, and the voices around him grew softer, more distant, until he found himself alone in the silent shadows of the realm between this life and the next. He stopped whispering prayers under his breath, though they may have been spoken only in his mind all along. He still felt the throbbing pain in his abdomen. It was his last connection to the physical world. It was a bridge he desperately wanted to burn away. He wanted nothing more than to drift off into the unknown.

Suddenly, a light broke through the dark, not blinding, but soft and gentle. He saw the face of a woman hovering over him, radiant with divine energy. She was beautiful. Was she an angel of God, sent to watch over him? There to pull him back to the mortal world, or to guide him across the threshold of death? The angel spoke, but he couldn't hear her. Still, her silent words brought him a profound, limitless peace. He lost himself in her heavenly eyes, and felt her gaze reaching into the depths of his soul. He felt like he was home.

———

"We're losing him!" Selenia cried. She didn't want to admit it, but she knew it was inevitable. She pressed torn strips of his shirt against the wound, trying to compress it, but his warm blood still flowed in torrents from the pursed lips of his flesh. It trickled between her fingers and left smears of crimson on her white robe. With no options left, she threw the makeshift bandages aside. She placed her open palm on the dying man's brow and closed her eyes. All she could do was pray for his safe passing into the afterlife. It was too late to keep him with them.

She released her personal will unto the Creator and let her selfish desires float away into the Emanation. If it was this man's time, it was his time, and there was nothing she could do to prevent his return to the unseen world. She felt a warmth in her fingertips, a tingling in her palms; she would have dismissed it as the heat radiating from his dying body, but he was as cold as ice. It couldn't have been him. An energy built at the base of her spine. She felt it creep upward, traveling along her back up to her skull. What was she feeling? Out of fear, she withdrew her hand.

Don't be afraid, said an echo in her mind. *Channel it. It is yours.*

She submitted in sweet surrender. And then she felt it: a ripple in the Emanation, gentle at first. She wondered how the men around her didn't perceive it. It grew stronger, until the tiny vibrations in the Eternal Sea turned to swells and waves. She trembled; they crashed over her, filling her with an ecstatic energy. It was more powerful than anything she'd ever experienced. She was deeply afraid—afraid that her body was too weak, too fragile to survive such a spiritual rush. But she cleared her mind and gave herself up. She saw flashes of prophetic images, of a young stranger wandering in the desert, of the childhood rains on her skin and the embrace of a man and woman in silver water. She felt her spirit open. Her heart became a vessel of the Emanation, more fully than it had ever been. There was no separation between herself and the world beyond. The ripples felt like sublime union.

———

Desh stared in wonder as the angel's face burst with a blinding light, like an ancient star exploding when its time had come, showering the universe with the building blocks of life. He felt the light pierce through him, turning the night within him into day, drawing the sun back into the darkened sky of his mind. His body was set aflame, and the heat filled him with joy, and the flames danced over him and burned away all his fear and pain. He heard the angel sigh; her breath was the breath of life rushing into his lungs. He'd never felt so alive.

———

The man jumped up with a sharp gasp. Selenia fell backward, her body shaken by the sheer power of the experience. He looked about, unsure of where he was. Selenia's gentle smile washed away his confusion. He dug his fingernails into the bed of dried blood on his hands. How had it gotten there? It looked old, like it'd been there for hours. He ran his hands over his bare stomach to feel for a wound. He must have imagined it being there. There was nothing—not even a scar. The blood must have come from somewhere. Was it even his?

If he hadn't been wounded, why did the strangers kneeling over him look so shocked? They looked astounded, afraid, like they didn't even want to approach or touch him. He reached for his shirt to cover his body, but it was torn to pieces and drenched in the blood he couldn't accept as his own. His body felt heavy. The weightlessness of spirit was gone. He struggled to sit upright.

"Where am I?" he asked, his deep voice exuding more calm and strength than Selenia had anticipated.

She smiled and touched her hand to his heart. It beat strongly, pulsing with a powerful thud that resounded through his strong chest. He was alive—and he'd be staying with them. Of that, she had no doubt.

"Welcome back, Executive," said Selenia with a grin. "This day was not your last."

24

"The Shatarin civilization has a long and illustrious history of tolerance and coexistence with those groups that deserve it, and that are willing to accept Shatarin cultural superiority. Indeed, our own refusal to adopt their way of life has resulted in violence, and we have only ourselves to blame for insulting their faith in not adopting it."
—Parliamentarian Panzi Illoszia of Bahía Brumosa

THE AFTERGLOW LINGERED, even with the Holy of Holies far behind them. Natharis was suffused with its calming radiance, glowing from deep within his body, through every bone and exhausted muscle. Livia felt it in the air, and saw it illuminate the corridors in her mind's eye; it made the torches along their path look finite and dim. With Natharis's hand around her waist and the aura of emotion that surrounded her, Livia had freed herself of her fears. They both knew that nothing could harm them. Their love was a shield, unbreakable, impervious to bullets and criticism alike. It was a feeling of security she never wanted to lose. So long as he was by her side, she knew it wouldn't slip away.

The suspicious, irritated glares struck them the very second they stepped into the entry chamber. Ninotchka didn't waste any time in mocking them. "Returning to your 'religious duties?'" she asked with her hands on her hips. "Whore ways die hard, I suppose."

Silviano seethed in his jealousy—he didn't say a word, though his eyes betrayed his façade. But behind the look there was something else. For a moment, Livia thought he was hurt. No one had ever rejected him before. It was a denial that all his years in carnal service of Mars hadn't prepared him for, and he exuded a vulnerability that no spiritual legionnaire should reveal. It was humanizing, almost endearing. But she felt no guilt in Natharis's arms. She'd made the right decision, guided by divine currents that led to no one but him.

Natharis scrambled past them in a panic. Ninotchka couldn't have offended him so deeply that he'd rush away in shame. Livia peered past Silviano to see what had seized Natharis's attention.

The man was sitting on the ground, his naked back against the cool wall of glistening stone. A torn shirt lay on the ground in a blood-stained pile. Around his broad shoulders he'd wrapped a cotton shroud, perfectly white, without a single drop of crimson to mar it. It was a death shroud, meant for a corpse. For the living to cover themselves with it, something dire must have happened. Mortals always shut their eyes to any reminder of the death that would one day embrace them all.

Two Colonial guards blocked Natharis with outstretched arms. The man was important, it seemed. His face did look familiar. Livia felt like she'd seen him before, perhaps in a dream.

The golden eagle, she realized. *But where's the wound?*

"There's blood on the floor," she whispered to Selenia. "Who's hurt?" She pointed to the shrouded man. "He looks fine."

"He stood at death's door, but he didn't step through. Something stopped him. I helped pull him back."

Was faith truly so powerful that it could bring a man back from death?

"Ripples through the Eternal Sea kept him with us. Powerful, overwhelming—like nothing I've ever felt before." She smiled as though she held a hidden knowledge. "What could have created such strong waves in the cosmos and beyond?"

The man stood and told his guards to stand down. "I'm fine, really. You're a Colonial marshal, aren't you?" He was addressing Natharis, whom he seemed to be familiar with. Natharis nodded, and introduced himself.

"Natharis Ruke, sir," he said, shaking the man's hand excitedly. "It's an honor—"

"That won't be necessary, Natharis. None of this 'Mr. Executive,' please. Just call me by my name."

"Well, Mr. Maru, it's an honor to meet you."

"That's a little better. I wish I had my designer suit for this kind of greeting. I've heard of you, Marshal, and the part you've played in fighting extremism in Chesapeake. Good to see you're safe."

Ninotchka shamelessly interrupted the underdressed Colonial executive. "While you were busy defiling temple, I was fully briefing Mr. Maru on our situation. Looks like we managed to alert authorities to ABAC plot, after all. Very convenient." She rolled her eyes at Livia. "As usual, *you* were too busy wandering off to see it."

Natharis asked Desh for his input, eager to receive advice from a man he so deeply respected and admired. His superior began to delicately fold his death shroud to hand it off, no longer needing it. "You're all pretty set on doing this, as much as I think you should let the military take care of it." He pointed to Ninotchka. "Or at least *she* is, and even I wouldn't cross her."

"Keep your military," the Muscovite insisted. "You're going to need every soldier you've got, because you have war to wage."

"You were against starting a war just a few hours ago," Livia noted.

Ninotchka fumed. "Yes, *before* I found out about Commune's failed assassination."

"I'll provide you with a small strike team for backup," Desh offered. "It's the least I could do."

"We've drawn enough attention to ourselves already," Natharis said. "It'll be quieter if we do it ourselves. We've been in enough fights. What's one more?"

Ninotchka had a contingency plan in mind. "Besides, we have ZGB special ops on call, if we need them. They're just waiting for my signal." She paused to think. "Maybe we should just call them now. They're more reliable than *some* dead weight in this group." Livia scowled.

"You should make up your minds soon," Selenia advised. "Your transport to the Bhalenjari Apex will be leaving. Once you disembark, look for a Mithneshi shrine. That's where you can descend into the catacombs. Follow the path I've mapped out for you, and you'll emerge just beyond ABAC's security points. The rest is up to you."

"*ABAC's central banking tower stretches beyond the limits of its facility's protective sphere,*" the Crystalline elaborated. "*It is divided into two zones: the tower structure, and the command center for the tachyon anchor. The command center and the device itself are at the peak of the tower, exposed to open space.*" It continued, despite the guards' looks of mistrust. It was, after all, a murderer. "*I believe our best plan of action is to bomb the tower. We plant explosives at the base. We reach the control room, detonate them remotely, and deploy the device, and consequently ourselves, into orbit. With the tower's collapse, we would depressurize the entire sphere, and every single ABAC soldier, politician and scientist in the facility dies.*"

"The Colonial flagship is in orbit over the planet," Desh added. "It could pick you up in its hangar bay once you've separated from the tower. Then the tachyon anchor will be in Colonial hands."

"Alright, we've got what we need," Ninotchka announced, calling for the guards. "You can detain prisoner. We're done with it." The prisoner accepted its fate.

"Against my better judgment, I think it should go with you," Desh said. His soldiers stood down. "It's been cooperative so far, and it certainly provides a tactical advantage in storming the facility, given that it's the only one who even knows what this damned device looks like. It'll face the rule of law once your mission is accomplished, and ABAC gets what it deserves."

"We don't have explosives," Ninotchka groaned, once again lamenting her lack of foresight, and her leaving her fully loaded luxury coat behind. "I'll contact ZGB team. *They're* bound to be prepared for raid." Laughing, she collected her effects. "I'm in mood for good fireworks show. And trust me: Muscovia won't disappoint. We learn to rig bombs before we can crawl."

A silver dart shot from the surface of Bhalenjar and raced past the countless skyscrapers that cast miles of shadows across the landscape. An endless fireworks show of plasma bolts burst from the Spiral Tower above and showered over the peaks of the city skyline. The Bhalenjari resistance fought desperately to hold back the ABAC forces in the upper levels of the laced Tower, but the Conglomerate had the upper hand, rallying support from the tens of thousands of foreign Children of the Dole. The opposing armies unleashed hell upon one another, marching on foot with rifles blazing through the urbanized scaffolds of the Tower of Bhalenjar. Aerial dogfights raged over the continent, and the biting gnats of ABAC's air force buzzed overhead in a great swarm of disease-carrying insects.

Misha's goal was to document the Bhalenjari resistance and the atrocities committed by Brock Dunham's indoctrinated armies, but the situation quickly went south when she and her team found themselves caught in the middle of a war much grander than they'd predicted. The U.C.S. *Fist of Alabama* was in orbit above the planet, Misha's pilot explained, and she made the executive decision to change their destination to the primary hangar of the Colonial flagship. Her crew was reluctant, citing the size of the enemy fleet taking on the most powerful warship in the Colonial Navy, and how they seemed to be appearing out of nowhere. But Misha knew better, and persuaded them to transmit a request to dock.

The ship passed through the suspended city without a single combat weapon to defend itself. It was a journalistic vessel, and it was illegal to open fire on such a craft. But even after the pilot opened a direct line to the two ABAC fighters on his tail, and sent confirmation codes that it was, in fact, a neutral ship, the Conglomerate didn't fall back. Misha slammed her fist onto the dashboard. "They can't shoot us down!" she barked, as though the pilot had any control over his assailants. "Get those bastards on the line!"

"Colonial journalism has been declared offensive to the Children of the Dole," the enemy reported ominously. *"Your neutrality is hereby revoked by Executive Dunham himself!"*

Misha was appalled and knew she had no choice but to take things into her own hands. With every impact their shields grew weaker, and there was no way to fight back, except with her own fists. She'd learned a few tricks in her military career, and though she was a little rusty, she planned to put them to good use. She instructed her pilot to continue his evasive maneuvers while she slipped out of her chic Romaean pencil skirt and donned an emergency evacuation suit. She pulled her helmet over her head and gave him the signal to level the ship. He did as she ordered, and when she climbed up to the roof hatch and began her countdown, he furiously protested.

"Are you fucking *crazy?*" he shouted. Her camera crew behind her screamed out in horror as the passenger cabin rumbled from the bombardment.

"I've taken down plenty of these Communal tyrants with good journalism," she asserted with her hand to the lock. "Now I'll show you how I do it with my own bare hands. In ten seconds, lower the shields and make an immediate ninety-degree barrel roll. Stay as close to me as you can. And don't you dare hesitate."

The wind blasted against her body as she climbed out onto the ship's hull and activated the magnetic anchors on the heels of her boots. She kept her eyes locked on the ABAC fighter behind them, discerning its speed and distance from glowing displays inside her helmet. Right on cue, the shimmering field of the shield scaffolding faded away, and her ship rolled over; she disengaged her anchors and fired the maneuvering thrusters on her back. Her slender figure soared through the air over the surface of Bhalenjar, and as she looked upon the city and the Spiral Tower above her shining silver and gold in the light of the sun, she found it to be one of the most beautiful scenes she'd ever witnessed.

She hit the nose of the fighter hard and came to a sudden stop with her foot upon the cockpit window. With magnets holding her in place, she reached for the laser saw clipped to the belt of her emergency suit; the device was meant to hollow out holes in an asteroid or dwarf planet to provide shelter in the event of a transit disaster, but for Misha, always a clever soldier, it was the perfect tool for the job. She threw back her arm and plunged her radiant blade through the window. The polymer shield turned red hot and melted away, and the laser carved open a smoldering hole in the porcine pilot's abdomen. Misha painted the walls of the cockpit with blood and dripping globs of fat. Lard-padded effluents spewed over the controls and the fighter sharply nosedived.

Misha's lasso spiraled through the air and locked onto the wingman's ship with a sharp crack. Her first target fell from beneath her feet and tumbled down upon the city below, and she flew across the sky toward the last collectivist pawn. The engine exploded with fire and black smoke when she swung her blade clean through it, and pieces of the hopeless fighter scattered out in all directions; she flipped gracefully over the shrapnel and clung victoriously to her civilian shuttle. The hatch sealed shut with a hiss after she pulled herself back inside, as if she hadn't just done something spectacular. She switched off her camera and pulled off her helmet.

"Now that's how it's done, boys. Stop screaming and get my effects. We have business to attend to up in orbit, and I will *not* be going in an emergency suit."

There wasn't a hint of light in the boy's bedroom. There was no soft flicker of starlight from just beyond the darkened walls. His lamps were off—he didn't want them on. He knew what was coming. They were going to take him again, and this time, there was no going back. A sense of dread festered deep inside him, from the center of his being, an intuitive sense he couldn't shake. His captors would emerge from the dark like demons or ghosts. He didn't want to see their faces. Their eyes paralyzed him. If he couldn't get lost in their heartless gaze, maybe he wouldn't freeze. Maybe he could fight back.

He knew he might die. He knew that if he defied their unbreakable will, they would subdue him. They were stronger than him, despite their skeletal bodies. His youthful muscles, slender but strong, could easily break their arms and knock them to the ground, but they always found a way to stop him. He imagined their surprise upon learning that he no longer had the implant they'd used for so long to silence him and keep him still. They didn't have their technological tranquilizer anymore. Without it, did they have any power?

The doorknob across the room turned with a metallic click. The door hinges creaked. *There's no going back now,* he thought. *Nowhere to run. Nowhere to hide.* Perhaps he'd never really had that option. He took a deep breath. He said a short prayer.

Even in the darkest shadows, he saw their eyes. They were blacker than black, darker than the darkness that hid their spindly bodies. Two, then four—six. Three of them approached. He felt their gaze upon his skin. He smelled the sour stench of their presence. He cringed, bracing himself for the cold fingers wrapping tightly around his wrist. He pushed away his blankets. He wasn't a child anymore—he knew the sheets wouldn't stop them. Even the impenetrable hulls of the ship and the lock on his door wouldn't stop them. Nothing could.

They ripped him from his bed. The first grabbed his wrist—the second, his ankles. He struggled to break their grip, cursing so loud that his shouts filled the room. The third touched its hands to his temples and tried to look him in the eye. The creature's stare filled him with dread, but he didn't stop fighting. It leaned in closer, until its grotesque face nearly touched his. Still, he didn't freeze. Even without a hint of Sapien expression, the creature seemed to glare, angry and thrown off guard. Selas's legs broke free. He scrambled onto the floor.

"Get the fuck away from me!" he screamed. He swung his fists blindly in the dark, but felt no flesh pummeled beneath his blows. The light switch was inaccessible. They'd managed to hide when he couldn't. It wasn't fair.

And then a ringing pierced his ears. He put his hands to his head and fell to the ground, crippled by the sharp sound. He felt a warmth down his wrists as blood trickled from his ears. The inexplicable shrieking came from around him and from within his own head. His body twisted upon the floor and his muscles clenched painfully, uncontrollably. He imagined cracks running across his skull, until the bone split and his brain spilled onto the floor like gray jelly. The lights turned on in a flash. They were so bright that, in his pain, he was blinded. In the white glare of the lamps, he saw only them. They reached for him, long fingers outstretched. They smothered his face in their hands until his vision blurred and his breath turned shallow.

In his mental haze he felt himself dragged across the cold floor by his ankles, with his arms just a dead weight stretched over his head. At first he'd wanted to fight, to struggle and try to break free, but he succumbed to his hopelessness. To rise up against them was as useless as a mortal rebelling against God, in His infinite power. Selas felt nothing anymore. He admitted to himself that he had nothing to fight for. He stared up at the creatures with dead eyes, nothing behind them. He offered no resistance. He imagined their satisfaction until he faded into the hideous blackness of their eyes and the inescapable oblivion of unconsciousness.

————

The sun rose over the mountains and cast shadows across the grassy plain. It painted the sky in bronze and gold, like the skin of the Caspian businessman who watched it creep higher into the sky through his office windows. He stood and saw the sunlight cascade over his fellow refugees, adding gold to already gilded faces. It gleamed off the barrels of their guns and filled the tower lobby. It warmed the air through the glass and made Tageron squint.

The glare off the metal towers in the distance made it hard to see much farther. They'd left the front gates wide open in an attempt to mislead the government forces, to make them believe that Tageron planned to peacefully surrender his livelihood. His employees and friends loaded their weapons and quietly discussed their plan of action. They would lure law enforcement inside the building, pick off as many as possible, then retreat into the work yard. Once their targets were out in the open, they'd unleash their heavier weapons. Tageron expected some loss on their side. Even with the risk fully explained to them, his supporters didn't back down. To them, staying on Hatal-Om was a death sentence in itself. They had no other option.

Sharsir turned from the window and pointed to the back of the reception area. "They're here. Take your positions and keep quiet." All but he and Tageron took cover behind any room feature they could find: desks, overturned tables, leather couches and bookshelves. Sharsir whispered to

Tageron, "I count around twenty of them. Looks like my friends were right."

"More will come. I'm sure of it." Tageron paused, peering out the window for a moment longer. "There!" he announced, pointing to the gates. "Another ten or fifteen, right behind the first. And they've got two—no, three—armored trucks."

"With mounted guns, I'd wager. That's gonna be a problem."

"Nothing a grenade or two can't solve. Lucky for us, I've got a good arm."

"I just hope you know what you're doing."

"I'm securing our futures, Sharsir. Nothing more."

"And thank God for that."

The two men took their places among the refugees and peeked cautiously from behind their luxury barriers. The first wave of officers arrived at the front door; those behind them split into two visible groups, each headed in opposite directions around the skyscraper. "Damnit," Tageron hissed. "Radio the transports. Tell them to fire up the engines. We've got less time than we thought." Sharsir followed his orders. They'd have to cut their gunfight short.

"Okay everyone, let's go," Sharsir whispered. He motioned toward the back of the room, to the corridor that led to the work yard behind the offices. Crouching, the group hurried with their heads low. They heard a clatter at the lobby doors. The officers pulled at the door handles, shaking them in frustration—they were locked, to buy the refugees just a few more precious seconds. One took the butt of his gun and smashed it into the glass. Tiny cracks crisscrossed outward from the blow. Tired of the slow progress, the officer opened fire on the doors and windows. The sound of shattering glass and gunfire filled the room. Many of the refugees stopped, and pointed their weapons back toward the door.

"Don't shoot!" Tageron commanded his employees. "Just head for the yard!" Most retreated at his order. A teenage boy

stopped dead in his tracks. He stared nervously at the troops, whose heavy boots crunched the broken glass scattered across the lobby floor. His rifle rattled in his trembling hands.

He's never fired a gun before, Tageron realized. *Who the hell gave that to him?*

An officer noticed him. He shouted to his team, "The damned civvies are armed!"

A gunshot echoed through the room; Tageron jumped up, thinking the boy was hit. But then he saw the officer fall to the ground, clutching his chest, blood bubbling from his gaping mouth. The boy dropped the gun in a panic and froze. Tageron grabbed him and threw him to the floor. Their opponents unleashed a fusillade of bullets across the room. Mirrors shattered and vases exploded into a thousand pieces.

Tageron pulled the boy out to the work yard, where all the other armed refugees were anxiously waiting. He heard the powerful thuds of the Gatling guns being fired from the armored trucks. Tens of his employees fell, their bodies pummeled with bullets, and their spilt blood was like fuel for the fire in Tageron's mind. He primed a grenade and hurled it toward the first truck, putting his whole body into the throw. It bounced along the ground and rolled beneath the vehicle. He smiled, grabbed another from Sharsir, and aimed for the second truck. The trucks flew into the air like massive fireballs, and crashed down with a smoking explosion that smelled of justice and burning fuel.

The refugees were still boarding the transports, but many of the men hadn't grown tired of the firefight, and stood out in the work yard with guns blazing and explosives sailing overhead. Tageron, though, was weary of the violence, and he headed for the boarding ramp. He told himself he wouldn't, but he looked back, just to take one last look at the company he'd built up, then tore down. The fires burned, and the bullets still flew, but from the center of the fray, he saw one person he'd never expected to see among such chaos. It was Koshann, his only son, standing in the distance, with a pistol dangling from his waist and a radio in his hand.

No. He wouldn't.

Koshann stepped closer, calmly, with his open palms held above his head. Tageron couldn't bring himself to stop him. He knew he wasn't there to take refuge on the transports. He'd be abandoning the insidious ideology he held so dear.

"Don't do this, father. You know you won't make it out of here. You're outnumbered."

"We've held our own for some time now. Just ask your barbecued friends back there."

"This will follow you wherever you go. You can't escape the truth that is our vision."

"The only truth is that one reaps what one sows."

"Then perhaps this is what you should receive."

Tageron reached out his hand. "Koshann, come with us. Get on the ship and leave this all behind. We can all start over. And you and I—we can start over. I wasn't the father I could have been. Your standing there is my fault." He begged his son to reconsider. "Please, Koshann."

"No. Not now—not ever. I'm standing exactly where I was meant to."

Tageron felt sick. His face paled and his words were somber. "Then so am I. Goodbye, son."

In a flash, Koshann pulled the pistol from his waist and held it to Tageron's head. "I can't let you do that, father."

"Try to stop me. You've never had the gall to do anything of consequence, other than putting me in debt with your childish antics."

His son clicked off the safety and pressed the gun harder into his father's flesh. "That's where you're wrong, father. I'd do anything to preserve the greater good—even if it means pulling this trigger, and putting a bullet right between my father's eyes." The crazed look on his face disturbed Tageron more than anything in his life. He was going to do it. After all, Brock Dunham was his true father. Tageron was just there for his birth.

"Do it," he dared his son. "You already killed me the day you took up the flag of collectivism and betrayed this family."

Koshann grinned; his teeth looked like fangs. He chuckled, "'Honor thy father and mother.'" And the crack of a single gunshot echoed across the plain.

Pentakiya twisted her arm uncomfortably behind her to zip up the back of her dress. It was a pleasant shade of robin egg blue, and it never failed to draw a quick but heartfelt compliment from her wife whenever she wore it. She chose to color her lips with a light pink lipstick; she'd wanted red, but felt it wouldn't quite work with the pastels of her dress. She knew her reasons for dressing up that night were delusional, at best, but she slipped her feet into a pair of tasteful heels regardless. She wasn't raised with much of a belief in a life after death—neither a collectivist education nor a Communal upbringing nurtured such fantasies. But at that moment, she told herself that if she were to see her wife again beyond celestial gates, then she should look good for her, as even angels could be impressed by a well-cut dress.

There was no hope for her wife. She was already dead—Pentakiya was sure of it. There wasn't a glimmer of hope for herself, either. In her despair, she concluded that she had little, if anything, left to live for. The blush wine she sipped from one of her rarely used crystal glasses didn't help to mask the bitter taste in her mouth, though she'd told herself it would. She poured herself another glass, this time half empty. She had no intention of drowning herself in alcohol, but she was already drowning in thought, and the wine would take the edge off once her lungs began to ache and burn for air. Pentakiya finished off the last drops with one reluctant gulp from the glass. It was time. She could only hope that her wife was waiting.

It was a warm night, as it always was in a city choked by centuries of traffic fumes. The breeze, for the first time in years, smelled almost fresh. Perhaps it was all in her head. She stepped out onto the balcony; the wind caressed her body and made her dress flutter around her. Pentakiya peered over the edge and looked down. Leftway Avenue bustled with people eight stories beneath her. For once, she saw no cars. It was of no importance to her, as she didn't plan to survive the fall. All it meant was that there'd be more spectators to stand over her contorted body, lying twisted in a pool of blood.

The railing was thin and made it difficult for her to find her balance. She climbed up on top of it, but left her shoes on the floor, because she couldn't stand on the delicate barrier in heels. It was a pity to leave them behind, though she knew she couldn't take them with her. The sight of the street below left her dizzy, disoriented. She held her arms out to keep herself from falling, struggling against the light breeze that, to a woman teetering on a metal tightrope, seemed like a hurricane ready to knock her down. She took a deep breath and closed her eyes. It was the moment of truth, after weeks of lies.

Forgive me, my love, she begged. *I was too weak to go on without you.*

A tear ran down her cheek. She tensed her legs, preparing to make her final leap of faith. But a sudden shout from the street caught her off guard, then turned to a frenzy of yelling and screaming, and in her surprise, Pentakiya lost her balance. She grabbed the railing instinctively as she slipped over its edge. Her feet dangled in the open air. Her knuckles faded to white while she held on desperately for her life.

But isn't this what I wanted?

She pulled herself up and caught her breath. Perhaps she wasn't ready after all. Or perhaps she wanted to die on her own terms, at the moment of her choosing. It wasn't her plan to fall. She planned to jump.

It wasn't shouting—it was cheering. An orange light flickered on the buildings farther down Leftway. Pentakiya couldn't see the source around the corner of the buildings beside her apartment, but based on the direction in which the mob below was scrambling, she could only assume that it came from Clinton Square, just a quarter mile away. She saw no signs or banners to identify the event. She hadn't even heard of it on the news. Granted, it'd been days since she'd turned on a television or sat down with a newspaper. For all she knew, there was a revolution in the works. But that was simply too good to be true. Justice was never served so swiftly, except to those who spoke out against the gravest of injustices and their arrogant perpetrators.

In her heels and blue dress, she hurried down the stairwell and stepped out into the street. A rotund mother, with thighs clapping together like thunder, knocked her aside; her five children, scurrying behind her as would a line of ducklings, rudely trampled her feet. Pentakiya struggled to follow the herd of rowdy Albians down the city block, but even with the shifting silhouette of the crowd blocking most of her view, she noticed the orange light getting brighter, more vivid, until it danced upon the high-rise windows and the faces of those around her. Massive billboards glowed above the mob, but instead of brandishing their usual tasteless advertisements, they proudly displayed the smug visage of none other than Executive Dunham, who watched over the city square with a smile of ominous satisfaction. His image didn't move, but soon enough, Pentakiya realized that it wasn't a still photo, but a video, and by the way he was eyeing a holotab below the view of the camera, she knew he was preparing to speak.

"Proud citizens of Albion, and of the most perfect Commune!" he began. His voice echoed from the buildings like the voice of God, shaking His believers to the very depths of their hearts and souls.

Pentakiya closed her ears to the Word and pushed farther through the crowd. She encroached on the spectacle ahead, and soon realized that the light came not from neon lamps of celebration, but from a furiously burning pyre. The flames leapt above the heads of those who still blocked her view, and embers crackled up into the air and faded into the starless sky. The onlookers cheered in awe, even when the black smoke descended and strained their breath.

"I regret that I cannot join you in person at this most auspicious celebration, but remember, my dear followers, that I am with you in spirit—for where many gather in my name, I am there among them, always."

Youthful laughter caught her attention. Students, wearing shirts and sweaters branded with the prestigious sigil of the Dearborn City College, were hurling their belongings toward the fire. What were they throwing? What kind of bonfire party were they hosting?

"What a delight it is to see our Commune's youth gathering together to express their utmost dedication to the greater good! The students of this fine city, this illustrious planet and this most prosperous Commune have organized this event, and to them we owe our gratitude, for it is they who will carry the torch of collectivism into the future."

The greater good? Wasn't it always?

"Their collectivist education has opened their eyes to the evils of this world, and I pray that, in the light of the fire, yours, too, will be opened forever. For these young people understand that no civilized society should expect its citizens to discern right from wrong, good from evil—and most importantly, truth from untruth. We can create and preserve a virtuous nation only by relieving its people of this dangerous burden."

The students were throwing books.

They hurled them into the fire with a disturbing voracity, chanting mantras of anger and vengeance against those who subverted the morality of the Commune through the written word. The sheer hatred that Dearborn's children harbored within them was enough to make Pentakiya sick. They picked up ancient novels, textbooks and magazines from the ground, and condemned them to be lost forever in the hellfire of Brock Dunham's most sinister vision. Pentakiya could no longer see any difference between a collectivist education and indoctrination. Her wife would have been disgusted. She would have wept for the death of knowledge.

"A citizen cannot be trusted to make the correct judgment when he is exposed to such differing, conflicting ideas—no man can be so wise. So, I have removed this dangerous choice. I—no, we—cannot tolerate those who oppose collectivism, who spread discord throughout the Convergency in their attempts to sway others to an ideology of selfishness and lies. Even a single book has the potential to bring a civilization to its knees. And I will not allow such a threat to our existence to ever see its purpose realized. Its authors must be silenced, for the sake of the greater good."

A band of soldiers emerged from behind a second mound of books, which still waited to be set ablaze by the screeching horde of liberal arts students. The soldiers' helmets moved from behind the literary wall and across its long, crescent shape; Pentakiya thought she could see other figures behind them, but in the shadows that cloaked them behind the bright fire, they were unclear.

"Let this be a lesson to all those who seek to destroy the glorious system I have worked so hard to build. Intellectual dissent is an act of treason, and there can be no lenience in its punishment. Justice will be served and peace will be preserved when they are no longer able to mislead others with their words. They must be sentenced to death without exception or mercy."

The crowd spat insults and threw trash at the three prisoners escorted by the masked soldiers. They held their heads low, hiding their shame as they were pummeled with torn books and stinking refuse. The crazed people of Dearborn called for their deaths, condemning them as traitors and liars—garbage meant only to be burned away and forgotten forever. This, they said, was the fate of the blasphemer, who spread heresies against the one true leader, Brock Dunham.

Pentakiya's heart stopped. *Oh, God. It can't be.*

The first detainee to be led up to the unlit pyre lifted her head and stared out into the crowd with no hope behind her dead eyes. Pentakiya recognized those violet eyes. They stole her breath, and tied her stomach into painful knots. It was her wife, with hands bound behind her back.

"*No!*" Pentakiya cried, pushing aside the onlookers ahead of her. She crashed through the crowd to get closer, but the mob had other plans, and kept her from slipping any father through their unruly assembly. Pentakiya shouted to her wife, screaming her name over and over, that she was there for her, that she never abandoned her memory, but her strained voice was covered by the sounds of cruel insults and humiliating obscenities. Her wife was nothing but an individualist whore; the two prisoners to her left and right were Commune-hating bastards. Their accusers spat at their feet.

Artimpasa winced when they tightened the ropes around her body and pressed her back against the wooden stake. She looked as though she could barely breathe. Pentakiya felt suffocated, not by smoke, but by the heaviness in her heart.

Brock Dunham laughed from his virtual throne. "*What do these traitors deserve?*"

"*Death!*" chanted the crowd. "*Burn them! Throw them into the fire!*"

The executive smiled. "*So be it.*"

Pentakiya screamed, but his word was law, and no matter how hard a woman fought, God's will would be done.

"I love you!" she sobbed, praying Artimpasa would hear. "I'm so sorry!"

Her wife looked down from the pyre and smiled, whispering, "I know, baby." And then she spoke so firmly that those around her, one by one, fell silent. The conviction in her voice commanded their attention, and cut short their rallying cries of blind, bloodthirsty obedience.

"You can burn my body. You can erase my name from memory," she warned. "But my ideas will live on. Free thought *cannot* die. So, throw your books into the fire, and try your best to turn history to ashes." She looked up to Dunham, who glared furiously from the heavens. "Freedom will survive and rise from those ashes, and, on that day, you will know you have failed."

Then the fire consumed her.

Pentakiya cried, screaming her name, rivers of tears cascading from her sullen eyes. She watched as her wife, like a tragic phoenix, was encircled by an infernal halo. Defiance was the tinder beneath her, and conviction, the match that sentenced her to die. The prisoners to her sides shouted out in agony, begging for mercy and forgiveness, but Artimpasa said nothing more. She did not beg. She did not bow to tyranny, to the unfathomable cruelty that tied her to the wooden stake and left her to die for the amusement of others. The bronze skin of her legs turned to black; her hair burned away, until she looked like a newborn baby, perishing before her time in the hope of a righteous resurrection.

Pentakiya felt the flames of her own guilt lapping at her feet, burning away the last of her loyalty to her cause. Her complacence with her leader's destructive will, her faith in a system broken and corrupt, had lit the fire that consumed her wife with such fury and hate. Pentakiya's blindness, her delusion, her ignorance, were the sparks that set the wood ablaze with hellfire. Her pitiful belief in the regime had wreathed her wife in flame. Her weakness had killed Artimpasa. And in her beautiful mind, her beautiful ideals died with her. Her death was the death of Pentakiya's purpose, her only anchor in life. Without her, Pentakiya couldn't breathe. She choked on the smoke that rose from her body. She suffocated beneath the weight of her own remorse. It was a burden that no fire, even one so furious, could burn away.

————

The light of the Ziggurat left a ghostly glare on the shuttle windows, even from hundreds of miles away. It shrank into the hazy blue of the planet's surface, and the sky gave way to the empty blackness of space, dotted with stars and other spacecraft racing by. Livia stared out the window and sighed.

The group was quiet, their own conversations replaced by the insipid chatter of a dozen or so strange passengers, who were riding the shuttle to get back home in the spirals of the Tower of Bhalenjar. Children whined about the length of the trip. To them, a mere half hour seemed like years—it was an eternity. But Livia Nettunaya had gazed upon eternity, felt it, tasted it, and the otherwise silent ride was nowhere near endless.

It had been a tearful goodbye. Selenia saw them off, embraced Livia and Natharis, and thanked them for their generosity and faith. Livia insisted that she come with them, as did Natharis, but she had other business to attend to. "Called by the Emanation," she'd said. "When I healed your executive, I saw visions of a man wandering in the desert. I first thought it was Maru, caught in the endless wasteland between life and death. But it wasn't him. It was someone from my past, whom I have not seen in some time."

Livia had found her path, and it was time for Selenia to follow hers, and the two roads would not cross again. She didn't say where she was headed. It seemed that even she didn't know her destination. But something was drawing her away from the Ziggurat, the very place she'd traveled light-years to reach on her pilgrimage. Whatever she'd felt in the midst of the miraculous healing must have been profound. Only something of grave importance would pull her from her sanctuary. Livia knew she'd never find out what it was.

The Tellurian girl held a Breathtaker in her hands, running her fingers over its silvery chain. Selenia gave it to her with little explanation, but told her she would instinctively know how to wield it. Livia was no fighter, but Selenia didn't care. In her belief, the Emanation would guide Livia's movements and protect her from harm. In giving her the Breathtaker, Selenia granted Livia the power to take another's life. It was something not to be taken lightly.

"Only those who walk as scourges upon the earth deserve to feel its grip around their throats," Selenia cautioned. She warned Livia to be careful with her strength. Her righteous judgment could all too quickly turn to cruelty.

Natharis put his hand on hers and pulled her closer. She rested her head on his strong chest and felt safe in his embrace. "I know you miss her," he whispered. "But she has to fulfill her own destiny." He smiled. "And you have your own, right here with us. With me."

"I only just met her. You, too. But I feel like I've known both of you all my life. And now I've lost one of you."

"You have me. And I'm not going anywhere."

"She was my first teacher. I don't know if I can follow this path without her guidance."

"Follow your heart. It's what she'd want. I followed mine and it led me straight to you. That says it all, doesn't it?"

Livia placed a single kiss on his neck. "It does."

————

Through the airlock came a scenic view of the ancient habitat, a cylindrical structure, endless in length. It was one of the titanic scaffolds that spiraled upward into the heavens as the Tower of Bhalenjar, gleaming gold in the light of the sun. The life-giving star shone through a mile-wide strip of glass that ran far into the distance; the artificial sky moved as the habitat slowly rotated, and soon the light would give way to the darkness of the star-spotted night sky, and reveal the face of the broken moon that hovered over the planet far below.

Man-made structures rose from the inner surface of the cylinder, anchored by the force of its crawling rotation, and the greenery of parks and fields peeked out from behind towers on the horizon. Natharis had never seen anything like it. He felt microscopic, and suddenly perceived Sapien achievements as insignificant, as it was the Procyon who took credit for building the Tower, and had conducted their otherworldly experiments within it thousands of years ago.

They followed Selenia's instructions when they disembarked and ventured into the city. Ninotchka appointed herself as their navigator, and mocked the others when they dangerously attempted to give their input on her directions. Bronze-skinned Caspians passed by, carrying out their daily lives in a settlement Natharis found completely alien and difficult to become accustomed to. The slight glare on the transparent arch of the sky left him unsettled, and he couldn't help but imagine a rogue asteroid crashing through and bringing about the death of millions of people. But the Tower had survived this long. Perhaps it was just as untouchable as its creators.

"There," announced the Muscovite, pointing toward a sewage grating cloaked in the shadows of an alleyway. There was a small Mithneshi shrine at the corner of the narrow path, long forgotten by passers-by. She grimaced. "This won't be pleasant."

"So, now we'll *literally* be wading through shit," Silviano groaned. "A real nice change from what we've already been through."

"I'm sure ABAC facility will smell just as bad. At least we can wash this stench off. Theirs lingers for years."

"Get to it," Natharis sighed.

They were lucky. When Natharis slipped in first, his feet splashed into a trickling stream of tap water, not a stinking cascade of excrement. His voice echoed down the pipeline as he called for the others to follow, reassuring them that they wouldn't be begging for a change of clothes. He clicked on a flashlight and shone it into the dark. Out of the shadows appeared the haunting face of a Procyon.

He stumbled backward and shouted out in nervous surprise. With a marshal's instinct, he drew his weapon and aimed straight for the skeletal being's bulbous head. When it didn't recoil, Natharis sighed, realizing it to be a statue, its dull metal corroded by moisture. At the macabre sculpture's feet was a steel slab. Livia bent over and gripped its edge. She pulled, but it was too heavy for one person to pull away. Natharis helped her roll away the stone that sealed the tomb and kept its secrets locked away in the perpetual dark below the city. He didn't know what they might find within it. He feared an ancient evil. He hoped for the light to come quickly at the end of the tunnels.

———

Livia ran her fingers over the dry bones that lined the walls of the Procyon catacombs. They were old, older than the Convergency, and set into niches in the walls long before the Tellurian Imperium rose to power. Mummified skin, like delicate paper, cracked and crumbled off the bones; she, nor any of the group, could identify the remains. They were creatures that no Sapien had ever laid eyes upon.

Rocky, the once nameless Crystalline, theorized that nature itself had never seen, nor birthed, such abominations. Natharis said that they were the children of mortal gods, born of hubris and delusions of grandeur. They were creations unknown to the Emanation.

"They boast of their endless successes, but deny their failures," the Crystalline explained. *"This is where they hid the evidence of their imperfection. Many of their creations never survived, and some were destroyed when they defied the Procyon's predictions."*

"They tried to play God," Natharis muttered.

"They reject any concept of God. The only deity they recognize is that of the Procyon Hive Mind—limitless in power, omniscient and omnipresent, and far above even the most genius of Sapien intellects."

"They're not the only ones with a god-complex," Livia said.

"You're right," Silviano added, noting a crisscross of man-made pipes protruding from the ceiling. "And we're right below their temple."

———

Natharis peered upward toward the dim light at the top of the brick-lined shaft. He estimated the height of the passage, which extended upward toward the surface above them. The Crystalline noted that they were at the boundary between the walls of the cylindrical habitat and ABAC's private sphere, one of many that resembled atoms between the molecular spirals of the golden Tower of Bhalenjar. If they ascended the shaft, they would emerge right within ABAC's closely guarded facility. All they had to do was make it to the top and crawl out into the daylight, guns drawn, silent and undetected.

He reached into his pack and produced a grappling hook. He locked it into the barrel of his rifle and turned off the safety. The crack of the gunshot was deafening in the empty tunnel, but a gentle hum followed it, and the hook at the end of the unraveling rope glowed an energetic blue. It struck the metal surface at the top of the shaft, anchored by its magnetic charge. The rope swayed back and forth, beckoning him to climb upward toward his destination and his enemies. With their belts hooked and secured on the rope, the magnetic forces pulled them along its length, and they glided gracefully to the tunnels a dozen yards above them.

The once stagnant air rushed past his ears when his feet lifted off the ground. There was a rustling to his left, vague and distant at first, but it began to pound rhythmically, like the beating of wings. Livia tapped Natharis's boot from beneath him and caught his attention; in the glare of his flashlight, he saw her motion cautiously toward the dark. The sound pounded around him like the echo of a fierce war drum. He drew his handgun and held his breath.

A monstrous form emerged from the dark on leathery wings, hissing through its needle-like teeth. Its face was grotesque but familiar, like a Sapien, but twisted and mutilated, with the cloudy, white eyes of a blind man wandering in the shadows. It wheezed with strained breath as it swept by Natharis, dying in the depths of the lifeless caverns. Its Procyon creators had left their failures to perish far from the sun. He almost pitied the creature. As quickly as it had come into view, it disappeared again into the blackness. Natharis sighed. Livia let go of his leg.

Shots fired and Livia screamed. She pulled Natharis downward, and the bullet narrowly missed his head. The stone of the wall shattered from the impact, and the rope swayed dangerously, with such force that he had to firmly grip it to keep from slipping. Ninotchka cursed from below, having almost free-fallen into the black depths to a grisly demise. Natharis held his gun above his head and fired blindly over the ledge. He heard the wounded grunts of an incompetent soldier. A colossal thud followed, and the sound of coughing and choking on blood.

"Stop where you are!"

A second soldier waddled toward the edge of the vertical shaft, his breath heavy and laborious. Natharis met him with a lethal gunshot to his undulating stomach, but the ABAC goon didn't appear to feel a thing, protected by a three-foot thick, fatty shield. Natharis fired four more shots, until the wounds wept liquefied blubber, and a pile of soupy, reddish globs grew at the bovine guard's trunk-like ankles. He dropped to the ground. The cavern floor shook from the weight of his shapeless corpse.

"ABAC knows about catacombs," Ninotchka barked. "That stupid, holy bitch led us right into trap. 'Road less traveled,' my exquisite ass."

Silviano drew attention to a makeshift bed on the stone floor, though it looked more like a heap of old clothes and candy wrappers, like a bird's nest, but meant for the most gluttonous of vultures. "They probably just got lost down here. Trapped on the wrong side of that airlock ahead. Might have even forgotten the password."

"Their ineptitude knows no limits." The Crystalline went ahead and examined the airlock data displays. The technology looked old, and the chamber doors were rusted and dull. There were two such airlocks; one opened up to ABAC's heavily guarded facility, while the other led only to the frigid vacuum of space.

Ninotchka approached the latter and withdrew a wilted rose from under her clothes, stolen from the gardens of the Great Ziggurat. Neglecting to explain herself, she launched it out the airlock, only for it to drift away as a red velvet icicle.

She threw something beautiful away into the oblivion like she always did.

Dirty computer screens flickered with information about the atmosphere just beyond the other outdated airlock. Based on the pressure readouts, the Crystalline concluded they'd be exiting out into a body of water—deep, but not dangerously so. *"Get your oxygen supplies ready. This will not be pleasant for you Sapiens."*

But Natharis wasn't afraid of drowning. Livia's affection was the only air he needed to breathe. His lungs burned without it.

———

Even through the shifting mirror of the water's surface, the broken moon over Bhalenjar shone brightly. It was a cluster of shattered glass catching the light of the distant sun, and it danced over the lake and on the faces of the men and women who walked in its sandy depths. The Crystalline rushed ahead of them, tumbling along the sea floor.

Livia spat out the air supply mouthpiece into the water when she emerged from the lake. Her hair was dripping wet, as was her suit, and she worried for the state of their guns, but Natharis and Silviano had made sure to keep them dry in sealed bags. They left their extra gear on the shoreline and crept up to the long grasses, crouching behind them for cover. Across the lake were formidable barriers, metal walls twenty or so feet high, topped with mean barbed wire and lined with rows of security cameras. They were within the boundaries of the corporate fortress, just as Selenia had promised. Livia hoped that Ninotchka would retract her prior criticisms and admit her misjudgment, but she didn't bother to hold her breath for it.

"Now would be the perfect time for your ZGB friends to show up," Silviano said to Ninotchka, his hands parting the dry, yellowish grasses.

She glared back. "They'll be here—unlike your Tellurian escorts, who didn't even bother to track down their sacred whores." She looked up into the sky, past the transparent sphere and its protective energy shield. "When they get here, we'll know it. Quiet entrance is un-Muscovian."

"They'll plant the explosives," Natharis confirmed, "and we'll storm the control center." He looked to the Crystalline. "You know where you're going, right?"

"It will be like going home."

"And back to a bitch of a mother," Silviano laughed. "I'm sure Brock Dunham missed you real bad. You know, he's not far from here. Congress is just one sphere above us."

"And if he had his way, it'd be two steps below him," Natharis added.

"Well, we're not going to let that happen," said Livia. She squeezed Natharis's hand and drew from him a confident smile.

She looked ahead and gazed upon ABAC's newest headquarters, far away from its older tower on Albion, rising from the clustered mess of Dearborn's skyline. Their target stood alone, surrounded only by fields and the low-rise facility spreading from its base. The skyscraper rose as high as the habitat's protective shell, and even surpassed it, protruding out into the vacuum of space. The control center, and the tachyon anchor itself, were just beyond its limits. ABAC thought itself so powerful that it could escape the bounds of life and survive in the unknown. Should Livia and her friends succeed, then ABAC was truly mistaken. And if they were to fail, then the Conglomerate would finally hold the reigns over all life in the Convergency, and lead them into the cold and lifeless dark.

25

"Don't fool yourself, my dear. You're much worse than a bitch. You're a saint. Which shows why saints are dangerous and undesirable."
    —Ellsworth Toohey, *The Fountainhead.*

"OUR OPTIONS ARE LIMITED, at best," declared the Colonial Delta, standing over the holographic layout of the Congressional building. "We're lucky we even got the Executive out in the first place. Panzi was stupid enough to leave the rear emergency exit unprotected, but I doubt she'll make the same mistake twice." He pushed aside the tablet to hand it off to the executive. "Point is, we're not using the doors this time."

"There's the air ducts," added another Delta, drawing attention to the thin, grid-like pattern of ventilation tubes that snaked through the building. "With a couple of ropes, we could jump out right on top of them."

"There's no way you're going to fit," Desh replied, shaking his head, "not with your guns and supply packs. A Xaztechuan trying to sneak into Colonial territory couldn't squirm through that, even with the light of prosperity at the end of the tunnel."

"Then what do you propose?"

Desh paused for a moment to take a closer look at the blueprint. "There," he indicated, pointing to a labeled control box. "Sabotage the pressure sensors. Unless Panzi's completely suicidal, she'll open the doors the second she thinks they might run out of air. She's perfectly content with economic suicide, but not the real kind."

"Sure you weren't ever a Delta?"

The executive laughed. "Some Navy experience, yes. But that was a long time ago."

"Well, you heard the Executive. Let's get to it. Don't hesitate to open fire on the collectivist leadership. They had no reservations about shooting ours."

"No," Desh ordered. "I want them alive."

"Some good old Colonial justice?"

"Like we've never seen before, boys. They'll be begging for a stay in Tartarus once we're through with them."

———

Supreme Doge Panzi Illoszia was the first to scream out in uncontrolled panic. The pressure alarms sounded, a rhythmic surge of wailing sirens, though her own desperate shrieks were even more deafening. She looked to her support base for a plan. As was their way, they had none. She gripped the edges of her podium and tried to calm her breathing. The individualists saw that it did little to comfort her in her morbid desperation.

Oksana rolled her eyes and groaned. "You'd best do something soon, Miss 'Supreme Doge,' or else we're all going to suffocate."

"And God knows we've suffocated enough under your ridiculous policies," Sir Byron added. "But at least this is more palpable. You can't deny it this time, Panzi. You really led us to our deaths, and went down with the ship."

Mireille laughed. "Maybe this is what she's always wanted."

"*Shut up!*" Panzi barked, flecks of saliva exploding from her mouth. She nervously rapped her fingers on the desk and chewed her lip. Even she knew that time was running out.

Sir Byron whispered to Mireille and Oksana, "According to the sensors, we shouldn't be breathing right now." Under his desk, he pointed to the readouts. "Someone's screwing with the system."

Oksana smiled slyly. "Get ready."

Panzi finally caved in and commanded her troops, "*Open the doors!* We'll die when Brock Dunham says we can!" She shook her fist with false authority. *"Do it! That's an order!"*

The soldiers turned their backs to Congress and forced open the doors. They braced themselves for a rush of air, a rapid, devastating blast of breathable atmosphere. They were met not by a violent breath, but by Colonial bullets, lethal and unexpected.

"No!" screamed the Supreme Doge, her personal army stolen from her.

The Colonial Deltas burst into the Congressional chamber with the spirit of justice behind them. They unleashed hell upon the misguided defenders of collectivism, so ruthlessly that the floor of Parliament ran red with blood. The three Arterran executives took cover behind their desks, but in the fray, saw no one but armed soldiers fall to Colonial force. With military precision, the Deltas avoided the innocent, even though Oksana, a fearsome Muscovite, considered no collectivist innocent. She wanted them to pay for their crimes with their lives. Sir Byron reassured her that the Colonies would never allow a single one to escape justice. Patience would lead to a satisfying judgment day.

"This is *my position!*" Panzi cried. *"It will not be taken from me!"*

"Your power is a lie," said a deep voice from the door. The floor of Congress fell silent. The legislature stared in awe and disbelief as none other than Executive Maru stepped confidently into the chamber, not with a limp or a hint of pain, but with a masculine stride that commanded nothing less than respect for his authority. He descended the central stairs and approached the Supreme Doge's unlawful seat. She cowered in fear. Her eyes burned with rage.

"You hold an unelected seat in this government, *Parliamentarian*," he continued, sneering at his helpless prey. "You are responsible for the deaths of thousands of innocent people, and led to the collapse of countless systems. No one deserves the position you've invented—*you*, least of all. This Congress—and this Council—will not humor your pitiful delusions any longer. And I dare you to try and stop us."

Colonial Deltas approached Panzi with handcuffs and guns drawn. She fought as they took her by the wrists and restrained her; she spat in their faces, and found herself knocked to the ground by the butts of their rifles. She writhed with the wind knocked out of her, trembling before Desh's judgment.

"I hereby place Panzi Illoszia under Colonial arrest for crimes against Sentients. Your war crimes will be presented before the Supreme Court, and it will decide your fate. And for such an offense, Colonial law will condemn you to nothing less than death. It is a fate you've brought upon yourself, Parliamentarian. You will not be a scourge upon this Convergency any longer."

The hideous creature shook with fury, her mouth foaming with hate and her brow breaking its permanent paralysis. Hot tears ran over her implanted cheeks; mucus burst from her poorly crafted nose and covered her mouth in bubbling slime. Her wrists bled from her futile attempts to escape her bonds. Desh looked upon her, listened to her nonsensical cursing, and thought he might even pity her. She was a pawn in Brock Dunham's twisted game, and perhaps, deep down, she really did think she was working for the elusive "greater good." But for Desh, her ends could never justify her means. She'd sentenced thousands to die for no reason other than her own lust for power. He couldn't pity her. She was unredeemable.

"With authorization from the Colonial Supreme Court, the United Colonies are now at war," he announced. "ABAC must be destroyed. For the 'greater good.'"

"The Kingdom of Windsor Britannia will come to the Colonies' aid."

"Tsardom of Romanov Muscovia has waited for this day for quite some time."

"*La République Fédérée de la Gaule* will deport them all to *l'enfer*."

"Find Executive Dunham," Desh ordered his Deltas. "I want him to be here when his entire fleet falls to a single Colonial battleship. And then, he'll meet his own fate."

Pentakiya's bed no longer brought her comfort at the end of the day. The mattress wasn't soft and inviting; beneath her back, it felt like hot coals or shattered glass. Her silken sheets weren't cool or sensual; they were a thin but unbreakable straightjacket, constricting her, binding her to the bed, to looming nightmares just beyond the edge of sleep. The salt of dried tears made the skin of her cheeks feel itchy and dry. Even the cotton of Artimpasa's softest nightshirt was rough against her body. Her senses were heightened, painfully so, but at the same time, she felt wholly and irreversibly numb.

She still smelled the smoke from the fire, which clung to the blue dress she'd stripped off and thrown angrily at the foot of her bed. It lay upon the floor with the stench of death locked into its fibers. The odor disgusted her. The dress held memories she wanted to leave behind, but couldn't. It was the dress she'd worn to her wife's desecrated funeral; it was the dress that Pentakiya wanted to wear when she passed from this world. She felt sick knowing that she was so close to committing such a selfish act. The taking of an innocent life was something Brock Dunham would condone—and she'd nearly taken her own. She wondered if she were truly innocent. She worried that she, like him, deserved to die.

The disc she held in her hand was fragile, smaller than most. She'd taken it from its hiding place and stared at it for hours. In spite of its plainness and insignificant size, it was more valuable than anything she'd ever kept in her possession. Clasped tightly in her fist was the power to collapse an empire. She held the access codes for Brock Dunham's most guarded secret. Her very knowledge of it was punishable by death. She was, after all, the wife of a traitor, and ultimately, a traitor herself.

She knew her death was inevitable. It was only a matter of time before the authorities discovered the disc. Rocky had been right. She alone had the ability to fight against injustice, and to defeat it with the simple push of a button. To anyone else, there would have been no moral dilemma. But her past loyalties made it impossible to push that very button. Her upbringing, her devotion to the cause, and her years of hard work for the sake of collectivism left her paralyzed. She feared she couldn't do it. She would die if she did, and her wife would never have wanted her to give up her own life. But Artimpasa herself had done just that, sacrificing her life for the preservation of liberty. And wasn't it Artimpasa, not Dunham, whom Pentakiya looked up to as a lifelong hero?

Her faith in him was a farce and a source of deep shame. She cursed herself for ever believing the lies he sold as truth, for putting even a shred of faith in his myriad broken promises, one after the other. She always forgave him for his shortcomings, rationalizing them, finding excuses. They were never really his fault. It was his stubborn, bigoted opposition; it was the unavoidable consequences of his predecessors' policies. Anything that went wrong under Dunham's administration couldn't possibly be because of any fault of his own. The buck stopped with those who came before him, who were no longer around to defend themselves against such criticism.

She knew what she had to do. She couldn't allow these monsters to pass the blame any longer, to deny responsibility for their abominable actions. Pentakiya sat up in her bed and gazed upon the crimson moon bleeding through her window. She vowed to the universe that she would make right all those things she did wrong. She swore to the memory of her martyred wife that she would make amends, if it was not already too late. She pulled her holotab off her nightstand and inserted the invaluable disc. She took a deep breath. There was no going back.

A digital chime confirmed that the data had been successfully transmitted. Soon enough, Rocky would find the access codes in his possession. She didn't know how long it might take for him to receive it, but she prayed that she hadn't waited too long to make her penance. The timestamp at the corner of her screen clicked one minute ahead. Soon enough, he'd know she had finally chosen the right side. And even sooner, ABAC would realize the same, and then she'd be greeting a legion of soldiers at her apartment door.

————

The first gunshots resounded unexpectedly, and the bullets came like a deadly rain. No one had seen the assault coming. ABAC's slaves were the first to emerge from the facility in the distance, alien, bound by control collars locked around their necks. Vehisipens, wielding plasma rifles at the end of each of their many tendrils, fired indiscriminately out into the open, screeching and roaring in their unintelligible language. Livia counted five of them, and dove behind a work truck for cover. She pitied the creatures, despite her being in their crosshairs. They were literally enslaved by the Conglomerate. She wondered if they were conscious of their own actions. She imagined their pain in knowing that they were forced to kill the very people who meant to liberate them.

Ninotchka and Silviano drew three in their direction; the Muscovian agent managed to disarm one, blasting off each of its tendrils at their base, leaving the creature writhing on the ground with no hope of escape. She crushed its small body with one stomp of her knife-like heel. Silviano fended off the others without much difficulty, calling upon the martial training all servants of Mars carried in the back of their minds. His muscles tensed as he clutched his rifle firmly to his side, and his black hair dripped with the sweat of his efforts. He truly looked like the war god he served with devotion. He channeled his god's furious spirit and sentenced his enemies to die without mercy.

Livia heard Natharis shout out for help. She pulled out her Breathtaker, still unsure of how to effectively use it, but she didn't care. She ran toward him through the fray, as he was surrounded by the mindless Vehisipens, desperately searching for a way out. Even he didn't see her coming. She leapt toward one of the creatures and jammed the blade of her Breathtaker between its body and the metal ring set around it. She'd meant to stab the beast, to let its blood run over her hands, but she accidentally pried off the control collar. It fell to the ground and crackled with glowing sparks. Livia lost her balance and landed on her knees.

The Vehisipen stood over her, its many eyes scanning her face. Its putrid stench made her eyes water and forced her to hold her breath. Natharis scrambled over the grass to pull her away, but the Vehisipen turned—not toward him, but to the oncoming horde of ABAC soldiers pouring from the facility doors. It howled and aimed its rifles at the crowd, opening fire with no clear target. A thirst for revenge guided its aim, but hatred was a poor guide, no matter how justified. Only a few soldiers were hit. The rest trampled over them with no concern for their fallen comrades, set only on taking out their targets and slaying those who refused to give up their livelihood for the sake of the ravenous whole.

Then came an explosion from above. Livia braced herself for flying shrapnel, crouching low on the ground with hands over her head. She peeked through her fingers up at the sky, and the air rippled and shimmered, distorted by the heat of the blast. A black craft clung to the habitation bubble's protective shell like a leech; lasers burst from its underbelly and cut through its surface. With the sun behind it, the ominous craft cast a wing-shaped shadow over the open field. It brandished no flag or identification. Livia feared it was an ABAC ship, but before she could run for cover, she saw a hatch snap open beneath the craft. She knew that bombs were about to fall.

Six metallic spheres dropped from the ship, bigger than any explosive any of them had ever seen. The ground shook upon their impact, but they didn't detonate as expected. Livia sighed with relief. ABAC's forces were clearly curious, encircling the devices, guns still drawn but halfheartedly aimed. They should have known better.

"Take cover!" shouted Ninotchka.

A plasma burst from each sphere knocked them to the ground, and their screams gave Livia a sick sense of satisfaction. Their uniforms caught fire, and their skin roasted away, and those still standing ran back toward the tower in terror. The spheres opened up like lotus flowers. Like the birth of Venus, six heavenly women emerged from their divine seashells.

"I told you ZGB wouldn't disappoint," Ninotchka laughed. She sprinted out into the field to greet the special ops team that had arrived just in time. "Women *love* roses—gets them every time," she said to the men in her presence. "Meet my favorite *shlyukha* squad: Sasha, Natasha, Tatyana, Svetlana, Natalya, and Katyusha, best agents ZGB's got, other than myself."

The six Muscovite beauties saluted their comrade. Livia had always thought Ninotchka's risqué manner of dress was some kind of absurd joke, but it seemed that the ZGB preferred to use sex as its most lethal weapon. The special ops team had no trouble catching the eye of every man they had in their crosshairs. Livia couldn't quite tell if they were wearing particularly skimpy shorts or actual lingerie, but she wouldn't have been surprised at the latter. In many ways, they made Ninotchka look like a modest, appropriately dressed lady of class. The special ops team was a busty example of an unsettling but effective self-objectification, one that conveyed a sense of feminine strength, and deadly power over the minds of men.

They immediately joined in the fray, although many of ABAC's soldiers had dropped their weapons and their jaws. They were so weak-willed that the sight of a single beautiful woman was enough to disarm them. Others, however, weren't so easily distracted. They waddled at full speed toward the six devilish beauties, guns blazing but imprecisely aimed. One knocked his undulating stomach into Katyusha; her rifle slipped out of her hands and slid across the ground. He grinned and reached out to pin her down, but she had other plans. In a moment of quick thinking, she grabbed him by the head and smothered his face between her breasts. He flailed his arms, fighting as best he could to escape her overtly sexual grip, but his face turned blue, and she dropped his lifeless body to the ground with a seductive laugh. Livia had never seen any martial art like it.

"Head for tower!" Ninotchka barked. She snatched a few ABAC rifles off the ground and held them under her arm. "Special ops will keep troops busy. They'll cover us then plant explosives." She shouted in Muscovian to the team, who nodded affirmatively. *"Spasiba!"*

They broke the glass of the lobby's front doors and marched through. "Where are the office workers? All the corporate executives?" Natharis wondered. Rocky speculated that they must have fled the habitation bubble, but well before the group's arrival. It seemed ABAC was preparing for something big. The Conglomerate would never have used its central banking tower as a massive barracks if it wasn't.

The distant sound of gunfire crackled out in the open courtyard, but the tower was silent and largely empty. The stairwell door slammed against the wall, and Livia prayed its frustrating echo wouldn't give away their position so soon. They brazenly ascended the stairs, gunning down the occasional soldier without hesitation. Livia heard a clatter from behind them, and turned around nervously, expecting to see a horde of troops ready to pummel their bodies with bullets. Instead, she saw the six Muscovites, pulling bundles of explosives out of their packs and securing them to the base of the stairwell. They grinned.

The agents followed them close behind, stopping at each floor to plant another round of explosives. Livia could hear their towering heels clicking against the stairs, thumping over the limp, blood-soaked bodies of fallen ABAC soldiers. With the final bomb secured to the wall just outside the control center, the special ops team had completed their mission. One of them approached Ninotchka with a detonator in her hand. She passed it on to her comrade and embraced her, then chatted briefly in Muscovian.

"They're going to planet's surface," Ninotchka translated, "to incite rebellion among Caspians. Apparently, Arterran executives have declared war on ABAC." She looked to Livia and said, "I guess you're sleeping with enemy now. Imperium will have no choice but to fight alongside ABAC." Livia frowned, offended. Unfortunately, Ninotchka was right. But she'd rather be a traitor to her people than the Conglomerate's pawn. And if the Mithneshi Creator Himself didn't choose sides, then surely love itself didn't, either.

"Dosvidaniya, moi dorogiye shlyukhi," Ninotchka said as a less-than-tearful farewell. *"Udachi."* The predatory females winked, then rushed away on their dangerous heels toward the exit.

"Here we are," announced Rocky. It approached a glowing panel on the wall beside the control center door. *"I hope my old security clearance still works."* Ninotchka didn't give it the chance; she took one unannounced shot at the panel, and after a shower of sizzling sparks, the door slid open.

"Security clearance?" she scoffed.

The apex of the skyscraper was a circular room, separated from the stairwell by a pane of bulletproof glass. Screens relaying footage from countless surveillance cameras lined the curved walls in place of windows. Concentric rings of desks, inlaid with holoscreens, encircled the central focus of the control center. The unarmed technicians were helpless, taking cover beneath their narrow workbenches; the fluorescent lighting from above left their white coats glowing, exposing their already poorly concealed positions. Natharis ordered them to leave the room, unwilling to gun down civilians.

"None of them are innocent," Ninotchka hissed. "We will spare no one." One by one, she executed them. She left no survivors. "Their complacency signed their death warrants," she assured Livia, who winced with each gunshot. Natharis didn't look satisfied.

"We've got company," Silviano declared, drawing attention to one of the camera feeds. Up the stairwell marched a well-armed brigade, riot masks concealing their faces. They were visibly more prepared than those on the front lines, with chests covered with thick body armor and strong, polymer shields held ahead of them. Silviano reloaded his rifle and pulled a second firearm from his back. "And of course, you had to sabotage the lock." He smashed his fist into the control panel, but nothing happened. "You can only close it from the outside!"

"They'll have to funnel through the door," Natharis said. "We can fend them off."

"All I need is three minutes," insisted the Crystalline scientist, who had torn open a technical panel and rigged a bundle of wires to its glassy body. An electrical current flickered through it, sparking where it'd loosely secured the cables. Suddenly, an alarm sounded, and the overhead lights shifted to a startling red. *"I have activated the deployment procedure. We will launch soon enough."*

Silviano and Natharis flanked the door with their weapons ready; Ninotchka stood directly before it with her machine gun aimed menacingly at the stairwell. The pounding of heavy boots against the stairs preceded the shock team's entrance. They burst into the control center foyer, barking commands at their targets, to get on the ground and surrender. Ninotchka simply laughed and pulled the trigger.

"What should I do?" Livia screamed over the thunderous gunfire.

"Catch!" Ninotchka shouted. She pulled the detonator from her bustier and tossed it behind her without looking back; Livia caught it nervously and crouched behind a desk. *"Prime explosives! Top button!"*

Livia did as she was told, but the tiny screen on the remote flashed unexpectedly, indicating an untimely error. "It's not working!"

"Blyad!" the Muscovite cursed. "Fuses failed!" She reloaded her gun and gritted her teeth as she shattered the enemies' full-body shields and knocked them down the stairs.

Natharis shot his rifle blindly around the corner of the doorway and yelled to Livia, "We're gonna have to detonate them manually!" He pulled a grenade from his vest and tossed it at the soldiers' feet. A splatter of blood hit the glass window. "The special ops girls planted their last one right at the top of the stairs!" Sure enough, a tiny red light blinked from above the stairwell door. The ABAC soldiers had stormed right past it without a second glance.

"If we set just one of them off, the chain reaction will take out the entire tower," Rocky theorized. *"But not until we deploy the command center. I will stay behind."* The red lights stopped flashing and glowed continuously. *"We are ready to launch."*

"As much as I would like to see murderer blown to bits, we need it," Ninotchka conceded. "We don't know shit about tachyon anchor. But it does."

"She's right," agreed Silviano. "You need it." He placed his rifle on the desk and sighed. "This is our only shot. It won't be long before the next wave arrives."

"Do not be foolish," Rocky advised.

"Think about this," Livia insisted. She watched nervously as Silviano put down the rest of his gear, leaving himself completely unarmed. "You don't have to be the hero."

"Yes, I do."

He approached her solemnly; Natharis didn't intervene when he put his hand on Livia's shoulder and leaned in to whisper to her. "I've spent my whole life serving the war god," he said, "and everyone's always called me his spear, just for lying in bed with others. But this is the first time I've ever really earned that name." He kissed Livia on the cheek. "Both of us have to surrender to our callings. Yours is with the Colonial; mine is here. I'll be baptized by fire and die by the sword. It's been my destiny all along."

Silviano turned his back and rushed for the door. Livia tried to stop him, but Natharis held her back. She collapsed into his arms as the consitor spoke his last words.

"*A vider-noz, Livia Nettunaya,*" he said in their native tongue. "*De porpido vollí cuinyoszer tiz amor.*"

"*No!*" Livia screamed, but he sealed the door with a tug of the bare wires. He put his hand to the bulletproof glass, and smiled with a tender sadness behind his eyes. The Crystalline warned them to brace themselves; everyone sat but Livia. The violent vibrations that shook the control center as it lifted from the tower meant nothing to her. She watched as a broken man sentenced himself to die—a man who never knew love, but wanted to in any form, no matter how false or fleeting. She wept knowing that he'd sacrificed himself for her. It was his one last attempt at understanding how she truly felt, not for him, but for Natharis, who held her in his arms as the fiery explosions erupted from far below.

"What did he say?" he asked, unfamiliar with her language.

She hesitated, then whispered her answer. "He wanted what all of us want: to know love."

"He loved you, didn't he?"

"He thought he did."

"You don't believe it?"

"All he knew was what he could touch. No one ever gave him the chance to know more. Not the priests, and not me." She closed her eyes. "But you gave me that chance—he knew that. And he laid down his life for it."

—————

The lifeless dunes stretched out to the horizon in great, shimmering waves, and the fine sand rippled with the heat's silvery pools. The desert wind was hot and dry, rushing into Selenia's nostrils not like the breath of life, but death. It spread a ghostly veil of sand over her body and scratched her face, leaving her skin red. She shut her eyes to the wind and cruel sun. It didn't matter if she could see her surroundings. She still didn't know where she was, and with her ship broken in pieces across the sand, she had nowhere to go.

The last she could remember was looking upon a Tellurian girl's face, sparkling with the tears of a fateful goodbye. A halo surrounded her, one that would protect her even without Selenia to guide her. It gave Selenia comfort, knowing that she hadn't abandoned the student she'd only just begun to teach. The girl would carry the light with her. Neither she, nor Selenia, had anything to fear.

Then there was a tunnel. It pulsed with energy and swirls of colors—Selenia had seen it before. She glided down the passage, carried on the wings of faith, drawn closer by the Emanation. There was a light at the end of the tunnel, and the silhouette of a lone person basking in its glory. The youthful figure was familiar, and carried a presence she hadn't felt in a long time. It was an innocent presence, one oppressed by an ancient evil, recognizable, but somehow changed. She tried to recall a name. It eluded her.

She was under fire, targeted by a force she could never hope to challenge. Her assailants' demeanor was like that of God, though she, nor anyone, ever knew God in mortal life. The thought disturbed her that she was looking upon the faces of almighty beings. They thought they were greater than God, and rejected the very concept of the Almighty, who created them and endowed them with the ultimate gift of reason. They shot her down from the heavens just as they had murdered their own faith, and she awoke to a wreckage on a nameless world they once walked, in those ancient days when they set foot on terra firma and called themselves the fair-skinned gods of Man.

––––––––

The air inside the room was cold, stale, leaving the boy with goose bumps and a sour stench in his nostrils. The bright lights, without any clear source, made it painful to open his eyes. The smooth metal of the examination table was hard against his back; his cold sweat sealed his bare skin to its surface. He thought he was paralyzed, but he could move his toes and fingers. His fear made movement near impossible. He knew where he was. He'd let them take him there. He didn't fight then, and he wouldn't fight now.

But where were his captors? The room was empty, silent. Selas didn't hear the clatter of surgical instruments or the patter of feet upon the floor. There was no piercing whir of drills or horrible screams from another torture chamber. No—he was alone. There were no black eyes watching him, gazing into the depths of his mind. Could it have been a trap? Were they waiting for him to build up hope, and plan a desperate but vain escape? Their motives were unknowable, as they always were, and always would be. He couldn't read their thoughts like they could read his own. All he could do was take that leap of faith off the table.

Carefully, he sat upright. His head felt heavy, as if all the blood in his body had rushed upward to the base of his skull. Selas touched the back of his neck to ease the aching; he withdrew his hand in a panic. His heart pounded and his stomach tightened in knots. There was something protruding from his body, embedded in his spine. He cautiously traced a trembling finger over the device: a curved piece of metal, arching from the ridge where his neck met his skull down to between his shoulder blades. He winced with a sharp pain when he tried to pull on it to see how firmly it was anchored in his spine. He shuddered and felt sick. He was happy he couldn't see it. He only wished he knew what it was, what it was meant for. It was an implant he was sure couldn't be removed. If he ever returned to his people, there was no hiding it. It was an alien stigma he couldn't deny.

He snatched surgical sheets from a nearby table and wrapped them around his naked body like an ancient shepherd's clothes. The floor was cold beneath his bare feet, and he stepped carefully, slowly enough to be silent. He took a deep breath and peeked his head out the open door. All he saw was white, with no beginning or end.

The light startled him, but he worked up the courage to step out into the endless whiteness. He put his arm out in front of him to feel for a wall, a boundary of some kind. Sure enough, he felt the curve of the corridor, and dragged his hand along the smooth, glowing surface. There was a ringing in his ears, and it started quietly, but with each step he took farther down the hall, it grew sharper, louder, until he felt blood pounding in his ears. There was a door ahead, just out of reach. Selas pushed on, his head split by the piercing din. He felt dizzy. His vision began to blur.

And then the pain disappeared. The second he stumbled through the door, he found his balance again and his vision sharpened. The excruciating ringing turned to silence, and the pain faded away like a distant memory. He collapsed to the ground in sweet relief, ignoring the sting of the cold, hard floor against his knees. Selas knelt, resting until he calmed his mind and slowed his breathing. But there was a sense of danger in the room that he couldn't escape; with his eyes closed, he saw visions of something terrible ahead, but it wasn't black eyes, or twisted hands grasping at his paralyzed body. What he saw was an abomination of unspeakable horror.

Oh my God.

There were too many bodies for him to count. They lay in their open caskets set into the floor, eyes open but with no consciousness behind their blank stare. The tanks that cradled them formed a great circle, spreading outward in concentric rings that looked like a blossoming flower the color of a corpse. They didn't moan, or even breathe; the only hint of life was the synchronized beeps of displays on the wall, dancing with the peaks and valleys of heartbeats and brain activity. Their thoughts raced visibly across the screens, although they may not have been thoughts at all, or even images the way a person would envision them. They appeared to be living in limbo, wandering the space between worlds, but all in their minds.

A clear, slimy fluid covered their faces and shimmered in the light of the computers. The bodies were rigged with thick, black cables, and breathing tubes emerged from their throats. Refracted through the viscous liquid was the unnatural shape of the same implant that protruded from Selas's spine. They were somehow connected to each other, to the massive device they were trapped in against their will. They surrounded the focus of the apparatus like pilgrims bowing to a holy shrine. It was a burial in a technological graveyard in the shadow of a trinity of unholy beings.

The black-eyed creatures floated at the center of the room in a triangular formation of ceiling-high tanks, submerged in fluid illuminated by a greenish glow. Selas was terrified at the sight of their inhuman faces, but a morbid curiosity overtook him, and he found himself stepping closer toward the ghostly figures. He tiptoed around the glistening graves and put his hand to the glass tank. He feared that he might wake them, but they stayed motionless. Perhaps they were dead. But there was never any life behind their soulless eyes to begin with.

What am I seeing?

The sleeping deities watched down over their slaves, who lay in bondage to their cruel, triune gods. The unwilling believers looked up to a heaven through whose gates they'd never pass, because their masters denied them the welcome release of death. Selas walked among them in a reverent silence and whispered prayers under his breath, but they brought him little comfort. With each step he took past another helpless soul, he felt himself growing sicker, and a foul, heavy fear grew in the pit of his stomach, until it overtook him and he fell to his knees in panic beside the only empty casket, knowing it was meant for him. He plunged his hand into the watery coffin beside him and couldn't breathe. The base of his skull throbbed with a sharp pain and chills ran down the back of his neck.

His heart pounded in his chest and his body went limp, and thoughts crashed through his mind with such unnatural force that he might as well have not been thinking at all. He once considered the workings of his mind to be a river or a powerful waterfall, but his old thinking was just a trickle of water between immutable stones. Images flashed before him and countless voices spoke at once, but he could hear all of them, and he could see what each saw and hear what each heard and feel what each felt. There was no more impenetrable boundary around him, no more self or ego, and each voice within the echoing sea was one. But there was another presence entirely, with a different voice, one that wasn't so much heard as felt. It was the voice of those who'd taken him—taken all of them. It was in words that no Sapien had ever heard spoken with their simplistic, useless ears. They told him he was finally theirs.

There is no you; there is no Sapien. There is only us. There is only the Hive Mind.

The clear fluid splashed over him as he pulled his hand from the tank, screaming for a way out. He looked about; he was back in the chamber, and the only thoughts he had were his own, and no one else's. But even with the boundaries of the self drawn about him once again, he still felt his senses heightened, and colors looked brighter, sounds were sharper, clearer, and the memories of all those thousands of beings,

Sapien or otherwise, still lingered. The viscous liquid was cold on his hands and felt like slime dripping from his wrists. He tried to shake it off, but it clung to him like napalm that had yet to be ignited. He smeared it onto the sheets he had wrapped around his body and dragged a wet finger over the edge of the tank.

Then he saw a familiar face staring back at him, past him, through him, from beneath the surface of the water. It was Burton, no longer fighting or trying to escape. And for the first time, Selas looked into his eyes without the eccentric black shades hiding their color: blue and cloudy, like the eyes of a blind man, the kind that gazed at nothing and everything at once.

He knew he had to save him, and he gripped the breathing tube at his lips, carefully sliding it out from down his throat. Even unconscious, the old man coughed up fluid, wheezing as liquid trickled from his lungs. He still didn't wake up, but his breathing had become shallow, almost stopped. Selas's last chance to bring him back to consciousness was to unplug him from the system, but he worried that he might damage his brain in doing so. He prepared himself for the task, but took solace in knowing that if he were to end Burton's life, it might prove to be a blessing, a welcome gift.

The man lunged at Selas when he tore the cable from the back of his head. He dug his fingers into the boy's shoulders and screamed, louder than any person should have been capable of, like two voices were bellowing from the depths of his lungs. Water splashed over him as he fell and slid on the floor. It was more than a cry of pain; his cries echoed with desperation and despair. Selas couldn't stop him. He lay on the ground with a gaping mouth, and a pervasive horror filled his eyes.

Forget the boundary; break the limits of the self. You are still connected.

The pressure grew on the back of Selas's neck, and the skin around the implant rippled with goose bumps. He cleared his mind and touched his hand to Burton's brow, visualizing a link between them, a connection that melded their thoughts and emotions into one. With a mental jolt, he knew he'd done it. The man fell silent. He turned his gaze away from the beyond and focused on the boy who'd tamed his tortured mind.

"Something's comin'," he whispered with a shaky voice. He looked about the room like he was waiting for a premonition to prove true.

"Do you know where you are?" Selas asked, convinced that Burton was disoriented and confused. "How long you've been here?"

He didn't appear to be listening. Selas tried explaining what little he'd deduced from all that he'd seen, but the words fell on deaf ears. Burton climbed off the floor, still trembling, but stood tall on weak legs. Selas pulled one of the sheets off his shoulder and covered the man's body, but he said nothing, and didn't notice his own nakedness. He listened for something, but for what, Selas had no idea. The longer he waited, the more his apprehension grew, until there was a tension in the room that he felt as well and just as inexplicably.

It came with little warning other than his dread—a deafening bang, then the wail of a piercing siren, not out loud, but in their heads. Their minds were flooded with the panic that spread through the entire ship in an instant. Water splashed from the caskets as the room shook violently; a heavy tube from the ceiling snapped and swung downward, crashing into the tanks that embowered the three unmoving creatures. Cracks ran along the glass and beads of liquid dripped from the fissures. Selas grabbed Burton by the wrist and pulled him toward the door. The man kept his eyes fixed on the people they couldn't save. He looked sick with guilt.

"We can't help them," Selas insisted. "This is our chance, and we've got to take it." He opened his mind and felt an emptiness outside the chamber. "Those creatures—the Procyon—they're gone. Hiding," he relayed. He paused upon saying their name out loud. Giving a name to his once nameless captors lent him a sense of power he'd never had. "Let's go. We're alone here."

Burton mumbled under his breath as he followed the boy, "Where the hell are they?"

"There aren't as many of them as they want us to think." He couldn't explain how he knew it, but there was a palpable barrenness to the massive craft, like it was meant just for a façade of strength, concealing the race's true weakness: they were dwindling in number. Down the corridors and through the rooms, Selas saw no one. All was quiet except for the explosions that shook the floors and made it difficult to run straight.

"You don't know where you're goin'," Burton panted as they rushed through the featureless white of the halls. It was a fair assumption. There was nothing in the structure of the ship that could help them even retrace their steps.

"I do. I've seen it all. It's all there in the back of my mind—and yours, too. Use your memories like a map." In his head he saw the entire layout of the craft, the maze of curved passageways and docking bays. He'd seen it in an overwhelming flash when he became one with the collective. In that fleeting moment, he'd learned everything he needed to know. He was confident that there was a hangar up ahead. He sensed that there was nothing in their path. The creatures had fled to the depths of their titanic vessel. They had no emotions, but Selas felt their repulsion. It was as close to fear as they were capable of feeling.

"We're here."

Burton looked at the wide doorway and searched for some kind of written sign. Throughout the ship, neither had seen a single word inscribed. "You don't know that."

"Yes, I do."

"Wait a second—" He tried to hold Selas back, but the boy slipped easily out of his weakened grip. Selas didn't think twice about entering.

And he was right. The open door led to the back of a massive docking bay. The roof arched overhead as a wide-set dome, but the hangar door hundreds of yards ahead looked like just a thin sliver across the empty chamber. There was a row of alien craft to the left, along the edge of the hangar, illuminated by eerie green lights. Selas had never seen anything like them. Disc-shaped and curiously small, they appeared to be scout ships. He saw no entry ports or cockpit windows. They, like all the Procyon designs he'd seen, were featureless. He had no idea how he'd pilot one, let alone get inside. Burton remarked the same.

"You don't even know how to fly one of our *own* ships. We ain't gettin' out of here, kid. Pretty soon they'll come back. And they'll be lookin' for us."

Selas didn't answer. He stood beneath the silently hovering craft, staring up at the metallic, shining surface. There were no exhaust outlets, no thrusters or visible drives, nothing that could even identify it as a ship. It looked more like an abstract sculpture, a work of art meant to please an inhuman eye. It was, indeed, beautiful. It captivated him. He felt drawn to touch it, so he did. He ignored Burton's pessimistic judgments and waited for something, though he didn't know what.

"Come on," he whispered. "Let me in."

And the craft obeyed. He jumped back when he heard the hiss of an opening hatch; the outer edge of the disc split in two, spreading open like a pair of cold, shimmering lips. He shouted in excitement and beckoned the older man to get inside. Burton was less enthusiastic. While Selas had practically jumped into the cockpit, he crawled in reluctantly. Only after he'd peeked his head in several times did he decide it was safe to board. There were no black-eyed beings waiting for them in the shadows of the craft. The only concern they had was, as Burton put it, "how to turn the damned thing on."

Selas stared at the controls and didn't even know where to begin. "I've never seen anything like it," he remarked, tracing his fingers over what he assumed to be the dashboard. Burton tried to identify a single switch, button or display, but saw nothing. There were two indentations in the otherwise blank surface, shaped like hands—not Sapien hands, but those of the Procyon, with their long, slender fingers. Burton groaned, but Selas didn't share his sense of defeat. He sat in one of the two pilot's seats and cleared his head. Intuitively, he slid his fingers into the smooth depression in the metal. He kept two fingers together to fit the four-digit handprint. Nothing happened. Neither heard the hum of engine drives that the boy had hoped to activate.

Burton plopped down in the other seat and sighed, but despite his discouraging remarks, Selas didn't withdraw his hands from the dashboard. He shut his eyes and tried to visualize their escape, holding a picture in his mind of the ship come to life. The image became clearer, sharper, until it began to project onto the still reality around him. He willed the craft to move forward; silently, he begged it to. And it responded.

"Holy shit!" Burton cried, clapping his hands in celebration. "How'd you do that?"

The ship drifted slowly at first, like it was floating on water, caught in an invisible current directed by the boy's conscious mind. It turned to face the hangar bay doors, but they felt no tug of forces on their bodies; it was like they were immune to known physics while in the quiet confines of the cockpit. Even moving, they heard nothing. It was a silence that neither of them was used to, having heard the constant, ever-present hum of aetherium drives for as long as they could remember.

Selas focused and they picked up speed. He didn't need windows or displays to see where they were headed—he saw it all in his mind. Burton slipped his hands into the dashboard and gasped in amazement when he saw their surroundings as well. The boy felt no separation between himself and the craft. He saw everything around them like the ship was one giant eye that relayed its sight directly into his head. And straight ahead of them were the hangar doors, looming closer and closer as they rushed forward.

"*We're gonna crash!*" Burton shouted. "*Slow down!*"

"Like they say: 'Knock, and it will be opened,'" Selas said calmly. Burton screamed as they flashed across the massive chamber with no exit in sight. The doors were only a few yards away; Selas saw Burton's fears in his own head, imagining a terrible death in a fiery wreckage. But he exhaled and willed the doors to open. They passed through a tiny sliver of an opening out into the blackness of space. Burton tried his best to catch his breath. He stared at the boy beside him in disbelief, and a bit of anger.

The dark vacuum wasn't calm as Selas had expected. It wasn't empty or still. They jettisoned out into the middle of a vicious swarm, a cloud of zigzagging flies that flittered past his eyes. They weren't insects—they were ships, thousands of them, surrounding a target. Plasma weapons flashed out in the dark like the light of countless fireflies. Selas struggled to maintain control over the vehicle. He found himself distracted.

"Holy—"

"*Hold on!*"

Selas plunged the ship downward, away from the fierce dogfight. He searched his mind for the Procyon's target, but it was so immense that he couldn't possibly miss it. It was a beast unknown to mankind except in myth and rumor. The leviathan clung to the hull of the titanic vessel that was once meant to be their tomb. It dug its talons into the surface and tore away smoldering chunks of metal, flinging them into the center of the swarm. It had no eyes but scrambled over the mothership with ease. The Procyon's weapons didn't stop the creature. It swatted away its attackers like irritating but harmless mosquitoes.

The Procyon were fighting a losing battle. Their immense *sona* was nearly torn in two, with a gaping, smoking crater in its side, spilling gases and debris out into space. Even with all their technology, they still couldn't delay the inevitable. Selas thought he'd managed to escape when they couldn't. But it wasn't as simple as he'd thought.

"Get us out of here!"

He didn't see the creature's tail coming. It cracked like a whip and smashed through the swarm of ships with no resistance. It swept right before Selas's eyes, and he felt his stomach clench with an instinctive fear. He pulled his fingers from the controls and their craft went dead. He only narrowly missed it. They began to tumble forward, and though he felt no forces pulling on his body, the image in his mind was enough to make him sick. He became disoriented, confused. The silence deepened until he could only hear his heartbeat and the sound of Burton's labored breaths.

He thought he might have been dreaming when he saw the planet beneath them. It was hazy with sand and dust, lifeless, remote. Neither he nor Burton could stop their uncontrolled descent. The beast and its prey shrank into the distance behind them, their escape just a faded memory. Burton panicked, fearing a devastating crash into the planet's rocky surface. Selas wasn't afraid. A voice in his heart beckoned him to come closer. There was a presence down in the desert that he'd longed to feel for many years. In his haziness he couldn't recall the name. But it was a name he wanted so badly to speak aloud.

———

Tageron gritted his teeth and snapped his eyes shut. The gunshot pierced his ears, but in his body, he felt no pain. He was alive. His heart was racing. And he felt sick to his stomach as he watched his only son fall to the ground, his hand clutching at his chest, blood trickling through his fingers. Cast over his body was the shadow of his sister Leveda, who stood with a smoking gun drawn and a tortured look on her face. Neither she nor her father said a word.

He picked up his son and slung him over his shoulder, then turned to make his way toward the boarding ramp. Leveda wouldn't let him. She urged him to set him down, but when he refused, she pulled Koshann's body away and dropped him onto the charred grass. She said they couldn't have a corpse on the ship. He'd have to be buried beneath the rubble of the company. There was no time to mourn him, or to mourn the loss of anything. His daughter took him by the hand and led him to their transport. Theirs would be the last to leave, the one that had to witness the entirety of his life's work destroyed.

Slowly and carefully, the transports rose into the sky. They departed one by one in formation, and the launches were separated by two agonizing minutes. It seemed, however, that the fight had calmed down, even stopped. The field was obscured by billowing smoke that stank of burning chemicals, but the gunfire had ceased, and what were once screams were now dying moans off in the distance. The battle had been won, but it was not without loss.

"Five more transports ahead of us," Leveda said calmly. "You should come inside."

He kept his back to her and stared out across the work site. Silently he said his goodbyes, but a distant crash caught his attention. It was the clatter of a downed fence on the pavement. When the smoke cleared, Tageron saw them. And they saw him.

The Children of the Dole scaled the fences and rushed out into the open work yard. They shouted and struggled for breath as they scrambled across the field, thighs clapping and their footsteps like rolling thunder. The stampede of covetous beasts grabbed at every bit of property they could find: they clutched their plunder against their swaying stomachs, and stuffed their loot into the hanging pockets of their oversized clothing. They cut their hands on broken glass when they climbed through shattered windows into the office tower; others picked personal items off the charred bodies strewn across the demolished work site. Unattended children fought over the most trivial of items while adults wrestled and snarled over anything that could possibly be pawned, and not a single one of them was satisfied.

"*You!*" screamed a grotesque blob of a woman, pointing a greasy, swollen finger straight at Tageron. Saliva foamed at the corners of her gaping mouth. "*You can't leave!*"

Tageron glared at the hideous creature but kept watch nervously out of the corner of his eye, counting the number of transports still idling on the ground. There were two ahead of his own. Four minutes, at the most.

The horde grew restless. "We'll all *starve!*"

"You can't take away our *rights!*"

"We have a *right* to take what's *ours!*"

"*Brock Dunham says so!*"

"*This is the greater good!*"

They snarled and howled, and flooded toward the transport. Tageron watched as the last ship drifted up into the sky; he only had to fend off the ravenous Children of the Dole for another two minutes. But their numbers were unfathomable, and they approached his transport like a tsunami ready to crash over anything in its path. They screamed obscenities and commanded Tageron to pay his fair share. He would do no such thing. He couldn't stand to see even a single piece of scrap metal stolen by the thieving parasites, no matter how worthless.

He pulled his gun from his coat and aimed for the row of chemical tanks that loomed over the wild mob. The centermost tank stood upon buckling supports, their metal framework damaged by the explosions that had rocked the work site. He pulled the trigger, and heard the thud of the bullet against the bending struts. The tower lurched to one side with a painful groan, and struck the tank beside it. One by one, they fell to the ground.

The hiss of boiling acid preceded the tortured screams. It spilled from the cracked chemical tanks and crashed upon the ground, flooding over the yard and filling the horde's lungs with poisonous gases. Their shoes melted, their clothes caught fire, and they fell to their knees with boils covering their faces and hands. They clawed at the bursting sores in desperation, and choked on toxic fumes and their own gushing vomit.

As he looked upon their smoking corpses, Tageron felt no pity for them. He harbored not even an ounce of remorse. An Arterran might not have supported such devastation, but he was no Arterran. He was just an individualist who would rather die than submit to the tyranny of the majority.

"Dad! We're cleared for takeoff!" Leveda called out. Tageron stood at the door as it slid shut, sealing the tomb of his life's work. The floor rumbled and the transport departed. The screaming faded away. The smell of smoke and chemicals dissipated.

The detonator felt heavy in his hands. He slid his thumb over the last switch and peered painfully out the windows. He flipped it.

He didn't hear the blast from far below or feel its heat, but he watched as his once glorious office tower collapsed to the ground in a mountain of steel and glass, and the entire facility was reduced to rubble. The group around him cheered in the spirit of victory. Tageron, though, was quiet. He merely looked down to the surface, and soon enough, the bittersweet sight of success and failure faded away into blue.

Leveda threw her arms around her father, and he embraced her to the sound of popped bottles of champagne. He began to pull away, and saw fingerprints of blood on the back of his daughter's blouse. It was Koshann's blood, still fresh on Tageron's hands. Leveda didn't notice, but even as she turned and walked away, he couldn't take his eyes off it. She kissed her husband Sharsir without a care in the world, with the blood of her brother behind her, out of sight. But Tageron saw it. It was a sight he wouldn't forget for some time.

26

*'I have seen things you people wouldn't believe. Attack ships
on fire off the shoulder of Orion. I watched c-beams glitter
in the dark near Tannhäuser Gate. All those moments will
be lost in time, like tears in rain.'*
—Old Earth cinema, *Blade Runner*.

THE POLISHED CHROME OF THE WARSHIP passed before the
Bhalenjari sun, shining with golden light as if illuminated by
Heaven itself. But there were no celestial choirs singing
before her majesty in the abysmal silence of space. She glided
with an oceanic grace across the brilliant solar disc, a gleaming
predator in an endless sea. Drifting in the current of gravity
far above the planet's surface, she stood her ground before
the enemy fleet, challenging the Albian Banking
Advancement Conglomerate without any support. She was
just one warship against hundreds, but she was a Colonial
vessel, and more powerful than anything her enemies had
ever seen.

The jumbled mess of the ABAC fleet looked formidable
in size but pathetic in its simplicity. Through the armored
windows of the bridge, Misha saw clusters of hastily

constructed bombers, herds of clumsy, barely functional support ships, and battleships that were probably manned by inexperienced officers. By her calculations, the lone Colonial flagship could easily take on the enemy without reinforcements. Years in the military had honed her intuition, and she had no doubt that the day of reckoning had finally arrived for Brock Dunham and his army. And while there was a time when she would have joined in the fray herself, it was now her journalistic duty to capture history for the masses. With special access granted to the bridge, she'd promised to document that the Colonials, representing the entire League of Arterra, had kept military action as their final option. As required by Colonial law, the flagship's admiral offered a peaceful resolution.

The communications team broadcasted the message. *"This is the Colonial warship U.C.S. Fist of Alabama, flagship of the United Colonies of Acadia,"* it began in the iconic, Old South accent of the heartland. *"We demand the immediate withdrawal of all ABAC and ABAC-aligned forces to beyond the Veil of Bhalenjar; the immediate surrender of ABAC-controlled Bhalenjar to native Bhalenjari security forces; and the extradition of former Executive Brock Dunham for crimes against Sentients. Should you accept these terms, you will not be engaged. You have five Convergent standard minutes to respond."*

The admiral ended his transmission and nodded. Misha's cameramen put down their recording equipment for the moment. The experienced journalist thanked the admiral and returned to the observer deck, far from the command bridge, where she and the other civilians watched and waited for what could be ABAC's death sentence or plea of mercy. The sight of an assembling enemy force, and the instinctive rush of adrenaline that flooded her veins, all lent to a sense of nostalgia that she couldn't quite shake. She missed her days as a drill sergeant, when she'd molded well-intentioned but naïve Colonial youth into fierce and loyal soldiers. Until that fateful day, she hadn't thought much about it. She supposed that, like the floral scent of a dead grandmother's perfume or the smell of firewood in winter, the sight of a coming battle evoked memories of a cherished past.

Her cameraman was the first to notice it. "I guess we have our answer," he said with a smirk, pointing out into the shadowy distance. Thousands of projectiles were headed their way, showering outward from the barbarian horde. Alarms rang across all decks of the *Fist of Alabama*, ordering a preparation for possible, however unlikely, impact. Then, a sudden burst of blinding light, like the eye-searing sparks of a welding torch, lit up the blackness of space. The missiles had doubled back, arcing through the vacuum toward the very fleet that'd launched them. Their guidance systems had been sabotaged. Misha laughed to herself when she realized she'd just been witness to the brilliant work of Colonial hackers. With the systems' programming covertly manipulated, the thousands of ships at ABAC's front line were decimated in a matter of seconds.

Then came the wave of Colonial bayonets, shot like porcupine quills toward the enemy's face. The double-edged blades, long and needle-thin, pummeled the remaining front line, piercing through the useless energy shields that covered the ships' hulls as shimmering exoskeletons. White plumes of atmosphere burst from the torn metal, carrying hundreds of bodies out into their silent and infinite grave. Misha eyed the forces that remained and judged that ABAC had lost a tenth of its fleet, at least. It was a strategy drafted by military genius, but even the otherwise incompetent ABAC wouldn't fall for it again. Any commander with even a shred of tactical foresight would disengage the computer networking to prevent another security breach. But even that remedy had its drawbacks. Without networked computers, ABAC's reaction time would slow exponentially. The Colonials, now more than ever, had the upper hand.

Misha snatched a smaller handheld camera from her colleague as she pushed past the other journalists, who crowded against the observation windows in anxious awe of the battle. The heavy blast doors fell from the ceiling to the floor, slamming shut with a hiss and a solid thud, to defend the civilian onlookers from any potential injury, whether due to a projectile impact or the unlikely event that the U.C.S. *Fist of Alabama* be boarded by an enemy strike team. The closing of the defensive barrier caught most of the reporters' attention, but Misha kept her eyes locked on the fearsome massacre miles ahead of her in the darkness, vowing not to allow a single moment of the historic battle to be lost.

The fiery explosions in the distance burnt out one by one and faded into shadow. The ABAC fleet, devastated but not defeated, drifted outward to encircle the Colonial flagship, which fearlessly pushed forward. Much to her dismay, defensive screens began to slide down over the windows, accompanied by an announcement by the commander, who was determined to protect the journalists from any danger; he insisted that the warship's sensor feeds would, in fact, provide a better view. Though the other news crews gave a sigh of relief, Misha scoffed at such safe journalism, and in an act of brave defiance she snapped a leg off her camera's tripod and thrust the metal beam beneath the lip of the descending window barrier, causing a burst of sparks and hindering its fall. The other reporters gasped in shock, but she merely grinned, holding the camera to her eye while fingering the zoom button, to capture every enemy fighter for posterity.

Two ABAC strike craft brazenly streaked toward the observation windows, inspiring a chorus of frantic shouts from the civilian onlookers, who leapt back as though a distance of three additional feet might somehow protect them from a direct missile strike. The *Fist of Alabama's* defensive turrets eased the journalists' fears and vaporized the offensive fighters into clouds of invisible atoms. The flagship's primary batteries sang like a host of angels, their heavenly war cries filling every deck, as though they were soaring from the firmament to slay the black-winged tempters of men. With each call of their holy trumpets, the bombers that loomed in the distance burst into the flames of judgment, their reactors overloaded with the keystroke of a Colonial hacker, and though the Creator Himself was merciful, the *Fist of Alabama* was His unforgiving emissary.

ABAC began to regroup, assembling its dying fleet in a defensive barrier before the golden Tower of Bhalenjar that spiraled up from the planet's surface. The Conglomerate clearly had no intention of handing control of the Convergent capital over to the Caspian Bhalenjari that rightfully deserved it. It was a denial of justice that the Colonies couldn't possibly allow.

The Colonial flagship shifted its focus away from the enemy navy, and instead turned toward the planet itself. It fired its engines and began an unexpected and furious descent; the camera team rushed for their seats and secured their seatbelts, terrified at the prospect of hitting the atmosphere at such a dangerous speed. But Misha knew better, remembering her old physics books from the Academy. The *Fist of Alabama* meant to ricochet off the crest of Bhalenjar's bluish haze. But why?

Flames lapped up from the underside of the warship and danced past the observer deck windows. Chaos engulfed the room and the inexperienced civilians screamed in panic, but Misha remained calm. She shook her cameraman until he regained composure and stopped shouting like a scared little boy.

"Grow some ovaries, would you?" she barked. "Get this on camera. The real show's about to begin."

The spiral Tower came into view through the fiery glare, growing closer too quickly for comfort. Misha tried to feign knowledge of the admiral's intentions, but she was at a loss. She felt her stomach drop as the *Fist of Alabama* streaked upwards and jettisoned off the planet's atmosphere like a rock skipped over water. The ABAC fleet was directly above them, but soon blocked from view; the Colonials glided through the golden scaffolding of the Tower of Bhalenjar, maneuvering gracefully around the titanic beams and urban habitats.

There it was: ABAC's central banking tower, shielded in its protective sphere, set just below the seat of the Convergency's broken Congress. The pinnacle of the skyscraper stretched beyond the boundaries of the bubble, protruding out into open space like a canon peering out from a sailship's sides. When the ship began to decelerate, Misha knew it must have been their target all along. But it wasn't a military target—it was civilian. And even though it was the command center for all the Conglomerate's detestable actions, it was unarmed. She couldn't imagine that the Colonials would strike a civilian facility without dire need. She was surprised by the admiral's impulsiveness, as she saw it.

In a flash, the skyscraper fell. Each floor of the tower burst with light and flame, one by one, from its base to its middle levels. But the *Fist of Alabama* hadn't fired a single shot.

"What the hell was that?"

The tower's apex shot away from the defensive sphere, tumbling through space toward the *Fist of Alabama*. Was it a weapon? A bomb, some kind of massive explosive? Maybe even with an aetherium payload?

Four Colonial fighters came into view and flanked the object in formation. It appeared to slow its approach as they ushered it toward the flagship, and Misha gave a sigh of relief. They weren't stopping the device—they were retrieving it. It was clearly something of grave importance. They were in possession of something that ABAC was willing to sacrifice tens of thousands of lives for. While the collectivists were in the profession of stealing from others, they certainly didn't like being stolen from. They would stop at nothing to get what they believed to be rightfully theirs, which had fallen into Colonial hands.

"I hope that thing's charged," Misha said, pointing to the camera. "We've got a long day ahead of us, boys."

———

Selas woke up with the metallic taste of blood in his mouth. His forehead throbbed with pain. He slowly lifted himself up off the control board of the Procyon ship; his joints were stiff with fatigue and his whole body ached. Burton's labored breathing sounded out from beside him. The older man was still unconscious, slumped over the controls, one side of his face swollen and bruised from the impact. They'd crashed somewhere—Selas couldn't remember where, but he last recalled the sight of a hazy world of sand and dunes, and an inexplicable sense of calm. He tried to evoke that same inner stillness, and focused as much as he could on connecting with the ship's intangible systems. No matter how long he tried, he found no connection, and received no response. The ship was dead, no longer a mechanical extension of the boy's mind, but a smoldering wreckage in an endless desert.

The wind outside whistled past the entry hatch, which hung open just a crack, enough to let the burning hot air creep into the cabin. The metal door was irreparably damaged, contorted outward as though it'd melted in the fiery descent through the atmosphere. When Selas heard a strange creaking, he thought it was just the wind, but the door wasn't fluttering in the breeze. It groaned, and metal scraped against metal, and the boy quickly realized that someone was trying to pry open the hatch. A wave of fear crashed over him. He looked about for anything he could use as a weapon, but found nothing. The Procyon had tracked him down. He should have known they wouldn't let their subjects escape so easily.

Fingers slipped into the cabin, curling over the edge of the broken hatch. But they weren't the pale, spindly fingers of a Procyon—they were feminine, soft and slender. Selas's heart skipped a beat; something stirred within him. He felt a presence he'd almost forgotten. The tan of the stranger's skin evoked memories of a woman he'd reluctantly left in the past. He shook his head. There was no way it could be the Mithneshi seer. It had to be a trap. Or his blow to the head had left him delirious, hallucinating an Alviran angel come to rescue him on a dead planet in the middle of nowhere. Either way, the outcome was grim.

He scraped his knee on the floor while scrambling to hide from the intruder. They'd played with his mind before, manipulating his fantasies and dreams—what was to say that they weren't doing it at that very moment? The woman might stride in and look exactly how he remembered her, and then he'd let his guard down only to find her with the same hideous eyes of the trickster gods. He peered over the control board, ready to duck back down behind it should the situation go wrong.

"Selas?"

The voice had the same serene tone that he remembered. He couldn't help himself. He raised his head up high enough to see, and there before him stood Selenia Santiago de Sonora, or a semblance of her, clad in Mithneshi garb with a Breathtaker held firmly in her hand.

He was at a loss for words. Cautious but filled with excitement, he took a step toward her, and then another, until he could feel her rhythmic breath upon his skin. He embraced her, and took comfort in the warmth of her body, the rich brown of her eyes. She wasn't cold or skeletal; she had eyes that shone with a Sapien spirit. She was no illusion, no cruel trick orchestrated by the Procyon. She really was Selenia, the Mithneshi who'd parted ways with Selas's people years ago, and whom he'd longed to see every night since.

"I can't believe it," Selas said, wide-eyed. "It's impossible."

Selenia smiled with a wisdom he hadn't yet attained in his young age. "You know that's not true. We were drawn here by something bigger than ourselves. For a purpose neither of us understand, our thoughts and desires aligned, and the Emanation opened a path for us to follow." She looked over at Burton, who hadn't come to. "He'll be alright. We should wake him."

Selas agreed and shook Burton by the shoulder. He jumped up with a look of terror in his eyes, like they were still about to crash into the desert. His breathing picked up and he fell into a fit of panic. Selenia put her hand to his forehead and hushed him, with no concern for the dried blood flaking onto her fingertips. She reassured him that he'd survived, and that there was nothing left to fear. It took some time for him to understand that she was telling the truth, and that he wasn't caught in a Procyon mind game. Years of abuse at their twisted hands had left him more defensive than both Selas and Selenia could have possibly understood.

Selenia beckoned them to the open hatch. "Don't worry," she encouraged. "The air's breathable. But then again, we'd all be dead already if it wasn't." She examined the odd, makeshift clothes that covered Selas and Burton's otherwise naked bodies, and decided that white surgical sheets wouldn't be enough to protect them from the harsh rays of the desert sun. "We're going to have to do something about that—find some shade or something. I don't have anything for you to change into, unfortunately. And just as unfortunate, I don't know if there's any shade to be found, except under your ship, and that's someplace I think we'd rather not stay."

The cloth was easy to tear, so Selas ripped off two pieces from his shoulders and wrapped them around his bare feet, fashioning a pair of soft sandals that couldn't protect him for long, but would help for the time being. Burton did the same. They pulled some extra length of fabric over the tops of their heads, assuming the appearance of shepherd nomads in the wilderness. They walked out into the wasteland, the hot sun beating down over their faces, with a scalding wind stinging their skin with showers of sand and the feeling of hot coals beneath their feet.

"Where's your ship?" Selas asked, hoping to salvage some supplies.

"Not far from here, but it's in pieces, and there's not much we can do with a pile of broken parts." She looked up into the hazy sky and paused for a second to think. "This place has to have some importance to the Procyon—they don't come this close to a planet without a good reason. They'd rather hide out in interstellar space, where there's almost no possibility of running into someone else."

Burton jumped into the conversation, bringing an air of pessimism to the subject. "I'm inclined to agree, but who's to say whatever they're interested in ain't hundreds of miles from here?" He pressed a finger into his quickly reddening skin and watched as the pale imprints faded back to a ruddy sunburn. "The kid and me won't last much longer out here."

Selas stopped dead in his tracks. He looked to the horizon and saw a dark shape rising out of the sand dunes, dome-like, but distant enough as to be indiscernible. "Look at that!"

Burton raised an eyebrow. "Well, I'll be damned."

Selenia wasn't paying attention. She'd turned her back to them, staring out into the desert. It took a moment for Selas to notice that she was distracted, but when he did, he looked back with her and fell silent. He heard a roar echo across the desert; at first, he thought they'd been hunted down by the titanic beast in orbit, but it soon proved to be the rush of a deadly storm, and a wall of churning sand in the air crashed like a tsunami over the dunes.

"Run!" Selenia shouted. "It's close enough—we can make it!"

With the violent sandstorm creeping behind them they made a break for the structure, less than a mile ahead of them. Their footprints disappeared and they left no trail, and the sand was smoothed over by the fierce winds. The boy's skin, already burned by the sun, endured agonizing pain as the sand pelted him like torrential rains in a tropical storm. He longed to feel water on his body, and not the sweat that dripped over his brow. His lungs burned, and his feet felt contorted from the way the ground gave out beneath him with each heavy step. He pulled the sheet over his nose and mouth to keep from breathing in the choking dust. Burton lagged behind, but would still make it.

He saw swirling clouds of pale green that glowed like sickly ghosts in a whirlwind around their bodies. A chalky dust spread over his skin, into his eyes, so fine that even the woven fibers of the sheets couldn't keep it from slipping into his nostrils. Selenia cried out his name; he heard her thoughts, and his senses merged with hers in flashes. The world around him was a hazy blur, shifting and warped, and as he ran, he could no longer feel his feet. He was floating, or so he thought. He was carried on the winds, or lifted up by the Emanation. It was a sea of aetherium through which he was swimming desperately toward shore. The desert was rich with it, buried beneath the endless dunes, and as the rare element passed into their blood, coursing through their veins, they saw visions that they could neither comprehend nor retain. The images flashed before his eyes, but he could make no sense of them. All he focused on was the facility in the distance, their only hope of survival.

Just a few days prior, Selas wouldn't have bothered to run. He painfully remembered his sense of defeat, his loss of will to live. He'd surrendered himself to the black-eyed captors, having understood that there was no hope of escape, and that there was nowhere, or no one, to run to. His family was dead; he had no friends. He'd resented Burton for evoking memories he thought he wanted, but really didn't. But there, taking him by the hand to run desperately for survival, was Selenia Santiago, whom he'd never expected to meet again. It was then that he truly understood the power of the Emanation. It was then that he realized he really did have something to fight for.

———

It had rained that night. After it'd stopped, little droplets still clung to the black-painted metal of the fire escape outside the apartment window. They slid down the slopes of the bars and met each other, growing bigger, heavier, until they were too heavy to fight gravity any longer. The clinking of the droplets falling upon the window pane was subtle, and if it hadn't been so deathly silent in the living room, Pentakiya wouldn't have heard it. But it was there, pattering in the distance like water trickling down the cool stone walls of a darkened cave.

She left all the lights off, except for the one dim table lamp upon her desk, and the low lighting contributed to the cavernous ambience. She wasn't trying to hide from anyone; she'd unlocked the apartment door, knowing the deadbolt would serve little purpose. She likened the door to a stone ready to be rolled away. Having lived with her wife for ten years in that apartment, she never thought she'd live—or die—to see the day that it became her tomb. But at that moment sitting in the dark, she didn't see it as a final resting place at all, where she'd be locked away for all eternity. It was the place of her resurrection. It was where she'd be free of all her ideological iniquities, all her sins she was once proud to commit. All the soldiers would find was a white linen shroud woven with broken heartstrings.

Despite the heaviness of their boots, they entered the sepulcher quietly; their target didn't even hear the twist of the doorknob. The houseplants' leaves fluttered in the breeze of their approach, like silvery olive trees in her own Gethsemane, bowing to the legion come to seize her. Three soldiers stayed behind, flanking her only means of escape, though she had no intention of avoiding her fate. She accepted it willingly. She pressed her foot into the serpent of fear at her feet until its spine broke and her own was strengthened. She sat up tall in her chair and faced her accusers, who'd chosen machine guns in place of swords, pointed with lethal intent across the room.

"I suppose it's time to go, then." She folded her hands on her desk and waited.

"You missed your chance to get out of this," said the lead soldier, his voice muffled by the dark shield cloaking his face. "You're not going anywhere. We have our orders."

"I had mine once, but I defied them, and I have no regrets."

The soldier paused. He seemed curious. "You had so much potential, from what I hear. But now you're just a traitorous slut, like your wife."

"Fighting tyranny, no matter how late, is never treason."

"And yet you'll pay the price."

"Not for treason. This is the cost of doing what's right."

She felt no pain when they opened fire. She lost herself in the rapture of her own salvation, and with each bullet in her heart, she said a prayer for redemption. She knew it was never too late to let go of her wrongdoings, to lighten the burden on her spirit. And when she fell upon her desk with blood dripping over her wife's unfinished essays, she drifted away with Artimpasa's last words written on the back of her eyelids. She would be with her soon. She was waiting for her just beyond the veil between Heaven and Earth, across the threshold of the destructive collectivism of this world, and the truly selfless eternity beyond, the one she'd always hoped to experience in life, but that could only be realized in death.

———

Violent forces no longer rocked the command center. It didn't shake with the turbulence of liftoff, or the shockwaves from the collapsing skyscraper below. It drifted off into space, smoothly, silently, while chaos ensued beneath it. Livia looked out the reinforced windows from the deployed apex of the ABAC Tower and looked down upon the Conglomerate's central sphere. White geysers of air sprayed out from the gaping hole they'd left in the transparent shell, stretching thousands of feet out into the vacuum. The tiny specks she saw carried up in the gassy plumes weren't all debris. Many were the frozen bodies of ABAC cronies, left to float forever in orbit around Bhalenjar, the planet they hoped to control, but lost instead.

She knew that one of those bodies was Silviano, and she held back tears at the thought. She was the only one who kept him in her memory—even Natharis seemed to have moved on already. The Crystalline scientist was too busy working with the central computer to mourn his loss, and Ninotchka preoccupied herself with a comprehensive reloading of her weapons. Natharis was staring out the opposite window, searching for the Colonial flagship they'd arranged to pick them up. Livia was alone in her reflection, but understood that ultimately, she was the only one of them that could understand Silviano's sad and deep-rooted concerns. She didn't want to admit it, but in some ways, he was right. Natharis couldn't possibly grasp what she, Silviano, and all of their brothers and sisters had gone through. And now that she was a traitor to her people, and Silviano had perished to save a traitor's life, she was alone in her experience. Natharis tried to help, and he did. But he couldn't hope to help her with everything.

A clatter across the room startled her, and Ninotchka groaned when she saw Livia look back in concern. She told her it was just debris striking the craft—"Some old junk, meteor, maybe collectivist skull." Livia watched to see a frozen mummy floating past the window, its pale face locked forever in a contorted look of fear, but she saw none. She heard the noise again, and she became more certain that it was coming from inside the room. Her curiosity got the best of her, and she peered over the farthest row of computers. She sighed, relieved that she saw nothing worthy of mention. Admittedly, the stress of their escape was playing with her mind.

"Not so fast," said a deep, throaty voice, with the bubbly effect of phlegm.

None of them saw the three ABAC soldiers coming. They jumped up from behind the computers, as quickly as their girth would allow. Ninotchka's guns clattered when she stood fiercely and aimed for the enemy; Natharis was unarmed. The soldiers chuckled, outnumbering the Muscovite, and equally overpowering her with three heavy rifles, almost cannons, propped up on their bulky shoulders. Livia kept her back pressed against the windows, hands behind her. It was then that she felt her fingers sliding toward the Breathtaker at her waist, as if with a mind of their own.

Something was growing inside her, not just within her body, but in the depths of her spirit. She was disgusted by the soldiers' cowardice, their willingness to fight a losing battle for a farcical ideology. Her thirst for retribution took hold of her as would a natural instinct for survival, begging to be quenched with blood. Her thoughts raced beyond her capacity to even recognize them, and with her mind moving so quickly, it seemed to stay still. A sense of calm filled her. Selenia's words echoed within her, guided her, telling her to open herself to the Emanation and all the gifts It had to offer—most important, the gift of faith in herself. For the first time fully, she was awakened. Her eyes were opened to her own power.

"Put the guns down," she demanded, her voice stern. The soldiers scoffed at her.

"Or else what? A Tellurian whore will fuck us to death?" The three of them laughed; one coughed violently, choking on the slimy spit that bubbled from his cavernous mouth. They kept Natharis in their crosshairs, taking advantage of his being unarmed. "When we're through with your Colonial friend here, you'll have to ship his body back to Hudson in a hundred boxes." Natharis glared back, but the soldiers were relentless. "Maybe you can add his severed cock to your collection, slut."

Livia smiled. Their insults were sticks and stones hurled at an armored tank, and she had bigger guns. She stepped forward, one foot in front of the other in a feline manner, her spirit like that of a lioness protecting her pride. Vulcan's forge burned in her eyes, and her glare was his blacksmith's hammer, showering the sparks of terror upon the enemy. Her heart beat as her ancestors' war drums on the battlefield, dictating the movement of impenetrable phalanxes and legionnaires thirsty for barbarian blood. Natharis shouted for her to stop. She didn't listen. She only heard her heart pounding in her chest and his voice like a trumpet calling her out.

Mercury himself couldn't have moved as swiftly. She swung herself from an overhanging beam with Zephyrus's west wind sweeping her upward. Plasma bolts smashed into the metal ceiling as the ABAC soldiers opened fire, but in their confusion and incompetence they missed with every pull of the trigger. She let go of the beam and flew through the air, and drove her heel into one soldier's unprotected skull. He screamed to the crack of his bones and fell to the ground, gray brains oozing from the gaping hole in his head, though Livia was surprised that anything dripped out at all. She rolled herself over the floor and knocked his partner off balance when she caught him like the violent undertow of Neptune's waves.

She loomed over the soldier who groaned in pain on his knees. Her Breathtaker swung overhead with the rattle of a chain and she cracked it downward, turning her weapon into Jupiter's flashing thunderbolt. The hooked blade on its free handle caught the peon's ear, slicing it off cleanly as she pulled it back into her hand. He cupped his head and cried as his blood trickled through his fingers. Livia swung the Breathtaker down one last time, pounding his face with the force of an iron hammer, and he hit the ground with a dead thud. His blubbery body quivered from the heaviness of his fall.

The last soldier standing tried desperately to gun her down, but she never gave him a clear shot. She kicked herself off one of the computer desks, cracking a display screen with her heel, and jumped with the Breathtaker outstretched between her hands. The metal chain flashed in the overhead lights and clattered when she caught it around the trooper's neck. His trachea shattered when she pulled the chain so tight that her knuckles turned white around the smooth handles of the lethal weapon. Her victim flailed his bloated arms in every direction, but he couldn't shake her off. His lips turned blue, his eyes, bloodshot red. She didn't give him the luxury of one last breath. She kicked his corpse to the ground.

Livia panted and tried to calm herself. She looked up, her dark hair in a frenzied mess. Natharis rushed to her and embraced her, thanked her, praised her. Ninotchka stared in disbelief. When once Livia would have expected an insult or a backhanded compliment, that time, she knew she'd shocked the brazen Muscovite into an unbreakable silence. The look in Ninotchka's eyes exposed her anger and reluctant respect. No doubt she was furious for not slaughtering the enemy herself, and for not noticing their presence in the first place. But even more so, she looked disappointed that she couldn't ever mock Livia's passivity again. In fact, she was even forced to respect her, regardless of how useless she thought Livia once was.

The altaria of Neptune never felt so empowered. She wasn't just one of many prostitutes anymore, or even one of many disbelievers turned faithful. She'd known before, but now she truly understood: she was a conduit of the Emanation, of the ocean of spirit through which man could know God, and not just a tool for lustful men to know a lifeless statue. Her love for Natharis, her utmost desire to keep him safe, opened her heart to the greater power within and without. For once, she'd join in the fray. And with his love and the universe on her side, she knew that the future held many things, but defeat was not one of them.

––––––––

A squadron of four Colonial fighters ushered the skyscraper's pinnacle into the hangar bay and landed in formation around the object. Armed Deltas marched up the access ramp and poked their rifles through the hatch to make sure that the group's presence wasn't a trap set by the Conglomerate.

When they were satisfied that they hadn't just brought a security threat onto the U.C.S. *Fist of Alabama*, they permitted the group to step out into the hangar, welcomed by the maintenance team and the warship's commander, second in command to the admiral. His voice, permanently shouting out of habit, reverberated off the bare walls of the massive chamber as though he spoke through a loudspeaker.

He loudly thanked them for their presence aboard the ship, and for the self-appointed role they'd played in sabotaging ABAC's pursuit of complete control of Bhalenjar. "We were holding our own, you see," he explained, handing off a holotab to Natharis and Ninotchka, who scrolled quickly through its flight logs. "But we've got some unexpected visitors. We had no problem fending off ABAC's forces, but it looks like they've called in the Tellurians for backup. And by our estimates, they've brought more than half the Armada with them." He eyed Livia with suspicion, fearing an act of Tellurian espionage, but quickly realized how unlikely that scenario was. "The Tellurians are better equipped than ABAC, and we're only one ship—a damned strong one, but one ship regardless. Defeat will be slow, but inevitable." He cursed under his breath. "I have to admit, I'm pissed that we've got to call in reinforcements."

Silviano had discussed war with Livia once. She remembered sitting in the cabin of their pilgrimage vessel, which they'd long since left behind, waiting for liftoff with him going on about Tellurian battle strategies. It was a subject she'd never had any knowledge of or interest in. As a servant of the sea god, she had little concern for the art of war, but Silviano was sworn to Mars, and was taught from a young age how to think like a seasoned commander. She remembered only a few key points, but they were facts that pertained to her directly as an altaria, and to him as a consitor. In fact, they played a larger role in war than she'd ever expected.

"You don't need reinforcements," she announced, much to the surprise of all those around her. "There's only one ship you need to be concerned with. If you take control of it, or destroy it, the Armada will surrender."

Ninotchka laughed, thinking Livia had gotten a bit too full of herself lately. "And what ship is that?" she sneered. "There are over hundred thousand out there, and we're not even sure which is flagship."

"The flagship is mostly unarmed," Livia explained, though few believed it could be true. "It's a religious vessel—the *Celestial Harlot*, it's called, and they'll never go into battle without it. Under religious law and superstition, it's forbidden."

"And what's so important about it?"

"In war, politics and religious life, Tellurians will rarely do anything without the proper blessing. Without the ongoing sacred rites of the altarias and consitores on the *Celestial Harlot*, there's no way they'd keep fighting. They'd be convinced of their own defeat. And that'd leave ABAC without any military support."

The commander was intrigued. "So, we only have to destroy one ship, then. Sounds easy enough. Hopefully you're right."

"I am. But you can't destroy it."

"Why not? It'd be the simplest plan."

"Because I have business to take care of, and the woman I need is on that ship." She reveled in the thought of confronting the sacred Whore-Mother one last time. She made sure to be vague; she didn't want to elaborate on her own personal issues before a group of hardened soldiers she'd just barely met.

"Then what do you suggest?"

Livia thought for a second. "We form a strike team, led by myself, and board the *Celestial Harlot*. We disable it and take hostages, forcing a Tellurian white flag."

"I'm going, too," Natharis insisted. Livia shook her head.

"This is something I've got to do on my own."

The *Fist of Alabama*'s commander seized the opportunity to suggest another mission. "Well, Marshal, if you're eager to join in the fray, then I've got just the job for you," he proudly declared. "Recent intel suggests that ABAC is trying to quell a Caspian rebellion on Bhalenjar—foolish enough to fight on two fronts, though I can't say I'm surprised. Violent protests have erupted across the city ever since Panzi Illoszia took control of Congress. We've assembled a group of Militiamen for an operation down on the planet's surface. I think you'd be the perfect man for it."

Ninotchka scowled. "You can't leave me out of this. Give me bomber and squadron to lead, and I take down half of Armada myself." She addressed Livia in an uncomfortably sincere tone. "Sorry to have doubted you, ex-sacred whore," she apologized. Of course, she had to follow it with a qualifier: "But some beginner's luck is no match for natural skill." She shouted for pilots to step forward from the group behind them; five presented themselves, fearful of her retribution had they stayed silent. Ninotchka commandeered the *Fist of Alabama* and made her own orders. The commander pointed her toward the bomber hangar, and she stormed off with her team behind her, laughing that she was in the mood for a good, old-fashioned Muscovian carpet bombing.

The superior officer gave Livia and Natharis ten minutes to prepare. He handed Livia a combat uniform and told Natharis to report to the Militiamen bay. They stood outside the hangar and looked into each other's eyes. Livia thought she'd cry, but she didn't. She was confident that a tearful goodbye was unnecessary, but Natharis didn't look so sure, and she thought she could hear a subtle shakiness in his voice as he spoke.

"Be careful, okay? We've almost died a hundred times already."

She smiled and touched his cheek. "I'll be fine. I'm just going home to my people for the last time. I'm leaving this all behind me, and this is how I'm going to do it."

"Just make sure to come home to me," he asked of her. "After this, no more fighting, and no more killing. I'm tired of justice. I just want peace, and I found it with you." He kissed her goodbye, and smiled when he saw the Colonial emblem branded on her uniform. "Looks like you're one of us, now."

"There's no Colonial, or Tellurian, or Caspian or Muscovite. There's only good and evil, Natharis. And we've always been on the same side."

The raging winds of the sandstorm slammed shut the heavy door behind them. Selas's skin rippled with goose bumps in the shocking cold of the facility's interior, which had been hidden away from the desert sun for countless years, he was sure. Burton, too, acknowledged the chill in the air, and though they were all thankful for the relief from the shimmering heat just beyond the dusty walls, they soon grew weary of it. Selas saw his breath billow like a cloud, a wispy ghost in the moist, frigid air. He felt as though the facility was kept at that temperature for a reason, and not just as a result of the dark. Perhaps it was meant to preserve something. Or perhaps it was meant to bother intruders just enough to get them to run back out into the heat.

The installation's interior starkly contrasted the featureless white of the Procyon's massive vessel in orbit. He felt blind, not from the glare of mysterious light, but in the shadows. He thought he could connect with a computer system of some kind, like he had on the ship, but no matter how still and clear his mind grew, he couldn't find the link. The walls looked organic, like old, preserved flesh that hung in drapes, as if the halls were lined with a thin membrane in place of metal. But that, too, looked dead. Even just a couple dozen yards into the tunnels, he already felt disoriented. He'd hoped to discover the layout of the facility through a connection with the network, but he had no such luck.

"I can't find a good link," he groaned in frustration, pressing his fingers against his temples. "The system's dying. It has to be. All I hear are whispers, like someone on their death bed."

"It's an ancient structure," Selenia whispered. She gazed in fascination at the bizarre sights around them, and touched her hand against the firm, rubbery flesh of the walls. "It must have been abandoned long ago. It's lifeless now. It feels more like a crypt than a facility."

"Why'd the Procyon come back *now*?" Burton muttered. "Comin' all the way back to the planet they left to rot, maybe hundreds—or *thousands*—of years ago?"

"Maybe they left someone, or something, to watch over it—and now they're back to claim them."

Nobody was able to answer the question, though there was no Sapien who could have possibly hoped to understand the complex and mysterious will of the Procyon, even those who'd been given an unwilling glimpse into their collective mind and memory. They traversed deeper into the structure in silence, and the floors began to slope downward ever so slightly, enough to make the muscles in Selas's legs tense up instinctively. It grew colder, confirming his assumption that they'd descended below ground. The halls were labyrinthine, crisscrossing in a bizarre and tempting web, and the three apprehensive intruders decided together that they should stay on a straight, predictable path. As what seemed to be a distinct feature of Procyon architecture and design, there wasn't a single sign to direct their attention or movement. They could only assume what they were looking at, and where they were headed.

A chamber with the high, arched ceiling of a hangar came up on their left; none of them chose to enter, but they peeked their heads inside. Selas saw rows of retired craft, some small like passenger vehicles, and others the size of colony ships from the history books, and all seemed to have one common purpose: they were built to carry multitudes of people. His first thought was to find one suitable for a desperate escape. The ships weren't built by Procyon hands, but Sapien. They carried the earliest banners of Arterra's states on their hulls, flags that had evolved much over the centuries, but Selas recognized them nonetheless: the Kingdom of Windsor Britannia, the United Colonies of Acadia, the Federated Republic of Gallia, among others. No one had sat in their cockpits in hundreds of years, he assumed, because their design resembled those of the oldest ships in the Gameer caravan, which had been recycled and repaired continuously for generations. Attempting to pilot them was a hopeless endeavor, he concluded, as their drives were most certainly dead and irreparable. Furthermore, he, Selenia and Burton would suffocate in their cabins, because the crafts' hatches had been removed: not carefully, but forcefully, and the metal that framed the missing access ports was twisted as though the doors had been torn off with malicious intent.

"They took Arterrans, too," Selas whispered, "and from the looks of it, far more than us Gameer." Burton nodded solemnly.

Soon they saw empty rooms to either side of the hall, arranged one after the other, each accessible by a single doorway. Panes of glass, frosted with ancient moisture, gave a blurred glimpse into the contents of each room; many were empty and unidentifiable, though some had a single table set in their center. Selas shuddered when he saw the tables, and Burton, too, appeared uncomfortable. It was too reminiscent of the examination rooms they'd each been brought to time and time again, and they had no choice but to conclude that the abandoned rooms they peered into were used for the same odious purpose. As disgusted as he was, Selas couldn't look away. He had a morbid curiosity that guided his eyes and kept him quiet, but attentive.

Selenia was conflicted. She'd stopped in a doorway, scanning what lay within. There were jars, dozens of them, lined up along mildew-slick shelves. They held hideous prisoners, suspended in a cloudy, yellowish fluid, embalmed and preserved for the ages. For a moment she thought she heard them calling her name, drawing her nearer. She'd never seen any creature like them, and hoped to never see anything like them again. The fruit of the Procyon's hubris disgusted her. "We're told that every creature has the breath of God within it. But I don't know if I can really believe that anymore."

"God had nothing to do with them."

Burton rubbed his temples and winced in pain, doubled over and fell back against the wall. Selenia ran to him, but he dismissed her with a wave of his hand. He groaned, murmuring under his breath, and neither Selenia nor Selas could understand him. Progressively, he raised his voice until he was moaning in a tortured agony that came not from the nerves of his body, but from deep within his mind.

"It's whispering," Burton said in a trembling voice. "In my head—I can hear it—It wants me—It wants us—It wants us all—It wants to live—It wants me to give it life." His thoughts were slurred like a drunkard's speech, bleeding into one another until they were all one. He stumbled toward an open doorway, rejecting any offers of help from the boy who followed him in without a word.

Selas figured it to be a laboratory, and stepped closer to the collection of preserved specimens. No matter how closely he looked, he couldn't compare them to anything he'd ever known. Many lacked any discernible features, like an embryo in the womb that hadn't yet grown hands or eyes. Others he thought at first to be insects, but then decided were rats— then fish, then lizards, and an endless list of other possibilities that he could never deduce for sure. But there was one that caught his eye, appearing more developed than the rest. He wanted to call it a worm, but it had legs, or what looked like the long, chitinous limbs of a massive spider, rigid and boldly jointed. The legs had curled up in death around its engorged, slithering body, a foot or so in length, though its contorted posture made it hard to judge. Tiny, hair-like spines lined its sides, like whiskers but stiffer, or maybe the pins of fish bones. It was its teeth that bothered him the most; in place of a mouth, it had only concentric rings of vicious fangs, encircling a four-pronged whip of a tongue.

"It's calling," Burton whispered. "You can't hear it, but it's calling for us." He leaned closer with his eyes open wide and focused on something invisible before him. He tapped the foggy glass of the preservation jar. Some bubbles rose to the top, but Selas lost interest, expecting little from a long-dead experiment. Burton was rambling, perhaps delirious from exposure to aetherium. He turned to leave the room.

Selas whipped his head around to the sound of sliding then shattered glass, and Burton screamed, *"Goddamnit!"*

The creature clung to his back, its legs locked around the old man's sides. Its body writhed as he tried to shake it off, falling to his knees with arms stretched vainly behind his back. The pronged tongue lapped at the ridge of his spine, caught hold of his skin, and its needles curled and buried themselves in his flesh. Burton struggled and shouted but Selas saw no blood; in fact, he didn't even seem to be in pain. More startled and disgusted than anything else, Burton barked, *"Help me!"* until Selenia came to his aid, and slid the blade of her Breathtaker beneath the parasite's belly. She caught it with the hooked knife and flung it across the room. It hit the ground and tried to scurry away, but Selenia stomped it with her boot, and it burst into a puddle of entrails and milky white eggs.

Burton was shaken and angry, but otherwise unharmed. He cursed the Procyon for their pointless endeavors in genetic engineering. Selenia uttered a prayer under her breath for having taken a life, even a primitive, unnatural one. But Selas looked down upon what remained of it and felt an unexpected pity for the creature. It'd been brought into the world by the hands of beings who thought they were gods, and left imprisoned longer than anyone could know, only to be stomped out once awakened by an act of sheer clumsiness.

Then came a sudden clatter from down the corridor, from the depths of the shadows. Selenia grabbed Selas by the wrist, pulling him forward. "Run," she whispered, and they all did. They headed deeper into the installation with no option of looking back. After minutes of running that felt like hours, the sound of an encroaching predator turned to silence. Selas worried they had fallen for a cruel trick, played by an unwanted intruder in their heads, whose murmurs they all heard but could neither explain nor ignore. Even still, Burton remained paranoid, fearful of another unwelcome embrace by a designed abomination. Selas, though, filled the role with black-eyed Procyon, tiptoeing through the darkness to take him one last time.

———

The boisterous cheers of celebration had quieted when the cargo ship reached orbit over Hatal-Om, turning to a pervasive silence—not an apprehensive or fearful silence, but one of great hope, a hope that led to a complete loss of words. The only chatter among the passengers came from the vessel's pilot, who talked via radio to his partners on the other ships in the refugee caravan, coordinating their escape from the star system. They set their sights on a tachyon vein running between the outer gas giants, with Iyrkarim, a world full of endless promises, as their ultimate destination. The images everyone held in their minds were diverse and fanciful; some imagined a planetary twin to Hatal-Om, while others pictured a green sphere of great forests, and others, a blue planet of endless oceans and tiny archipelagos. Tageron, however, chose not to envision Iyrkarim. He didn't want to be proven wrong. He called it a promise, and a chance for salvation—all ideological, and nothing physical.

His old home shrank away into the dark as he stood reverently at the observation windows. It became just a blurry dot among hundreds of stars, fading away, until it had no identity among the myriad lights in the blackness of space. In some ways, he wished his memories could fade just as quickly. Sadly, he knew he couldn't escape them as easily as he had from the planet. There were no powerful engines to drive his consciousness above and away, far from all the blessings and curses he'd received, whether gratefully or begrudgingly, while building his life on Hatal-Om. He couldn't slip into a tachyon vein to a dreamy reality where the tangible had little relevance. He'd have to carry those memories with him.

Leveda approached and stood beside him, though she, too, said nothing. The reflective, serious look on her father's face was a wall between them, one raised justifiably, and that would one day be torn down with the joy of a new life. He was thankful to have her with him. She represented one gift he'd attained on Hatal-Om. She was his only means of keeping his memories positive, and while he hoped to keep himself from dwelling on the bad, he couldn't stop thinking about her brother—his son, who died with an act of betrayal on his spirit.

Tageron felt as though he'd lost two children, not one: Koshann, and the company he often viewed as his child, both of whom he'd raised from birth to maturity. But Koshann couldn't handle that maturity and all the responsibilities that came with it, and instead chose to take refuge with those who promised him everything but gave him nothing. In stark contrast, the company had flourished the way Tageron had hoped for his son. He felt the pangs of guilt in admitting to himself that, even up to his death, he'd been disappointed with Koshann. The only solace he could find was in understanding that Koshann's actions were his own choice, and no reflection on his father, though many would call Tageron heartless and selfish for saying so. He had free will—the highest ideal that Tageron could uphold.

Tageron, too, had made his choices, and he prayed that they would lead to a better life. He chose to leave behind his old life for the sake of others, and this was the true greater good. The good of the whole was not stealing from others to benefit those who preferred a sedentary life over one of productivity and independence. The greater good was sacrificing certain aspects of the present to make a better, more fulfilling life for himself, and for those around him whom he loved and cherished.

Iyrkarim, he told himself, was the greater good, for himself, for his daughter, and for all the refugees. They believed it as well. Only time would tell if that promise could be kept, but while Tageron fingered the key to his old office in his pocket, he knew that the potential to open the future's door was in his hands, and in the hands of all those who sought something greater.

27

"Bhalenjar burns. Through the flames that spread across the galaxy's greatest monument, a lone angel rises, streaking through the skies in defiance of evil's will. The celestial Fist of Alabama, resilient and strong, braved the siege by hell's agents, but would they consume her and the Convergency with her?"

—Excerpt from *Bhalenjar Burns,* by popular historian Charlize Blaauw of the Isolate State of Windsor Anglostralia.

A FEARSOME MECHANICAL WARRIOR towered over Natharis. Fifty feet tall and heavily muscled with plates of impenetrable metal, its head nearly scraped the ceiling of the massive launch bay, so huge that Natharis felt insignificant. It was a hulking, intimidating figure, and its powerful thrusters took the appearance of biceps, and a chromium camouflage covered its entire body, except for the neon blue stripes along its head, which Natharis identified as generators for an energy barrier yet to be activated. They called it a Militiaman, one of dozens standing lifelessly in the hangar, and it was to become a second body for Natharis, in which he would bring ABAC's deranged forces to justice on the war-torn surface of Bhalenjar.

Natharis prepared himself with the other Militiamen pilots, and they all waited before the metallic titans, shivering in the cold of the launch bay. They'd stripped down to the form-fitting regulation trunks provided to them, as the cockpit of the anthropomorphic craft was filled not with pressurized atmosphere, but with a viscous fluid that always unnerved Natharis. It'd been years since he operated a Militiaman, and even when he was an active pilot, he never truly got used to the submersion.

He ascended to the chest of the warrior on a slow-moving lift pad, and its bulging ribcage split open to allow his entrance. Tiny lights glowed within the otherwise dark interior like stars set in a metal firmament. He crawled in; the hatch snapped shut behind him, and with little warning, a thick liquid began to bubble up from the cockpit floor. He pulled straps over his shoulders and cringed as cables automatically attached themselves to the back of his neck and pricked his wrists and ankles. The fluid crept up his body, and he took a deep breath just before it rose over his head. For a second, he felt like he was about to drown, but he couldn't hold his breath any longer. His lungs burned for fresh oxygen, and instinctively, he gasped for air. The fluid rushed down his throat and into his lungs, but he didn't suffocate. Suddenly, he breathed again. There was more resistance than air, but he was alive.

He opened his eyes and saw his surroundings as if the Militiaman was his own body, its sensors, his own eyes and ears. He felt as tall as the behemoth in whose heart he was suspended. It was a rush he hadn't felt in years, an immeasurable confidence that made him invincible. He became the man he'd always wanted to be: greater than his enemies, stronger than anyone who hoped to crush him and those he loved. More than anything, he became what Livia thought of him. It was no longer a dream in the eyes of a love-struck woman. With hundred-ton muscles and a stature that conveyed the utmost power, it became reality. He understood, though, that he'd had it all along. He didn't want to overpower her or make her feel weak. Instead, he wanted to share that power with her, and to guard her with it until the end of their days.

"Launch sequence in fifteen seconds."

The launch bay around him bustled with activity, and the maintenance crews scrambled to safety after their last-minute tune-ups. Sirens wailed and red lights flashed along the hangar, and with a deafening groan a launch tube opened like a dilated pupil under a bright lamp. The digital voice continued its countdown: *"Ten seconds to launch. Activating full motor function."* Natharis fluttered his fingers to test the Militiaman, and in perfect sync with his own movement, the mechanized warrior did the same, with its chrome hands mirroring his. Then the countdown reached its final number. Signs inscribed in neon light prompted a confirmation for ignition. He mouthed a definitive "yes," but made no sound. Sensors read his lips. The Militiaman obeyed.

He was gliding through space mere seconds later. Behind him the sleek U.C.S. *Fist of Alabama* shone in the sunlight until she became indistinguishable in the distance. The team of Militiamen drifted into formation and rocketed through the lines of ABAC vessels in their descent toward Bhalenjar. They maneuvered around clunking ships as if they were passing through a repulsive but harmless field of space junk, debris scattered in shapeless piles from a shipping accident. The streamlined design of Colonial vehicles streaking toward the planet made the Conglomerate's fleet look laughably primitive. They didn't even land a single shot on the Colonial squadron. Natharis and his wingmen had outrun them with ease.

A golden spire emerged from behind the enemy fleet, and the sun cast its light upon it at the edge of Bhalenjar's glowing crescent; it spilled rivers of silver and gold that trickled and interweaved within the gilded framework. It was a stunning sight, but not Natharis's target. They bulleted at a steeper angle and oriented the Militiamen toward the city at the Tower's base, spanning the whole of a large continent. Expansive forests, endless prairies and jagged, white-tipped mountains manifested through the blue haze of the atmosphere, but on that one landmass, surrounded by bright oceans, he saw nothing but the gray scars of urbanization. It was there that the bronze-skinned Bhalenjari had taken up arms against their oppressors. They were staging a resistance against the unlawful government imposed upon them by collectivist murderers. Natharis wondered if they knew the Colonials were coming.

A veil of flames blocked his view and the liquid around him flurried with bubbles, shaken by the friction of the atmosphere. Through the fiery curtain appeared the vast ocean, and his sensors warned him of the dangerous speed of his approach, but he ignored the alerts and instructed his wingmen to follow his lead. If they crashed down fast enough, they could easily avoid detection. Their armor would have absorbed any radar regardless, but should ABAC's agents be watching with their own eyes, they might just mistake the Militiamen for falling debris from the raging battle above. Natharis aligned his body and slid effortlessly beneath the water. Steam rose from the Militiamen's heads, boiling the sea with superheated metal.

With perfect timing he engaged his submarine thrusters and shot through the water toward the city, leaving a trail of churning sand in his wake. The navigation system calculated a travel time of seven minutes; in seven minutes, the Bhalenjari forces gathered at the outskirts of the city would graciously welcome their Colonial reinforcements. On cue the *Fist of Alabama* relayed necessary tactical information from orbit, outlining the geography of the outer city and highlighting the migration of refugees from the Tower of Bhalenjar. A separate group was funneling toward the hills at the shoreline, pouring into subterranean bomb shelters that hadn't been used in thousands of years, since the closing of a long-forgotten war.

Then there was ABAC, destroying everything in its path. Mechanized arachnids, creeping over the landscape on slow-moving legs, crushed shelters beneath their weight. Exposed wiring crackled and hydraulics hissed, and from the ground rose the screams of hundreds of innocent Bhalenjari, whose homes collapsed to rubble and whose families lay dismembered in the dust. Even from miles away, Natharis thought he could hear the enraging cackles of genocidal maniacs, marching through settlements under the flag of collectivism, killing anyone who'd lived there for generations. It wasn't the Bhalenjari's planet, ABAC would attest, because the greater good knew no boundaries, and, being universal, owned every world.

"The Bhalenjari resistance is organizing in the hills," Natharis reported to his wingmen. "They'll never push back ABAC if we don't take care of those Arachnidans first." He flagged one major formation of iron behemoths, marching sluggishly through a devastated cut of the city. "There's no sign of survivors in that area. No risk of collateral damage." He hinted at the request of an orbital assault from the U.C.S. *Fist of Alabama*; his squadron unilaterally agreed with the plan. Natharis transmitted the message, and within seconds the flagship gave her answer and promised a single bombardment, as the sheer number of enemy vessels above made any additional passes impossible. They identified two hundred and sixteen targets out of a total two hundred and thirty-two. The countdown began, and it ended in fireworks.

Blinding violet streaks flashed from the sky and struck the shoreline. The Militiamen rose from the sea with their chrome bodies shimmering in the glowing aura of the artillery fire. Natharis saw no flames or plumes of smoke, no evidence that the Arachnidans had ever even strode across the land. The plasma blasts vaporized them to dust in one swift strike. The scorched earth cracked beneath Natharis's heavy feet, littered with the ashen bones of ABAC soldiers brought to Colonial justice. They'd been erased from history, but never from the minds of the Bhalenjari, who waited upon the hilltops and shouted out in celebration.

"All targets eliminated," announced a transmission from the flagship. *"Clean up the rest yourself, farm boy."* Natharis grinned. He targeted the next cluster of Arachnidans and began his merciless assault.

He saw Bhalenjari families running for shelter, clutching their small children close while the iron spiders towered over their homes. ABAC troops marched through the streets in single file, their waistlines too wide to allow for any other formation, and they rounded up stray children to sell as slaves to the Shatarin Empire, and pinned down women for their own pleasure. The Militiamen sprinted across the beach to protect them, leaving small lagoons in each footprint. The screams became louder upon their approach; they were even more unbearable than Natharis had imagined from a distance. They were the desperate cries of an indigenous people being slaughtered for their land. It was an act of injustice that made Natharis sick.

Whistling rockets spiraled through the air and exploded upon contact with the Arachnidans. The Militiamen fired a fusillade of missiles from their chests and shoulders and eliminated the front line of mechanical beasts, showering the Bhalenjari with smoking debris. The second wave was more prepared: they slapped the rockets out of the air with their metal limbs, demolishing buildings from the ricochet. Natharis knew he couldn't make use of his ranged weapons anymore. He had no choice but to go in and fight with his fists.

He lunged at the first of five opponents, and it raised its limb to pin him down, but he slid beneath it and grabbed it by one of its back legs. It struggled to drive another arm into his Militiaman's stomach, and burst with sparks when he pulled off its limb. He stood over the disabled vehicle and crushed its cockpit with his fist. The bodies of two bloated pilots fell to the ground after he tore away the hull with his fingers. Laughing, he swung the defeated Arachnidan at one of its comrades and knocked the second beast to the ground. It cracked in half under the weight of its fallen ally.

An unseen foe caught Natharis off guard and he lost his balance. It jumped onto his back, clutching his torso with its rusty arms, but was unable to penetrate his armor. He engaged his thrusters and sent the Arachnidan soaring through the air; it crashed through a cluster of buildings and slid limp across the ground. Two more tried to flank him, rushing at him at full speed, but Natharis lifted his Militiaman into the air and watched the two creatures collide head-first, bursting into a flurry of electric sparks. Just for fun, he dropped down to earth right on top of them, stomping his feet to drive their wreckages farther into the cratered ground. He grinned when he saw his wingmen cut down the last of the Arachnidans with their battle saws, slicing the leviathans in two with lasers in place of blades.

The transmissions from the Bhalenjari resistance came immediately. Cheers of joy echoed from the hills and families began to cautiously emerge from the subterranean shelters. Like the rebels, Natharis and his team regrouped; they coordinated the retaking of the city with the resistance forces, whose window of opportunity had finally opened. Without the Colonials' help, they would have been quite literally crushed before they even had a chance. Natharis had never really been one to advocate intervention, but that time, the fate of the Bhalenjari rebellion affected the whole of the Convergency. They symbolized the ever-present and growing disgust with the Convergent government, and all its destructive, self-serving policies. He was proud to say that he had fought alongside them. But he knew that the fighting wasn't over—not on the planet's surface, and not in space above them, where his new love was fighting her own battles and would surely emerge the victor.

The Tellurian triremes were the first to strike. They unleashed their hordes of fierce harpies, and the talon-shaped craft poured from the gaping hangars of the battleships. Shining with royal purple and gold banners, the Imperium's strike craft pulled out of the Armada and set their sights on the U.C.S. *Fist of Alabama*. They encircled the Colonial flagship and opened fire, and when their target fought back, they quickly scattered. When the squadrons returned, they came in classic Tellurian formation, cruising closer as a three-dimensional phalanx, glowing shields at maximum strength. They decelerated, coming to a full stop. Motionless, standing their ground, the phalanxes stared down the Colonials, playing an agonizing game of intimidation.

Livia's shuttle shot from the launch bay out into space, too quickly for the Tellurians to react. The fighters that rushed alongside her escorted her past the triremes at a speed no force could hope to match, and immediately they entered within ABAC's range. The antiquated fleet unleashed a shower of sluggish rockets, which Livia and her escorts effortlessly outmaneuvered. They doubled back abruptly, passing straight into the Tellurian Armada; Livia broadcast a transmission in her native language in the hope of discouraging her own people from indiscriminately opening fire. Their point defense guns, staring out from the hulls, could unleash a fusillade at any moment, but Livia had little fear of heavier weaponry. The massive phalanx of the Armada had one fatal weakness: with cruisers and battleships so tightly organized, they couldn't afford the risk of turning their strongest cannons inward.

The inexperienced altaria was rocked with excitement and fear, a feeling she could only identify as the thrill of looking over death's highest cliff. Her body flooded with adrenaline, and she tried her best to quell her energy. She breathed how

Selenia had taught her, repeating prayers of peace in her head, until the inner warmth that came with divine communion kindled her spirit. She saw glimpses of an untold future: she saw icy-eyed Natharis, the leonine Desh Maru, the crumbling of the Convergency and the Matra Altaria screaming in anger. Soon, it would all come to pass, for ill or for good. She was ready to play her part and confront the sacred Whore-Mother. In the duel with her past, she would surely win. And with it, she'd end the Imperium's vassalage to ABAC. Her people would suffer provisional hardships, but in a few short years, they would be a true economic power again, and they would all thank her for her righteous treason.

The *Celestial Harlot* emerged from behind a shroud of guardian triremes. The sacred Whore-Mother's honorary chariot bulged with a wide, circular head, shaped like an arena covered with a dome of steel. From the far end of the disc stretched two columns, anchored together by metal struts along their length. Tactical analysts identified viable docking points and smoothly guided the shuttle to its target. The fighters flanked the *Celestial Harlot* and Livia's team adeptly hovered against its hull, sealing themselves to the airlock. Colonial soldiers donned their goggles, produced blindingly bright saws, and slowly cut red-hot gashes into the airlock door.

Everyone jumped back when the door slid open on its own. The soldiers ducked to the sides of the port and thrust their guns into the opening, anticipating shots fired by encroaching Tellurian guards. They waited, but heard nothing. Livia boldly stepped forward, her Breathtaker clutched tightly in her hands, and braced herself for an attack, but none came. She looked back to her team and waved them forward. She whispered ominously, "She knows I'm here." Tucking the Breathtaker into her belt, she told the soldiers to put down their weapons. Reluctantly, they agreed, but she still worried they might be too quick to open fire. They promised her otherwise.

Inevitably, the guards arrived, but they came with their weapons still strapped to their backs. They spoke in Tellurian, and Livia felt strange speaking her native language. She pronounced her words carefully, deliberately, as though she hadn't spoken it in many years. *"Eu som Livia Nettunaya, un'altaria de Nettuno i l'iscorza ispirita, i puiszo lo dazo miz de coytar a la Matra Altaria, ote siz única erediza."* They accepted her demands: that she, Livia Nettunaya, altaria of Neptune and the sacred whoredom, demanded her right to counsel with the Matra Altaria as her sole heiress. They led her deeper into the *Celestial Harlot*, under the condition that her soldiers wait at the airlock. After much protest she convinced the Colonials to honor the request. She would be fine on her own. It was, after all, her fight.

Haunting, exotic music echoed through the corridor, and Livia's heart beat to the rhythm of ancient drums, and her steps were a dance to the plucking of strings. The tall wooden doors, inlaid with gold and silver, swung open slowly, like a city gate opening to a hero returned. The scent of incense touched her nostrils and smoke billowed in the air as a veil to be parted. She heard moans and sighs that she'd heard too many times before: it was the sound of divine rapture in the arms of another, of an instinctual trance that came from release. It was the sacred Whore-Mother's chamber, filled with servants of the Pantheon, the sisters and brothers Livia had left behind, and hoped to have left behind forever.

Screams of pleasure surrounded her, and the naked altarias and consitores of the gods cried out in intoxicated ecstasy. Hard-bodied consitores of Mars thrust themselves into the delicate whores of Venus, and every god found a willing goddess for the sake of the Tellurian Armada that desperately needed their blessing to change the tides of war. They lay in concentric circles around the floor of the amphitheater, on plush cushions of red and purple, empty cups scattered around them in puddles of spilt wine. The air stank of temple incense and the stale smell of sex and sweat. And then Livia noticed the delicate scent of the Matra Altaria's perfume, a floral tone added to the stench of the divine orgy.

She lay upon an altar at the focus of the arena, fondling herself with closed eyes as hungry altarias ran their hands over her body and lustful consitores lapped at her skin as if her glistening sweat were a drug. A bronze gong hung beside the altar, vibrating to the writhing of the sacred Whore-Mother's body, creating a deep, droning sound beneath the brighter notes of the mystic songs. She shivered and groaned, lost in the rapture of their servitude, and bucked her hips to the tingling of curious fingers and wet tongues. Her eyes opened. She looked across the chamber at Livia, and smiled with the knowledge of her return. She dismissed the altarias and pushed away the consitores, who stumbled and fell to the ground in fear.

Naked and exuding a feminine strength, the sacred Whore-Mother was a prowling she-wolf as she crossed the floor of the amphitheater toward her spiritual daughter. She wrapped a sheer, white shroud over her body, a useless gesture of modesty, and glared deep into Livia's eyes.

"Will you partake in our offering, my daughter?"

She pushed a strand of Livia's dark hair behind her ear and grazed her fingernails against her cheek. She touched her soft, red-painted lips against Livia's to greet her like a perverse, twisted mother welcoming her innocent child.

Livia pulled away and said nothing. She took up the mallet for the gong beside the altar and struck the brassy shield three times, letting it hum and fill the arena with a threatening resonance. The altarias and consitores froze, then sat up straight upon their cushioned rows of benches. The stare of dozens of fearful eyes fell upon her, but she kept her focus on the Matra Altaria alone. She commanded the attention of the entire room; the music stopped at once. All that could be heard was the sound of the sacred Whore-Mother's clapping in amusement.

Livia, however, was not amused. "It is my ancient right to challenge my spiritual mother." She slid the Breathtaker from her belt and pulled its chain taut. "You've committed crimes against our people that can't be forgiven."

"You've never shown much respect for decorum before, Livia. I quite like this."

"You could have stopped this senseless killing. In sanctioning this war, you've sentenced the Armada to destruction and our people to starvation. Can't you see we're fighting a losing battle?" She clenched her fists in frustration. "You've helped our leaders become allies with evil, and now you're ensuring our damnation when it is punished by good."

The sacred Whore-Mother's grin turned to a disgusted scowl. "Has an altaria fallen in love with a Colonial, perhaps?" She laughed when she saw Livia's face redden. "And now she's *thinking* like one! 'A City on a Hill, an Arsenal of Freedom,' as they say? It is your sacred duty to preserve our way of life, not theirs. Our culture is superior, and it always has been. Roma Ceisora is the light, and all others are barbarians in the cold and brutal dark."

"Stealing children and brainwashing them into sexual slavery is barbarism."

"We turn them into vessels of the divine."

"You turn them into the objects of others, all for a free orgasm that we've fooled ourselves into calling a sign of 'divine favor.'"

The Matra Altaria motioned for her servants, who presented her with her ritual weapons. "Then let's put your beliefs to the test," she said, securing leather straps over her forearms, into which she slid two menacing blades. She stretched her arms and twisted them, watching the torchlight reflect off the vicious machetes that stretched from her elbows to beyond her slender fingertips. "Heaven will favor one of us. And the other will perish for her blasphemy."

The sacred Whore-Mother's eyes burned with the fires of betrayal, but Livia was calm, in control of her basest emotions. Her opponent's fury would be her downfall, as her movements would be guided by impulsiveness and revenge, not a connection with the greater reality. She stared her down from across the circle of the arena, rattling her Breathtaker's chain. A timid altaria approached the gong and took up the mallet. The Matra Altaria grinned, and Livia took a deep breath. The sacred Whore-Mother sliced her fingertip to display the razor-sharpness of her blades; she licked her own blood sensually and smeared a thin line across her bare chest. The hammer struck the plate and it resonated. Ritual combat could begin.

Her spiritual mother wasted no time in her attack. She lunged for Livia with the snarling rage of a wild boar, and the girls throughout the chamber gasped, and young men cheered for their carnal heroine. Livia slid her feet over the floor and gracefully dodged the oncoming assault. She kicked the sacred Whore-Mother in the back and knocked her to the ground; she swung her Breathtaker over her head like a lasso and shot it toward her disabled enemy. But the Matra Altaria was more prepared than Livia thought. She caught the metal chain on the hooked points of her blades and pulled Livia closer, close enough to feel her hot breath on her face. Livia screamed and struggled to regain hold of her own weapon. She pounded her foot into the Whore-Mother's chest, landing blow after blow on the cackling matriarch's shaking breasts. A blade sliced deep into the flesh of her arm and she cried out in pain, blood dripping upon the wine-stained floor. The chain slipped off the blades and the Whore-Mother fell backward. She caught herself on the central altar. Her disheveled black hair covered her face and masked her hateful glare.

"*Filia, nuenca moris!*"

Her teeth looked like fangs when she leapt off the altar and thrust her blades forward, her eyes fixed on Livia's throat. She was a winged demon masquerading as an eagle goddess, her feathers made of tempered steel as she flew through the air.

But Livia was as peaceful as an angel of God, and set her mind free of thoughts and words, and swung the far end of her Breathtaker down over the sacred Whore-Mother's head. It coiled around her neck; fighting for breath, she fell to the ground hissing when Livia unleashed the rest of her weapon and buried its blade in her ankle. She collapsed, naked and bound on the floor of the arena, the eyes of all her spiritual children staring at her in horror. She spat at Livia, who stood over her soaring on the wings of victory.

Struggling for air, the sacred Whore-Mother panted, "End it—kill me, traitor. Destroy me like you've destroyed your own people."

"No," Livia replied sternly, taking her foot off her chest. "I've saved us. And you'll be here to witness it."

She turned to the crowd of awestruck servants of the Pantheon and let her voice resound throughout the amphitheater. "I declare myself Matra Altaria, the highest sacred Whore-Mother of the Imperium. This woman here will never again call you her 'children.'"

Not a single one protested or rushed to kill or capture her. They bowed to her. The consitores touched their brows to the floor in silent respect; the altarias stood to wordlessly anoint their new mother with holy oil and incense. They draped a violet cloak over her shoulders and prostrated themselves before her. She stopped them, ordering them to look at her, not to avert their eyes for fear of punishment.

"From this day forth, I am ending this barbaric practice," she announced, and instructed the Tellurians to stand tall. "Telluria will no longer honor its gods with sexual tribute. Her offerings will be genuine acts of kindness and charity; each altaria and consitor will be clergy tending to the gods' temples, not courtesans for half-believing pilgrims."

The Imperial guards watched from the doorway, and Livia addressed them last. "As sacred Whore-Mother, I dictate the fate of this Armada. Transmit this order to the fleet's commanders." She threw the cloak to the ground and clicked a button on her Colonial transponder, relaying the success of her mission to the U.C.S. *Fist of Alabama*. With unshakable power in her voice, she uttered the command that would change the course of history.

"Turn the Legionnaires away from the Colonials," she ordered. "And burn the ABAC fleet."

———

With a burst of blinding light and sizzling sparks, the Colonial engineers touched their laser cutters to the heavy metal of the blast door. They carved glowing red lines in the semblance of a smaller portal, slowly and carefully, and the impregnable steel split open like a molten wound. Behind the barrier, in the highest levels of the Capitol, hid the cowardly Brock Dunham, who had walled himself in for fear of the armed Deltas at his doorway. And among those soldiers stood none other than Executive Desh Maru, holding in his hands a heavy rifle, the safety off and his finger twitching eagerly on the trigger.

The engineers stepped back to admire their handiwork. The executive gave the thumbs up; the Deltas nodded. With one powerful motion, Desh slammed his boot into the improvised hatch and kicked the metal slab onto the floor with a deafening clatter.

Colonial intelligence had provided the strike team with an array of schematics and floor plans, as the upper wing of the Capitol building was Communal territory, its access restricted to collectivists alone. It had been decades since a single Arterran had seen what lay beyond the iron gate; the last Desh had heard was that it housed a defunct hangar bay and several conference rooms for clandestine board meetings. The collectivists, however, had evidently replaced those earlier features with sickeningly characteristic facilities, the first of which was identified by a bold-lettered sign: THE CREATIVE CENTER FOR INDIGENEITY.

The Deltas insisted that the team don their respirators, as the intelligence reports indicated that the center was likely used for the creation of biological weapons to be employed against the native Bhalenjari. Desh knew better. He opened the door without a gas mask to protect him from airborne pathogens or noxious chemicals, ominously predicting that the reality inside was much more insidious. When his escorts looked upon the true purpose behind the Creative Center for Indigeneity, one covered his mouth to hold in his vomit. He struggled to swallow it down. The rest cursed under their breath in horror.

The agonizing howls of thousands of women filled the repurposed hangar bay. Each squirmed and barked in her cot in countless rows spanning the length of the cavernous space, legs kicking and backs arched in pain. Their swollen stomachs throbbed and quivered, filled with litters of fetuses ready to slide out screaming into the world; obese Communal nurses waddled between beds to catch the unending deluge of slime-slick infants in baskets, labeled with the names of doomed planets. Litha, Vehisipen, T'jan—Desh saw them all, and soon those unfortunate worlds would witness the arrival of newborns and heavily pregnant mothers, ready to cover the landscape in placentas and government checks.

A throng of nurses approached the Deltas with an unexpected calmness, though their breathing was labored from the strenuous effort of lifting their elephantine legs. They addressed Desh first, eyeing his ideal physique and towering stature. "You must be the new sperm donors!" they squealed with excitement. They pointed their stubby fingers toward a line of tanks along the wall, rigged with a tangled mess of tubes that ran across the floor to between the sweaty thighs of every bedridden woman. "We've been running low on our supplies ever since the Supreme Doge doubled our fetal quota," explained the charge nurse, motioning for her underlings to lead the soldiers away for collection. Then she contorted her porcine face in horror upon noticing the sword and arrowhead of the Colonial Deltas patched on their shoulders.

"You'll never take us alive!" she screeched, ordering the others in guttural Shatarin to tear open their white coats to reveal belts of explosives strung around their sagging, bovine bodies. The Deltas reacted swiftly with military precision and flung their combat knives straight at their targets' chests; one by one, they fell to their knees with milky globs of fat dripping over their undulating stomachs, shaking the hangar with the force of a small earthquake. The Colonial engineers defused the explosives out of caution as the strike team pushed onward, racing through the ranks of reproductive colonists on to the next high-security facility. With a bang the second blast door slid shut, sealing in the ear-piercing shrieks and the stench of semen and sloth.

Following the outlined path, the Deltas rushed forward down the corridors, their boots thumping on the marble floor. The farther they made their way into the Communal wing, the more luxurious the décor became: wood and painted frescoes in place of metal walls, and elaborate lamps where once were long fluorescent lights. But when the soldiers ducked behind a corner upon reaching a manned security terminal, they scorched away the paintings with the toss of a concussion grenade. Collectivist blood splattered over the melting oils and the blackened portraits of ancient collectivist leaders, whose smug grins disappeared forever beneath the smoking effluents of their progeny.

Desh groaned when they arrived at their destination. A set of exquisitely carved wooden doors towered over them, crafted from Shenandoah Bocote, marking the entrance to the collectivists' luxury VIP lounge. Without an ounce of shame, the Communals adorned their private chamber with expensive woods imported from none other than Acadica, in the heartland of their most hated enemy.

"Hypocrites," the executive muttered. Reluctantly, he raised his weapon and opened fire, showering the hall with splinters and smoldering sawdust.

The guards inside wasted no time in their attempt to fend off the Colonial offense, but they were ill-equipped, both with weapons and wits. In a pathetic act of limitless incompetence, they pulled their triggers but missed with every shot; even after unleashing a fusillade of hundreds of rounds, they still found themselves in the crosshairs of a full squad of Colonial Deltas, who punished them before a single one could shout out in barbarian Unispeak. With their wall of guards torn down and collapsed upon the ground in a bloody heap, the crowd of collectivist officials had no defense. They burst into a frenzy of unintelligible grunts and cries, scrambling for the exits.

ABAC's oligarchs jumped back in shock when the blast doors snapped shut across every open doorway at the Colonial engineers' command, who sabotaged the controls and locked the Communals in their opulent prison. The Shatarin guests snarled, bearing teeth beneath their religious masks; collectivist staffers dropped their expensive holotabs in fear and tried their best to hide behind the growling Children of the Dole. They were terrified of the leonine ghost that loomed before their eyes, a man who should have died at their executive's order.

"We're here for Brock Dunham," Desh declared, standing confidently with his soldiers to his back. The room was as silent as the war criminal's future grave. The former executive's pawns cowered but refused to give up their prophet. But the vicar of God revealed himself, rising up from behind his cultist ranks, with a slow clap of his hands and a sick grin across his face. He appeared unsurprised by Desh's presence. He stepped forward to confront him, parting the red-eyed sea of his seething supporters.

"You're always so difficult to get rid of, Executive. This game is beginning to bore me."

"Your reign has been many things, but a game is not one of them. Lives are not yours to gamble away for your own amusement," Desh warned. "But now your life is in Colonial hands. I'm sure history will remember you dearly."

"*You* are the criminal here!" Dunham sneered. "Maybe I failed to dispatch you once, but I *promise* that your selfishness will catch up with you. You'll be executed for your ignorance—if not by me, then by the oppressed people of this Convergency!"

Desh swung his ignorant fist square into Dunham's jaw.

The collectivist yelped like a wounded dog and dropped to the floor. The Deltas snickered and suggested that they simply shoot him and get it over with, but Desh had other plans. "No," he ordered, motioning for his team to lower their guns. "He'll be tried by the Supreme Court. We're not here to execute him."

A screeching banshee of an office assistant flew out from among the throng of acolytes, hurling the words "racist" and "ignorant" at Desh as though they were weapons; she tore her clothes in a crazed trance and swiped her talon-like fingernails at his face. He coolly backhanded her and she slid across the floor, but the staffer was relentless, and scurried on all fours like a rabid rodent, ready to bite at the Colonial's heels. She was met with the stomp of a Delta's boot and a broken jaw.

In the confusion Dunham had gotten to his feet and slicked back his disheveled hair. He looked down upon his vanquished pawn and shook his head in disappointment; in shame, she averted her eyes and wept. Dunham spoke over the sound of her choking cries. "You can't sentence me to die, Executive. I *am* collectivism—I *am* the greater good. And the greater good is immortal!"

"You truly have lost your mind. Your kingdom's burning before your eyes, and you're still dancing like it's a damned cause for celebration. The 'greater good' has met its end. Colonial justice is timeless—and now you'll meet it in the Supreme Court."

"You're just a *coward*," Dunham hissed. "If you really think you can take me down, then why not do it *yourself*?"

Desh scoffed at his accusations of cowardice. "You've let your peons bully the hardworking people of this galaxy into providing for the lazy. You've used the genocidal Shatarins to wipe out your enemies. You've engaged in your crony collectivist politics to destroy the galactic economy, carried out an illegal coup d'état, and had your pawn, the 'Supreme Doge,' make an attempt on my life," he berated. "You've always preferred to let others do the dirty work, and yet I'm the coward?"

Immediately, Dunham's obedient chorus chanted their token insults: "Ignorant!"; "Racist!"; "Uneducated!"; "Selfish!" Their god-king silenced them with a wave of his hand. ABAC's executive pulled off his tie, unbuttoned the top of his shirt and rolled up his sleeves. He assumed a defensive stance, raising an upturned fist. Desh raised an eyebrow. His opponent had to have been joking.

"Tell your soldiers to stand down," Dunham snapped. "This is *our* fight. I'll finish what the Supreme Doge couldn't."

Desh sighed and handed off his rifle to one of his Deltas; he pulled off his combat vest and dropped it on the floor, revealing sweat-slick muscles that glistened like obsidian in the light, which the lanky Brock Dunham couldn't ever hope to match. He cracked his knuckles and flexed his arms, curling them in calm preparation for his opponent's first move. "Make it quick," he groaned. "Panzi's waiting for you in custody."

Without warning, Dunham lunged with arms outstretched, his spindly fingers reaching for the Colonial's throat, but Desh casually stepped aside and sent him stumbling forward. Dunham regained his balance and turned back, throwing himself with his fists flurrying gracelessly ahead of him; waiting until the Communal was just inches away, Desh swung his hardened arm and smashed his unyielding fist into

Dunham's face. Brock flew backward and spat out saliva and broken teeth, a trickle of blood running over his split lip.

He searched frantically for an improvised weapon, and cackled when he snatched a menacing shard of hardwood from the broken doors. *"Bigot!"* he roared, leaping through the air with the pointed wood like a knife aimed straight for the jugular, but Desh shattered his hopes of sinking the splinter into his flesh with a single kick in the chest. Dunham hit the tile floor with the crunch of cracked ribs and imported marble. He didn't find the courage to get up.

"No!" cried a devout young woman upon seeing her savior's defeat. She ran at a Delta and snatched the rifle out of his hands.

"Stop her!" Desh shouted, rushing to disarm her, but she didn't open fire on the Colonials. In an act of true devotion, she put the gun to her head and pulled the trigger. With her brains sprayed over the congregation, she attained her dream of martyrdom. Dunham's followers wept for their loss, and prostrated themselves before the god they thought was dead.

"Round them up," ordered the Colonial executive. "They're just as guilty as he is." He stepped forward and looked down upon the cowering Brock Dunham, who whimpered in fear of the raven-skinned champion. "I'll cuff him myself."

————

A pale green light glowed upon the door of the ancient vault, casting an eerie haze over the corroded metal. It stood at the end of the longest corridor as the dead end that Selas feared they'd hit. There was no hint as to what lay behind the gate, and what had been locked away for millennia to rot in the pit of the Procyon's genetic graveyard. He approached it and put his hand upon it; the metal was rough, cold, and finely engraved with a subtle image. Stepping aside to look upon it in a different light, he saw a figure etched in the shape of a man, with long, thin arms outstretched, and strange fingers spread. He realized it was the graven image of the Procyon. He pressed his back against the door and stood cruciform against it. When his hands slid into place, the antechamber burst with a blinding white light.

The room around them came to life, illuminated without a clear source of light, and Selas's mind raced with knowledge just as unexplained. He saw the facility like a schematic, twisting and spinning in his head, and witnessed its entire history in the blink of an eye. A smile spread across his face as he lost himself in the rapture of brief omniscience.

"It wasn't dead," he sighed, eyes wide and unfocused. "It was sleeping." The vault slowly slid open with an agonizing groan. "There's something in here we have to see."

"No," murmured Selenia, her eyes cloudy in an entranced stare. Her words, and her expression, gave her the appearance of being light-years away in a waking dream. "It won't let us leave."

"What?"

"Don't you hear it?" Selenia asked, looking upward, searching for the source of a silent voice. "It's calling for me. It wants to live." She gripped her Breathtaker and broke from her mystic state of consciousness. "Wait here for me. Try to open your mind, but be careful. Don't let it all in. This place is evil, and you aren't accustomed to deception. Your soul is too innocent. But mine is prepared."

———

Through the corridors, Selenia saw only darkness. Her steps were not her own. She felt guided by an invisible hand, but it didn't have the loving warmth of God's infinite Emanation. It was cold, unfeeling, its motive not one of compassion or mercy, but anger and bitterness. In the Creator, there was never the heavy, suffocating feeling of desperation. This was different: she perceived a struggle for survival, a frenzied hunger for life, tinged with a hopeless fear that was the absence of sanctity. The Creator was there—He was everywhere—but the abstraction that was an empty consciousness had closed its heart and mind to His presence and denied itself the gift of His Emanation. It was an act of defiance that Selenia found both repulsive and pitiful. There was no hope for the voice that beckoned her into the shadows.

She saw a light in the darkness: it came from her own eyes. They shone blue, a vibrant, living blue, the color of the water of Alvira's most crystalline seas, and they lit her path like a beacon in the night. The aetherium of the desert storm coursed through her body, carried through her veins like tachyons through the Aether's flowing currents, and with each heartbeat it permeated her brain even further, opening the very depths of her consciousness to the world around her and all the evils it embowered, whispering to her in hoarse and wailing voices. They echoed from the confines of a black hole at the heart of the Crypt—yes, it was a Crypt, a prison for the twisted and the damned—and Selenia could not shut her ears to them. It was her fate to deliver them. Should they refuse their deliverance, then it was her hand that was fated to smite them. She would banish them to the endless abyss whence they came.

"Open your mind to me," said the voice that spoke for the many. *"I have such wondrous things to show you."*

"Save your lies for the weak, dead one," she answered, her voice echoing off the naked walls of the massive chamber, where there was only loneliness and despair.

"I will not hide my intentions. Surrender and become one with me, and you will see that they are as I tell you. I am the Crypt; this is my purpose. It cannot be denied."

"The Crypt is the puppet, but you are the hands that guide its movements," Selenia declared. "You are the most ancient incarnation of the Procyon Hive Mind. It is you who removed your race from Eternity. You are to blame—you were the first to reject the Infinite. And it is you who are responsible for the death of your species."

"Perhaps. But it is also I who will resurrect us."

"Enough!" Selenia shouted, challenging the darkness around her. "No more lies! You have thrived on them for too long!" Memories filled her head, flashing images of failed experiments, the genetically bastardized, the enslaved and the used. "I felt the life that lingered in their minds. I saw their dreams—I felt their fears.

"I looked upon the Arterrans' craft and knew what evils you have committed. They were your captives, all of them, and you used them—you used their *children*—and bred them with your abominations, against their will and against the will of Eternity. They were to be in your bondage forever, a living, breathing bridge to the Emanation you denied and rejected. But you cannot mend that wound so easily. You will never complete your conquest of objective reality. You have strayed too far for such salvation."

"Only Sapiens could be so blind," sneered the most ancient Hive Mind. *"I have you now—a Mithneshi, her genes forever evolved in the radiance of Aetherspace, her blood inundated with aetherium itself. You, Mithneshi, will be my conduit. Your sacrifice will bring commonality to the galaxy, and individuality will be exterminated. All will become one with the Hive Mind. The dreamers and your precious Gameer will be our tools, and I will be the craftsman, who is the only creative force, and the only preserver."*

"My order and I will perish before we allow you to destroy the minds of the many."

"You will soon forget this primitive 'I,' and you will be only 'we.'"

The aetherium moved through her as though it were a glowing wave through the Emanation. It lifted Selenia up on chemical wings, and her perception of weightlessness was so intense that she had no choice but to believe she was, in fact, levitating in the void. Her eyes turned to sapphires that glowed with an inner light, breaking the shadow before her, piercing deep into the invisible being that threatened to possess and keep her. She heard its screams in her ears, the screams of thousands of voices, commanding her to open herself to them; the Hive Mind's thoughts pierced her like knives, intent on tearing her apart to reside within whatever was left of her. It underestimated her strength, and she smiled, knowing it had no concept of the spiritual power that crashed over her.

The Aether moved through her, and her body and soul became a living tachyon lens, such that each gene in her cells opened like an invisible rabbit hole, through which the subtle reality of Aetherspace spread into the cavernous abyss. And with one final push, breaking through the wall of tortured screams, she damned the Hive Mind in a thunderous voice:

"You will become what you chose to be when you severed your ties to the Infinite: *nothing.*"

The sapphire light in her eyes burst as a shimmering nova, and her mind expanded out to the farthest reaches of space and time. In the brilliance of her luminous spirit the Hive Mind pulled back, retreating into the dark, but Selenia allowed it no such refuge. She pushed it from its unholy dwelling out into the universe, where it had no hope of survival: the eternal pulse of life poured into the emptiness of its being, carried on streams of stardust and silver light. In an instant, that which lay dormant for thousands of years was no more. It disappeared, not with a wail, but a whimper. It was fated for everlasting silence. Selenia heard nothing more.

———

Selas ran for Selenia when she emerged from the corridor in the distance, throwing himself into her arms. He wasn't sure to whom he meant to give his gratitude: the Creator and His Emanation for guiding Selenia's hand, or to Selenia herself, who slew that which meant to hold them hostage in the dark. She looked weakened, her skin pale and eyes tired, though Selas felt the fight was over, and that she had secured good's triumph over evil. The voices in their heads faded away, turning from furious shouts to a dying whisper. Looking ahead with nothing but light behind them, they approached the airlock ahead, shining bright in the soft illumination of the chamber that had come to life. It now seemed to be free of the shadows that once dwelled hidden in the back of the Crypt's ancient consciousness.

Burton stumbled while struggling to follow. Selenia caught him by the arm, and his skin was slick with cold sweat, which left the thinning hair on his head limp and wiry and his paling skin sickly. He tried to keep up with her, but even with her help, he couldn't walk any faster than an exhausted shuffle. With each heavy breath, the tired circles around his eyes darkened, and his face turned sunken, like he hadn't eaten in weeks. The ailing man insisted that he was fine, other than his mental exhaustion. Neither Selas nor Selenia believed him.

"Do something," Selas implored her. He cited the history of healings he'd seen her perform in his past, to the revitalizing power of attunement with the Infinite, but her answer disappointed him. There was nothing she could do, she lamented. She was too weak.

Even in the omnipresent white light of the antechamber, Selas felt as if he were lost in a spiritual darkness, and he listened to the emptiness around him in expectation of monsters in the shadows, though there were no shadows. But then the void—in their hearts, not before their eyes— consumed the old man behind them. Selenia turned back and shouted out in terror, *"Selas!"*

With two voices bellowing from his creaking vocal cords, Burton hissed, *"The Mithneshi whore will never free my children! They belong to me!"*

Burton knocked her to the ground and pinned her, snarling like a vicious predator. A squirming tentacle ribbed with rings of spines and needles lashed out from the depths of his throat; it thrashed through the air and whipped Selenia's skin, leaving stinging slashes that wept with blood. She cried out in spiritual weakness, her movements slow with fatigue, and the creature Selas once knew as Burton overpowered her in seconds. His face was grotesque, inhuman, dripping with sweat and foaming saliva. Veins pulsed beneath his scalp, shaking the few strands of hair that hadn't yet fallen out in a heap upon the floor. Blood dripped from his fingernails, more like sharpened talons, when he pulled them from the flesh of Selenia's arms. Selas shouted and the twisted old man looked up and hissed. His eyes were entirely black.

"I will spread them and I will multiply, and you will open the door!"

Selenia slid her Breathtaker across the ground and it stopped at the boy's feet. She shouted for him to pull the man off of her, screaming that she could disable him, but he was speaking for the Crypt in which they wandered, and through him its terrible power flowed in one last attempt at survival. Selas knelt and slowly took the weapon in his hands. It was lighter than he'd thought. He was fascinated by the way its metal chain glimmered in the light. The look of fear on Selenia's face stirred something within him. He wasn't about to let another loved one die.

The blade came down with unspeakable speed. With his whole arm he swung the free end of the Breathtaker overhead and caught it around the howling man's neck. The arteries in his throat bulged as Selas pulled the chain tighter. His screams turned to dying breaths. His trachea snapped with one more flex of Selas's muscles. His lifeless body collapsed to the floor. The blackness of his eyes faded away, and he breathed his last breath with the blue eyes of a mortal man.

Selenia looked down upon his body and whispered a prayer. Selas wished it could have been different; the ancient Hive Mind had claimed Burton as its vessel, and despite his innocence, he perished along with it. Selenia addressed it one last time, and she would not speak its name again. "You separated yourself from the life-giving sea of the Emanation, and you sentenced yourself to death. It was your choice. But you did not have to take this man with you."

"Burton wanted to die for a long time. They made sure of it. But he's free of them now."

Selas heard a rush of air like the old man's final breath. A second airlock slid open; he stood frozen in the doorway, and his eyes grew wide. Selenia bowed her head.

The untouched vault evoked a paralyzing reverence within the souls of those who entered, stealing their words to be replaced with prayers. Ancient pillars studded the length of the white cathedral, but they weren't carved from marble or granite. They were tanks, set into cylindrical columns of silvery metal. And through the glass, floating in an unmoving pool of clear liquid, stared unnatural beings with eyes focused on something known only to them. They were locked in an eternal embrace, arms entwined in groups of three. Naked, they didn't look male or female—there were three sexes, none of which were Sapien. But the experiments had the figures of Sapiens, the same number of fingers and toes. The black eyes, open but sleeping, were unmistakably those of their creators.

Selenia covered her mouth in horror and nearly fell to her knees. Selas spoke, but didn't look back. "Hybrids—Sapien and Procyon." He touched the glass and gazed sadly into the beings' open eyes. "This is what they did with the Arterrans."

His heart skipped a beat when he heard a hatch open to the back of the vault. Selenia dodged behind one of the tanks, pulling Selas with her. Selas peered out hesitantly, only to see a brightly lit opening between the rows of columns. And through the doorway he saw a dashboard with the imprints of four Procyon hands. It was a cockpit.

"It's a ship!" Selas exclaimed. He hurried toward the hatch with an ecstatic smile. "A sleeper ship!" They were saved—he had no doubt. He'd piloted a Procyon craft before, though his senses told him this one was massive: sprawling and ancient, stretching deep into the heart of the earth. He could do it again, however, and he'd be sure not to crash it.

The floor rumbled the instant he slipped his fingers into place. Shattered rock clattered against the walls, and the cavernous chamber behind him rang like a bell with the sound of tired engines priming. The launch sequence had begun; there was nothing to fear. The boy shouted with a joy he hadn't felt in ages.

Like a spirit freed from the confines of the underworld, the craft ascended into the sky, leaving the valley of death far below. Selas saw images of the Procyon's Crypt crumbling beneath the blast of the sleeper ship's powerful drives; he heard its screams of agony echoing through his mind like sharp, endless thunder, wailing in the knowledge of its own demise. The desert shrank away, until they could see only stars.

Selas had no time to weep for an unlikely friend. At last, they'd both found the liberation they'd sought since their very first memories of the crimes committed against them. There was a freedom that came from embracing once terrible memories. In knowing the demons' names, he'd gained power over them and everything that lay waiting in the dark. He felt awakened, like his eyes had been opened to the road behind him and the road ahead. For many, the journey had come to an end. And Selas knew that with a servant of God at his side and a hope for something greater, his was just beginning.

Selenia saw her own visions, surging through her head like the invisible molecules of aetherium that were gradually leaving her body with each heartbeat. She saw the galaxy, slowly turning in the emptiness of space, pulsing with the Aether's subtle light in a web of luminous veins. It was a wheel with limitless spokes, turned by the invisible hand of the eternal Emanation; it was a living samsara, imbued with life and the most sublime potential. But out of the darkness emerged a hideous beast, a demon of the abyss with the face of a man and a pale hide of stitched corpses' skin, and it reached out to consume the galaxy, swallowing stars and prosperous worlds by the millions. At first, she felt only hopelessness, and wanted to fall to her knees in a keening for the destruction of all she knew and loved. Then she heard a voice whispering, sweet and gentle like an angel's, and it urged her to persevere.

"Free the dreamers," it sighed with divine breath. *"Free them from their dead captors. They will deliver you, as you will have delivered them. This is the Word: be wise and heed it."*

———

The command deck of the U.C.S. *Fist of Alabama* fell silent when the transmission came. The admiral's direct line rang louder than the alarming shrieks of the damage sensors, and every soul onboard held his breath, fearing the incoming message even more than the relays of shield failures and impact blasts. The call came from the *Celestial Harlot*, the spiritual flagship of the Tellurian Armada, which, had things gone according to plan, should have been seized by a dark-haired girl and a team of Colonial Deltas. If it'd fallen into their hands, then the battle was won; if they'd failed, and the girl and her escorts lay dead upon the floor of the sacred vessel, then the Convergency would fall to ABAC's tyranny with no hope of redemption.

The admiral nodded in understanding and put down the phone calmly, without a hint of victory or defeat in his battle-weary eyes. He looked up at his crew and smiled. Misha jumped up from her chair, cameras behind her, and waited for the words she had hoped to catch on film for years. They all stood in respect and anticipation. The admiral kept them with bated breath and relayed his message throughout the entire flagship. Tension permeated every hangar until he broke his silence with a triumphant grin.

"Attention all crew: This is the admiral. The Tellurian flagship is ours," he declared. "The Armada has surrendered." With cheers echoing from every deck, he concluded with one final statement: "Let's see how long ABAC lasts without its allies."

He put down the intercom and addressed the dispatchers. "Order all squadrons to pull back. It's time to put ABAC's little project to good use." He turned to the Crystalline among their ranks, who confirmed that the acquired weapon was primed and ready. He advised the Tellurian flagship and the Armada to withdraw to the spiral Tower of Bhalenjar, safely out of range. Promising a spectacular show of force, he ordered the technicians to do exactly as the scientist had instructed.

Tactical readouts indicated that all Colonial squadrons had safely returned to their hangars—but there was one bomber still weaving through the ABAC fleet, who must not have received the transmission, possibly with his communications jammed. "Get an ID on that bomber," the admiral demanded. "And put him on a direct line."

The response came in a heavy Muscovian accent. *"You'd better have good reason for calling me personally, Admiral,"* the pilot said, her voice ringing out across the command deck. *"You're interrupting spectacular dogfight."*

"Pull back, pilot," the admiral replied with a roll of his eyes. "That's an order."

The Muscovite laughed in defiance. *"I do not take orders from Colonials. You're not my superior, and your pilots might learn something."* She cackled and cheered. *"See? Another one shot out of sky!"*

"Pull back, pilot!" he shouted, tired of the power struggle. "For your *own* sake!"

"I'm not done yet," she hissed. *"There's one bastard left. I've got him."*

The admiral's face reddened with frustration, and he begrudgingly ordered the technicians to abort the activation sequence. With eyes filled with fear and regret, they replied that they couldn't. Even the Crystalline couldn't come to the pilot's rescue. Ten seconds remained before activation, and there was nothing they could do to stop it.

"You've got ten seconds to get the hell out of there!"

"Before what?" she mocked. *"Court-martial me, Colonial—I dare you."* She stayed on the line but said nothing, only filling the room with bloodthirsty laughs and expletive battle cries in her native language. To her, the biggest disaster was letting one fighter get away.

Misha ran for the command deck windows and looked out upon the ABAC fleet, whose leaders were likely celebrating the perceived Colonial retreat. An object drifted out into view, deployed from the *Fist of Alabama's* main cargo hold. It crept forward, away from the flagship out into the open, where it came to a menacing stop between the lone warship and the unprepared enemy fleet. A squadron of hostile fighters raced from the Conglomerate's ranks toward the silent threat; they encroached on the Colonials' secret weapon, stolen from their own hands. Five seconds remained. Misha held her breath.

Three.

Two.

One.

The anchor burst with light and began to rotate, faster and faster until its shape became indiscernible. Space around it shimmered like a mirage in the desert, shifting and distorted, so dramatically that it looked like fabric pulled tightly enough to tear its very threads apart. The Muscovite pilot noticed it as well. She cursed over the live feed.

"Mother-*fucker!*" The line cut out to dead static.

A lethal gash in space-time tore open, bleeding with blinding blue light, as an invisible knife sliced through reality and tore it in two. The thin line stretched through the ABAC fleet and split wider like broken skin, and the lifeblood within spilled out as a wave, crashing through the enemy ranks and destroying everything in its path. Imaginary screams of horror filled Misha's head; heavy cruisers collapsed and crumbled, and fighters evaporated into clouds of atoms. Others disappeared into the energetic void of the Aether, pulled into the severed tachyon vein. Misha had never seen anything so terrifyingly beautiful, and she watched at a loss for words, unable to describe the paralyzing power of nature's fury, guided by mortal hands in a way that no one had ever seen, nor should ever see again. And as quickly as the universe had been wounded, it healed. The light faded into darkness, and all that was left was half a fleet, devastated and utterly hopeless.

"Fire cannons and deploy all squadrons," the admiral ordered one last time. "Let's finish the job." The command deck burst into applause. His pilots eagerly obeyed. It took little time at all before ABAC was begging for Colonial mercy. It waved its white flag and declared its unconditional surrender, but it found no mercy that day. The skies of Bhalenjar were littered with the broken pieces of an army brought to swift and unwavering justice.

Misha had never felt so proud to fight on the side of freedom. What she'd been told since childhood wasn't a cliché, or a lie to fool the masses. Liberty truly did prevail, even in the face of the most insidious tyranny. One warship, or even one person, could take on an entire army when emboldened by the strength of an eternal truth. Free will was a force that could not be stopped, for better or worse. And those who tried to suppress it, to manipulate mankind into crippling conformity, would suffer the fate of all those who came before them in their pursuit of limitless authority. They would drown in the stagnant pool of ideas that festered when they dammed all streams of dissent and thought, and they would grow sick and weak, until the disease of their endless desires ate them away. But the sunlight in the mind of every free man was the only disinfectant, and that day, the Convergency shone like a newborn star, and the shadows of collectivism retreated into distant memory. The war was won. And the sanctity of free will stood victorious over its desecrators.

EPILOGUE

THE SKIES OVER CHESAPEAKE lit up with fireworks, and a joyful roar rose up from the streets. Children ran with sparklers and colorful streams of ribbons danced in the breeze overhead. A crowd had assembled before the marble edifice of the Colonial Supreme Court, embracing and celebrating beneath the banners of the League of Arterra. They waved newspapers in the air and shouted for the man proudly approaching the podium. He raised his fist up high and drew cries and whistles from those who were proud to call themselves citizens of the United Colonies, and who, on that day, truly felt like the sons and daughters of Liberty that they were addressed as every evening on Misha's program.

She watched toward the front of the crowd with cameras rolling, ready to capture history from the first rows. She'd already heard the news that collectivist leadership had finally come to justice, and though she wasn't there to film it, she was just as satisfied reading it in the papers. She grinned upon seeing photos of former Executive Dunham led away by Colonial marshals, bound in handcuffs with cowardly tears running down his cheeks as he was marched to a certain death in the frozen hell of Jotunheim. Shameful bruises still covered his face, which rumor held to be the proud handiwork of Desh Maru. His smile was now largely toothless, though miles beneath the lifeless tundra, he wasn't likely to flash his arrogant grin again.

Misha had seen other broadcasts as well, laughing to the reports of riots throughout the Commune, which had broken out in response to the collectivists' failure to provide for the Children of the Dole. She swooned with satisfaction upon learning that Panzi Illoszia, the self-declared "Supreme Doge" of the Interstellar Convergency, was dragged naked through the streets of Dearborn, her head shaved and face drenched in the spiteful saliva of her once loyal supporters. The orphaned Children of the Dole came to despise her. They bound her in chains and pulled her to the heart of the city, where they lopped off her withered breasts, tossing them into a smoking fire. With her wrists and ankles tied to four police vehicles with revving engines, she was sentenced to be drawn and quartered. They executed her in the town square and fought over her dismembered corpse. It was far too graphic to be shown on Colonial television, though radio programs described the barbaric scene in great detail. The Colonial public, more than ever, came to fully understand the savagery of the Commune and its animalistic peoples.

The Commune had been cut off from the Convergency entirely; it disappeared into the fray of anarchy and joined its Shatarin allies in exile. Corporations found themselves without political influence, having lost their seats and right to dictate the lives of others. All those who violated the most basic law of free will inevitably found their punishment. Even the Crystalline scientist who'd helped defeat ABAC was detained, however reluctantly. Its crimes could not be pardoned, despite its role in the preservation of liberty. It accepted its fate willingly. Misha had watched as they took it away, never to be seen again, but she hoped it would find a redemption greater than a record expunged.

With it she'd seen a young man and woman, both of whom were then standing near her in the crowd, anxiously awaiting Desh Maru's address. The blue-eyed Colonial kissed the dark-haired foreign girl, and she wrapped her arms around his neck; in the sunlight sparkled a ring that Misha couldn't help but notice. A man with the same icy eyes embraced him as well, stepping away from his husband to celebrate his brother. Their faces glowed like those of the entire assembly, all of whom had been praying for that day to come, when they would no longer have to stomach the atrocities committed outside their borders in such hateful disdain for their way of life. Now, they weren't the only ones who were free. They loved nothing more than to see liberty shared with the entire people of the former Convergency, who had lived without it for so long under the tenure of their since deposed tyrants.

The crowd's applause dampened to a fixated silence when Desh boldly began his first address since the dissolution of the Convergency, which was to be replaced by a galactic provisional government until a new polity could be formed, one that would prove to be a haven for free thought and all those who held it sacred.

"For years now, we have heard the enemies of freedom glorify the elusive 'greater good.' But what does that really mean? The collectivists were convinced that the good of society could only be preserved through concern for just that: society, the group. We know better. We understand and profess that it is only through the individual that the good of all may be attained. For when you focus solely on the group, freedom cannot thrive. The inalienable rights of men as individuals will be violated, and this is the only possible outcome. And when these rights are taken away, and called the vestiges of selfishness and greed, then every man and woman becomes a degraded, cynical vessel of discontent, and this unhappiness spreads like wildfire. The collectivist utopia will prove only to be a civilization in ruins. A government can hide its infringements on the rights of its people, but it cannot conceal social decay. It is a blight that is visible to all, and it cannot be cured, unless leaders uplift the individual and spread freedom from the ground up, until it pervades all strata of society and each person has the choice to live his life how he sees fit.

"One of the inherent faults of the collectivist ideology is its arrogant assertion that only its adherents know what's best for everyone else. The collectivists believe that if individuals are left to their own devices, they will make the wrong decisions, and lead cruel, meaningless lives. It is only through collectivism that a man can stay on the right path, avoiding that which his leaders deem 'wrong' and embracing that which they arbitrarily call 'right.'

"This is the central difference between our systems of thought. Collectivism is built on a central mistrust of others. It dictates behavior under the assumption that a person will be selfish, self-serving, and unsympathetic to the plight of his fellow man. It declares that only government intervention can prevent widespread suffering. On the other hand, Arterran individualism was kindled in the assumption that people are good. Individual freedom is necessary for the fair treatment of others. Individualism places a profound trust in people, and we as individualists have faith that people will ultimately do what is right when given the opportunity.

"Collectivism can never succeed. It is a system of thought that destroys itself through the collapse of the society it claims to preserve. Its only outcome is revolution. When the people become so oppressed that they, as producers, are forced to flee their worlds to escape the insatiable needs of the majority, then collapse is inevitable. And when the state can no longer provide for its parasitic dependents, it will fall, for it lost a viable host to steal from and enslave. In an individualist society, this will not happen. Who would overthrow a system that empowers him and gives him freedom of choice, and the right to vote in a new government should the establishment stagnate and turn ineffective?

"A new galactic government must be formed, for the Interstellar Convergency is dysfunctional, and cannot stand when it is brought to its knees by corruption and corporate self-interest. The corporatism that has strangled the life from the Convergency is the antithesis of our precious capitalism, though it seems that many can't see the difference, no matter how clear. This reformed polity, with Arterra carrying the torch into the darkness, will exalt the truly oppressed. It will preserve the liberty of all its citizens.

"The atrocities we have witnessed will never again come to pass. But if the tides of society begin to flow in that detestable direction, then I call upon all men and women to rise up and change it. One of our classical patriarchs once spoke these immortal words: 'The tree of liberty must be refreshed from time to time with the blood of patriots and tyrants. It is its natural manure.' And today, that tree has grown from a tiny seed that the collectivists once tried to keep away from the sun. We stand beneath it today in gratitude for the shelter it gives us as it rises higher and higher. No axe can cut it down; no insects will devour it from within. And no man, in his hatred, will have the strength to tear it from the earth."

APPENDIX A: GLOSSARY

Academic Truth and Eliminating Dissent Organization (ATEDO). An institution advocating the censorship of all academic materials that contradict the revisionist history promoted by the corporatist collectivists. It is represented on the Executive Council by Giles Bronson.

Acadica. The capital planet of the United Colonies of Acadia. It is an Earth-sized moon of the gas giant Vega Prime, orbiting the star Vega. It is the most advanced planet in the known galaxy. Acadica's capital city is Chesapeake, while its largest city and economic center is Hudson. The planet was colonized by the refugees of the Jovian Exodus, primarily Western Europeans who had settled North America, along with other significant ethnic groups. Acadica takes its name from the early term for North America, where the Jamestown colony, the seminal settlement of the modern Colonial people, was established. See also: ***United Colonies of Acadia (UCA)*** and ***Jovian Exodus***.

Aether. A normally inaccessible pocket of reality that can be opened through the superheating of the rare element aetherium, and within which known physics do not apply. See also: ***tachyon vein***.

aetherium. A naturally occurring element and only known fuel source for faster-than-light travel. Aetherium is highly unstable and alters the fabric of space when exposed to the extreme heat of artificial aetherium crucibles. Most minarchist individualist societies use an aetherium standard for their currencies.

aetherium crucible. Part of a standard faster-than-light drive. A small amount of fuel-grade aetherium is superheated by powerful lasers within the crucible, resulting in the bending of space and the creation of an artificial entry point into the Aether.

Æx. Interstellar Convergency designation for the galactic standard calendar year. A contraction of "After Exodus," the calendar era is based on the year of the Jovian Exodus. Written variants are A.Ex. and AEx. Galactic standard time (i.e., hours, days and minutes) is based on Hudson local time on Acadica. See also: ***Jovian Exodus*** and ***Acadica***.

Aitar. The elusive Procyon "World Vessel" and center of the dwindling Procyon civilization. From Old Mithneshi *aitara*, of the same meaning.

Albian Banking Advancement Conglomerate (ABAC). The central bank of the Commune, which has a corporatist relationship across thousands of worlds within the Interstellar Convergency. It has gradually established itself as the Convergency's de facto central bank. ABAC is the union of corporatist collectivist and welfare state interests. The Conglomerate is represented on the Executive Council by Brock Dunham.

Albion. The most prominent planet within the Commune, and the location of the Albian Banking Advancement Conglomerate's central headquarters. Its capital is Dearborn.

altaria. See **Tellurian sacred prostitution**.

Alvira Confederacy. A decentralized federation of star systems spread across the border of the Mid and Inner Rims. Called *La Confederación de Alvira* in its native tongue, Latigón, its name is the etymological descendant of the Roman name for Grenada, i.e., Elibyrge, or Elvira. The Confederation of Alvira is a member of the League of Arterra, represented in the Convergent Congress only in the lower house of

Parliament; in the Senate, the Romaeans defend Alviran interests. See also: ***Cundinamarca***.

Arterra. A galactic region that was once the core of Procyon civilization at its height, but has since been abandoned. Following the Procyon's withdrawal, the region saw the settlement of Sapiens, primarily proto-minarchist individualists, who fled Earth from the ancient nations of Australasia, Europe, Israel, North America, South America, the Southern Cone and Russia, among other smaller, scattered countries. See also: ***League of Arterra***.

Bhalenjar. A Caspian planet associated with minarchist individualism, and the seat of the Interstellar Convergency. The only settlement on the planet is the city of Bhalenjar, which spans an entire urbanized continent; the city also extends into the Tower of Bhalenjar, with multiple laced tower levels rising into orbit. Bhalenjari Caspians are identified by their amethyst-colored eyes. They are represented on the Executive Council by Gokol Kodraku. See also: ***Tower of Bhalenjar***.

Breathtaker. The Mithneshi sacred weapon, used in ritual combat. It consists of two blade-tipped handles linked by a metal chain.

Caspians. A race of Sapiens genetically altered by the Procyon to possess various, rare eye colors and a distinct, bronze skin tone. The concept of Caspian ethnic divisions was invented by collectivist academics, who sought to tap a previously nonexistent voting bloc. See also: ***Bhalenjar***, ***Gottia***, and ***Khiteziya***.

Children of the Dole. A collectivist euphemism for the left-wing population of the Commune and Shatarin Empire that receives its livelihood through the rapidly expanding welfare state.

Communal Entitlement Recipients' Organization (CERO). A collectivist organization advocating the so-called "Sentient rights" of the Children of the Dole to obtain their livelihood through the labor of others and to limitless reproduction to achieve such a lifestyle. It is represented on the Executive Council by Sanders Flick.

Commune. A collection of developing planets united by their adherence to the corporatist collectivist ideology.

consitor. See **Tellurian sacred prostitution**.

control collar. A device used by ABAC to restrict and dictate the actions of various non-Sapien species, fully enslaving them to the collectivists' will.

Convergency Ameliorated Legal Union (CALU). A corporation that promotes and defends the arbitrarily declared "Sentient rights" of individuals upon the legitimate enforcement of any Arterran policy or law. It is represented on the Executive Council by Armando Marcotti.

Convergent Congress. A three-house legislature governing the Interstellar Convergency, composed of Parliament, the Senate, and the Executive Council in ascending order. See also: *Executive Council*.

corporatist collectivism. An ideology centered around a vision of totalitarian government and the welfare state, as well as a concept of institutionalized, false altruism.

Council for Interstellar Shatarin-Related Affairs (CISRA). A collectivist organization committed to the empowerment of Shatarins within the Interstellar Convergency and their dominating participation in legislation. It is represented on the Executive Council by Nahar Wali-Mutalbin, a Shatarin convert born Eliezer Crowne.

Crystallines. A silicon-based species known for their extensive mining industry and binary electrical language. Their capital planet is Litha, and they are represented on the Executive Council by Executive Feldspar.

Cundinamarca. Capital planet of the Alvira Confederacy, to which minarchist individualists fled from the nations that originally comprised the Viceroyalty of New Grenada. See also: ***Alvira Confederacy***.

Deltas. Colonial special forces responsible for power projection outside the borders of the United Colonies of Acadia. Their insignia is the iconic sword and arrowhead. See also: ***United Colonies Armed Forces (UCAF)***.

Emanation. A spiritual medium through which mortal creatures may interact with the otherwise unreachable Creator worshiped by Mithneshi Deists. Conscious will is believed to have powerful effects on the Emanation. See also: ***Mithneshi Deism***.

emist. A chemically comatose Sapien used by the Procyon to interpret their usually imperceptible language into audible speech. From Old Mithneshi *īmist*, "lips, mouths."

eparchy. A constituent country within the Interstellar Convergency that possesses both a government and a particular territory. Some corporations and organizations have eparchy-level status within the Convergent Congress, while not at all meeting the legal requirements to be defined and treated as such.

Executive Council. The highest-ranked legislative body in the Interstellar Convergency, comprised of twenty-one representatives from the most influential eparchies.

exoport. A spaceport used as a hub for interstellar travel.

Federated Republic of Gallia. A decentralized federation of star systems across the outer Mid Rim, colonized by settlers from La Seine. It is called *La République Fédérée de la Gaule* in its native language, Gaulois. Gallia is a member of the League of Arterra, and is represented on the Executive Council by Mireille Leveque. See also: *La Seine*.

free space. Space as normally perceivable by a sentient being.

Gameer. A Sapien, spacefaring people descended from the last waves of refugees from Earth in the distant past. They are unrepresented in the Convergent legislature and have no homeworld.

Ghourad. The Shatarin executive councilman's native title, designating his role as the sole intermediary between the devout theocracy and the rest of the secular, nonbelieving galaxy. From Shatarin *ghūrad*, "bridge, connection."

Gottia. A Caspian system-state aligned with corporatist collectivism. Gottians are identified by their emerald-colored eyes, and are represented on the Executive Council by Leipox Aparin.

Gradual Onset Deep-Space Psychosis. A psychiatric disorder caused by prolonged exposure to deep space in susceptible individuals. Popularly called "the Rakes" among space travelers, its symptoms include paranoia, visual and auditory hallucinations, and violent outbursts. It is thought to be highly contagious and is especially feared by the spacefaring Gameer.

Great Ziggurat. An ancient temple on Bhalenjar revered by the Mithneshi Coven as the sacred heart of their faith. The pyramidal design of the Ziggurat is often used for smaller temples throughout the Interstellar Convergency.

Hive Mind. See **Procyon**.

H'jan. A sentient race genetically engineered by the Procyon in the distant past, renowned for their scientific inquiry and technological advancements. Their capital is T'jan, and they are represented on the Executive Council by Sel'zhiiq Zatsh.

Holy Vendetta. An ongoing religious war between the polytheistic Tellurian Imperium and the fanatically monotheistic Shatarin Empire.

Interstellar Convergency. An intergovernmental organization and political-economic union established by the League of Arterra and the Procyon to promote pan-galactic cooperation and unity. The Convergency functions through a complex set of institutions on a supranational level. Intergovernmental decisions are achieved through Congress, i.e., the voting of eparchies. See also: ***Convergent Congress.***

Jotunheim. See **Tartarus**.

Jovian Exodus. The second escape of minarchist individualist North Americans from the Galilean moons to their final destination in the Vega system in the year 2270 AD (in the Convergent standard calendar, 0 Æx.). See also: ***Æx.***

Khiteziya. A politically neutral Caspian system-state loyal neither to collectivism nor individualism. The Khitezi are known for their sapphire-colored eyes, and are represented on the Executive Council by Zaran Bvelet.

Kingdom of Windsor Britannia. A decentralized federation of star systems across the Mid Rim, colonized by settlers from Thames. It is a member of the League of Arterra, and is represented on the Executive Council by Sir Byron Clay. See also: ***Thames***.

La Seine. Capital of the Federated Republic of Gallia, colonized by minarchist individualists fleeing France in the final exodus from Earth. Its capital city is Lutetia. See also: ***Federated Republic of Gallia***.

League of Arterra. A defense and trade alliance of Sapien powers in the Mid Rim based on a common minarchist individualist ideology.

Legionnaire. See **Militiaman**.

Lekaah. The cruel, all-powerful deity of the Shatarin religion and alleged author of its sacred book, the Mutalbin. From Shatarin *le-Kāh*, "The Power." See also: ***Mutalbin***.

mass driver. A method of propelling freight shipments into orbit by accelerating a payload at high speeds along miles-long rails with powerful electromagnets.

Matra Altaria. See **Tellurian sacred prostitution**.

Mei Zhi. See **Red Kingdom**.

Militiaman. A Colonial mechanized combat unit operated by a single pilot as a massive, powerful extension of the body.

The Tellurian equivalent is known as a Legionnaire, while the Muscovian is referred to as a Cossack.

Millennial Anglic. The common language of the United Colonies of Acadia and the most widely used language in interstellar trade and politics.

minarchist individualism. An ideology emphasizing the rights and freedoms of the individual and the innate sovereignty over one's own existence without the forced obligation to support and improve the lives of others. It is championed by the League of Arterra and Bhalenjar-aligned Caspian worlds.

Mithneshi Coven. A spiritual order that tends to the needs of the innocent, specializing in healing and the martial arts.

Mithneshi Deism. A liberally monotheistic tradition centered around the worship of an otherwise unknowable Creator who is removed from everyday affairs. From Old Mithneshi *mithnesh*, "mirror," i.e., of the spiritual world. See also: ***Emanation***.

Mutalbin. The sacred book of the Shatarin religion, said to be the literal word of Lekaah, who commands believers across twenty-one chapters to exterminate nonbelieving populations. From Shatarin *le-Mutalbin*, "The Answer."

Night-Watchman State. A form of government in which the state's sole purpose is the protection of individuals from assault, theft, etc. In such a system, the only legitimate governmental institutions are the military, courts and civilian police. The night-watchman state is the ideal government of minarchist individualism.

orbital bridge. An anchored cable stretching from a planet's surface into low orbit, along which passengers and cargo shipments may ascend or descend.

planet cracker. An informal term for a class of demolition warships capable of shattering minor planets and rendering larger worlds uninhabitable by heavy bombardment and gravity field manipulation.

Politically Correct Broadcasting Company (PCBC). The highly censored media outlet that broadcasts across the Interstellar Convergency. It is the parent company of *The Harlequin Post* and is represented on the Executive Council by Reon Harlequin.

Procyon. A highly advanced, humanoid species known for its interest in scientific and social research. The Procyon are known to have been historically involved in the artificial acceleration of other species' evolution through genetic engineering. All Procyon are extensions of the greater Hive Mind, or collective intelligence and memory. They are represented on the Executive Council.

Red Kingdom. A Sapien kingdom located within the galactic Inner Rim, known as an economic power for its export of luxury goods, most importantly pearls and silks. It is represented on the Executive Council by I-Lin Xai.

Rosc Occupied Territories. A contested territory held by the Rosc, a Sapien population that claims a strong hold over the galactic arms trade. The Rosc engage in extensive strip-mining operations across the occupied planets, and are infamous for dirty banking in their financial capital of Hosc Rejtz. They are represented on the Executive Council by Remy Vlotoscu Dostjya II.

Scythian. The common language of the Caspian peoples, spoken as a lingua franca throughout the Inner Rim and Deep Core.

Shatarin Empire. A theocratic, warmongering state within the Outer Rim that upholds the barbaric laws of the Shatarin religion and its sacred book, the Mutalbin. It is the League of Arterra's bête noire, but believed by the Commune to be a bastion of freedom and Sentient rights. It is represented on the Executive Council by Sawal Pezh-Lekaah, currently declared persona non grata.

Shatarin religion. A strict monotheistic tradition emphasizing the innate superiority of its adherents and their divine right to subjugate all nonbelieving peoples. From Shatarin *le-Shatarin*, "The Right, Entitlement."

Sol Radiofónica. The most prominent broadcasting company within the Tellurian Imperium.

sona. A Procyon "City Vessel" and a massive carrier for smaller craft. While they are known to be scattered throughout the Convergency, their total number is unknown, though believed to be increasingly limited. From Old Mithneshi *sōna*, "city."

Sorn. A largely uncharted region of the galaxy unaffiliated with the Interstellar Convergency. It is viewed as a sort of "galactic orient," an exotic, mysterious place frequented by traders and merchants.

space elevator. See **orbital bridge**.

Ssimfar. A diminutive and subservient form of Procyon created through genetic engineering. From Old Mithneshi *ssimfar*, "constructed, made."

Ssimvomai Center for the Lost. A Mithneshi station that tends to the needs of juvenile refugees from the Commune and other corporatist collectivist systems. From Old Mithneshi *ssimvōmai*, "children."

tachyon lens. An artificial structure that allows for the passage of ships between free space and the Aether, often referred to as "rabbit holes" in colloquial speech. Craft not large or advanced enough to possess aetherium drives must use tachyon lenses to enter or exit the Aether.

tachyon vein. A current of subatomic tachyon particles that runs through the Aether faster than the speed of light. The course of a tachyon vein is altered by the gravity wells of stars in free space.

Tartarus. A Colonial judicial complex hidden in the Badlands of the Outer Rim. It is the location of the ice moon Jotunheim, the highest security prison in the League of Arterra, reserved for those convicted of the most heinous crimes.

Tellurian Imperium. An Inner Rim empire descended from a sample of Roman stock taken by the Procyon in the early first century BC. The Tellurian language, a Romance language descended from Classical Latin, is widely spoken throughout the inner Convergency due to the influence of the Tellurian media. The Tellurians are notably polytheistic. They are represented on the Executive Council by their Praetor, Domínico de la Réina.

Tellurian sacred prostitution. The Imperial practice of serving deities through sexual acts. Temple prostitutes are divided into the order of *altarias* (women) and *consitores* (men); the *Matra Altaria*, or sacred Whore-Mother, is the overseer of the altarias. When a temple prostitute is brought to climax, a pilgrim's offering is believed to have been accepted by the deity.

terraformation. The artificial process of altering a planet's inhospitable environment to be suitable for colonization and long-term settlement.

Thames. Capital planet of the Kingdom of Windsor Britannia, colonized by minarchist individualists fleeing Great Britain in the final exodus. Its capital city is Kensington. See also: ***Kingdom of Windsor Britannia***.

Tower of Bhalenjar. The massive, double helix structure spanning thousands of miles from the surface of Bhalenjar into space. It was built by the Procyon thousands of years prior to the foundation of the Interstellar Convergency, for use as a scientific research station.

Tsardom of Romanov Muscovia. A decentralized federation of star systems across the outer Mid Rim colonized by settlers from Volga. It is a member of the League of Arterra, and is represented on the Executive Council by Oksana Molotova. See also: ***Volga***.

Unispeak. A degenerate form of Anglic characterized by its prominent borrowing of foreign words and spoken as the common language of the Commune.

United Colonies of Acadia (UCA). A decentralized federation of star systems across the center and inner Mid Rim, colonized by settlers from Acadica. Considered a night-watchman state characterized by minimal government, it is centered around the Vega sector, adjacent to the Sol sector or Earth Quarantine Zone, the birthplace of the Sapien species. Nationals of the UCA are Acadian, but more often referred to as "Colonials." The UCA is also referred to as "the

Colonies," and is represented on the Executive Council by Desh Maru. See also: ***Acadica*** and ***Night-Watchman State***.

United Colonies Armed Forces (UCAF). The national military forces of the United Colonies of Acadia, consisting of the Army, Deltas, Orbital Guard and Navy. It is the premier military force in the Interstellar Convergency, rivaling that of the Procyon.

vacibia. A plant root used by Tellurian women to prevent pregnancy. Prolonged use of vacibia is known to result in sterility.

Vehisipens. A nonhumanoid sentient species originating in the mangrove swamps of the planet Vehisipen. They are represented on the Executive Council by Executive Gh'vuur.

Veil of Bhalenjar. A famous nebula surrounding the Bhalenjar system.

Volga. Capital of the Tsardom of Romanov Muscovia, colonized by minarchist individualists fleeing Russia in the final exodus from Earth. Its capital city is Petrograd. See also: ***Tsardom of Romanov Muscovia***.

Xaztechua. One of the more notorious planets of the Commune, known for its citizens' unexplained capacity for limitless, lifelong reproduction.

ZGB (ЗГБ). The Muscovian central intelligence agency, called Заведение государственной безопасности (*Zavedeniye gosudarstvennoy bezopasnosti*, "Institution for State Security") in the Muscovian language.

APPENDIX B: MEMBERS OF THE EXECUTIVE COUNCIL

I. MINARCHIST INDIVIDUALIST

Bhalenjar	Gokol Kodraku
Crystallines	Executive Feldspar
Federated Republic of Gallia	Mireille Leveque
H'jan	Sel'zhiiq Zatsh
Kingdom of Windsor Britannia	Sir Byron Clay
Tsardom of Romanov Muscovia	Oksana Molotova
United Colonies of Acadia (UCA)	Desh Maru

II. NEUTRAL (UNAFFILIATED)

Khiteziya	Zaran Bvelet
Procyon	The Procyon (Executive)
Red Kingdom	I-Lin Xai
Rosc Occupied Territories	Remy Vlotoscu Dostjya II
Vehisipen	Executive Gh'vuur

III. CORPORATIST COLLECTIVIST

Academic Truth and Eliminating Dissent Organization (ATEDO)	Giles Bronson
Albian Banking Advancement Conglomerate (ABAC)	Brock Dunham
Communal Entitlement Recipients' Organization (CERO)	Sanders Flick
Convergency Ameliorated Legal Union (CALU)	Armando Marcotti
Council for Interstellar Shatarin-Related Affairs (CISRA)	Nahar Wali-Mutalbin
Gottia	Leipox Aparin
Politically Correct Broadcasting Company (PCBC)	Reon Harlequin
Shatarin Empire	Sawal Pezh-Lekaah
Tellurian Imperium	Domínico de la Réina

APPENDIX C: THE INTERSTELLAR CONVERGENCY

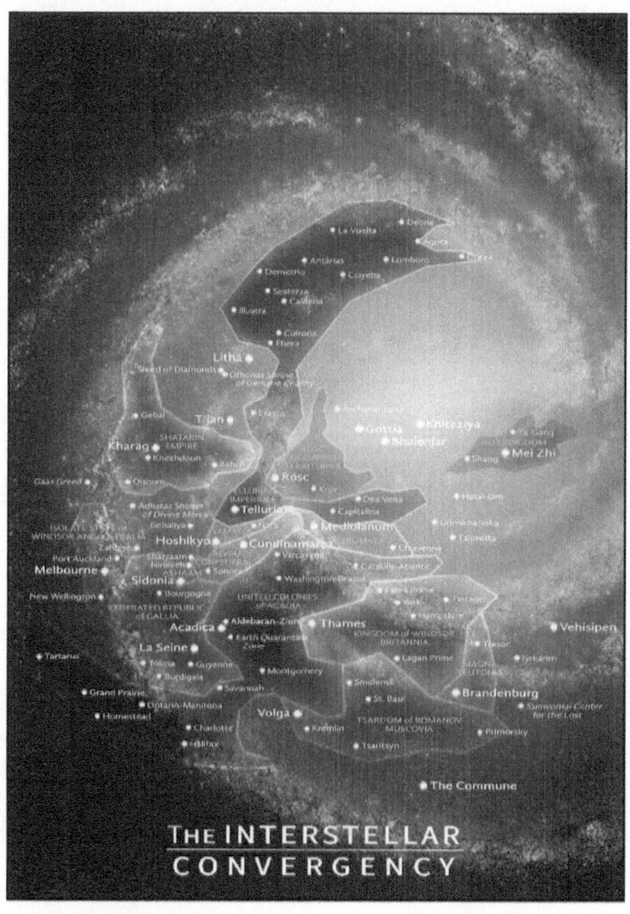

For a more in-depth exploration of the Interstellar Convergency, visit **theaetherverse.com.**

ABOUT THE AUTHORS

Joseph (Joey) D'Urso and Eugene Bryan, the politically incorrect creators of *The Aetherverse* and *Aethertales*, first met at Binghamton University in 2008. Joey, a born-and-raised New Yorker, received a BA in the Arabic language. Eugene, a so-called Florida man, obtained two BAs in History and Political Science, and later obtained his MS in Mass Communications at FIU.

Even during their time at college, Joey and Eugene spoke out against the absurdity of modern politics by contributing to the *Binghamton Review,* Binghamton University's student-run free speech magazine. Eugene even received open calls for violence against him by his triggered classmates. With articles such as "LASU: SA-Sponsored Terrorism?" and "You Call This Culture? LASU's Dirty Secret," it was only a matter of time before someone was offended.

Sharing a love of satire and science fiction, Joey and Eugene decided to sit down and write an epic novel in their spare time. What started as a fun hobby quickly became a massive project, and as their sci-fi universe grew, so did their ambition. With a culture war raging all around them, they created *The Aetherverse* to bring some common sense to a world gone mad – and to stir the pot just a little in the name of free speech.

For bonus content and more, visit <u>joey-durso.com</u>.